Bruce looked to his right and s far right, heading toward Jake. Jake let off a burst that hit the runner in the chest, slowing it down. Then Jake lowered his weapon and kicked the runner in the chest, sending it across the living room, slamming into the far wall. Bringing his weapon up, Jake put a burst though the runner's head. "Contact down," he called.

Jake, Bruce, and Buffy continued to clear the first floor when Debbie called over the radio, "Contact." Bruce listened for the shots but didn't hear any and was fixing to run upstairs when Debbie called out, "Contact down."

Pissed, Bruce keyed his radio, asking, "Care to elaborate on that contact?"

"Walker locked in the bathroom. Didn't want to shoot it and damage the stuff inside, so I stuck a knife in his skull," Debbie said.

Shaking his head, Bruce informed her in a really pissed-off voice, "Next time, throw some hate at 'em. Screw damaging shit."

Debbie politely said, "Fuck off. Mary is pissed that she didn't get to stick a knife in it or shoot it. Be damned if I'm going to listen to shit from either of you."

"I'm sorry, baby, please don't shoot or shank me," Bruce apologized.

"I'm not promising shit," Debbie replied, ready to beat members of her family.

In less than ten minutes, they called the house clear. Bruce, Buffy, and Mary took up watch on the back. Debbie, Jake, and David took the front. Bruce had put Mary with him since they had pissed off Debbie. He was not in the mood for Debbie to start spanking kids or him. Being honest with himself, Bruce figured he could throw the kids at her one by one, and by the time she got to him, she would be too tired to bust his ass.

BLUE PLAGUE

PLAGUE

TWO: SURVIVAL

THOMAS A. WATSON

A PERMUTED PRESS BOOK

ISBN: 978-1-61868-725-8

Blue Plague:
Survival

© 2017 by Thomas A. Watson
All Rights Reserved

Cover art by Christian Bentulan

PERMUTED
PRESS

Permuted Press, LLC
permutedpress.com

Published in the United States of America

CHAPTER 1

With a startle, Bruce woke up looking at a ceiling and immediately reached for his SCAR but grabbed only blankets. Sitting up and quickly looking around, Bruce saw his bedroom. Realizing he was home, he looked down at his side to see Buffy and Debbie beside him. The memories of the night before started coming through the sleepy fog that clouded his brain.

The entire family had been in a group hug around Buffy. After she had fallen asleep in Bruce's arms, he stood up to take her to his and Debbie's bed. Before he made it to his bedroom, Danny stopped him and told him to put Buffy in her room. Bruce looked at her for a minute then nodded. Buffy had been so close to him the last few days that he really had gotten used to her being beside him. He gently laid her on the bed. Danny took off Buffy's shoes and crawled in bed beside her. Bruce watched Danny pull Buffy close to her and smiled before he left the room.

Debbie was in the hall, waiting on Bruce as he left Danny's room. Grabbing his hand, she led him down the hall to their bedroom. Once they got to the bedroom, Bruce started stripping off clothes. He wanted nothing more than to burn the top layer of skin off of his body in the shower.

Debbie was going to join him until she saw him turn only the hot water on. Steam boiled out of the shower. She would wait; second degree burns were not fun to endure. Shaking her head, Debbie couldn't understand how Bruce could take the heat without blisters covering his body. The heating element for their shower was set at one hundred and thirty degrees and burned the shit out of her if she didn't run cold with it. Bruce would just get out red from head to toe.

1

When Bruce got out of the shower, he felt a lot better and saw Debbie at the end of the bed, waiting on her turn to shower. Walking over, she put a new dressing on his leg then put the bandages back under the sink and turned back to face him. Smiling, she ran to him, jumped, and wrapped her arms and legs around him as she locked him in a passionate kiss.

With a big grin, Bruce carried her to bed, where they played for an hour. As they lay in each other's arms, breathing heavily, waiting on a second wind. Bruce heard a thump on the door. Reluctantly getting out of bed, Bruce went to see who it was. Bruce was going to answer the door butt naked, just to let whoever knocked know they had interrupted playtime. Debbie told him to put on some underwear as she covered herself with blankets. Bruce grabbed some underwear, not wanting to irritate Debbie.

Bruce cracked the door but didn't see anyone in the hall. About to close the door, he noticed Buffy lying at the base of the door. She was fast asleep, curled into a ball. Opening the door, Bruce pointed at Buffy and told Debbie they had company. He told Debbie he was taking her back to Danny's room when Debbie told him no. Climbing out of bed, Debbie put on a t-shirt and told Bruce to put Buffy in their bed. Letting out a low growl as he picked up Buffy, Bruce did what Debbie asked.

Remembering last night and in no hurry to get out of bed, Bruce sat watching the two as they slept. Debbie had an arm around Buffy, holding her close. It was then that Bruce noticed Danny lying on the other side of Debbie. Bruce wondered when she had come in. *Damn, no wonder I didn't have any room to turn last night*, Bruce thought.

Debbie woke up with Bruce looking at her. "Hey baby, did the girls wake you up?" she asked.

"When did Danny come in?" Bruce asked, glancing over at Danny.

"About an hour after you went back to sleep," she responded.

"Told ya last night I should've put Buffy back in Danny's room," he said, reaching over and stroking Debbie's face.

"I can't believe that you would do that to her. This is her family now, and she looks at you like some kind of demi-god," Debbie said.

"She's going to have to learn to sleep in Danny's room sooner or later," Bruce said.

"Bruce, Danny slept in this bed with us almost every night until she was fourteen. She still comes in to sleep on a regular basis," Debbie reminded him.

"Yeah, beatin' the shit out of us in our sleep."

"Part of being a mama 'n daddy," Debbie said then continued, "Buffy will learn to sleep on her own but not until she's ready."

"We were busy last night, hot mama, and I wanted to continue," Bruce said with a slight whine in his voice.

"We can play later, stud muffin. The babies needed us last night," Debbie replied, smiling.

"When?" Bruce asked hopefully.

"Later, big daddy," Debbie replied, laughing.

"Well, I'm goin' down and gettin' some coffee and something to eat. We have a busy day today plus the next couple of weeks coming up." Bruce said, leaning over to kiss her then Buffy and Danny.

"Bruce, I want'cha to take the day off, baby. I can see it in your eyes. You're tired. So is everyone that you brought in yesterday," Debbie said, concerned.

"Babycakes, we don't have time to relax. We have to get everyone settled in and trained to fight. This farm could be hit any minute by raiders or a mob," Bruce told her as he got out of bed.

"Okay, baby, but at least go easy for a few days. On yourself and the others."

"I will try, but I can't promise. When everyone comes down, I want to go over what I've planned. I need you and Nancy to get everyone's names and start on a guard duty roster," Bruce said, putting on fresh tiger stripe BDUs.

"We did that yesterday, big daddy one," Debbie said as he put on another tactical vest.

"Figured as much. My wives like runnin' a tight ship here. See ya downstairs, baby," Bruce said, walking out of the bedroom, grabbing his SCAR.

Closing the door behind him, Bruce headed down to the kitchen. The wound on his leg was sore but tolerable as he went down the stairs. He could hear someone down there rattling pots and pans. Walking into the kitchen, he saw Lynn starting breakfast. Heading straight to the coffee pot, he poured a cup then walked to the den. It looked like a massive sleepover. There were people lying everywhere from the game room, through the den, and into the dining room. *This has got to be fixed soon*, he thought as he headed to the basement.

Walking over to the gun storage area, Bruce grabbed the parts to turn his SCAR to selective fire. Taking the gun apart, he took out the factory components and put in the ones he and Mike had made. When he was finished, he put the SCAR back together and rotated the fire selector around. Now, he had single, three-round burst and full auto. Feeling better now that he had options on how much hate he could send downrange, he headed back upstairs to the kitchen. Sitting in his spot at the table, Bruce took a sip of coffee.

He almost turned to get his laptop but remembered Jake had told him that the farm lost internet service two days ago. They still had satellite internet, but Bruce decided he was not in the mood for more bad news right now. So he grabbed a notebook and started making a list of the tasks that needed to be done. While Bruce sat writing, the rest of the farm started waking up. While making the list, he heard a rooster crow from the backyard. Bruce got up from the table and walked out of the back door to the pool patio.

As he sipped his coffee, the rooster crowed again. He started to have serious thoughts about killing it when he heard a cow moo. *That's a lot of noise coming from the farm. How can I make the animals shut the hell up?* he wondered. Hearing the door open behind him, Bruce glanced over his shoulder and saw Debbie, Buffy, and Danny walking up to him.

"Hey guys, sleep well?" Bruce asked.

"Yeah, after I found Buffy. When I woke up and she was gone, I ran down to Mission Control to ask Tonya if she'd seen her. She told me that besides the pigs in the field, nothing was movin' outside. I ran back to my room and looked everywhere. When I couldn't find her, I went into everyone else's room. Let me tell ya, Jake is so pissed at me about that too! Anyway, after searchin' all of our rooms, I stopped, and I knew where she went. That's when I found her in your bed. By then, I was tired again, so I just slept with y'all," Danny said. "I mean, I finally got a little sister, and I thought I'd lost her," Danny added as she put her arm around Buffy.

"I'm sorry, Danny. I just wanted to be by Daddy and Mama," Buffy said, giving Danny a sad look.

"Don't be sorry. Just wake me up next time, and we'll both go get in their bed," Danny said, hugging Buffy, who was smiling at her.

"Thanks a lot," Bruce stated dryly.

"Oh, you know you like it, Daddy," Danny said.

"Yeah, I like gettin' the shit beat out of me, pushed to the corner of the bed, and having no cover for the night," Bruce said, looking at her.

"Daddy, you're hot when you sleep. I thought I was sleepin' by a fire last night, and Danny is the same way. Why do either of you need blankets? I was sweatin' when I was beside either one of ya," Buffy said, looking at them.

"Thank you, Buffy, for finally telling them the plight I've had sleeping between both of them. I swear, with the heat you two put off, I could melt lead," Debbie said.

"I always wondered why the covers were on the floor when Danny slept with us," Bruce wondered aloud.

"Who in the hell needs covers when you have a furnace on each side of ya?" Debbie replied.

"If you stay so warm, why do I get woken up with two small, ice-cold feet in my back?" Bruce asked, crossing his arms.

"Well, you are a furnace, but my feet do get cold, so I stick 'em in the fire. I can't do that to Danny because she's my child."

"I've fallen out of the bed at least three times movin' away from you because ice cubes have hit me in the back," Bruce stated, not smiling.

"You do warm my feet up good, baby, and those times you fell outta bed. I did feel bad—for a little while," Debbie said with a smile.

"Let's get inside, guys, and go over today's activities," Bruce said, heading to the door.

As they followed Bruce inside, Debbie noticed Conner sitting in Bruce's chair, drinking coffee. Bruce kindly told him to move his ass. Sitting, in his now vacant spot, Bruce started going over his list. Looking up, he saw Debbie point at his and Mike's spots, whispering to Conner. Lynn was telling others to wake everyone and get the dining room ready for breakfast. Between the breakfast table and the dining room table, they could seat thirty. For now, everyone else would have to sit in the den and game room to eat.

Jake sat a plate of food down for Bruce then sat down beside him with his own plate. They were joined by Debbie, Buffy, and Danny on Bruce's right; they all sat down with their own plates and started eating. Debbie handed him a list with everyone's name on it. Bruce stood and told everyone to be quiet. They could continue eating, but he wanted their attention.

Raising his voice, Bruce started. "Mike, Debbie, Nancy, and I are the bosses. What we say is to be followed. If you think you are being treated unfairly, take it to another boss but only after you've completed the task at hand. First, the loft of the barn has to be prepared to make a sleeping area. Nancy and Debbie are making a new guard roster, and only the little ones won't be on it. If you miss a shift or are caught sleeping, punishment will be harsh. Next, Mike and I will be laying out a training roster that will be followed. Nancy, Debbie, we need a list of where people are sleeping now. If someone needs to be woken up at night, I really don't want to wake everyone up to find 'em."

Steve stood. "Dad, Tonya and I are movin' back to my old room with Pam. The Stewarts can have the guest room we are in, and Angela, Alex, and Cade can have the other guest room," he offered.

"Well, son, since you've put that much thought in where people should sleep, draw up a list for the Mamas. You have an hour," Bruce said, grinning.

"Thanks," Steve said sarcastically, wishing he had kept his mouth shut.

Bruce laid out the rules of the farm one last time so there could not be any misunderstandings. Then, he asked if there were any questions. Only Marty asked when they could eat. Bruce turned to the chubby little boy eating his breakfast. In the trip to the farm, he had lost weight but still had a round appearance. Bruce said, "Everyone can only eat when food was set out on the table. Only those on kitchen duty are allowed to go in the refrigerator or pantry. With the extra people we have, our food supply is going to be put under strain, so no raiding the food supply." He looked at his family and said this went for everyone. They all nodded in agreement.

Lynn spoke up. "I want to be assigned to cook all the time for the group. I'll still do guard duty and train, but could it be at night please?" Lynn stared at Bruce, waiting on an answer when Nancy stood.

"If Lynn cooks, then she has no guard duty. That's too much to ask of anyone. Cooking for forty people is a lotta work," Nancy said, looking at the family.

"I agree; if she cooks, no guard duty. Nancy and I can train her on an individual basis, but I think she needs at least one helper assigned a day," Debbie said, looking around the table.

"Second that motion," Mike said from his end of the table.

"Motion passed. One person will be assigned to help with each meal, and no guard duty for Lynn," Bruce said, thankful he would not have to perform cooking duties.

"I don't want Bruce or Mike assigned to be my helpers either. Don't get me wrong. I love both of y'all, but neither one of ya listens worth a shit unless it comes from your wives' mouths," Lynn said, looking at Bruce then Mike.

Nancy said that was fine, thankful that someone had volunteered to cook. Mike did complain that if he got to help, then he could sample the food. With a scowl, Nancy told him to shut up before Lynn changed her mind.

Bruce then read out names for work details around the farm. First group was cleaning out the loft. Second group was moving equipment and supplies off the vehicles, separating it, and then putting it up. He reminded everyone to look at the board in the kitchen to find out what they had to do on the duty roster and told them it was their responsibility to know when they had duty.

Bruce walked to the dining room. Paul and his family were sitting with the group from the gas station. Walking over, Bruce said, "Paul, I want you to get three M-4s with suppressors and show your family how to use them. Just the basics. You can continue their trainin' later. Then, I want you to look at the animals, gardens, greenhouses, and tell us what'cha think. This evening, you can tell us where our shortcomings are." Paul assured him they would have it done by that evening.

Walking back to the kitchen, Bruce told everyone that it was time to go to work and that lunch was at noon. Everyone was to be in the house unless they were on guard duty. Looking over at the gimp, Bruce told him he was to eat lunch on the patio, and after he cleaned up that evening, he might eat inside. Gimp only replied, "Yes sir," never looking up from the floor. Bruce shook his head, asking Mike to show gimp what to do before heading to his area. Mike said it would be his pleasure. It was a few minutes after 7 a.m. when everyone left the house to go do their assigned duty.

Around 10 a.m., Bruce told Joseph and Lance, the two teen boys from the gas station, to get an electric buggy and deliver water to everyone, and they took off. After finishing, they returned to finish unloading the trucks. Bruce smiled at the two then looked at the five young girls they had rescued who were unloading trucks. It made him mad to think what those kids had been through. Mindy, the oldest at seventeen and in charge of the little group, was lean and pretty. They all worked hard to get the task accomplished.

At noon, everyone headed to the house covered in sweat from the oppressive heat. Those not in BDUs and vests had stripped down to t-shirts. It didn't really matter in Louisiana; you could walk around naked and still sweat to death. Pam stayed in Mission Control during the day since her injuries kept her from heavy work for now. As the others worked outside, Susan watched her kids, and Cade while helping Lynn with lunch. As everyone filed in to eat, the family and soldiers stripped off vests and weapons, putting them in the racks.

When Bruce sat down, Debbie told him, "I want gun racks in the den, dining room, and another in the kitchen on a different wall."

"Why do ya want another one in here?" Bruce asked, looking at the big gun rack on the wall.

"Just do it." The family laughed, remembering the calamity yesterday when Danny screamed.

After Bruce got comfortable, Conner walked up to him and said, "The loft is done." Bruce looked up at the four women, who were also rescued, at the counter fixing their plates. They were all very pretty. A chill ran down Bruce's spine as he looked at them. Everyone they had rescued was pretty, even the two boys. The gang had killed anyone that did not fit that mold. Bruce looked down at the table, suppressing the anger that was trying to fill him.

Conner, seeing Bruce look down, thought he was disappointed. "We worked really hard and did it as fast as we could," he assured Bruce. Bruce told Conner that they had done an excellent job; he was just thinking that this was a shitty world now. Agreeing with him, Conner went to get some food.

Bruce shoveled his food down then stood. Raising his voice, he asked if everyone could hear him. Everyone said they heard him throughout the house. Even Tonya in the fort said she could probably turn off the intercom and still hear him.

"After lunch, everyone will be assigned a weapon. I'm making groups, and those needing training will report to them. From now on, you will be responsible for that weapon. Today, we work on weapon training until two. In one week, you'll be tested on the weapon you're assigned. If you pass that, your weapon will always stay loaded. If you fail, you'll retrain. If anyone fails three times, they'll be given a butter knife for a weapon and put on shit detail with the gimp until they pass."

Everyone who did not have a weapon looked at each other, knowing they were going to train hard. They wanted to learn so they could defend themselves, and they had seen the gimp all day with his wheel barrel full of shit roaming the farm. Nobody wanted that job and secretly hoped the gimp would hold up so they wouldn't have to do it.

Bruce continued, "In no way will training interfere with the daily chores. We have a lot of work to do, and it has ta be done. Starting tomorrow, everyone's goin' to start morning workouts at 5 a.m. before starting the day. After weapon training today at 2 p.m., everyone will finish unpacking the convoy. Mary and Jake have been makin' an inventory list as stuff is taken off so we can pass out gear. Work today will stop at five, and we are goin' swimming and relax before supper." When Bruce paused, everyone cheered at the thought of swimming in the Olympic-sized swimming pool after working in the heat all day.

Bruce told them those without a weapon were to come down to the basement after eating to pick one up from him. To clear the matter up, he informed everyone the only people that would not carry weapons were gimp, Cade, Cassandra, and Joshua. He wanted everyone armed at all times. The new kids were excited that they were gonna learn how to protect themselves. Heading to the basement with Buffy in tow, they each kissed Debbie when they walked past.

One at a time, they came down to the basement to get a weapon and magazines. Then, they went back to the kitchen to see which teacher they had. The teachers were Danny, Jake, Matt, Mary, and David spread around the house. Those who already had weapons went back to work unloading the convoy. At 2 p.m., the rest of the clan showed up to finish unloading. By 3:30, they had unloaded everything. Bruce told several people to get the soldiers' backpacks and duffel bags that had been unloaded from one of the Duce and halves and unpack them. He wanted the ACU uniforms and equipment put in stacks by sizes on the back patio. He turned to Conner and told him to make sure that he and the other two soldiers had all of their stuff separated from the packs that the group was going through. Conner, Campbell, and Kenner grabbed their packs and duffel bags from the pile.

In less than an hour, there was a long line of clothes in piles laid out along the back patio. Bruce had them put all the NVGs, thermal scopes, and other delicate equipment in the basement. Then, he told those from the gas station to go and pick out one uniform, a pair of boots, and a tactical vest. As they ran to the piles, Bruce told them no fighting; if someone was left out, they would find them something. Once everyone had gotten one set that fit, Bruce told them to grab a backpack and move back. Then, Bruce told Paul and his family to do the same thing. Bruce told Lynn and Maria to take the school kids and find some clothes.

After they had finished, Bruce kept sending people back to get another set of digital ACUs until everyone had three complete sets and an extra pair of boots. Some of the smaller teens' uniforms were big, but Nancy and Debbie could fix that. Several would have to wear extra socks to make the boots fit, but everyone had boots now. Then, he told everyone to put their stuff in their backpacks, and this pack was to stay where they slept. Just as he was fixing to give out more orders, Matt and Jake ran up to him.

"Dad, hold on, okay? We have somethin' we want to show ya," Jake said with a grin.

"Son, we have a lot to finish up," Bruce said, looking at him.

"Daddy Bruce, you're going to love it," Matt assured him.

"Let 'em show us, Bruce; they've been put off for two days showing us what they've made," Debbie said, helping several of the girls put stuff in their packs.

"Alright, men. Let's see what you've made then," Bruce said, smiling as the boys took off to the workshop.

Mike came over to stand beside him. "Nancy said they worked for over two days, still pullin' guard duty and not sleeping much."

"Ya think we should hide then?" Bruce asked, looking toward the shop. "Because that means whatever they worked on is dangerous."

"You know those boys wouldn't make somethin' that would intentionally hurt us, Bruce," Mike said.

"What about unintentionally?" Bruce asked, cutting his eyes at Mike.

"Maybe we should step back a little," Mike said as they overhead the door to the shop slide up.

"Too late," replied Bruce as Matt and Jake were running back to the patio with several laptops and boxes with joysticks and buttons on them.

They stopped at one of the covered patio tables and started setting up computers and plugging the boxes into the computers.

Bruce and Mike went over to stand behind them, watching the two set up the maze of wires and turning on computers. They had no idea what the boys were doing, but it looked cool as hell. The boys pulled up chairs and sat behind computers, each with a box with a joystick. Looking at one of the laptops in front of Jake, they could see the house. Mike and Bruce looked up at the shop and realized that there was a camera in there. Neither could fathom what the boys had built. Then, Jake turned around.

"I want to introduce everyone to 'warlord,'" Jake said then faced his computer, grabbed the joystick, and purposefully moved it.

By this time, everyone was standing behind them, looking at the shop. They saw the scissor lift come rolling out with a damn turret on one end. The turret held a gun with several cameras mounted on it. Jake drove the vehicle past them and stopped it, looking into the hay field to the east. Then, he flipped a switch, and the platform started to rise.

Mesmerized, Bruce looked at the warlord then back at the computers. In front of Matt, he had a view from the top of the platform with crosshairs. As Matt moved his joystick back and forth, the crosshairs moved across the hay field. Then, Matt flipped another switch, and his screen had a thermal view of the field with crosshairs. Jake turned around to explain as Matt started doing system checks.

"Dad, we took the civilian M-240 you had and mounted it on the platform. I know you were going to convert it to full auto, but it's belt-fed, and we needed it. Then, we put it on the robotic arm we built for the science fair last year. We put servos on the lift operating board to drive it and operate the platform remotely. Next, we mounted the suppressor you made for the M-240. Now, whoever is in Mission Control can send the warlord out to check on any motion detected without havin' to send people out. If you look on top of the barn, we put the other thermal camera up there. It'll be operated from Mission Control," Jake said with a grin from ear to ear.

Bruce looked at the top of the barn, and sure enough, there was a small tower with windows on all sides. Looking at the boys then at the computers and equipment in front of them, Bruce sat there speechless. Then, a mischievous grin spread across his face. "How does it shoot?" he asked.

"We thought you'd never ask, Dad. We could only test it at night at the back of the property, when everyone was asleep. We could barely hear it at the barn, and it can't be heard from here shooting at the catfish pond. We have accuracy out to five hundred yards on a head-sized target," Jake said, still grinning.

"Five hundred yards? We only have fields of fire that big on the east 'n west side," Mike blurted, staring at the equipment.

"Who cares? That thing is awesome," Bruce said. "Fire it, Matt. Let's see what she can do."

Matt zoomed in on the far side of the hay field, which could only be seen from the house with the platform forty feet in the air. Seeing a small animal inside the tree line, he zoomed in. Once Matt zoomed in, they could tell it was a small, wild hog. Moving the joystick with his right hand, he moved the crosshairs on the screen while his left hand hovered over a button. When the crosshairs settled on the pig's head, he pushed the button. They all heard the suppressed shot and saw on the screen the bullet hit the pig in the head, dropping it in its tracks.

"Holy shit!" David said, and neither mother told him to watch his mouth. They were staring at Matt and Jake in disbelief and a little fear as Matt turned around, smiling.

"How far can we send the warlord out?" Bruce asked in amazement.

"It only has line of sight capabilities. We set up relays so it can go anywhere in the fence, but it can't leave the property. We didn't have the transmitters or receivers to make it long-range. With all the cameras and servos, it only operates for roughly six hours before it needs recharging," Matt said with disappointment in his voice.

"Boys, that doesn't matter. This thing will help us out a lot. The warlord can take out small groups of either blues or bandits without having us expose ourselves. I for one will speak for the other parents and everyone else. We're very proud of you," Debbie said as she hugged each of them, secretly thankful they did not build an atomic bomb.

Matt and Jake explained that they had wanted to be able to send it out to check around the area. Conner told them to hold on as he took off running to the Stryker. He returned a few minutes later carrying a large case. Setting the case down, Conner opened it up, taking out what looked like a laptop. He handed it to Jake. Then, Conner started taking pieces out, putting them together. When he was finished, he was holding a small airplane.

"Shit. That's a Raven," Jake said, standing up.

"Jake, watch your mouth," Debbie scolded.

"Mom, that's a micro UAV, like a predator only smaller. It can fly for ninety minutes, sending back digital video, thermal, or high resolution," Jake said, setting the laptop down and walking over to Conner.

"Think you can operate it?" Conner asked.

"Give me and Matt three hours, and we'll be able to do anything with it," Jake replied confidently. Conner reached back into the case and pulled out a large user's manual and handed it over.

"Make that thirty minutes," Jake corrected, grabbing the manual and sitting down by Matt. They started to speed read the manual until Nancy broke the spell.

"You two need ta put your baby back to bed before you start another project," Nancy said, pointing at the video screens. As Jake lowered the platform to drive warlord back, Bruce walked up to them.

"How long will it take for you two to set up a control station in Mission Control for warlord?" Bruce asked.

"We can have it set up in less than an hour, but we only have twenty-inch LED monitors left. The gun sight really needs to be on somethin' bigger. Plus, the desk in Mission Control is already crowded with all the radios, computer, and monitor control board," Matt said as Jake was driving the warlord back.

"Take the fifty-inch LED TV out of the shop; then, get one of the old desks that we brought out of the top of the barn and set up a complete control system tonight. I want y'all to label every control, and starting tomorrow, you two will take turns givin' classes on it," Bruce said.

"Alright," they said together.

"Now, it's time for everyone to relax. I still want noise discipline from everyone. No yellin' period, okay?" Bruce turned to look at everyone. He was met with lots of nodding as everyone was ready to get in the pool. Bruce told everyone to find a family member that was close to their size and get a swimming suit from them. Weapons were to stay outside, where they could be grabbed if needed. Looking at Buffy and Cassandra, he told them Danny had some old swimsuits in storage that they could use.

Everyone ran to the house, grabbing their packs and taking them to the area where they would be sleeping. The family grabbed shorts and bathing suits, laying them out in the kitchen so the rest of the clan could find something to swim in. Danny grabbed Buffy and led her outside to one of the storage containers that held clothes. When they returned, they each had an armload of clothes. Danny dropped several of her old bathing suits and several others on the table as she and Buffy took the rest of the clothes upstairs to her room.

Little Angela had to wear a two-piece bikini that Danny had worn when she was twelve. Bruce giggled at her as she walked through the kitchen wearing it. It still amazed him she could not weigh more than ninety pounds on her childlike frame. Yet she had carried a pack weighing at least forty pounds with another fifteen pounds of equipment and sometimes carried Cade, who was over three quarters of her body weight. She had done it, kept up, and held her own. Bruce knew any of the girls in the family could do that, but they had practiced and trained for it. Angela had just done it without training or preparing. He watched the small woman walk out as Debbie came up beside him, already in her bikini.

"What are you snickering about?" she asked. Bruce told her what he had been thinking.

Debbie replied, "That young woman is somethin' else. She may be small, but she's filled with fire. I like her a lot. She and Alex make good additions to the family. Plus, with her here, I'm not the shortest adult now."

"I love my five-foot-tall woman though," Bruce said, picking Debbie up and kissing her.

"You damn well better love me," Debbie said as Bruce put her down. "Come on, stud muffin. Get some shorts on; let's swim," she said, hugging him and walking out to the pool.

Bruce went to his room to change, passing Danny and Buffy as they headed to the pool. When he stepped outside, he caught his breath. There were scantily clad women everywhere. *We could almost shoot a music video here*, he thought. He ran and jumped in the pool.

Bruce swam for a while, playing with the kids. For the most part, they did stay quiet. He only had to remind the kids once or twice to keep their voices down. Bruce then got out and joined Mike at one of the patio tables.

"Bruce, if anyone sees all these women here, they'll hit us hard," Mike said, looking around.

Bruce had not thought of that. "Well, from now on, everyone will wear their uniform unless in the house or here at the pool. That also means we have to prepare and train harder," Bruce replied with Mike nodding in agreement.

Paul came to join them at the table, followed by Conner a few minutes later. Bruce saw Conner following Danny and Mary around with his eyes. Following Conner's gaze, Bruce turned to look at his daughters. To say they were knockouts would be an understatement. They were toned and had women's bodies even though they were sixteen. Though they would be seventeen next month, he would always see them as little girls but knew others wouldn't. He liked Conner, but he would have to have a talk with him later. Chuckling, Bruce knew the girls already had boyfriends.

Looking past the patio, Bruce saw the gimp standing in his underwear at the water hose, washing his clothes off. Bruce called Lance over and told him to tell the gimp to come over and to move it. Lance ran over to the gimp then talked to him, pointing at Bruce. Gimp took off at a dead run toward Bruce, stopping beside the table.

"Gimp, you had some not so nice thoughts today. They weren't bad, but they weren't nice either. Didn't you?" Bruce asked, looking at the gimp, who had a shocked look on his face.

The gimp looked down at his feet and said, "Yes sir, I had some bad thoughts but not to hurt anyone, just bad thoughts of throwing shit at people. I'm sorry."

"I'm not going to hit you now. Not because the wives said not to but because I'm tired, and you did do some good work today." He saw relief ripple over the gimps' body and pride from the compliment. "Now, don't let it go to your head. Anymore bad thoughts and we'll have a score to settle. Get down on your knees. You don't ever look down at me," Bruce snapped. Gimp dropped to his knees so fast Bruce felt the impact through the concrete. Bruce cringed inside, knowing that had to hurt.

Looking at the gimp kneeling, Bruce said, "After you clean up, I want you to go over to the piles of clothes and pick out three ACU sets, two pair of boots, tennis shoes, underwear, socks, and t-shirts. Then, put 'em in a backpack. From now on, that is what you're to wear: clothes like the rest of us. Do you understand?"

"Yes sir," gimp said with tears in his eyes. He liked being treated like everyone else. "I won't think bad thoughts anymore, sir," he promised.

"That's good because tomorrow, you'll learn how to work in the garden after shit detail. The more you make yourself useful, the better the treatment you'll receive."

"Thank you, sir," gimp replied with a look of determination.

"Now, throw those old clothes away, and do what you're told." Gimp jumped up and ran off.

Mike laughed as gimp ran off, "Alright Jedi master, what's on the plate for tomorrow?"

Bruce turned to Paul. "Well, what does the farm look like to you?"

"Well, first, let me say this is the best operation I've ever seen much less heard of. Y'all are prepared here for a lot of stuff. But I hate to tell ya y'all are not farmers. First, in your garden, you have planted your plants too far apart. There should be double what you've planted on each row. I know what it says in the books, but this is good soil, and that twenty-acre garden is goin' to put out literally tons of food per acre. But it could've been doubled. Second, you're overfeeding every animal on this farm and wastin' a lot of food. You have several years' worth of chicken feed alone if you feed them correctly, not nine months as Nancy had projected. Same thing goes with the quail, pheasants, and ducks. Your horses and cows are fat from overfeeding. They require about two percent of body weight a day. For the horses here, that's about twenty pounds of hay or grain a day. Not both like y'all are feedin' 'em. They waste what's not eaten. You have the hay trough off the ground and one for each animal, which is good. Your goats and rabbits are so fat they can barely move. They need their food cut in half. You need ta harvest your catfish pond soon. There are way too many fish in there, and we had to fix the aerator in the pond. Let me tell ya when we got in that pond to fix it, I was actually scared with all the fish around us. We all got stuck with a fin at least once. Your greenhouses are in top-notch shape; you just need a better watering system. I figure we should get close to a ton a month from each of them."

Paul looked at Mike and Bruce before continuing. "If we could seal off this land, we could stay here for a while with the supplies and what is already set up here. We only have ta worry about others coming here, be they infected or raiders. The chain-link fence around the property is in excellent shape, but it can be climbed easily. I noticed several piles of razor wire by the barn and wondered why it wasn't put up. I figure with a few more milk cows and chickens, we could seal this place up and try waitin' it out."

"Well, it's good to hear your mistakes from a man who knows what he's talkin' about. We all may have grown up on farms, but you're right; we aren't farmers. If you could, would ya set up a feeding schedule for the animals? When we replant for fall crops, we'll do what ya said. Now, as for the razor wire, I for one didn't want to put it up after puttin' up that damn fence. Then, if any hunter or someone had seen a ten-foot chain-link fence with razor wire on it, they would have wondered what was inside. Now, it doesn't make a difference with the end of the world shit going on," Bruce said.

"I'll get several of the others and put up the razor wire. It is the least we should do," Paul said.

"We'll get to that later, but first, we have to get the loft ready for this group to live in. It'll need plumbing and a septic system for showers, sinks, and toilets. Then, it needs to be wired in so we can get A/C and heat up there. We'll raid several empty houses around here to get what we need. There's a Boy Scout camp thirty miles from here where we can get bunk beds. Before anyone says anything, I want bunk beds in case we find more people. I want the loft to be able to hold up to fifty people," Bruce said.

"Why not wait a little while before goin' out? Let's see if it gets better," Conner offered.

"Hold that thought for a second," Bruce said, waving to Debbie, motioning her to get Nancy, Angela, and Alex. When the four got to the table, Bruce related everything that had been discussed so far as they all pulled up chairs. Seeing everyone at the table, Stephanie came over and sat down beside Bruce and Debbie. After Bruce finished bringing everyone up to speed, he turned to Conner.

"I feel it's goin' to get a lot worse sooner, and it'll be decades before it gets better if it ever does. I want to be prepared for a siege real soon. Whether it comes from blues or a gang, I want this place ready. We have ta get everyone a spot to live in and reinforce the fence all around the property," Bruce said.

"You told us to prepare for a zombie apocalypse; that's why I wanted the fence and bought it, Bruce. You even said it would work in a zombie apocalypse," Nancy whined at him. She was damn proud of her fence.

"We did try to prepare for a zombie apocalypse, Nancy, because anything else would seem easy to live through. No one could have predicted that we would be surrounded by evil Smurfs, some with rocket engines in their asses, wantin' to rip you to pieces and then eat ya. If one of you had told me this was comin', I would have packed my bags and left, afraid that you'd stab me to let the demons out while speaking in a demonic voice."

"Okay, I thought you were makin' fun of my fence," Nancy said, sounding an awful lot like a kid.

"Making fun of your fence, baby girl? If Mike wouldn't get jealous, I'd come over there and kiss you with tongue," Bruce said, making everyone laugh.

"Come down to our room later tonight, Bruce. We can share, brother," Mike said, winking at Bruce and blowing him a kiss. Nancy slapped him on the arm, laughing.

"Being serious again, tomorrow, a small group will go out in trucks with trailers to maximize our hauls. I'll be in the Beast, leading the raid. We will ransack houses close to us first. Then, make a run to the scout camp, stopping at that man's house who installs septic systems and get some of his stuff after we leave the camp. If we run into survivors and they look ok, we'll invite 'em here; if not, we'll move on. We will not kill anyone unless they act against us or hurt others. If the man that sells septic systems is still home, we'll try to barter. If it's a no go, then we'll move on. We will not become marauders here. Period. Is that clear? We will help who we can but won't endanger our clan unnecessarily," Bruce said, looking at everyone. Each nodded in agreement. Then, Stephanie spoke up.

"Actually, fewer than eighteen percent of infected attacks result in pure cannibalism. They bite to infect and most of time leave you alone after biting. Sometimes—"

Bruce held up his hand. "Stephanie, I love you with all my heart, and I'm going to let you give a full dissertation and briefing on whatcha know about the virus and the infected but not right now. Once the loft is done, we will all gather in the game room and let cha explain what you have found out, okay?" Bruce said, putting his hand on her leg and patting it.

"Okay, deal. I will get a good presentation together for you," Stephanie said, glad she had been given a task she knew she could handle.

"Conner, you and one of the other troops will be in the Stryker ready to roll out if we get in trouble. We'll gather over three days then build. I want this project completed in two weeks because we have more stuff to do," Bruce said.

Mike chuckled. "You know, Bruce, it never ceases to amaze me. No sooner than we leave the hospital the entire family reverts back to 'Southern Grammar,'" Mike said.

"Well, we have no one to impress. Let's just be country boys now," Bruce agreed, laughing. Bruce stood and told everyone, "It's time to eat and get some sleep because we're fixin' to get busy."

CHAPTER 2

They couldn't leave the next day because Mike wanted several of the SAW machine guns to have suppressors. Bruce had given in, kicking himself for not thinking about that. Getting up early, Mike and Bruce made suppressors for three SAWs and one M-240, which was just a larger version of the SAW. It just fired the bigger 7.62 ammo. Then, Bruce made suppressors for the 50 cal machine guns on the Stryker and the Hummer. He almost attempted to make a suppressor for the Mk-19 grenade launcher but decided against it since that thing made enough noise to be heard twenty miles away.

With the adventure put off for a day, Jake and Matt put up a large antenna on top of the barn for the Raven to extend its range. Then, they pulled out a large satellite dish that the previous owners left on the farm. After running wires from the dish into the house, the boys would run outside and move the dish then run back inside. Just watching the way the two were acting, Bruce did not even want to guess what they were up to.

Everyone now had at least an M-4 with a suppressor and a pistol. Buffy had gotten some of Danny's old BDUs, combat boots, and a tactical vest that Debbie had made for her using one of Danny's old ones. Now, she carried a compact Glock 9mm pistol with her UMP 45 submachine gun. The first time Bruce saw her dressed in camo, he thought she looked like Shirley Temple going to kick someone's ass.

Jake and Matt sent the little Raven up the next day while Bruce and Mike worked on suppressors. The small village of Castor, fifteen miles to the east, had blues running around everywhere. Several blues were seen around the farm on the roads. Switching to thermal, the closest survivors they found were on the Snead farm fifteen miles to the northwest as the crow flies. It was over thirty miles by road. They had seen several vehicles traveling on the highway forty miles to the west. They could not tell if they were gangs or survivors.

With the suppressors done, Bruce and Mike pulled out the Beast and put the steel plates over the windows. Then, they loaded it with extra ammo and fuel after making sure the video cameras worked so they could drive it with the plates over the windows. The Beast was then moved to the front of the house.

Sending the Raven out several times during the day, Jake and Matt had found two houses ten miles to the south, sitting close together with another one beside them under construction. They loaded up Bruce's, Mike's, and Steve's trucks along with Debbie's SUV with tools to take what they needed from the houses. Matt would be the only kid not going with them on the first run. Bruce wanted him at the house to run the Raven. Mike was also staying to run defense in case the farm was hit. He did not like it and voiced his opinion about it to everyone. Debbie was coming along with Paul, Alex, Angela, and Mindy with the four women from the gas station, seventeen total counting Buffy. The three soldiers were staying behind in the Stryker for backup. Bruce told everyone else to stay alert and do whatever Mike said.

The next morning, Bruce put at least one family member in each vehicle in case they came under fire. He, Debbie, and Buffy rode in the Beast. At 5:30 a.m., he called out over the radio, "Everyone, load up. Mike, do you see anything with the UAV?" When Mike replied that the coast was clear, Bruce told them to open the gate, and the small convoy left. They kept the speed at thirty-five mph so the vehicles would stay quiet.

They reached the houses without incident. It was not until Matt had to bring the Raven home to change its batteries that the first few infected hit. After Bruce, Buffy, and Jake cleared the house, they took the front of the house to stand watch. Debbie, Danny, and David took the back while everyone else went inside to get what was needed. Ten minutes after the group had gone into the house, a group of infected came down the road from the direction they had come. Without pause, Jake raised his AR-10, dropping the entire pack of nine in less than fifteen seconds before they got within a hundred fifty yards.

Watching Jake shoot, Buffy ogled at him with an open mouth. Bruce smiled at her reaction. "We taught all the kids how to shoot, BB, but nobody can shoot better at long distance than Jake. Matt is almost as good but not quite."

"He may be able to shoot, BB, but all the brothers still have trouble taking me in hand-to-hand. I can take everyone else," Danny called over the radio.

"I beg to differ on that," Mary came over the radio.

"Drop it, and keep the radio open; we have infected coming through the field behind the house," Debbie yelled over the radio. This froze Bruce's blood.

"How many, and do you need backup?" Bruce asked, fighting the urge to run to her.

"Five, and we have them," Debbie said as the three of them opened up with suppressed single shots. Then, he heard someone open up on full auto. Worried, Bruce called them and asked again if they needed backup. Debbie popped off, "We trained also, Bruce. You don't have to hold our hand. One was a runner, so I went full auto and sprayed his face."

Chuckling to himself, Bruce keyed his radio. "Good job, baby. Stay alert." He was glad everyone had a radio on this raid; it was already making a world of difference. Hearing the inside team ripping out showers, sinks, and toilets, he turned back to the road. "Mike, when is the Raven coming back?" Bruce asked over the radio.

"Matt's outside changing the batteries now."

Hearing something behind him, Bruce turned and saw several girls bringing out a sink and putting it on the trailer of Steve's truck. Debbie came on the radio. "Inside team, grab all the clothes, shoes, food, towels, toiletries, blankets, and everything else we might need." Bruce almost said something but decided not to; they might as well get what they could. In less than an hour, they had two showers, two sinks, and two toilets on the trailer. The back of the truck was full of clothes and other stuff. Bruce even saw a large, flat-screen TV sticking up from the front of the bed. When he saw the team coming out empty-handed, Bruce told everyone to load up, and they moved to the next house.

Pulling over to the next house, Bruce walked up with the clearing team. Pointing for Jake to take the lead, he moved to the door to find it locked. Kneeling, Jake went to work. Bruce and the others readied to enter as Jake picked the lock. When it opened, Jake swung the door open and pulled up the P90. With his AR-10 across his back, he entered with Bruce, Buffy,

Mary, and Debbie behind him. Danny stayed at the door with David. As they entered the main living room, Bruce motioned for Debbie and Mary to head upstairs. They moved up the stairs while Bruce and the others took the first floor. Then, Bruce heard Jake call out, "Contact front."

Bruce looked to his right and saw a runner come out a door on the far right, heading toward Jake. Jake let off a burst that hit the runner in the chest, slowing it down. Then Jake lowered his weapon and kicked the runner in the chest, sending it across the living room, slamming into the far wall. Bringing his weapon up, Jake put a burst though the runner's head. "Contact down," he called.

Jake, Bruce, and Buffy continued to clear the first floor when Debbie called over the radio, "Contact." Bruce listened for the shots but didn't hear any and was fixing to run upstairs when Debbie called out, "Contact down."

Pissed, Bruce keyed his radio, asking, "Care to elaborate on that contact?"

"Walker locked in the bathroom. Didn't want to shoot it and damage the stuff inside, so I stuck a knife in his skull," Debbie said.

Shaking his head, Bruce informed her in a really pissed-off voice, "Next time, throw some hate at 'em. Screw damaging shit."

Debbie politely said, "Fuck off. Mary is pissed that she didn't get to stick a knife in it or shoot it. Be damned if I'm going to listen to shit from either of you."

"I'm sorry, baby, please don't shoot or shank me," Bruce apologized.

"I'm not promising shit," Debbie replied, ready to beat members of her family.

In less than ten minutes, they called the house clear. Bruce, Buffy, and Mary took up watch on the back. Debbie, Jake, and David took the front. Bruce had put Mary with him since they had pissed off Debbie. He was not in the mood for Debbie to start spanking kids or him. Being honest with himself, Bruce figured he could throw the kids at her one by one, and by the time she got to him, she would be too tired to bust his ass.

Matt called them over the radio. "Raven overhead." Bruce looked up, trying to find the little plane when Matt added, "A large group of at least fifty coming down the road from the other direction."

"Anything behind the house?" Bruce asked.

"Some deer about half a mile away," Matt replied.

"Keep an eye out back here," Bruce said. "Angela, Alex, come to the back of the house, and stand guard. We're moving to the front," Bruce called over the radio as he led his group to the front.

"We have it, Bruce; stay there," Debbie popped off.

"If this is a group of runners, they will be on you before half are down."

"Well, get your ass up here, and quit talking," Debbie replied, making Bruce grin.

Arriving at the front, Bruce looked down the road to the left. He could see over four hundred yards down the road where it ended in a curve. "Jake, set up in the middle of the road. Debbie, you and your group get in the ditch on this side, my group the other side," Bruce said as he moved across the road and knelt in the ditch. "Everyone, shoot any that try to get in the ditch. Keep them on the road, and funnel them to Jake. Buffy, you watch our back. Everyone in the house, keep working, but be ready to leave."

Matt radioed, "They're almost at the curve." Bruce told Buffy to watch their back. Raising his rifle to his shoulder, Bruce sighted down the road. He only had to wait a few seconds before seeing the first blues come around the corner. In his scope, he had the distance at four hundred and eighty yards, way out of his range. Just then, he heard Jake's rifle cough and watched one drop.

Jake ran through his first twenty-round magazine fast, dropping eighteen before the entire group had even cleared the curve. Aiming toward the group, Jake would gently squeeze off shots at a steady pace until his bolt locked open. Slamming in another magazine when he ran dry, he just kept squeezing the trigger. When Jake slammed in his third magazine, Bruce brought his rifle up and looked through his scope. He only saw six more blues coming down the road. That was when David called over the radio. "Hey, Jake, save some for everyone else."

From back at base, Mike came over the radio, "David, shut the hell up. Jake, finish 'em off." The mob that had attacked them in the woods was still very fresh in Mike's mind. Jake dropped the last six in seconds. When Bruce looked back down the road, he saw no movement. The closest body was barely three hundred yards away. Jake had started the engagement at over four hundred yards and ended it three hundred yards away. Now, this was the kind of fighting Bruce could get used to. He was tired of looking the damn things in the eye.

Matt reported that nothing was even close to them now. The work crew brought out the stuff and filled the trailer up behind Steve's truck. Then the work group filled the bed of Mike's truck with clothes and stuff from the house. Once everything was loaded, they moved to the house that was under construction. Only the frame was up. Several pallets of 2x4s and plywood were stacked around. They loaded them and opened the steel container beside the house. It was full of plumbing supplies, wire, conduit, screws, and nails along with other supplies to build a house. Matt called over and said Raven had to come home for new batteries.

After hearing that, Bruce spread his security team out. He really wanted another Raven. That kind of blanket over you made you feel good. In two hours, they had loaded up everything they could, not leaving much they needed behind. The Raven was back overhead, and Matt reported all clear.

It was 10 a.m. when they pulled back into the farm. The excursion had taken less than five hours, and Matt had steered them around several groups on the way home. That little airplane was worth its weight in gold to Bruce. With that kind of intelligence, they could avoid a lot of problems.

As they walked back to the house, Debbie stopped, Bruce telling him, "Mike needs to lead the next mission out. If you don't let him, it will be slap in the face." Bruce knew Mike could do it, but if it got bad, Mike would think with his head and not his gut. Bruce trusted him with his life and the life of his family but worried about Mike when it got bad.

When they reached the house, everyone came out to hug them. Bruce turned to Mike. "Mike, prepare and prep a team by 4 p.m. for the next mission." The same group was going out except Bruce, Debbie, and Jake. Mike, Nancy, and Matt would take their place.

The rest of the day, guards in the fort shot blues that moved down the road, and warlord shot over a dozen in the east field that had moved off the road. No infected made it within a hundred yards of the farm.

True to form, Mike planned everything down to a tee for his patrol. Before they left the next morning, Bruce hugged them all, telling them to stay alert. Mike's mission was taking him twice as far away as Bruce's mission. The group left at 5:30 a.m.

Mike had told them to hold the Raven until they got closer to the scout camp. He wanted it there a few minutes before they got there and to stay on station as long as possible. Bruce just wanted the little plane in the air, giving him information. Mike tried to deploy his surveillance to maximize the time overhead on target.

As the convoy neared the camp, Mike called for the Raven. Jake launched the Raven, flew it toward the camp, and spotted a large mob heading toward the group. "Big Daddy Two, you have a large group heading at you, about fifteen miles away," he reported.

"That's okay; we will be gone in thirty minutes. We will take the alternate route home," Mike called back. Looking at his dad standing beside him, Jake sent the little plane down the road as the group pulled into the camp. It was two miles down the road when they saw another mob, this one huge, heading toward the camp. Mike and the group were cut off by two large mobs, one coming from each direction down the road.

Letting out a string of curses, Bruce called on the radio. "Big Daddy Two, you have another mob coming at you."

Bruce paused to make sure Mike heard him as Mike came over the radio. "We have time, Bruce. They can run fast, but fifteen miles."

Fighting the urge to yell, Bruce calmly keyed the radio. "Mike, shut up and listen. You have a group coming from each direction. The one following you is about a thousand. The one coming from the other way looks close to three thousand and are much closer, like two to three miles." With that, Mike told everyone to load up; they were leaving. "Mike, you can't leave. There are too many to drive through. Move your team to the field beside the parking lot, and set up a circular defense. Have the heavy weapons hit the blues in the legs, and everyone else, pop them in the head when they stand up." Looking at Debbie, Bruce told her to immediately launch the Stryker with the backup team. Mike deployed the team in the field as Bruce and those in Mission Control watched.

Not taking his eyes off the monitor, Bruce asked how much longer the Raven could stay on station, and Jake replied forty minutes. *Well, by that time, it would be over one way or another,* Bruce thought. The runners from the larger mob reached the group first, and everyone at the farm watched the battle unfold.

They watched as three people opened up with heavy machine guns, making the two hundred plus runners fall as the group picked them off while they were down. Bruce saw the runners from the smaller mob coming through the parking lot, heading down into the field. Bruce called on the radio, "Right flank runners," because no one had engaged them yet. Then on the screen, Bruce and everyone at the farm watched someone open up with a heavy machine gun on the right, knocking the fifty plus runners down, and then, the group began picking them off as they crawled toward them.

When the right flank runners were down, the large mob had made it to the field, and the group started to open fire on them. Just then, Bruce saw a tracer race across the screen and told Jake to pan the camera out. The backup Stryker was behind the smaller mob, blasting away with the 50 cal. When a 50 caliber bullet hits someone, they explode. With targets this close, each bullet was hitting three to four infected, causing them to blow up. Bruce called over the radio, "Watch your fire, Conner; you have already sent several over their head." Conner replied that he understood. They watched the Stryker blast a path through the infected to drive through. It pulled into the parking lot and down onto the field with the group.

Bruce called over the radio, "Everyone, hold your position, and don't run toward the Stryker, and try to leave, or you will die." Conner moved the Stryker beside the team as its M2 completely decimated the advancing blues then ran dry. They saw someone pop out of the turret on the monitor, reloading the fifty caliber while someone jumped out of the back of the Stryker, opening up with a heavy machine gun on the right side. Once the M2 was reloaded, the entire left flank was down, and only a few hundred were on the right. The ma deuce or M2 made real short work of them.

Mike called over the radio, "Everyone load up; we are leaving."

"Mike, you can't leave. With the noise y'all have made, we won't be able to leave the farm for weeks. Continue the mission," Bruce yelled over the radio. They could see no blues walking around them. Though a lot of infected were crawling in the field, they were not a problem. Bruce told them Raven had to come home now but to get what they had gone after. Mike copied.

Still looking at the monitor, Debbie slapped him on the shoulder. When Bruce put the mic down, Debbie yelled at him, "You tell them to come home now!" Bruce told her to shut up so he could think. Mike radioed back and said they had the trailers loaded. After thinking it over, Bruce told them to head out the direction the large mob had come from, making a large loop to pick up the septic system. Then Bruce told the Stryker team to stay with them. When they reached the house that sold septic systems, finding nobody home, they loaded four systems and equipment from the shop then started home.

Bruce sent them further out in a loop after seeing a mob building behind them. He then had the Stryker separate from the group, telling them the roads to follow. The group pulled into the farm at 5 p.m. almost out of ammunition. When the Stryker pulled back into the farm at 7 p.m., it was almost out of fuel, having traveled almost three hundred miles.

With everyone home, Bruce sent the Raven back out to fly a large circle around them. They saw several large groups to the east where the group had been, but they were all headed away from them. The closest mob was over twenty miles away and heading south. Only a few scattered infected were even close to the farm. The closest was over a mile away, chasing a deer.

The next morning, Mike found Bruce at the kitchen table before the rest of the clan woke up. Plopping down in his chair, Mike said, "I screwed the pooch on that run."

Shaking his head, Bruce stared at him. "How do you figure? You completed the mission and brought everyone home."

"Bruce, I lost control and was just fighting the battle, not leading it. Actions like that get people killed," Mike replied.

"Brother, you might have made a mistake or two, but so have I. Don't worry about. Just don't make the same mistake twice."

"I should have sent the Raven out earlier like you did. Then, we would have found the groups before we even got close to the camp. I over planned, Bruce. I don't want to take another group out."

Bruce sat there, studying his brother and best friend before replying. "Mike, if the drone had been up, we might have found them, but the mob could've changed direction and hit you elsewhere. Even worse, it might have followed you home. Hindsight is 20/20, and you can't play 'what if' in this game."

Mike shot back, "Bruce, I don't think I could live with myself if I lost someone. These are our kids and family, not troops in the military. From now on, you are in command, and I'm your second—the way it's always been."

"Let's get something straight right here and now. We are going to lose people, probably some of the family, maybe even you and me. We can only do our best, giving it everything at all times, taking only manageable risks.

Fight battles on our terms or as close to our terms as we can get them. This is the last time you and I will speak of this. If I'm in command, you will lead groups again. Now, let's go over the work schedule."

Then, they pored over the supplies, making lists for everyone to complete. Bruce could see from the look on Mike's face that it was not over, but he would fix that later. Bruce could not afford to have Mike sit on the sidelines.

Sixteen days later, at 4:30 a.m., Bruce collapsed in his chair at the kitchen table. No one was awake yet. He even beat Lynn to the kitchen. Looking down at his notepad, he replayed in his mind what they had done over the last two plus weeks.

It had taken ten days to get the loft ready for the new members of the clan. Twenty bunk beds lined the walls to the right and left with foot lockers under each one. At one end of the room was a men's restroom and at the other end a women's. Each restroom had toilets, showers, and sinks, two of each.

Paul had taken the backhoe to the machine shop and built a shroud lined with insulation over the engine and put a muffler damper on the exhaust. Unless you were within 20 yards, you couldn't hear the engine. Paul told them he had seen a man do that in Baton Rouge when he was in college studying agriculture. The man had a field beside a suburb and got several noise complaints, so he designed a way for his tractors to run quietly. They did tend to overheat, so they had to watch the temperature real close in the heat of the day. Bruce and Mike copied his design on the tractor then on several of the ATVs. That made the ATVs very quiet. You could hear the knobby tires before the engine.

Paul used the backhoe to dig the hole for the septic tanks and the hole for the A/C units for the loft. Then, he leveled an area to put up the rest of the solar panels that were stored in case of an EMP. Bruce had told everyone that if they were hit with an EMP, then it would be back to the pioneer days, and they would all die. Intelligence and technology were how they were going to outlast the blues and fight the gangs.

Bruce shook himself out of his daydream, looking down at his notepad for the day's activities. It was September now, but the heat would stay until November at least. It was not uncommon to wear shorts at Christmas here.

Today, he was leading a group to the Snead farm to give them ten M-4s, twenty Berettas, and a SAW, all with suppressors. They were also taking thirty thousand rounds of ammunition and NVGs to give them. He had watched the Snead farm with the Raven as it was slowly beginning to turn into a walled camp. They were cutting down trees to build a fence around the house and barn. Bruce could not tell how high the fence was with the Raven, but it looked well over ten foot.

The Raven was sent out two times a day, once in the morning and once at dusk to see what was close before work started and what had been attracted by the work of the day. So far, only sixty-two infected had found the farm, and all were shot before making the fence. After the area was called clear, they would take out an electric buggy or modified ATV with a trailer to load the bodies and dump them in the scrap pond. Bruce had seen several alligators in the scrap pond before the plague, but after they started throwing in bodies, holy shit. The alligators must have called their friends. Yesterday, when they had thrown in the three infected that had been shot, he could see several dozen sets of eyes across the water. The alligators must have liked them because the bodies that had been thrown in over the last few weeks were gone. Bruce hoped the virus did not affect them. Just the idea of an alligator that could run that fast made his skin crawl.

With that thought, Bruce felt something bump his arm, making him jump. Looking up, Bruce saw Lynn setting down a cup of coffee. She had scared the shit out of him. Bruce thanked her, looking at the clock and seeing it was almost 5 a.m. The rest of the clan should be up soon, and he knew several were already in the gym. He was going to wait until Mike came down before working out. Breakfast was served at 6:30 a.m., after workouts. Everyone listened to the day's briefing while they ate breakfast.

Matt and Jake were turning into quite the little intelligence team. Mission control now looked like a true command center. They had put a huge ten-by-ten foot satellite map of the fifty miles around the farm on the wall marking infected sightings, moving vehicles, and points of interest, like fuel tanks on local farms and such. They had seen several biker gangs move along Louisiana Highway 1. The range of the Raven after the boys put an antenna on the top of the barn and boosted the signal output was almost forty miles out, then it had to come home. It was not the signal that was the limiting factor now; it was the battery life. When they found the limit a few days ago, the Raven did not make it back home but landed on the road a mile from the farm. Bruce and the boys jumped into the Beast, driving like a bat out of Hell to get the precious equipment. The normal range was only line of sight or roughly seven miles. Leave it to the two computer geniuses to improve that.

The next time the boys sent out the Raven, he told them to send it to the dam. Bruce wanted to check out the military check point. Since the check point was twenty miles away, it took several trips to video the entire area. At the west end of the dam was a large collection of military and police vehicles. On the north side of the road was a large collection of civilian vehicles. Bodies surrounded the entire site with the largest pile from the road leading to the dam. Nothing other than animals had moved at the scene in the four days they had watched it.

It was the military vehicles that Bruce wanted, two HEMTTs, three Strykers, four Hummers, and one RG-33L. The RG-33L was a monster of a vehicle, weighing in at twenty-eight tons. It was a 6x6 MRAP or mine-resistant ambush protected. Twelve troops could sit in the back and look out of bullet-resistant windows. The HEMTTs were cargo haulers, and both were loaded down. With what, he didn't know. Also, Bruce knew if the position was overrun, then the equipment should still be lying around. With the clan giving the Snead farm all the extra M-4s, they needed replacements, and new equipment never hurt anyone. Not to mention Bruce wanted more toys. Bruce also did not want a gang to take the equipment. He knew there was military equipment lying around everywhere, but this was too close and needed to be secured for the clan.

They would bring back all the military vehicles, but if the HEMTTs were loaded with crap, then they would leave them. Bruce figured it would take them several hours to gather all the equipment and jump off all the military vehicles. He had called Marcus yesterday and told him to expect company at 8:30 a.m. He told Marcus they would call and give him the name of his wife before turning into his farm in case someone was listening on the CB. Marcus said he understood.

Bruce was taking a team of twenty-one in both of the SUVs and the kid mobile SUV, all with trailers. Mike, Debbie, and Nancy were going to the Snead farm to drop off supplies and to check on their status in Nancy's SUV with a trailer. They were going to stay at the Snead farm for two hours then come to the dam, drop off Nancy's SUV, and take one of the loaded

SUVs home to make sure the road was clear. When the area was loaded up, the vehicles unloading the police cars would head back across the dam to the farm. The rest of the military convoy would head the opposite way, making an eighty-mile loop around the lake back to the farm.

Bruce would love to just travel back across the dam, but there were twenty-seven patrol cars parked on it behind the checkpoint. That was too many cars to move, and the vehicles they were bringing back made a lot of noise. The Stryker was quiet for a military vehicle, but as quiet as the world was now, it could be heard from a mile away. Bruce had never been around the RG-33L, but it just looked loud, and he *knew* the HEMTTs were loud.

Mike walked up beside him, casting a shadow over his notebook as Bruce was making notes. "Let's go, little girl. It's time to work out. It's going to be a big day, so you can go get more toys," Mike said with a grin.

"Toys," Bruce said, throwing his pen down and standing. "We need that equipment, so quit your bitching, and put your skirt and high heels on because we're going shopping. Daddy needs new shoes." He walked out to the gym.

"I only wear my high heels for Nancy, baby. You're not that special," Mike said, following him out.

"Damn, and I thought I was goin' to get you dressed up sexy tonight." Bruce put his arm across Mike's shoulders.

"Maybe some other time," Mike said as he opened the door, and they went into the gym to start their morning workout.

CHAPTER 3

Bruce was in his room, checking his equipment over. He had removed the pistol drop holster on his right leg and made a holster for the P90. He still had the XDM with its suppressor on the left side of his vest in the cross draw holster. He had four magazines for the P90 strapped to the front of his right leg. He took off the four magazine MOLLE pouch on the right side of his vest and put on a six magazine pouch. Then Bruce, added another six magazine holder to his left leg drop platform, giving him eighteen magazines for his SCAR. After the mob in the woods, Bruce wanted to make damn sure they had ammo. Making sure his weapons were good, he motioned Buffy over to him.

Buffy walked up to him dressed in tiger stripe BDUs, like his, and little combat boots. All of it used to be Danny's, just like the little tactical vest. He had taken her magazine carrier and mounted it on the front of her vest, and she had a four magazine pouch on her left thigh. Now, she carried fourteen magazines for her UMP submachine gun plus the one in it. She had her Glock 17 compact pistol on her right in a drop holster with a suppressor in a pouch on the holster. It used to be Debbie's concealed carry gun, and Bruce had put the threaded barrel on it for her. Buffy still had the switch blade he had given her clipped on her left shoulder.

Scanning over her equipment, Bruce made her jump up and down to see if she made noise. When she didn't, Bruce smiled at her. Her hair was pulled back into a pony tail as she looked up at him, returning the smile. Bruce told her to put on her tinted safety glasses, and like her gloves, she was not to take them off unless it got dark. Then, she was to put on the clear ones. Grabbing her glasses, Buffy put them on and tightened the lanyard. Making sure her earbud for the radio stayed in place and her glasses were secure, she looked back at Bruce. Bruce picked up Buffy's boonie hat and set it on her head, smiling at her.

"You ready, BB?" Bruce asked. He had started calling her BB for Buffy Baby, and she loved it.

"Let's get some, Daddy," she said.

"Hopefully not, but let's be ready just in case. Grab your pack, and come on. Until we get back, you stay at my side unless I tell you different," Bruce said, and she gave him a thumbs up.

Buffy picked up her pack, which also used to be Danny's. It was a small, black, tactical backpack with a Camelback in it. It held extra magazines, ammo, and a couple of FSR meal packs for emergencies along with a few other items. Bruce's pack held the same, just with more. He was carrying what he called an assault pack; it was heavy on ammo. Picking up his pack, they headed outside.

When they got to the vehicles, Matt and Jake were there waiting on him. They were staying and were in charge until Mike and his team got back. Tonya was going to stay in the fort with one other person also until the group returned. Matt and Jake did not like being left behind but understood the need to have them here. Jake came up to Bruce as he threw his pack in the Beast and turned around to look at Jake.

"Dad, the area is clear. There can't be more than twenty blues in a thirty-mile radius. We sent the Raven to the dam and seen several people at the Snead farm but no blues. The check point is the same: no movement except a lot 'a dogs eating the corpses. It's really weird," Jake said, concerned. There were usually over a hundred in the area.

"Well, wherever they moved, I hope they build a house and stay there. Blues suck as neighbors," Bruce said.

"Oh, hell no. If they start building houses, I'm moving to the arctic tundra," Jake said.

"Yeah, I'll probably be there with ya. When was your last flight?"

"Fifteen minutes ago."

"Keep the flights between here and the Snead farm, and once every three hours, make a loop around the area. No one is to be outside unless you or Matt approve it," Bruce said.

"Are you kiddin'? Everyone is already in Mission Control waiting to see how everything goes," Matt said, standing beside Jake.

Bruce hugged both of the boys as Danny walked up. She had on the same style BDUs and tactical vest. Her Glock 17 was in a cross draw holster with a suppressor attached. On her right thigh was an Uzi with a suppressor.

"What are you trying to be, an Israeli storm trooper, sweet pea?" Bruce asked since both the Uzi and Galil were from Israel.

"Not my fault they know how to make good weapons. Besides, there're no more P90s. Mom took the last one," Danny said.

"Sweet pea, Daddy'll get you a P90. Are you ready otherwise? It's going to be a long, hot day."

"Thank you, Daddy. This Uzi weighs a ton with the suppressor, but yeah, I'm ready," Danny said, hugging Bruce with difficulty because of all the weapons and gear.

Bruce said, "That's why teams knuckle bump while wearing gear." He keyed his radio. "Remember, the equipment we're getting is contaminated keep your gloves and glasses on. Don't touch any exposed skin. Radio check, sound off by numbers."

Everyone counted off their assigned number with Buffy answering last with twenty-one. Bruce called Mike and asked him if they were ready. Mike didn't answer but held out his arm, giving a thumb up. Bruce told everyone to load up over the radio then told Buffy to sit on the console between the front seats. With people and gear crammed in each vehicle, there was no extra room. As Bruce pulled out, he called radio check to Mission Control and got the loud and clear reply. Pulling out, Mike was driving Nancy's SUV, David was driving Debbie's SUV, Steve was driving the kid mobile SUV, all were pulling trailers, and Bruce was leading them in the Beast with Danny driving.

Keeping the speed at forty miles per hour, Bruce called Mike. "Don't forget to call Marcus and tell him his wife's name is Carroll."

"I will, and be careful. If things get bad, you better leave. We will find you some more toys," Mike said. Bruce said he would and signed off.

The soldiers were with them, so there was no one to come rescue them. Bruce had no choice; he needed the soldiers with them. He was sure that the batteries in the vehicles were dead. All military vehicles had what was called a slave cable. It was large cable that plugged into one vehicle then into another, nothing more than a fancy jumper cable. The plug was the same on all vehicles, so a Hummer could jump off an M-1 Abrams.

Everyone had been assigned a vehicle to leave in, and those who were driving had been taught on the ones at the farm. Two of the Strykers were going to have manned weapons along with one Hummer in case the shit hit the fan. Fifteen were staying with the military vehicles, and six were driving the SUVs and Beast back.

Bruce passed the parish road leading to the Snead farm at 8:18 a.m., and Mike at the tail of the convoy turned down the road. Bruce heard Mike over the radio. "Marcus, your wife's name is Carroll. See you in five."

"Copy, boys at the gate," Marcus replied.

Bruce would love to see his friends again, but they needed those weapons and vehicles on the dam. He continued on for another ten miles then slowed down to twenty mph as he reached the dam. He called over the C/B to Mission Control since the radio was out of range.

"Sunny sky," Bruce called out.

"Clear sky, one cloud seen five miles south of weather station, stationary," Matt replied. The code was in case someone was listening in on the radio. Clear sky meant nothing by the road. One infected was seen five miles south of the Snead farm and was not moving.

"Thanks for the weather report. Call if changes. Out," Bruce replied, pulling onto the dam.

When he was fifty yards from the last of the patrol cars, Bruce told Danny to let the convoy pass. Opening his door, Bruce motioned them around, and they turned the SUVs around, backing up, which was not an easy feat. Turning around on the dam with a trailer was nearly impossible, but they did it. David stopped twenty feet from the last car in Debbie's SUV, and Steve had backed up the kid mobile SUV beside it. Motioning everyone to get out, Bruce reached back to get his backpack as the smell of decomposed bodies hit him like a brick wall. It was a close call if the blues stunk more alive or dead.

Steve's group got out and started emptying the patrol cars, loading the trailers. Bruce's group headed to the military vehicles. Walking by the police cars, Bruce noticed state cars and several from other jurisdictions. One even looked like a federal car. There were police Suburbans and pickup trucks and even two motorcycles. Those assigned to Bruce moved in single file behind him to the military vehicles.

When they reached the road block, Bruce stopped and looked around. Guns were lying everywhere. Except for a dozen or so infected inside the ring of military vehicles, there were no bodies. Bruce sent Danny, Mary, and David out on watch and told everyone to start gathering equipment. Just looking around, Bruce saw twenty M-4s easy.

Leaving his group to gather them, Bruce went to the area to the right of the checkpoint, where they had seen the civilian cars. Walking closer, he saw a huge pile of something under a tree. Getting closer, he realized they were guns. The pile was almost as tall as he was and thirty yards around. *There must be thousands of them*, Bruce thought, feeling all tingly. Looking closer, he realized they were all civilian weapons, not military. Fuck it, they were taking these also, and Bruce called the group on the radio. "I just found a small mountain of guns, and we're takin' 'em."

"What about what's in those vehicles?" Stephanie asked, pointing to the cars parked off the side of the road.

Bruce turned and looked across the sea of cars and trucks. There was over a thousand easy. "Too many to check out. I'm gonna check the area out here real quick. Keep on task," Bruce called. Everyone copied.

Looking at the rows of parked vehicles, Bruce noticed a brand new black Chevy 2500 diesel quad cab parked by itself. He walked over admiring it, almost drooling. It had a huge front bumper with a winch, at least a 4-inch lift, and huge Super Swamper tires. Bruce had always wanted one, but these damn things cost over eighty grand stripped, and this one was loaded. Walking around it, he saw it still had the window sticker on the passenger window and almost passed out at the price with all the extras. Yeah, that's why he always bought used. Walking to the driver's door, he pulled on the handle, expecting it to be locked, but it opened. The key in ignition chime started. He looked, and sure enough, there was a dealer key with two sets of keys and remotes. Grabbing the keys, Bruce put them in his back pocket. He was so coming back for this one day.

Grinning with his find, Bruce turned around and started walking through the sea of cars with Buffy following like she was told and, as always, on his left side. Hearing something, Bruce stopped and listened carefully, swearing he heard gunfire from far off. "Anyone hear that?" Bruce called.

"It's gun fire comin' from the other side of the lake. It's at least ten miles away," Steve reported over the radio.

Bruce continued his sweep of the cars, trying to make sense of the area. From his best guess, the guards stopped people and took their weapons from them. Then, they took them behind the patrol cars to be picked up and transported. But picked up by what and transported where? Bruce gave up trying to be a detective and walked back to the checkpoint.

Looking at the area in front of the Strykers and Hummers that formed the check point perimeter, it was piled high with bodies, but the road had very few bodies. *The Strykers must have cleared it between engagements,* Bruce thought. Turning around, he headed to the HEMTTs to see what was on them. Reaching the first one, Bruce saw it had ten pallets on it. Climbing up on the bed, he pulled Buffy up then made a small hole in the plastic shrink wrap on the first pallet. Bruce saw it was 5.56 ammunition. He didn't even check the rest. Instead, Bruce jumped to the other HEMTT's bed and did the same to the last pallet and found it was fifty caliber ammo. He called over the radio and said both HEMTTs were coming. Campbell and Kenner would drive them since they had driven them before.

Bruce keyed his radio. "Conner, see which vehicles need to be slaved off. I'm heading to the RG-33L."

Conner replied, "Okay," as Bruce jumped off the HEMTT. Walking up to the monster-sized 6x6 truck, Bruce stared in wonder. He wanted to drive it through a house just because it could. Walking behind it, Bruce saw the rear hatch was open, so he climbed up the steps to find the back was full of backpacks and ammo cans. "Buffy, climb over this crap, and open the front doors if they are locked," he said in case the combat lock was on.

As Buffy crawled over the equipment, Bruce walked to the driver's door and found it opened up when he tried it. Bruce climbed in just as Buffy made it to the front. She was looking at the big truck in amazement. Bruce looked at his watch, and they had been there for two hours.

"Does it really drive, Daddy?" she asked, looking around the truck in wonder.

"Yes it does, Buffy, and we're drivin' it home," Bruce said, looking at the controls.

"Can we run over somethin'?" she asked with hope in her eyes.

"Maybe," Bruce replied, smiling. She may not be his child by birth, but she damn sure was in spirit. He flipped the toggle switch on, and the panel lights came on. The battery was still charged, and the glow plugs were warming up. Bruce waited for them to warm up then turned the switch off. He radioed Conner and said the RG was ready to go.

Conner replied, "Only one Hummer is ready. The Strykers and the other three Hummers had radios left on. The batteries are dead, and have ta be slaved. Both HEMTTs are live and ready. We'll use the one Hummer to slave off the one beside it. Next, we will use those two to slave off the other Hummers. Then, three Hummers will slave off the Strykers at the same time while one stays on watch."

"Copy that. How much longer till the pile of guns by the cars is collected?" Bruce asked.

"That pile alone will take several hours, boss. I don't know if we can get all of them. The Hummers and Strykers are loaded with packs, gear, and ammo along with the stuff we are puttin' in them. There won't be much room left," Conner explained, and Bruce told him to hold.

"Steve, how many trailers will the cop cars fill up?" Bruce asked over the radio.

"One trailer is almost loaded. We might need half of one of the other trailers."

"Big Daddy Two, we are ready for you. Do ya copy?" Bruce radioed Mike.

"Copy, Big Daddy One. We was just fixin' to call you. Family here says they miss ya," Mike replied.

"Copy, tell 'em I'll come and see 'em soon," Bruce said.

"We're rolling to you now," Mike called.

"Little foot, call and get a weather report," Bruce radioed Angela. Looking around, he saw Stephanie walking among the piles of infected, picking up weapons and taking pictures. Watching her, Bruce wanted to tell her that this wasn't a sightseeing tour; they had work to do. Just as he was about to radio Stephanie, Angela came over the radio.

"Big Daddy One, sky is still clear. Small clusters of clouds to the east of outpost moving north. No clouds near weather station. You copy?" No infected were near the Snead farm.

"Copy, Little Foot," Bruce said then called Steve.

"Son number one, how many more presents do ya have left?" Bruce asked.

"Only a few more presents left," Steve replied

"When Big Daddy Two gets here, we're gonna form a line to transfer the pile of goodies here to the sleds. You copy?" Bruce called out as he looked around.

"Copy. Big Daddy Two is here. We're moving around back here, and he's comin' to ya real quick," Steve replied.

"Copy. I see him. Get all your teams, and start a relay to move the goodie pile. Leave two people to clear the rest of the presents out of the cars."

Steve said he understood as Mike walked up to him.

"Hey, brother, just wanted to tell ya Eric and Darrell were out raiding empty houses yesterday along the south side of the lake and saw a mob of thousands pass them. It took over three hours for the mob to pass them by. There has been gun fire and explosions on the north end of the lake. They think that's where they were headed. So don't go around the lake. Just rough calculations, they were puttin' the number close to ten thousand," Mike said, making a shiver run up Bruce's spine.

"No shit. We will take the short way home and pray we don't hit a parade that size on the way," Bruce said, wondering what a group that size was doing out in the middle of nowhere.

"Didn't want to say anything over the radio in case bad guys might be listening. We're staying here to help. Three more bodies means we can move that much faster."

"Well, let's get moving then," Bruce said, jumping down and joining the relay line.

By two o'clock, they had finished, and Bruce told everyone to drink some water then move to the vehicle they were riding in. Paul called him over the radio and said he needed to talk to him. Bruce told him to meet up at the RG. As Bruce drank the last of his water from the Camelback, he threw his pack in the front cab. When Buffy had finished hers, he threw hers in as Paul came up to him.

"Bruce, I want to take my family to the house and grab some of our stuff please," Paul asked as Cheryl and Chad stood beside him. Bruce looked at the family, knowing he would ask the same thing if the roles were reversed. But he had to think of the group's safety also.

"Paul, we are leaving here in thirty minutes. That's how long Conner says it will take to slave off all the vehicles. If you get into trouble, I'll only be able to send one Hummer to help, and if it meets a large mob, it will have to back out and leave you. We're spread too thin in a lot of vehicles, and we need the supplies we've gathered."

"If we see anything, we'll bug out, but we accept the risk. So can we go please?" Paul asked with a pleading look.

"Down there in that group of cars is my new truck. It's a black Chevy 2500. Take that, but please don't hurt it, okay? You have until the vehicles are ready. Then, we're leaving with or without you. With this many diesel engines running, it's bound to attract attention that we do not want." Bruce told him and handed Paul the keys he pulled out of the truck.

"We'll see you in twenty minutes," Paul said as he grabbed the keys and took off running to the truck with his family behind him.

"Son Number One, three of your return parties are making a side trip. Have Mama ride with you, Little Foot and her other half together in another vehicle. Big Daddy Two and wife will ride together. David and Danny will still lead y'all in the Beast. I want you gone in five minutes; do ya copy?" Bruce ordered over the radio.

"Copy. We are rolling in five minutes. Good luck, Big Daddy One," Steve replied as Bruce watched the big Chevy pull out to the road and head to Paul's house.

"Corporal, start the slaving now," Bruce told Conner.

In fifteen minutes, all the Hummers were running. It took another twenty to get the Strykers running. During that time, seven runners had shown up along with a large group of joggers, and all were cut down. Bruce was on the radio telling everyone to load up when he saw Paul and his family return. The bed of the pickup was full of stuff. When Bruce started the RG, he could almost see the ground shake. He pulled forward, telling everyone they were taking the alternate route and that he had the lead. Bruce told Paul to get between the two flatbeds as he pulled forward.

He headed west to Highway 71. When he reached it, he turned south, heading home. When Bruce came around a blind corner, he saw a mob of a hundred or so walking down the road. Seeing the vehicles, they started moving toward the convoy. Bruce called contact and floored the RG. He didn't even feel the impact as he centered the mob. They had moved right at him, not even trying to get out of the way. What he missed, the Strykers and HEMTTs got. In his rear-view mirror, he only saw four or five still standing. He was glad Paul had not hit any in his truck. Bruce turned to look at Buffy, who was just shaking her head.

"What?" Bruce asked.

"They're crazy as a shit house rat, Daddy. They just ran right at this big truck," Buffy said, looking out the window.

"That's what worries me. They have no fear, BB. If they were afraid, they would avoid us," Bruce said as he continued down the road, heading home.

CHAPTER 4

It took three days to unload the vehicles from the checkpoint. They had to make a lot of crates for all the weapons. Then, they numbered each one and stacked them in the bottom of the barn after each weapon was wiped down in oil. Keeping his promise, Bruce gave Danny a P90 from one of the police cars. Then, Buffy started whining she wanted one too, so she got one. Bruce got four more SCARs from the escapade. Three were selective fire, found in the squad cars. The other was a single shot like his used to be. His and Mike's now fired single shot, three round burst and full auto, using the equipment from the buried cases.

They had scored big time with the convoy. They now had over half a million rounds of 5.56 alone. Ammunition could now be measured in tons. One of the pallets held a crate of AT-4s, which were rocket launchers used to take out armor or fortifications. From the Strykers, they pulled out ten Javelins, fire-and-forget rocket launchers. Once one locked on a target and fired, it would chase it down. It could take out an Abrams tank. In the back of the RG were two cases; one held another Raven, and the other held a Puma. The Puma was a larger micro UAV, but you could move the camera in flight instead of turning the whole plane to look at a target. To Bruce, those alone made the trip worth it.

The convoy had attracted a lot of attention from the blues but only forty-six found the farm. Those were quickly shot and fed to the growing gator population. It started raining the day after they finished storing equipment, so everyone stayed inside, learning weapons. Bruce had everyone get an M-4, and several had the M-4A1. The military M-4 came standard with a 14.5-inch barrel unlike the civilian one, which had a 16-inch barrel. Bruce told everyone in the family they had to get two military

M-4s and one had to be an A1. The A1 had a heavier barrel and could be fired on full auto instead of three round burst.

Now, they had fourteen 40 mm grenade launchers and hundreds of rounds of, HE (high explosive), HEDP (high explosive dual purpose), tear gas, some XM1060 thermobaric grenades, and even buckshot rounds but no practice rounds. That was why only the people who had fired the M-203 were given one. The three soldiers each had one, and Paul had one. Mike and Bruce each had two, one on their SCARs and one on an M-4A1. Everyone would train on the M-203 but not fire it. Shooting the weapon was not really loud, but the grenade exploding did make a little noise. Bruce had never fired the thermobaric grenade since it was new to the inventory, and he was really fighting the urge to. When Danny found out she couldn't shoot the grenade launcher, she started throwing a fit. After Debbie had calmed her down, Debbie gave Bruce the "look."

"Your child," she told him as if that explained everything.

They did not find many pistols at the checkpoint on the ground like they did rifles. Bruce figured from the rifles and packs there had been fifty-five army personnel at the checkpoint. Then, he figured about fifty cops with them. They had only gathered thirty pistols, most being police issue. He figured that number should be doubled at least.

This did not include the mountain of weapons that had been taken from civilians. In that mountain, they had gotten over three thousand two hundred rifles and shotguns. Everything from high quality civilian assault rifles to black powder muskets in hundreds of different calibers. There were over sixteen hundred pistols: again, everything from high quality weapons to pieces of crap. From pea shooters to hand cannons. Also in that pile were hundreds of pounds of ammunition in everything from Wal-Mart bags, boxes, ammo storage boxes, and loose rounds on the ground. The calibers the clan did not use went in boxes and were moved to a storage shed. Some of the weapons from the pile Bruce had only seen pictures of, and others he had never even heard of.

They had put all the high quality weapons in the basement in racks they had made. It turned the open area of the basement into a maze. Bruce issued everyone a pistol because now, everyone had tactical gear. He told those not trained on the pistol yet not to load it until they were trained on them. He would make suppressors for them later.

Lynn did voice her opinion about giving the kids pistols. "Bruce, I can understand about the rifles, but pistols are much more dangerous. The kids could hurt themselves or others."

"Lynn, the days of childhood are gone. The kids have to learn how to fight and survive just to live. What if we're attacked, and something happens to us, and they manage to escape? If we don't teach them, we're killing them. The same as if you took a gun and shot 'em yourself." Looking at the kids, Bruce said, "Anyone caught playing with a weapon will be beaten. Then, they will be the gimp's bitch for a month. I don't care if it is child or adult."

Lynn looked at Bruce in shock as she replied, "That's a little harsh, but you're right. I didn't look at it from that point of view." Bruce was glad she agreed because that woman could cook, and he wanted her to keep doing it. With her doing the cooking, it freed up a lot of people to do other things.

It rained three straight days, then one afternoon at lunch, Bruce made an announcement. They were moving some of the vehicles off of the farm to the dead end area of the road, and tonight was movie night for the clan. Both the HEMTTs and the convenience store gang's trucks were going to be left down there because it was getting a little crowded, and they served no useful purpose. After the vehicles were moved and everyone was back at the farm, preparations started for movie night.

Only those on watch didn't come to watch movies in the game room on Mike and Bruce's high definition projector. After the first movie, they stopped and ate supper then returned to watch another. It was such a big success in boosting morale that Bruce declared every Saturday night would be movie night.

The next morning, everyone was eating breakfast and relaxing. Bruce had told everyone that Sunday was a day of rest if nothing came up. Workouts were not required even though most did, just later in the day.

Bruce was eating and making notes in his notebook when Stephanie called his name from the middle of the table. It wasn't until Debbie kicked him under the table that he finally looked up. "That hurt, damn it," Bruce said, glaring at Debbie as he rubbed his leg.

"Stephanie has called your name several times, baby. It's my job to keep you alert," Debbie said as she continued to eat.

Bruce grumbled at Debbie then turned to Stephanie. "Yes, Stephanie?"

"I'm ready to give my report now. How about this afternoon in the game room?" she asked.

"Sounds good to me. Let's say one o'clock after lunch," Bruce said.

"Okay, I will get ready," Stephanie said, getting up.

After lunch, Bruce went into the game room for the briefing. On the small table between his and Mike's recliners was a projector aimed at a sheet on the wall. Bruce sat down in his recliner as everyone found a place to sit. He took out his notebook to make notes and questions to ask Mike later because he was sure he wouldn't understand much of what was said.

Stephanie walked up to the front and set a stack of papers on the coffee table. "Can everyone hear me okay?" she asked. Everyone said they could; even two voices from the intercom replied.

"First, I want to tell Matt and Jake thank you for getting the information from my e-mail account. Before anyone asks, yes, some of the net is still up, but we only have connection here via satellite, and there are people trying to trace signals down. We don't know if it's government or someone else, but when Matt and Jake went to my e-mail, someone tried to track them. Whoever it was tracking them was not able to, so we are safe. Until the tech team says so, no one is allowed online." She saw happy faces that at least others were out there. It was going to break her heart to kill that little bit of hope.

"The tech team downloaded my account that a colleague at the CDC, Sandy, sent. It is the information about all the research that was being done on the blue virus. It has been over a month since the outbreak began. After I left the CDC, Sandy agreed to send research information every day. She did until a few days ago. Since then, nothing. We should assume the CDC is down."

Stephanie continued, "Now, let me start on the virus. The virus—" she stopped as Bruce spoke.

"Hold on a second there, pretty woman. I want you to explain this virus and infection using words that don't make me feel like a dumbass. Just use words I can understand." Mike, Nancy, and Debbie stared at Bruce with astonishment on their faces.

"Bruce, you are not a dumbass, so what are you talking about?" Stephanie asked, looking at Bruce.

"Stephanie, when you start talking about viruses and DNA, you use words I can't even find in a dictionary. Well, I might could if I could spell 'em. Molecular density of the helix strand, the 'whatever' transfers to the 'do hicky' to change the genetic makeup and code for that gene complex. I can understand the verbs and conjunctions you use. After listening to you talk, I run to Mike, Nancy, or Debbie to get them to explain what the hell you said. I've even bought several books to try to get a grip on what you're saying, but I'm still lost," Bruce admitted out loud for the first time. He could not understand something that he had tried to learn.

Debbie got up from the couch, ran over, and jumped in his lap, hugging Bruce while Mike was patting his shoulder. "I'm so proud of you, stud muffin. In the lifetime we've been together, you finally admitted you didn't understand something for the first time," Debbie said, kissing him.

"What, you're proud I'm a dumbass and no matter what I try, I can't wrap my brain around the molecular world? It's too small for that much crap to be taking place. Once you go smaller than a single cell, it gets complicated for me," Bruce said, disgusted with himself. He had not wanted to admit it out loud, but he really wanted to know what they were up against with the virus.

"Bruce, other than Stephanie, you are the smartest person I have ever met. You commit things to memory easily and know lots of information. You can explain how a medication works to someone, take apart a car and put it back together, cook a gourmet meal, then fight a battle. I'm proud you admitted that you're human, baby," Debbie said.

"You mean in the four, almost five years I have known you, all the times we have talked about my work, you did not understand, Bruce?" Stephanie asked with shock on her face. "You know everything; why didn't you tell me sooner? I would never make you feel bad on purpose, Bruce," Stephanie said, on the verge of tears.

Mike looked at Stephanie as he was holding Bruce's shoulder, proud of him. "Stephanie, it has nothing to do with you, baby. I've watched Bruce read those books and throw them in disgust. Last year, he took two books, Physics of Atoms and Molecules and Advance Molecular Biology, on our hunt to Canada. I watched him over the period of four days try to read both books in a huntin' blind, waiting on a bear. When he was three quarters of the way through one and half-way through the other, Bruce started ripping pages out, yellin' the whole time. Then, he burned the pages along with the books as our guide just stared at the crazy man. Not one time did Bruce ask me for help. Bruce wants to teach himself and understand somethin' on his own."

"I wondered what happened to those books. They were pretty good," Nancy said to herself.

"Oh yeah, just rub it in, Nancy, that I'm an idiot that should be kept in the basement wearing a rubber helmet, playing with crayons," Bruce snapped.

"Bruce, if you think I understand everything Stephanie says, you're so wrong, ninety-nine percent of the people on the planet don't understand the molecular world. I only understand the nuts and bolts of what she says. Then, I research what I don't understand, big man," Nancy told him.

"Those damn books might as well be written in hieroglyphics to me," Bruce replied, pissed off that everyone knew he was a dumbass now.

"I never meant to make you feel bad, Bruce. Please believe me. I would have helped you to understand me," Stephanie said with tears in her eyes. She loved this family more than her own. They always treated her like one of their own. Bruce was her idol. He treated her the same as everyone else. He taught her how to shoot, change a tire, hunt, fish, and so much more.

Debbie got off Bruce's lap as Nancy got up from the couch, and they went to Stephanie. "This is a boy thing, Stephanie, and Bruce is the king of the boys' club. Until you came, he thought he could learn anything on his own. He doesn't realize that it's a lot easier to be taught something by someone who knows the subject. In college, he would read the night before class until he understood the next day's lecture. When he got to class, it was only to reinforce what he'd already learned. He graduated with a 3.7, but if he would've asked for help sometimes, he would've had a 4.0. Most men have that stubborn streak of not wanting to admit that they can't understand everything. Bruce's streak is just a mile wide. That is why most men don't read instructions; they just do it," Debbie said.

"Mike had it, but medical school knocked that out of him real fast," Nancy said.

"That's no shit. The four years of college in pre-med, I just bulled my way through, but the four years of med school and the information you have to take in made me humble very fast," Mike admitted. "We all knew Bruce was lost every time you talked about your work. Bruce would come up to one of us later and steer the topic toward what you had talked about. We would then tell him our understanding of it," Mike added.

"Why didn't you tell me? So I could have tried to explain it a different way?" Stephanie asked.

"Because you would've tried to teach someone who has never admitted until today that he didn't understand the details of the topic. Don't get me wrong; he understands a lot more now about the molecular world since you came along. Like my mama said, 'You can lead a horse to water, but you can't make him drink,'" Debbie said.

"So now I'm a dumbass horse," Bruce said dryly.

Mike jumped out of his chair and turned toward Bruce. "If you refer to yourself as a dumbass one more time, we are fixing to fight. Not spar or wrestle but a knock-down, drag-out right here," Mike yelled, balling up his fist. Everyone close by cleared the area, seeing the anger on Mike's face. "You are a Ranger, trained sniper, and a registered nurse. Then, you taught yourself to be a gunsmith, mechanic, carpenter, machinist, landscaper, the list goes on and on. You read one fucking book on how to make bio-diesel then go to the barn and in one day made a machine to do it. Everyone in this family looks at you like the greatest thing since mayonnaise, including me. I have never met or heard of anyone as smart as you until Stephanie came along. For you to say we would hold a dumbass in such high regard pisses me the fuck off!" Mike yelled, looking at Bruce.

Looking at Mike, Bruce thought he was about to tote a gold medal ass whooping. He never knew they looked at him like that; he was just Bruce. He always considered himself the least intelligent one of the group. Bruce realized that Mike was mad because Bruce had degraded himself not because he didn't understand something. "I'm sorry I made you mad, Mike," Bruce said, looking down at his lap, hoping Mike wouldn't start the beat down.

Mike let out a puff of air, thankful he was not going to have to fight Bruce and get his ass kicked. "Bruce, you are only human, brother, and you were the only one who did not know it. Bruce Wayne Williams, you are a hero to this family and to this clan. People do not take kindly to their heroes being put down even by the hero himself. I would kill to be like you, brother, and I do try, but the mold was destroyed after you were made."

Bruce stood and embraced Mike in a bear hug, which Mike returned. "I love you, brother," Bruce said.

"I love you too, brother," Mike said. Bruce let Mike go and walked over to Stephanie, who was still being held by Debbie and Nancy. They let

Stephanie go as Bruce came over, wrapped his arms around her, and pulled her to his chest.

"I'm sorry. I didn't mean to hurt your feelings," he said.

"I would never intentionally make you feel stupid, Bruce. I promise. I would die first," Stephanie said, looking up at him.

Bruce looked at her tear-streaked face, explaining, "It's a guy thing called 'pride.' Us guys like to think we can at least learn everything. We don't like to admit we can't."

"Well, you should start wearing a bra and drop some testosterone. If I had known how it made you feel, I would've never spoken about my work. You do believe me; don't you?" Stephanie asked.

"Yes, I know you would never hurt anyone's feelings in this family. As for wearing a bra, I'm gonna decline. I swallowed my pride today for the first time admitting I couldn't do something in front of others. Now, I want you to start this briefing, okay?" Bruce said, kissing her on the forehead.

"Okay," Stephanie said as Bruce let her go. Debbie hugged him as he turned around, and Nancy hugged him from the back.

"We are so proud of you, baby," Debbie told him.

"I almost choked to death swallowing that much pride," Bruce said.

"That's okay; we could've saved you," Nancy said.

Bruce kissed Debbie then turned to Nancy, kissing her on the head. Then, he walked back toward his chair. When he reached it, he stepped over to Mike, who had sat back down. Reaching down fast, Bruce grabbed both sides of Mike's face, kissing him on the lips. Mike struggled to push him back. Finally breaking the embrace, he started to spit in the air.

"You used tongue, dude," Mike hollered as everyone started laughing.

After the laughter died down, Bruce said, "I just wanted you to really know I love you too."

"You can't kiss me like that in front of the wives. Only when we're alone. In front of them, just pass me a love letter," Mike said, sending everyone into another round of laughter.

Bruce sat back down in his chair, looking around at everyone. When he got to Angela, she was just staring at him. "What?" he asked her.

"Bruce, it's not just here. Everyone at the hospital knows and respects you. If someone wants to know something or wants something done, then the answer is usually 'find Bruce.' I always knew you and Mike were great, but on the trip here, if you had walked on water, I wouldn't have been surprised. It's refreshing to know you're human after all," Angela said.

"Well, now you know," Bruce said, smiling.

"I think I can speak for everyone here when I say we don't want to be led by someone who is perfect. That would set the standard way too high, not that we can reach it now but at least we can see it," Angela pointed out.

"Thank you, I think, Little Foot."

"Bruce, I love you, and so does everyone else here. If you pointed at someone here and told them to go beat their head against a tree, they would do it. Everyone here for the most part would be beating their head against a tree before the thought even crossed their mind to ask why. Have you not noticed everyone that you brought here eats with their non-dominate hand, me included? The ones from the convenience store were told you said to do it, and Mike said it was to train your weak side. Train it to do what, we don't know, but we were told by the duo, so we do it," Angela said as Bruce stared at her in gratitude. Angela returned his stare and said, "Just to show you how much I love you, tonight, you can sleep with my husband."

"What?" Alex cried out as everyone started laughing again.

"Thank you, Little Foot, but Mike would get jealous if I slept with another man," Bruce said then turned to Stephanie. "Start it up, girlfriend."

Stephanie stood in front the group again and started, "First, the virus is a single-strand DNA virus. Now, before you say DNA is two strands and RNA is one strand, let me finish."

"I knew that," Bruce whispered to Mike.

"Good boy," Mike whispered back.

Stephanie looked at the two as she continued, "DNA viruses attack the cell nucleus, infecting the host DNA. Unlike any virus we have ever seen, this virus targets and invades every cell in the human body. If you want my hypothesis on how it does this, see me later. Right now, I'm only going into general terms," Stephanie said, holding up a ream of typed pages then put it back on the table.

Holy shit, Bruce thought, *she would have read that to them if I had not spoken up. Understand, hell, I would have had trouble staying awake. There is an easy three hundred pages in that stack.*

As if Mike was reading his mind, he whispered, "I owe you one."

Bruce whispered back, "We're even."

With a smirk on her face, Stephanie looked at the two of them, shaking her head, and continued, "The virus incorporates into the host DNA and changes the genetic makeup of the cell. Normally, the body would kill the cell, but it still recognizes the cell as normal. The actual cell structure and genetic makeup is changed after infection. The infected running around out there may look human, but we actually have more in common with chimps than with the infected. They are a new order of species. The rate of infection through the body is extraordinary and unlike any DNA virus known. There are fifty trillion cells in the average human body, and it takes at most three days for the virus to infect every cell. Now, as for the reason we have walkers, joggers, and runners. Walkers are infected people that turned fast, in some cases less than an hour. Let's get something clear first; those infected are alive. I know there were reports of the dead rising, but that's bullshit. The virus slows the body's metabolism, vital signs, increases muscle density, chemical makeup, and actually reverses the aging process, which I will come back to later.

"The virus attacks parts of the brain first but only the lower function areas, none of the higher function areas. Then, it goes down the line from respiratory, vascular, and so on. Now, don't think that the virus is smart when I say this. All the systems are under assault at the same time, but the lower functions of the brain turns first. By lower functions, I mean the lower portions of the brain that maintain homeostasis, our normal body metabolism. It alters the pituitary and lower portions of the brain to keep running as the body turns. Now, in a walker's case, the person turned before the virus was finished turning the whole body. Now, the virus will continue to infect the uninfected cells, but they are dying off with the decreased oxygen and the chemical change of the body. For example, a human's pH is 7.4; an infected runs at 6.2. A human will usually die at 7.0. All the chemicals in the body of the infected are off the charts and are incompatible with human life," Stephanie said, looking around.

"Now back to the walker. As the normal uninfected cells are dying off with the changes going on, the infected cells are reproducing, making new infected cells. If enough of the cells are left for a frame, the walker will survive through the infection. It all depends how many cells the virus infects to have a foundation to work with." She pushed a button on her laptop, and the projector came on, putting a picture of a dead blue on the screen.

"Look closely; there are no injuries on it. This was a walker that not enough cells were turned, and it died because like us, it takes a lot of cells to make us work. Unlike us, though, they are very hard to kill once infected. At one of the labs in the CDC, there was a severed infected head on the table. The head was alive, and it even ate a rat. It would even follow you with its eyes. Sandy told me it took seven days for it to die. When the virus takes over a cell, there are several new structures we have never seen before. We found out one stores ATP and a lot of it. ATP, or Adenosine triphosphate, is what life uses for energy. It is referred to as the currency of life, and we don't know how it does this since ATP is inherently unstable. In a normal human body, at any given time, there is roughly eight ounces of ATP. In an infected body, ATP averages over ten pounds or a hundred and sixty ounces. Humans store fat to make ATP later; infected just skip the process and store ATP. Now remember; infected run at a lower temperature, around eighty degrees, so they need less energy at rest. If you shoot an infected in the heart, it will die, if enough of the heart is destroyed, in about a week. The rest of the cells in the body have that much ATP, energy stored, to run that long without getting blood supply to make more ATP. Now, if only a small portion of heart is damaged, it will repair itself. The infected rates of healing are off the charts." Stephanie paused, letting that sink in, then continued. "I have the report right here where two runners were shot in the heart. One was shot with a shotgun, the other with a 9mm. The one shot by the shotgun died in six days; the other one actually healed. It just sat down like it went to sleep then woke up two days later, healed."

"That gives them quite an advantage," Mike admitted with a frown.

"Oh, I haven't even got to the best part yet," Stephanie said then continued. "Back to the walker on the screen, it died because there were not enough cells infected at the turning or reproducing to keep the system running. Does everyone understand so far?" She asked and saw nodding heads everywhere.

"As we understand the virus now, twenty-five percent of walkers will die eventually. It may take up to six months, but they will die. Forty percent will live and slowly develop into joggers. If they can feed, they will live. The remaining thirty-five percent will stay walkers. Now, several scientists think they will die off not being able to feed, and I disagree with this. With the slow metabolic rate, they can go a long time between meals—I mean weeks not days—and they have been observed eating bugs. So I think most will live," Stephanie said then continued.

"Now, with our current understanding of the virus, the walkers that move to a jogger cannot progress into a runner. Too much damage at the cellular level has occurred. Too many holes in the framework to be filled. An infected jogger means most of their system was turned, and up to ninety-five percent will progress into runners. Studies predict anyone taking at least ten hours to turn would develop into a jogger. What the CDC called midlevel infected, which estimates put seventy-five percent of those who were infected.

"Now, runners. First, this is what the virus is trying to reach. They are carnivores, make no doubt about it. Studies have already confirmed that their teeth are harder than ours, and the fingernails are thicker and harder than ours. Their speed is actually increasing, and pound for pound, they are three times as strong as humans. Now, I'm going to go over some of the examinations that have been run on the infected.

"Intelligence is at the animal level. No complex thought, but they do learn. They have been observed to set ambushes like lions and use stealth to kill prey. They have been observed using rocks and sticks to beat prey with like chimps but nothing more. They will even cover themselves with something when they are cold like leaves and boxes. They will not put on a coat, and once the clothes they have on are off, they stay nude. Several have been observed chewing their shoes off, not being able to untie them.

"Now about cold, they don't like it. At fifty degrees, they will group together, usually in a structure, until it warms back up. This has been tested and confirmed in a lab. They threw several infected in a large, sealed room with a small building placed inside the large room. Then, the researchers dropped the temperature, and the infected broke a window out of the small building, crawled in, and huddled in a corner together. They never used the door even after seeing someone else use it. They always went in and out the window unless of course the door was opened. Interestingly, when the door was opened, they never closed it either.

"Another part of this experiment, they froze an infected, dropping the temperature to minus twenty degrees. All signs of life were gone, no brain activity, heart, lung, nothing. Thinking they had killed it, they warmed it up, and one of the scientists was infected when she was bitten when it woke up. Only frogs and some lizards are known to do this. Frogs will flood their system with glucose before they freeze so the ice crystals do not rupture the cells. Infected glucose levels average 2,500 while humans average 80.

"Infected try to infect others to spread the disease. This is their goal. They have been videoed running up to someone, biting them, and then leaving. In China, we have started getting bad reports. The infected are purposely killing humans and no longer trying to infect. The hypothesis is they no longer see us as potential members but as competition. The same way a lion will kill a hyena and not eat it just to get rid of the competition. Now, any questions so far?" Stephanie asked.

Several hands shot up, and Stephanie pointed at Mindy, the oldest teen from the convenience store. "Do they remember anything from before they turned?" Mindy asked in a small voice.

"No, the higher cognitive areas of the brain are dead. After they turn, it's like they were just born. Nothing of the previous person remains," Stephanie said then asked for the next question, and no one asked anything.

Stephanie continued, "Now, infected are more active at night, like most predators, but will hunt during the day. Runners' night vision are a lot better than ours. We do not know how, but they seem to be able to detect heat in the visual field. Scientists took a runner, burned its nasal passage and ruptured both ear drums, then put it in a dark room with a dog. If the dog stayed still, the infected could find it, but when the dog moved, the infected could not see it until it stopped. They repeated the process to determine that a runner's sense of smell is the same as ours, but their hearing is better. They are visual predators. They hear something, go to it until they see it, then attack it.

"Bruce and Mike have an interesting hypothesis. They think infected stay near roads because they associate roads with food and more people to infect. I believe that they use roads for the same reason we do. It's the fastest way to travel. Now, if you look at this slide," Stephanie pushed a button, and on the screen was a thermal picture, "you will see a group of thirty-four moving through the woods at night to the east of us. There is no prey around them, and they are not moving fast. The little spy plane watched them for twelve minutes, and they were just moving through an area. Now, they do not like moving through heavy brush and seem to have a mortal fear of water."

Stephanie changed slides again. This one listed countries on the left and had three columns with numbers in each one across from each country. At the top of each column was Infected, Dead, and Survivors. Then, she continued, "This slide is the three-month prediction from the infection rates. In America, they were using the population projection of three hundred and twenty million. In America, two hundred million infected, eighty million dead, forty million survivors. It is worse everywhere else in the world as you can see. In Britain, they will only have a million survivors in three months. Current predictions are that in one year, there will be less than twenty million humans in America. The only reason we are lasting longer with better survival rates is that guns and food are everywhere in America. But most people don't stock the amounts of ammunition and food that is needed to survive this and will run out. In most countries, the population can only hide and wait. In the war-torn, third-world countries, they might have guns but not the food stores. This means over seventy percent of the world's population, almost five billion, will become a new species."

"How many do you think will be runners in a year, here in the states?" Debbie asked.

"About a hundred and fifty to a hundred and eighty million," Stephanie replied. Hearing that number, Debbie slumped down in her seat.

Bruce interrupted and asked, "Stephanie, I know they age slower than us and heal faster than us, but what is their shelf life? When are they gonna die?"

"Bruce, you have not been listening," Stephanie said then enunciated, "The-virus-infects-every-cell."

"Yes, I've been listening, and I know that. Every cell lasts for a real long time, but how long?" Bruce asked.

"Bruce, they can reproduce," Stephanie said, and everyone stared at her as it hit home. Man was no longer the dominate species.

Bruce broke the silence first. "Well, fuck me."

"Sideways," Debbie added.

"With a monkey holding a broom," Angela added.

"And wearing high heels," Mike added, shaking his head.

"Yes, it's bad. They artificially inseminated one female in the lab with infected sperm. Human sperm was not genetically compatible, believe it or not. Not that a human male could mate with her because she would tear him apart," Stephanie said.

"Where did this virus come from?" Nancy asked.

"The outbreak began in the Congo, but I can tell you one thing; this virus did not come from nature," Stephanie stated with certainty.

"You said that before. What makes you think that?" Debbie asked.

"The CDC and USAMRID, the army version of the CDC, started to break down the virus. They found gene sequences in infected DNA that come from several other species. Humans use twenty percent of our DNA; infected use fifty percent. Let me just list some of the infected viral makeup. Super healing, age regression, strengthened immune system, boundless energy, and super strength. What comes to your mind?" Stephanie asked.

"Genetic research for the fountain of youth," Mike answered.

"Exactly," Stephanie said.

"Why not a bio weapon?" Angela asked.

"My director at the CDC said the same thing. Do you really want to infect your enemy with something that makes them age slower, heal faster, run fast, have super strength, is a carnivore, and has an infection rate of 99.9%? Meaning if it gets in your bloodstream, you will get it. When you develop a bio weapon, you find a cure while you develop it," Stephanie explained.

"What about drugs?" Maria asked.

"It would take at least a decade to find a drug to stop the infection if you got bit. We do not have the understanding to reverse the process. It would be like me trying to make a drug to give you blue eyes. The infected have been changed at the genetic level," Stephanie stated.

"You mean someone made this virus but can't undo it?" Danny almost shouted.

"Danny, just because you can do something is not a good reason to do it. Genetic research is the most dangerous thing in the world. Screw nanotechnology and atomic weapons. This is how life was formed, and screwing with DNA is wielding God-like powers," Stephanie answered, looking at her.

"How long does the virus last outside the body?" Nancy asked.

"Not long; it's very fragile. If it is kept warm, out of light, and moist, the virus has been recorded to stay viable for five hours. That is the extreme limit. The virus usually is not viable after ten minutes when exposed to the elements. Direct UV light kills it. It must enter the body quickly, through blood or mucus membrane exposure."

"Okay, so what can we expect the infected to do? I just want your best guess," Bruce said.

"In China and India, the infected are not staying in huge groups but are breaking down in groups of several hundred to hunt. They will converge en masse on a large target of humans to kill them. I feel we will be seeing that soon here. They will then try to just kill us, not infect us. We will be seen as competition. We are hearing fewer reports over the radio of infected breaking into groups and infecting people. I pray that they will start to fight each other for resources, but as long as we're here, I don't see that happening. Humanity is on the verge of extinction," Stephanie said.

"Mankind may be going extinct, but let's get one thing straight. One thing mankind has proven time and time again is we can kill shit on an astronomical scale. Starting tomorrow, we start hunt and kill patrols. Let's start makin' a dent here," Bruce said, standing up.

"Bruce, we may have almost a million rounds here now, but that's not even enough to make a dent in North Louisiana, much less America," Nancy said, trying to rein him in.

"The military orders over two billion rounds each year of 5.56, and the civilian market produces half that much. The government stockpiles several billion rounds of 5.56 not to mention everything else. We just have to get it. We aren't gonna just sit here holding our dicks waitin' on a mob of infected or a gang of raiders to hit us. I want ideas on how to strengthen the fence fast. Training is to be three hours every day, including hand-to-hand starting tomorrow. This is a war, and we're gonna fuck something up," Bruce said, looking around.

"Hell yeah; let's get some!" Jake yelled, jumping up. Danny jumped up with him and gave him a high five. The rest of the clan started jumping up with excitement.

"Okay, Bruce, but don't you think this might be inviting trouble here?" Nancy asked. Everyone got quiet.

"Trouble has already gotten an invitation. All that matters now is how we fight it when it gets here. Let's make everyone and everything fear us," Bruce said, smiling.

Nancy looked at him, knowing he was right but scared for the battles that were coming and what they would cost. Then it hit her; sitting there doing nothing, they had no chance. By fighting, they at least had a small hope.

Looking Bruce in the eye, she grinned and said, "Let's get some."

CHAPTER 5

While the family was listening to Stephanie, forty-seven men were walking around the checkpoint at the dam with five sitting in pickup trucks. One was kicking bodies and yelling at the top of his lungs.

"Warren, what happened to the stuff? It was here just a few weeks ago," a man asked the one kicking bodies.

"You dumb fuck, someone came here an' took it! Do ya think it just disappeared, Ed?" Warren yelled at him.

"I know someone took it, but who?" Ed asked his older brother.

"Oh, I know who took the stuff. I'm just not gonna tell ya. How in the hell am I supposed to know who took the shit?" Warren said, walking toward Ed. Then, Warren punched Ed in the mouth, knocking his little brother down.

A man came running over to Warren and looked down at Ed. "The patrol cars are empty too. We found some drugs in the cars parked together, and the only gun we found was that machine gun under the pile of bodies," the man told Warren, sending him into another yelling fit.

"What'cha you want us to do, Warren?" the man asked.

"Carl, I'm fixing to hit you," Warren told his brother.

"Warren, you're the one who said we can't stay out in the open long because the blues will start gathering," Carl said. Warren was the oldest, smallest, and meanest. Carl was the biggest, and he was the middle brother.

"Tell everyone we're leaving," Warren said.

Looking around, Warren was mad as hell. They had driven sixty miles from the hunting camp on Toledo Bend Lake and had nothing to show for this trip. He and Ed had driven up several weeks ago after the checkpoint was overrun. From the east end of the dam, they had seen thousands of infected at the checkpoint running around. Pulling back, Warren told Ed that they would come back in a few weeks after they went to Fort Polk and collect the stuff at the checkpoint.

Warren told Ed to drive to his house; he wanted to get some more stuff when they came back to see the checkpoint. He didn't think he had killed Pam with her beating, and if she was there, then he could beat her again. If she was dead, he didn't care; there were dozens of bitches at camp. When they got to the house and didn't find her body, he knew where she had gone. Grabbing the stuff he came after, Warren got back into the truck. Then, they went in search of that shaved-head son of a bitch's place.

Warren had never been to Bruce's farm, but he had an idea where it was. When Warren started thinking of that shaved-head fucker, it made him mad enough to kill. Warren wanted to kill him, but first, he was going to hurt Bruce by torturing and raping his family. How dare he judge Warren and interfere with his family? Pam had to be beaten regularly because she tried to tell him what he could and couldn't do. That bitch could not even give him a son.

That day years ago, when Bruce had come over, Pam had stopped Warren from fucking Tonya. She was his daughter, and he could do whatever he wanted to her. Pam had jumped on his back while Tonya had run out of the house, heading to Steve's house. Warren beat the hell out of Pam that afternoon after Tonya left. Then, the asshole showed up. After Warren got out of jail and finished going to counseling, Pam continued to threaten Warren with calling Bruce to the house.

It had taken them an hour that night driving around, but they finally found the farm. Then, Warren told Ed to head back to the camp. Now, Warren knew where to find them.

The next week, Warren had taken sixty men to Fort Polk, but it was still manned by the military. Warren had lost a lot of men just trying to get away alive and did not get any weapons. They were down to a hundred and seven men at the camp, who were mostly drinking and hunting buddies and friends of friends. They had scored a lot of food and hit several police stations and pawn shops but had only a few military weapons. He had not worried about returning to Fort Polk because he knew the checkpoint was still there. But everything was now gone, and he had wasted a lot of gas getting this crew up here for nothing.

He was pretty sure the biker gang at the state park on the north end of the lake had taken everything. Warren's group had come across them twice. Each time, his crew had gotten the better of them. The plan was when they got the military weapons, they were going to roll over there and wipe out the bikers. There were only so many women left, and he didn't want to share. Now, the other gang had all the weapons.

On the way back to the camp, he saw a gas station on the left and told Ed to pull in; they would refuel here. His convoy followed him. Warren got out, grabbing his shotgun, and looked around for blues. Not seeing any, he walked to the store. He stopped looking at seven decomposing bodies lying in front of the door. Each had its hands and feet bound. Walking into the store, he saw bodies everywhere and bullet holes on the walls. The shelves were empty of food, but the liquor behind the counter was still there.

Warren ran back outside then walked around, looking at the ground. Warren called Ed and Carl over. He was the boss, and they were his captains. They hurried over to Warren and stopped in front of him.

"How many men do we have with us now, Carl?" Warren asked, still looking at the ground.

"Fifty-two, includin' us." Of the three brothers he was the smartest. That was why Warren hit him a lot, to remind him who was boss.

"I want ten people on guard duty while we fill up; then, we're leavin'," Warren said, looking around the gas station again.

"What's wrong, Warren? We can empty the store and get a lot 'a fuel here—" Carl started until Warren kicked him in the stomach. Carl fell to the ground, holding his stomach. None of the other gang members even liked getting close to Warren. He just shot them when they pissed him off. One man had tried to kill him after Fort Polk, and Warren had tortured him for three days until he died. Warren had made every person in camp watch. After that, he had no problems from anyone.

"Don't ever question me in front of the others again. You may be my brother, but I'll kill ya," Warren said, standing over Carl.

"It's okay, Warren. What's wrong?" Ed asked, wanting Warren to quit hitting Carl.

"The military or police have been here, not that there is any difference between 'em now. Those at the door were bound hand and foot with ties. All those at the corner were taken out by snipers like that man on the roof.

Inside, it looks like a team rushed 'em. I put the number here over thirty; that means the attackers were double that." Warren had watched a lot of programs on the military channel. "These are military tire tracks, and shell casings are everywhere. You can still see jail house tattoos on several of the bodies, so they weren't civilians. The military came through here a few weeks ago and wiped this gang out. If it would've been a gang that wiped them out, then the liquor would be gone along with the smokes. We need to leave here fast."

Ed was getting scared and replied, "Okay, I'll get some guys out. It shouldn't take long to fill up." Ed trotted over to the vehicles and sent men to stand watch.

Warren looked down at Carl. "Get up." Carl got up hoping not to get hit again. "Get a couple of guys to get the liquor and tobacco out of the store while we fuel up. No one is to use the CBs for any reason unless they see something. Ya understand?" Warren asked, and Carl nodded. "Then go."

As Carl ran to do what he was told, Warren stood by the road, watching the guards take up positions. If the military showed up, it would not be much of a fight. All Warren could hope for would be to outrun them. They had the one machine gun that they had found at the checkpoint but no belted ammunition for it. Out of the one hundred and seven men he had, they only had nine M-16s, which they had gotten from cops. They did have a lot of the civilian knockoff weapons taken from pawn shops and a fair bit of ammo. He had an AK-47 in the truck, but it too was a civilian model. They needed machine guns to fight the blues, other gangs, and the military.

Warren knew if the military caught them there or at the camp, they were dead no matter what. Someone whistled and said they were finished. He watched as they pulled the hose out of the ground tank that was connected to a hand pump. He ran for his truck and jumped in only to find Ed was already at the wheel. They would hit the gang at the state park in a few months unless the military hit them first. Then, he would take care of his wife and daughter. Those thoughts made him happy as Ed drove them back to camp. Warren would never forget Bruce and had a score to settle with him.

There were other places to get weapons, and they would find them. Warren would get more men for his growing army. He truly loved this new world. Never would he have believed that he would control this many men, and he could have any bitch he wanted. If someone pissed him off, he could kill them and not have to worry about anything.

"Yes, I'll find some weapons. Then, we're coming back. He'll be sorry he ever messed with me, and he will be scared of me before he dies," Warren said out loud, smiling as Ed drove the truck back to camp. Ed just drove, praying Warren wasn't talking about him.

CHAPTER 6

Leading his patrol, Bruce held up his hand for the group to stop as he looked and listened to the area around him. They were twenty miles south of the farm, looking at a clearing with several trailers in it. He motioned for the team to spread out along the tree line but not to enter the clearing yet. Matt had told them there were over forty blues on the other side of the trailers.

They had crossed the land bridge between Saline Lake and Black Lake at 9 a.m. This was the largest group not near a town or a village. The populated areas were full of infected, but Bruce was not quite ready to take them on just yet. So they stayed out in the country and slaughtered any infected they could find. On patrols, the group maintained a five-mile-an-hour pace on foot, carrying fully loaded tactical vests, weapons, and backpacks full of ammo plus water. The family could do this because of the physical condition they stayed in. Conner and Buffy were holding up pretty well. Granted, the family never believed they would have to do what they were doing now. They had stayed in shape to enjoy an adventurous lifestyle, but they were all glad they had trained for it.

It was October, only two weeks after Stephanie had given her presentation. Danny and Mary had birthday parties the last week in September and got presents. The first week of October, the family threw a birthday party for Buffy, each giving her presents. Bruce had given her a small ghillie suit he had made for her so she could train as a sniper.

They were going out every morning between 4 and 5 a.m. in five-man patrols that stayed out all day. Jake or Matt would guide them onto any infected in the area. They had already killed a little over two thousand infected, all in small groups. They no longer tried to avoid them but hunted infected. Bruce led patrols on Monday, Tuesday, Thursday, and Friday with Mike leading a patrol on Wednesday. It was Friday, so after today, Bruce could rest for two days.

Thinking about his upcoming two days off, Bruce wiped the sweat off of his face and grinned. It was only 10 a.m., but it was already over eighty degrees. It would stay in the nineties until November if the weather stayed true to form for Louisiana. It was real bad when you called ninety degrees a cold spell.

Bruce looked down the line at his patrol. Today, it was Danny, Debbie, Jake, and Conner. He never counted Buffy because as far as she was concerned, she was part of him. The only time she was not at his side was when she was with Danny. Looking at her on his left side, her face was covered in face paint like everyone on the patrol. He had made her take an M-4 with a suppressor to get used to it. The weapon did look big across her little chest, but Bruce didn't think she should carry a submachine gun for her primary weapon. With the stock opened only halfway, it fit her reasonably well, and unlike the submachine gun, she could take out targets far away. After she had fired a thousand rounds through it, Buffy could hit a head-sized target at fifty yards with ease. She could hit a target at a hundred yards, but it usually took several shots and a lot of steadying herself. Buffy, like everyone else, had been learning to speed-shoot targets with both her rifle and pistol. Infected provided real life target practice, and everyone on the farm was using it. Today, Buffy was keeping up very well just like Conner. But, a five-mile-an-hour pace was a good jog for her. Her little legs kept moving, and she never complained.

Bringing himself to the here and now, Bruce called Jake on the radio. "Spook One, what do you see?"

"See several moving around in between the trailers, Big Daddy," Jake replied as Matt came over the air.

"The trailers form a semi-circle, and the group is in the middle of 'em. They're just laying around."

Bruce was making plans to move the group around to the front of the trailers and let Jake take them out from a distance. That was when he heard a sound that always made his blood run cold. A roar split the air. The trailers were over a hundred yards away, but it was still loud, and he felt it in his chest.

Everyone brought their weapons up, and Buffy spun around to face the rear at the sound of the roar. Bruce did not think a human could even make that sound. It sounded like a lion's roar, but it was at a higher pitch. Everyone now had heard it while on patrol. They still didn't know why blues did it, and so far, they had only seen males do it. Sometimes, they did it when chasing after prey, but often, they roared while sitting around.

Looking through his scope, Bruce told everyone not to shoot unless they charged. All confirmed. He saw the group move up the road that led into the trailer park but were looking south, at the opposite tree line. Several kept roaring as the group moved further up the road and stopped, still looking south.

Bruce counted forty-six in all with their backs to the patrol. He knew if they looked this way, it was going to get interesting real quick. He called Matt and whispered, "What are they so interested in, Spook Two?"

"I can't see anything, and the battery is goin' out, so I can't fly that way. I'm calling the Raven home and sending the Puma out. It'll take ten minutes to get to you, so don't go startin' shit yet, Big Daddy," Matt answered.

"Copy that. Tell me when you're on station," Bruce said. They had covered the twenty plus miles in just over six hours, and Bruce was happy with everyone's performance. They had taken out twenty-nine infected on the way, but he wanted this group. Just then, the group took off running to the tree line across from them. Over half of this group were runners and looked like Olympic sprinters.

"Engage from the rear, and work forward," Bruce told the patrol as he fired a shot, taking down a walker.

The rest of the patrol opened up on the group, and in thirty seconds, it was over. They had taken down twenty-one, but twenty-five had gotten away. Bruce lowered his rifle in disbelief. Those runners had cleared the hundred-plus-yard distance from the road to the far tree line in less than 10 seconds.

Stephanie had told them that at the CDC, the scientists had put one on a treadmill, and it had run at thirty-one mph for eighteen hours before collapsing. The reason it didn't run faster was that was the top speed of the treadmill. It then lay on the floor for five hours like it was asleep then jumped up ready for more.

"Let's go after them, single file behind me. Conner, you have the rear," Bruce said as he moved into the clearing and started jogging across the field. Conner had the SAW to hit runners in the legs when they charged. Every patrol had at least one SAW with them.

Debbie radioed Bruce as they moved across the field to the road, "Bruce, we're chasing runners. We have no hope of catching them on foot; you do know this right?"

"Yes, I know that, little mama. I think they're hunting, and they have a one-track mind. If what they're after is not far, we can take them at the kill," Bruce replied over the radio.

"You think! If those things turn around on us in the woods, it'll go hand-to-hand, up close and personal, real fast," Debbie shot back.

"That's what my gut feels, and you can take two in hand-to-hand any day. Now, be quiet; you're messing up my breathing at this pace," Bruce said as he kept his jogging, pace steady.

They followed the runners' trail through the woods at a jog for thirty minutes until Matt called them over the radio. Bruce held up his hand for everyone to stop. "The group you're following is four miles ahead of you."

"Where are they headed, Spook Two?" Bruce asked then started to drink some water from his Camelback, controlling his breathing.

"They're headed south, toward Nantachie Lake," Matt said.

"Well, is there a party there that they're late for or what?" Bruce asked and took a long drink.

"I'm a thousand feet above them now, and the lake is another seven miles, I'll be there in a minute," Matt replied. Bruce walked in slow circles, waiting for the update.

"Big Daddy One, this is Big Daddy Two. There're several hundred blues along the bank of the north end of the lake with a lot more on the way. There are people on an island about eighty yards from the bank. We're having problems keeping the Puma on station because of the distance. Do ya copy?" Mike asked.

"Copy, Big Daddy Two. We're going to see if we can help," Bruce said.

"Big Daddy One, your radio signal is gettin' weak. You're fixin' to lose contact with base. Your group is over thirty miles away now," Mike said, and Bruce could hear the worry in his voice. They were now using the military radios they had gathered at the checkpoint, and they had just found the range.

"Copy that. What side of the lake do we need to come over on?" Bruce asked, pulling out his map.

"The island is on the east side of the lake, about a mile from the north end. Let me get another patrol headed your way in case ya get in some shit," Mike said.

"Negative on the patrol; you'd be too far away to help, and I don't want to spread surveillance too thin. Movin' out now. Will call when we can. Big Daddy One out," Bruce said, not wanting to get in a debate.

Bruce looked at the satellite/topographical map and saw the island. There was a road that ran along the east bank with houses on either side. There were several houses along the east bank and across the little road with one overlooking the area. Bruce guessed from the map it was less than a hundred and fifty yards from the bank. He called everyone close so they could see the map. "We're makin' for this house," he said, pointing, and continued. "We'll set up on the roof and kill everything not human. Then, I'm going to this boat house and see if they have something I can paddle to the island to get the people. After we get 'em, we'll head to this pipeline to the east and follow it back to Saline Lake. If we get separated, the pipeline is the rally point. If it's compromised, head home. We will stop here at this pond to refill our water before headin' to the house. Any questions?" Bruce asked, looking at everyone.

No one asked anything, and he moved out at a jogging pace. They lost radio contact with base at thirty-eight miles. It was almost three times the distance of their old radios. When they reached the pond to refill water with the filter pump, they could hear roars off in the distance. Bruce looked at his watch; it was almost 1 p.m. They had covered thirty-eight miles in eight hours. He looked around at the group, and they were soaked with sweat. Smiling, Bruce saw they still had a lot left to give and was glad because it was a long walk home.

It took another hour and a half to cover the last mile because they moved slowly and carefully. They approached the house from the back, through the woods. Stopping ten yards inside the tree line, Bruce could see the backyard of the house. Then, looking to his right, he saw a mobile home. He motioned to the mobile home and moved toward it inside the tree line. The smell could gag a maggot. Unbelievably, it got worse the closer they got to the infected, but it didn't make his stomach reverse gears. Either they were bathing or he was getting used to it. Bruce thought it was the latter.

When they were directly behind the mobile home, Bruce led the group toward the back of it. They were keeping the trailer between them and the mob as they moved toward it. The noise coming from the mob was so loud it was hurting their ears. Growls, yells, and an occasional roar came from the mob. It reminded Bruce of being in a football stadium. He was sure they could speak in normal voices and not be heard, but he wasn't going to find out.

When they reached the back of the mobile home, he moved a trash can over and motioned Debbie to get on the roof. He sent the rest up one at a time with him being the last. Everyone was spread out on the roof with Conner on the far right end and Debbie on the left. Bruce went prone beside Buffy, who was next Debbie. Keeping his movements slow, he took off his pack and opened the top. Inside, he had ten more loaded magazines. The back edge of the mob was about sixty yards from them. He hoped the crest of the roof would hide them. To make matters worse, the metal roof was hotter than nine kinds of hell as he set up his gear.

Bruce radioed everyone, "Get your magazines out and ready. When we start, it'll be from the back, and move forward. Give me a thumb up when you're ready." Everyone pulled off packs, getting ready as Conner set the SAW to the side, pulling his M-4 off his back. Bruce pulled out his binoculars, scanning the mob and the island.

Conner just stared at Bruce in disbelief then turned to look back at the crowd. There were so many he could only pick out individuals on the outer edge. Looking back at Bruce as he studied the crowd through his binoculars, Conner wanted to say something but couldn't think of anything to say except to ask Bruce if he was insane. Seeing everyone stacking magazines, Conner did the same with fear gripping his chest.

Scanning the mob, Bruce saw it was eighty yards deep from the bank to the back edge and stretched over a hundred and fifty yards along the bank. Bruce was guessing the number was close to two thousand. Looking toward the island, he could not see all of it because of the houses along the bank. On the map, the island looked almost a hundred yards long and fifty across. Looking back at the mob at the water's edge, Bruce noticed none were in water deeper than their ankles. Putting his binoculars in his pack, he looked at everyone as they gave him a thumb up.

Bruce called over the radio, "When we start, there will be no stopping until they're all gone or we get overrun. Keep calm. When you see me fire, open up, and keep fire discipline. There're people on the island in front of this group, so watch your fire. The first two who empty half of their magazines call reload, and reload what you've shot so we don't all run out at the same time. If you copy, give me a thumb up." Bruce got thumbs up from everyone and raised his rifle.

Bruce sighted on a female blue that was probably pretty before turning blue. He slowly squeezed the trigger and watched her head explode. Then, the others opened up and kept firing at a steady rate. Moving his rifle from head to head and watching them disappear as he pulled the trigger, Bruce smiled. Several in the mob turned to the sound of the suppressors but turned back around toward the island. None charged them or even moved toward them. Danny called reload first, followed shortly by Jake. When Bruce put in his fourteenth magazine, he looked out in front of the group toward the mob. Bodies were laying everywhere, stacked four to five high in places. They had to pick the shots carefully now. Trees and houses along the lake edge were blocking their shots from the rest of the blues.

Looking around, Bruce figured there could not be more than sixty along the bank and behind obstacles. Bruce called everyone on the radio. "I'm reloading and heading to the dock. Danny, I want you with me. Buffy, I want you to reload your magazines then move to each person and reload theirs. Jake, you are to cover me and Danny until we are on the water. Debbie and Conner, keep killing. Any questions?" Bruce asked and did not receive any. He had expected an argument from Buffy, but she just started to load magazines and smiled at him. He reloaded and put the ten extra magazines back in his pack and the others in his vest. Turning around to get off the roof, he saw two infected come out of the woods. He pulled up his rifle and snapped off two shots, hitting both in the face. Then, he waited to see if they had friends.

"Two just came out of the woods behind us. Keep an eye out," Bruce said.

"Bruce, at least forty have come out of the woods since we started shooting. They just run right by us to the mob," Debbie informed him. Conner reported the same thing on his end.

That didn't make sense; the blues should have easily seen them on the roof. Bruce called over the radio, sliding on his pack. "Buffy, you cover us when we get down; then, get back to loading magazines. Debbie is in charge until we're back together."

Bruce slid off the roof and crouched down when he landed, burning his arm on the hot barrel of his rifle. Danny landed beside him, and he led her to the boat house. Bruce stopped at the corner of mobile home. What was left of the mob was to the left of it. The boat house was a hundred and twenty yards to the right. Not seeing anything between him and it, he took off running with Danny hot on his heels.

When they were halfway there, Bruce heard a growl from his right and saw a runner coming at him full speed. Fear gripped Bruce as he turned toward it, raising his rifle when the blue's head exploded. The body collapsed, sliding across the asphalt toward them from its forward momentum. Bruce put his head down and ran like the devil himself was behind him. He saw movement to his left and turned just in time to see another runner's head explode. As the body fell, it did a complete flip in the air and slid a foot before coming to a stop. They reached the boat house out of breath and turned around just in time to see two more runners drop.

Looking back in the boathouse, Bruce saw a fourteen-foot aluminum boat on the dock. He walked up and saw two paddles inside. He and Danny picked it up and set it gently into the water. Bruce got in the back as Danny got in the front. He grabbed a paddle and paddled out of the boathouse.

Out on the lake, he could see the island, and what was left of the mob could see them. The remaining infected ran toward them, moving from behind the obstacles, but they were cut down by the group on the roof. Bruce watched in amazement as the numbers just melted on the shore as he paddled the two hundred yards to the island when Danny turned around.

"Look at the other bank, Dad," she said. Six hundred yards away, he did not see what she was talking about. The trees ran up to the water's edge. Then, he saw the infected moving between the trees. They lined the bank on the other side of the lake. Bruce started paddling faster in case they figured out to go around the lake. Bruce had once read a paper that said if a human could run at sixty-seven miles per hour, they could run on water. He just prayed that the blues could not run that fast because if they did, he was digging a hole and staying in it.

"Jake is one badass sniper. Isn't he?" Danny asked, looking at the island.

"Yeah, he is. I thought the first one that slid toward us after he shot it had us," Bruce said, paddling hard, still thinking about blues running on water.

"Dad, that one was the third one he had shot. You didn't even see the other two."

Bruce could not believe he had missed two. *It might be time to raise Jake's allowance,* Bruce thought as the boat hit the bank on the island. "Danny, be careful. We don't know who's here. Stay frosty," Bruce whispered. Danny nodded, jumped out of the boat, and pulled it further onto the bank.

Bruce got out and walked into the small stand of trees on the island with Danny on his right. As he moved forward, he swore he could hear a kid talking and another answer. He stopped to see if he could hear an adult but didn't and moved closer. Then, he saw six kids sitting around a tree. There was a little girl no more than seven playing with a baby doll and talking to a boy who looked about nine.

He motioned Danny to stay beside him and raise her hands. They walked toward the kids. When they were less than fifteen yards away, the girl gave a little squeal and grabbed the baby doll to her chest. The little boy she was talking to turned around with a small knife.

Bruce held up his hands and said, "We're not going to hurt you. We're here to help. My name is Bruce, and this is my daughter Danielle, but we call her Danny." The little boy put himself in front of the kids, holding out his knife. Bruce looked closely at the kids. They all looked like skin and bones with sunken eyes. The little boy looked at Bruce.

"How do we know you won't hurt us?" he asked, looking at them suspiciously.

"Because you'd be dead already, young man," Bruce answered. "We just killed all the blues on the bank to help who's over here," Bruce said, pointing to the bank that was blocked by the trees.

The little boy lowered his knife and said, "There're a lot of monsters over there."

"Yes, there was, and we still have people over there killing them, so we could help you," Bruce said. Two little girls ran toward Bruce and latched onto his legs. Looking down at them, Bruce saw they were identical twins around four.

The rest of the kids came over to them. When the little girl with the doll came over, Bruce froze. "Oh my God, that's a real baby," Bruce cried out, walking to the little girl. The baby was lying limply in the little girl's arms. The little girl turned away from him. "Little girl, I'm a nurse, and I help people. Please, give me the baby," Bruce said in a kind but firm voice. The little girl slowly handed the baby to Bruce.

Bruce grabbed the baby, thinking it was already dead, and stripped it down. It was a boy about six to nine months old. He was breathing rapidly, not moving his arms or legs, lying like a rag doll and not opening his eyes. Bruce could tell the baby was dehydrated, in shock, and close to dying. Turning to the boy that had the knife, Bruce asked, "What's your name?"

"Frank," he replied, watching Bruce with the baby.

"Sit by me right here; everyone else sit around us. No one is to talk but me and Frank unless I talk to you. The baby is close to dying. Danny, take your pack off now, and give me your first aid kit. Then, start feeding the kids slowly. Water first but also give it slow." Bruce dropped his pack, pulled out a blanket and his first aid pouch, then took off his gloves. He put the baby on the blanket and opened his pouch, getting IV supplies. Debbie called him over the radio.

"Are you two alright over there?" she asked.

"Can't talk now, a baby's dying in front of me," Bruce said, kneeling by the baby then looking up at Frank.

"Frank, I need you to find a stick that's as tall as you and bring it to me fast," Bruce said, and Frank took off.

Bruce wiped the baby's arm off with alcohol then put an IV in the bend of his little arm. The baby never even moved. That made Bruce real nervous. Then, he reached in his first aid bag and pulled out a small, 250cc IV bag of normal saline. He hooked up the tubing to the bag then connected to the baby's IV. He held the bag up so that the fluid ran into the baby as Frank ran back with a stick. Bruce shoved one end into the ground and hung the IV bag from the top. Then, he turned to Frank. "Where are your parents?" Bruce asked, looking at the skinny kid. Bruce grabbed a vial of dextrose from his kit. Doing some rough calculations, he grabbed a syringe.

"Don't know. Bad men shot at the bus we were on, and it crashed. The driver told Paul to take us and run after we wrecked," Frank replied, looking at Bruce with hope.

"An adult sent you out by yourself without anyone older?" Bruce asked, looking at the kids and wondering which one was Paul as he drew up 10ccs of dextrose. Then, Bruce slowly pushed the dextrose in with the IV fluids.

"Paul's sixteen," Frank said with an angry expression.

"Where's Paul now so we can get him?" Bruce asked.

"A blue man bit him before he brought us here. He swam us over here and said he had to go and for us to wait here for him. He was going for help. He told me to protect everyone until he came back," Frank said with tears running down his cheeks.

"How many days ago, Frank, was it that Paul left?" Bruce asked with tears running down his own face.

"Two days ago, and we saw Paul this morning. He was over there, and he was a blue monster," Frank said, pointing toward where the mob used to be.

"Frank, you're a great leader. We're the help Paul was looking for. We're going to take you to someplace safe, but we'll have to fight to get there. Do you know the names and how old everyone here is?" Bruce asked, and Frank nodded. Danny was still feeding the kids, breaking off small pieces of food for each one. "I want you to point to each one here and tell me their name and how old they are. Okay?" Bruce said, checking on the baby, who had started to move around.

"This is Emily and Sherry; they are twins, and both are four," Frank pointed at the two little girls who had run up to Bruce. "This is Nathan, and he's six. This is Robert, and he's seven. This is Alice, and she's seven, and I'm nine," Frank finished as Bruce watched the baby.

"What's the baby's name?" Bruce asked.

"Don't know," Frank said, shrugging.

"Aren't you family?" Bruce asked, shocked.

"No," Frank said.

"Where did you come from, and how did you get here?" Bruce asked, trying to keep his questions simple.

"We went to the building the army men told us to. Then they said we had to leave and go to the mountains. We got on some school buses, and I think it was five days ago bad men shot our bus, and it crashed," Frank said eating a piece of food Danny had given him. Then, Danny lifted his shirt up and felt over his body.

"So the bus driver told Paul to get you kids and run. Someone just gave Paul a baby; then, Paul took off with you kids. On the way here, Paul was bitten by a blue monster. He led you here and swam each of you to this island. Then, he left and showed up this morning as a blue monster?" Bruce asked, trying to make sense of the child's story.

"Yep, but Paul did kill the blue monster after it bit him 'cause it was tryin' to get Sherry," Frank said, glad Bruce had finally got all his story. He ate more food.

Bruce looked at the baby, who was now awake and moving around. Half of the IV fluids were in as the baby started moving around kicking and cooing. Bruce figured the baby at fourteen pounds or six kilograms, and the 250cc was double the bolus he needed—Bruce knew the baby needed it all. He opened one of his FSR pouches, taking one bar of food out, broke it in half, and handed the rest of it to Danny. He opened some gauze out of the first aid kit then picked the baby up in his arms. Wetting the gauze with water, Bruce wiped the baby's dry mouth out.

"Danny, I want you to tell your mother what's going on here. We need another thirty minutes before we can move," Bruce said as he bit off a piece of bar and chewed it up. The IV bag was empty, and Bruce clamped the tube. Taking some of the chewed food out of his mouth, Bruce put the paste in the baby's mouth. The baby started kicking and laughing, sucking his fingers. "Does the baby have a bottle?" Bruce asked the kids.

"I'll get it," Alice said and ran to the tree. She pulled the bottle out of the only backpack he saw. "Here you go, Mr. Bruce," she said, handing it to him.

Bruce thanked her and opened the bottle to make sure it did not smell like spoiled milk. It smelled okay, so he put a little water in it and rinsed it out then filled it up with water. Reaching in his pack, he took out a powdered sports drink mix and poured it in the bottle. The baby started pulling his goatee as he finished. He took more of the chewed up bar out of his mouth and put it in the baby's, which made him happy again. Bruce picked up the bottle, shaking it to dissolve the powder, and put the nipple in the baby's mouth. The baby grabbed the bottle and started to slam the water down, sending huge bubbles up the bottle. The baby needed the electrolytes and sugar, but Bruce had to keep taking the bottle out of the baby's mouth so it wouldn't get sick. This action really pissed the baby off big time, and it cried until Bruce put the bottle back in its mouth.

Danny had told Debbie the story, crying through the whole thing. Debbie came over the radio. "Bruce, baby, what do you need from me?" Debbie asked, and he could hear tears in her voice.

"I need you to cover us until I can get these kids ready to move. It shouldn't be much longer," Bruce said, looking at the baby then at the kids.

"God as my witness, you take as long as you need. You will not be disturbed," Debbie said in a tone of determination that sent shivers up Bruce's spine, making him proud.

"Frank, did any of you drink out of the lake or have you been bitten or scratched by the blue monsters?" Bruce asked.

"No, Paul told us not to drink the water, and we gave the baby our last water this morning. Paul didn't let the blue monsters near us," Frank replied.

Bruce nodded as tears ran down his face. Bruce wished he could have saved Paul from his fate. A sixteen-year-old kid protected seven kids who he didn't know and led them to safety. Knowing he was infected, he took them to a safe place and left so he wouldn't hurt them then died alone. Bruce prayed to God to let Paul know the kids were okay.

Bruce could feel the anger building as the tears dried on his face. He took deep breaths, calming himself. *Now is not the time,* he reminded himself. Maybe later, but not now, Bruce wanted to unleash the rage but needed to stay focused for the surviving kids. *Rage would come later,* he promised himself.

Glancing at his watch, Bruce saw it was after five p.m. He told Danny to get ready to go and called the kids around. He put the baby in Alice's arms as he cut the blanket down to make a sling so he could carry the baby across his chest. While he worked, he talked to the kids. "We are fixing to leave. It's too dangerous here; blue monsters are coming. We are going to your new home. If you see anything that scares you, don't yell or make noise because the monsters can hear real good. We can fight the monsters, but if you make noise, more will come, okay? And we could run out of bullets, and they would get us," Bruce said as he tied the two ends of the sling together.

All the kids told him okay except the twins; they just looked at him with wide eyes, standing at his side and holding his pants legs. Bruce took the baby from Alice and put it in the sling. Taking the IV out, Bruce put a band aid on the spot. He put everything back in his pack and grabbed several powdered drink mixes then put his pack on. Putting the empty baby bottle in his left thigh pocket with the drink mixes, Bruce looked around as he put his gloves on. He told the kids to follow him and for Danny to bring up the rear. When they reached the boat, he radioed Debbie.

"We're coming back. Keep us covered," Bruce said as the last kid got in the boat. He pushed the boat out to ankle-deep water then motioned for Danny to get in. Then, he turned the boat with the back to him and pushed it out, climbing in.

"Take your time, baby. We haven't seen anything in twenty minutes," Debbie said as he started paddling.

"Dad, the blues are gone from the other side," Danny said as he started paddling hard and fast.

Looking between strokes, he saw nothing was on the far bank. He radioed Debbie. "Meet us at the boat house now. We're goin' to have to move fast. I think we're about to have company, more than we have bullets for," Bruce said, paddling hard with the baby just smiling up at him.

When he reached the boat house, the others were there, waiting on them. They helped the kids out of the boat. Bruce was the last one out as he tied the boat up just in case they needed it again. Danny was making introductions as Debbie came over to Bruce and looked at the baby with tears in her eyes.

"Bruce, what are we going to call him?" Debbie asked, holding the baby's hand.

Bruce was looking at her playing with the baby and said, "He has a name, baby. It's Paul."

CHAPTER 7

Bruce called everyone around, "Kids, we're going to have to carry each of you because monsters are coming, and we have ta move fast." Bruce could feel goose bumps on his arms, knowing the infected were getting close.

"Conner, carry Frank. Jake, carry Alice. Sling your rifle, and carry your P90. Debbie, carry Nathan, and Danny, carry Robert. Emily and Sherry, come here. I'm carrying both of you," Bruce gave out orders.

"Daddy, I can carry the baby," Buffy volunteered.

"No, BB, you have to protect us. If they make it by you, we all die," Bruce said.

"Nothing will make it by me, Daddy. I promise," Buffy answered in a hard voice.

"We are moving out fast. We aren't stopping for at least two hours. If someone has to stop before then, everyone else keep going. Remember; if you give out, the child you're carrying dies with you," Bruce said as he knelt and picked up one twin's leg, putting it through his left backpack shoulder strap as she straddled his hip. Then, he did the same to the other twin on his right. Even if they let go, they wouldn't fall. With his arms wrapped around the twins and his rifle in his right hand, he took off at a fast jog.

The others fell in behind him. The pipeline was a mile from them, and they reached it in seven minutes. Turning down the pipeline, they settled into a quick jog. Bruce glanced down at Paul as he turned down the pipeline. Paul was just smiling and clapping his hands. Bruce looked up, staying in the middle of the pipeline. He didn't want to get too close to the wood line on either side. Sweat poured off his body, raining down on Paul and soaking the twins as they held onto him with a vise-like grip.

79

Conner was the last man in line, running at the pace Bruce had set. When Conner was on the roof, he had questioned himself. Why was he following this crazy man? Bruce was waging a war with hopeless odds against the infected and against any others that preyed on the weak or helpless. Hearing Danny tell the story of the kids on the island, he knew now why he followed Bruce. Bruce thought of others and would fight until the last breath escaped his lips. Running down the pipeline, Conner looked at the small boy he was carrying. Conner knew in his heart that the only reason he would stop running would be if he died from exhaustion. Smiling, Conner knew he would die for his clan, and could kill a lot before he died.

They had been running for over an hour when, fifty yards in front of them, two blues popped out of the wood line on their left. One second they weren't there; the next, they just materialized. Without even breaking stride, Buffy raised her M-4, sending a three-round burst into each blue's face. They just jogged past the bodies and down the pipeline. Fifteen minutes later, Bruce heard someone scream over the radio. "Get off the fucking pipeline now; move to your right fast."

Without hesitation, Bruce turned and plowed through the thorn bushes into the woods as everyone followed him. The twins squeezed Bruce when the thorns hit their legs but never made a sound. After he had run about thirty yards into the woods, Bruce turned back north. Then, he heard in his ear, "No. Go further east, to your right." He followed the instructions and headed east, getting pissed. *Whoever is giving instructions had better have seen something because running through the woods sucks,* Bruce thought as he jumped another log.

He wanted to ask what they had seen but was having trouble keeping his breathing in rhythm. It had been a male voice, so he thought it was either Jake or Conner. He just kept running. For how long, he didn't know. The voice came back over the radio. "Alright, head north again. You're fixin' to come to a road that heads northeast. Take it, and I'll tell you when to turn."

That could only be Jake. "You memorized the map that well, son, and can run it from memory?" Bruce asked in amazement between breaths.

"This is Mike, motherfucker! There're infected all around you. We watched a mob of at least thirty thousand pour out of Natchitoches. I know you're tired, but you have to keep going. I hope it was worth it, chasing that group down," Mike said, pissed.

"Seven kids on the island, oldest nine, youngest about nine months. Had to save baby. He was dying," was all Bruce could say as he gulped down air.

"Okay, brother, here's the road now. Take it for a mile. Then, I'm takin' ya through some fields and roads to the levee on Saline Lake," Mike called back. He felt bad about yelling at Bruce after hearing about the kids. Since the group was carrying them, he didn't see them with the UAV.

When he reached the road, Bruce turned down the road and just concentrated on moving his feet. He glanced down at Buffy and noticed she was wobbling with her stride. Their fast jog was a good run for her little legs. Bruce reached over, grabbing her M-4. She just let it go. He put the strap over his neck and slung the rifle over his back. He called on his radio and asked if anyone needed to stop. Hearing roars in the distance, everyone replied, "Just go."

As Bruce was reaching down to try to carry Buffy also, he heard from his side, "I have her, Dad." He saw Jake run up beside Buffy, picking her up with his right arm with Alice on his left. "Alright, little sister, you hafta wrap your legs around me and Alice and hold on," Jake said as he set Buffy on his right hip.

"Thank you, bubba," Buffy said. She was out of breath but doing her best to hang on.

"Alright, I want you to head right, through this field," Mike told Bruce.

Never stopping, Bruce followed the directions he was given for another hour, only slowing down to wade across several large creeks. Reaching the levee, they ran on top of it. It was dark now, and off to the west and south, they could still hear lots of roars. They just kept running until Mike came over the radio.

"Okay, you can rest here. The closest infected is over a mile away. Get you NVGs on; you have two more large groups to get by. Take twenty minutes," Mike said.

Dropping to his knees, Bruce let the twins' legs out of the straps. He pulled off Buffy's rifle and set it down then lifted the sling off with a sleeping Paul in it. Laying Paul gently on the ground, he then dropped his pack. Unclipping his SCAR from its sling, Bruce laid it on the ground. He got up walked two steps, fell down on all fours, and puked. As his stomach muscles continued tightening five minutes later, Bruce was expecting his boots to fall out of his mouth any minute. After he stopped puking and never seeing his boots come out, he sat up on his knees. Wiping his face, he looked at the rest of the group.

They looked just like he felt: like hammered shit. His entire body was numb, but he stood up and wobbled to his pack. Dropping down beside it, Bruce pulled out his NVG and two bottles of water, handing them to the twins, telling them to drink. One held her bottle out to him. At just the thought of drinking, Bruce would swear for years to come, he felt boot laces at the back of his throat.

He shook his head then dug out an FSR and pulled two bars out, handing them to the twins. They took them and started eating right away. Bruce watched them, thankful they didn't offer him any. He took out his thermal scope and mounted it. Buffy walked up beside him, picked up her rifle, then took off her pack and started doing the same thing as Bruce.

Bruce took the last bottle of water out of his pack and made Paul a bottle of sports mix. Then, he slowly drank what was left. Putting the last bar from the FSR in his thigh pocket with the bottle for Paul, Bruce started tightening his vest since it had become loose with the run. Then, he started to drink the last of his water from the Camelback. Looking at his watch, it was just after 9 p.m. *Holy shit, we moved twenty miles in just over three hours,* he thought. That had to be some kind of record while carrying kids and full combat gear. *Well, knowing you could get eaten and/or infected did give you a large amount of determination.*

Taking slow drinks, Bruce studied the twins, who were standing together, watching him, eating their food in unison. They had blond hair and green eyes with heart-shaped, china doll faces. Bruce turned around, asking in a low voice, "Everyone drink some water?" He got four yeses and one fuck you. Knowing who had said the 'fuck you,' he said, "Debbie, you better drink one liter, or I'll pour one down you."

Turning back around, Bruce found the twins still staring at him. He hated to admit it, but it was starting to freak him out. One stepped toward him, holding out the uneaten half of her food bar, and Bruce shook his head. Then, the other one stepped forward and held out hers. Again, he shook his head. They both stepped forward together, putting the food bars on his lips. Somewhat afraid they were fixing to voodoo his ass, Bruce took a bite of each, chewing it slowly. At first, his stomach growled in protest, threatening to invert itself, but he slowly continued chewing. Once his stomach quit protesting, Bruce thought this was the best food he had ever eaten. Swallowing it, he took another bite of each as the twins held the food in front of his mouth. They each fed him half of their food bars. After he had finished, they both hugged Bruce's neck, kissing him on each cheek. Then, they sat down at the same time beside baby Paul, who was still sleeping.

Checking on everyone, he saw they had put on NVGs and were putting their packs on. Sighing, Bruce pulled on his pack and looked down at Buffy, who was just staring at him. What was it with little blond girls just staring at him tonight? Reaching up, Bruce turned on his monocular. There was a lot of light out, but he still lowered it over his left eye. Looking back down at Buffy, she had lowered her eye piece, still looking at Bruce.

"What, Buffy?" Bruce asked. He just wanted to lie down and sleep for a year.

"They really love you, Daddy," Buffy said.

"Don't ask right now, BB. Daddy is ready to lie down and die, and we still have a long way to go," Bruce said just as Nancy came over the radio.

"Okay, you need to move, but do not run. Keep a sixteen-minute-mile pace. Any faster and you could run up on blues. Now, come home."

Bruce knelt, motioning for the twins to come to him. They walked to him, stopped in front of him, then, without a word, switched sides. They pulled out his shoulder straps, putting their legs in. Bruce looked at the twin on his left.

"Weren't you on the other side last time," Bruce asked, and she nodded. "Your leg hurts from the straps, huh?" he asked, and they nodded in unison.

"Don't worry. We'll get home, but it'll almost be daylight. Which one are you?" he looked at the twin on his left. "Emily," she replied in a soft, meek voice.

"Let's go, girls," Bruce said, picking up a sleeping Paul and slinging him across his abdomen. From that point on, Bruce could tell the twins apart. Everyone else would have trouble. Even Danny and Debbie would paint their fingernails different colors to tell them apart.

Adjusting his rifle, Bruce started walking home, keeping the pace he was told. After walking an hour and twenty minutes, they were in a field, still heading north. Buffy was starting to fall down a lot as her little legs started giving out. But she would get back up and keep going. Wobbling with each step, Bruce glanced down at the twins, and both were asleep, holding onto him. It always amazed him how and where a child could sleep. As that thought went through his mind, Nancy screamed over the radio, "On your left now!"

Bruce spun to the left, flipping his SCAR to full auto. He saw runners coming out of the woods forty yards away. Not able to bring his weapon to his shoulder, he sprayed and prayed as did the rest of the group. Seeing some infected fall down and get back up, he started getting worried. As his bolt locked, he dropped the magazine and was having trouble getting another one out from under Emily's butt. When he got it out, Bruce slammed it in and released the bolt. Two were still coming. He pulled the trigger and walked the rounds up one runner's body until he got to its head blowing it off. Buffy dropped the last one. Knowing he was almost empty, Bruce dropped and dug out another magazine then slapped it in. Conner had finished a two-hundred-round belt and set Frank down to replace it. Buffy moved over, shooting the crawling ones in the head, then wobbled back to Bruce.

For the first time, Bruce noticed Paul was crying. Bruce reached in his pocket and handed the bottle to Sherry, telling told her to put it in his mouth. As soon as the bottle touched Paul's lips, he stopped crying and went back to sleep, drinking from the bottle. Bruce knelt, picking up his magazines, and handed them to Emily. He told her to put them in his shirt, which she did. Bruce watched the woods as Nancy came over the radio. "Four more coming; they will come out where those did."

Bruce knelt again, aiming the best he could in the direction where the other blues were lying. Then, he saw them running through the trees. When they broke the tree line at a dead run, he heard four rapid bursts, and all four dropped as if they were told to stay. Tracing the source of the shot, he saw Jake lowering the P90. *He is so getting a raise in his allowance*, Bruce told himself.

Nancy came over the radio. "Sorry, they changed direction. I thought they were going to pass you. Only a little further. Move it, guys."

A little further? Bruce wanted to scream at her they were still over fifteen miles from home and still had a lot of rough terrain to cover. His pace had slowed to a twenty-two-minute mile, and it was almost 11:30. Physically, they couldn't go any faster. They were all worn out and moving on determination. It was going to be morning before they got home, and he could not feel his legs.

Nancy came over the radio. "At the road up ahead, stop in the ditch and wait." Not in the mood to talk, Bruce did as she told him. Ten minutes later, she came back on the radio. "You should be able to see Mike and his team coming down the road now."

Bruce looked down the road and saw four electric buggies coming at him at their top speed of thirty miles per hour. Mike came to a stop in front of them. "Need a ride?" he asked, smiling.

"I love you, man," Bruce said, kneeling down. He told the twins to get off. They both shook their heads. "Both of you can sit by me, and I'll hold you," Bruce said, and they climbed out of the straps. Bruce sat beside Mike. He put Emily between him and Mike, and then Bruce sat Sherry between his legs. Bruce keyed his radio. "Conner, make sure you're covering our ass. Runners go faster than our rides."

"Already doing it, boss," Conner replied.

The thirty-minute trip home was uneventful as Mike and his team floored the buggies. When Mike stopped in front of the house, Bruce got out, grabbing the twins, putting one on each hip. When someone opened the front door, Bruce was almost blinded by the light. He still had his NVG on, and the light wasn't bright enough to throw the safety shutoff. Hearing several groans from behind him, Bruce knew he was not the only one.

Stumbling into the house, everyone rushed forward to hug him and then hugged everyone else as they walked in. Lynn called him into the kitchen, telling him to sit down; she had cooked them something. Bruce tried to set the twins down, but they wouldn't let go. "Girls, we're home. I'm sitting down with you right there," Bruce said, pointing to his chair, but they wouldn't let go. Lynn ran over and put two chairs beside Bruce's, one on each corner. The twins finally let him set them in the chairs.

Bruce started dropping equipment, letting it hit the kitchen floor. Last, he took off his tactical vest while holding Paul; then, he dropped down in his chair. Paul was awake, clapping his hands and laughing. Taking him out of the sling, Bruce held up the naked baby boy. Paul was covered in baby poop. Bruce had never stopped to wrap something around him for a diaper. Bruce held Paul up in front of him.

"You shit on me? How could you shit on me? Then, you rolled around in it. Paul, that's disgusting," Bruce moaned. Paul was just laughing away and clapped his hands. Just then, Paul peed on Bruce's chest, making everyone laugh. Even the twins giggled. "Then, you pee on me. We have to work on your manners," Bruce said. Paul thought that was the best thing in the world as he smiled and laughed. Susan came over, took Paul, and told Bruce she would give him a bath and put a diaper on him. When Paul left Bruce's hands, he started crying, or more appropriately screaming, and continued as Susan took him to the bathroom.

Standing up, Bruce started stripping off clothes. His tiger stripe top and t-shirt were so soaked in sweat that he couldn't see where Paul had peed on him. After his shirts were off, he just looked down at his boots. He decided they were not worth the effort. Maria and Angela came over and started unlacing them. Bruce looked at the table as they worked on his boots.

Conner, Danny, Jake, Buffy, and Debbie were sitting in their underwear sound asleep with plates of food sitting in front of them. The kids they had rescued were spread around the table, asleep in their chairs. Buffy had her head lying on the table fast asleep, her food untouched. Maria and Angela pulled off Bruce's boots and pants. He sat down and looked at his plate. The next thing he knew, it was empty, and Bruce didn't remember eating it. Looking across the table with a fog over his brain, he saw Danny snoring with her head on the table. Jake, Debbie and Conner were leaned back in their chairs, asleep. As were both the twins, but they had just curled up on the seat of the chair and went to sleep. Bruce thought he was the last one awake from the patrol until he heard Paul crying as Susan brought him back. When Paul was back in Bruce's hands, he stopped screaming.

Bruce looked around the kitchen. The rest of the clan was awake, looking at the patrol group. With a herculean effort, Bruce stood, wobbling with Paul in his arms. Stephanie rushed over and supported him, making sure he didn't fall. Bending down to pick up Sherry to carry her upstairs, Mike grabbed his hand. "Who do you want, and where do you want them? We will carry them," Mike said as Stephanie held him upright.

"I want me, Danny, Buffy, the twins, Paul in my room. Oh, and don't forget Debbie. Put Jake and Conner in Jake's room. Find the kids a place together," Bruce said. Stephanie guided him upstairs.

Bruce never remembered lying down.

CHAPTER 8

Coming out of the void of sleep, Bruce felt something slapping his face, and it was cooing. Opening his eyes, Bruce looked toward the sound. Paul was propped up on his shoulder, smiling and drooling on him. Not in the mood to get up, Bruce pulled him down into the crook of his arm, hoping Paul would go back to sleep. Paul was having none of it and he crawled back onto Bruce's chest then started hitting him in the face again. Bruce glared at Paul, who was still smiling and drooling on him.

"I saved you, carried you across north Louisiana at a dead run, and how do you repay me? You piss, shit, and drool on me then wake me up when I feel like a whole football team gang raped me," he protested. Paul must have thought that was funny because he started to laugh, slapping Bruce's chest and face.

He moved to get up when he glanced at the clock on the night stand reading 9:18 a.m. To his surprise, a baby bottle with milk was beside it. *You are a kind and merciful God,* Bruce thought as he grabbed the bottle. He laid Paul back down in the crook of his arm. Paul was starting to voice his displeasure with that move; he wanted to get up. When the nipple hit Paul's lips, as Bruce shoved the bottle in his mouth. Paul shut up, attacking the bottle. Bruce was back asleep before half the bottle was downed.

Bruce felt something hard and hollow-sounding hit his right cheek. He didn't want to open his eyes, thinking Paul would leave him alone. Then, he noticed a heavy weight pressing on his abdomen and felt something lying on his cheek. He probably could have gone back to sleep, but his bladder was full, and Paul was trying to make Bruce wet the bed. Then it occurred to Bruce; Paul was not that heavy or that big. Bruce opened his eyes and saw a dirty little foot resting on his cheek in front of his right eye. *How the hell did that get there?* he thought as he grabbed the dirty little foot, feeling it was connected to a little leg. He moved it off of his face. The foot no sooner cleared his face than Paul hit him between the eyes with the empty bottle.

Bruce took the empty bottle from Paul and snapped, "That's enough." Paul sat back, looking at Bruce like, "Who the hell do you think you are talking to me like that?"

Bruce traced the owner of the foot down to find it was Sherry. Emily was lying across his abdomen with her head hanging off the bed. Bruce extracted himself from the mass of bodies as his muscles screamed in protest. He stood at the side of the bed, fighting the muscle cramps with his joints popping and heard a squeal behind him. He turned around as Paul crawled over the mass of twins toward Bruce. Picking up Paul, Bruce put him on his hip and looked down at the bed. He did not see Debbie at first because Buffy and Danny were sprawled across her.

Looking down at his body, Bruce saw it was covered in a fine layer of dried mud from his sweat. He had drool all over his right side and felt in his ear with a finger. Yep, there was drool there too. He was going to move Buffy and Danny off of Debbie, but he had to shower first. Debbie would have to fight her own battles for now. Heading to the bathroom, Bruce closed the door so he wouldn't wake anyone. Laying a towel on the counter, he put Paul on it then took his diaper off.

They had no diapers at the farm but did have hundreds of bath towels. Several were sacrificed to make diapers for Joshua, and Susan had put one on Paul the night before.

Peeling the diaper back revealed a baby poop paste with a toxic odor that made Bruce gasp. "Oh man, that's disgusting. Those FSR bars don't come out of me looking and smelling like that," Bruce said, who just started kicking his legs and laughing.

Bruce tried to clean Paul up fast before he started playing in it. "I don't think any of my kids acted like this," Bruce told Paul, who didn't seem to care. Trying to wipe the poop paste off, Bruce was convinced it was part toxic waste and part Velcro. Bruce wiped Paul down and then set him on the floor as he opened the shower door and turned on the water. Taking off his watch, he noticed it was 10:41. Well, at least Paul let him sleep a little longer.

"I have to take a cold shower because of you. I hope you're happy," Bruce told Paul, who was on the floor, looking up at him. Apparently, it did make him happy as he started laughing and squealing as he crawled to Bruce. Taking off his boxers, Bruce picked up Paul and got in the shower.

It was a large shower with three shower heads: one above and one on each side. The shower controls were on the wall facing the door with a mirror above them so Bruce could shave. Bruce sat Paul down on the marble tile, and he immediately started splashing in the water at the bottom of the shower.

Bruce quickly washed and shaved. Then, he picked Paul up and washed him down. Paul didn't like the water hitting him on top of his head. He would try to look up to see where it was coming from and get drowned as the water hit his face.

"Well, quit lookin' up, goober," Bruce said as he turned off the overhead shower head and heard the bathroom door open and close.

"Come on in, Debbie. I'm just washing a mean baby in here," Bruce called out as Paul kept trying to put his face in the stream of water coming from the right.

Bruce turned around to open the door for Debbie and he saw the twins standing in front of the sink in t-shirts and panties, holding hands. Their t-shirts had at one time been white but were black now. Their skin was dusky from caked dirt and dried sweat, and their hair was matted and sticking out.

Bruce sat Paul on the shower floor, and he again started slapping the floor, splashing water everywhere. Stepping out of the shower, Bruce stripped Emily and Sherry. Looking at their legs, he could see the mark his pack straps had put on their thighs. He pointed to the shower, and they both stepped in as Bruce followed.

Bruce scrubbed Sherry down then Emily. Then, grabbing one of Debbie's bottles of shampoo, he turned off all the shower heads and lathered Emily's head. Paul started yelling when the water stopped. Not crying, just yelling in a baby voice like, "Hey, idiot, I was having fun."

"Knock it off, Paul," Bruce growled, looking down at him. Paul slapped the water on the shower floor, making it splash while looking at Bruce like, "That could be you."

"I'm so scared," Bruce said in a sarcastic tone as he lathered up Sherry's head. Paul started laughing as he slapped the water. Bruce pushed Sherry in a corner, picked up Emily, and turned one shower head on. Paul started squealing in delight.

Holding Emily with her looking up so the soap wouldn't get in her eyes, Bruce rinsed the shampoo out of her hair. Putting her down, he repeated the process with Sherry. Then, Bruce heard the door open and close.

"Debbie, that had damn well better be you 'cause if it's not, I'm flushin' someone down the toilet," Bruce threatened.

"Well, hell yes it's me," Debbie said, stripping, and opened the shower door. She saw Bruce holding one twin, the other behind him in the corner, and Paul having a blast on the shower floor, trying to beat the water into submission.

"When are you going to give me a bath?" Debbie asked, smiling at Bruce.

Bruce cocked his head to the side and asked, "Are you going to help me or what?"

"Well, move so I can get in and thank you for not boiling the kids alive," Debbie said, getting in. Paul didn't care; he was having a blast crawling around, splashing the water.

"I've washed everyone, but the girls need another scrubbing down. They're filthy," Bruce said.

"Bruce, you didn't put any conditioner in their hair, and it needs to be washed again," Debbie said, scrubbing down a twin.

"Debbie, I haven't used shampoo in over twenty years. I'm sorry that I've let you down. Please forgive me. You need to scrub the bottom of Emily's feet. I haven't checked them. I knew Sherry's were dirty because I woke up with one in my face," Bruce said, scrubbing Sherry.

"Which one is Emily?" Debbie asked.

"The one you're scrubbing," Bruce said in a smart ass tone. Debbie let it slide.

Bruce and Debbie scrubbed the girls down two more times. Then, Debbie washed Emily's hair, and Bruce washed Sherry's hair with Debbie telling him how to do it correctly. Bruce mumbled something bet kept his comments to himself. If he had to do this many more times, he was going to convince the girls to shave their heads like him.

When they were finished, Debbie opened the door, leading the twins out. Bruce was bending down to get Paul when he noticed the baby had pooped on the shower floor.

"Paul," Bruce whined. Bruce picked Paul up then aimed one shower head at the toxic spill and stuck Paul's butt in front of another one. This just made Paul laugh. Bruce turned his head toward Debbie, who was just looking at him holding the baby's butt up to the shower head. "What? It's like a bidet," Bruce said. She shook her head, mumbling something about men.

They dried everyone off, and when one of the girls reached for her shirt, Debbie told her no. "That's Sherry," Bruce said, which earned him "the look." Bruce scowled right back at her as if daring her to say something. He was sore, tired, and pissed. Plus, he thought Paul had something wrong with him. Babies shouldn't shit toxic waste that stuck to everything it came in contact with.

Wrapping Paul in a towel, Bruce walked out of the bathroom to his dresser and put on some boxers. He grabbed two of his t-shirts, walked back to the bathroom, and laid Paul on the floor. Bruce put the shirts on the girls. They could have used them for tents. Turning back around, Bruce went to Debbie's dresser and looked until he found two t-shirts. He went back to the girls, pulled his shirts off, and put Debbie's on. They were big, but the bottom stopped at their ankles. Debbie finished towel drying her hair and wrapped it then wrapped a towel around her body. Then, she and Bruce started brushing the twins' hair. They walked into the bedroom as Bruce looked at Buffy and Danny lying across the bed.

Bruce put on shorts and a t-shirt as did Debbie with the twins just looking at them. Bruce kicked the bed, telling Danny and Buffy to get up as he heard the trash can hit the floor in the bathroom with a squeal of delight. Unable to run, Bruce hobbled quickly back to the bathroom to find Paul playing in the spilled contents

"Paul, quit that," Bruce said, standing in the door. Paul looked up at Bruce as if to say, "I didn't do it." Then, Paul reached out to Bruce. Bruce picked him up and wrapped him back in the towel. "You aren't getting me today, buddy," Bruce said as Paul smiled. Bruce walked over and kicked the bed again, saying, "Get up, troops. Drop your cocks, and grab your socks. Daddy is up so, everyone else has to be up."

Buffy raised her head. "Daddy, I hurt everywhere, and my legs are tingling," she wailed, dropping her head to the bed.

"It's called pain. Like and love it, BB. Pain lets you know you're alive. Let's go," Bruce said, walking to the door.

"Daddy, I don't want to move," Buffy complained in a whiney voice.

"Buffy, reach down, find your balls, grab 'em, then squeeze 'em hard and get up," Bruce said, walking out of the room with Paul in his arms and the twins following.

Buffy sat up fast. "I have balls?" she asked.

"It's a figure of speech, Buffy. You don't have like real balls, like boys, but you do have balls, little sister," Danny said, her head buried in a pillow.

"Well, what are real boy balls for?" Buffy asked, causing Danny to sit up fast and Debbie to look at her.

"What?" Danny said.

"What are balls for?" Buffy repeated.

"BB did your Mama tell you about boys and girls?" Debbie asked.

"Yeah, she said if a boy touches you wrong to call the cops," Buffy said, looking at Debbie.

"Do you know were babies come from?" Danny asked her.

"Duh, the hospital," Buffy replied not believing Danny had asked her that.

"Have you ever seen a boy naked?" Danny asked.

"Yeah, when we were at Mr. Marcus'," Buffy answered.

"Didn't you play with other kids?" Danny asked Buffy.

"Only at school. Mama worked a lot, and Ms. Miller watched me. She wouldn't let me go out and play because somebody might take me," Buffy said.

"Danny, you and Buffy take a shower fast; then, you and I are going to have a girl talk with Buffy," Debbie said. While they showered, Debbie stripped the bed then sprayed it down with Lysol. After taking new sheets and blankets out of the closet, she made the bed. Danny and Buffy came out of the shower wrapped in towels, and Debbie pointed to the bed. They all sat on the bed as Debbie explained the birds and bees to Buffy with Danny telling Buffy what the slang terms were. This was making Debbie mad, but after an hour, Buffy looked at Debbie.

"That's what boobies are for?" Buffy asked.

"Yes, BB, to feed babies," Debbie said.

"Then why does Daddy say his...you know...girl part hurts?" Buffy asked.

"His pussy," Danny supplied, which earned her "the look" from Debbie.

"Daddy just means he's tired, sore, and in a bad mood," Debbie said.

"Like when Daddy told you to grab your balls, he meant reach down and be strong. Laugh at the pain," Danny said then continued. "Like when I tell someone to suck my—"

"Danny, watch your mouth," Debbie snapped, not able to tolerate it anymore.

"Mom we have to let her know this; it's important. You can be here now, or I can tell her later," Danny said, wondering why her mom was being so weird. *It must be a Mama thing*, she thought.

Debbie looked at Buffy. "Don't use any of those words after we leave this room," she said.

"Now, when I tell someone *that*," Danny emphasized, "It means I'm about to kick their ass and I'm better than them," she finished.

"You understand, Buffy?" Debbie asked, looking at her.

"So you mean we bleed then get cramps that hurt so guys copy us saying their…hurts. A guy may have balls but not have 'balls,' being weak, and a girl can have balls meaning she is tough?" Buffy asked, twisting her face, trying to understand what she was saying.

"That's it," Danny said, smiling.

"How come girls are referred to as weak?" Buffy asked, a little angry.

"It's just society, Buffy. Women are not as physically strong as a man, and we have those hormones we told you about. Always remember: Behind every great man is a greater woman. Behind a great woman, you hardly ever see a man," Debbie said.

"Okay, Mama," Buffy said, hugging her then Danny.

They got up, leaving the bedroom. Danny and Buffy headed to their room to get clothes, and Debbie headed downstairs to the kitchen. Bruce was in his chair with a twin on each side, eating eggs, bacon, and pancakes. Bruce had Paul in his lap, trying to feed him. Paul was actually eating pretty well even though he was making a mess, and Bruce was arguing with him. Debbie stopped as Bruce continued to argue with the baby. Not yelling or using harsh tones, just arguing like the baby understood him. Debbie reminded herself why she loved Bruce and how much she loved him. She could tell the mood Bruce was in and knew why he was in it. Taking a deep breath, Debbie let it out slowly. She was sore, had no feeling in her feet, and the baby wouldn't let anyone but Bruce hold him. She would not fight with Bruce today because that's what he was wanting. Tomorrow was a completely different story though.

Grabbing the plate that Lynn handed her and the cup of coffee, Debbie walked over to her seat. Sitting down with a twin between her and Bruce, the twin turned, smiling at Debbie as she ate her pancakes with syrup, which was all over her face. Shaking her head, Debbie saw another shower in the twins' immediate future. Mike, Nancy, Angela, Alex, and Stephanie were at the end of the table, watching Bruce argue with the baby with shocked expressions on their faces. Lynn and Susan were in the kitchen with the same expression. Debbie just ignored Bruce and started eating.

"I swear feeding you is like teaching a pig to sing. It pisses you off and annoys the pig," Bruce said to Paul, feeding him another bite of eggs. "You respect nothing and drool too much. I'm not even going to talk about what comes out of your butt," Bruce continued as Paul clapped his hands.

"Emily, don't put a piece that big in your mouth," Bruce told the twin sitting next to Debbie as he reached over, cut the large piece of pancake in half, and continued. "Look at both of ya: syrup everywhere and it took an hour to wash you last time. I'm going to have to give you another bath and get yelled at by the Great Hairdresser because I'm not doing your hair right. Sherry, you just heard me tell Emily not to take big bites." Bruce reached over to cut her piece in half and kept right on arguing as Paul let out a baby yell to get Bruce's attention.

"I hear you. You see me feeding someone else? Well, do ya?" Bruce asked Paul, who was smiling and looking at Bruce like, "I know you are crazy, but feed me." "I haven't even had a chance to eat because oh no, someone has to scream like a girl when anyone but me holds him. Then, two girls from the Village of the Damned follow me around tryin' to voodoo my ass," Bruce said to no one and everyone as the twins looked at him at the same time, smiling at him as if saying, "You are insane, old man, but we love you."

"Alright, you two; don't be doing that movin' in unison thing, okay? It freaks me out. I swear if your eyes start glowing, I'm packing my bags. I will swim the Pacific Ocean until I find a deserted island. If Robinson Crusoe is on it, I'll kick his ass then feed him to some sharks just so everyone will leave me the hell alone," Bruce continued as Paul clapped his hands to remind the crazy man to feed him.

"You hear me talkin'; don't interrupt, and let me tell you: We're fixing to start potty training you." Angela was going to say something, but Debbie looked at her, shaking her head as Bruce kept on. "I have no idea what the hell you ate, but keep that toxic waste spillage up, and I won't change ya. You can do it yourself. I will leave that diaper on till it rots off. Let me tell you another thing; you keep demanding me to feed you, and I'll take you outside and put a goat's tit in your mouth. I'll tie you to the bottom of the goat and not let you off until you can walk," Bruce threatened, which Paul must've thought was hilarious because he started laughing. Everyone except Debbie was looking at Bruce like he was insane. He was carrying on an argument with a baby who couldn't talk and four-year-old girls who didn't know what the hell he was saying but smiled at him anyway. Bruce never yelled at them or spoke harshly; he was just arguing with himself and losing. Bruce looked up at the adults and used a smartass, harsh tone at them. "What the hell are you looking at me like that for?" They all turned away looking in different directions.

"What, all of you going to take their side? Huh? Just 'cause they're kids? Think my balls have fallen on the floor and I've started lactating?" Bruce looked toward Debbie. "What took you so long? I'm covered in eggs, and little poop machine here threw eggs in my ear. Emily and Sherry both are bound and determined to put a whole bottle of syrup in their hair. But I'm glad you look good though and graced us with your presence," Bruce popped off. Debbie just looked at him, shrugged, and went back to eating. Seeing Debbie not taking the bait, Bruce was fixing to unleash on someone else as Paul let out a huge, wet-sounding fart and laughed. Bruce sat straight up. "That better be sweat I feel on my leg because if you shit on me again, I swear I'm going to pick my nose and wipe a booger on ya," he threatened. Bruce stood, never looking down, and walked to the bathroom. Buffy and Danny passed him in the hall.

"I'm glad you two finally got up," Bruce said.

Before he could start bitching at them, Buffy yelled with enthusiasm, "Daddy! I reached down and squeezed my balls and jumped out of bed after Danny squeezed her balls to show me how."

"Now, that's what I'm talking about! Hell yeah, girls. Now, go in the kitchen, and find mine. I think they fell off under the table," Bruce said, his voice fading as he went down the hall. Danny and Buffy grabbed plates and just started eating at the bar.

"Debbie! Shit fire is he bitchy! He walked in and started bitin' anyone's heads off. I popped back off, but he got hostile with me. Then, he sat down and started arguing with the kids. Never raising his voice but arguing, and they think it's funny as hell. Is he okay?" Mike asked.

"He's fine. Leave him be," Debbie said in a warning voice.

"Debbie, we'll watch the kids. Take him upstairs, and give him some. If you won't go, let Nancy, or hell, I'll go give him some, but make him stop," Mike offered.

"It's not sexual frustration, Mike," Debbie said.

"What is it, Debbie?" asked Nancy.

"I can't say right now," Debbie said, looking at the twins.

"Why didn't you say something to him when he started on you?" Angela asked with everyone else agreeing, wanting an answer.

"That's what he wants. Let's all get something straight right now. I love you all and will die for you. If anyone starts an argument with Bruce today, that person and myself are going outside. I'll walk back in. The other person will crawl back in," Debbie warned, sipping her coffee.

"Debbie—" Lynn started, but Debbie held up her hand.

"Angela, sneak down the hall to the bathroom. Don't let Bruce hear you, and come back and tell us what you see," Debbie said. Angela got up, left the kitchen, and came back shortly.

"He is playing with Paul, talkin' baby talk," Angela reported with a confused look on her face as she sat down.

"Debbie, please just say it. I'm a man, and I don't understand what you are saying," Mike said.

Turning to Buffy and Danny at the bar, Debbie said, "Danny and Buffy, I want you to take Emily and Sherry upstairs and wash them off, and I want you to do it now." Hearing her tone, they ran over to the girls and rushed upstairs with them.

"You've seen this before with Buffy to a lesser degree. Now, don't take this the wrong way for those that have not lived in this family. I'm going to talk fast, so keep up, and don't interrupt. Mike's family, our family, Stephanie, Cassandra, Joshua, and Angela's family, because they are his residents which Bruce sees as his kids, are his close family. If anything happens to them, it'll hurt him something horrible because each one has a piece of his heart, and that piece will die with them. Everyone else is next to his heart, and he loves you. If something happens to you, it'll hurt him, but he'll be able to continue. Then, Buffy took a piece of his heart. Now, he has two little girls and a baby that are demanding a piece of his heart. Bruce doesn't want to give it to them because he's scared. We are living in a war here, and Bruce doesn't want to lose a piece of his heart. He feels if he does, he won't think straight, and he will lose someone else he loves until he's alone. That's Bruce's greatest fear: being alone," Debbie said, looking at each of them.

"He wants someone to argue with him so he can get mad and not let those three kids have a piece of his heart," Debbie said. Stephanie was fixing to say something, but Debbie held up her hand, reading her mind. "It's totally a guy thing, Stephanie. Mike does it, and so do the boys though not to this degree, but they do the same thing." Nancy agreed, saying Mike just pouted. Mike disagreed.

"How long will it last, and what can we do besides not argue with him?" Stephanie asked, wanting to help.

"It will be over by this evening. The ones that are going to stop it are upstairs washing syrup off of two little girls. Bruce will pop off at one or both of 'em, hurting their feelings. They'll do that Daddy's little girl thing, and he will feel like crap and give up. He will tell the girls he's sorry; then, he will be the Bruce you know. We will get our apologies tomorrow," Debbie said as Mike just stared at her. She knew Bruce better than Bruce knew himself. Then, Mike saw the bigger picture. Bruce never got away with anything. Debbie just let him think he did. Mike looked at Nancy, and she was observing him with a smirk. He knew it was the same way for him.

"Paul—not the baby, Cheryl's husband—wanted to go over some upgrades today," Mike said.

"Tomorrow," Debbie said as Bruce walked back in, arguing with baby Paul.

Bruce continued to argue with the kids and trying to pick a fight with anyone. Then, it played out just like Debbie said it would. He yelled at Danny and Buffy, causing tears to come to their eyes as they sat on the couch. Feeling like a total piece of shit, Bruce went over to them, carrying baby Paul, and sat down with them. He told them he was sorry and called the twins over as they all hugged. Resting on the opposite couch in her shorts, Debbie smiled with her sore feet propped up. Bruce got up with baby Paul and walked over to Debbie, moving her pillow he sat down, putting her feet in his lap. Bruce put the baby on her chest, and Paul started to cry as Bruce snapped, "That's your Mama, so drop it, boy." Paul cried for a minute as Debbie talked to him; then, he started playing with her face and hair.

Bruce started rubbing Debbie's feet, which hurt like hell at first, but the pain went away, and her feet felt so good when he was done. Sitting up, Debbie kissed Bruce then took Paul to the kitchen to feed him before movie night started. She did not notice the two women looking at her like she was a mortal deity. Angela and Stephanie could not put into words the awe they felt. What they did not understand was Debbie and Bruce did not have secrets from one another. The love they shared was a love that many would never know.

CHAPTER 9

Hearing a baby cooing, Bruce slowly woke up. He opened his eyes, rotating to the sound, moving little bodies off of him in the process. Paul was sitting up by Debbie's head and slapping her in the face.

"PJ, quit that! You'll wake up Mama," Bruce scolded, reaching for Paul, who just looked at Bruce like, "I wasn't doing anything."

The night before, Debbie asked Bruce if they could call the baby Paul Jack Williams after her father, Jack, who had died two years ago. Bruce told her that was a great idea and started calling Paul PJ. PJ didn't care what anyone called him as long as Bruce and Debbie fed him.

Bruce picked up PJ, who started giggling as Bruce shushed him. This only turned the giggling into laughter. Bruce rushed PJ into the bathroom to change the toxic diaper he could smell. After changing PJ, he walked back to the bedroom and looked at the bed.

He could not even see where he had been sleeping. The twins had the most room followed by Buffy then poor Debbie. Bruce didn't even see Danny in the bed and started looking on the floor. He found her asleep on the floor on Debbie's side of the bed. Grabbing a blanket, Bruce covered Danny then, smiling to himself, left the bedroom and headed to the kitchen. It was Sunday, and if they wanted to sleep late, then that was okay.

Entering the kitchen, Bruce saw Lynn making breakfast. Lynn turned around upon hearing a baby babbling behind her. "There's a bottle at your place on the table, and I will get you some food for Paul," Lynn said, smiling.

"It's PJ," Bruce reminded her as he headed for his spot. PJ was leaning out of Bruce's arms, reaching for the bottle before Bruce even sat down.

"Knock it off, PJ. I'll give you your bottle," Bruce said as he sat then put the bottle in PJ's mouth.

PJ grabbed the bottle like he had not eaten in weeks. Bruce made him take breaks so he could breathe, which of course PJ did not like at all. Lynn set a plate of food and a bowl of oatmeal down. Taking the bottle out of PJ's mouth, which made him mad, PJ started yelling at Bruce. Ignoring the outburst, Bruce started mashing up eggs to feed PJ. With the first spoon full, PJ shut up and started eating, forgiving Bruce for taking his bottle away.

Debbie walked in as Bruce was feeding PJ. Walking over to Bruce, she kissed him on top of his shaved head then kissed PJ. PJ regarded her with a scowl on his face like, "You are interrupting my food, woman." Debbie grabbed a cup of coffee for her and Bruce. Taking PJ from Bruce, Debbie continued the feeding. During the exchange, PJ voiced his displeasure about having his food interrupted again.

Thankful for the relief, Bruce dove into his plate as Debbie talked to PJ, shoveling food in his mouth. Within an hour, everyone was up in the house and the barn, sitting at the tables, eating breakfast. Bruce looked at the clock reading 7:30 and felt cheated. He would've liked to sleep late.

The twins pushed chairs to either side of him. Smiling at their effort, Bruce sat them in the chairs and brought both of them a plate of food.

They each had on outfits that were a little big for them with flip flops. Danny and Buffy had gone through the clothes that were gathered from the houses the clan had grabbed supplies from. Lost in thought, Bruce was just staring at Debbie until he heard Mike calling his name.

"Bruce, can you hear me?" Mike asked for the third time.

"Yes I can, Mike," Bruce replied turning to look at him.

"I was saying Marcus called yesterday and said they found more survivors. Darrell brought over a map yesterday with the locations. Marcus didn't want to say over the CB. They found sixteen more, and they relocated to Marcus' farm. Those survivors told them where others were. Most want help, but a few want to stay put. Darrell told me they have over fifty people over there now and asked if we could take in the others. Also, the log fence around the house and barn is almost finished."

"After breakfast, we will have a meeting in the game room. Debbie said that Paul had some ideas he wanted to run by us. We can make plans then. Let's just enjoy breakfast now," Bruce said, looking again at Debbie, who was now playing with PJ. Mike nodded his agreement and continued eating.

Danny looked at Bruce and said, "I don't know if I like PJ, Daddy."

"Why?" Bruce asked with a serious expression.

"He pulled my hair this morning at three o'clock, waking me, and wouldn't leave me alone until I fed him a bottle. That's really unfair. I mean, both you and Mom were there. Why'd he wake me up?" Danny asked as Bruce started laughing.

"Well, sleep in the Momma and Daddy bed, you have to take care of the baby. It's part of the job," Bruce told her.

"Sleep. Y'all killed me last night."

"Y'all?"

"Yeah, you and Mom could've got on the floor so I could've at least outrun everyone as they tried to lay on me," Danny replied between bites.

Bruce looked at her with a traumatized expression but said nothing. He was not in the mood for a teenage daughter argument today. Whatever he said was going to be wrong, but be damned if he was sleeping on the floor in his own room.

After breakfast, Bruce put on BDUs, grabbed his tactical vest, and went down to the game room. After laying his vest on the coffee table and putting his rifle in the rack on the wall, he sat down in his chair and waited on everyone else. Bruce pulled out his notepad as the twins climbed in his lap. After everyone showed up, Bruce called the meeting to order.

"Okay, everyone, unless you have the floor or have been told by the person that has the floor you can talk, don't. For those of you new to this clan, this is how we decide what's going to happen. It is a limited democracy. You will get to speak your mind and add your input, but it will be done in an orderly fashion. Since I have the twins in my lap, I'll conduct this meeting sitting down. Nancy, how are the food stores coming with the added mouths and the chore schedules?" Bruce asked.

Nancy stood, looking at her notebook, "Well, Lynn has gone over our food list and is makin' a menu months in advance. She has assured me the stores we have could feed the clan for one hundred days easily with replenishing from the garden. Lynn was having trouble puttin' it in the computer. Lynn is now just writing it down, and Debbie and I've been taking over putting it in the computer," Nancy reported.

Damn, we went from eighteen months to a hundred days with the extra people, Bruce thought. Jake spoke up, looking at Lynn. "Why don't you just write it down in the computer?" Jake asked Lynn.

"Jake, I can't type worth a damn. I did try, but I can only use two fingers," Lynn replied.

"Well then, just write it down for the computer. Don't type it," Jake said.

"You can't do that with a computer," Lynn said. Everyone in the family groaned as Jake stood up and marched out of the game room like he had been insulted.

"Lynn, don't ever tell him you can't do something with a computer," Bruce said when Jake had left the room. Then, he added, "The last time that was said in this house. Jake hacked into the President's e-mail. Just because someone said it couldn't be done." Bruce turned to Mike.

"All I said was nobody could do it. How was I supposed to know it could be done?" Mike stated, turning away from Bruce.

"That's saying it can't be done. He handed you a printout of the President's e-mail in less than an hour," Bruce replied. Mike was not looking at him or listening to him. Jake came back into the room carrying a touchpad notebook, but before he could hand it to Lynn, Bruce spoke up.

"You can show her how to use it later, Jake. Nancy, how about the chore lists. Any problems?" Bruce asked.

"Everyone is doing excellent. No missed shifts on chores or training."

"Everyone, that's great; let's keep that up. Now Debbie, how about guard duty?"

Debbie was trying to get her notebook away from PJ, fighting a losing battle. Rushing over, Danny and Buffy helped wrestle it away and took PJ from her. At first, PJ started crying, but he was soon being entertained by the girls.

"No missed guard shifts, but Jake and Matt have brought up a valid point about adding another person in Mission Control. With warlord shooting any blues that get in the fields, it takes one person just to operate that. They've been teaching people how to operate the UAVs. If the UAVs are up, it's too much for one person. I've put Pam on dayshift only until I've released her for other duties. I'm not giving those with night duties time off, but I am allowing for sleep time after their shift," Debbie finished, looking up at Bruce.

"Jake, you and Matt are to make a list of people who're trained for UAV operation. They'll pull four-hour shifts in the morning and afternoon, and we will add another for the warlord. We have thirty radios. I'm putting out a list today for fifteen people who'll always have a radio unless in the house or the loft. Now Mike, what's the news from the Snead farm?" Bruce asked.

"They have over fifty people there now." This news brought smiles from others in the clan. Mike continued, "They've been sending out scavenger runs every day. Since we brought them weapons, they feel safer goin' out to gather supplies. I gave them another twenty thousand rounds yesterday when Darrell came over. Darrell gave me a map that they have marked out with places where survivors might still be. They got this information from others they've brought in. One of the locations is outside of Jonesboro. It's what's left of the Homeland camp after it got overrun. The survivors are in a large, metal building on the outside of town that was used for supplying the camp with food and water. If the blues have not gotten inside, then they're okay. The rest are people holdin' up in farms. Marcus said in his letter that they got this information from some survivors that escaped from the camp. All but one of the farms is too far away for them to get to easily."

"Marcus doesn't want to send out his patrols any further than fifteen miles out. The farm in question is twelve miles from him and has two families there. They have no fence, two guns, little food and water. They said that they would stay there. Marcus wrote…" Mike looked down at a piece of paper before continuing. "'Bruce, will you see if these crazy, stupid white people will listen to you because they won't listen to an old black man,'" Mike read. "This farm is fifteen miles from here with the two families totaling nine. The estimated count at Jonesboro is around thirty-seven with the other two locations having at least eighteen between them. I don't think we will get those nine in Marcus' letter to join us if they wouldn't join Marcus. We estimate fifty-five at least, which I think is low. If they all come here with the forty-one we have, that's ninety-six. It'll start getting crowded here, and this will put a huge strain on our supplies, like food. We go from a hundred days to less than fifty. I'm not sayin' not to get them, but I want everyone here to realize that. We will have to bring in more supplies fast if we get 'em," Mike said, looking around the room.

The clan was talking in little groups with each other. They all wanted to help, but they could survive here now without much trouble. Adding that many mouths to feed to the clan would change the situation. Then, Cheryl stood up. Asking to be recognized as her husband, Paul was trying to make her sit back down. Bruce pointed to her as she slapped Paul's hand.

"If these other people are brought here to *your* farm, would they work like the rest of us?" Cheryl asked, looking at Mike and Bruce.

"Cheryl, this is the clan's farm now. We're a big family here now. When each of you agreed to come here and stay, you became part of the family and clan. The answer to your question is yes. They either work or they are sent on their way," Bruce said with Mike agreeing.

"What if we send them out and a gang picks them up and finds out where we are? Every night on the HAM radio in Mission Control, we hear people talkin' about the lawless groups out there. Just two nights ago, we heard someone get attacked while they were on the radio," Cheryl said.

Bruce was glad they were listening to the HAM radio and writing down everything, but it was also a source of fear for them. Not having an answer for that, he addressed Cheryl's question. "I will not keep people here against their will. If they want to leave, then they can. If they become a danger, they'll leave, but only their spirit, the body, will stay behind. I will kill anyone who threatens this clan. We have safety here, which is rare right now, and I will not let anyone endanger that," Bruce said.

Mike added, "We're not fools. Nobody will get a free ride here unless they're sick or injured. Once they can work, then they will help or leave, not taking any of our supplies with them. Now, when Bruce and his patrol came back, we gave them a day off to rest—"

"Yeah, but they picked a fight with every blue in central Louisiana then ran like a hundred miles through the day," Maria interrupted. "If they hadn't taken a day off, I for one would've thrown a fit." Everyone agreed with her.

"Thank you, Maria, and I might have you do that if the need arises. Now, if I would've gone and told Bruce that I needed him to attack a large group headed toward us, what would he have done?" Mike asked.

Angela replied without hesitation, "He would've taken off to fight, sleep or no sleep."

"That's right, and that's what we expect from everyone. If you can, do what is needed," Mike said then continued. "Those that come here will be expected to do the same. We can use the extra help, especially if we're hit by a gang or a large mob." The clan talked quietly amongst themselves until Stephanie spoke up.

"What do you and Bruce think about bringing more people here?" Stephanie asked Mike.

He replied, "I think if we can get some of these people without endangering ourselves too much, then we should." Bruce nodded his agreement.

"That's good enough for me," Stephanie replied, writing in her notebook.

"We only have room for around fifty as we stand right now. We're gonna have to build a shelter for the rest. Or more accurately, they'll have to build it," Mike replied, and everyone agreed.

"We'll have to bring in even more supplies with that many more people and soon. Just remember, boys: We designed this farm for just a small group. Don't think I don't want to help but don't bring in more than we can supply and feed," Nancy said as Mike sat down and Bruce spoke up again.

"Okay Paul, tell us what you have in mind," Bruce said, looking at him. Paul got up from beside Cheryl and walked in front of the fireplace.

"I have a list, which I will go through one at a time. We need to expand our storage area, bring in more animals, expand our garden, reinforce the fence, and add towers around the property. Now first, the storage area that I have in mind will be underground. We will dig out five acres on the west side of the property. Dig the hole fifteen feet down then concrete the bottom and walls. Then, cover it with a concrete roof, and cover it with dirt. We can still put a garden or greenhouses on top with the three feet of soil there. That will give us over two hundred thousand square feet of storage area with a ten-foot roof," Paul said, and Bruce and Mike started in.

"Hell yeah! Now we're talking. You're the man, Paul," Bruce yelled, high fiving Mike.

"Go big or go home, baby!" Mike shouted, high fiving Bruce. The twins held up their hands so Bruce and Mike could give them high fives too.

"Boys," Debbie shouted, which made Mike and Bruce shut up.

"Don't you think that two hundred thousand square feet is a bit big, Paul?" Nancy asked, looking at him. Having experience with dealing with Bruce and Mike's adventures, the women prepared for the verbal battle to rein them in. Very rarely did they get mad and scream at the two; they used common sense.

"I told him it was," Cheryl replied.

"Well, we don't have to worry about cost, and with that much space, we should be okay for a long time to come for storage," Paul replied, avoiding looking at Nancy or Debbie by looking down at his notes.

Hearing that, Debbie almost wanted to laugh. She could hear Mike and Bruce say the same thing. "Cost isn't what I'm talking about, just moving that much dirt then finding that much concrete laying around to build it, not counting the metal beams, will be challenging. You're talking about thousands of yards of concrete for the floor and roof. We can't begin to move that much concrete out of the city with blues and gangs about," Debbie stated.

"Concrete won't be a problem; there's a warehouse outside of Castor that has several thousand pallets of eighty-pound bags of concrete. The oil and natural gas drilling rigs store it there for concreting the wells. We have one back hoe, and on a farm we have to go to for more animals, there's another one and a bulldozer. I can make those quiet too. Working straight, I believe we can have it done in under twelve weeks," Paul said, reading from his list, not wanting to look up. He had already had this fight with his wife and lost. Cheryl was used to this as well: like most wives.

Bruce spoke up. "Come on, you two; it'll be huge—like our own super warehouse." Mike agreed with Bruce. Thinking about having a building that big on the property made him tingly inside.

"Turn down the testosterone, boys," Nancy said, looking at the duo then turning to Paul. "What the hell are we going to put in there? I'm not saying we don't need to make another storage area, but two hundred thousand square feet? Don't you think we could go with something smaller? We have a lot to do besides build a super boy toy storage area." Watching Bruce and Mike, she felt like she was trying to talk her kids out of buying a stupid toy when they were young.

"Well, Bruce and Mike said they wanted an area to store large amounts of ammo and weapons," Paul replied, finally looking up at the two women, trying to defend his idea since Mike and Bruce loved it.

A few minutes passed as Debbie scribbled in her notebook. "I have run a few numbers through my head," Debbie replied, and Bruce mumbled, "Oh shit." Debbie glared at him before she began. "The average ammo crate of 5.56 is 4'x5'x5' and contains a little over eighty thousand rounds, weighing a ton. I know it holds more and the dimensions are off, but let's round off for now. In a two-hundred-thousand-square-foot building, you could have eighty rows with two hundred cases in each row. That's leaving a big aisle between each row. We're not even talking double stacking yet. I come up with sixteen thousand crates, that's over a billion rounds. There isn't that much ammo nearby first, but let me continue. If there was, you could still double stack the rows and still have over a hundred thousand square feet of space to fill. I'm not even going to mention triple stacking. Now, is that not a bit much?" Debbie asked the three men with almost every woman agreeing with her. Only Danny, Mary, and Buffy were with the Daddies. The twins just wanted more high fives, and PJ wanted his chew toy that Debbie was writing in.

"Debbie, we wouldn't have to worry about storage for a while," Mike told her with a grin on his face.

Nancy spoke up. "Okay, I've just run a couple of numbers here myself. If we assigned fifteen people a day to work on this testosterone storage area, I put it over ninety days before completion. That's with nothing but good weather."

"Why the hell weren't you two accountants?" Bruce asked. He loved the idea of a huge ass underground storage area, but leave it to the women to bring rational reason to the table like always.

"Did you say something, baby?" Debbie asked in a dangerous tone.

"No, baby, I didn't say a word," Bruce replied, trying to look innocent, but nobody bought it.

Debbie turned away from Bruce to look at Paul. "What about clearing most of an acre and building an eighty-thousand-square-foot area underground? Using my calculations, we can still store over five hundred million rounds in one level even without double stacking."

Before Paul could answer, Nancy spoke up. "That size we could do in four weeks."

"Well, I guess so," Paul replied.

"Okay, that's settled. Next item please, Paul," Debbie said, tired of that argument and getting ready for the next if the need arose. She knew the boys meant well, but someone had to keep them under control. This was a never ending fight for her and Nancy, but she had to admit they were getting very good at reigning in the two.

"I want to get some 4x8 three-quarter-inch plywood and circle the fence on the inside with the plywood then brace it with 2x4s. Next, build an earthen berm behind the plywood. My rough calculations figure about eight tons per foot across the fence. Not only would it stop a mob from knocking over our fence but also gun fire or someone trying to knock it down. The five-acre hole we were going to dig was going on the fence," Paul replied, trying for the big area again.

"See, he's thinking ahead. Let's do the big storage area," Mike said hopefully.

"No, we will get the dirt from elsewhere. This's a great idea, Paul. Debbie and I were just talking, and we want at least ten more forty-foot cargo containers buried on the property," Nancy replied matter-of-factly.

"With a big storage area, we won't need those other containers," Mike said.

"If for some reason your man cave storage area blows up because of your boy toys that you men want to put in there, we want to make sure we have stuff left to survive on. Don't put all of your eggs in the same basket, remember? One is none, and two is one," Nancy said, looking at the duo.

Damn it. Bruce hated it when the wives used his own words to win an argument. He finally gave up. "Okay, we won't build the coolest storage area ever. We will build the small, punk one, and we'll be happy with it. Next, Paul," he said. Debbie and Nancy looked at him with eyebrows pinched together, not sure if he had insulted them.

"The towers. I was just goin' to get some hunting towers and place them around the inside of the fence. Mike said we could use them for blues and lay behind the berm if we're attacked by a gang," Paul replied, putting his notebook down.

"What about the animals?" Debbie asked.

"They're all at the same farm where the backhoe and bulldozer are at. I was thinking ten more milk cows, a hundred more chickens, and a few dozen pigs," Paul said. Debbie and Nancy clapped with joy as the rest of the family bowed their heads, groaning. The Mamas had finally won the pig vote. The farmer wanted them here. "Y'all have a hundred and ten acres fenced in here. You have two twenty-acre fields in the back to rotate livestock. Adding the garden, buildings, orchard, chicken house, quail, rabbits, pheasant, and the pond, you have over fifty acres that aren't being used. We need every square foot inside the fence producing."

"Fine, bring the damn pigs in. I don't care," Bruce said as the wives clapped. Sure, they got their damn pigs, but did he and Mike get the cool storage area? Oh no. Bruce was convinced it was a conspiracy. Bruce turned to Jake. "What's the area like after our little hike?"

"South of us, the blues are dispersed over a large area. We have several thousand around us with the closest being less than a mile. Warlord has taken out blues that haven't come down the road; those are taken out by the guard in the fort. In the last forty-eight hours, the count is at one hundred and twenty-eight blues shot. This afternoon, we need to gather up the bodies. We have only shot four since change of shift this morning. In our twenty-mile circumference, I put the number at five thousand give or take," Jake reported.

"Matt, what intelligence reports do you have to add?" Bruce asked.

"Nothing much, just on the radio, the remnants of government are in Colorado and telling survivors to go there. It's just a recording. No live broadcast in two weeks. There're a lot of gangs on the move. People are reporting the blues are getting smarter. They're ambushing now, and they're killing people and not trying to infect. No reports of using human intelligence but definite increase in animal instinct. They now wait around for a large group to take on a large concentration of humans," Matt stated.

"Okay, order of action," Bruce said, standing up and moving the sleeping twins off of him. "First, we're sending out four teams. One each direction of the compass to set up on the roof of a house, the team will make noise and kill whatever shows up. Each team will take at least ten thousand rounds of ammo and set up for three days unless we run out of targets. Conner, I want you to have all three Strykers ready to roll out in case the teams get in some serious shit. Have teams ready to roll in ten minutes of a call.

"The four teams will each have four members. I will post teams later today. Matt and Jake, you will both be here manning Mission Control. After we return from our hunting trip, two teams are goin' shopping, and another is going to secure the survivors.

"It's mid-October, and the first frost usually comes around Thanksgiving. I want the buildings and fence done before the end of the month. We have a lot to get done during the winter. Check the board in the morning to see where you're assigned for this mission. I have fort duty from six to midnight, so don't bug me. Don't think because I don't send you on a team I don't think you're ready. Someone has to guard the farm and be ready to pull our asses out if it goes bad. Everyone here will have to learn to be a warrior and do their part. Now, is there any other business that needs to be addressed?" Bruce asked. Frank raised his little hand, and Bruce pointed at him.

Frank lowered his hand. "Can we go swimming, Mr. Bruce?"

Bruce smiled at Frank, wanting to thank the little boy for reminding him kids were there. "Yes, Frank, after lunch, we can go swimming, but no yelling. Everyone must be quiet, okay?"

After lunch, everyone that was not on duty was by the swimming pool. Bruce and Mike were sitting at the picnic table with an umbrella, both wearing full combat gear. Most everyone else was wearing bathing suits but had weapons and gear set in piles on the back side of the house. Danny was teaching Buffy hand-to-hand fighting on some mats that they had spread out. All the wives were laid out in the sun. Bruce was looking at Debbie in her bikini. Bruce was mad that he had kids sleeping in his bed as he inspected Debbie's sexy body and drooled.

Reluctantly, Bruce turned to watch Danny teach Buffy how to punch correctly on a punching bag. Danny and Buffy were in shorts, t-shirts, and tennis shoes. Letting out a low growl, Bruce watched Conner walk over to his girls. From the look in Conner's eyes, Bruce could tell he wasn't looking at Danny in admiration of her fighting style. Yep, he was going to have to say something to that boy. Granted, Conner was twenty, and Bruce did like him, but don't be drooling over his baby girl. Bruce just wanted to tell him he had better treat his girl with respect or he would break his legs. Since the last paintball game, Bruce knew for certain who had Danny's heart. Bruce sat listening to the conversation.

Conner walked up to Danny and Buffy. "Want me to teach both of ya a few techniques?" he asked.

"No thank you. I know more hand-to-hand than you. I hold two black belts in different forms plus the extra stuff Daddy and Daddy Mike have taught me," Danny replied politely and honestly to Conner, never taking her eyes off of Buffy as she continued to hit the bag.

"I'm not saying you aren't good, Danny. I saw you with the gimp, but he's not much of an opponent. I will show you how to bring down a man," Conner stated.

"You think I can't take a man down?" Danny asked, pissed. She held up her hand for Buffy to stop then turned to Conner.

"You're a teenage girl," Conner pointed out.

"I weigh one hundred and fifty-six pounds at 5'6" with 12% body fat. I can bench press my body weight more than once. I may be built like a girl, but I can kick your ass all over this farm," Danny stated as matter of fact.

"I doubt that. I've studied martial arts for ten years," Conner said with an air of confidence.

"Okay, let's have a full-contact match. The first one that taps out has to shine the other's boots for two months," Danny said, crossing her arms across her chest.

"I don't want to hurt you, Danny, and you would get hurt," Conner said, folding his arms across his chest.

"So you are scared of me then," Danny said, smiling.

"I'm not scared of you. I just don't want to hurt you," Conner replied in a firm tone. Bruce got up and headed toward them before Danny beat the shit out of Conner.

"Danny, that's enough," Bruce told her.

"Listen to your dad, Danny. I don't want to hurt you," Conner replied, smiling.

Bruce turned to Conner, "I'm not worried about you hurting her. I'm worried that she will hurt you, son."

"She can't hurt me, sir," Conner replied.

"See, Daddy, let me show him this little girl can kick his ass. You can referee, and if one of us gets carried away, you can stop it," Danny replied, looking at Conner.

"If you get on that mat, Conner, I promise you: you'll lose," Bruce said.

"I doubt that, sir," Conner replied, taking off his BDU top then his boots and socks.

"I'm not going to stand between a man and an ass whopping. Danny, don't break any of his bones or put him out of action. We have a lot to do tomorrow." Some of the confidence washed off of Conner's face at that. Debbie, having heard the conversation, walked over.

"Conner, don't do it. You're about to get hurt," she said as she stood beside Bruce.

"Don't worry, ma'am; I won't get hurt, and I won't hurt your little girl. I'm a man after all. I outweigh her by thirty pounds, and I'm four inches taller than her," Conner replied, stepping on the mat with pride. Debbie just stared at the cocky young man with her mouth open.

Debbie looked at Danny and said, "Kick his ass, Danny, just don't hurt him too bad."

Bruce looked down at Debbie standing at his side and wondered who this woman was and where was his wife. Looking back at the mat, Bruce saw the two get in opposite corners. "When I yell break, you'd better break or I'm coming in there; is that clear, Danny?" Bruce told both of them, but was looking at Danny. Conner and Danny replied they understood, and Bruce said, "Go!"

Conner charged Danny to try and grab her and use his weight against her. Danny sidestepped and kicked him in the stomach. Then, she kicked the back of his leg, bringing Conner to his knees, where she punched him in the face, knocking him down. Before Danny could get on top of him and commence the beat down, Bruce yelled, "Break." Danny stomped her foot, glaring at her dad, and went to her corner.

Conner pulled himself off of the mat, shaking his head as he stood up. No one in the clan was swimming now. Everyone had come over to stand around the mat, watching the fight.

"Conner, do you yield?" Bruce asked him.

"No, she just got lucky," he replied, walking back to his corner. A look of anger washed over Danny's face.

"Young lady you watch your control," Bruce said in a firm voice then said, "Go."

Conner didn't make the same mistake twice. He advanced slowly toward Danny, this time throwing a right punch then a snap kick. Danny blocked both with ease then snapped a kick into Conner's thigh that made him wince in pain. Conner's next punches and kicks were full-force, but Danny blocked and dodged them. When Conner threw his next kick, Danny dropped and kicked through the leg that Conner was standing on, sending him crashing into the mat. Danny continued her kick but brought it back in an arc, driving her heel into Conner's solar plexus. Conner's lungs deflated.

Danny jumped beside Conner, grabbed his arm, and rolled him over onto his stomach. Danny put her foot in Conner's armpit, wrapped his arm around her leg, and then knelt on Conner's back. As his arm bent at an unnatural angle, the stars he had in his head left as the pain hit. Any way he tried to move sent waves of pain through him. Danny leaned forward, sending more pain shooting through him. Conner knew she could break his arm in two places and dislocate his shoulder if she leaned forward anymore. He was fighting through the pain when he heard.

"Tap out, or I'll break it before my daddy can stop me," Danny said. Conner tapped the mat as Bruce ran over to pull Danny off. Danny stood up, letting Conner go before Bruce made it to her. "I have three pairs of combat boots. The pair I wear for guard duty, I want you to make them shine. The others, just clean and polish them," Danny said as she walked away with Bruce watching her.

Bruce helped Conner up, making sure he was alright. Conner looked at him and said, "Damn, I was state champion three years in a row. When she hit me, I swear my insides shook."

"Conner, I've trained her since she was five. Besides myself and Mike, the only people here that can take her are her four brothers. Sometimes, I think she just doesn't want to hurt them. Debbie can take her but won't for the same reason."

"Sir, if I ever do somethin' that stupid again, I want you to shoot me with that Taser gun," Conner replied, moving his arm around to make sure it still worked.

"Every man must have a lesson in humility, Conner," Bruce said.

"I just got a whole semester of it," Conner replied then walked over to Danny.

"I apologize for underestimating you. Where're your boots?" Conner asked.

"Don't worry about it. You've apologized, so forget the boots," Danny said, grabbing a bottle of water and taking a drink.

"A deal is a deal. Where're your boots?"

Danny pointed to her pile of clothes. "Those are the boots I wear on guard duty."

"Have your boots down every night after supper, and I will polish them. I don't think your dad would like me coming upstairs to your room to get them," Conner said, heading to grab her boots.

"Why? You can't hurt me," Danny replied, stating fact as far as she was concerned.

"Danny, I'm now scared of you, but I'm terrified of your dad. If you can do that to a man, I don't even want to think what he could do to someone he thought might be sneakin' to his daughter's room," Conner said, picking up her boots. "You fight good, Danny, and I'll always be on your team," Conner said as he left to shine her boots. Danny smiled as he walked off.

After the sparring match, those who had been swimming went back. Buffy was looking at Danny with awe as they started the training session up again. Mike came back after leading a group to collect dead blues and throw them to a huge gator population. At five, everyone went in for supper.

Bruce ate fast. When he got up to start his guard duty, he saw Buffy get up. Motioning her to sit back down, Bruce told her no. She was staying in the house, and she was to watch the twins. With a discouraged look, Buffy told him okay and walked over to stand beside the girls. Bruce grabbed his equipment and headed to the fort.

As Bruce settled in, he took out his notebook to make the teams. Looking up at the monitors, he saw three blues walking down the road in the furthest camera on the road, almost a mile from the house. Grabbing his AR-10, Bruce opened up the window and waited until they came down the road. When the three came into view, they were four hundred yards away. Bruce squeezed the trigger three times, sending out three 7.62 go away requests. All three dropped.

Standing his rifle up in the corner, Bruce picked his pen back up. Watching the monitors while he wrote, Bruce noticed someone leave the house and head toward him. He glanced down at his watch, reading 9:30. It was not his relief. It was not until the person got behind the fort that he saw it was Debbie as she climbed up the steps to the fort. Bruce opened up the door for her.

"What do I owe for the pleasure of your company, ma'am?" he asked as she walked in, and he closed the door.

"The kids are asleep, and I just wanted to be with you," Debbie replied, walking to the far end of the fort, looking out the window.

Bruce sat down in the chair, looking at the monitors. "Well, pull up a chair, baby, and let's watch some monitors," he said.

"I saw you staring at me by the swimming pool today," Debbie said. Bruce looked up and realized she was wearing a bathrobe.

"Well, I really couldn't help it, baby; you were in a little bikini." Bruce grinned.

Debbie dropped her robe to the floor, still wearing her bikini, "I thought you might want a closer look."

"Baby, I'm not saying I'm not turned on big time, but I'm on guard duty," Bruce said, dropping the grin and looking Debbie up and down.

"Well, I guess we just have to be quick then," she replied.

"Quick is really not my style, baby. You know I like to bring a lunch and stay a while." Bruce couldn't believe what was coming out of his mouth. He was actually making excuses so his hot wife would not jump his body.

"I never said how many times we had to be quick, now did I?" Debbie replied, smiling at him with a naughty grin.

Bruce stood and started dropping equipment, saying, "Oh yeah, hot mama."

CHAPTER 10

Bruce woke to the sound of the alarm clock going off at 4:50 a.m. He hit the off button with the clock only letting out a few chirps. Looking around the bed, he saw everyone was asleep. He got out of bed and took a quick shower then dressed in the now familiar BDUs and tactical vest. Checking his weapons over, he slung his SCAR and grabbed his pack. Reaching back into the bed, he picked up a sleeping PJ, trying to hold him so something on his vest wasn't poking him.

Debbie woke up as he was situating PJ. "Is it time to get up already, baby?" she asked.

"Yeah, first team goes out at 10 a.m. then one team each hour after that. Wake the girls; it's going to be a busy couple of days," Bruce said as he went to the door. When he reached it, he turned and saw Debbie waking the girls. After three plus decades with her, Bruce was still struck by her beauty.

Feeling eyes on her, Debbie turned to the door and saw Bruce staring at her. "What? I'm getting them up."

"Just looking at the most beautiful girl in the world, baby," Bruce said.

Debbie laughed. "I don't feel beautiful right now. I think I have fur on my teeth, PJ spit up on me, and one of the twins peed on my side of the bed."

"You're always beautiful, sugar mama," Bruce said, walking back to kiss her as she put her hand on his chest.

"The rules haven't changed. No kisses until I brush my teeth. Thank you, stud muffin," Debbie said as she kissed his cheek and PJ on the head. She turned back to the bed and, not seeing anyone moving, yanked the covers off. This woke everyone up—maybe not in a good mood, but they were up.

"I love you, sugar mama," Bruce said as he turned to leave.

"I love you too, stud muffin."

Bruce walked downstairs, waking PJ in the process. When Bruce walked into the kitchen, PJ told everyone he did not like to be woken up; he liked to wake others up. Bruce ran for a bottle to shove in his mouth to stop the crying. He set his rifle and pack down, which took a lot of coordination while holding PJ.

Sitting at the table, Bruce pulled out his notepad and started going over notes. Mike, Nancy, Debbie, and he were the team leaders. Bruce put at least two experienced people with each team leader except his team and one inexperienced person. He would have Stephanie and Buffy as his experienced team. Maria and Mindy were his inexperienced team members. Bruce had been told by Danny that Mindy was the best of those training and was ready to go out. He knew Maria was ready. Bruce did not notice everyone else sitting down for breakfast. Nor did he notice Paul standing beside the table, looking at him. Mike coughed to get Bruce's attention. Hearing the fake cough, Bruce looked up at Mike then noticed Paul.

"Something on your mind, Paul?" Bruce inquired.

"Why am I not on a team?" Paul asked, looking at Bruce.

"I have to leave someone here that can run the farm and protect it. The garden needs to be tilled for the fall crops. If something happens to us, you're in charge here. After the Strykers leave, we will have no other backup. You're to seal the gate and ride out the storm. You can turn over responsibilities to Jake and Matt when you feel they're old enough to take them," Bruce said in a flat voice.

Shocked to the core, Paul just looked at Bruce with his mouth open for several seconds before speaking. "I really don't want that kind of responsibility. Why not let me take one of the wives' places?"

"You run this farm better than we do, and you have military training. You're our best bet if something happens to the teams. The clan needs you here just with your farming knowledge alone," Bruce replied, looking at Paul.

"At first, I thought I wasn't good enough to go out," Paul said, looking down.

"Far from it. I would have to take two team leaders off, and we still wouldn't have the farming and architectural knowledge you have. So I really didn't have much of a choice. Everyone in the family has been trained as a sniper and to speed shoot."

"I'll do my best; you just make sure that everyone comes home," Paul said, heading to the dining room table.

Mike spoke up next. "Bruce, I think we need to take more ammo, and each person needs to have one other assault rifle. If the mobs get pretty big, we're going to have to worry about the barrels overheating."

"Good idea with the extra rifles, but you do realize that each team will already be moving ten ammo cans," Bruce pointed out.

"We're staying in one place, and a truck will drop us off. We don't have to haul it in by hand. They will stay as we climb up the roof of the house we are assigned. If a team has to run, leave the shit behind. Better to have it and not need it than need it and not have it," Mike replied with determination.

"How much more are you talkin' about?" Bruce asked Mike, afraid of his answer.

"Double at least. I really want thirty thousand rounds," Mike answered.

"May I ask why?" Bruce requested, observing Mike. He wanted to know what was bugging him. "Bruce, we are going out to draw in blues. They come out of the woodwork, and if you add the population of the little villages and small towns close to us in a twenty-mile radius, it comes to over sixty thousand. That means over forty thousand infected easy. The large group that is still to the south of us is that many alone. I just don't want a team stuck on a roof and only using bad language on the blues."

Mike did not want to scare people too bad, but he could see this going bad real easy. He knew it needed to be done. Better to fight the blues in a place of their choosing.

Studying Mike, Bruce then glanced around the table before speaking. "Alright, we take thirty thousand rounds per team not counting basic load. It's not like we're saving them for Christmas," Bruce said, and Mike let out a huge sigh.

Nancy looked at Bruce and said, "I'm not one to critique your plan, but your team is the least experienced, yet you have taken the south. Care to explain why?"

"My team has five. I know I don't list Buffy, but she goes where I go. I really think if I would leave her somewhere without me, she would go into convulsions. Stephanie is very good with a weapon—as is Maria. Danny says Mindy will be okay. This is a sit and wait hunt, not a running gun battle. My only concern is one of us getting hit by a gang as we're laid out on a roof. If that does happen, drop your ropes, and get the hell out of Dodge. I want my team out back so I can go through equipment and get the truck loaded. Remember, you're not to make noise until the drop off team has been gone for twenty minutes," Bruce said, standing and kissing Debbie and PJ then the twins then headed outside.

Bruce went to the barn to grab several rolls of rope then headed to the ammo storage in one of the buried storage buildings. He pulled out thirty cans then tied them together, leaving ten feet between each one. This way, when he pulled them up to the roof, he was only lifting two at a time. Matt drove Bruce's new pickup around back with Mike in the passenger seat. When Mike saw how Bruce had the ammo cans, he smiled, thankful that they weren't going to make a shit load of trips up and down the ladder.

After loading the truck, they drove it back to the house with Bruce riding in back when it hit Bruce he had not even driven his new truck. When Matt pulled up to the back patio, Bruce jumped out and grabbed the keys from Matt and climbed in the truck, driving it around the property.

Paul had put a shroud on the bottom of the engine and made the muffler quieter. It amazed Bruce just how quiet it was. Looking around the cab, he smiled. This truck had it all. There was no way Bruce would ever pay what the sticker had for the truck though unless it came with several free stays at the Playboy mansion. He pulled back up to the patio where everyone was watching him.

"I never got to drive my new truck," he told them, calling his team over as Conner drove the Beast over.

Conner got out of the Beast, asking, "What on Earth possessed y'all to build this?"

"We wanted an armored car, and that's the best we could do," Bruce replied, stopping to look at him.

"Oh, I'm not complaining. I feel safer in that than I do a Hummer. This thing has some serious power. I went over it, and fuck a duck does it have some armor. Y'all even put a V bottom on it," Conner said, looking at the Beast.

"Yeah, we like the Beast. It has almost a ton of half-inch steel on it. The engine has aftermarket twin turbo chargers, giving you almost eight hundred little horses," Bruce answered proudly as the family came outside.

"How much money do you have tied up in this?" Conner asked, still looking at the Beast.

"Not much," Bruce answered quickly, seeing the wives taking an interest in the conversation.

Walking over to his team, Bruce went through everyone's pack to make sure they had packed what was needed. Next, he looked over each one. Only Buffy had her hair in a ponytail, and he told the others they needed to do the same. Everyone except Bruce had two M-4s with suppressors and night vision. Bruce was carrying his SCAR with the sixteen-inch barrel and the grenade launcher plus his AR-10. He was only taking twenty-five hundred rounds for it. He had his night vision and his thermal mount. Bruce had an extra thermal that could be clipped on and would rotate it through the team. Everyone had twenty magazines on them and twenty more in each pack. Bruce only wanted two days' worth of food in each person's pack.

They had two duffel bags with enough food and water for the three days they were spending out. As he was going over Mindy's gear, Bruce noticed she did not have a knife. Bruce called over the radio for Jake to bring one up from the armory. Jake came running out and gave him a Marine K-bar, which Bruce put on Mindy's vest. When Bruce looked up, he saw Danny, Matt, Jake, and Mary talking on the patio. Bruce reminded them they had work to do. They hugged each other, and it occurred to Bruce they were saying goodbye, making him grin. Bruce keyed his radio, and everyone stopped.

"This is Big Daddy One. Remember your training, don't do anything stupid, and listen to your team leaders. If you follow these rules, you'll be fine. I want a copy from everyone," Bruce said, and everyone replied.

Bruce looked at his watch, reading 9:30 a.m. He grabbed the ladder and put it in the back of the truck. The truck was going to back right up to the house, and they would climb the ladder from the back of the truck with the security team riding in the Beast. Everyone came out to tell the first away team goodbye. Debbie had PJ, and the twins were walking toward Bruce then took off running and crying.

"Don't go," they said in unison, hugging his legs. Bruce knelt by the twins.

"I have to go and kill monsters, you two. Mama Debbie will be leaving later today, and I'm counting on both of you to help Lynn take care of PJ while we're gone. If you go to the room with the radio, we will tell you good night every night, okay?" Bruce said, looking at the girls.

Emily looked at him. "The monsters are mean."

"I'm meaner than they are, Emily, and I have taught the family how to be just as mean," Bruce said, pointing to everyone around them. Emily and Sherry wrapped their arms around his neck.

"Who will protect us at night? Ms. Lynn can't," Sherry asked, crying.

"Jake will protect both of you while we're gone. He is my son," Bruce told them as the twins pulled back, looking at Bruce.

"Really?" they said together.

Bruce looked up at Jake. "Jake, the girls will sleep with you while we're gone," Bruce said in a tone that demanded compliance.

Jake looked at his dad in disbelief, mumbling, "Yes sir." The twins ran over to him and hugged his legs. Jake looked down at the girls, and some of the agony left his face.

Bruce walked over to Debbie, who was still holding a happy PJ. Bruce hugged and kissed her then looked at PJ. "You better know how to use the bathroom when I get back and get a job too," Bruce told PJ, kissing and hugging him. PJ just laughed and slapped Bruce on the face.

Bruce walked over to the truck as Buffy, Maria, and Stephanie came back from goodbye hugs. Mindy was still beside the truck looking at the ground. Bruce's heart hurt seeing tears fall from Mindy's face to the ground. She thought she didn't have anyone to tell her bye. Bruce walked over to her and stood in front of her until she lifted her head. She still had tears running down her face.

"They're waiting on you to hug them bye, Mindy," Bruce said, and shock appeared on her face. Mindy looked behind Bruce, not knowing who he was talking about; there were over thirty people there. Bruce turned her face to his and said, "Mike, Nancy, and Debbie are waiting on your goodbye hug. They were going to come over here, but since you didn't hug them, they thought you did not want one."

Joy spread across Mindy's face with the thought that someone cared for and loved her. Mindy took off at a dead run and almost knocked Mike on his ass as she hugged him. A shocked Mike returned the hug from the teenage girl crying in his arms. Then, Mindy ran to Nancy, hugged her, and then moved to Debbie and PJ as Bruce walked over to them. Mike looked at Bruce with a questioning look. Bruce just dragged his index finger across his throat, signaling no questions.

Bruce was standing behind Mindy when she let Debbie go and kissed PJ. Mindy turned around to see Bruce standing there. Bruce looked at Mindy. "We're your family here, your clan. We will love you, fight for you, kill for you, and die for you if need be. This is your family now. Let me show you." Bruce turned to Paul. "Paul, will you fight and die for Mindy?"

"Yes, I will," he replied without hesitation. Bruce was looking at Mindy as she realized that she was loved and not alone.

Everyone now understood why Mindy came over to hug them. Mike came over and picked her up, squeezing her tight followed by everyone else in the clan. When everyone was finished, Mindy looked at Bruce and ran at him with open arms, hugging him.

Bruce lifted her face up to look at him. "We have to go and protect the ones that love us now. Danger is out there threatening them."

Mindy stepped back, wiping tears off of her face, and said, "Let's go and kick something's ass." Then, she took off to the truck and jumped in the back.

Bruce motioned Debbie, Nancy, and Mike to him and whispered, "Make sure everyone knows they're part of this clan. I don't want anyone out there thinking if they die, nobody will care."

Nancy promised, "That's going to be taken care of right fucking now."

"Wait until we leave please," Bruce said, running for the truck.

Bruce jumped in the back as Matt drove off. Conner was driving the Beast in the lead and had two others to help guard while the team got in position. Bruce told Jake to get a UAV up as they pulled around the house. Before the trucks cleared the gate, Jake replied he had eyes on them and was moving forward.

When the team was halfway to the house where they were going to set up, Jake told them he counted an easy thousand within a mile. Bruce replied that was good because he was not in the mood to sit on a hot ass roof and wait too long.

When Matt reached the house, he pulled into the driveway and backed up to the front of the two-story house. Conner and his crew got out to protect the team as they climbed to the roof. It took less than ten minutes to get all the gear up. Bruce was the last one up as Conner and his team jumped into the Beast after helping Matt lower the ladder back down. The two vehicles slowly pulled away, leaving the first team out.

The roof was not steep and had no windows that opened to it. Bruce told everyone to move the gear up to the crest of the roof as Jake called over the radio. "Have a mob of several hundred moving down the road toward you. I think they heard the trucks," Jake reported.

"How far away and how long until contact?" Bruce asked.

"Two miles. I figure you have four to five minutes. They're not running," Jake replied, and Bruce told him to keep the UAV close for now then turned to his team.

"If that group gets past us, they'll hear the trucks when they take off with the next group and find the farm. It's time to get some," Bruce replied. He took off his pack and laid it on the roof then took out a knife, driving it into the roof. He then put one of the straps of his pack around it so it could not slide off. Then, he took out his extra magazines.

The rest of the team copied him. Buffy was trying to stick her knife in the roof but was not having much luck. Bruce grabbed her knife and drove it in the roof for her then turned around. It was only eighty-nine degrees, but the roof made it a lot hotter.

Bruce turned to look down the road, hearing roars coming toward him. The house they were on sat a hundred yards off the road. With the exception of a few trees in the backyard, they could see at least four hundred yards in every direction. Lifting his rifle and looking through the scope, Bruce could see movement about three quarters of a mile away on the road heading toward them.

"Remember, they can't get us here unless a shit load come. Just don't fall off. I was going to make us some safety lines, but we have business to attend to. When they're four hundred yards away, I'm goin' to hit them with a grenade to get their attention," Bruce said, and they all nodded. Buffy was just looking down the road, waiting. The other three were shaking badly.

When the group was four hundred yards away, Bruce brought up the grenade launcher and sighted on the leading edge. Bruce pulled the trigger and heard the *plump* as the grenade left the tube. A few seconds later, he was rewarded with a small explosion, and a few on the front row went down. Then, they were run over by those behind as the group broke into a run.

"That's all that damn thing does?" Stephanie blurted.

"Yeah," Bruce replied with his feelings hurt. He liked his grenade launcher.

"In the movies, that damn thing blows up buildings. It's just a wimp," Stephanie said, looking at the grenade launcher with disappointment.

"It can blow up buildings if it hits a box of dynamite inside," Bruce replied in a wounded tone.

"Bruce, I was just saying—"

Bruce held up his hand. "I'm not talking to you right now, Stephanie. You hurt big SCAR's feelings. The mob is almost here. Engage when they hit two hundred yards. My wimpy weapon and I are moving to the end of the roof," Bruce said, walking off and loading another grenade. There are some things you just don't do, like call a man's weapon wimpy. Bruce raised his rifle and fired another grenade when the mob was at the two hundred mark. Bruce turned to his team. "Are y'all going to send them invitations or something? How about shoot 'em like my wimpy gun here," Bruce snapped.

The four were sitting on the peak of the roof with their weapons on their knees as they opened up with single shots. The mob quit running in front of the house. They just stopped, looking around as the team continued dropping them. The mob could hear the suppressed shots and looked at the house but did not come toward it.

Bruce swore he saw several blues look right at him but then just kept looking around. He lined up his sights and dropped two dozen with thirty rounds. He changed magazines, and the mob just kept standing there, looking around. Moving his scope from head to head, Bruce continued to drop blues until his bolt locked back. Then, several started taking off down the road. Bruce yelled as he replaced magazines, and the ones leaving stopped. Then as one, the mob turned, moving to the house.

Lining up his sights, he started squeezing the trigger as his crosshairs settled on a head and continued firing quick single shots. As his bolt locked back, he dropped his magazine and loaded another one. There were only eight left in the mob, and they were just looking around the house, sniffing the air after stopping halfway down the driveway. Bruce yelled, "Cease fire." As soon as the words left his mouth, the remaining infected started running toward the house. Bruce raised his rifle and fired a grenade at the group. It hit right in front of them, showering their legs with shrapnel, causing six of the eight to fall. Bruce snapped off eight shots, smiling at his weapon. "You're not wimpy," Bruce said, patting his rifle.

"Buffy, ask Stephanie why they acted like that," Bruce said over his shoulder, and Buffy relayed the question.

"I'm right here, Bruce, and I'm not sure," Stephanie said as Bruce just sat there. Stephanie and Buffy looked at each other. Then, Buffy turned back to Bruce and replied, "She's not sure."

"Buffy, tell her I think that the heat off of this roof confused their vision. Since man is a predator and sight is our primary sense, next is hearing. They could not see us since they have a type of thermal vision. We made a noise that they understood and connected to prey, like voice, and locked on to us," Bruce stated, and Buffy relayed.

"Bruce, you are acting like a five-year-old, but I think you are right about your conclusions. But I think you are acting immature, taking offense with me disrespecting your weapon. It's an inanimate object," Stephanie yelled, and Buffy relayed every word.

Bruce called the farm over the radio. "Spook One, this is Big Daddy One. Come in."

"This is Big Daddy Two. What went on there? Over," Mike asked.

"I do believe that the blues couldn't see us on this roof because the heat up here masked us. I have relayed this to Stephanie, and she agrees. We dropped almost two hundred, and they never charged until they heard us talking. I fired several 40mm grenades, but they didn't even try to follow the sound down," Bruce reported. Then, he heard Mike yell for someone to go and get him some 40mm rounds. He was shooting some too.

"This is Mama One. What do you mean 'relayed with Stephanie.' She's right by you on the roof; I can see her," Debbie said.

"I'm not talking to her right now," Bruce replied, sullen.

"Bruce, what the hell is goin' on out there? You're in the middle of a war zone and acting like a child," Debbie stated harshly, and Bruce wouldn't answer her.

"Mama One, this is Stephanie. I called his weapon wimpy."

"Why in the hell would you do that, Stephanie?" Debbie yelled.

Stephanie jerked back from the comment. "After he shot a grenade, it made a little bang, but on TV, they blow up whole buildings, and I said that it was wimpy," Stephanie replied.

"Baby, you don't do that. It would be just as bad if you pissed on his car. When we get back here, you and I are goin' to have a talk about boys," Debbie said.

"They get mad if you pee on their car?" Stephanie asked, not understanding the opposite sex at all.

"Stephanie, don't say anything else. Bruce, I love your grenade launcher on big SCAR. When we get back and you're on guard duty, just you and I will clean it together, okay?" Debbie said.

"Really?" Bruce inquired, perking up.

"Yeah, stud muffin. Now, you have more coming. Mike is fixin' to leave, so the UAV is moving off. Stephanie didn't mean it, baby. You and big SCAR forgive her for me. I will meetcha in the fort for guard duty."

With a grin on his face, Bruce was thinking about calling and asking someone to put him on guard duty Thursday when he got back in three days. Then, he heard Mindy ask, "Who's big SCAR, Mr. Bruce?"

Bruce held up his rifle. "This is big SCAR. It has a sixteen-inch barrel, and little SCAR is at home, and it has a fourteen-inch barrel," he replied.

"Do all of your weapons have a name?" Stephanie asked, and Bruce never even turned around. Stephanie walked over and sat down beside Bruce. She reached over, patting his assault rifle, saying, "I'm sorry, big SCAR."

"See, that's all you had to do. Now, come here," Bruce said, picking her up and sitting her between his legs and putting the rifle up to her shoulder.

Stephanie was caught off guard. As soon as Bruce pulled her close to him, he showed her how to aim the grenade launcher. It was Heaven to her, feeling his arms around her, holding her close. When Bruce put his chin on her shoulder, pulling her face next to his, showing her how to aim down the sight, Stephanie almost stopped breathing. It was over a hundred on the roof, but Stephanie felt chill bumps on her arms. Bruce told her one was coming down the road and to take it out. He wrapped his legs around her so she wouldn't slide down the roof.

When he did that, Stephanie's heart almost stopped. If she died now, she would be happy. She smiled to herself. Bruce moved with her, aiming down the road at a lone blue walker. When the blue was two hundred yards away, he told Stephanie to pull the trigger, and she did, having no idea what she was shooting at. The grenade arced toward the blue, hitting it in the chest, blowing him apart.

"Holy shit! You blew him apart. Now, that's rock'n," Bruce said, kissing her on the cheek.

"That was fucking awesome," Stephanie said in a dreamy voice as Bruce helped her stand up. When she got to her feet, she wobbled, drunk with excitement.

"You okay, little red?" Bruce asked.

"Just got a little hot. I need some water," Stephanie said, walking to the supplies, trying to cover her emotions.

"I'm sorry. I forgot how hot it was. Lay down for a second. I'll set up the tarp." Stephanie wanted to tell him it could have been below freezing and she would still feel this way but kept her mouth shut.

Bruce set down his rifle and pulled a tarp out of one of the bags with several poles. He took out a hammer and nails and made a tent on the back side of the roof in front of the chimney. Bruce then nailed down a blanket and made Stephanie lay down. Then, Bruce took her boots off, loosened her vest, wet a towel, and placed it on her neck. She smiled at him as he went over to shoot several more blues coming down the road.

Stephanie lay on the blanket, reliving the experience. She had loved Bruce from the moment she first saw him. He treated her like a person, picking and joking with her, making her laugh. She was a little annoyed about the wedding ring, but then, she met Debbie. Debbie was just a female version of Bruce. Stephanie liked her and grew to love her, knowing she would never hurt Debbie. That would kill her soul. Not that Bruce would ever cheat on Debbie. Stephanie had seen many women try, but none ever succeeded. Bruce belonged to Debbie and Debbie alone. Stephanie would watch Bruce stare at Debbie like a kid in school day in and day out. This only made Bruce better in Stephanie's eyes. Stephanie would just follow along. Being close to him was enough for her.

Another large group came down the road and was wiped out like the last, but this time, Bruce threw a hand grenade after making everyone get on the opposite side of the roof. The explosion almost made Stephanie run off the roof. The girls agreed the hand grenade rocked. Bruce taught each one how to shoot the M-203 grenade launcher, letting each of them fire several shots. Bruce even got to fire a thermobaric grenade, and even he was surprised by the explosion. In between mobs, he taught them how to throw grenades. Since each one had four, over the next three days, he let them each throw them, which made noise to bring in more infected.

At 6 p.m., Bruce was showing Mindy, the last one of the group, how to shoot the M-203. When Bruce put the weapon on her shoulder and pulled it back, Mindy turned around. "Mr. Bruce, am I ugly and dirty now?" she asked. The question caught Bruce totally off guard, and he didn't know what she meant.

"Mindy, you're not ugly, and you have sweated some up here, but we all have. If it will make you feel better, you can wash off. I'll stay on this side of the roof," Bruce replied, looking at her.

"That's not what I meant, Mr. Bruce. Those men you rescued me from did things to me, so am I ugly and dirty now?" Mindy asked. Bruce jumped back in shock at the question, but Mindy took it the wrong way. Seeing that, Bruce leaned forward and hugged her tight as she quietly sobbed. Bruce pulled her face to look at him.

"Mindy, your question caught me off guard, baby. You're not dirty or ugly. Now, I'm going to tell you some secrets about boys. You have to promise to never say anything I'm about to tell you to any man, okay? I will get in trouble." Bruce looked at her as she nodded. Bruce turned around and saw the other three looking at him. "That goes for you too," Bruce told them, and they also nodded.

"First, those were not men who took you. They were subhuman, cock sucking pieces of shit, and each time I drove a knife into one, I almost had an orgasm," Bruce said, and Buffy interrupted.

"Daddy, what's an orgasm?" Stephanie turned beet red and almost put her hand over Buffy's mouth, not wanting the information to stop. This was classified info Bruce was fixing to give.

"Ask your mother when you two are alone," Bruce answered, and she sighed. "Now, before I start, why do ya think that you're ugly and dirty?" Bruce asked.

"In high school, all the boys would ask me out and hang out with me. But now at the farm, they act like I'm not even alive. They just play with guns, lift weights, and train to fight," Mindy said, looking at Bruce for an answer.

"Okay, hold that thought. First, when you asked me, how did I respond? I thought you were talk'n about here and now, not the past. This is how boys think. I jumped back because boys don't like talk'n about stuff that will make us sad or cry. We think it makes us weak. I know it's stupid, but this is boy stuff. I'm being honest; even if you think it's stupid, I don't,"

Bruce said. "Now, let me say you're beautiful, Mindy. I've seen several of the boys lookin' at you back at the farm. You don't see it because they are doing it out of the corner of their eyes, reflections off a window, things like that. Because if we get caught looking directly at a girl, we get embarrassed, and boys don't like being embarrassed. Next, what happened to ya. Every boy at the farm would love to kill those people again. They care that those men hurt you but could care less what was done. By that, I mean boys don't think less of you. No one sees ya as dirty, Mindy.

"Now, when boys are together and have lots of toys, we do tend to be single-minded. I know guns 'n stuff aren't toys, but to boys, they are because we're very simple. Now, remember that; boys are simple. We love our toys, and they're important to us. I'm not saying girls aren't important to boys, but girls are a mystery to boys because y'all are very complicated. Toys are very simple." Bruce continued through the night, stopping only when blues came around.

If Bruce had been paying attention, he would have noticed the girls were shooting the blues at incredible distances just to put them down so Bruce would keep talking about the male half of the population. He talked all through the night and even during engagements. In the early morning, a huge mob showed up and could see the team fairly well since the roof had cooled down, and it took most of two hours to put them down.

Each girl would ask a question to make sure Bruce would keep the information coming. No one was tired the next day as Bruce kept answering questions about boys. It was late the next evening that Bruce told them he needed a nap. The girls let him take a nap as they gathered in a circle, going over what had been said then came up with more questions. They would stop and shoot blues when they showed up, pissed off that their conversation was interrupted.

They woke Bruce up at 1 a.m. when a large mob showed up. After it was put down, the girls took a short nap in shifts. At least one was up asking questions, usually Stephanie, and the days flew by. Thursday morning, the last day, the house was surrounded by bodies on every side, and the road was clogged with bodies for over two hundred yards. The smell was beyond bad, but they had become accustomed to it now.

Looking around the house in a daze, Bruce did not remembering killing so many. They used over twenty-four thousand rounds, all the hand grenades, 40mm rounds, and there was no more ammo for the AR-

10 sniper rifle. The girls could clean a rifle in record time, and clearing a jam was now second nature. They all loved the hand grenades, and each one wanted an M-203. Bruce could only guess at the count, but he was sure it was around sixteen to eighteen thousand bodies around the house. Looking at the bodies, Bruce was very glad they had brought more ammo. He told the girls to keep watch as he took down the tarp and for them to pick up what brass they could and put it in the empty ammo cans.

The girls went to the other end of the roof picking up brass and decided to keep this information to themselves. It was too valuable to just tell everyone. Then, Stephanie pointed out if boys found out girls knew that much about them, they would probably change. Everyone agreed that they would only tell their daughters.

As the little group broke up to grab their equipment, Stephanie stood up. She did not believe she would ever have kids, so the information would stay with her. She smiled to herself, understanding Bruce now in a whole new light. She knew she would never disappoint him again. Stephanie would tell Debbie because she did love her, and Debbie needed to know this stuff. Stephanie figured Debbie knew most of it anyway, but she would make Bruce happier, and that would make Stephanie happy.

Bruce called over the radio, telling them to bring the RG and that even it might not make it through the bodies. Bruce turned to his team. "I'm very proud of each of you. Remember, no talkin' about what we talked about on the first night, okay? Boys would really hate me for that."

"But Daddy—" Buffy started as Mindy yelled, "Is that a blue running?" This caused Bruce to turn around to look where Mindy was looking. Leaning over, Stephanie whispered in Buffy's ear not to say anything. Bruce never realized that he talked about boys the entire time. Buffy understood and shook her head as Bruce turned back around.

"Probably one we wounded. Now remember; ya promised," Bruce reminded them.

Maria answered, "We have sworn to each other never to tell anyone but our daughters."

Bruce liked that answer. He had really enjoyed the time up there with the team. When he heard the big diesel, he told everyone to grab their stuff. Then, Buffy looked up at Bruce. Stephanie had to fight the urge to put her hand over her mouth. That would draw too much attention, and she was just a little girl. Stephanie really did not think she should have the information now and would talk to her in private later.

"Daddy, does Mama know that stuff about boys?" Buffy asked him.

"BB, I'm a boy, and your mama knows more about boys than I do," Bruce said, watching the big truck head into the field, driving over piles of bodies. It pulled up to the house, and they just stepped onto the top of the RG then climbed down into the back.

Stephanie smiled to herself as she sat down beside Buffy. She left just enough room for Bruce to sit between them. Boys were creatures of habit, and this was her first chance to test her information. Bruce had said over and over boys were simple. Stephanie just shook her head in disbelief that boys were so simple, they were complicated. Bruce walked back from the front and sat down between Buffy and Stephanie.

Stephanie laid her head on Bruce's shoulder, smiling. He had told them the truth. She did feel a little guilty that Bruce did not realize that he talked about the male half of the species for three days, but she pushed that thought from her mind. Stephanie closed her eyes and had to be woken up when they reached the farm.

CHAPTER 11

Bruce was sitting in his chair in the game room, rocking PJ, waiting on Mike to finish with his shower. All the teams were in and reporting huge kill numbers. Bruce was very optimistic about getting the other survivors and supplies for the upgrades. Bruce looked over on the couch, watching Jake play with the twins. Jake, feeling his Dad stare at him, looked up.

"What, Dad?" he asked.

"Nothin', son, just watching you play with your sisters," Bruce replied, smiling.

"Let me tell ya; they may be little, but they beat the hell out of me every night when we went to sleep. Then, Ms. Lynn brought me PJ to see if I could make him shut up. That little turd can scream, but he finally shut up, and then I was stuck with him too," Jake said while looking at PJ then continued. "He may not walk, but he can get into anything. I had to pull him out from under my bed several times. Everyone here tried to help with PJ, Emily, and Sherry but they had to stay up my butt," Jake replied.

"That's what I call stepping up to the plate, son. Words can't describe how proud I am of ya for that."

"Thank you, Dad. It wasn't that big a deal," Jake replied as he filled with pride.

"The hell it ain't. I've done it, and I think they are tryin' to see if they can drive me crazy. I want to ask you; did Emily and Sherry do that moving in unison thing to you?" The only twins he has experience with were David and Mary, but they were obviously fraternal.

"Yeah, Dad, all the time, and it kinda freaks me out," Jake replied as the girls hugged him.

Bruce and Jake continued to talk until Mike came in and sat in his chair. Debbie came and took PJ and sat on the couch to feed him oatmeal. Debbie had not even sat down when the twins ran over and jumped in Bruce's lap. Bruce let out a long sigh, convinced he would never get to sit by himself ever again. When everyone was in the game room, Bruce called the meeting to order.

"Okay, everyone, I want this meetin' to be short. We have ta move fast tomorrow before more blues show up. We have people to rescue and supplies to gather. Now my team will be goin' to the survivors, and Paul will be leadin' one supply mission. Mike will lead the other for food. There will be no backup. Matt and Jake tell me they have several people trained to run the UAVs. Angela and Alex, you are now assigned to find placement for those that are comin' here. Get their names and what they can do. Pam, you'll run Mission Control tomorrow. Start time for mission is 7 a.m. tomorrow." Bruce wanted to get up and walk around, but the twins were snuggling into his sides, going to sleep.

Bruce continued, "My team will take two Strykers, one deuce and half with a trailer, and the RG. With those four vehicles, we can haul seventy plus back. My team will be myself, Buffy, Debbie, Jake, Danny, Conner, and Matt. We'll start with the farm that the idiots are in first then move to the other farms then to Jonesboro. Jonesboro still has blues in strength. The camp there was big accordin' to Marcus, holding between six and seven thousand. With around thirty somethin' people left, that means lots of blues. If we get compromised, we leave. I don't care if we have the survivors or not. I don't want a battle of attrition when we're on the ground without cover," Bruce said, looking at each member of his team before continuing. "We'll stop four miles from town, then Matt 'n Conner will watch our rides. The rest of the team will move in on foot. Once we have all the survivors, we'll head home. I figure we should be done around three.

"There will only be three adults here at the farm once we leave. If the farm calls, everyone is to stop and come a runnin'. I don't care if we haven't got anything or anybody. I want Paul's group finished before my team gets back. Any questions?" Bruce asked. Lynn raised her hand, and Bruce motioned to her.

"Leavin' just me, Susan, and Pam with a few teenage boys seems a little risky; don't cha think?" she asked.

"I'm only worried about gangs right now after the slaughter we had over tha last few days. We'll see them long before they get here so I'm not really worried. Risky yeah but very necessary and we need ta move fast. Saturday and Sunday we'll be goin' out again for more supplies," Bruce said, and Lynn nodded. "Any other questions?" Bruce asked, and little Frank raised his hand.

"Mr. Bruce, we still get to have movie night, don't we?" he asked. Bruce looked at his little, hopeful face then looked at the other kids and a few teens and saw the same look on their faces.

"Yes, we'll still have movie night," Bruce told him, and all the kids started clapping. Bruce held up his hand for them to quiet down. "We have a lot of work to do, so no whining when you have to do it, Jake and Matt, what do you have to tell us?" Bruce asked, turning to them.

Matt pointed to Jake, and he stood up. "We don't have an actual count, but our figures say the teams that went out put down approximately forty thousand blues. This number is close plus or minus two grand. The twenty-five-mile radius around us is clear. We have not seen any on thermal. There might be a few, but we can't find them," Jake finished then looked at everyone in the game room. Each person had a smile on their face.

"Thank you, son," Bruce said. "It is 5:30 now, and Lynn has supper ready. We need to eat and get some sleep because not only tomorrow but the next few weeks will be very busy. Anyone have anything to add?" Bruce asked, looking around. No one raised their hand, so Bruce told everyone to eat and get some sleep.

The clan moved to the tables to get some food and talked amongst each other. Bruce noticed Mindy talking with David, who had a grin from ear to ear. Bruce made sure the twins ate while Debbie fed the toxic poop machine, who kept yelling to make sure everyone knew he was there.

Bruce and Debbie had everyone upstairs showered and in bed before 7:30. To Bruce's delight, Danny and Buffy were sleeping in their room. Bruce read to the twins and PJ until they fell asleep, which did not take long, and took Debbie with them. Bruce put his book down and was soon fast asleep.

When his alarm clock went off at 4 a.m., he swore he had just laid his head down. Bruce still got up, put on some workout clothes, and headed to the gym. He was not in the gym long before Mike showed up. By 5 a.m., the gym was crowded as everyone wanted to get warmed up for the day ahead.

Bruce and Mike finished their workout then went to shower and dress for battle. They really didn't eat; it was more of just shoveling food into their mouths. Then, they went to Mission Control to see what the UAVs had found.

One of the teenage boys from the gas station was running the UAVs and reported no sightings in twenty miles but found several large mobs of blues around Jonesboro. Bruce almost canceled the mission, but the blues were on the east side of the village, and the building was on the west side. Bruce figured that the blues were about a mile away, so the rescue was still a go.

With his team in the Stryker, Bruce put Buffy in the gunner's seat of the one he was driving. With the large suppressor on the end of the mounted 50 cal, it looked like a different weapon. When Buffy had shown Bruce she knew how to operate the weapon system, he stepped out the back. It was false dawn at 6:30. Bruce called over the radio for everyone on his team to load up; they were leaving early.

By 7:30, they were pulling up to the first farm. Bruce pulled up in his Stryker. Debbie and Danny pulled up in their Stryker. Bruce and Debbie got out of the Strykers holding their hands up and walking up to the little farm house. Buffy and Danny covered them with the weapon systems on the Strykers.

A clean-shaven white man in his early forties came out carrying a shotgun. Bruce and Debbie tried for thirty minutes to get the man to bring his family to the farm, but he refused. When Bruce told him he needed to put a fence around the house, the man just said that would be too much work and lower the value of the house. Debbie gave him a CB radio and told him to call if they got in trouble. The idiot thanked her, and the rest of the families came out on the porch as Bruce and Debbie climbed into the Strykers.

As Bruce pulled out, he took one last look at the families, knowing they were as good as dead, and felt pity for them. Bruce called Debbie on the radio and told her his thoughts. She reminded him you can't cure stupid.

The other farmhouses were more than happy to leave. Bruce told them to only grab a small bag of clothes and weapons to take with them. Most didn't have anything but the clothes on their back and ran for the vehicles.

At 11:10, the team had reached the point where they would leave the vehicles. Bruce, Debbie, Buffy, Danny, and Jake would go to the building with the survivors while Matt and Conner watched the group and vehicles. Before leaving, Bruce called Pam for an update on the area.

Pam told him the blues were still on the other side of town, and a few people had come out of the building but went back in. Bruce told her if anything changed to call back, and Pam said she would.

Bruce led the team in single file through the woods, walking parallel to the road that lead into Jonesboro. Moving slowly, it took them over an hour to reach the large, brown, metal building that held the survivors. Bruce stopped the team in the tree line with the building less than fifty yards from them. He was studying the area as Debbie came up beside him.

"How are we goin' to let them know we are here because you are *not* just gonna walk up and knock on the door," Debbie said, looking at the building.

"I was just wondering the same thing, sugar mama," Bruce admitted when a thought hit him. Bruce looked at Debbie. "Give me the extra radio in your pack. See those windows at the top of the walls?" Bruce said, pointing to a row of windows under the edge of the roof fifteen feet off the ground. They were four feet long and about one and half feet tall.

"I'm going to wrap the radio in a shirt, shoot out a window, and throw the radio through it and call them," Bruce said, proud of his idea.

"That's a good idea, but Buffy and I will throw the radio in, and before you say anything, shut up and listen. You, Jake, and Danny are better at long-distance shooting. If the group in there see a woman and a little girl, they are less likely to shoot at us. Now, you can talk." Bruce wanted to argue, but she had valid points, and he nodded.

Bruce lined the others up to cover them as Debbie got the radio ready to throw. When everyone was ready, Bruce told Jake to shoot out a window. Jake raised his AR-10 and squeezed off four shots, hitting the window and shattering it. Bruce set his radio to monitor the team channel and the channel Debbie had set on the radio she was throwing in. In case the people inside were hostile, Bruce did not want them to listen in on his team. Debbie and Buffy cleared the distance to the building fast, threw in the radio, then turned around and ran back to the wood line.

Bruce called over the radio, "Hello, is anyone there? Over." He repeated it four times before getting a reply.

"Who's this?" a male voice replied.

"This is Bruce Williams. I have a team here to take you to a more secure location if you want to leave," Bruce answered. The man on the other end tried to say something else, but the radio was taken away when a female voice came on.

"How do we know you aren't with the gang that hit us a week ago?" she asked in a smartass tone.

"Ma'am, if that was the case, I would've thrown grenades through the window and not a radio. We don't have much time," Bruce replied. The woman keyed the radio, and Bruce could hear arguing and fighting. Then, the first man came back on.

"Mr. Williams, where are you? We can't see you," he asked.

Bruce let out a sigh. "We are in the tree line. We really don't want to be out in the open right now with those fast blue fuckers around. We can't run that fast. Now, do you want to leave or not? Hold on," Bruce said as Pam came on the radio.

"You have four blues coming toward you from the back of the field. You should see them in a few seconds," Pam said. Jake moved his rifle to the back of the property, and sure enough, thirty seconds later, four blues came out of the tree line about a hundred yards away. Jake squeezed the trigger four times. As the first one hit the ground, the last one died.

"That was good shooting," the man replied over the radio.

"Thank you. Now do you and your group want to leave?" Bruce asked, looking at the building and seeing faces at the windows.

After a few minutes, Bruce was about to tell his team they were leaving when the man came back on the radio. "Can you send in one of your team? I have some questions to ask, and I want to see who we are dealing with," he replied.

Bruce expected this but still didn't like it. He would not just leave with someone until he could look into their eyes. Bruce replied, "One of my team is coming in. Have the door on the side of the building open where we threw in the radio. If you hurt my team member, no one in that building will live to see the sunset today. Don't think you'll be able to use them as a hostage either because the same thing will follow."

"If your man shows no hostility to us, I give you my word none will be shown to him," the man replied.

The man was a poet, Bruce thought as he turned to the team. "Buffy and I are going in. If something happens, kill everyone," Bruce said and took off with Buffy in tow before Debbie could say anything.

When Bruce and Buffy were ten yards away, the door opened, and they ran in, and the door closed behind them. Bruce looked around and saw filthy men, women, and children standing around. A man in a dirty deputy uniform, holding the radio Debbie had thrown in, walked up to Bruce.

"Hi, my name is Bill Thompson. I was a deputy at one time. Who are you?" Bill asked, looking at Buffy behind Bruce.

"I'm Bruce, and this is my daughter, Buffy. Now, do you people want to leave?" Bruce asked Bill.

"You aren't military," Bill stated, looking at Bruce then to Buffy as she held her M-4 ready for action.

"Good call, Bill," Bruce said, smiling.

"Where do you want to take us to?" Bill asked as Debbie told Bruce over the radio that Jake had just shot two more infected.

"We have a farm that is secure not far from here, but those that come will have to work to help make it more secure and learn to fight. This is no free ride; we have killed over forty thousand infected just this week. There are several large gangs moving around this area, and those that come will be expected to work and fight. We have food, shelter, and water. Now, if you don't like it, you can leave, but you will live by our rules, which I will tell you when we get there. Buffy and I are leaving in three minutes with or without you."

"We're coming with you," Bill said, turning to tell people to get ready when a woman hollered, causing everyone to stop.

A woman about fifty and a man a little younger walked over to Bruce. Unlike everyone else, they were clean. Bruce did not like them from first sight. With them were two state troopers carrying M-4s. They were clean also, but their uniforms were dirty. "We have not given anyone permission to leave here, and that includes you," she told Bruce.

"Listen, bitch, I don't follow orders from you, and if you try to stop me, you'll die," Bruce said, and one of the troopers moved his hands on his rifle. "Move another inch, and I'll give you a one-way ticket to hell free of charge," Bruce said, and all the survivors watched.

"You can't threaten them. I am district judge Carla Owens, and this is Congressman Mitch Tanner," Carla said, pointing at the man beside her.

"I don't care if you're Donald and Daffy Duck. If he moves any more, you will be the first to die. We leave in two minutes," Bruce said in an emotionless tone as the other survivors grabbed what little they had.

"We are in charge here, Mr. Williams, not you. You will do what we say," Mitch said, finally speaking.

"I wouldn't follow you out of a burning building. If you want to stay, that's fine, but if you try to stop anyone from leaving, your day will go to shit fast, boy," Bruce said, flipping the selector switch to auto on his SCAR.

Bill came up to Bruce. "We're ready." Bruce studied the group. He saw five soldiers with M-4s. Besides Bill and the state troopers, they were the only ones armed. None of the other people had guns, a few had bats, and one even held a sword.

"Soldiers, spread out in the line of people, and don't fire unless we are gettin' overrun. My team will cover us as we move. All of our weapons are suppressed. If you shoot, we will die. There is a mob of several thousand on the other side of town. They're spread out looking for you. We have a UAV up and can see them moving around. No talking or crying. Keep in single file one arm length from the person in front of you. We have five miles to go to get to our rides," Bruce said and saw relief on their faces. Bruce turned to Carla and Mitch, who were talking. Mitch turned to the group.

"Do what he says for now," Mitch told everyone.

Bruce did not give a shit; he wanted out of there. He looked at the two state troopers. "Hey, dumb and dumber, that goes for you too. Don't fire your weapons. If you do, you'll be shot. I'll shoot ya in the legs just so the blues can get you," Bruce said, and he could see anger wash over their faces.

"They were assigned as our bodyguards by the governor, and you will address them with respect," Carla said.

"That is strike two, bitch. If you tell me to do something again, you'll spit teeth. No one is to shoot except my team."

"Silencers are illegal, and I will make sure you are punished later," Carla promised Bruce.

"Mine aren't. Well, some of them aren't," Bruce replied, heading to the door. Bruce called Debbie over the radio and told her to lead the group to the vehicles. Danny and Jake would flank the group; he and Buffy would cover the rear. It took ninety minutes to reach the vehicles because they had to go slow for the survivors. Just before they reached the vehicles, Bruce called his team over the radio, telling them they were going to disarm the state troopers at the vehicles then laid out his plan. Bruce told Matt and Conner to put the women and kids in the Strykers and the RG then put the rest in the duce and half and trailer. Bruce received affirmative from everyone.

When Bruce reached the vehicles, Carla and Mitch were telling everyone they were riding in the RG with their escorts. Bruce yelled, "Now," and suddenly, the troopers, the judge, and the congressman were looking down gun barrels.

"If you move, you'll die," Bruce told them. "Now, slowly raise your hands." They did. Bruce took the M-4s from the troopers and turned to Bill. "You know how to run one of these?" Bruce asked.

"Seven years Atlanta SWAT. I should," Bill replied as Bruce threw him one M-4 and handed the other to one of the soldiers. Then, Bruce took the pistols out of their belts and backups off their ankles and looked at the troopers.

"When I trust you, then you'll get them back. If you are seen with a firearm until then, you will be shot. Now, get in the trailer or stay here; I don't care," Bruce said. "Let's move out."

It was 3:30 when they got back to the farm.

CHAPTER 12

Glancing at his watch as the last of the supply trucks pulled into the farm, Bruce saw it was 4:10. The newly arrived survivors were on the back patio eating. Lynn had set up a table with food and would use a pen to write on each person's hand as they grabbed a plate. This was done to make sure everyone got something to eat and people could not keep coming back. Mike had dropped off Alex and Angela at the farm at 2 p.m. after one of the supply runs to prepare for the survivors.

When the vehicles had stopped, Alex came over and told everyone that they needed their names so they could find everyone a place to sleep. Standing beside Alex, Angela told everyone that families should come up together. Then Angela told them food was being prepared and for everyone to sit in chairs on the back patio and that the pool house had a bathroom for those that needed it. This caught many off guard since they had not seen a working toilet or running water in months. Chairs were set around the patio with folding tables that the family kept for parties. There was almost enough for everyone leaving only a few kids sitting on the ground.

Watching the new group and shaking his head, Bruce looked at the piece of paper that Alex had given him with the number of people and the break down. The group had young, old, males, females, white, black, Hispanic and Asian. The total was seventy-nine new survivors and they did not have places for all of them to sleep. This brought the number of the clan to over a hundred. Mitch, Carla and their two guards had not given their names to Alex and Angela. Bruce asked Bill to stay with him as Bruce led him around the property.

141

While the group ate, Bruce looked at the mountains of supplies that were scattered all over the property. It looked like a supply depot had gone out of business. Huge piles of lumber from several construction sites were set up in massive stacks, with more pallets of concrete than Bruce had ever seen. There was heavy equipment parked in front of the barn. Bruce saw a diesel fork lift with a boom arm, back hoe, bulldozer and pieces of construction equipment that he did not know what the hell they did, but they looked cool as hell.

Mike and Paul came over to join him and Bill. Paul gave them a rundown on what else was needed as Bruce gave them the numbers.

Paul was the first one to speak when Bruce finished. "We need to get the barracks built and I want to build a community building where everyone can eat. It can be put behind the patio at the back of the house. We can put a kitchen in it and use it as the meeting room and class room. The barracks I designed will house a hundred and twenty people in small cubicles, sixty people on each floor. With the two semi-trucks of cinder blocks we found today, the first floor can be put under ground to save on cooling power. Those two projects need to be started tomorrow. Then we can start on the storage area," Paul told them while making notes in his notepad.

Bill looked at Paul in amazement asking, "Are you an engineer?"

"No, I'm a farmer but I have a master's in agriculture, a bachelor's in structural engineering, and I minored in architecture. Farmers hafta build. It's cheaper to do it yourself, plus I designed small buildings on the side," Paul told him, not looking up from his notebook.

"Damn, makes me feel like a little bitch with my associate's degree in criminal justice," Bill replied, looking at Bruce and Mike.

"Wait until you meet Stephanie. She has four doctorates and six master's degrees and she's only thirty," Mike told Bill.

"Is this a genius colony for Mensa?" Bill asked Mike.

"No, knowledge is power and everyone here will learn or they'll leave. We are going to have classes on everything from welding, gardening, sewing, computers, survival, firearms, combat, advance chemistry and anything else we need to know," Bruce told Bill as he looked at all the stuff the supply teams had brought back.

Turning to Mike and keying his radio, Bruce started talking, "Everyone with a radio listen. We have at least two problems. The clean white lady is a judge and the clean white man is a congressman. They believe that they are in charge and don't have to listen. The two troopers with them have been disarmed but might be a problem. I want the two troopers because they have firearm experience, but they follow the two dipshits hook line and sinker." Bruce was fixing to continue but Bill interrupted.

"Let me tell you about those assholes," Bill replied, Bruce moved toward him, taking off his throat mic so everyone could hear. "Those two are responsible for more deaths than I care to remember. They are prejudiced to no end. Not really evil but indifferent, believing they're better than everyone else. They ruled jointly, using fear from the bodyguards and the soldiers. The soldiers stopped listening last week after the two got twenty of their buddies killed. Let me put it this way. With the limited water supply we had, both of them took a bath every day, to 'maintain appearances.' Then they made others wash their clothes every three days. The bodyguards got to bathe every other day.

"The soldiers never did anything bad to the people, but that cannot be said about the two troopers. I have watched them beat and falsely imprison people. They would force others to leave on supply runs or just leave the group. There used to be four bodyguards but two got killed when the Homeland camp got overrun. The majesties keep them close now. I can't prove it but I think they've killed several people at the camp before it was overrun. They would tell everyone that they were escorting someone out of camp, then return alone. You'd think that two cops wouldn't follow the idiots but I think they like being next to power and being the enforcer." Bill stopped, looked at Mike and Bruce, then continued.

"I was trying to lead the group out with the soldiers, leaving the four to boss each other around. I knew if I did that, it was going to come to gunplay. You have no idea how much I and the others appreciate what you've done. Disarming the troopers before getting here, that was a stroke of genius. They would've caused a big problem otherwise," Bill finished.

Bruce put his mic back on and asked everyone if they copied that, getting affirmatives from everyone. Then Debbie came over the radio.

"I've told them to sit down three times. They keep walking around trying to boss everyone around. Steve threatened to shoot all four of them when Carla snapped at me. Lynn told them she'd shoot them when they commanded her to prepare a meal just for them. This needs to be handled soon or I'm letting Steve shoot them," Debbie told him.

"On the way over. I'm giving my rules speech and be ready to back me up," Bruce replied, heading to the patio with the others in tow.

When Bruce reached the patio, he called to everyone, "May I have your attention please." After all talking stopped and all eyes were on him, he continued.

"I want to welcome you all here. There isn't much safety in the world now but we've made a little haven here. Please hold your questions until the end. My name is Bruce and I'm one of the leaders here," Bruce said as Mike came up beside him and interrupted.

"Let's get this clear, he's the boss, the wives and I are next," Mike said then stepped back behind Bruce.

Bruce just shook his head, not wanting that, then continued. "First, the rules of the farm. There is no stealing, period. If it's not yours, leave it alone. Punishment will be dealt out fast. Next, everyone has to work. If I'm out here working, then every swinging dick and pair of boobs will be working too. If you're sick we have doctors here that will see you. If needed, you will be given another task until you're better. Anyone caught trying to get out of work will be given jobs that no one else wants. Remember, if you don't work, you don't eat.

"Only Ms. Lynn and those assigned to help her are allowed in the food storage areas. You will get enough to eat, but only what is prepared. There are now over a hundred people here and this is goin' to put a massive strain on the supplies we have now. Teams will be going out to get more, so don't worry. We have arranged for six thousand calories a day per person. That's a lot but it's earned with work for the clan. If you stay, you will be a part of the clan. We love, fight, care and will die for each other here. That's what I expect if you stay.

"This is a limited democracy here. People are assigned to jobs based on abilities, not on vote. Every Sunday we have a group meeting for problems to be addressed. If you pose a danger to the clan you will be dealt with, and if you pose an extreme danger you'll be shot. Talk to the others that are here; this is not a bad place and if you think it is, carry your punk ass elsewhere. We don't need you. If you follow the rules you'll be happy here. These rules are simple. Treat others here with respect and they will do the same for you.

"Since I have now been put in full command, my word is the final word. I do listen, but when my mind is made up the decision is over. If you think I'm wrong then on Sunday bring up your argument, and if the other three think I am wrong, then that's the way it will be. If you don't like the language I use, I'm sorry but I'm not going to change." Bruce paused and looked around before continuing.

"Alex and Angela will be handing out paper and clipboards. Everyone will write their name on the top. List what education you have, what you did for a living, and all the jobs you have held. Then I want you to list what you know how to do and your hobbies. If you know how to sew, we want to know. If you can write on a grain of rice, we want to know. If you know how to make illegal drugs, hot wire a car or break into a building, we want to know. We don't care if you've been in jail. With that being said, if you screw up here, your life will become an instant living hell. The clan must know what skills are here and all skills are needed. We don't care if you have been in prison, everyone has a clean slate now and you can truly start over.

"Now, the punishment for rape is death in this clan. The punishment for murder is death by torture, and I promise ya, I can come up with some medieval shit." Bruce paused and looked around again. Most were just ordinary people and nodded in agreement. Only a few had questionable looks. The small kids were just looking at the swimming pool.

"All kids fifteen and under will have four hours of class a day. Then they, along with everyone else, will have two hours of class on learning how to fight and to survive. You'll learn guns, knives and hand to hand. Everyone is required to work out four times a week, an hour each time. This is to make sure you can fight when the time comes and that you can work at peak performance.

"Once you're checked off on a weapon, you'll keep it with you at all times. If you look around, there are several twelve-year-olds that are armed. Everyone is expected to fight after they learn how. I can see worry on some faces, so let me clear something up. Nobody will be asked to go on supply runs until they've been checked off on weapons and training. You would endanger the rest of the team otherwise. We fight and die for each other here. If something happened to you, the team would die trying to save you," Bruce said, seeing relief on several faces.

"For the next few weeks, it'll be very crowded. If you need clothes, shoes, or other necessities, see my daughter Danny later, after your list is done. Until you're cleared to carry a firearm you aren't to touch one, period. You have a right to them but until we see you are safe with them you can't touch one. Training on them will start tomorrow, along with a lot of work. Tomorrow morning there will be an assignment list for different jobs for everyone. Unless you're dying, you will report for work. I truly wish we had time to let this new group rest, but we don't.

"Crops have to be planted in, weapons need to be taught, buildings need to be built, and the list goes on and on. Life as we knew it is now gone and we have to rebuild the world. Make no mistake: there are almost two hundred million infected out there, and lots of gangs raping and pillaging what they find. I'm sure everyone here has lost multiple loved ones and for them you should do your best to survive to carry on their memory. We have a long hard battle ahead. I can't promise you we'll make it but we will do our best. I'll not ask anyone here to do something that I will not do. I will fight for you and if necessary die for you. This is America and I say let's take it back." Bruce stopped and glanced at those around him. He could see hope and determination on their faces now. One person stood up and began clapping, joined by another until everyone except the four problem children were clapping.

Bruce's face turned beet red and he held up his hands for everyone to stop, which only made them clap louder and start cheering. Debbie gave PJ to Buffy and ran over to Bruce, wrapping her arms around him. Bruce returned her hug, wishing he had guard duty tonight but it would be another week. Letting Debbie go, he kept his arm across her shoulders as she stood beside him. Bruce held up his hand for everyone to sit down so he could continue. The clapping and cheering slowly stopped and everyone sat back down.

Bruce continued on. "I will try to answer some questions but remember we have a lot of work to do so please keep it short. If I don't get to you today, you can ask Sunday at the weekly meeting, before we start the work day. I want you to wait until you are called on. I want this to stay orderly." Bruce pointed to an elderly black lady who had her hand up.

She stood up and asked, pointing at the judge and congressman, "Are they going to be in charge in any way and do they have to work like the rest of us?" Everyone just stared at Bruce waiting on his answer.

"No ma'am, they will not be in charge in any form or fashion. From my observations, they're both idiots. If they want to eat, then they'll work or starve," Bruce told her, getting another round of applause.

146

Mitch jumped out of his chair and pointed his finger at Bruce, his face going from red to purple. "Listen, country boy, I have had enough of your mouth. Carla and I were appointed by the governor to oversee this area for the federal government. Not you and your militia family. I could have you shot now for using military equipment and for your own admission of killing infected. Only the military and police are allowed to address the infected problem. I'm responsible for that military equipment, not you. It has been assigned to me. The President of the United States declared martial law over the entire nation. No citizen is allowed to own property and must follow the duly appointed representative of the federal government. That means Carla and I own this farm, not you. I am the executive branch and she is the judicial. By your own account, you have also killed law enforcement officers and citizens. We have the authority to authorize summary executions. We have done in the past and will do again in the future. You are playing with one right now!" Mitch finished yelling at Bruce.

Debbie felt Bruce's body turn to rock under her hands as soon as Mitch stood up. The more Mitch spoke, Debbie could actually feel the anger pour off of Bruce. She looked up at Bruce's face and saw no emotion at all. Taking her arms off of Bruce, Debbie stepped back behind him. She had never seen this expression and knew hell was coming and she was not going to stop it. Not that she really wanted to. If anyone was asking for a beating, it was this asshole. In all the years she had known Bruce, he'd always threatened to rape a man before he got in a fight. It was only psychological warfare, to install fear in his opponent. Being raped by another man is what most men were afraid of. Glancing up at the side of Bruce's face, she was almost certain this time she might have to watch a rape. Thinking it over for a second, Debbie decided she would help hold Mitch down.

Bruce glared at Mitch for several seconds after he quit talking. A grin spread across Bruce's face before he spoke. "Who's going to shoot me, bitch? Who are you going to call before I rape you?" Debbie smiled from behind Bruce. She knew her man.

"The government is in Colorado and we have been in contact with them. It is only a matter of time before the military gets the upper hand," Mitch told Bruce smugly.

"There hasn't been a live broadcast in weeks. Shit fucks like you wasted any opportunity to save people," Bruce replied, and he saw shock on both of their faces. The grin took an evil appearance and spread across Bruce's face. Seeing his expression, many were certain that it would have made Satan cry. Then he spoke. "You didn't know that because you've not had a radio for a long time. I declare you a danger to the clan." Those sitting anywhere near Mitch got up swiftly, knocking over chairs in their haste and clearing the area. Debbie watched the people move away; many were smiling. They had listened to Bruce's speech and rules.

Carla jumped up to bring order to the madness. She was a judge after all. "Listen Bruce, Mitch did not say you were going to be executed, but if you threaten him again I will sign the order myself," she threatened. Bruce slowly turned to Carla, looking into her eyes. Carla took a step back in shock; she had seen that look before from those she had sentenced. It was the look of death. Carla fought off a shiver, not wanting to show weakness. She turned and spoke to the crowd. "If anyone here follows this man's orders you will suffer the same penalties. Any that do not follow our orders will face execution," Carla said, pointing over her shoulder at Bruce. She had done this once before with that dumbass colonel. His own troops did not even protect him as she had him executed. She only had to scare one person with a weapon. She turned back to Bruce.

"We were going to put you in charge of the security, Bruce, but you have fucked yourself out of that. You will now give your weapons to my bodyguards. Mitch and I will be taking the master bedrooms upstairs. No one else will be sleeping in the house. I will appoint certain people to jobs in the morning. Bruce, you will leave these premises now and do not return because you will be shot on sight. Next—" Carla began as Debbie ran up to her.

"Whoa bitch, you don't come to another woman's home making those demands and saying you are throwing people out. Especially this house, because I will monkey stomp your ass right here!" Debbie yelled in Carla's face.

Carla, who was six inches taller than Debbie, looked down at her. "Little woman, get out of my face before I hurt you," Carla told her. Carla knew she could beat the shit out of this woman.

Hearing that, Debbie's blood froze as the anger washed over her body. Without thinking, Debbie palm punched Carla in the abdomen. Caught off guard, Carla staggered back from the punch as all the air escaped her lungs. Debbie reached up with both hands and grabbed a handful of hair on each side of Carla's head. Still in full combat gear with her elbow and knee pads on, Debbie pulled Carla's head down while she brought up her right knee. Carla's face met the point of Debbie's knee at the center of the hard shell over the pad and everyone heard her nose crunch on impact. Letting go of Carla's hair, Debbie let Carla fall to the ground, blood pouring out of her crushed nose.

One of the troopers ran toward Debbie, pulling out his baton as Carla fell to the ground, but Jake cut him off. Seeing movement, the trooper raised the baton, swinging it at Jake's head. Jake blocked the blow with his left hand as he grabbed the officer's wrist, and struck out with his right, hitting the officer in the throat. Then Jake brought his right hand back, still holding the trooper's wrist. Jake brought up his right palm, hitting the elbow and pushing through it. The officer dropped the baton, screaming as his elbow crunched, bending ninety degrees the wrong way. Then Jake jumped up into the air and struck out with the side of his right foot, hitting the officer above his right knee. As Jake's body weight came down, the force of impact caused the end of the femur to snap. Still holding the broken arm, Jake let the officer go. As he fell to the ground Jake yelled, "That's my Mama, bitch boy!"

The remaining officer had started moving to assist his buddy when Jake caught the first one's wrist. Steve was on him before he even got close. Snapping out his right foot, Steve caught the officer in the gut, bending him over. Steve brought his right leg back and jumped up with a left snap kick that caught the officer in the face with Steve's steel-toed combat boots. The officer's head snapped back, leaving an arc of blood in its wake. The officer threw out his arms to try to get his balance but Steve grabbed his right arm and pulled the officer toward him. Steve punched the officer above the bicep, breaking the end of his humerus, then stepped back as the officer hit the ground.

Jake and Steve had put both officers down in less than fifteen seconds. They both turned to check on their mama and saw her on top of Carla, beating the ever loving shit out of her.

Debbie was not slapping or pulling hair. She was punching Carla in the face, alternating with dropping elbows. Then Debbie would do a hand stand and bring her knees into Carla's stomach, Debbie was still screaming obscenities at her as she monkey stomped her ass. Carla was begging and pleading for her to stop. Nancy ran over, trying to pull Debbie off of Carla and she yelled, "Damn it Debbie, stop, I want a piece of this bitch's ass too."

Speechless, Bruce just gawked at his family as they dished out a major ass whooping. Feeling left out, he turned to Mitch. Then, out of the corner of his eye, he saw Danny in a dead run jump into the air, lean back parallel to the ground and kick out with both feet at the same time in a textbook drop kick.

Mitch turned just in time to catch both booted feet to his face, sending him flying. Unlike the gimp, Mitch was a big man of six foot two and pushing two hundred and sixty pounds. Granted, most was flab, but it was still weight. Danny did not sail through the kick but stopped at the point of impact, hitting the ground in a roll and springing to her feet.

To Bruce's surprise, Mitch also rolled to his feet just as Danny charged. Mitch swung a wide right hook that Danny ducked easily. Then she jumped up, extending her right arm in an open palm punch which caught Mitch square on the nose, sending him backwards.

Bruce heard a yell from his side. "Don't you fucking touch her!"

Before Bruce could turn to see who'd said it, Matt flew by him in midair. He was spinning in a flying round house kick. Matt's heel hit Mitch in the chest and those closest to the fight heard ribs crack. Mitch landed on his back as Matt landed on his feet. Then Matt took two running steps, leaping into the air again toward Mitch. Matt was already on his descent with his knees pointed down when Mitch saw him. Matt's knees hit him in the lower rib cage, breaking more ribs. Matt then rolled over Mitch's head to his feet. As Matt was readying his next assault an unsuppressed gunshot went off behind Bruce.

Dropping down, Bruce pulled his pistol. Rolling his body to the threat as he aimed his pistol, he found Mike holding his pistol in the air with his right hand. The suppressor was in the other.

"I think they have had enough," Mike told the family.

"Bullshit! This bitch still has to deal with me!" Nancy yelled at him. She had finally pulled Debbie off so she could get a piece of Carla's ass.

"Baby—" Mike started.

"Don't you fucking 'baby' me! This bitch wanted to throw me out of my house and my room. Debbie wouldn't get out of the way so I could beat this bitch's ass!" Nancy screamed at him.

Mike just looked at his wife, as everyone else did. No one had heard one word she said. All they could hear was a banshee scream. They all knew Nancy wanted to do something to Carla, just from the expression on her face and the screaming, but what exactly they had no idea. When Nancy let Debbie go to scream at Mike, she dropped back down and went back to hitting Carla. She was showing everyone what a monkey stomping was about.

Nancy looked at Mike and in a flat voice said, "Torture this bitch." Debbie finally quit hitting Carla when she heard Nancy say that. Then Debbie stood up by Nancy as she tried to catch her breath.

Mike looked at Nancy, frowning. "Nancy, that's enough."

Before Mike could say anything else, Nancy cut him off in a calm voice. "I'm going to tell you something, Mike, and I'm going to use little words so even a man can understand. You don't come to a woman's home and tell her you're throwing her and her family out. Then go sleep in her bed. Especially when those women have let their families risk their lives to help others. I don't care if something happens to me, but if something happens to the kids or you, I know I'll die. When this started, I wanted to close that gate, build a moat and just stay right here until the earth stopped turning.

"You and Bruce brought others here with you. I do see it's the right thing to do now. There are good people out there and they do need our help. But after risking our family's lives to rescue these people, to open up our home to them and offer what we have to them, to then have them come here threatening to throw us off this land or execute us after all we have done is wrong! I believe that's just too much for Debbie and me to swallow. But it's not just our house anymore. Look at these other women; it's their home now also and this bitch wanted to throw us out of it!" Nancy finished in a scream as Mike walked over to her.

Nancy paused for Mike to process what she had said then continued speaking calmly again. "For a woman to do that makes it even worse. Now this bitch is going to suffer, then I will drag a knife across her throat and feed her to the gators. I want this bitch raped, stabbed, burnt, skinned, and beaten. You can use a stick to rape her, I don't care. But help me do it!" Nancy again ended in a scream.

Bruce looked around at the clan as they watched the exchange. Then Bruce noticed women coming to stand by Nancy and Debbie. A few even kicked Carla as they walked by her as she lay on the ground crying. Grinning, Bruce thought to himself, *Don't fuck with a woman's family or her house. She will get seriously medieval on your ass.*

Mike just gazed at Nancy with a bewildered expression, not knowing what to do. His wife had just asked him to rape, beat, stab, and burn a woman. Not to mention that woman had already been monkey stomped by Debbie.

Yanking her knife off her vest, Nancy snarled, "Fuck it, I'll do it by myself."

"I'll help," Debbie told Nancy, turning toward Carla.

Bruce heard several other women saying, "Me too."

"Grab her arms," one said as the women started pinning Carla down.

Seeing it go far enough, Bruce took a deep breath and yelled, "HEY!" It was not a scream, but a loud, deep-throated bellow. Everyone recoiled from the sound. Several of the women who were holding Carla fell backwards on the ground. Even Debbie and Nancy jumped in the air and Nancy's knife hit the ground. They all turned as Bruce calmly strode over toward them. All of the women backed far away from Carla, seeing Bruce still wore that evil grin with an expression that held no emotion. His eyes were what scared them the most. They were the eyes of a predator that did not have a problem killing.

Nancy and Debbie never took a step back. They had no fear of Bruce, but his expression did make the anger leave their bodies. Reaching them, Bruce stopped in front of the wives and just studied them.

Looking at them, Bruce could see in their eyes that they were almost on the wave, but were not enjoying the edge of the rush. They were only running on the anger. They only wanted to use the anger to hurt, to ease their fears, not hold onto it and distance themselves. It was only a target. They could not focus the rage onto a target and feel it course through their veins. Anger built and unleashed the rage, but you couldn't hold onto the anger. Anger would just burn you out. With the rage unleashed, there were only targets to be dealt with as you rode the wave. No pleasure or remorse when the target was dealt with. You just moved through it, riding the wave. Feeling the rage course through you was ecstasy, the peak of the wave.

Looking at Bruce, Nancy cautioned, "Don't try to stop me, Bruce."

"Oh, I am going to stop both of you. Not to save the whore, but because I love you," Bruce told her, still no emotion showing on his face.

"Y-you-you have no right to stop me," Nancy stuttered as Mike walked up beside her.

"Yes I do," Bruce told her. Then Bruce leaned forward and said, "You don't know how to ride the wave." Debbie gasped, taking a step back. Nancy just looked at Bruce as a chill passed over her body. Then Bruce spoke again. "Don't get me wrong, if I thought you could ride the wave, I'd let you cut this bitch to pieces. But you'll feel guilty about it tomorrow and the rest of your life," Bruce told her then turned to Debbie. "You would too.

"It would eat at your soul, making ya feel guilty. You would remember the screams of this bitch because you don't understand. Targets don't scream. There's nothing but a target on the ground there. If Mike would've come over here and helped ya, you would've felt worse. Let me tell you something, he would have done it too, because he loves you that much. His soul and heart would die, but he would do it for you. All of you would start to question your actions, and sooner or later that would cause the death of one of the family," Bruce told the three standing in front of him.

"Me, on the other hand, could do inquisition-style torture to this piece of shit and never bat an eyelash or lose sleep. It's only a target, no guilt or remorse. Deal with your target then move to the next one. But I won't yet. Because y'all would feel guilty, you'd convince yourself that you were the cause of it. The only thing that can crash the wave is by hurting one you love, someone that has a piece of your heart, a teammate. That's why I won't do what you asked, because it would hurt all of you. When the wave crashed on me the pain would be unbearable. You can use hate to ride but the same thing happens. Then you have to live in the hate." Bruce looked up and closed his eyes before speaking again. "It's a rush, let me tell you, and you don't want it to end. No drug can compare to it. But when you hurt one that you love, your teammates, the wave turns on you because you are killing a piece of yourself. I'm not going to kill them even though I want to, but a lesson is called for." Bruce lowered his head with his eyes still closed. His breathing was getting harder.

If Bruce had been looking at Debbie he would have seen tears running down her face. Debbie had never seen him on the wave he had told her about. She had only seen what it did to him afterwards while he was in the Army. He always wanted to go back out on missions, volunteering for anything dangerous to do. Bruce had a kind heart and the wave was killing it in her eyes. Mesmerized, Debbie could see it on his face now and in his breathing. He was bottling up the rage inside to ride the wave.

Snapping his eyes open, Bruce made the three jump back. Then with a drill sergeant's voice and attitude he started barking orders out. "I want every list completed in thirty minutes and I had damn well better be able to read them. Angela, make sure everyone has their sleeping assignments. Alex, get some duct tape and boards then put splints on the two little pussies over there crying. They are not to get any pain medication for any reason. Jake and Steve, tie up Mitch, drag him by Carla, then do what you were told. It is now 1800, or 6 o'clock for those that can't tell time. I want every man, woman, and child showered and in bed by 2030, or 8:30 for those of you who are special. Wake up will be 0500. I will let you guess when that is. I want Mike, Debbie, Angela, Alex, Nancy, Jake, Stephanie, Bill, Paul, and Cheryl at the kitchen table at 2030 to go over tomorrow's schedule. Danny and Buffy, get the twins and PJ upstairs washed and in the bed. Gimp, get over here now. Now move like you have a purpose, people, or I will move you," Bruce finished with his voice still echoing off the buildings.

People took off in every direction, not wanting to face the wrath of the evil Mr. Clean. Most of the lists were completed in fifteen minutes, with some of the finest penmanship ever seen. People jumped in showers, scrubbing down real fast, and then ran naked past those in line for the shower. They dried off, heading to where they were sleeping. One of the new soldiers just washed under a water hose outside, then ran to his sleeping area. The gimp ran over to Bruce, falling to his knees and hoping not to feel the pain again. Only three people did not move: Debbie, Nancy and Mike.

"Move," Bruce told them, stepping forward as they parted.

Bruce kneeled beside Carla, who was curled into a ball on her side crying. Jake and Steve moved Mitch where they were told and took off. Never looking up at them, and with a gentle voice, Bruce asked Carla as he gently stroked her arm, "Are you in a lot of pain?"

"Yes, it hurts. Please no more. I'm sorry," she said, crying.

"My wife only hurt you a little bit. The pain I was going to put you through would've been bad, but you would've survived," Bruce told his target in a soft voice, still caressing Carla's arm. Reaching down, Bruce pulled his sheath knife from his boot, laying it flat on Carla's arm. When she felt the knife on her arm, her body became rigid.

Moving his hand up to her head, Bruce started stroking Carla's hair. Speaking in a soothing voice, he told her, "You brought out something in the people I love that they were not ready for. Now I have to give you pain that you'll not believe. See what you have brought on yourself? Even now, I can't do what I really want to do because they would feel guilty about it." Carla started crying again.

"Stop crying right now," Bruce snapped, grabbing a handful of her hair and yanking her head up. The three spectators jumped with the sudden change in his tone. The gimp was still kneeling with his head down, not making a sound. Carla stopped crying out of fear. Letting her hair go, Bruce started talking to her again in a soft voice. "See, you can listen. Now remember that lesson when the pain starts. Now lay on your back with your arms and legs straight."

"Please don't! I'll leave, but please don't do anything else t—" Carla started to beg as Bruce hit her in the back. Then he started raining down finger strikes over her body till she rolled onto her back. Bruce then grabbed her throat and held the knife over her face.

"See what you made me do to you?" Bruce asked her, calmly smiling. "Targets don't talk. They only do what they are told. You are a target; you have no name and your only purpose is to be knocked down." Carla wanted to scream and cry but she couldn't breathe. She wanted to raise her arms but they were numb and wouldn't move. She wanted to beg the wives to get Bruce to stop, but all she could do was nod her head while looking at the knife.

Relaxing the hand over her throat, Bruce continued holding the knife over her face. He lowered the point of the knife over her right eye and she closed her eyes. "If you don't open your eyes, I will cut off your eyelids off. But I promise I won't hurt your eyes when I do it. I have so much to show you," Bruce told her, leaning over her face as Carla opened her eyes.

"You're listening. That's good. Now lay flat on your back like you were told," Bruce said, and Carla laid completely flat. Bruce leaned over her, his face only inches from hers. He closed his eyes, his breath washing over Carla's face as he breathed though his nose and out his mouth. "You feel that? That's the fear and pain in your soul and it carries your thoughts to me. You want to beg my wife for me to stop. You want to beg for forgiveness. It's intoxicating." Bruce opened his eyes and looked at her shocked and frightened eyes. Carla's face was covered in blood, and Bruce stuck out his tongue, licking her from chin to forehead. Carla never moved as he finished; then Bruce lowered his head to her neck, breathing deeply through his nose again.

"I can feel, taste, and smell the fear and pain in your body and it's great," Bruce said, rocking back onto his heels and then standing up. He looked down at Carla as she just waited to be told what to do. "Don't move at all, no matter what you feel," Bruce told her.

Bruce leaned over, dragging his knife across her clothes, cutting them off and throwing them to the side. When he was finished, the only thing Carla still had on were her loafers. Bruce looked down at Carla, seeing little strips of blood where the knife had nicked her; she had never moved. For an older woman she looked pretty good. Bruce could see where she had gotten a face lift and breast implants on her toned body. Granted, it was covered in bruises from Debbie beating the shit out of her. Then, with a flash of movement, Bruce stomped on her stomach. When she tried to turn over he kicked her in the back.

"I didn't tell you to move. Targets do what they're told," Bruce told her and Carla made herself lay flat even as the pain threatened to make her pass out. "I'm not crazy and don't think that again," Bruce told her. Carla jerked her head over, looking at him in abstract fear. Dropping to his knees beside her, Bruce put the knife under her right breast. "If I was crazy I'd cut your tit off and make you lick it, wouldn't I?" Bruce asked her and Carla just nodded her head. "Am I crazy?" Bruce asked her and she shook her head no. Bruce stood up and rolled his head to the left and right, popping his neck. Looking behind him, Bruce saw the three just staring at him in shock.

"Leave," Bruce told them, motioning to the house with his head.

"Bruce. Brother. They're scared now, just come on inside," Mike pleaded with him.

Debbie was just watching Bruce. She felt awe, wonder, disgust, amazement, loathing, joy, and desire all at once. She could actually feel him on the wave. The energy he was giving off was intoxicating. Not once did he ever refer to Carla as a human, only a target. Debbie could see it on his face. He was with a target, not a person.

"Leave now," Bruce told them again.

156

"Bruce, you were right, I'll feel guilty tomorrow. Please come inside," Nancy begged him.

Closing his eyes, Bruce took a deep breath. He could feel the rage ebbing from his body at their request. Bruce opened his eyes and looked at them. "Mike, you're a good man, with a good heart. That's why I cherish you. When push comes to shove you are a good warrior and my best friend. Nancy, I love you dearly. You always give me your honest opinion. You have always stood up for the family and you're a true friend. But you are wrong, you won't feel guilty tomorrow. You now know I'm doing this because I want to, for bringing anger into your heart. Anger that you were not ready for," Bruce told her, then turned to Debbie, "My true love. You're the best thing that has ever happened in my life. Everything good in my life has come from you or by you. I want you to leave with Mike and Nancy now. Start on the schedule. I will be in shortly. Nobody is to come out the back door. If they need to go to the barn, tell them to take another door."

They all just stared at him as he said, "Leave now. Please."

The three started taking small steps toward the door, all of them wanting to grab Bruce and pull him inside. When they reached the door, Debbie stopped and turned around. "Bruce, when you come inside I want 'YOU' to come inside. I want you to leave the rage out here for me, baby. Will you do that for me, baby? Get off the wave?" Debbie asked him.

Bruce looked at her and replied, "Yes baby, I will. Now please go inside."

After the three went inside, Bruce turned to Mitch. "Now, where should we start, big boy?"

Two hours later, Bruce stood over the last one, the state trooper with a broken arm. All four were naked except for shoes and had felt pain few thought possible. Their spirits were almost broken, but he would probably end up killing Mitch and the trooper with the broken arm and leg. Bruce did not think those two would stay broke and he could not do this too many more times in front of Debbie. When she left, he did not like the way she looked at him. It looked like half of her wanted to join him and the other half wanted to puke at the sight of him. He could take the easy route and just kill the three, but he wanted to give them the chance to rejoin the human race.

All four were crying softly; they lay on their backs with no restraints but that would change shortly. He turned to the gimp who was still bowed down in the same spot. Bruce was amazed that anyone could stay in that position that long. "Gimp, come here," Bruce said, watching the gimp get up and almost fall down several times as he came over.

"Yes sir," Gimp said.

"I have to admit, I'm proud of you. I know several of the others are talking to you and showing you kindness, but I have not punished them or you. How do you like it when someone shows you kindness?" Bruce asked him.

Gimp was not surprised that Bruce knew others were being nice to him, but he was shocked that he was not going to be hit for it. Gimp took a deep breath. "It makes me feel good, sir."

"I'm going to see if you can join the human race again and be a man. You now have a new job. These four will start shit detail tomorrow. You'll oversee them, even the police officers with their broken arms and leg. The cops' names are Dumb and Dumber. The others are Bitch and Bitch Boy. That is how they are to be addressed. They are to remain naked until I say otherwise. They are not to use shovels, hoes, rakes, or pitchforks when they work. They are only allowed to use their hands until I say otherwise. Until they work half a day, none are to eat or drink until I say otherwise. Do you understand what I've told you?" Bruce asked him. Gimp just stared at Bruce, not believing his ears; he couldn't make his voice work so he just nodded his head 'yes' with tears in his eyes. "Gimp, I would like a verbal response," Bruce said firmly.

"Yes sir, I understand," Gimp replied, crying.

"You are not to hurt these four unless they try to hurt you or others. If they're not doing their job, you find me or one I have put in charge. Now go over there and bring me those policeman's holsters," Bruce told Gimp, who ran to grab them and brought them back to him. Bruce grabbed the four sets of handcuffs from one belt and handed them to the gimp. Bruce looked at the other belt. It still had the taser, pepper spray, keys, cuffs, and baton. Thinking about it for a minute, he handed it to the gimp. "Put this on and wear it always. If you're going to enter the world of man again, you'll start to act like it," Bruce said. Gimp looked at the belt then put it on. It didn't have a gun but that did not matter. "You're still not allowed to talk to Susan or the kids. Is that clear?" Bruce asked.

"Yes sir, I will never bother her again. I have hurt them too much to be forgiven," Gimp told him.

"You will handcuff these four to one of the gates on the pastures every night. When they work, their hands will be cuffed in front of them. This continues until I say otherwise," Bruce said.

"Yes sir," Gimp replied, feeling like he was in a dream. He was being given a second chance.

"When we're alone, you may call me Bruce," Bruce told him.

Gimp took a step back and looked at Bruce. He *must* be dreaming. He replied meekly, "I-I can't, sir."

"Your choice, but when we're alone I'll call you Jim," Bruce said. Tears started rolling out of Jim's eyes. It had been almost three months since anyone had used his name.

"Thank you sir," Jim replied fervently.

"You're now in charge of these four. Use my name for discipline and tell them about your story," Bruce told him.

"Yes sir," Jim replied.

"Now, do what you're told. Let's see if we can get some more people back in the human race," Bruce told Jim as he headed to the door.

Bruce turned back and watched Jim lead the four to the back pasture. Bruce closed his eyes as the wave left a void in him. Feeling drained of energy, Bruce took a deep breath as he grabbed the door handle and walked in.

CHAPTER 13

Debbie, Mike and Nancy walked in the house and found the others all at the table working. They each grabbed a chair and sat down, gazing off into space. The others just stared at them, wanting them to say something, anything.

Mike was the first to break the silence, "Holy ass balls."

"Second that," Nancy said.

Stephanie put down her pen and looked around the table, finally asking, "What the hell was that?"

"He was riding the wave," Conner replied in an offhand tone as he wrote on his list. They all looked at him as he continued writing. Feeling everyone stare at him, he looked up. "What?" Conner asked.

"Care to explain?" Stephanie asked.

Conner put down his pen, "Look, I have only one combat tour, but I was ready to apply to Ranger school. I've met a lot of meat eaters and most of them talk about it. I have only experienced it once. Other than that, it's all secondhand information," he informed them.

"First, I don't care if it's secondhand information. Second, everyone here is a meat eater," Stephanie told him.

"Ma'am, in the military, meat eaters are the warriors at the top of the list. Your apex predators, they live for the job. Rangers, Special Forces, SEALs and Recon, those elite forces that live on the edge," Conner replied.

"Okay, it's the boys that are really full of testosterone. Now what is the wave? I've heard Debbie mention it a few times, but what she described bordered on sociopathic behavior," Stephanie said, not liking the fact that anything about Bruce could be bad.

160

"I'll try to explain it, but until you experience the wave, it's hard to describe. In my case it started as panic, then it moved to anger. I could feel goose bumps over my body and I was filled with a rage that I have never felt before. It wasn't really directed at anything. It was just there. You feel like you can do anything, and you can actually feel the world around you," Conner told her.

"Then you start killing?" Bill asked.

"Yeah," Conner said.

"That's sociopathic, Conner," Stephanie said, leaning back in her chair.

"It would be. But you don't get pleasure from the act. They're just targets, Stephanie. If you get pleasure from it you release the rage and you don't want to do that. The first ambusher I shot, I started to feel happy about it and I could feel the rage leaving. I stopped feeling happy or sad and just engaged the enemy. Don't think about it; you just move through one target to find another one. That's riding the wave. You hold the rage in. If you let it out like retribution, you slide down the wave. Let's get something straight. These aren't nuns and Boy Scouts we are fighting. They want to kill us. We have to kill them first. How you feel when you do it is splitting hairs on morality," Conner replied, looking down the table at her.

"What about what Bruce said: 'We have a piece of his heart?'" Nancy asked Conner, but Debbie spoke first.

"You can't hurt your team because you love them," Debbie said.

"My platoon sergeant was a Ranger. He told stories of men riding the wave, jumping in front of bullets, jumping on top of grenades to save the team. Among meat eaters, it's better to hurt yourself than a teammate with your actions or your inactions," Conner told everyone.

"I can honestly say I never felt threatened by Bruce out there. I did feel some pity for those four, but it was only for a few seconds," Bill admitted.

"Like I said, once you feel it, you never forget it and you do want more," Conner told everyone before picking up his pen and writing again.

"There is a down side, Conner," Debbie told him and he looked up at her.

"You want the wave more and more like a drug addict. You start to push those close to you away if they do not ride the wave. It slowly eats at your soul until all you want is the rage. That's the only thing that has ever come between us. I almost left Bruce when he was in the service because of it. Haven't you ever wondered why the divorce rates are so high in the elite forces?" Debbie asked everyone.

"You almost left Bruce? Are you shitting me?" Nancy asked; this was the first time she'd heard this.

"Yes. He was changing each time he came back from an assignment. He was getting more and more distant. His eyes were getting cold to anyone we met and he was indifferent to the world. I told him if he did not leave the Army, I was leaving with Steve and Jake. He chose us, but for the first year I was ready to kill him. None of you have seen him that bitchy and it lasted a whole year. Then he returned to the man I fell in love with," Debbie told them and everyone was in shock.

"When y'all came back home from the hospital I could see it in his eyes. It had happened again. I had not seen that look in his eyes in over fifteen years but it was there. Until tonight, I'd never seen him 'riding the wave.' I'm not going to lie, part of me wanted to join him. I could feel the energy he was giving off. The air around him was alive. I could see at that moment that he could and would do anything to protect us. The rage came because someone threatened his family, his team. That being said, the other part of me wanted to take off running and puke," Debbie said, stretching her arms out on the table and laying her head down as Mike spoke.

"Debbie, I can honestly say if it was not for that wave, we wouldn't be here now, and that goes for all the survivors also," Mike told her.

"I know, Mike, that's why I didn't say anything and have just tried to make him let it go until he needs it," Debbie said, lifting her head up, tears running down her face. "Part of me wants to go out there right now and tell him to unleash it, live in it and move through the land like a second plague. I know we will be safer if he does, but I can't because I don't want to lose him."

"I'll help you," Stephanie promised, grabbing her hand.

"I will too," Angela said, placing her hand on top of theirs. She was followed by Nancy, then Mike, as they all placed their hands on top of one another, pledging to help Bruce keep the wave in check.

Then Angela asked her, "How do you stop it?"

Debbie looked at her. "Ask him to let it go. Now I said ask, don't tell. Then avoid him for a little while, but not too long. Then make him smile and laugh, just to shock him back to himself."

"Damn, that's what Angela and I did after we were hit by that mob," Mike admitted in disbelief.

"It's not hard, unless he's been in it for a long time. The second time Bruce went to Africa for six months was the worst ever. When he got home, I could tell he'd been on the wave the entire time. Don't ask what he did because he never told me. That's when I gave him the ultimatum," Debbie said quietly as she relived the event in her head.

Then Angela asked, "Debbie, how did you meet Bruce?"

Debbie laughed. "I've known Bruce my whole life. I remember him from Sunday school and first grade. He was so mean to me, always pulling my hair and making fun of me. When he was in sixth grade and I was in the fifth grade, I knew he was the one I wanted to marry."

"So he was nice to you then?" Stephanie asked her.

"Nice, hell. That son of a bitch still pulled my hair and hit me with spit balls. But I could see something in him even then that just made my heart stop," Debbie told Stephanie, which shocked her.

"How in the hell did you catch him then?" Angela asked.

"One day I asked him if I could come over to his house so he could teach me how to play basketball. When I helped him with his homework that first time, he invited me over again. After the third time, I asked him to come over to my house and he did." Debbie smiled with the happy memories.

"You ambushed him," Mike said in a shocked voice.

"Well, yeah," Debbie replied, looking at Mike like he was an idiot.

"Did he ever try to go out with any other girls?" Nancy asked curiously.

"Yeah, in ninth grade there was a dance and I couldn't go because I was in the eighth. A girl named Wendy German asked Bruce to go to the dance with her but somehow her dress got all torn up," Debbie said and they all started laughing. Then Debbie told them about their first date, Bruce's first hickey Debbie put on him, and several other funny stories. The laughter continued until Bruce walked in the door and everyone stopped laughing and looked at Bruce.

"What? Did I fart?" Bruce asked.

Debbie leaned her head backwards until she saw Bruce upside down. "No, baby. If you had we'd all be on the floor."

Bruce leaned over and kissed her then sat down in his seat. "Jim is guarding them and they're to stay naked until further notice," Bruce said. All eyes locked on him, except Bill's.

"Yes, I called him Jim, but no one else can. I have to make sure he's broken and is ready to join the human race again. I also gave him an empty gun belt. The others will be on shit duty and can only use their hands, no tools, and Jim is their supervisor," Bruce told them.

"Damn, that's good," Bill said after Nancy informed him what shit detail was.

"Now, let's start making list of work crews and a training schedule," Bruce said.

"Here they are," Stephanie said, handing several pieces of paper to him. "Angela and I made them after looking at what everyone could do."

"Well, let's get some laptops in here and get these lists on the computer," Bruce said.

"Done, Dad," Jake said, lifting his head off the table.

"Okay then, I'm going out on the supply runs tomorrow, so let's—" Bruce started but Nancy cut him off.

"Already done. I have Danny, Jake, Buffy, Matt, and Conner for fire team," she said.

"What the hell do y'all need me for then?" Bruce asked.

"Well, your shaved head is really sexy, Bruce," Mike said, winking at him as everyone laughed.

"I'm going upstairs to bed and get my ass kicked by a bunch of little girls and a baby boy," Bruce said, standing up and stretching.

"No you're not, brother," Mike told him.

"Why the hell not? Everything's done," Bruce demanded.

"Cassandra is sleeping with Susan tonight, so you and Debbie are sleeping in our bed. Nancy and I will sleep with the kids," Mike told him.

"What does Cassandra sleeping with Susan have to do with this?" Bruce asked, totally lost.

"Cassandra and Joshua sleep with us at least five times a week and has since she got here," Nancy said smiling.

"I'm her daddy after all," Mike said, smiling. That smile let Bruce know he forgave him for that.

Everyone got up and headed to bed. Conner had to wake Jake up to get him moving. When Mike opened the door to Bruce's room, he looked at Nancy.

"You go in first. There're bodies everywhere," Mike told her.

Bruce just laughed, heading on to Mike's room. After he stripped, he went and took a quick shower with Debbie. Since Mike didn't have a mirror in his shower, Bruce shaved at the sink. When Bruce was finished, he cleaned the sink out and headed to bed. Debbie was sitting on the corner of the bed waiting for him.

Bruce thought he was in trouble until she said, "You're mine, buddy."

Bruce smiled. "Bring it on if you think you're bad enough, girlfriend." Debbie ran and jumped up on him, wrapping her legs around him.

"I can take ya," she replied.

CHAPTER 14

Bruce struggled to wake up; it felt like something was sitting on his stomach. With a lot of effort he slowly opened his eyes to find Debbie sitting on him. Debbie leaned down, kissing him on the cheek, then squeezed him in a long hug.

"It's time to get up, stud muffin," Debbie said next to his ear.

"What time is it?" Bruce asked, not wanting to get up early but he felt he could be persuaded.

"Fifteen till five. You slept through the alarm twice." Debbie rolled off of him and got out of bed. *Well, so much for being persuaded*, Bruce thought. He rolled over and sat on the edge of the bed as Debbie opened the door and left. A few seconds later Nancy walked in.

"It looks like you had a good night's sleep, big guy," Nancy told Bruce as she went to her closet.

"Yeah, I didn't have to fight to keep my spot in the bed," Bruce said, getting up to gather his stuff.

"I feel you there, Bruce. Those girls and PJ made us work for our sleep. Around two, PJ crawled from one person to the next, hitting them with his empty bottle, hollering," Nancy told him from inside her closet as she got dressed.

"How did you get him back to sleep?" Bruce asked, wanting to learn the trick. He always had to go and get another bottle.

"Mike got him another bottle," Nancy said, stepping out of the closet dressed in ACUs.

"Mike got up at 0200 to get PJ a bottle?" Bruce asked her.

"Yeah, he got up. I did have to push him out of the bed first. When he hit the floor I asked him since he was already out of the bed if he could

166

get another bottle," Nancy said with a straight face as she sat down to put on her boots.

Bruce laughed. "Let me go and check on my husband."

He walked down the hall to his room and saw the door was open. He heard Mike grousing, "Oh man! What the hell are they feeding this kid? That's nasty. Be still PJ. No, don't put your hands in it. Quit laughing, that's disgusting. Nancy, come here!"

Bruce laughed and headed in to rescue Mike. He found Mike on the bathroom floor trying to figure out how to put a cloth diaper on PJ. PJ was not cooperating at all. When Mike rolled PJ on his back, PJ would promptly roll over and try to crawl away, laughing as Mike groaned each time.

"I'm fixin' to tape you to the floor. Now be still," Mike threatened PJ. He grabbed PJ and laid him on his back, swiftly trying to get the diaper on. PJ rolled over, taking off again. "You little nudist, come here. You *will* wear a diaper. If that toxic stuff hits the floor, we'll have to burn the house down to sanitize it," Mike told PJ as he picked him up and laid him back down.

"Need some help, brother?" Bruce asked, standing in the door.

Seeing Bruce in the door, Mike picked up a naked PJ and handed him over. "Here, you do it. That kid has something wrong with him. I'll never drink goat's milk again, I can tell you that. That's not crap coming out of his ass. The military could use it in toxic warfare."

Bruce grabbed PJ and Mike got up off the floor, groaning.

"You know he doesn't understand, Mike," Bruce told Mike as he laid PJ on the bed and put on the diaper.

"The hell he doesn't. Watch," Mike said as he walked over to the bed. "You know you irritated the hell out of me, don't you?" Mike asked PJ. PJ squealed in delight and started laughing. "See? I think when we aren't around, he talks. Then he finds small dead animals and puts them in his diaper to gross us out." Mike walked out into the hallway, then spun around to face Bruce. "You want to know when the rise of man occurred? It occurred when we made disposable diapers. That was the rise of man.

"Those things could be put on fast and held a lot of the smell in and didn't need to be changed every ten minutes." Mike spun around and walked toward his room, still talking about the rise of man related to the invention of the disposable diaper.

Bruce picked up PJ and dangled him over his face. "That wasn't very nice." PJ just blew Bruce a raspberry, slapping his face.

Debbie stepped out of the closet, giggling. "That was some funny shit."

"You could've helped him," Bruce told her, setting PJ on the floor as he headed to the closet.

"No, I couldn't. See you downstairs. I have PJ," Debbie said as she left.

Bruce got dressed and headed downstairs. There were people everywhere as he weaved his way through the crowd to the kitchen. He looked to make sure his chair was empty. It was, with a twin on each side. Bruce saw the line for the food and headed toward his chair.

When he sat down, the twins looked up at him, smiling. Three women walked up to the edge of the table, stopped and just stared at him. Bruce looked up at the women, wondering what the hell they wanted. Since they had not spoken, he did.

"Ladies, can I help you with something?" Bruce asked.

"Yes Bruce, we want to help Lynn cook," the one standing in front said. Bruce remembered her from last night at the speech. She was the black lady in her sixties. The other two were white; one was about the same age, and the other a lot older.

"Can you cook?" Bruce asked.

"I might not be able to beat Lynn's cookin' but I could at least tie with it in a competition," the lady told him.

"What's your name?" Bruce asked.

"Millie," she replied.

"Millie, if you three join Lynn in the kitchen you have to do what she does. She has to show those that are assigned to her how to milk a cow and goats, how to collect eggs, prepare game, and a lot more. When the crops are ready, she'll teach you to jar and can what is harvested. Most people here do not know this stuff, so she will have to teach them. Lynn is in charge of the kitchen; she has set out the menu months in advance," Bruce told the women to make sure they knew what they were asking.

"Bruce, we all growed up on farms and we waz still on 'em until the military came and drug us off. I can do evrathang you said plus them pigs y'all got. I can slaughter, boil down, render the fat for lye soap, then butchers 'em in quality cuts. Any animal you brings me I can slaughter it and they can do the same. We's country folk," Millie said proudly.

"Can you teach others to do it?" Bruce asked.

"I teach'd my young'uns and grandbabies," Millie said in a soft voice, her eyes downcast.

"Millie, look at me, please," Bruce told her. When she met his eyes, Bruce looked at the twins and PJ, with Millie following his gaze. "You have kids and grandkids here that need to learn what you know or they'll die. Like I said, this is your family now. But I doubt if you want them to sleep with you. They beat the ever living hell out of you," Bruce said, looking down at the twins and PJ. They just ignored him.

"I had ta stop dem grandbabies from sleepin' with me. I thought they gonna break my bones," Millie said, laughing. Then looking back at Bruce, she asked, "Can we have tha job? Y'all are working tha hell outta Lynn over there, even with that little girl helping her."

Bruce called over to Angela, who was sitting about halfway down the table. With almost a hundred people talking at once, she couldn't hear him. Bruce yelled, "*Angela!*" The entire house became silent. Angela looked at Bruce like a deer caught in the headlights, wondering what the hell she had done.

"Take these three off any work detail. They're assigned with Lynn to cook for this mass of humanity," Bruce told her, then looked at Lynn and could see relief wash over her face.

"Okay, but don't yell at me like that. I think I peed my pants," Angela said, glad she had not disappointed Bruce. Several others chuckled.

"How many on my scavenging team?" Bruce asked.

"Ten, not including your fire team," Angela replied and Bruce told her thank you.

Millie came around and hugged Bruce. "Thank ya and I just wanted to tell ya something. If you'd raped and tortured that bitch, I'da made sure no one would've touched ya. If I'd been made to wash that evil woman's clothes one mo' time, I was gonna hit her. She woulda had me shot, like so many others. If ya don't believe me, look in those police officers' wallets. She or Mitch would sign an execution order. They'd take 'em out and shoot 'em. They kepts the order so they couldn't get in troubles later."

Bruce stood up and hugged Millie back. He then asked everyone to please keep it down for a few more minutes because he was going make an announcement shortly. The room quieted.

Bruce called out, "Susan, come here please." Next Bruce asked Danny to go and get the officers' wallets out of the clothes he'd cut off them. Susan came out of the dining room with Joshua on her hip, followed by Cassandra, who took off running to Mike.

So that everyone could hear, Bruce told Susan in a loud voice, "If Gimp keeps proving he is worth something, I'm going to give him his name back. Last night I put him in charge of the prisoners and he's to supervise them on shit detail. They're not to use any tools, only their hands. None of the prisoners are allowed to wear any clothes at all. This isn't to change until I say so. Is this okay with you, Susan?"

"I don't care, Bruce. This is my family now," Susan said, motioning to the folks seated around the table.

"Then why the hell aren't you sittin' here with us?" Bruce asked, since she usually ate with them.

Susan averted her eyes and started to blush as she grinned, acting like a teenaged girl. "Conner asked if we would sit and eat with him."

"You tell Mr. Conner from now on y'all are to sit in here. Mike and I have to make sure he's good enough for you," Bruce told her, smiling. He was glad she'd found someone good.

"Oh he is, Bruce, but we will start joining you. And thank you for asking me my opinion. It means a lot to me," Susan said, turning and heading back to the dining room. She called out for Cassandra to follow and Cassandra said "No," from her spot on Mike's lap.

Before Susan could say anything, Mike grabbed her hand. "Leave her here, Susan, and she can sleep with us whenever. After last night, I feel like I fell asleep in a wrestling match and lost against little girls and a baby. Cassandra is no problem. Go in there and sit with Conner."

Before Susan could move, Nancy stood up. "Give me Joshua and go sit with him," Nancy said, holding her arms out. Susan was fixing to say something but Nancy cut her off. "Sweetie, don't say anything. My Depo shot has worn off and I'm fixing to start that time of the month. I haven't felt this in years and I'm leaning to the bitchy side today," Nancy told her, and Susan quickly handed her the baby. As Susan went back to the dining room, Nancy sat down and started talking to Joshua.

We are hitting every pharmacy around here today, Bruce thought. Every female in the family was on Depo. He didn't think he could survive if all the women started having super raging hormones. Then Bruce called for everyone's attention as Danny came back in and set the wallets in front of him.

"I hope everyone heard what I told Susan. No one is to hit the prisoners unless they're a threat to you or someone else. If they try to escape, let them make it through the razor wire Paul put up before you shoot them. You can make fun of them, but no one is allowed to give them food or water until I've taught them some manners. This is nonnegotiable. Any breach by anyone and you'll take the prisoners' place for at least one day," Bruce told them and then asked for any questions. He did not receive any, but Bruce did get some clapping and yelled thanks.

Bruce sat back down and opened the wallets. In each wallet he found stacks of papers that had been folded four times. Bruce unfolded each, laying them on the table but not reading any. After he had all of them on the table he counted sixty-seven handwritten notes.

Grabbing one, Bruce read it: *I do here by authorize the execution of John Walter Smith (age 16) for stealing food from the camp population. Second offense.*

Bruce sat there in disbelief, then read it again slowly. Then he started leafing through the pages. The only things different were the date and the names. The ages ranged from thirteen to fifty-one. At the bottom of each document was either Carla's or Mitch's signature. Under that was the officer's signature and the date and time the execution was carried out. Bruce's breathing sped up as he continued flipping through the papers. Stopping, he closed his eyes, dropping the papers and putting his hands on the table as the world wobbled in his vision.

Gripping the table hard, Bruce stood up so fast his chair hit the ground, causing everyone at the table to stop talking and turn toward him. Bruce was leaning over with both hands on the table. His fingers tried to claw through the wood as they closed into fists. This was an anger Bruce had not felt in a long time. Everyone was asking him what was wrong, but they sounded like they were in a tunnel and he couldn't hear the words. Keeping his breathing under control, he finally released the anger, holding the rage.

Bruce turned around and headed to the back door. He hit his leg on the chair he'd knocked over. Bruce kicked it, sending it spinning into the wall as he opened the door and slammed it behind him. Debbie and several others were fixing to follow him until they heard someone yell out. They all turned to the source of sound and saw Millie in the kitchen.

"Read them papers before you go out that door!" Millie yelled.

Debbie grabbed a sheet of paper as everyone rushed to grab one. Debbie could not believe what she was reading. Then she looked over at other pages people were holding, reading over their shoulder. She started getting light headed. *They were the government. How could they do this?* Debbie turned to the door.

"Don't stop him, baby," Millie told her.

"Stop him? I'm going to join him. No one is to follow me," Debbie said as she slammed the door.

As Bruce neared the barn, Jim came around the corner. Seeing Bruce, Jim ran over and told him, "Sir, they won't do what I told them. I told them I was coming to get you and they didn't care."

Bruce never broke stride but just said, "Follow me," as he led Jim to the barn. In the barn, Bruce grabbed a whip, a cattle prod, a dog chain and a jug of gasoline. The cattle prod and the whip had never been used. The family had only bought them because they lived on a farm. Lifting the prod up, Bruce pulled the trigger and saw sparks. Smiling, he handed all the stuff to Jim and headed out the back door.

It was still twilight outside, so the prisoners didn't see Bruce until he was very close. When they did see him and the hate on his face, the look on their faces became one of terror. Mitch was the first one to speak.

"Okay Bruce, we'll do it, but please give us some gloves at least and something to cover up with," Mitch begged.

Bruce walked up and kicked him, then went down the line kicking each one. When Bruce came to the officer with the broken arm and leg, the man tried to kick Bruce first. This brought a flurry of blows that rained down on him, knocking him to the ground. Then Bruce jumped in the air, landing on the man's other leg and breaking it. Bruce knew this guy was the one he was going to have problems with.

Finally, breathing heavily, Bruce stood in front of all four. The officer whose leg he'd just broken was still screaming out in pain.

Bruce turned toward him and said, "If you don't shut up, I'm going to make you eat one of your own balls." The officer shut up immediately. No longer did Bruce have hate etched on his face as he turned to look at Mitch and Carla. There was nothing there and that terrified them more.

"How many executions did you authorize?" Bruce asked in a flat voice.

Mitch replied, "We were just doing what we were told. We got orders from Washington to get rid of anyone who was a dissident, who questioned authority, refused to disarm, leave their property or failed to follow orders. Go to the camp, the briefcase is still on my desk. Those orders gave us the means and authority to do it."

"How many?" Bruce asked again.

"I really don't know. All orders were to be handwritten for the officer in charge to hold, so no criminal prosecution could be brought against him," Mitch told Bruce.

"If you don't answer the question, your life will be measured by how much pain you can go through, motherfucker," Debbie screamed, walking up behind Bruce.

Bruce turned around and stepped in front of Debbie. "Go back to the house," Bruce told her.

Debbie pulled her knife from her vest. "Fuck that and move," she said. Bruce stepped out of her way as she walked toward Mitch. Mitch, seeing the small woman coming at him with the knife, tried to move. But when you are handcuffed to a cattle gate there is really nowhere to go.

Debbie stopped in front of him. "I'm going to ask you the same question. If you don't know the number, it better be a good guess. When I ask those inside, if the number they give me is not close to yours, I'm finding a blow torch. When I ask you a question, you will answer it. If you try that political dodging I'm going to cut shit off. Do I make myself clear?" Debbie asked him and Mitch nodded his head.

"How many?" Debbie asked.

"Between a hundred and thirty to a hundred and fifty," Mitch replied quietly.

"Was this going on at other Homeland Security camps?" Debbie asked.

"Yes," Mitch answered, shaking.

Debbie walked back to Bruce, put her knife away and turned back to face the four. "How could you do that? You're Americans. This is the holocaust all over again, during a plague outbreak," Debbie yelled at them, fighting off the urge to just run up and start stabbing.

Carla answered, "We had a duty to get rid of those that would cause problems, no matter if they were in camp or at their home. If we didn't, we would have been executed."

"That argument was tried in Nuremburg and it didn't work then either. Doesn't look like it's working real good for you now," Debbie said. "How did you know who to go and get from their homes?"

"The FBI and ATF had a list for every region, those who had bought a lot of food, supplies, or guns. A police officer would be sent out to bring them in. If he returned without them, a SWAT team was sent to collect them or kill them," Carla told her.

Debbie's heart skipped a beat as she broke out in a cold sweat. The cop that had come to the house would have taken them to be executed. The only thing that had saved them was killing him first. The family would now be dead if they had not killed him.

"Those people came to you for protection, and those that had supplies could have lasted for a while in this. What right did you have to decide for them to die?" Debbie asked.

"By taking some freedom and getting rid of some troublemakers, we can protect the masses," Mitch said, trying to justify their actions.

"When you started taking weapons and supplies from people, you took away their chance to save this country and millions of lives," Debbie told them.

"You are a fine one to talk. Your husband tortured us last night and you did nothing to stop him. We are trying to rebuild America," Carla told her.

"Oh, sweetie, he didn't torture you last night, he was just trying to teach you. But we are fixing to do things to you that will cause others to remember what their actions can bring on them. The only difference between you and the gangs out there is that everyone knows *they* are evil. They don't hide the fact. Both of you killed innocents. They just rape them first and you don't," Debbie said. Mitch darted his eyes away.

"No," Debbie gasped. "You didn't." She started toward Mitch, pulling out her knife as Bruce grabbed the back of her vest. "Let go, Bruce," Debbie said, feeling tears coming to her eyes. Bruce yanked her back hard and spun her around. Grabbing the front of her vest, Bruce lifted her off the ground until they were face to face. Debbie was fixing to start kicking him until she saw his eyes.

"Watch and learn. Hold it. Don't let it out. When you cry, you let it out. Control the anger; let it move to rage at everything and nothing. You cannot hold anger against a person because it hurts later. Those are just cardboard targets lying on the ground, nothing else. No pleasure, no anger, no remorse, no sorrow," Bruce told her. He could see the rage in Debbie but it was wild; she had to control it. Debbie listened as she looked in his eyes and slowly relaxed. "Feel it? Hold it? That tingling in your back making you breathe harder, bringing chill bumps up," Bruce asked her with a dead voice. She nodded her head as she felt the rage course through her body. "They're targets; nothing more. You get nothing from it except dropping a target or the wave ends. Ride it, don't let it go. Now watch me and learn," Bruce told her as he put her down.

Bruce walked over to the officer with the broken arm and asked, "How many has he raped?"

"You keep your mouth shut," Mitch yelled.

Debbie started moving quickly toward Mitch. Bruce told her to stop, which she did. Bruce walked over and grabbed her vest. He looked into her eyes. "That was anger making you move. Anger builds the rage, and if you attack with anger you get pleasure then sorrow. Hold it, that's just a paper target talking. You're trying to see them as people. Now follow me," Bruce told her, letting her go and heading back to the officer.

Debbie felt drunk as she did what Bruce told her, yet she wanted to explode. Anger flooded her body and she wanted to kill to let it out, but Bruce made her hold it. She was breathing like she was running a marathon. Looking at the four, she did not see people anymore. She saw targets. She could see clearly even though it was dark. Her body felt like it was vibrating as she walked up beside Bruce.

"Mitch, if you talk again out of turn you will get my undivided attention for the day," Bruce said, looking at Mitch. Then he turned to the officer, who was cowering in front of him.

"How many did he rape?" Bruce asked in a calm voice.

"Two that I know of," the officer replied as Mitch yelled, "He fucked them after me."

The officer looked up at Bruce. "He told me I had to," he said, crying.

Bruce spun around, putting his mouth by Debbie's ear and hugging her tight as he whispered, "Hear that? They raped women and enjoyed it. The targets love to hurt others. People don't do that, only targets. Do you see now?" Bruce could feel her trembling with rage; then suddenly her body became hard as a rock. Her breathing slowed down and emotion left her face. Bruce smiled as Debbie hit the wave. "That target thinks it has a name and it's Mitch, but targets don't have names. Only weapons do. Go to the gimp and take the baton off of his belt and teach the target it has to do what it's told. Remember: Don't let it go. You don't let your anger out on a target; it's only a target. There are no enemies in the world; only targets. Now, ride the wave." Bruce let her go.

Debbie turned and walked over to the gimp. He was still holding the stuff Bruce had given him. When the gimp saw Debbie's face, he wanted to run. But he had not been told to run, so he just stayed put. She was so pretty but had no emotion on her face or in her eyes. When she reached him, she took the baton off of his belt. When she reached out, Gimp could barely follow her hand. Before she turned around, she looked right in his eyes. For a brief second, Gimp saw a flash of ecstasy in her eyes then she turned away.

As Debbie walked back, she felt like she was floating. She could smell a hundred different smells. When she got close to Mitch, she smelled something she had never smelled before. Stopping in front of him, she closed her eyes and breathed deeply through her nose, inhaling the smell. Suddenly it clicked. It was fear. The target reeked of it. Flipping her wrist, Debbie snapped open the baton and the target curled into a ball, crying words at her but she did not understand them; a target could not speak unless given permission. Looking down, she understood what Bruce had been saying. They were targets; nothing more.

An hour later, Bruce was standing in front of the remaining three prisoners watching Debbie drag her knife over Carla's head, shaving her hair off. The other officer was almost dead, but he did finally quit screaming to stop the pain. When Debbie finished, she walked over and stood by Bruce.

"That ends the lesson for now. Jim, you will take Bitch and Dumb on shit detail. If they do good, bring them to the back patio. I will let them have food and water. If they don't, bring them back here. And Jim, don't try to fool me or you will switch places with them. Bitch Boy gets nothing today. He gets his first chance after a full day's work tomorrow. When Dumber dies, drag him to the pond and let the gators have him," Bruce told him. Jim nodded his head.

Bruce grabbed the stuff and headed to the barn with Debbie at his side. After putting the stuff up, he turned to Debbie. She was wavering from side to side, blinking her eyes and trying to focus on him, because his image was fuzzy. "Bruce, what's wrong with me?" Debbie asked, feeling her energy draining out of her.

"The wave is over. You don't have any more targets. You let it go too fast," Bruce told her. Debbie turned around and headed back to the prisoners. Bruce grabbed her arm before she got to the back door.

"Let me go! There are three targets out there," Debbie said, pulling against him.

"Those targets have been knocked down. You're chasing the wave. Don't. Let it come to you when you need it. If you chase it, you want the pleasure and it's not the same. Let it go for now. I'll show you later how to hold it and release it slowly. The first time you hit the wave it's too wild, so just let it go," Bruce said and Debbie just sank to her knees.

"I feel like we had sex for days. I have no energy," Debbie replied, gasping for air.

"It'll pass. Now come on, it's almost 0800. We have a lot of work to do," Bruce told her.

"Work my ass. I'm going to bed," Debbie informed him.

"You can't do that. If you're in a battle and during a lull the wave leaves, you will want to sleep then and you'll die. Now come on," Bruce said, pulling Debbie to her feet.

"You can't make it last?" Debbie asked, leaning heavily on Bruce as they came out of the barn.

"Yes, you can. There are several different ways. I used the worst one, and when I did, you made me choose," Bruce told her, helping her to the house.

"Bruce, why was I moving so slow? They should've dodged everything I threw," Debbie asked, trying to make her feet work.

"Baby, I couldn't have dodged you with how fast you were moving. It only seemed that way to you," Bruce said as they walked across the yard to the patio.

Bruce opened the door and led Debbie inside. Everyone turned to them as Bruce closed the door. Bruce guided Debbie to her chair. She just plopped down, sprawling out in the chair. "I want work to start now. My team, be ready to leave in thirty," Bruce said as people started filing out to start the day.

Debbie was looking around at everyone and the world was swaying in her vision. She looked at the table real hard. Sitting up, she swung her right arm in a wide arc, throwing place mats and the center piece off on the floor. Debbie climbed onto the table and rolled over on her back and looked at the ceiling. "That was fucking great," she yelled out. Those still in the house just stared at the five foot tall woman, wearing full combat gear, sprawled out on the table. Mike turned to Bruce.

"What the hell happened back there? We heard a lot of screaming," Mike asked, not really wanting an answer.

"We were teaching assholes and having surfing lessons," Bruce told him.

"What happened to Debbie? She acts like she's on drugs," Mike asked, feeling Debbie's face and checking her pulse.

When Mike looked up at Bruce he saw Bruce grinning as he answered. "She rode the wave."

CHAPTER 15

It was 1430 when the supply team left the fourth location on this run. They had already dropped off five loads at the farm. Bruce was in the lead, driving the Hummer with the Mk-19, a fully automatic grenade launcher. Danny was in the passenger seat with Buffy sitting in the middle. Behind them were five pickups with trailers and a diesel forklift with a boom arm. This was the gathering group. Matt, Conner, and Jake were at the rear in a Stryker. They had left the Beast because Mike was mounting a machine gun on the roof.

The fire team was responsible for protection, but since no blues had been seen near the farm, they took turns helping load the trucks. They had finished gathering all the lumber at construction sites within a twenty-mile radius. Then they hit every store they came across even though half had already been ransacked. They had emptied four pharmacies. Three others they found were empty. When the group hit a store, they literally took a trash bag and raked a shelf into it until it was full. Then the full garbage bag was taken to the trucks and trailers. The trucks looked like garbage carriers going down the road.

Bruce had emptied out two machine shops of all the stock metal they had. He now had enough metal to make more suppressors than they had military guns. Next, they emptied out two gyms of workout equipment. The gym at the farm was big, but they only had one of each workout station; that was all the family had needed. Before this last group got to the farm, you would have to stand in line for equipment. The new group had not even hit the gym yet. With the extra equipment, workouts should move faster.

When the supply team had returned for the first offload, Bruce went to check on Debbie. He found her running one of the back hoes. She assured Bruce she was alright, but wanted to go out with him on his run the next day. Bruce finally gave in and told her she could.

Bruce pulled his mind back to the here and now. They were getting ready to hit farms now, but there was one more store to the south. Bruce saw it on his right and he started slowing down. This store sat on the main highway and was also a truck stop. Bruce could see at least thirty big rigs. *We so have to check those out*, Bruce thought as he keyed his radio.

"Same as last time: Fire team forward. We clear the area. Matt, you stay on thermal in the Stryker. Any contact, supply team you head home, we will follow."

He pulled into the parking area. The Stryker pulled in beside him, and Matt started scanning with the gun turret. The fire team got out and looked around. Seeing nothing, they headed to the door. The team flanked the door, putting their backs to the wall. Bruce keyed his radio to call out assignments.

"Buffy, you'll be point, Danny shotgun, next Conner. Jake at the back of the stack. I'll keep a watch on the outside and door," Bruce finished giving assignments.

They all smiled at each other. This was the first building Bruce was going to let them clear without him. Buffy pushed her M-4 to her side, pulling her P90 off her back. Then she moved to the door and pushed against it with her hand.

"Locked," Buffy said over the radio.

Bruce grumbled as he let his rifle drop to his chest, reaching for his lock picks. "Cover," Bruce called over the radio as he kneeled in front of the door and inserted his picks. Mike could open a door with his picks faster than most people could use a key. It took Bruce two minutes to get the lock turned.

"Open," Bruce called as he stood up and put his picks back in his vest. Raising his rifle off his chest, he scanned the area.

Buffy eased the door open, aiming her P90 into the gap as she slipped inside. It was killing Bruce not to turn around and watch them, but he kept his area covered. Over the radio he could hear them clearing the building, calling out rooms. Twenty minutes later, Buffy called the all clear. Danny told the supply crew to bring the battery lights because it was really dark inside. The supply team moved the vehicles closer.

Bruce headed into the store. It was big and he smelled rotten food from the diner. Danny walked over to him. "Dad, this one store is going to almost fill up all the trucks. The store room for the restaurant is slap full."

"We're taking the liquor also. We can use it to barter with, if we need to," Bruce told her as he glanced around. They usually left the alcohol, taking just a few bottles. In this store, there were cases stacked everywhere.

"Well, the trucks will be all full then," Danny said.

"Danny, you and Conner keep cover here. Jake, Buffy, and I are goin' to check on the rigs." Bruce told her and then radioed Jake and Buffy to meet him outside.

Bruce walked over to where the trucks were parked in a line. When he got closer, he saw there was another row behind the first. There was a truck with an excavator and another with a big front-end loader. Several trucks were hauling lumber, one was loaded with cinder blocks, and there were several tanker trucks. The rest were box trailers so they would have to open them to see what they contained. Bruce headed toward the closest trailer. As he approached the first one, Bruce saw it was secured with a combination lock.

"Supply team, can any of you drive a semi-truck?" Bruce asked over the radio. He received two yeses in reply.

Danny, Jake, Matt, and he could drive a semi, and with the other two they could drive back six. They would take the two trucks with the excavator and the front-end loader, a dump truck, then three of the trucks carrying lumber. Bruce called over the radio, telling everyone his plan. Then Bruce called Danny.

"Danny, pick someone to drive the Hummer back. How long will it take to empty the store?" Bruce asked.

"Dad, this is a big ass store, with that supply room for the diner. I'm just guessing but I say two hours at least," Danny replied, doubting her answer.

"You have ninety minutes. I want all these trucks back at the farm today," Bruce told her.

"Okay Dad, we'll do our best."

Bruce waved Jake over to him and asked, "You remember how to hot wire a vehicle?"

"I'm going to act like you didn't ask me that, Dad," Jake replied, looking at Bruce like he was stupid.

Bruce shook his head. "You're turning into a smartass in your old age."

"I had the best teacher in the world. You," Jake popped back.

"Okay, you win," Bruce laughed. "I want those six trucks." Bruce pointed them out. "I want you to help get them open then see if they have keys. If they don't, get them ready to hot wire but don't start them. It will make too much noise and we're past the edge of our safe area. We really don't want company."

Jake said he understood and ran off to start opening trucks. Out of the six trucks, only one was unlocked with the keys in it. Bruce showed Buffy how to pick a truck lock then hotwire it. After he showed her how on two, he made her do the last one. It took her fifteen minutes but she did it by herself. Then Bruce told Jake to go help in the store as he and Buffy went to pitch in.

At the ninety-minute mark, Bruce called a stop and told everyone to load up. The store was not empty, but it was close. Then Conner called contact. "Blues south side, heading toward us, approximately fifteen," he reported as he started firing.

"Jake and Danny, head to Conner. Buffy and I are taking the north," Bruce instructed the team, cursing himself. Matt was parked on the north side of the building in the Stryker and had no one to drive him since he was manning the weapon station. Matt would have to climb out of the gunner's area, drive around then climb back in the turret.

Reaching the front, Bruce could not see any blues and told the supply team to hold inside. Danny called clear then reported, "Dad, they came out of a clearing to the southeast, not along the road. But that's not the bad news. They were using cover, trying to sneak up on us."

Her words sent a shiver down Bruce's spine. That was thinking on a whole new level. "Let's get the hell out of here. Conner, you drive Matt, and you two better cover our ass. Order of march: Stryker in the lead, three semis, supply trucks, three semis then the Hummer," Bruce told everyone and they ran to the vehicles.

After the six trucks were started, Bruce called for them move out. They were twenty miles from the farm as the crow flies but it was almost forty by road. When the convoy was on the road Bruce told Buffy to keep a look out as he turned on the CB then turned it to the base channel.

"Base, this is Big Daddy One," Bruce called.

"This is Base," a reply came back from a voice he didn't recognize.

"I need Big Daddy Two on the horn *now*," Bruce said brusquely.

"Copy," Base replied. Bruce waited for a several minutes until Mike came over the radio.

"This is Big Daddy Two," Mike called over the radio; he sounded out of breath.

"Big Daddy Two, I need ten people that can drive semis. They need to be ready in fifteen. Will lay out plan on arrival to Base, and Farmer Boy can't be one of the drivers. Have area on east side clear," Bruce told Mike.

"Copy, see what I can do," Mike told him.

The convoy drove as fast as they could on the little roads, which for big trucks was not very fast. It was 1630 when they arrived at the farm. Bruce called to have the gate open then told the truck drivers to take it easy and not hit the fence.

Pulling around to the back, he stopped in front of the barn. Bruce had only taken out one flower bed. Parking the truck, he got out followed by Buffy. Mike came running up to him as the other trucks pulled in slowly.

Mike looked at the trucks carrying the heavy equipment and lumber. Then he turned to Bruce, "Nice work, brother. I have twelve plus the family still here. That's sixteen total," Mike told him as Nancy and Debbie walked up.

"Steve, go to the shop and grab a pair of bolt cutters and bring them," Bruce called over the radio.

"What's the hurry, Bruce?" Nancy asked.

"The truck stop on Highway One has over sixty semis that we're bringing here," Bruce said, then called the fire team and the two supply drivers to him.

"It's kind of late now, let's just get them tomorrow," Mike suggested.

"We had contact there. Those trucks need to be here today. There will be no supply run tomorrow; maybe a patrol but no supply run. Get those drivers over here," Bruce told Mike then turned to Conner.

"Get six people that can drive the Strykers and the RG. That's what we'll use to ferry us back and forth. You have eight minutes because we leave in ten," Bruce told him then turned to the group gathered around him.

"Look, I know some of you haven't been trained yet, but I need you. There's a truck stop twenty miles from here with over sixty trucks that I want here. I don't know what's in them and we are only taking the ones that are loaded. In a quick glance, I saw nine tanker trucks and let's pray they hold fuel. Those not trained will stay in the armored vehicles until your truck is ready. Once you're in your truck you will lock the door and not open it until we're back here. If you don't want to go, I'll understand. I wouldn't ask but we need those supplies and trucks." Bruce hoped all of them would go.

A man in the front asked, "When do we leave?"

Bruce looked at his watch. "Six minutes."

"Let's go then," the guy said.

Mike spoke up. "We don't have room for that many trucks here, Bruce."

"I know that, Mike. We're going to park them past the house on the dead end road. Turn them around at the dead end and park them on the side of the road," Bruce told Mike as the Strykers and RG pulled up.

"Bruce, it's only a mile to the dead end," Mike said.

Bruce looked at Mike, wanting to strangle him, "Mike, you can fit over a hundred semis in a mile."

Mike just huffed at Bruce. Ignoring him, Bruce started pointing at people then to vehicles for them to get into. Bruce and Buffy were the last ones in as Bruce told the driver to go. On the way to the truck stop Bruce called out the plan.

"When we get there, I want the Strykers on the north and south. Debbie and David will take the east. Nancy and Mary will take the west. Mike, Jake, Steve, and Matt will start opening trucks and hotwiring them. Start on the tankers and the last truck with lumber. Danny, Buffy and I will start checking the trailers. If the trailer has something in it, we take it. We can take twenty-two in a trip. Keep on your toes and call out contacts. Conner, you'll escort each driver to their truck. Any questions?" Bruce asked, finishing his briefing. Nobody said anything. Afraid nobody had heard him, he asked if everyone understood and everyone said they did.

They pulled into the truck stop and everyone went to the task they were responsible for. The convoy was pulling out in less than thirty minutes and heading home. Dropping off the trucks at the end of the road, they loaded up and did it again.

The third time they pulled into the truck stop they only had eighteen more trucks to get. The others were empty. As the perimeter team moved into position, the blues hit them hard.

The calls came out, "Contact east," "Contact south," "Contact north," "Contact west." Bruce divided up his hotwire team to each post. Then Bruce called on the radio to those in contact.

"I need numbers and direction," he yelled over the radio. He needed to know where to send back up, which was just him and Buffy.

"North clear now, seven down," reported one of the Strykers.

"West clear, nine down," Nancy reported.

"South, too many to fucking count," Conner yelled over the radio as he fired at the wave of blues coming at him.

"East is the same," Debbie called.

"Hot wire team, southeast," Bruce yelled over the radio as he took off.

Reaching the southeast, Bruce saw blues coming out of the store and the tree line behind it. Bringing his rifle to his shoulder, Bruce started firing on full auto into their legs, trying to get some breathing room. When his bolt locked back, he launched a 40mm grenade toward the doors of the store where the blues were still pouring out. The grenade exploded, sending shrapnel into the blues' legs, those in the front falling and causing those behind to trip over them.

Slamming another magazine in, Bruce started firing bursts at the blues' heads. The fifty cal on top of the Stryker at the south didn't have a suppressor. The noise it was making hurt his ears, but, Bruce just kept aiming and firing. Ejecting an empty magazine, Bruce slammed in his sixth and brought his rifle up. There weren't any blues running toward him, but he saw some crawling toward him and even some trying to crawl away from him. Lining up his scope, Bruce started shooting the crawlers. When he put in his tenth magazine he couldn't see movement anywhere.

Bruce keyed his radio. "Report off." North, east, west and south reported clear. Bruce glanced at his watch. The attack had not even lasted four minutes. Keying his radio, he said, "My team, get those trucks started. I want to leave this store. The prices are ridiculous." Then the family started popping off over the radio, making him smile.

Mike came back. "Yeah, the sodas are flat."

"The bathroom was filthy," Danny radioed back.

"There were no candy bars," Mary whined.

"There weren't even any video games," Jake cried out.

"They don't even rent videos," Matt chimed in.

Debbie called out, "Well, the boy at the checkout was kinda cute."

"He was probably gay, Debbie, to be that cute," Nancy replied over the radio as Bruce heard trucks starting up behind him.

Jogging around the area, Bruce tried to get a count. It looked like at least sixty to seventy blues had come out of the store. The store had been cleared, so the blues had moved in between pickups. To the south, the bodies were torn apart by the big fifty but they covered the forty yards to the wood line. Bruce guessed the total number was around three hundred and fifty blues. Looking at the brass casings on the ground, Bruce knew the ammo they had used was enormous for that number.

The blues had waited for them to stop and get out. Then they'd launched a four-point attack. The only way they could do that was if they had watched them take the other trucks. They'd clearly planned the attack. Bruce wasn't sure if the south would have held without the fifty cal on the Stryker. He didn't even want to think about what would have happened if they'd used similar numbers on all fronts.

Mike called out on the radio that all the trucks were started. Conner escorted the drivers and the convoy was soon on the road. Bruce called on the radio for an ammo-expended count. After the last person reported in, he lowered his head. It had taken almost nine thousand rounds to take out four hundred attackers. By military standards, that was great, but they did not have the reserves for that kind of exchange ratio. In the past engagements, the ratio had been three rounds for one kill. Now it was over twenty for one kill.

The group pulled back into the farm after parking the semi-trucks. Bruce got out of the RG-33L, thinking hard as Mike walked up to him. "What was the hurry to get home? I didn't even grab a beer at the store," Mike grinned.

"All they had was cheap beer. Don't forget, it's movie night," Bruce informed him.

"It'd better be a good one. I want to at least see some boobies," Mike told him.

"We can't watch that kind of movie. Too many kids. Plus if I see boobies it'll give me false hope of gettin' some and that's kind of hard with so many kids in that bed," Bruce said.

"Well, let's watch a cartoon and at least laugh," Mike offered.

"Deal, brother. Let's go," Bruce said, slinging his arm across Mike's shoulders and heading back to the house, Buffy beside him.

CHAPTER 16

Sitting up in bed, Bruce glared at PJ. He wouldn't quit hitting Bruce with his empty bottle when he tried to go back to sleep. Disgusted, Bruce looked at the clock. 0640. *It's Sunday and I still didn't get to sleep late*, he thought grumpily, getting out of bed. He reached back and picked up PJ.

"You're supposed to wake Mama up, not Daddy, PJ," Bruce instructed him.

"I heard that," Debbie said, her face buried in a pillow.

"That was PJ talking, baby. We're going to take a shower," Bruce said, moving to the bathroom and fearing the wrath of Debbie.

After he and PJ showered, Bruce went to the closet and set PJ on the floor. Bruce put on clean ACUs, missing his tiger stripe BDUs. Almost everyone in the clan had this pattern so the family would wear this for now. Grabbing another tactical vest, Bruce walked out of the closet, leaving PJ behind. PJ yelled from the closet. It was probably something like, "You forgot me, butthead."

Bruce turned around and told PJ, "You can move on your own. Hell, you crawl all over me every night." PJ let out another yell, thereby letting Bruce know he meant business.

"I'm not kidding, PJ. Come on out or I'll close the door and leave you in there all day. I don't think anyone would even miss you," Bruce predicted, walking over to the dresser. Taking equipment from his old vest, Bruce loaded his new vest. The other one needed cleaning bad; he was fairly certain the blues could smell it. PJ crawled out of the closet, stopping at the end of the bed, sat up on his knees and started blowing raspberries.

"I'm serious. I don't think anyone would even miss ya," Bruce said, looking at him. PJ squealed and clapped his hands.

"Well, maybe in a few hours someone would start to look for ya," Bruce told PJ. PJ laughed then crawled to Bruce babbling. Reaching Bruce, PJ grabbed his pants leg and started pulling on it as he babbled.

"You know I wouldn't leave you in a closet. Even though sometimes I want to flush you down the toilet," Bruce said. PJ started laughing. "You're a mess," Bruce said, reaching down and picking him up. With PJ in his arms, Bruce started tickling him, making him laugh and squeal. Feeling someone looking at him, Bruce glanced at the bed. The twins and Debbie were watching him and smiling. "What? I'm torturing him into submission," Bruce told them with a serious face, but PJ was still laughing.

"OH, you scare me so much," Debbie said as she faked a frightened expression.

Bruce tucked PJ under his arm like a football. This only make PJ laugh more. "You will fear, me woman," Bruce told Debbie.

"Yeah, like that'll happen," Debbie replied sarcastically.

Putting PJ on the floor, Bruce dove on the bed and started tickling Debbie. The twins watched Bruce tickle Debbie and they laughed at Debbie's expense. Swiftly, Bruce reached out, grabbed both of them and started tickling them. The little girls were just squealing with laughter with arms and legs flailing about. Emily tried to escape but Bruce grabbed her by the ankle. Pulling her back, he made her pay for that. Then Bruce pinned all three down between his legs. Hearing yelling from the floor, Bruce reached over the side of bed and picked up PJ, who had been sitting on the floor yelling, "Ahh" over and over like "Hey, I want some too."

"Now I have you all and you will all suffer the tickle torture," Bruce stated as he slowly lowered his hands to them.

Trying to catch her breath, Debbie sputtered out, "Please—quit—I—have—to pee."

"Tickle torture does not care about pee," Bruce informed her as he started tickling all of them.

Debbie started kicking her legs, laughing and screaming. She tried to grab Bruce's hand but he kept moving all over to different spots on her body. She kept crying out, "You are going to make me pee," between giggles. The twins had tears running down their face, they were laughing so hard. After five minutes of pure laughter. Bruce stopped and got off the bed. PJ was at the head of the bed, bouncing up and down and sitting on his knees. He was yelling and clapping like he was saying, "That was great, do it again."

Bruce turned to the dresser to get his vest and head downstairs when he heard the twins say in unison, "More, Daddy." Bruce stopped in his tracks. They had never called him Daddy. Bruce slowly turned around.

"You want more tickle torture?" Bruce asked them.

"YES Daddy!" they squealed together.

"They do, Bruce, I don't. I have to pee. Please Bruce, not again," Debbie pleaded, trying to catch her breath. Squeezing her legs together, she scooted to the edge of the bed.

"Does Mommy want tickle torture too?" Bruce asked the girls.

"Get Mommy too!" they yelled together.

Bruce ran back to the bed just as Debbie had reached the edge. He grabbed her, pushing her back on the bed. Pinning them all between his legs again, Bruce started tickling all over again. There were actual screams this time with the laughter. Except for PJ, each of them begged Bruce to stop, with Debbie also screaming she had to pee. PJ was just laughing; to him this was the best thing ever. Bruce looked at Debbie and told her, "If you had to pee you wouldn't be laughing."

In between the tickles and trying to catch her breath, she gasped, "If—you—would—stop—I would stop laughing." Bruce told her he didn't believe her and continued tickling all of them.

"Stop it Daddy!" Bruce heard behind him.

Bruce stopped and turned to the door. The twins and Debbie didn't care why he stopped. They just tried to breathe during the reprieve. PJ sat up, looking for more. Standing in the door were Danny and Buffy, both wearing his t-shirts and boxers. Behind them were Mike and Nancy. "You two wear my clothes and try to stop me? I am the tickle torture king!" Bruce cried out with a mocking evil laugh. Then he started tickling Debbie, the twins and PJ again.

Debbie screamed out, laughing, "Make him stop! I have to pee!"

Buffy yelled, "We'll save you Mama!" Running to the bed, Danny and Buffy both jumped on Bruce, trying to pull him off.

Letting go of the twins and Debbie, Bruce pinned Danny and Buffy and tickled them until they were having trouble breathing. The twins and Debbie just lay there trying to breathe, thankful for another reprieve. PJ crawled over to get more. When one of the three would try to move away,

Bruce would reach over with one hand and tickle them until they lost their breath.

Standing in the door and laughing at the sight, Mike turned to Nancy, "Ten bucks Bruce doesn't stop until Debbie pees."

"If you ever do that to me again, I'll kick your ass," Nancy warned, watching Debbie begging Bruce to let her pee.

Suddenly, Mike grabbed Nancy, dragging her to the foot of Bruce's bed and forcing her to the floor. Then Mike started tickling her until Nancy screamed out laughing, begging for him to stop. The other kids came down the hall upon hearing the laughing and screaming. Seeing what was going on, they ran to try to help their mothers. It was a valiant effort, but doomed to failure. They only brought fresh bodies to be tickled.

Steve just stood in the door with Tonya. With disappointment on her face, Tonya looked at him and said, "Aren't you going to help your poor mama?"

Steve looked at her in shock. "Are you insane, girl? That's tickle torture. Dad doesn't stop until someone pees on themselves."

"That's your mama and she needs to pee. Help her," Tonya said, pushing Steve in the room.

Steve turned around, yelling, "You have never had tickle torture." Grabbing Tonya, Steve forced her to the floor, tickling her until Tonya too, screamed along with Debbie that she had to pee. And so the tickle torture was passed on to another couple and another generation.

After twenty solid minutes of laughter, everyone stopped almost at the same time, collapsing and breathing hard. If anyone would have come in the room, they would have sworn that every person in there had run a marathon because of all the heavy breathing and sweat pouring off their bodies.

Bruce was lying beside Debbie. The twins dragged their numb bodies and bellies sore from laughing so hard across the bed. Each movement was a test of will, but they crawled inch by inch until they were both lying on Bruce's chest. Bruce looked down at Sherry with Emily beside her. Looking in his eyes, Sherry informed him as she gasped for air, "That was great." Then her head collapsed on his chest followed by Emily's.

After several minutes Debbie announced, with great urgency in her voice, "Bruce, carry me to the bathroom, now. I'm not kidding. Please baby, now, hurry."

Bruce started to get up when he heard Nancy from the floor at the foot of his bed, "You owe me ten dollars, butthead."

"Check her panties," Mike said as Bruce picked up Debbie, who was squeezing her legs together tightly.

"Shut up Mike!" Debbie yelled at him, causing Bruce to laugh and then wince, his stomach muscles sore.

"Bruce, I'm serious. I don't want to give Nancy my last ten bucks. Help me out," Mike pleaded, trying to catch his breath.

Bruce carried Debbie to the bathroom and stood her in front of the toilet. He lifted the lid and before she sat down, Debbie started peeing. "Nancy, you owe Mike ten bucks," Bruce yelled out the door. It caused everyone to laugh, even though they didn't want to. Debbie slapped Bruce's butt as he walked out of the bathroom.

Looking at the bed, Bruce noticed Jake gasping for air. He wondered when he'd come in. Then he saw Mike and his whole family on the floor. Turning to the door, he saw Steve and Tonya. *How and when did all these people get in here,* Bruce wondered. Then Bruce shrugged, figuring it was one of those mysteries in life you never figure out.

Picking up his vest, Bruce weaved through the bodies to his closet where he grabbed his boots. He slid his feet in, but didn't tie them because it hurt too much to bend. Reaching over to the new gun rack he and Mike had put up last night, Bruce took out little SCAR.

Debbie and Nancy had demanded last night that all gun racks were to be moved four feet off the floor. Every room, including the bathrooms, had to have at least one. They said by the time the kids could reach four feet, they would know about guns rules. Bruce, Mike, and several others missed movie night and worked on gun racks for two hours. That was why Bruce didn't feel bad about the tickle torture. He had missed Roger Rabbit.

Before he left to go downstairs, Bruce saw PJ passed out on the pillows. "Oh no, you don't, PJ. You woke me up. Guess what," Bruce said, picking him up. "You gotta wake up and eat."

"Bruce, you let that baby sleep," Debbie yelled from the bathroom.

"No!" Bruce replied like a two-year-old as he headed out of the room. Then PJ let Bruce know he didn't like being woke up. He hollered and whined, a grumpy expression on his face.

"Little PJ doesn't like being woke up," Bruce teased PJ, not helping the situation at all. Walking into the kitchen, Bruce grabbed the bottle that was being handed to him. PJ forgave him as soon as the bottle hit his mouth. Millie sat a plate of food down for Bruce and PJ.

"You should be ashamed of yo'self, tickling that poor woman likes that. I almost went to help her," Millie said over her shoulder.

"I would've thrown you down and started tickling ya," Bruce told her. Taking the bottle out of PJ's mouth, he started spooning in food.

"Yeah, that's what I thought you'd do. I'm a little too old in the tooth to be tickled like that," Millie told him, giggling.

Bruce kept feeding PJ as the victims came down the stairs with the other torturers to the kitchen. The twins walked in, holding their stomachs but smiling. They climbed into their chairs and stood up on them, wrapping their arms around Bruce's neck and hugging him. The twins leaned dangerously over the side of their chairs. Bruce almost dropped PJ as he threw his arms out to support them. He slid PJ between his legs and held him with his thighs as he held the twins so they wouldn't fall.

"We love you Daddy," they said in unison. PJ didn't care if they loved Bruce. He tried to reach up and hit them, yelling each time he swung at them. They were interrupting his food, and after he got woke up too.

"I love you too, girls. Is Mama okay?" Bruce asked as he squeezed his legs together in an attempt to shut PJ shut up and quit swinging at the girls. That only turned PJ's wrath on him and PJ started hitting his legs.

"Mama's okay. She's gettin' dressed," Sherry told him as Danny and Buffy walked in, moving very slowly.

"Danny, Buffy, help the girls sit down so they don't fall. I have a pissed off baby between my legs," Bruce told them. Buffy ran to get Emily.

"Let 'em fall, they need to get tough," Danny said then saw the expression on Bruce's face. Danny grabbed Sherry, sitting her in her chair. Buffy did the same for Emily. Danny sat and laid her head down on the table as Debbie came down with the last of the others.

"Mom, I am never going to try to save you again," Danny told Debbie as she sat down.

"How many times have I thrown myself down trying to save you when Daddy tickled you?" Debbie asked her.

"I don't know, but I remember when I used to ask for more. Now I'm willing to wear those stupid dresses Daddy buys me for Easter every year. Just to make him stop," Danny admitted.

"Really?" Bruce asked, looking up hopefully.

"I'm not talking to you right now, Daddy. Unlike Mom, I didn't have someone help me to the bathroom. I did pee on myself," Danny told him then turned her head the other way.

His feelings hurt, Bruce looked at Buffy. "Did you like the tickle torture?" he asked.

"I didn't know you could laugh that long, but I will still try to save you, Mama," Buffy smiled, looking at Debbie then Bruce.

"Traitor," Danny said.

"Danny, after Daddy left you said that was fun," Buffy said. "Does your pussy hurt?" she asked with a serious face, causing several people to almost choke on the food they were chewing. Jake just spat his on the table. Unfortunately for Mike, Nancy was drinking coffee and sprayed it on him as she started to laugh.

Everyone was laughing on sore stomachs and the more they tried to stop, the more they laughed. Once they got control over their bodies, they started to breathe again.

Debbie looked at Buffy, struggling to look stern. "Buffy, don't say that word. It's not nice," Debbie said, praying Buffy didn't make her laugh anymore.

"Why not? It's just another name for a vagina," Buffy said defiantly.

"It's not a nice word, especially out of a little girl's mouth," Debbie said, trying to hold back her laughter as was everyone else at the table.

"Everyone says it, Mama. I even heard you say it," Buffy told her, getting sassy. Down at the other end of the table, Mike was holding it in and turning blue. Nancy grabbed his hand, trying to give him strength as she rocked back and forth, holding her laughter in.

"Buffy, that's different. I'm grown up," Debbie replied in a high pitched voice, trying not to laugh. This was important.

"Yesterday when those blues came out of that building, you were hollering 'suck my dick' as you shot them. Then you would ask them if their pussy hurt. You don't even have a dick. Danny said girls can have balls, but she never said we have dicks," Buffy said, shaking her head, blonde curly hair bouncing everywhere. Jake fell out of his chair, trying not to laugh out loud, and curled up in a ball on the floor.

Grabbing PJ's bottle, Bruce shoved it in his mouth and started sucking on the nipple to keep from laughing, and he hated goat's milk. Stephanie, who was sitting beside Buffy, was just staring straight ahead with tears rolling down her face as she tried to hold it in.

Debbie had to wait a few minutes before answering Buffy. She never took her eyes off of her, knowing if she looked at someone else, it was all over. Debbie took a deep breath before saying, "Buffy, that was in the heat of battle. I'm a little crazy then."

"You said dick, not penis. So when I'm shooting at people, I can't ask them if their pussy hurts?" Buffy asked, waving her hands in the air. Lynn and Millie hugged each other in the kitchen to keep from falling down. Angela tried to stand up and leave, but fell down on the floor beside Jake. Bruce just kept drinking the bottle, PJ hitting him and telling Bruce that was his.

Debbie started again, "Buffy—" then stopped as she took a deep breath to keep from laughing. Then she continued, "Buffy, a firefight isn't the best time for you to be yelling out words."

"So I can't yell at blues to see if their pussy hurts before I bust a cap in their ass?" Buffy stood up indignantly. Danny hit the floor, rocking back and forth as she tried not to laugh out loud.

"Buffy—" was all Debbie could manage to get out as her body shook with laughter.

"It's just words, Mama. I should be able to tell those bitches anything I want before I bust a cap in their ass," Buffy said, shaking her head and hips back and forth. Steve was holding Tonya up in her seat to keep her from falling, but Tonya still collapsed to the floor, trying desperately to hold the laughter in.

"Bu—" Debbie said several octaves too high and stopped. Bruce coughed, milk shooting out of his nose but he kept the bottle in his mouth, sucking down the last of the milk. Unable to stay in his chair, Alex slid out, joining Angela on the floor.

"I can show you in those medical books of Daddy's and Daddy Mike's that dick and penis is the same thing, I read about it. Just like coke and soda are the same things," Buffy told Debbie, putting her hands on her hip, showing her sassy attitude. "So I can't say soda either. But I can say vagina and coke, is that it? So when we are attacked I have to yell out 'Hey blues, does your vagina hurt today?'" Conner slid out of his chair and under the table, guffawing fit to bust a gut.

Debbie was rocking back and forth in her chair, afraid to answer. Buffy mistook that for her shaking her head yes.

"So while everyone else yells dick and pussy, I have to yell 'Hey blue, suck my penis! I have erectile dysfunction, come and get it.' Whatever that is," Buffy said, cocking her hip with her hand on it and flipping her hair. Mike's head hit the table and Nancy hit the floor. Muffled shrieks and snorts filled the air.

Debbie managed, "Not—nice—words," through gritted teeth, tears of mirth rolling down her face.

"What, now I can't say vagina or penis? That's not fair. I know what they are, you told me about them. I have a vagina and I can't even yell it out?" Buffy cried out, waving her index finger in the air, now bordering on open rebellion. "I guess I can't tell you my pussy hurts now," Buffy said as she sat back down in her chair, folding her arms on the table and laying her head down. Matt and David hit the floor and flopped bonelessly, holding each other and laughing hysterically.

At the other end of the table, Cassandra was sitting in Susan's lap while Susan was shaking with silent laughter. Cassandra looked at Mike and asked, "What's a pussy?"

The dam broke. Bruce spit out the bottle on the table, laughing. Debbie hit the floor, laughing so hard she looked like she was having a seizure. Those listening in the other rooms fell about, laughing like crazy people. Bruce stood up, set PJ on the floor, and dropped down beside him laughing, his head turning purple.

Buffy just sat at the table sulking, thinking everyone was laughing at her because they could use those words and she couldn't. Bruce grabbed her leg, pulling her to him; she tried to fight him but he pulled her down anyway. Wrapping his arms around her, Bruce hugged her tight as he continued to laugh. Still laughing, Debbie managed to crawl across the floor to Bruce and Buffy. Bruce opened up his arms then he and Debbie hugged Buffy tight. Then she returned their hugs. She didn't care if she could use those words. Mama and Daddy loved her.

Several hours later, everyone was gathered on the patio for the Sunday meeting. Bruce had to move it back because he wasn't in the mood to do anything after all the laughing he had done that morning. Buffy was sitting in Debbie's lap with PJ.

"Buffy, look at me," Debbie told her. "Don't say anything right now. I can't laugh anymore today. You can use those words but only outside the house and not in front of the little kids. They don't need to say them and you don't either. But you're old enough to make your own choice on the use of your words. You go willingly to fight and are fighting for this family. In a fight, I don't care what you say as long as you stay safe. Do you understand?"

"Yes Mama," Buffy said, smiling at her. "I'm sorry if I hurt your feelings," Buffy added.

"Thank you baby, but you didn't hurt my feelings. You are one of the princesses and I want the best for you. Now, before the meeting starts, go tell Cassandra not to say those words. Don't say them to me," Debbie warned her as Buffy was fixing to clarify which words. "I'm not kidding. If I laugh anymore today, I might die." Buffy looked at Debbie in shock. "Not really die, Buffy. But I can't laugh," Debbie told her. Then Debbie leaned in real close and whispered in Buffy's ear, "My balls hurt."

Buffy understood. Wrapping her arms around Debbie's neck, she hugged her tight, then jumped out of her lap and ran over to Cassandra, who was in Mike's lap. Debbie looked up in the sky. She would not be able to stand straight for days. Her abdomen hurt so much from the laughing but she'd needed that. Looking around at everyone with smiles on their faces, Debbie knew they'd needed it too.

Bruce was at the table getting his notes together. Debbie was glad they had laughed this morning. Last night she had read Bruce's notes after he went to sleep. They were full of his predictions and assessments so far, and none of them were good. Bruce did not mind her reading his notes, but she wished she hadn't read them and had found out like everyone else at the meeting. She hadn't slept worth a shit last night after reading them.

Bruce called the meeting to order as Buffy ran back to Debbie, getting in her lap as PJ chewed on his fist. "I'm glad everyone is okay after this morning," Bruce told everyone.

"Baby, don't make me laugh anymore. I'm not kidding. If you make me laugh anymore today we are getting a divorce, for at least a week," Debbie threatened him.

"Okay, sugar mama," Bruce said.

Then Bruce started the meeting, "For those new to this, we start on projects we are working on now and those next in line. Then we get updates on blue activity and action reports of engagements fought during the week. Next we go over supplies and duty assignments. At the end we ask for ideas, complaints and anything we forgot. Now I'm going to turn it over to the project man, Paul." Bruce sat down as Paul stood up.

"First, I want to say that yesterday everyone did an outstanding job. If the work continues at this pace, we will be done way ahead of schedule. Now, the barracks we are building will hold one hundred and twenty people with two people to a room. Each room will be ten feet by ten feet with a closet and drawers on each side. Each side will have one plug in, with four outlets. This is to limit power consumption. The solar panels can only produce so much and the batteries can only hold so much. The barracks will have two floors with male and female bathrooms on each floor and a washer area. The first floor will be underground to save heating and cooling. Also, this is so the barracks will not throw a shadow across the solar panels. There will be a dryer but we prefer if you hung your clothes in the hall to dry them. We do this now in the loft and in the house. The Community Center will be three thousand seven hundred square feet total. The common area will be two thousand five hundred square feet where we'll eat, have meetings and classes. The kitchen will be large at twelve hundred square feet; it'll run off propane and we'll be able to prepare meals for two thousand at a time. The storage area will be eighty thousand square feet with a fifteen foot ceiling all underground. We're going to put greenhouses on top of it." Paul paused as Bruce raised his hand.

"Yeah, Bruce," Paul said.

"Paul, I only see a couple of hundred pallets of cement here. The areas you're talking about are going to take like a thousand pallets. Where are the rest going to come from?" Bruce asked.

"At the warehouse where we got the first ones from," Paul answered.

"You didn't get them all?"

"Bruce, there were over sixteen hundred pallets of concrete. We don't have the storage area here for that, and we need to keep them out of the weather. We're going to start pouring the community slab today. I was just going to have the supply teams bring them as we need them," Paul finished, looking at Bruce and wondering what he was getting at.

"Go on, I'll cover that in my briefing," Bruce said.

Paul continued on. "With the trucks of lumber that Bruce found yesterday, we have lumber for all the projects with a lot left over. We'll start the framing up of the fence today. Two pieces of plywood will be screwed together then sat against the fence, with long side on the ground. Then we'll brace it with two by fours and build an eight-foot earthen embankment behind it. Even a tank can't knock it down. Now, with the razor wire all the way around, the fence is twelve foot tall. When we're done, I'm going to take a dozer and dig a slopping ditch away from the fence to increase the height to fifteen feet. The only weak areas will be the gates. With current progress, I'm giving us a completion time: community building complete two weeks, barracks complete three weeks, storage area four weeks and fence two weeks. These times are concurrent, meaning in four weeks all will be done if we keep working like this. Any questions?" None were asked, so Paul sat down. Next Matt and Jake got up and gave their report on blue activity.

Bruce looked down at his notes, then threw his notebook down on the table. He didn't want to give the clan the information he had.

"It's okay baby, tell them," Debbie said gently. Everyone looked at her, then back to Bruce.

Taking a deep breath, Bruce started. "It's worse than I thought. The blues are getting smarter. Yesterday at the truck stop they hit us in a coordinated attack. They had watched us, then spread out, covering all sides of the kill area. Then they attacked simultaneously on all fronts, using cover to advance on our position. Stephanie, before you say other predators do the same thing, I know, but there are two hundred million blues out there. Before yesterday, we were averaging three rounds per kill. By military standards that's unbelievable. Yesterday we went to over twenty rounds per kill, which by military standards is still outstanding. Most everyone out there at the truck stop was in my family, which does include Mike and his family because we are one and the same. We practiced a lot before the shit hit the fan. Long range shooting, speed shooting, CQB or close quarter battle, ambush and the list goes on. The adults and our kids have been doing this for years. What I'm getting at is that the rest of you will not be able to shoot that good in a short period of time. We will train you, but this type of precision takes years of practice.

"For arguments sake, let's say we can teach all of y'all to shoot like us in ten days. It still doesn't matter. In the Shreveport-Bossier metro area, with a seventy percent infection rate, there are over four hundred thousand, just eighty miles away from us. With our current ammo expenditure, it will take over nine million rounds to take that one city. On the radio, they've reported mobs of hundreds of thousands to millions moving amass, which they're calling hordes. We aren't even going to talk about Dallas, just a hundred and eighty miles away or Houston, Baton Rouge—you live here, you know the big metro areas.

"Paul, that's why I wanted everything here. We cleared the area close to us, reducing our risk for a little while. I didn't believe they'd get that smart, and it's the numbers they're in. Even if we had the ammo, we don't have the weapons. M-4s have to replace barrels at fifteen thousand rounds. After we took supplies from the checkpoint at the dam we had almost a million rounds. We've already used a quarter of that. We used over eighty thousand rounds killing blues sitting on roof tops. With our current usage, if everyone shot as well as we do, we can barely take forty-two thousand now in a mass attack."

"What about hunting them like we did before?" Maria asked hopefully.

"I'm going to try, but I don't think it'll work again. If it does, I don't think it will work as well as the first time," Bruce answered.

"Let's finish the fences first then!" someone yelled.

"Has everyone here seen a football game on TV? Imagine if those fans charged the field, how hard it would be to stop them. They would just pile up at the fence until they built a ramp with bodies and come over the top. Remember that a stadium usually holds about fifty thousand. The reason I want the fence is that it'll give us time and breathing room. Until we get more ammo and weapons, if we get hit by a large mob our best chance is to run. That isn't really an option for us. If we must, then this family has a farm in North Dakota. It doesn't have a fence and is nowhere near ready, but if we leave, that's where we go. Until then we have to kill 'em away from here. That means actively hunting them."

"Let's go get some ammo and guns," another voice called out.

"We can't yet. It would cause too many blues to get on our travel corridor. Stephanie gave a report that blues hibernate in the cold. When we have frost two days in a row, we're going to load up several semis and bring shit in here until we have no room for a frog to take a dump. Until then, supply runs will be few and far between and only in areas where a hunting patrol was the day before. Patrols of search and destroy will be almost every day. The blues have already started moving back into the area we just cleared.

"We took out the predators, then deer and other animals moved in. Guess what is following them back in? Nancy, Debbie, Angela, and Stephanie, I want a two-man patrol inside the fence around the clock starting tonight. Danny, today I want you to check off the new soldiers, Bill and anyone else with police or military training, work will not interfere with training.

"Next, after what that judge and congressman told me yesterday, if the government shows up we'll fight them to the death, theirs or ours. They informed me, with a little persuasion, that as the plague was hitting they sent out officers to bring in those that had weapons and large stockpiles of food. Before anyone asks, yes, one did come here before the world went to hell. But he was shot by my son Steve at Debbie's command." Nancy gasped at Bruce's words. "Yes Nancy, he came here to take this family in. If Steve hadn't have killed the officer, he would've told Homeland you were here, and they would have sent a tactical team here. That was from both the judge and congressman. They were told to execute anyone not following instructions, basically anyone who didn't kiss their ass. They want sheep to lead, not wild horses. Now if you want to leave after I've told you we will fight the government, that's fine. We will give you a truck, some food, and a weapon, and we'll hold no hard feelings. If you stay and they come, I expect you to kill anyone who threatens this clan. Does anyone want to leave?" Bruce asked, looking around.

Millie stood up and walked toward Bruce. He'd expected a few to leave, but not Millie. His heart sank but he remained expressionless.

When Millie got to the table, she handed Bruce a piece of paper, "That's the execution order for my son. They told me that they made him leave buts in my heart I know'd better. The officer you burnt is the one who did it. I broke your order; he was still alive when I finds him spread out. I took a knife from the kitchen. I puts a rag in his mouth and just started cuttin 'im until he died. You said not to touch 'em and I brokes your rule. Whatever punishment you decide, I'll do. If ya wants me to leave, I'll leave." Millie stood up straight, waiting on Bruce's decision. Everyone held their breath, waiting.

Bruce grabbed his notebook, tore out a page and wrote something on it. Then he handed Millie the page and said, "Here, you're excused, you can go back to class." Millie looked down at the note. It read, "You're excused." She looked at Bruce in disbelief then hugged him and went back to her seat. Several people clapped for her.

"Millie," Bruce called and she glanced up. "When it slows down a bit, ask my beautiful wife what she did to him. I have to admit, at times I was aroused." Millie looked at Debbie, blew her a kiss and Debbie returned it.

"It was good, Millie," Debbie said, and the memory of the wave hit her, making her breathe faster. Not the memory of the actions on the targets, just the wave. Bruce smiled at Debbie as she closed her eyes. He knew what she was thinking.

Danny jumped up. "That's my mama!"

"I would ask others to hold off on any actions against the three that are left. I'm not finished yet. Now to continue, if you stay and the government comes, you'll fight. If you don't fight, I will kill you myself. That means you've just been going through the motions. Eating the clan's food and using the clan for protection. This is your last chance. If you stay you're in for a pound. We live or die together," Bruce said, expecting someone to leave. Then Bill stood up.

"Bruce, I think I speak for everyone here when I say your family is the only sign of hope we've seen. You have taken us in, treated us as equals, given us food, offered us protection, and let's not forget rescued our asses. The only thing this family has asked is for us to pull our own weight. That was rare before the world changed. I'm sure it's almost extinct now. What you had set up before the world took a dive is amazing, and you're willing to share it with total strangers. I can't say if the shoe had been on the other foot if I could've left my family to rescue others. You not only leave, you take your whole family into battle. I'm proud to be a part of this clan," Bill finished, sitting back down as everyone agreed with him.

"Thank you, Bill. This family needed to hear that. Paul, is there any way we can work at night without drawing a lot of attention? Maybe we can use some huge work lights?" Bruce asked him.

"Yeah, the fence for sure. We could put the two pieces of plywood together in the bottom of the barn. Then we could bring 'em to the fence using one of the electric buggies with a trailer. I could rig up something to cut down on the noise of the industrial mixer. Yeah, we could run a night crew and I could keep the projects going, but it won't be as fast as the day work. You just need too much light and power. The array you have here must have cost a fortune. It puts out more power than the batteries can store. Right now, your batteries are the weak link. Each of your arrays put out at least five kilowatts an hour, but on a good day it averages eight kilowatts an hour and you have ten arrays. Your windmill was just turning because you didn't need the power. I stopped it to save wear and tear," Paul told him.

"Nancy, Debbie, Angela, and Stephanie, I want a ten-man night crew worked in also. Four for the fence and six for construction, doing what Paul has laid out," Bruce told them, each of them nodding. "I am going to be making fire team assignments. This'll be who you patrol with and fight with. If you have a problem with that team, let me know, I'll move you. They will be five- and six-man teams. I know I said man but women will be on them also. My team will only be on standby today in case blues hear the construction, but we'll be out tomorrow. Next, I have noticed several kids running around here. All of you adults, I want someone to adopt each kid. If it goes bad here, I want someone responsible for each one. Bill, I have a favor to ask and it's a big one. I want you to adopt someone," Bruce said to him.

"I would be honored. My wife and I never had kids," Bill said gravely. Bruce didn't ask what had happened to his wife.

"Frank, come up here, please." Bruce called up the little boy who had guarded the kids on the island. Frank ran up to Bruce, smiling. "Frank, Bill is the person Paul was looking for, just for you," Bruce said as Frank's smile broadened to a grin.

"Bill, this is Frank. He guarded seven kids on an island and he was the oldest at nine," Bruce told Bill. Frank took off at a dead run, locking Bill's leg in a hug. Bill reached down and picked up Frank and hugged him, then headed back to his seat.

Bruce looked over where Frank had run from and saw Nathan, the six-year-old boy from the island. The last of that group that nobody had adopted yet, as Paul's family had taken in Alice and Robert. Nathan was just sitting there looking at Frank in Bill's arms, tears running down his face.

Bruce looked in his notebook and asked, "Where is Thomas Caldwell and could he come here, please?"

A stocky man in his early fifties with gray hair stood up and walked to Bruce, stopping in front of him, "Yes sir."

"You are an ordained minister, correct?" Bruce asked Thomas.

"Yes sir, of the Catholic faith," Thomas said.

"You will fight to protect this clan?" Bruce asked him.

"Yes sir. Sometimes a shepherd has to protect his flock. I have seen with my own eyes what Satan has unleashed on this world. I'm not just talking about the infected. Satan's minions can come in the forms of lawless bandits and government officials," Thomas replied.

"I have a favor to ask you also," Bruce told him and leaned over, whispering in his ear. Father Thomas said, "I would be honored."

"Steve and Tonya, come here please," Bruce said as they walked up to him, wondering what they had done.

"I want you two married today. This world has gone insane and I want Tonya to carry the Williams name. If something happens to either of you I want you to have no regrets. We can have a formal wedding if we ever get a chance to breathe," Bruce told both of them. Tonya hugged Bruce then Steve hugged his dad.

"Dad, we need rings," Steve said. Bruce reached in his pocket and pulled out two rings.

"These are the rings your mother and I used, passed to me by my father. They were used by all his brothers and sisters going back eight generations. These rings have seen hundreds of Williams married. All I ask, since you are the first, is that you let your brothers and sisters use them. They are now yours," Bruce told him.

"I will guard them with my life," Steve promised.

"I know you will, son, and they'll fit. I snuck out to the machine shop last night," Bruce said.

"Everyone, I want you all to be witnesses to the marriage of my son to Tonya Stone," Bruce said loudly.

Debbie, Nancy, and Pam ran up to Tonya and started fixing her hair after Debbie handed PJ to Bruce. Danny and Mary headed to one of the flower gardens and brought back a bouquet of flowers. Jake and Matt ran into the house, coming back with cameras. Bruce told Buffy she was the ring bearer.

Tonya came up to Bruce. "Will you give me away, Mr. Williams?" she asked shyly.

"I would be honored to, but call me Mr. Williams again and you get a spanking. On your wedding day your husband's supposed to do that," Bruce told her.

"I'm sorry, Dad," Tonya told him, smiling.

After the wedding ceremony, everyone posed for pictures. Debbie walked over to Bruce. He was looking at Danny holding PJ with several other teenage girls gathered around her. "Never even heard of a wedding with everyone in full combat gear and assault rifles," Debbie said.

"Yeah, it's a first but I have a feeling it won't be the last. Not for a very long time," Bruce said as Debbie slapped the back of his head.

"How could you do this without telling me? It was the right thing to do but you should have told me," Debbie snapped at him, then hugged him.

"After that slap, I better get some tonight," Bruce said, hugging her.

"Maybe," Debbie replied in a not so convincing tone.

"I thought you slapped me for what I said," Bruce whined.

"About them staying in combat gear? Please. If they would've come to me right now wanting everyone to dress up, I would've beat both of 'em," Debbie told him. "Oh! She's going to throw the flowers," Debbie said, running to the group. Danny and Mary bolted away from the group.

Bruce chuckled at the sight. Then he looked closely at the group; several dozen women were standing ready to catch the flowers, many of them carrying assault weapons. *This can't be good*, Bruce thought. Tonya threw the flowers over her shoulder and Bruce watched them go through the air and land in Buffy's hands. Buffy started jumping up and down with the flowers. With a scowl on his face, Bruce yelled out, "Buffy, you're grounded until you're twenty-one."

The excitement washed off Buffy's face when she heard Bruce. She just stared at Bruce like he had lost his mind. She had won, wasn't that what Daddy always told her to do? Then Debbie leaned down and whispered in Buffy's ear and a look of horror crossed Buffy's face. With a look of disgust, Buffy handed Debbie the flowers, wiping her hands off on her chest. Debbie walked over to Bruce carrying the flowers. Steve and Tonya came over and Debbie gave Tonya the flowers back.

"I really didn't mean to throw them to her," Tonya said to Bruce.

"I know. Can I ask you two something?" Bruce asked.

"Sure," they said.

"You two are married now and I want y'all to have a kid," Bruce said. Debbie looked at Bruce with a shocked expression, not believing her ears.

"We had planned on it, Dad," Steve said blushing, looking down at his feet.

"No, I mean right here, right now," Bruce said, looking at the couple.

"Dad, there are people everywhere out here, they'll see us. And babies take nine months to get here," Steve said, not wanting to explain the facts of life to his father.

"Well, I'm glad you paid attention when I gave you your talk. That's not what I meant. Look at that kid sitting down by the back door," Bruce told them.

"Who, Nathan?" Steve asked, looking where Bruce had said.

"He's crying," Tonya said, bringing her hand to her mouth.

"Yes, Nathan. He's the last kid from the island that has not been adopted. He's crying because he and Frank were always together since they've been here. I want you two to adopt him," Bruce told them. Debbie had never shaken off the shocked look so her expression never changed.

Tonya and Steve looked at each other then back to Nathan. Looking at each other one last time, they turned to Bruce. Tonya said, "It's a wonderful idea. Will you introduce us, Bruce?"

"We'll watch him tonight so you two can have a honeymoon night," Bruce offered.

"That's okay, we already had our honeymoon night," Tonya said, blushing prettily.

Bruce smiled then turned to Debbie. "If you don't close your mouth and change your expression, the kid is goin' to think you farted."

Debbie started stuttering and shaking her head, "Wh—how—no—."

"English, baby, you speak it," Bruce said and called Nathan over. The boy came over slowly, never once looking up. He still had tears in his eyes and they had lots of friends running down his face, hitting the ground.

Bruce kneeled down, looking at Nathan who was staring at his shoes with tears still hitting the ground. "I found the people Paul was looking for to take care of you and love you," Bruce told him.

"Nobody wants me," Nathan told him.

"You are wrong, buddy. They couldn't adopt you until they got married. They couldn't have kids out of wedlock," Bruce told him with a serious face. Nathan understood married. He looked up at Bruce with his jaw hanging open in shock.

"Do I stink? Or maybe I'm not speaking English?" Bruce asked, looking up at Tonya and Steve. Debbie slapped him across the back of his head. Bruce looked back at Nathan. "It's my son and his new wife. They want you to join their family. Are you ready for it?"

Nathan turned his head, looking up at Tonya and Steve. Before they could kneel down, Nathan threw himself at Tonya's leg, holding on for dear life and crying his eyes out. Steve picked him up and hugged him and Tonya joined in. Nathan gave kisses all over their faces, telling them he loved them as all three cried.

Tears rolled down Bruce's cheeks as he watched the three. The last loose end from the island was taken care of. Steve walked over with Nathan in his arms, still hugging him. Tonya took Nathan from him so she could get some baby boy love. Steve watched Tonya take Nathan over to everyone so she could tell them she was his mama. "She could've let me hold him a little longer," Steve said with envy in his voice.

"Get used to it. I didn't get to hold you until you were one. Your mama just about went into conniption fits 'cause PJ wouldn't let her hold him. I think she broke out the Ouija board and put voodoo on my ass," Bruce told Steve as Debbie slapped the back of his head again.

"I know damn well I'm getting some tonight. That's the third slap today," Bruce told Debbie, dropping his smile.

"Dad, please don't, that's gross," Steve said, shaking his head to get those words out of his head.

"You do know that's how you got here, right? Even though I didn't get to hold you until you could walk. I think you just ran away from her and I just picked you up, not knowin' you were my kid," Bruce told him, wincing at another slap on the back of his head.

"Please Dad, don't say it," Steve said, knowing what was coming next.

Bruce looked at Steve as he remembered all of his first times to do everything. Pride filled him from head to toe. Bruce could remember taking him on base, showing him off to everyone. Then taking him down to the air field. Steve had loved watching helicopters. "I'm proud of you, son. A father couldn't ask for a better son; one who has turned into a good man. Every father wants to see their child to grow up better than them. You've succeeded tenfold. I'm sorry you didn't get the normal childhood. I just wanted you prepared for life, I hope one day you forgive me," Bruce told Steve, tears rolling down his face.

Steve wrapped his arms around Bruce, giving him a bear hug. Steve started to cry. "If I would've had a normal childhood, we'd all be dead,

Dad. Who would want it anyway? How many kids can say they shot a fully automatic weapon at the age of seven, learned how to blow stuff up, sky dive before they were a teenager, ride rapids, fix anything, shopping on eBay while yelling at the computer when someone outbids you, and all the hunting trips. Every friend I ever had in life wanted to be a part of our family," Steve said, letting Bruce go and looking at him. "I just hope I'm half the dad you are."

"Half, my ass. You have my and your mama's blood. You'll be ten times better," Bruce told him.

"I doubt that," Steve said.

"Get over there with your wife and son. They get pissed if you're not up their ass for the first five years," Bruce told his son, dodging the slap to the back of head that Debbie threw at him. Steve laughed and ran over to Tonya. Reaching them, he tried to take Nathan but she wouldn't let him.

"All right, are you taking drugs? Who are you and where is my husband?" Debbie asked, spinning Bruce to face her.

"What the hell are you talking about, woman? Have you taken your Depo shot? I did rob a pharmacy for you," Bruce said, trying to steer her away from the topic.

"I have known you since we were in diapers and this is weird even for you. I thought taking everyone to Panama so everyone could learn jungle training was weird. There aren't any jungles in the States but I didn't say anything. I'm not talking about the scuba diving, kayaking, mountain climbing and other stuff. Then two years ago you take us to Arizona for two weeks so we can learn defensive driving and learn how to drive formula one race cars. Now that was weird. Two of the kids didn't even have permits but you wanted them to do spin outs," Debbie stated, waving her arms at him.

"You liked Arizona, Debbie," Bruce said, looking at the kids. The twins were playing with PJ in Danny's lap.

"Bruce, you come out here today talking about how short ammo is; then you build fire teams and increase training. Then you stop supply runs and increase patrols. You marry off our son without talking to me. Keep wanting, no, let me rephrase that—*demanding* sex, not caring who's around. Finally, you make sure all the kids—" Debbie stopped in mid-sentence, looking up at Bruce and following his gaze.

Debbie grabbed his arm, pulling him along, and Bruce followed her. Debbie led him to the shop, opened the door, pushed him in and then closed the door behind her. "What is it Bruce?" she asked.

"Just a bad gut feeling, Debbie, that's all," Bruce said.

"Bruce, the last time you had a bad gut feeling, the fucking world ended!" Debbie yelled.

"I don't know, baby. Everything is going good but it feels bad. There's something wrong here," Bruce told her.

"A plague is loose on the planet turning people into evil overgrown super-powered smurfs. We are technically prisoners on the farm, but you know all of this so tell me what's wrong," Debbie pleaded.

Bruce looked at her somberly. "I don't know, but it feels bad, like we are fixing to walk into an ambush. I have done everything I know to do and I still feel off. Nothing I do will make the gnawing sensation in my gut go away."

"Are we going to be attacked?" Debbie asked.

"That's a definite, Debbie, by blues and gangs. Probably several times by each every year," Bruce told her.

That scared Debbie, the way Bruce said it with certainty. She had convinced herself they could stay hidden. "You're certain we will be attacked?" Debbie asked him, praying for at least an 'I don't know.'

"Debbie, we are going to be found. It's only a matter of time. Gangs are running out of drugs and victims. The blues will chase food and sooner or later a large group will find us. Don't build yourself into a false hope. If you do, when it happens you will be shocked and will let your guard down. Debbie, you're a warrior now, start thinking like one. If you get a funny nagging feeling, listen to it. You have ridden the wave, baby. You are different now," Bruce said, looking down into her eyes.

"What can we do?" Debbie asked, wanting to tell Bruce she had more than a nagging feeling.

"I have done everything I know to do and the feeling doesn't go away. So I think it's something we can't prepare for," Bruce admitted to her.

"We can prepare for anything. We can get some more supplies. The fence can be higher—" Debbie stopped as Bruce spoke.

"I think we're going to lose a lot of people, soon," Bruce told her.

"Wha—Why do you say that?" Debbie asked, her body going numb.

"When you get the gut feeling, you make small changes. If that does not make it go away, make bigger changes until it goes away. If it doesn't, then it means it's inevitable and the only thing that makes the gut feel like that is the loss of a teammate," Bruce told her, saying the last sentence slowly.

"How could you know that and just what is the wave?" Debbie asked fearfully, hoping Bruce did not feel what she knew.

"I have been in combat, baby, and I have lost teammates," Bruce said. Then he grabbed both of her hands. "Okay baby, let me explain something to you. Turn the female side of your brain off. The wave is called a lot of different things. Each Native American tribe has a name for it, along with every warrior culture. In the service it's called the wave, the thousand-yard stare, in the zone, and the list goes on and on. I don't go for the supernatural answer because I can't touch it or feel it. I think the wave is your body dropping tons of hormones into your system and awakening the primitive and higher thought areas in your brain. You can see better, hear better, move faster, and I think the gut feeling is your brain playing out scenarios days in advance with how your life is going and sees something coming that will hurt you or a teammate. You don't control that part of your brain, but it lets you know with the gut feeling.

"Like the plague: at the table that first morning after I woke all of you up. I had the gut feeling. I started making plans. When I got to: go out and buy as much shit as possible or do a massive stockpile, the feeling went away. I made the deduction that it was going to be bad because going out and buying a lot of shit made it go away," Bruce finished, hoping she understood.

"Let's go make some more lists until it goes away," Debbie asked hopefully.

"It won't; that's why I even mentioned the other farm. It didn't make my gut feeling go away, nor yours," Bruce told her.

Debbie leaned her head back. "What the hell are you talking about? I don't have a gut feeling."

Bruce looked up and let out a sigh, then looked back to Debbie. "Okay, turn off that female side again. That side tries to think rationally and the wave is nowhere near rational. Only the best warriors can get the wave, and you are now a true warrior. When you get this gut feeling it's damn near impossible to get mad at a teammate. I've been trying to piss you off all morning. The best you could do was pop me on the back of the head. You know something is wrong; that's why we are having this conversation. Besides me, there are three people on this farm who have ridden the wave. You, obviously; of course, Conner. He doesn't know how he did it but he really wants to ride it again. I saw it in his eyes the first day I met him. He was mad at the world because he could not call the wave when he was held prisoner. Now I want you to tell me who the other is. You know them very well," Bruce challenged her.

"Bruce, I can't do that," Debbie told him.

"Turn that shit off in your head. Close your eyes and just run through people in your mind, but don't think," Bruce said.

Debbie closed her eyes and tried to do as he said just to amuse him. Debbie took a deep breath then opened her eyes. "Buffy," she said immediately. Debbie looked at Bruce, who was just smiling at her. "That's not possible—" Debbie said, taking a step back and not believing what she had done. Then it struck Debbie who she'd named. "No, Bruce, she's just a little girl. Buffy can't feel that and be a warrior," Debbie replied.

"She can ride the wave like a pro," Bruce said with admiration.

"She can't," Debbie stuttered.

"Why do ya think she tried to pick a fight with you this morning? She knows something is not right but she can't get mad at you even though she tried. You couldn't get mad at her. If anyone outside the family would have tried that you would have ripped them apart. She's your teammate. Like me, Mike, Nancy and the kids," Bruce told her.

"Why?" Debbie asked.

"I don't know. The wave doesn't come with an instruction manual, baby, turn that side off again. It just does. Here's what I think: you know something is going to happen to someone you care about. But you can't get mad at them in case they get killed so your last days together were good. Then you have to look at it like this: you try to piss those around you off and if you can get mad at them you know it's not them. It's never worked for me, but I still try," Bruce told her.

"Can anyone be taught to ride?"

"I don't think so, but I'm not sure. Like anyone can be an athlete but only a few can be Olympic athletes and fewer still gold medal athletes. Most warriors get combat shakes or adrenalin rushes; they are the Olympic athletes. Few ride the wave and these are the gold medal warriors. You gain a lot with the wave but it does come at a price," Bruce said.

"Can you tell if someone can?" she asked.

"Yeah, but just because they can doesn't mean they will," Bruce replied.

"There are a few on the farm now, aren't there?"

"Quite a few. We have a lot of survivors here and yes, some are our kids. Before you ask, I can't read your mind. This is not Jedi shit. Just simple deduction," Bruce said.

"Which of our kids?" Debbie asked, not really wanting the answer.

"Tell me the one that won't and not because they can't," Bruce said.

Debbie did not even have to close her eyes. "Steve." Then she looked at the floor. "Have Danny and Jake ridden yet?"

"No, not yet, but they've come real close. Danny felt the edges the night she beat the gimp, and several other times in firefights. She felt the edge and knew there was more and wanted it. Jake will ride the wave better than all of us. He can snap up his rifle and by the time his eye is on the scope he is at the edge," Bruce informed her.

"Steve shot that cop," Debbie pointed out.

"Solders kill, baby. It's what they are trained for. Don't think Steve is not a badass and not a good warrior. But to ride the wave you have to give up part of yourself and most don't want to. Then you have to see your enemy as targets and not people. I think Steve sees that as being too inhumane. Debbie you know as well as I that Steve likes to feel in control, and the wave is not control. You act on instinct, not by thought. Most feel if they keep that part of themselves, then life is good." Bruce then asked, "Which of Mike's kids will ride?"

"Mary and Matt," she replied back without thinking. "Bruce, stop that, it freaks me out."

"Baby, if you think in a fight you'll die because you are reacting, not anticipating. Trust your gut even if you don't know what it's saying," Bruce said. "It's 1245. Work will be starting soon. We need to get back." Then he looked at her. "Debbie, if the world hadn't changed, I would do everything I could to try to make my kids not ride the wave, but in this new world it is a hell of an advantage." Bruce moved to the door.

"Why did you let me?" Debbie asked.

Bruce looked at her in shock. "Let you my ass. From the day I came back from the hospital you've wanted it bad. In every battle we've been in you were almost there. You could feel it in me and you wanted it. I would've had to shoot you the morning you followed me out to the prisoners. When you stopped at the edge of the barn, you were going to watch me to see how I did it. Debbie, the thing that worries me is that you like the anger. That's a double-edged sword; the rage does last longer and the wave will go higher, but guilt will follow unless you kill your heart. That kind of guilt doesn't go away, trust me, as long as you have compassion or love in you. I'm not going to say why either, so don't ask. When you're on the wave still trust your gut; if it feels wrong, don't do it even if you know the wave will go higher. You liked it, didn't you?"

Debbie closed her eyes. "Holy shit!" she said as the memory flooded over her. She leaned against the table, smiling.

"Feels good, just the memory, doesn't it?" Bruce asked.

"Hell yeah," Debbie said, still smiling.

Bruce leaned toward her. "Remember that feeling. When you do something in anger and hate causing unnecessary pain, taking joy in it, that's how the guilt hits you. You saw them as a person and enjoyed it," Bruce told her.

Debbie stood up fast. "You couldn't live with yourself if guilt hit you like that."

"Yes you can, baby. It just takes practice. You can either stay on the wave or you learn to live with it. You can't push it out of your mind no matter how hard you try." Bruce looked away before he spoke. "I always wondered why you chose a piece of shit like me, Debbie. You deserve to live in a palace. I want to give you everything and all I have ever given you is a crazy lifestyle." Bruce reached out, running his fingers through her hair.

"I love this crazy lifestyle, Bruce, and I can't imagine life without you," Debbie told him.

"I didn't want you to ride the wave. I always knew you could, but figured the need would never present itself. I was scared you would love the anger, not the wave, and if you ever had to deal with that pain I'd die," Bruce told her. Then he looked at her with fear in his eyes. "Debbie, the wave can be a two-edged sword. If you chase the wave you just become a killer, not a warrior. You have no thought but you get joy out of the act. You'll start to see your enemies as people, not targets. If you're chasing the wave, you will start to deliver pain just for fun. When that happens, you live with it or lose the ability to love and care for others. That is not living, because you no longer have a soul. Always be wary of those on the wave that refer to the enemy as human and not targets."

"You're right, I felt it and I wanted it. If you hadn't been there I would have gotten totally medieval. I know what you mean by the guilt. I wanted to hurt them just for the fun of it, Bruce, I felt invincible. Just the thought of what I wanted to do makes me sick. If those thoughts came at me like the wave I don't know what I'd do, but as always I have my stud muffin to save me," Debbie told, Bruce hugging him.

"Let's go, baby. We have a lot of work to do," Bruce said, turning toward the door.

"Where the hell do you think you're going?" Debbie barked behind him.

"Baby, we will talk more tonight," Bruce turned, seeing Debbie laying her weapon on the table and unbuckling her vest. "What the hell are you doing?" Bruce asked her.

"You told me not once but like four times that I had to give you some. So do you want some lovin' or what?" Debbie asked him.

Debbie watched Bruce turn around and locked the door before laying his weapon on the table. She started undoing her ACU top and pulled it off, dropping it to the floor. She turned back to Bruce and he was standing in front of her butt naked with his pants pulled down to his ankles.

"How in the hell did you get undressed that fast?" Debbie asked, looking at his equipment laid neatly on the table.

"It has nothing to do with the wave, baby. I'm just a horny man who wants some," Bruce told her as she got undressed.

"Well come here, horny man, let's get those evil spirits out," Debbie said as Bruce rushed her.

Twenty minutes later they snuck out the door like teenagers, trying not to get caught. They ran to the patio and stopped there, trying to act normal, but doing a lousy job of it. They watched the crew working on the community building as they started pouring the slab. Bruce pulled Debbie to the kitchen door as he headed inside.

Danny and Buffy were sitting in the game room playing with the twins and PJ. Danny looked up upon hearing someone walking toward her. "Where have y'all been? PJ was being a total brat outside. I have stuff that you told me to do, Daddy. I have fourteen people that are or have been in the military or police. I think they will pass with ease."

"Why didn't you get Susan to watch them?" Debbie asked, hugging the twins.

"I don't know," Danny said, shrugging her shoulders.

"Why are Emily's fingernails red and Sherry's pink?" Bruce asked, looking at the twins.

Danny grabbed both twins' hands to confirm what Bruce had said. "How'd you know which twin was which?" Danny asked, looking at the twins again and trying to find something different between them.

"Daddy could tell them apart since the night we brought them back," Debbie told her, admiring Danny's work.

"I painted Emily's nails red and Sherry's pink so I could tell 'em apart," Danny replied, still looking at the twins.

"Oh, that's good, Danny," Debbie said with admiration.

"Thank you, Mama." Danny smiled at the compliment.

Debbie smiled back at her. Then she noticed something. "Danny, where is your tactical vest?"

"By the back door with my rifle, Mom," Danny said with that teenaged girl tone. Debbie fought off the urge to slap her.

"Danny, from now on I want you to wear it at all times until I tell you different, okay," Debbie said, wanting Danny ready at all times.

"Mom, we're not at that threat level, plus the vest makes me look fat and it's uncomfortable," Danny whined.

"Matt doesn't think so," replied Bruce.

Danny whipped her head toward Bruce so fast her hair wrapped around her face. "What's that got to do with anything?" Danny asked in a frightened tone.

"Nothing sweetie, I was just saying when you wear all of your tactical gear around that boy, at times he makes me uncomfortable. Last week when we went on patrol and you had on your boonie hat, sunglasses, and your hair up in a ponytail with that P90 strapped to your hip, I almost slapped his eyes out of his head," Bruce told her.

"Really?" Danny asked with amazement in her voice.

"Danny, I know y'all aren't real brother and sister, but sometimes when that boy looks at you in full tactical gear ... I mean with knee and elbow pads, fully loaded vest, gloves, boonie hat, glasses, and weapon across your chest ... I want to get a water hose and hose him down then slap him around some. I love that kid, otherwise I'd beat the shit out of him. I think

Matt has a thing for badass women. I still want to take a water hose to him when he looks at you like that and probably will the next time he does. I don't even know why he looks at you like that, he's not your type," Bruce said, picking PJ up and playing with him.

"Daddy, you better not take a water hose to him. That would embarrass him and how do you know what my type is?" Danny spoke up for Matt's dignity.

"When you sit down by him in full gear, he turns beet red. Of all the boys that have ever liked you, Matt is the only one I ever liked and approved of. That's strike one there. Danny, all the boys you have liked are whiny, long haired, wanting someone to take care of them. That is strike two. Matt wants a girl that will stand by him and not try to take care of him. That's why I think he has a thing for tough women. The only upside about you wearing fatigues is when you wear the same camouflage pattern for a week he gets used to it. He still looks at you but I don't want to get a water hose. Then you change ACU or BDU patterns and it starts all over again. Since the plague started, with you being in fatigues all the time, I want to pop his eyes out of his head and eat 'em. I don't want to talk about it anymore because I want to break his legs now," Bruce said as he tried to get PJ's belly button, making him laugh.

"Daddy, don't hurt Matt, please," Danny begged, holding her hands clasped together in front of her chest.

"Baby, I love that boy and can't hurt him like that, even though I want to. I just don't like him checking out my daughter," Bruce said with a grumpy look on his face. Then Bruce turned back to PJ, trying to get the belly button.

Danny chewed her lower lip, looking at Bruce as he played with PJ. Then she jumped up. "I have to get ready to teach class." Danny said, then took off at a full sprint and headed upstairs. A few minutes later she came down wearing her knee and elbow pads, her hair in a ponytail, her Oakley sunglasses perched on her nose and her boonie hat cocked to the side. Danny grabbed her vest and weapon before running out the door.

Bruce looked up from playing with PJ at Debbie, who was looking at him with squinted eyes, studying him. "What was that all about?" Debbie asked Bruce.

"Nothing, sugar mama," Bruce said with an air of injured innocence.

216

"Bruce, the nonchalant verbalizations works on the younger form of girls, not the older," Debbie said. Bruce just looked at her, smiling. Debbie took a step back. "No!" she gasped.

"I'm surprised you and Nancy haven't seen it," Bruce told her.

"How long?" Debbie asked, feeling bad. Mamas should see stuff like this.

"You remember the last time we played paintball?" Bruce asked as he sat on a barstool beside the pool table.

"Yeah, we invited the boys you tried to kill at the paintball field out here to make it up to the girls because you embarrassed them," Debbie told him.

"Whatever," Bruce replied, waving his hand through the air. The attitude sounded so much like Danny, Debbie almost slapped him.

"So what about the boys at the paintball field?" Debbie asked him, still fighting the urge to slap him.

"The girls were using those punks to make the boys jealous," Bruce told her.

"Girls? Boys?" Debbie said out loud, looking to Bruce, who was just smiling.

"Jake and Mary?" Debbie asked in a shocked tone. Bruce just continued to smile.

Debbie just collapsed down on the floor. "I'm a horrible mother. My baby boy and my baby girl, falling in love right under my nose. I suck," Debbie said more to herself than Bruce.

"You're the best person I've ever met and as far as being a mother goes, none even come close to you. You never had much of a chance to catch them because the boys are covering the escapade. Secret looks, where to meet and stuff like that. Do you remember when you got to my first assignment, you and I were lying in the bed. You asked what the secret to boys was. What did I tell you?" Bruce asked Debbie and she closed her eyes, trying to remember.

"You said boys are simple, but that's bullshit. How do we handle the kids?"" Debbie asked.

"What do you mean?" Bruce asked with a puzzled look.

"Bruce, they are boyfriend and girlfriend with someone in the house," Debbie said.

"Yeah," Bruce said, wanting her to understand.

"We have to do something," Debbie said.

"See, there you go thinking complicated again, just like Danny and Mary. They devised this whole big plan to make the boys jealous. The plan was complicated, involving numerous people, leaving a lot to chance. All they had to do was talk to the boys and it would've been problem solved. I probably wouldn't have noticed it if they had done that, but the problem they had would've been solved," Bruce said then continued. "If you remember, when we all moved in here I told you Danny was going to marry Matt. I do admit, I never saw Jake and Mary. With Danny, I could see it in her eyes even as they played in the dirt together. I saw those same eyes follow me from Sunday school to sitting in front of me right now," Bruce told Debbie.

"Bruce, if I ask you a question will you give me a true, honest answer?" Debbie asked. Thinking about it for a second, Bruce smiled and nodded his head. "All the times you've gotten in trouble with me, how many were on purpose, just so I could catch you?" Debbie asked.

"Most, at least ninety-eight percent, but you know that," Bruce told her.

"I know, I know that, but that takes all the fun out of it, baby. If you know that I know, then why do it?" Debbie asked smiling.

"It makes you happy to scold me. You solved a riddle. That's good enough for me," Bruce told her.

"That's all, so I can scold you, that makes me even more dreadful," Debbie protested.

"No, you just like solving a riddle and giving me a scolding. Then you have to remember the making up part is really good. Girls have a guilty conscience. I always know two to three days afterward it is happy time," Bruce told her, walking over and handing PJ to her and kissing her on the head.

"I'm going to check the last UAV flight to make sure our friends stay away. Then I'm going to walk the property and just look around. Nancy, Angela and Stephanie will be here soon so you can make the list. Remember, I'm going out tomorrow to see if we can thin the blues. We will be on horseback, I want Danny, Jake and Conner, you can come if you want. I want seven on the patrol so two can stay with the horses if we dismount," Bruce told her and did not need to name Buffy. His shadow always followed him.

At 1500, Debbie, Nancy, Stephanie and Angela were in Nancy's room around a card table working on the schedules for projects, guard duty, night duty and patrols. The group had been working for an hour not saying much to each other as they concentrated on the task. Nancy set down her pen and closed her laptop.

"Debbie, you have to tell me, how was it?" Nancy requested.

"Bruce and I just walked around the farm after the wedding, that's all," Debbie replied, looking around nervously.

"What are you talking about?" Nancy asked. "What's it like, the wave?" she clarified as Angela and Stephanie stopped working and looked up at her.

"I can't even describe it, Nancy," Debbie told her.

"When you came in, you looked like you were on the best drug ever made," Nancy said, probing for more information.

"It *is* like a drug, but this is the most dangerous drug," Debbie said, wanting Nancy to stop asking questions.

"Debbie come on, you're killing me," Nancy begged.

Debbie looked at the closest friend she had ever known. The want on Nancy's face made her give in. She could see what Bruce was talking about now. It was in Nancy's eyes, but there was something that would not let the wave out. That could not be said with the other two.

"Okay Nancy, I'll tell you about it. The reason I don't like talking about it is some parts of the wave are very scary. You can do things you can't believe. You feel like you are moving in slow motion but you're really moving fast. You can see better, feel things around you and detect smells that you never knew existed. I could smell fear, not that I couldn't see that they were afraid, but could smell fear and it is intoxicating. This is where the bad part comes in. If you don't keep the anger in check you will do things just to hurt for your pleasure. That will haunt you and eat away at you. That has not happened to me; it almost did but Bruce stopped me each time," Debbie told Nancy and made sure she understood.

Debbie continued on, closing her eyes, leaning her head back and reliving it. "Nancy, just remembering the wave is vivid; it's nothing like riding the wave, but shit it's good. You can't dwell on it long because you want to find the wave. That is the bad part."

"Bad part, how can that be bad? Debbie, you looked like you were heading to ecstasy just then," Nancy said with envy.

"I was," Debbie said. "Imagine if you did a horrible act and that act came back to haunt you like an LSD trip every time it crossed your mind."

"That would be bad," Nancy admitted.

"You have no idea. It'll drive you insane or you learn to live with it, which in my opinion is just as bad," Debbie said.

"You said it has never happened to you, so how do you know?" Nancy asked.

"What is said here stays here." Debbie looked at each woman as they nodded their heads in agreement.

"It has happened to Bruce. I don't know what or how and I'll never ask him," Debbie told them.

"How and why did he learn to live with it?" Stephanie asked.

"The how: I have no idea and don't want to know. The why: I asked him to leave the military," Debbie said. "I see it clearly now. Bruce volunteering for everything to find the wave to block the pain for something he did out of pleasure to chase the wave."

Debbie answered questions for twenty minutes then she told them she did not want to talk about it anymore; she was getting a headache. Nancy told her it was because she had missed lunch. Nancy got up and told Debbie she would bring her a snack, something to drink, and something for her headache. Before Nancy left, Angela said she would help her bring the stuff back and they left.

As they walked out, Stephanie just stared at Debbie in wonder. She admired this woman so much. Debbie was everything she wanted to be: brave, pretty, smart, mother and a total badass. Yet she was in love with Debbie's husband. The guilt was killing her and had been since she met Debbie. When Debbie spoke it scared her.

"What is it, Stephanie?" Debbie asked, rubbing her temples and feeling Stephanie look at her.

"I have something I want to tell you. If you want me to leave after I tell you, I understand and I'll leave," Stephanie told her. Stephanie started taking deep breaths, working herself up to tell Debbie her harbored secret.

"You're in love with Bruce," Debbie replied, looking at Stephanie who was still taking in deep breaths. Stephanie was taking a breath in when Debbie spoke and she held it, forgetting to let it out.

Shock spread across Stephanie's face. Debbie knew, but how could she?

"Let the breath out, Stephanie, before you pass out, baby," Debbie told her, patting her hand, and Stephanie let it out, seeing stars dance in front of her eyes.

"I'm sorry, I don't know why or how but I do. I will load up and leave tonight. Debbie? Please don't think too badly of me," Stephanie told her, fighting back tears. She had brought this on herself and she would reap the consequences. She would probably be dead tomorrow but at least Debbie knew.

"If you try to leave over something that stupid, I'll beat the shit out of you. Stephanie, you're more than a sister to me, just like Nancy. I love you more than I love members of my own family. You're caring, loving, and kind; those are your strong points but also your weak points. That and you are smarter than any ten people I know," Debbie told Stephanie, holding her hand.

"I'm in love with your husband. How can you love someone like that?" Stephanie asked.

"When I met you that first day and I saw you look at Bruce, I knew. I'm not goin' to lie, when I first saw you I did feel threatened, for about an hour. Here is this younger, gorgeous auburn-haired woman, with a perfect body. She's smart, successful and a joy to be around. I'm not going to lie to you, I did think about shooting you and saying it was an accident in that first hour. Then I got to know you and saw who you really are. Stephanie, you have a stripe of honor that is a mile wide. I've never seen that in a woman before or since," Debbie told her.

"You are much prettier than I am, Debbie," Stephanie stated and Debbie started laughing.

"Please, Stephanie, don't make me laugh, my stomach hurts too much," Debbie told her.

"I wasn't trying to make you laugh. Why won't you make me leave?" Stephanie asked.

"I tell you what, Stephanie, tonight come to my bedroom. I'll get out of bed and you can get in. Wake Bruce up and have sex with him. You have my permission and he'll be half asleep. It won't be bad, I promise. Don't worry about Bruce; he won't realize it's not me for a while," Debbie told Stephanie, watching shock spread over her face.

"Debbie I—I couldn't do that to you. Even if you said to, it would hurt you, then when Bruce found out it would kill him," Stephanie told her.

"I rest my case," Debbie said. "Stephanie, you're probably the only woman on the face of the earth I would trust to sleep naked with my husband. You will not do anything if it hurts someone you care about. You'll suffer so others won't."

Stephanie looked at Debbie, not understanding her. "Thank you, Debbie, for not letting me leave and for letting me come and stay here," Stephanie said, smiling.

"Stephanie, if Bruce would've been here, we would have come for you. Stephanie, you mean a lot to this family because you're a part of it," Debbie told her.

"Thank you, Debbie, I love you," Stephanie said, looking down at the table.

"I love you too, Stephanie, and don't feel bad about loving Bruce. He's the best of the best," Debbie told her.

Stephanie looked up at Debbie. "When I was in Bruce's group on the blue hunt he talked about the male psyche for three days. He said you knew more about boys than he does. I made notes if you want to see them."

Debbie started chuckling. "Well you've learned the first rule on boys. When you want to know something, get their mind on a task and their mouth will ramble on. How did it start?" she asked, holding her sore stomach and giggling.

"Mindy, the teenage girl from the gas station, she asked Bruce if guys thought she was ugly because of what happened to her. Bruce told her boys really don't care about the act. They care about her being hurt but they don't think less of her for being raped," Stephanie said.

Debbie sat up. "Bruce has never gone over this with me. Keep going."

"I wrote it all down so you—" Stephanie started as Debbie held up her hand.

"How much did you write down?" Debbie asked her.

"All three days. Debbie, I will never make the mistake again of saying something about a boy's toy—" Stephanie stopped again as Debbie held up her hand.

"You mean to tell me you wrote down, from memory, the conversation that your group had over three days? How many pages?" Debbie asked with a look of amazement on her face.

"My handwritten notes are four hundred and seventeen pages, but the typed version is three hundred and seventy-four pages."

Debbie looked at Stephanie and a thought crossed her mind. "Stephanie, recite Bruce's speech last Sunday afternoon." Stephanie closed her eyes and recited Bruce's speech from last week. Debbie knew it was word for word because it held Bruce's attitude. Stephanie stopped speaking and opened her eyes as Debbie spoke. "Stephanie, you hold a true power. No man would argue with you with that memory. I want to read the notes but I would ask that no others do," Debbie said, still not believing what she had just heard.

"Don't worry, that's great information and it just can't be out in the open," Stephanie informed Debbie.

"You're able to do that with anyone? Just remember what they said and recite them?" Debbie asked her.

"Yeah, and I can remember where they were standing, who was sitting where and what they had on. Now once it gets a few weeks out, it does start to get fuzzy. That's why I have a journal so I can write down daily what happens," Stephanie replied in an offhand way.

"Stephanie, I have kept a journal since I was ten years old but it's only the highlights of the day's events, not a complete hour by hour dissertation of the day's events with accurate dialog," Debbie told her. Hearing Nancy and Angela coming down the hall, she said, "We'll talk later." The other two walked back into the room carrying drinks and food.

"Well, what have we figured out," Nancy asked as she and Angela set down the drinks and food on the table.

Debbie looked at Nancy and said, "Stephanie finally admitted she loves Bruce." Stephanie looked at Debbie in shock, not believing she had let out her secret.

"Thank God, I thought she was going to hold it in forever," Nancy said, sitting down. Stephanie jerked her head, looking at Nancy with a shocked expression. Nancy smiled at her and said, "Stephanie, everyone in this house, except Bruce, knows. It has been the topic of conversation many times here. I thought it was cute because the boys felt bad that they could not compete with a daddy with this hot, young woman."

Stephanie just looked at Nancy then to Debbie. Even the kids knew and they still loved her. She loved their daddy in a way more than a friend. Stephanie wanted to crawl under the bed and die.

Nancy could see that Stephanie was not dealing very well with it and spoke up. "Stephanie, let me tell you something. More than once Debbie has told me she trusts you implicitly. At first I was a little nervous with you here, when you first came to the farm, but after getting to know you, I realized you were too good of a person to hurt someone like Debbie. Debbie has told me before, she trusts you more than me around a naked Bruce. Not that the desire has ever crossed my mind but I have seen him naked a few times." Stephanie just stared at Nancy with her mouth open. Debbie had just told her the same thing.

Nancy mistook the look of shock. "We've been camping several times and the boys don't feel the need to cover up, baby," she clarified.

"No shit," Angela said, then looked at Debbie. "I want to ask you a question please."

Debbie looked skeptically at the small woman; she really didn't want to answer any more questions about the wave or fighting. Debbie had to admit she really liked Angela a lot and even loved her. This small woman had fought to defend her family and friends then proven herself a valuable asset to the family. Debbie finally nodded her head for the question.

Angela asked, "Did you take off running and screaming the first time you saw Bruce naked?"

The question caught Debbie off guard and she just started laughing, grabbing at her sore stomach muscles as Nancy joined in. Stephanie just stared at Angela.

"When did you see Bruce naked?" Stephanie asked with attitude.

"At the hospital and on the trip here," Angela told Stephanie, then looked at Debbie. "Well, did you?" she asked.

Debbie stopped laughing and replied, "No."

"Debbie, you're not much bigger than me. I can tell you, if I wouldn't have took off running, I would have shit twice and died," Angela informed her.

"Bruce was the first boy I ever saw naked, Angela. He was the one I played doctor and house with."

"That's what you had to compare the rest of the male population with?" Angela asked in disbelief.

"Bruce is the only man I have ever been with," Debbie replied.

"You have my utmost respect, Debbie. I would've chickened out," Angela replied and Nancy agreed with her.

Stephanie just looked at the women. They should not be talking about Bruce like that, and what was the big deal anyway? He was a boy; so what. Debbie saw the look on Stephanie's face. "Bruce is well-endowed, Stephanie," Debbie told her.

"That's no reason to run away," Stephanie replied, defending Bruce.

"The hell it isn't. Physics still plays a part in making love, girl," Angela told her smartly.

"Well Debbie didn't run so I think you are just exaggerating," Stephanie sassed back.

Debbie called the group back to order. "Ladies, we have a lot of work to do with a lot of people counting on us, so let's get this done."

The little group finished the list out for the next three weeks at 1900 and headed downstairs to eat. The laughter had done their souls good; it helped to hold back the grief and terror they all felt. Laughter was going to be scarce in the coming months and the memories would get them through some tough times ahead.

CHAPTER 17

It was 1700 the next afternoon when Bruce led his patrol home. They were all riding horses, which was the only reason they were alive. Several times the blues had tried to ambush them or charge them when the patrol ambushed them. Only with the horses did they stand a chance to pull back and cut the blues down.

Bruce adjusted little SCAR across his chest. He was sitting on his solid black Frisian stallion that was seventeen hands high. It was a war horse of old, and when he rode it, he felt like a knight riding off into battle. Bruce called his horse Nightmare. Several blues had found out that Nightmare was not afraid of them as he rode them down. When a ton of horse steps on you it tends to hurt and if he keeps doing it, you tend to die. One blue had tried to sneak up behind Nightmare only to be kicked in the chest and sent sailing ten yards. Nightmare let out a neigh that Bruce thought sounded like a laugh.

When they were a mile out from the farm Bruce called over the radio, "Base, Big Daddy One patrol returning, don't get trigger happy. Is the hunting team scoring yet?"

"This is Base, we see you Big Daddy One and are waiting on you. Hunting team is out and starting to score," Pam replied.

That morning Mike had dropped off nine people at a two-story house fifteen miles to the southwest. Then the group was put on the roof to see if they could thin the blues in that area.

Bruce's patrol had taken down almost two hundred since dawn when they left the farm. The groups were ranging in size from ten to fifty. Through the day, Mission Control would guide them to blues for them to hit. When the patrol opened up on them the blues would charge

226

them, only to be cut down, until the last group. The last group they had to chase down to kill them. While the patrol chased the blues, they kept roaring. It was only after Bruce and his patrol had taken them down that they were told by base that several groups of blues were heading to them. The pack they had chased had called for help and others had responded. That required thought, planning and worst of all communication; all that combined worried Bruce.

Leading his patrol into the farm towards the barn, Bruce stopped and watched his team get off their mounts. Buffy was riding a quarter horse the family had picked up for friends of the kids to ride when they came over.

Bruce climbed off his horse and spoke to everyone. "I want everyone to put your gear up and tend to your horse. If you don't know how, watch others and do what they do." Everyone took care of their horse then walked them to the field to feed them.

As Bruce walked to the house he could see the frame of the community building was already up as Debbie grabbed his hand. "I get the shower first, stud muffin," Debbie told him.

"That's not fair, sugar mama," Bruce told her.

"Well, you could take one with me but you can't boil me alive," Debbie replied, adjusting the pack on her back.

"I have to get clean, baby," Bruce told her.

"Clean yeah, not sterilize your body."

"Okay, you can have the shower first," Bruce said.

Debbie looked back at Danny and Matt. Debbie had put Matt on the patrol because she just wanted to see Danny and Matt together for herself. Matt always remained alert but would snatch quick glances at Danny and she would do the same. They were walking side by side now, talking to each other. Debbie could see they wanted to hold hands but did not want to give up the cover. If Bruce hadn't told her, Debbie still wouldn't have seen it. Now Debbie could see it plain as day. She leaned toward Bruce.

"They're so cute. They keep it very low key and I don't think they should. I wish we weren't the only ones who knew about them," Debbie told him.

"Yeah, they did very good today. Even in pitched battle they took care of business, and for teenagers in love that takes some doing. What do you mean we're the only ones who know?" Bruce said.

"Well, of course Jake and Mary, but I also meant them as well. Mary came running out of the house as soon as we rode in and I'm sure David knows," Debbie said.

"I was talking about Buffy," Bruce told her. Debbie stopped and looked at Bruce in shock.

Bruce saw the look and said, "No baby, she didn't see it. Danny told her and made her swear not to tell anyone."

"And Buffy told you?" Debbie asked.

"Hell no! I don't think she would tell me if she was dragged across hot coals. When we talked yesterday in the game room, she wouldn't look up. I knew then Danny had told her. I can also say Buffy will not tell Danny we know because Buffy will think Danny will blame her that we know," Bruce told Debbie.

"Bruce, we can't let the kids ever think that. It would really hurt Buffy's feelings," Debbie replied.

"That's why we aren't going to do anything. They will tell us when they're ready," Bruce told her.

Debbie started walking toward the house, a plan starting to form in her mind. Bruce could see the wheels turning in her mind. "Baby, please don't form some outlandish plan," Bruce begged her.

"Why not, I got you, didn't I?" Debbie pointed out.

"Well, yes you did," Bruce admitted, not able to argue that point.

"Does Stephanie know?" Debbie asked.

"Why in the world would she know?" Bruce asked.

"She sleeps in Mary's room with her," Debbie pointed out.

"Debbie, Stephanie is the smartest person I've ever met, but there is no way she'd see this. The kids know how close she is to you and Nancy so they wouldn't tell her," Bruce said.

"Stephanie is a lot like someone else in that matter," Debbie replied.

"Debbie, Stephanie is not in love with me. She might be infatuated with me but that's all," Bruce told her.

"Whatever," Debbie said, waving her hand.

"I almost slapped you just then. Debbie, you sounded just like Danny," said.

"Well, we learned it from you, so go and slap yourself," Debbie told him as they crossed the patio.

"Debbie, they will tell us. Give them time and don't force them," Bruce pleaded.

"I won't," Debbie promised as they walked inside.

The clan now ate in shifts; those that had already eaten were in the game and theater rooms. Bruce sat down in his chair, not really caring about eating; he just wanted to rest. He loved his horse but did not like smelling like him. Millie brought over plates for him and Debbie and sat them down in front of them.

Bruce looked up at Millie. "You don't have to serve us, Millie. I'm somewhat capable of getting my own food, as is Debbie," Bruce told her.

Millie just looked at him, hands on hips. "I know that, but in my kitchen I does what I want. If I wants to sit down and feed ya I wills, do I make myself clear?" Millie asked with iron in her voice.

Bruce pulled off his gloves and picked up his silverware replying, "Yes ma'am." Millie started back to the food line.

Mike, sitting in his chair at the opposite end, leaned forward. "I told her the same thing and she threatened to spank me with a wooden spoon. I don't believe most people but I think she would've done it," Mike told Bruce.

Millie yelled at Mike, "I hears you Michael, don't make me get my spoon."

"Yes ma'am," Mike replied to Millie then said to Bruce quietly, "See what I mean?"

"Shut up, Mike, before you get us in trouble," Bruce told him. He was not in the mood to get popped with a wooden spoon today. Millie brought the rest of the family plates of food and Danny was about to say something but Bruce shook his head no and Danny kept her mouth shut.

Millie walked over and filled Debbie's glass back up with tea and told her, "Girl, you needs to eat more if'n yous gonna hang with Bruce, going off to war."

Debbie just laughed. "I don't want to get fat, Bruce might not like me anymore."

"Girl, this boy thinks the sun rises just for you," Millie told her as she filled more glasses. "You can't weigh more than a hundred."

"I weigh a hundred and nineteen pounds," Debbie told Millie. Debbie did not like being reminded how small she was. Debbie pointed at Angela.

"I'm bigger than her." She sounded a lot like a teenager that had her feelings hurt.

"That's not saying much. Little Angela can't tip the scale no mores than ninety soaking wet. I don't knows how her little frame coulda had a baby as big as Cade," Millie replied.

Angela sat up, saying, "Well Debbie is a total badass. She can handle Bruce's big—" Angela stopped, looked at the kids around the table and just started eating.

Bruce blushing, changed the subject. "Mike, how was the hunting team doing?"

"They're getting some good kills but the blues don't advance until they turn on the radio," Mike answered. Jake had rigged up a radio to play recorded voices and screams that the hunt team had put in a car with the windows rolled down. The team could operate it with a remote control.

"I don't like it. Those fuckers are getting smarter," Bruce said, taking a bite.

Stephanie spoke up. "Bruce, they're following predictable animal behavior. I feel they will end up at the level of chimps. Chimps are some of the most aggressive hunters in the world."

"I know that, Stephanie, but chimps take years to learn hunting tactics that these assholes are learning in months," Bruce told her.

"Bruce, the higher areas of the brain are dead. They will learn to use bludgeoning weapons like chimps but the areas that make us human with complex thought are dead. In successive generations they might get that back. Since this is the result of genetic manipulation instead of hundreds of thousands of years, it might only take thousands," Stephanie said.

"Well, now we know we have to exterminate them from the planet. Once they can fight like us, we're screwed," Bruce replied.

"Bruce, we have to exterminate them anyway. They see us as competition and will try to kill us. Infected might be scared of us but they will still try to kill us. I can see now that they hate us, and animals are not supposed to have emotion. When they attack us, you can see and feel the hate they have for us. Other scientists would laugh at me for saying that. But that's what I feel," Stephanie told him, expecting Bruce to laugh at her for saying something so stupid.

"Stephanie, I'm proud of you. You followed your gut feeling and you're right, they hate us. This is going to be a battle of the species. Not only do we have to worry about blues, but also other humans—I use that term loosely—that want to rule us," Bruce told her and she smiled at the compliment.

The group made small talk and got updates on construction from Paul. Then Bruce and Mike went to sit in the theater room in their recliners. Debbie kissed Bruce and told him she was going to take a shower. Bruce and Mike played with the kids for an hour until Buffy came down and told Bruce that Mama wanted him upstairs. Buffy said she was to watch the twins and PJ and had to bring them up in thirty minutes.

Bruce smiled as he took off to the kitchen to grab his weapon then headed upstairs, unbuckling his vest. Walking into the bedroom, he saw Debbie on the bed, drying her hair with a towel. Bruce started shedding clothes. "Thirty minutes, baby? I still have to take a shower. I can't be snuggling up to you smelling like a horse," Bruce told her, stripping in record time and heading to the shower.

"Hold on, stud muffin, I want to talk to you," Debbie told Bruce as he looked at her in disbelief. Upon seeing his expression, Debbie asked, "Do you always think about getting some lovin' from me?"

"Pretty much, yeah," Bruce replied honestly.

"Okay, I want you to turn that part of your brain off and listen," Debbie told him. Bruce did not like that when it was directed at him. Debbie just smiled then said, "Stephanie is goin' to start sleeping in here with us."

Bruce just looked at her, stunned to the core. Then he replied, "I'm not enough for you anymore?"

"I'm going to ignore that. Now listen. The kids will be able to spend more time together now and will want to bring their relationships out into the open. I told Stephanie I wanted her to sleep with us to help with the kids. You and I are always goin' out on patrols and needed a little help but she bought it. Well, what do ya think of my plan?" Debbie asked.

"Baby, even the thought of you bringing another woman to our bed is intriguing. I'm not all that thrilled. I've known you almost my whole life so I can mark 'that' off. I asked you that once and I got popped with a little fist and yes it hurt. Now, I will have to fight more for my spot to sleep in. The twins, PJ and you think I'm part of the bed and y'all have to lay on me. Now there is another grown up to battle. Can I just sleep on the floor?" Bruce asked her, a little irritated.

"It's a good plan," Debbie told him with a pout. Bruce could see sadness spread across her face. He wanted to tell her that the plan wouldn't work because it left too much to chance and had no direction.

But looking at her expression, Bruce said, "It's a good plan, baby." He felt like the biggest sissy in the world but he couldn't disappoint her.

Debbie ran over and kissed him. "Hurry and get in the shower, baby," she told him and he went to the bathroom. Watching Bruce close the door, Debbie smiled; she had found a way to start her preparations without making Bruce suspicious.

Several minutes later, Debbie heard a knock at the door. She opened it to see Stephanie standing there and Debbie motioned her in. Stephanie was wearing a flannel pajamas and fluffy socks. Debbie pulled her over to Bruce's dresser.

"Hurry, take off those pajamas and socks. Bruce and the kids put off enough heat and if Bruce feels socks touch him he wakes up," Debbie told her.

"Debbie, this is too weird. Let me sleep on the floor," Stephanie whispered to her.

"Stephanie, I told you the kids won't bond with you if we don't do this. They have to trust you if something happens to me and Bruce. They have to have someone there for them. Aren't you going to help me with the kids?" Debbie asked her.

"Yes Debbie, but this is still very weird," Stephanie replied as she took off her pajamas and put on the t-shirt and a pair of Bruce's boxers. When she put on the t-shirt she could smell Bruce and thought this might not be so bad. Then she put on Bruce's boxers. Stephanie had always wanted to wear them. All the girls in the family wore them, except her; even Nancy and Angela wore them.

Buffy brought the twins and PJ to the room and put PJ on the bed. Buffy looked at Stephanie in Daddy's t-shirt and boxers and drew her eyebrows together. Debbie, upon seeing Buffy's reaction, kneeled beside her.

"Buffy, Stephanie is going to sleep in here now so the girls and PJ will accept her into the family. If something happens to me, you, or Daddy, they have to know someone is here for them," Debbie told her.

Relief flooded over Buffy's face. "That's good thinking, Mama," she said, then looked at Stephanie to give her some advice. "Don't get on

Daddy's pillow or he might roll on top of you, and whatever you do, don't wear socks to bed. Daddy yells out 'caterpillars' and wakes up kicking the covers. He really freaks out."

Stephanie laughed. "Thank you, Buffy."

Buffy headed off to Danny's room as Debbie got the twins and PJ ready for bed.

"Stephanie, you're in the middle. You are going to have to lay claim to your spot. PJ likes playing with my hair during the night, so don't freak out if he does the same to you. The twins take turns who they snuggle up to during the night," Debbie told Stephanie as she pulled the covers back. PJ was crawling from one side of the bed to the other and laughing at his game.

Bruce came out of the bathroom in his boxers as Stephanie and Debbie made room between the twins, giving PJ obstacles to crawl over. Bruce walked over to Stephanie, grabbing her legs and pulling her socks off. "When I feel socks touch me in my sleep, it freaks me out," Bruce told her.

"Sorry Bruce," Stephanie said, but Bruce was not paying attention as he looked at PJ.

"Not as much as getting peed on. Let me tell you, buster, if you hit me with that damn bottle in the morning, I'll flush you down the toilet," Bruce told PJ. PJ just squealed and held out his hand, palm up, and closed his fingers like he was saying "I will crush you like a bug."

"That does it, you sleep in the dresser tonight," Bruce said, moving toward PJ.

Stephanie grabbed PJ and put him on the other side of her, taking Bruce seriously, "Bruce, you can't put the baby in the dresser." Stephanie told him as PJ blew raspberries at him, taunting him to try something now.

Bruce just got in the bed, turning his back to everyone. Stephanie rolled over with her back to Bruce, lying PJ down next to her as Debbie put a bottle in his mouth. Stephanie rubbed PJ's head as he drank his bottle. Looking up from PJ, Stephanie saw the twins and Debbie looking at her. Stephanie reached out and played with the twins' hair. The twins at first moved back but then moved closer and drifted off to sleep as PJ dropped his bottle, fast asleep. Bruce was already asleep and breathing softly.

Debbie and Stephanie were the only ones awake when Stephanie looked at Debbie and smiled. Then Stephanie felt the heat radiate from

Bruce and could actually feel sweat on her back. Stephanie felt PJ start playing with her hair in his sleep and it made her smile.

Debbie whispered, "Not so bad, is it?"

"No, it's not but I think there is a fire over here. Bruce puts off heat like a furnace," Stephanie whispered back.

"Told ya. Just kick the covers off or you're going to sweat to death. Later tonight everyone will be over there by the fire," Debbie told her.

"I can't kick the covers off then Bruce won't have any on him," Stephanie pointed out.

"You're going to sweat to death then," Debbie whispered back, smiling.

Gritting her teeth, Stephanie took the heat for another few minutes before she kicked the blankets off. She felt the t-shirt sticking to her back and wished she'd kicked the blanket off when Debbie told her to. Just then Bruce rolled over, throwing his arm over her. Stephanie's body became rigid as she looked at Debbie, who was laughing silently.

"Don't worry, Stephanie, he only bites once or twice during the night," Debbie said matter-of-factly as Stephanie eyes widened. "I'm only kidding, Stephanie," Debbie admitted as Stephanie relaxed.

Bruce pulled Stephanie to his chest. Stephanie looked up at Debbie like a little school girl, grinning and blushing. Debbie just smiled at Stephanie then became serious. "You will take care of them if something happens to me, won't you?"

"Nothing is going to happen to you, Debbie," Stephanie assured her.

"Please, will you help take care of them if something does happen?" Debbie asked her again.

"Yes I will, Debbie. I will love them and protect them with my life," Stephanie replied, stroking the face of each child.

Debbie drifted off to sleep with a weight lifted off her shoulders. The beginning of her preparation was in place. Stephanie never caught on what was really being asked of her, thinking only of the small kids in front of her as she too drifted off to sleep.

CHAPTER 18

Stephanie woke up upon hearing a hollow thunk-thunk followed by a baby giggling. Struggling to open her eyes, she felt heat on her left side, weight on her legs and abdomen, and something wedged under her right side. Lifting up her head, Stephanie felt something hit her on top of her head. Turning to the source of the assault, she saw PJ sitting between her and Bruce, taking turns hitting them on the head with an empty bottle and laughing.

"Stop that PJ," Stephanie said, but PJ just hit Bruce again and laughed. Stephanie extracted an arm out and took the empty bottle from PJ. Immediately, PJ told her he wanted his drumstick back and Stephanie handed it back to him. She was rewarded with a whack to the head.

"I'm going to throw you on the floor, PJ," Stephanie warned him. PJ didn't care; he dropped the bottle and started clapping.

Stephanie looked down to her belly and saw both twins lying across her. Turning her head, she saw Debbie had burrowed under her right side. Stephanie pulled her body out of the tangle of humanity, crawling out of bed. She reached back, picked up PJ and saw the clock read 0432.

"Come on, I will get you another bottle," Stephanie told PJ, who laid his head on her shoulder, making her smile.

Heading to the door, Stephanie's body felt like she had run a triathlon. She realized she hurt in places she never knew existed as she walked downstairs into the kitchen. The ladies were already starting breakfast when she walked in holding PJ.

"That was nice of ya to get PJ so Bruce and Debbie could gets some sleep," Millie told Stephanie, handing her a bottle for PJ.

"Didn't have much of a choice, he was assaulting everyone with an empty bottle," Stephanie replied, taking the bottle and putting it in PJ's mouth. PJ started gulping down the bottle.

"Don't let him fill up on tha bottle Stephanie. Here's some foods you can feed him," Lynn told her, putting a plate on the counter. Stephanie took the bottle out of PJ's mouth, set it on the counter and handed him a biscuit.

"Stephanie, you hafta break it up first," Millie told her, grabbing the biscuit from PJ. "Did ya change him yet?"

"No, am I supposed to? He's a boy," Stephanie pointed out.

Millie laughed. "Yes baby, it's okay. Let me gets some stuff for us and I'll shows you how." Millie left and returned with supplies. She took PJ from Stephanie and he immediately started crying upon having his meal interrupted. She laid him on the table. Stephanie grabbed the bottle and shoved it in his mouth to make him shut up. This made Millie laugh. "It's okay for him to be cryin," Millie told her.

"Not with the way my head feels," Stephanie told Millie as she learned how to change a diaper. "Is that normal? Feces is not supposed to look and smell like that," Stephanie said, leaning back and wrinkling her nose.

"It's just baby poop, Stephanie," Millie told her. Stephanie looked unconvinced and made a mental note to ask Nancy since she was a pediatrician. Millie picked up PJ and handed him back to Stephanie. "Ain't you never been around babies befoe?"

"No, but I have read some books and they said nothing about nuclear waste coming out of their rectum," Stephanie said as she took the bottle from PJ and tried to feed him a spoonful of eggs.

Millie giggled at her. "Let me shows you, baby." She took the spoon and mashed up the biscuit, grits, and eggs together. Then, putting a little bit of food on the spoon, Millie handed it to Stephanie.

"That's disgusting, Millie," Stephanie told her, taking the spoon and raising it to PJ's mouth. PJ opened his mouth and emptied the spoon. Stephanie gave a shudder. "Your food selections should remain separate from each other and only be mixed together in your stomach."

Lynn laughed at her. "It'd take too long to feed a baby that ways, Stephanie."

Stephanie took the spoon and continued to shovel the food into PJ's mouth. PJ cooperated some but in ten minutes they were both covered in the mashed-up food. Mike and Nancy came in wearing workout clothes and carrying their vests and weapons. Nancy looked at Stephanie feeding PJ and noticed her wearing Bruce's t-shirt and boxers.

"About time you joined this family. Bruce's boxers make great pajama bottoms," Nancy told her.

Mike looked at Nancy. "You could wear my briefs, baby."

"I wear your t-shirts but your briefs cut into me," Nancy told him, making Mike laugh.

"I think I'm fixing to start wearing Bruce's boxers too," Mike replied.

"Mike, I have tried to get you to wear boxers for the last seven years. I would feel better about wearing my own husband's underwear but a girl has to stay comfortable," Nancy replied, grabbing a cup of coffee and heading to the back door to the gym.

Stephanie stopped Nancy as she started to open the door. "Nancy, I think something is wrong with PJ."

Nancy spun around, throwing her gear on the table and moving quickly to Stephanie. "What's wrong with PJ?" Nancy asked, feeling over his body.

"I think he has a gastrointestinal malformation. Feces should not look or smell like that coming out of a human. We need to run some tests on him," Stephanie told her in a serious voice.

Nancy laughed and began picking food out of Stephanie's hair. "I've looked PJ over and he's fine. Those are normal bowel movements for an infant." Stephanie just looked at Nancy as she grabbed her stuff and headed to the gym.

Stephanie continued the feeding process as those in the den and hallway woke up and headed to the gym for morning workouts. Bruce and Debbie came into the kitchen and were greeted with the sight of Stephanie trying to feed PJ. Bruce walked over to get PJ from Stephanie but PJ refused to come to him. Shocked, Bruce stared at him, this being the first time PJ had refused to come to him unless it was Debbie holding him.

"That does it, you sleep with the goats tonight, buddy," Bruce threatened. PJ just laid his head on Stephanie's shoulder for protection from the mean man.

Stephanie snapped at Bruce, "Bruce, you leave him alone or I will let him beat you to death with his bottle tomorrow." Bruce took a step back as PJ laughed and hugged Stephanie.

Bruce grabbed his stuff and walked out, afraid to say anything. Debbie started laughing. "That was good, Stephanie. Give PJ to me so you can go get cleaned up."

"No, I'll feed the twins; you go and work out. I will work out after breakfast," Stephanie told her.

Debbie walked over and hugged her and PJ. "I knew you were right for this. We'll rotate every morning on who gets up with the kids, okay? I never heard PJ or I would've gotten up."

"I heard him beating Bruce with the bottle and when I told him to stop he popped me," Stephanie admitted.

"When he does that to you, Stephanie, you need to pop his hand," Debbie told her.

"He's just a baby," Stephanie replied, shocked.

"A baby who was told to stop and hit you for telling him to stop. Babies have to learn to listen. I did not say hit him hard, just take his bottle away and lightly pop his hand. If that doesn't work, put him on the floor and let him cry so he knows he did something bad. He will get bigger, Stephanie, and he has to learn to listen to what we tell him."

"Does he stop when Bruce tells him to?" Stephanie asked.

"When Bruce uses his Daddy voice, he does. I have to pop his hand. In all fairness, when Bruce uses his Daddy voice toward the kids, I almost do what he says. Don't tell him that though. That doesn't work for Mamas unless we get mad," Debbie told her as the twins walked in and sat down at the table.

"Okay I will. Now go, I can take care of this," Stephanie said as she grabbed plates for the twins. Debbie grabbed her weapon and vest and headed off to the gym.

At 0610, Bruce walked back in and saw Stephanie at the table with the kids. He leaned over, kissing the twins then Stephanie and PJ on the head. Then Bruce walked into Mission Control to find Mike looking at the large monitor that was hooked up for the UAVs. He could see the hunting team on top of the house with infected several hundred yards away in the woods surrounding the house.

"What the hell is going on now?" Bruce asked.

Mike looked at Bruce. "The team leader said they'd killed about a thousand then the blues started hanging back. They have tried attacking from different directions at different times looking for a weakness. The team reported another fifty to sixty kills during each attack, but now the blues are just hanging around the perimeter in the woods," Mike told him.

"Shit, the blues are putting them under siege. There have to be a couple of hundred around the perimeter," Bruce said in disgust.

"It's worse. The blues are calling for reinforcements. Look," Mike told Bruce as the UAV operator panned out with the camera. Several small groups of blues were moving in to join the siege.

"We can use that for later, letting them call more to us, but for right now the hunt team only has enough food for two more days." Bruce told Mike as he closed his eyes to think of a plan.

"Let's just go in, get the team, and lay out an ambush," Mike offered.

"Won't work, the blues will be able to spread out and could outflank the ambush team. How many do you think will be there by 0900?" Bruce asked.

"With what's there now and with the rate others are joining, I'd guess about five, maybe six hundred," Mike answered.

"That's manageable. Get dressed, I'll lay out my plan at breakfast," Bruce told him while opening a filing cabinet and grabbing a ziplock bag. Then he headed upstairs.

Bruce jumped into the shower, washing and shaving quickly then got out to dry off. He was standing in front of the shower drying off as Stephanie walked in leading the twins and holding PJ. Stephanie looked up and gasped, taking a step back.

"Sorry Bruce, I was just fixing to get the kids cleaned up," Stephanie replied, looking down at the floor, Bruce never stopped dying off.

"Well go ahead, Stephanie, don't mind me," Bruce told her, grabbing his boxers off the counter before walking out of the bathroom.

Bruce put on his underwear as he headed to the closet. Throwing clothes on the bed, Bruce heard the sink in the bathroom come on. Bruce stopped and looked toward the open bathroom door as Debbie walked in. Debbie, seeing Bruce looking at the bathroom, asked, "What?"

"The sink is on," Bruce told her.

"Well you're a big boy now, you can turn it off all by yourself," Debbie told him.

Bruce headed to the bathroom, replying, "I think Stephanie is trying to wash the twins and PJ in the sink."

"She wouldn't do that. The twins are four years old," Debbie replied, following him.

When they reached the bathroom, Stephanie was washing the twins off with a rag. They still had their sleeping t-shirts on. Stephanie was washing only exposed skin, nothing that was covered up by clothes.

Bruce spoke first. "Why aren't you putting them in the shower, Stephanie?"

"They can take a shower?" Stephanie asked with relief.

"Yeah, with you helping 'em," Bruce told her.

"I'll get my clothes wet," Stephanie replied.

"Then take them off or hang them up to dry out," Bruce told her.

Debbie started pushing Bruce back. "Go get dressed, I'll meet you downstairs." Debbie pushed Bruce out and kicked off her shoes as she closed the door. Debbie stripped down as Stephanie watched, turning the twins around. Debbie walked over and started stripping the girls before looking at Stephanie.

"What?" Debbie asked.

"Debbie, you're naked in front of the kids," Stephanie told her.

"Stephanie, you've seen me naked before," Debbie told her.

"I'm a woman, though," Stephanie told her.

"Stephanie, these are our kids. We're not perverts, so what's the big deal? Didn't you take a shower with your mama or your brother?" Debbie asked as she stripped PJ.

"I've never taken a shower or a bath with anyone in my entire life," Stephanie admitted.

Debbie stared at her in disbelief then she said, "Arms up," as she grabbed Stephanie's shirt, pulling it over her head. "You sleep in a bra?" Debbie asked, not believing her eyes.

"Yeah, don't you?" Stephanie replied.

"Stephanie, I only own two bras to wear with dresses. I only wear sports bras. I would love to meet the asshole that invented the damn things so I could beat the shit out of 'im. Now take it off, we don't have a lot of time," Debbie said as she grabbed the boxers and panties Stephanie was wearing and pulled them down. Stephanie covered herself as Debbie moved to the shower and turned on the water.

Stephanie took off her bra, covering her breasts with one arm. The other hand was covering her crotch as Debbie turned to tell the girls to get in. "Stephanie, quit being modest. You're a doctor after all, and now you are also a mom. Now get PJ," Debbie said as she ushered the twins into the shower.

Stephanie watched how Debbie was acting and reached down, grabbing PJ and stepping into the shower. Debbie showed her how to wash the kids in an assembly line fashion, making sure to keep soap out of their eyes. In twenty minutes, everyone was showered and drying off in the bathroom. They dressed the girls and PJ then themselves and headed to the kitchen.

Bruce saw them coming and stood up and called for attention. "Okay, everyone, it's 0700 and we have a lot to do. The hunt team is surrounded and the blues have them under siege now. Danny, Matt, Jake, Steve, Mary, David, Debbie, and Nancy, we're going to wipe out the blues around the team. Mike, you'll run the operation from here. The reason all of you are coming is that you have hunted on the horses before. I want ammo, water, and one meal only. I want everyone to have at least thirty extra magazines in saddle bags and another bag to drop empty magazines into on your saddle. Buffy, you will ride with me." Bruce stopped and looked at the group then started again.

"We're going to attack the edges with hit and run, then pull back and engage at a distance. Team one will be me, Danny, David, and Jake. Debbie, you have the rest in team two. Steve, I want you to carry a SAW for team two and I will carry one for team one. We'll be moving all day on horseback so be ready. Work will continue here. Conner, you'll get people to man the two Strykers and the Beast for back up and extraction of the hunt team. Mike has overall command from Mission Control. Questions?" Bruce finished.

Conner raised his hand and Bruce nodded to him. "Why can't I be on one of the teams?" he asked.

"You aren't ready to ride like I need you to. Everyone here has thousands of hours on horseback, plus they've all hunted from horseback. We'll be moving fast and the horses will be jumping. I would really like to keep you around," Bruce informed him and he agreed with Bruce.

Bruce looked around for more questions as Bill asked from the den, "Why not just go and get the team with the vehicles?"

"The blues will follow us back. The blues are calling other blues to the site like they're bringing in reinforcements. I don't want them to follow us back here. Then we would have to go into the woods on foot to wipe them out. In close proximity and in numbers they have the edge, brute force. We have to fight on our terms, unless we have no alternative," Bruce replied, waiting on other questions. When none came, he continued. "Mike, I want you to get four people plus Bill to act as a defense team here at the farm. Everything else moves forward, people, we have to get this place ready. Now teams will meet at the barn at 0800. Get your gear and let's go hunting," Bruce told everyone, then leaned over to Stephanie, pulling out the plastic bag with several flash drives.

"Stephanie, I need you to go over this for me. It's about how to refine oil and a schematic for a small scale refinery. See if I'm at least close with what I have, okay. Will you do that for me?" Bruce asked her.

"You know I will, Bruce. You don't even have to ask, just tell me what you want me to do," Stephanie told him, taking the plastic bag away from PJ. Bruce kissed her on the cheek and headed to the basement to grab two SAWs for him and Steve. Those not going out on patrol went to work as the teams went to grab gear and ammo.

Bruce met the teams and found someone had already pulled the horses to the barn. Buffy was just looking up at his horse Nightmare with wide eyes. Nightmare was looking at Buffy waiting for her to do something, like give him a treat. Nightmare lowered his head to smell Buffy to see if he could find the treats. Bruce walked up to Buffy and Nightmare.

"He is lookin' for treats," Bruce told Buffy, handing her a carrot. Buffy held the carrot in the palm of her hand like she was taught and Nightmare ate it in one bite. Buffy reached up and petted his head while he chewed the carrot.

Bruce walked over to Steve, giving him one of the SAW's and a thousand rounds. "Only use it when they attack in groups and take out their legs," Bruce told him.

"I got it Dad," Steve said as he put on his saddle. Then he turned to Bruce saying, "Who would have dreamed we would be using assault weapons from horseback?"

"Not me," Bruce admitted as he went to saddle Nightmare.

When Bruce finished, he turned to Buffy. "We'll put your M-4 in the saddle holster. Keep your P90 across your chest. You'll be riding Nightmare and he's not like the horse you've ridden. He is gentle but wants to play a lot so hold the reins tight. I'm tying you to me with a belt so you won't fall off," Bruce told Buffy as he lifted her onto the saddle giving her the reins. Buffy just nodded at him.

Once everyone was mounted, Bruce climbed into his saddle and put a belt through the back of her vest and through the front of his. Bruce had his SCAR on his right side with the SAW across his back.

"Let's go," Bruce said as he squeezed his legs and Buffy steered Nightmare to the front gate. When they were on the road, Bruce radioed Mike.

"Which side has the fewest?" Bruce asked.

"The east side," Mike called back.

"Call the hunt team and tell them they are not to shoot toward the east at all," Bruce told him.

"Already did that. I told the team leader I would call out directions he could not shoot in. Who do you think you left in charge?" Mike snapped back.

"Sorry, boss," Bruce called back as he kicked Nightmare into a trot.

When the group was less than two miles away and they could hear the roars ahead of them, Bruce told Buffy to stop. Bruce pulled out his map before leading the team toward the house. The house sat in a field off the highway with trees several hundred yards away in any direction.

There was a field to the east side behind the blues, but he would have to move through a mile of trees to engage the blues. Bruce headed to the field, taking dirt roads and logging trails forming his plan of attack. When they reached the field, he called everyone close.

"Alright, I'm going to stir up trouble. Team two, form a firing line here directly across from the tree line and mow them down when they come out. This field is about a hundred and fifty yards across and two miles long, just watch your flanks. Team one will form up on the north side of the field. This'll put us in an L-shaped ambush. Once the blues get within twenty yards, we head north to the crossroad and will set up again. Let me tell all of y'all, if you fall off your horse you'll probably die. If you fall, call out fast. The closest person is to grab you and the attack is off. We leave then head back to the farm and I'll call out the backup force. Please don't shoot me when I come out. I will not be able to get Nightmare to run in the woods but we'll be able to gallop. The horses move faster in the woods than the blues can. Once I hit the field, I'm heading to my team. Team two, it's your job to keep my ass clear until I join my team," Bruce told them.

They all said they understood and Bruce headed to the tree line on the other side of the field as Mike came over the radio. "Bruce, the trees there have a large canopy. We're only catching glimpse of the blues. I won't be able to tell you how close you are," Mike said.

"We're good. Just don't let the blues circle the ambush site," Bruce said, reaching the far fence then kicked Nightmare into a run. As they reached the fence, Bruce squeezed his knees, telling Nightmare to jump.

Nightmare leaped into the air, clearing the fence and landing on the other side, Buffy pulled back on the reins, slowing him down. Nightmare shook his head, snorting about having to stop. Bruce leaned forward to whisper to Buffy.

"That was good, BB. Now wrap the reins around your wrist. If we need to jump something, yell at me so I can signal Nightmare to jump. When we find the blues, we are going to have to move fast. Watch the ground for holes and logs. If we lose our ride, we can't climb a tree that fast. When we find them turn Nightmare around. Don't wait for me to tell you, I'm liable to be busy. Try to take the path out that we take in," Bruce told her.

Buffy looked back wrapping the reins around her wrist and said, "Don't worry Daddy, I got this."

Buffy guided the horse through the trees. About a hundred yards in the smell hit them like a hammer. Nightmare let out a snort and Bruce leaned forward, slapping his neck to let him know to be quiet. They continued at a walk and the roars were getting closer. Bruce could feel Nightmare tighten up under him the closer they got to the roars.

A blue jumped out from behind a tree ten yards to his right, letting out a roar. Nightmare reared up, neighing. Bruce kicked his feet to get the horse down as he lowered his weapon, flipping the switch to full auto. Just when his sight rested on the blue, Nightmare's front feet hit the ground and Buffy wheeled away from the blue, heading back to the field.

Bruce squeezed the trigger, sending half a dozen rounds into the dirt behind the blue, who was now charging. Bruce swung around in the saddle to shoot the blue. As his rifle came across he just squeezed the trigger, seeing the blue less than five yards from them. The first rounds hit the blue in the shoulder, turning him, and Bruce walked the impacts across his chest up to his head. When the first round hit the blue in the face, Nightmare jumped forward into a run, catching Bruce off guard.

Bruce fell backwards, pulling Buffy back and causing her to pull the reins, stopping the horse.

The blue dropped beside the horse as Bruce scooted back into the saddle and Buffy started kicking Nightmare to go. Through the trees behind them, Bruce could see blues moving through the trees toward them. He changed magazines, dropping the empty one into a canvas feed bag on the saddle.

Nobody had told Nightmare that he couldn't run full speed through the woods because he was weaving in and out through the trees, almost taking Bruce's arm off on one. Just as Bruce was getting ready to tell Buffy to slow down, a blue jumped out in front of them. Nightmare never slowed and just plowed over it, churning the body under his hooves.

"Slow down some, Buffy," Bruce yelled.

"I can't, I'm pulling back on the reins and your stupid horse isn't listening," Buffy yelled back as a branch hit her in the face.

Bruce leaned to the side and saw Nightmare had the bit in his teeth. Bruce reached around with his left hand to yank the bit out of his teeth and saw the fence fast approaching. When Nightmare was within five feet, Bruce squeezed his knees, praying that the stupid horse would listen.

Nightmare felt the command and leaped into the air. They cleared the barbwire fence by five feet and flew another twenty. Nightmare landed and continued in a full gallop, churning up huge clumps of dirt, throwing them up in the air.

Bruce yanked the reins, pulling the bit out of the horse's teeth, making him slow down. Buffy turned to their team now that she had control again. Bruce turned around in the saddle and saw blues jumping the fence behind them. He raised big SCAR and fired off a grenade. The grenade did not hit anything but it did make the blues pause, letting them open up the distance.

Halfway across the field, Bruce heard team two open up as he reloaded another grenade. Buffy lead Nightmare to the end of the line their team had formed and spun the horse around. They were turning around when the rest of his team opened up on the blues pouring out of the tree line.

Once Bruce was facing the field he was reminded of the World War One movies of the troops running at the machine gun nest. The field was covered with blues running at both lines. He raised his rifle up switching to burst and started working with those closest to him, yelling for Buffy to watch the sides.

Feeling his bolt lock, Bruce just dropped the magazine, ramming in another one. Lining up the sight, he started squeezing off bursts. He yelled for Buffy to call over the radio to tell everyone not to worry about keeping the empty magazines now. Bruce dropped another magazine, replaced it and raised the rifle up. He saw a group of ten close together heading toward them and squeezed the trigger on the 203, putting a grenade right in front of them. Those in the front fell, making those behind trip over them.

Bruce started squeezing off bursts at the closest blues who were now less than fifty yards away, but he did not see more coming out of the tree line. Bruce just kept dropping empty magazines and firing until he had no more targets. Jake in the middle of the line was still shooting the wounded blues in the field.

Unbuckling from Buffy, Bruce dropped to the ground, picking up magazines, not remembering firing that many. Bruce put them in his bag and moved to each person and did the same for them as Mike came over the radio.

"You have really pissed 'em off now. The south and west groups are attacking the hunting team, but the north side is coming for you. The front edge will be to you in a few minutes. It's at least double what you just took out," Mike told him.

"Will they come out in the same area?" Bruce asked as he finished picking up the last of the magazines.

"No, this group will come out even with your group," Mike said as Bruce jumped back behind Buffy, buckling her to him.

"Team one, spread out in a forward firing line. Team two, swing down in a slanted firing line. We'll just reverse the L," Bruce told the group.

Bruce dropped big SCAR, letting it hang by its sling as he pulled the SAW off his back. He grabbed another two-hundred-round belted box and sat it in front of Buffy. Buffy turned around, undoing the belt, looking at Bruce. "Let me get behind you, Daddy. I'm going to sit looking backwards so they can't come behind us."

Before Bruce could answer, Buffy was sliding around behind him, feeding the belt through the back of his vest, attaching herself to him.

Bruce just grabbed the reins as Mike called out the distance over the radio. Then he yelled ten seconds.

Bruce looked at the tree line to see blues jumping the fence in a dead run. He raised the SAW and started firing low to clip the legs. The blues started falling as the bullets hit their legs. They did get back up but they were not running. Feeling the bolt slam forward, Bruce opened the feed tray, pulled the bolt back and placed in another two-hundred-round belt. He slammed the cover down and continued firing again as he heard Buffy start to fire her submachine gun from behind him then yell over the radio, "Mama, behind you!" Buffy screamed.

Glancing at the other team fifty yards away, Bruce saw four blues coming across the road behind them. One member of team two turned to take out the rear attack and Bruce turned back around and opened up on the advancing blues coming across the field.

Bruce felt Buffy moving behind him and he yelled, "Are more coming from behind us?"

"No!" she yelled back, still moving.

"Be still, you're throwing my aim off!" Bruce yelled at her.

"I'm getting a real gun, damn it, screw this little one!" Buffy yelled out, trying to pull out her M-4 from the scabbard on the saddle.

Bruce reached down, undoing the weapon for her, and Buffy pulled it out. Letting her P90 hang from its sling, Buffy raised her M-4 up, looking for targets. Bruce settled down to reengage the blues in the field as he heard Buffy open up with the M-4. Bruce turned around, watching a naked blue woman drop thirty yards behind them.

Buffy yelled at him, "Quit moving, these are mine back here, you shoot your own!"

Mike called over the radio, "More coming from behind you, looks like about twenty."

Bruce hit the voice switch and opened up on the blues in the field. "Thanks for the hot tip. How did ya miss those?" Bruce asked, taking out the legs of the runners.

Mike did not reply back as Bruce put another belt in the SAW and started firing again. Behind him Bruce could hear Buffy yelling at the blues coming out of the tree line behind them. When the SAW ran dry, Bruce opened the cover.

"Buffy, you need help?" Bruce asked her as he put in another belt.

Buffy hit the voice button on her radio and continued to fire, "I got these bitches, Daddy."

Bruce could not help but chuckle as he closed the feed cover. Smoke was pouring off the barrel as he raised the SAW up and started firing. Bruce said a little prayer that the barrel would not overheat as he swung it back and forth.

When the bolt locked back, Bruce lowered the SAW, setting it across the saddle so it would not touch the horse or him. He lifted big SCAR to his shoulder but did not see anything coming toward them. He looked down at the SAW and the suppressor was a dull cherry red. Bruce held his hand over it and he could feel the heat through his tactical gloves. Reaching into his thigh pocket, Bruce pulled out a barrel mitten. Putting it on over his glove, he unscrewed the suppressor, letting it fall to the ground. The suppressor was aluminum and he didn't want it fusing to the barrel. *That will teach me to make aluminum suppressors, trying to save weight*, Bruce thought.

"Steve, if you used the SAW a lot, take off the suppressor and just drop it," Bruce told Steve over the radio as he heard Buffy yell out from behind him.

"Your mama likes it like that, butt munchers!" Buffy yelled.

Bruce laughed. "Danny, gather magazines." Then looking over his shoulder he asked Buffy, "Where did you hear that from, Buffy?"

"From you," Buffy replied, changing magazines.

"When did I say that?" Bruce asked, changing barrels on the SAW.

"Just a few minutes ago," she replied.

"Buffy, I was shootin', not yelling," Bruce told her.

Mike came over the radio, "Like hell, I had to ask some people to leave Mission Control with the words you were using. It'd no sooner come out of your mouth then she was repeating it."

Debbie spoke up next, "He's right Bruce, I didn't hear everything because I was yelling too."

Bruce turned the voice switch off and keyed his radio, "Team two, come down here. Jake and Nancy, head out into the field and take out any still moving. We need to reload magazines." Bruce told Buffy to turn off her voice switch.

He and Buffy climbed off and started loading magazines. When the others came over they all got off and joined. In fifteen minutes they all mounted back up and went to help Nancy and Jake. In the direction of the hunt team they heard an explosion followed by another.

"What's happing over there?" Bruce asked Mike.

"They had several get real close and used hand grenades to take them out. The blues are pulling back," Mike reported.

"Keep an eye on 'em, I want to know where they go," Bruce said, heading out into the field, shooting surviving blues.

"Hey, let me shoot some," Buffy complained from behind him.

Bruce complied, leading the horse past some that were trying to crawl off. After clearing the field, Bruce told everyone to meet him in the middle of the field. Bruce told Buffy to unbuckle and get off. Then Bruce slid off, stomping his feet and rubbing his butt. Bruce looked up as Jake rode over and climbed off.

Bruce smiled as he looked at his son's face. He was on the wave. Jake had a small grin on his face. Snipers could ride the wave as few others could. They very rarely faced the anger and guilt with the way they detached themselves so they could shoot. Bruce always envied them that and they could ride the wave longer than anyone. Bruce walked over to him.

"It's good, isn't it?" Bruce asked Jake. Jake just looked at him, not understanding. "You're on the wave, son," Bruce told him.

Jake nodded and his grin broadened. "This is great, Dad. From the back of a horse I took out sixty-four with seventy shots. My weapon felt like it was part of me." Jake looked around as if he was seeing the world for the first time. "How long does it last?"

"For snipers it lasts a long time. Just don't let it take control of you. Drink some water, we're going to get some more," Bruce told him.

Buffy walked up to Jake. "Ride the wave hard, bubba," she told him and held up her fist for a knuckle bump.

Jake just looked at Buffy as Bruce told him, "She's ridden the wave too, son, and so has your mom."

Jake bumped knuckles with Buffy. "Cool."

Bruce headed over to Debbie, who was drinking water. She looked up as he walked over. "Bruce, this is bullshit. It was right there," Debbie said in a pissed off voice.

"Don't force it, baby. When you feel the tingling in your spine, quit yelling and just let it go. That being said, remember the rules," Bruce told her.

"Quit yelling. I thought that's what you were doing, working yourself into the wave," Debbie said.

"No baby, I was yelling so I wouldn't go into the wave. I didn't need it. You're too drained once it leaves and these were not worth the effort," Bruce told her.

"Yeah, I guess you're right," Debbie admitted, taking another drink of water.

"You could've told me that, Daddy," Buffy said from his side.

"This was not worth it, Buffy," Bruce told her.

"When I start to tingle, I'm not scared anymore," Buffy admitted as Debbie came over to stand beside her.

"Yelling almost does the same thing, Buffy. Sometimes you want to feel fear to remind you to be careful," Bruce told her. Buffy just sighed and took the bottle Debbie handed her, taking a drink.

Bruce looked at Debbie. "Jake is on the wave now."

"What? Why aren't you over there guiding him?" Debbie asked.

"Baby, he's a sniper. Snipers are a breed unto themselves. They face only one problem, they want to be alone. We can handle that easy enough," Bruce told her.

"He's alone now. Call him over here," Debbie told Bruce.

"He's in the field, baby. Leave him alone. When we get back home is when you have to be near him. He's riding the wave but not like I ever have. A sniper can throw themselves on the wave at will and stay there for days. I've talked to several and they've all told me the same thing. The longest I've ever managed is fourteen hours and I slept for twenty afterwards. Unless you sacrifice part of yourself, then you can ride a long time. Snipers don't have to," Bruce told her, looking around him, seeing everyone standing around listening.

"I want to learn to be a sniper," Debbie told him.

"Baby, you can learn to be a sniper but you can't learn to 'become' a sniper. That's something you are born with or without. I've been trained as a sniper and can hit targets at a mile, but I don't have the mindset of a sniper," Bruce told Debbie. Mary, who was standing close to them and had heard the discussion, turned to look at Jake with worry on her face.

Mary started to walk to Jake who was standing off from the group. Bruce grabbed her arm. "Not now, Mary. Never in the field, okay. Leave him alone until we get back. Give him a few hours then you can talk to him. Do you understand?" Bruce asked her.

Mary just looked at Bruce and then alarm spread across her face. Without moving her face, she cut her eyes toward the mamas as Bruce spoke to her. "It's okay, Mary, you're just worried about your teammate." Mary looked back at Bruce. Staring into his face, her heart skipped a beat. He knew.

Thoughts started racing through her mind to try to cover for them. Bruce just looked down at her and said, "Mary, I've not let Danny or his mama go to him, so neither can you."

Mary let out a long breath and hugged Bruce. Bruce was going to cover for her. Tonight she and Jake had to have a long talk, Mary thought. She turned and went to her horse, getting a bottle of water.

Nancy watched the exchange and as Mary grabbed some water asked her, "What's wrong, Mary?"

Mary just shrugged her shoulders as Bruce spoke up, "Just training my troops, Nancy. I know we're family but we have to remember we're also a team in combat."

Nancy walked over to Mary and hugged her, telling her Jake would be okay. Bruce called everyone over as he took out his map and called Mike over the radio. "Base, where are the party guests, and how many do we have?" Bruce asked.

"The guests have stopped five miles to the southwest of the house," Mike reported then called out the grid coordinates. "The group is sixty-three strong. I had to send out the home defense team. The second micro spy plane found a group of seventeen to the north east, only two miles from the farm. Sent them in my truck. The hostiles tried to chase it down and were taken out by those in the back," Mike reported.

Bruce found where the group of blues had run to on the map. It was a small group of trees in the middle of a field smaller than a hundred and fifty by two hundred yards. They would hit them there if they stayed. "In one hour come and get the hunting team; we're going after the party poopers. Keep us informed of any movements," Bruce told him as he looked at the group.

"We are going to attack the assholes. We're going to charge them and wipe them out. I want everyone who has one to load up the beta mags," Bruce told them. The beta mags were a hundred and twenty round magazines for the M-4s and SCARs. They did fit the AUGs that Debbie and Nancy carried but you couldn't aim the AUG for shit with them on. The beta did not fit the Galil that Danny carried.

The group mounted up and took off at a strong trot. In twenty minutes they were at the field and waited for the UAV to confirm that the blues were still there. While they waited, they watered the horses and tightened saddles until Mike called over the radio that the guests were still there.

"We're a half a mile from them now. We are going to charge them, moving through the little stand of trees and wiping them out. Stay in line, don't charge forward alone. I'm center and Debbie and Nancy will be on the ends. Let's see if we can scare them," Bruce said.

Everyone mounted and when Bruce got a thumbs up from all he kicked Nightmare into a run. They looked like knights as they entered the field. Instead of lowering lances, they lowered assault rifles. The blues saw them at a hundred yards from the trees. A group of eleven charged the patrol as the rest ran out the other side of the stand of trees, trying to make it to the woods a hundred plus yards away.

The patrol cut the attacking runners down before they even got close. They rode through the stand of trees, chasing the escaping runners. As one, the entire patrol opened up, cutting the escaping infected down. Then they shot the wounded in the head.

Bruce stopped and looked down at a blue. It was a nude female in her early twenties. He shot her in the head again then unbuckled from Buffy. Climbing off his horse, Bruce walked over to the female blue. Nightmare did not want to come closer but Bruce yanked his reins, pulling him over. Bruce kneeled by the body and studied it then stood up, calling Debbie over as Buffy jumped off Nightmare.

Debbie rode over to him as did everyone else. "Get off and look at this one and tell me what you see?" Bruce requested.

Debbie got off, handed Bruce the reins to her horse, and looked at the body. She reached in her pocket, pulling out nylon gloves, taking off her tactical gloves and put them on. Kneeling down, Debbie examined the body. "At one time she was pretty before she was infected. I think she is in her early twenties—" Debbie stopped as she looked at the breasts then felt the abdomen.

"Oh shit!" Debbie exclaimed.

"That's what I thought," Bruce said.

"What?" asked Steve.

"She's pregnant," Debbie said.

"Stephanie said they'd be able to reproduce," Nancy said.

"Nancy, hearing it and seeing it are two totally different things," Bruce told her. "Mount up, we are headed home," Bruce called and walked over to Jake.

Bruce stopped beside Jake's horse and handed him the map, "Take us home, you're in charge; I'm in the rear," Bruce told him.

Jake looked at the map. "I really don't want to, Dad."

"I didn't ask, son. I need to think some things over, now take us home," Bruce told him. Jake grabbed the map and studied it for a route home.

Buffy walked over to Bruce. "Daddy, when will I get boobies?" she asked.

"Buffy, you are to never ask Daddy about your boobies again, ever," Bruce snapped as he climbed into the saddle.

Debbie ran over to Buffy and whispered, "You don't ask Daddy about that ever. We will talk about it later. Daddy tries to always remember you as a little girl. When Danny got her first bra, Daddy wanted to blow up J.C. Penny's." Debbie helped Buffy up to Bruce and he made her sit up front to drive.

The whole trip back, Bruce sat lost in thought about what they had seen today and what still needed to be done.

Jake led the patrol home. It was a little after 1700 when they rode in and headed to the barn. Tonya and Nathan were waiting at the barn for Steve. They ran over to him as he climbed down from his horse. Steve wrapped both of them up in his arms then lifted Nathan up to the saddle as he led the horse to the barn.

Bruce looked up and saw Stephanie holding PJ with the twins beside her. She ran up to Debbie, hugging her then moving down the line, hugging everyone. They stopped at him as he climbed off. Bruce reached down and picked up the twins, hugging them then put each one in the saddle behind Buffy. They held on as Buffy trotted off on Nightmare toward the barn. Bruce held out his arms for PJ and he reached out for Bruce.

Grabbing him, Bruce gave him big squeezes and kisses that PJ really loved. Then Bruce looked at Stephanie. "Well, are ya going to hug me or not, woman?" Bruce asked her. Stephanie hugged Bruce as Debbie walked up.

"Hey, no tongue now," Debbie said.

Stephanie let go of Bruce and looked at Debbie, "How do you use tongue when you hug someone?" Stephanie asked Debbie.

Debbie laughed, shaking her head, "I was kidding, Stephanie, like when you kiss."

"I only kissed him on the cheek," Stephanie told her, not understanding. Debbie looked down, shaking her head.

"You bring another woman to our bed that doesn't know anything about hanky panky?" Bruce asked Debbie, shaking his head with a disappointed look.

Stephanie slapped his arm. "I know stuff like that Bruce," she told him in a sassy tone.

"Let me guess, you read about it in a book?" Bruce asked.

"Yeah, but I even saw a dirty movie once," Stephanie shot back, hoping to startle Bruce.

"Shocking, I never would've believed they made those," Bruce replied sarcastically.

Stephanie looked at Debbie. "He's picking on me."

"You asked for that one, baby," Debbie told her, laughing.

Bruce reached down, picking Stephanie up and throwing her over his shoulder. Debbie walked over and took PJ from him. Bruce put his arm around Debbie and they walked past the community building with Stephanie over his shoulder hitting him on the butt to put her down. Bruce stopped on the patio and whispered to Debbie, "Watch this."

Bruce put Stephanie down and while she was trying to tell him something, Bruce kissed her on the mouth. Locking his mouth to hers he thrust his tongue into her mouth. He then let her go. "That's with tongue." Bruce turned around, kissed Debbie and then walked into the house.

Stephanie was standing there with her eyes closed. She started to wobble on her feet as she opened her eyes. She took a step back trying to keep her balance. Debbie laughed as she caught her arm so Stephanie wouldn't fall. Stephanie looked at Debbie, who was still laughing. Why wasn't Debbie mad at her?

"It was good, wasn't it?" Debbie asked her, smiling.

"Holy shit!" was all Stephanie could manage to say.

"I take it that's good?" Debbie inquired.

"I will sleep somewhere else tonight, Debbie," Stephanie said, looking down.

"What?" Debbie asked in shock.

"Hello, Bruce just kissed me," Stephanie told her.

"Stephanie, Bruce has kissed Nancy and Mike like that. Granted, he has to fight Mike to do it," Debbie told her. Stephanie was just staring at her. "You don't get out of this relationship that easy, honey. Bruce is more than man for both of us," Debbie told her, grabbing her arm and leading Stephanie into the house.

Bruce was in his recliner, already dozing off with his vest on the coffee table. Debbie sat down at the table with PJ, then asked Stephanie, "Will you take Bruce's boots off, please." Stephanie complied and then sat down at the table with her laptop.

Danny, Matt, Jake, and Mary came in thirty minutes later, dropping down into chairs, except Jake, who just sat down slowly. Mary reached over and patted his hand. Jake looked at her and smiled.

Danny looked at Debbie, who was feeding PJ. "Thanks Mama. You and Daddy just left your horses. Don't worry though, we took care of it. Thank goodness Daddy Mike came out because the twins wanted Buffy to take them for a ride on that mountain Daddy calls a horse. I was tired of watching them. I want a shower. I love my horse but I don't like smelling like him. Then Jake is on some kind of drug. I just wanted to tell ya thank you for leaving us out there to take care of your and Daddy's horses and gear," Danny finished bitching.

Debbie looked up at Danny. "Did you say something baby girl?" Debbie asked.

Danny just dropped her head to the table. "No ma'am."

Debbie kept feeding PJ as others continued to come in. When the cooks called supper ready, Debbie told Buffy to wake Daddy so he could eat. Bruce came into the kitchen after Buffy woke him up. Bruce growled as Millie put a plate at his spot. Millie stopped and looked at him. Bruce just turned away, looking at something else as Millie went to help in the kitchen. Bruce reached down, grabbed the chicken breast off his plate and walked out on the patio.

Gimp/Jim was sitting at a table eating. When he saw Bruce come out he stood up. Bruce motioned him back down to eat. The three prisoners were sitting at the edge of the patio in the grass, still naked. Bruce called them over. They ran over to him, stopped, then looked down at their feet.

Bruce looked at them and said, "When you're around anyone in this clan you will kneel. When it's me, you will bow on your knees or we'll have another lesson." The three dropped to their knees like someone had shot them. Bruce looked them over as they kneeled in front of him. Bill was walking by but stopped, seeing Bruce with the three, and he sent Frank into the house. The three were covered in shit and smelled of it. Their skin was sunburned and Carla's shaved head was bright red from the sun.

Bruce cleared his throat after taking a bite of chicken. "I'm going to ask each of you questions. Some I know the answers to, some I don't. If you lie, and I will find out, you will see your colleague got off easy. If you answer truthfully you'll be rewarded. Do you understand?" Bruce asked.

"Yes," they said together.

"First, when you talk to me you will address me as sir or I will rape each of you right here with a blow torch. Now, do I make myself clear?" Bruce demanded.

"Yes sir," they replied in unison.

Bruce closed his eyes to fight back the anger, then opened his eyes. "Bitch Boy, you know where government stockpiles of supplies are located, don't you?" Bruce asked Mitch.

"Yes sir," Mitch replied.

"In what states do you know the locations, Bitch Boy?" Bruce asked him.

"Texas, Oklahoma, Kansas, Arkansas, Louisiana, and Mississippi, with several others in Montana, sir," Mitch replied.

"Do you know what each one holds?" Bruce asked.

"In general, but not a complete inventory, sir. If I had my laptop from the camp, I could give you a detailed list, sir," Mitch replied on his knees with his head on the ground.

"Bitch, what about you? Do you know locations also?" Bruce asked.

"Yes sir," Carla replied.

Bruce turned to the trooper. "How about you, Dumb? Do you know where the state police had stock piles of ammo and weapons?" Bruce asked.

"Yes, sir," the trooper answered.

Bruce tore off three bite-sized pieces of chicken and threw it in front of each of them. "Eat it off the ground; don't use your hands." Bruce told them and they did as they were told.

"You three have lost some weight since you've been here. Bitch, if you didn't have a shaved head and weren't covered in shit you just might look good. Now if you prove yourself useful to the clan you can join the human race again when I allow it. I will allow it when I see that you know you're part of it and not better than the rest of us," Bruce told them and turned to Bill.

"Tell Debbie I want three notebooks and pens. A bar of soap and three towels please," Bruce requested from Bill. Chuckling, Bill went in to get the supplies.

"Bitch, do you want to be raped and violated?" Bruce asked her.

Carla started crying. "No, sir."

"Do you think the girls that Bitch Boy, Dumb and Dumber raped wanted that?" Bruce questioned as Debbie came out to the patio.

"No sir," Carla said, still crying.

"Do you think these two need to be raped to show them what it feels like to have someone do that to them?" Bruce asked her.

Carla stopped crying and replied, "Yes, sir."

Bruce was watching the men and saw their bodies become rigid with her answer. "Well now boys, put your butts in the air for me then," Bruce said as he walked behind them. Both men raised their butts up in the air as they cried. Bruce knew they were broken now. They would only need a demonstration here and there, unless someone showed them mercy too early. Bruce smiled. He had saved three more back to the human race. *I should've been a warden*, Bruce thought.

"You two are lucky. I killed a lot of infected today and I'm tired," Bruce told them as Bill came back outside carrying the supplies.

"Now you three will take a bath under the water hose. Then each of you will sit down and write down what you know. If you make me a neat long list in the notebooks I'll let each of you have a meal tonight and cover up with a blanket. If the clan can use what you've written down I will give each of you a shirt and one pair of pants tomorrow. Now, do you understand?" Bruce asked them.

They replied in unison, "Yes sir."

"Bitch, tell me in your own words what I mean with these gifts," Bruce told her.

"If we are good and do what we are told, we get rewarded, sir," Carla told Bruce.

"Very good, Bitch. You two need to tell her thank you later. Tomorrow you can use shovels to pick up shit. If you piss me off again, you'll pick it up with your mouth. Do I make myself clear?" Bruce asked. They replied in the affirmative.

"Now, go bathe. You three stink, but boys, if you try to hurt Bitch because she told me the truth, I will become angry. Do you understand?" Bruce warned the two men.

"Yes sir," they replied.

"Now go bathe," Bruce told them. Carla and Mitch jumped up, running to the water hose. The officer continued to bow.

"Dumb, why are you still here?" Bruce asked.

"Sir, my writing arm is broken. I will not be able to do what I have been told. I'm waiting on my punishment," the officer replied, crying.

"Jim, write for Dumb after he bathes. Now move," Bruce said as the officer ran off. Jim replied "Yes sir," as he came over to Bruce.

"Jim, take the idiots the soap and towels so they can wash off. They are to keep the towels and soap. Each night they will bathe right there. Jim, in the barn at the far end is a metal cabinet. On the bottom shelf are wool army blankets we use for the horses. Grab three and give them to the idiots. I want each one at a separate table when they write down what they have been told. Do I make myself clear?" Bruce asked Jim.

"Yes sir," Jim replied.

"Do it, Jim," Bruce told him. Jim took the supplies, setting the notebooks and pens on a table. Then he ran to the barn after giving the idiots the soap and towels.

Debbie came over to Bruce, wrapping her arms around him. "I don't know if I could watch you rape a man," Debbie admitted.

"Baby, between me and you, I couldn't rape a man. I just say it because it scares the shit out of 'em. I couldn't even rape a woman, get medieval on one yeah, but not rape one," Bruce told her then looked at her. "You think I could rape a woman?" Bruce asked.

"No, I know you couldn't do that either. Torture one, yes, but not rape, that's not who you are. I know there are some lines you will never cross,"

Debbie told him. Then added, "But hearing you talk like that did make me hot." Bruce started looking around for a place to go as Debbie grabbed his face, turning it toward her. "Let's go take a shower. Just don't be so obvious, okay," Debbie told him.

"I will be a ninja," Bruce told her, crouching down in a Kung Fu stance.

"Come on, let's eat," Debbie told him, giggling and leading him back inside.

Bruce sat down in his chair, fighting sleep as he took a drink of tea. Mike asked, "Well, what did you do to them this time?"

"I let them take a bath under the hose," Bruce answered as he started eating.

"Thank you, Bruce, they stank to high hell," Mike said.

"They're making a list of government stockpiles tonight. If the lists are good they get clothes tomorrow and get to use shovels. If they piss me off again they have to pick up shit with their mouth next time," Bruce told Mike.

"Are they broken yet?" Mike asked.

"I told the men to put their butts in the air so I could rape them and they did it while they cried," Bruce told him.

"That's broken," Mike said.

Millie came over, put a piece of cake in front of Bruce and kissed him on his shaved head. As she turned to leave, Bruce stopped her. "Millie, I have to ask you something," Bruce said.

"If it's fo me ta stop bringin' ya and the others food, furget' it, I'll leaves the kitchen," Millie said. Several people at the table and the other cooks asked Bruce not to ask her that. Bruce held up his hand for everyone to shut up.

"No Millie, I have to ask you to be a terror. I want you to just talk and threaten those idiots out there. Tell them if you ever hear of them doing anything like trying to hurt someone or not doing their job, you'll me they were planning on doing stuff to the kids in the clan. You get the idea? I want them too terrified to even think of anything. I want them to be drones that just work. Then maybe they will see that they can be part of something without hurting others. They do jobs that no one else desires to do but the jobs need doing. I would understand if you don't want to," Bruce appealed to Millie.

"Why me?" Millie asked.

"They watched you kill the other one and are terrified of you," Bruce answered.

"I'll do it. I'll have thoz three so scared the first time I talks to dem they'll wets their pants," Millie told Bruce.

"Thank you Millie, but you can't scare someone enough to pee on themselves," Bruce told her as he continued eating.

"I'll tellz ya what Bruce, if they don't piss theyselves the first time I talks to 'em, I'll never bring you or anyone else a plate again," Millie bet Bruce.

"Thank you then, Millie for bringing us plates of food these past days, but I don't like the special treatment," Bruce told her. He didn't know that he was going to lose the bet the next day. Not only did they piss on themselves, two shit themselves.

Bruce kept eating as Millie went into the kitchen. Stephanie looked at Bruce and said, "Okay, I read what you gave me and have gone over your schematic—" Stephanie stopped as Bruce dropped his fork, which hit his plate with a loud clank. Bruce slowly turned his head toward Stephanie with his mouth open, full of food.

Grinning, Debbie told him, "Baby, close your mouth, that's gross." Bruce just pushed the food out with his tongue onto the table so he wouldn't choke.

"You read all those books on the flash drives in nine hours? Then went over the schematics too?" Bruce asked in bewilderment with his eyes bugging out of his head.

"I was finished with the books by noon, Bruce. They only went over chemistry, how to boil down crude oil to recover the hydrocarbon chains by the different boiling points. Then how to add or take away hydrocarbon chains with catalytic reforming or—" Stephanie stopped as Bruce interrupted.

"I know what's in them. It took me two months to read 'em, then another month to draw up the schematics. Stephanie, that's over fourteen gigabytes of information you read in four or five hours. You have to read over a thousand words a minute to do that," Bruce told her.

"Bruce, I can read almost three thousand words a minute but I already had the general idea from chemistry. I do have a masters in organic and biochemistry you know. It was interesting to read; I never thought about how gas was made from oil. Now after going through your schematic I made some changes which should increase the yield by twenty percent. Running at full capacity, I'm sure you could process ten thousand gallons a day. I'll be able to work out a way to use everything by tomorrow, except the contaminated salts and metals. Since the wells around here produce light sweet crude, we will get a large nominal yield." Stephanie stopped as Bruce closed his eyes and pinched the bridge of his nose. Stephanie looked at Debbie for guidance but Debbie was just laughing silently.

Bruce stood up, looking at Stephanie. "Thank you, Stephanie, for going over that. Once again, you've proven yourself invaluable to the family." Then Bruce turned to Debbie. "I'm carrying my dumbass to bed if I can remember how to get to my room and undress myself. Bring me some pretty yarn and crayons to play with." Bruce walked out of the kitchen, heading upstairs.

Mike stood up next. "It took me three months to read that shit and another two to understand what the hell Bruce had drawn up. I'm carrying my stupid ass to bed since all I have to do is follow Bruce. My room is beside his, if I can find it." Mike turned to Nancy. "Bring a diaper up for me, I don't know if I'll remember how to use the bathroom," Mike told her as he walked out. Nancy's body was shaking as she tried real hard not to laugh out loud.

Jake and Matt stood up, next heading to the door. Jake said over his shoulder, "It took us a week to get that drawing in the computer and we still have no idea what it does. Our dumb asses are following our stupid fathers upstairs. I'm just going to wet the bed."

Alex, Steve and David looked at each other, then around the table, then stood up and left, which left only Conner beside Susan at the table with the women. Conner stood up. "I'm carrying my dumbass with them because I don't even know what the hell y'all talking about," he said as he left the kitchen.

The women all busted out laughing. Several came over and hugged Stephanie, giving her high fives. Stephanie did not understand why the men left and hoped she hadn't hurt Bruce's feelings again. She closed her eyes and mentally went through the book she had written from Bruce about boys and couldn't remember anything about this.

Debbie realized she was reading the boy book from memory. "Stephanie, it's not in the boy book. You just reminded them that a girl can be, and is, smarter than the boys." Debbie added, "Thank you, it's refreshing to see them humbled. Nancy and I read those books and others like them and we have long arguments."

Danny asked Stephanie, "Can you teach me how to read like that?"

"I can try Danny, I never taught anyone to read like I do." Stephanie was starting to feel good about herself as pride rushed through her.

Angela asked Stephanie, "When you read a hundred thousand plus words an hour, what is your retention?"

"Over eighty percent," Stephanie told her.

"That's why she holds four doctorates and six masters," Nancy said.

"Damn, how old were you when you graduated medical school?" Angela asked.

"Twenty," Stephanie answered.

Debbie stood up and handed PJ to Danny. "I'm going up to rub it in. Stephanie, will you bring the kids up in twenty minutes. Bruce will probably use language that I want to limit their exposure to."

"Sure, just don't rub it in too much please," Stephanie pleaded as Debbie kissed her on the cheek and took off upstairs.

Debbie opened the door to find a naked Bruce waiting on her. "It took you long enough, sugar mama," Bruce told her.

Debbie stripped as she walked across the room to him. They ran to the shower, washed off, then made hot passionate love. After getting out, they dried off then ran to the bedroom, picking up clothes off the floor to hide the evidence. They jumped in the bed acting like they weren't talking when Stephanie carried PJ in, followed by the twins.

The twins ran and jumped on the bed, giving hugs and kisses. Stephanie put PJ on the bed and he crawled up to join the hugs and kisses. Stephanie watched PJ and the twins as she took off her combat boots and ACU's. She stood in her t-shirt and panties looking at Bruce's dresser, afraid to get out a t-shirt and a pair of boxers.

"They're in the top left drawer, Stephanie. You may take whatever you want anytime," Bruce told her.

Stephanie looked at Bruce, smiling. She opened the drawer, grabbing a shirt and boxers, then ran to the bathroom. She then ran back out wearing Bruce's t-shirt and boxers and jumped into the middle of the bed to join in on the hugs and kisses the kids were giving out.

Debbie put her hand on Stephanie's chest. "You took your bra off. Good girl."

"You slept in a bra? I haven't touched you," Bruce exclaimed.

"I always slept in a bra, Bruce. I thought you were supposed to," Stephanie told him.

"That's tough, stupid, but tough," Bruce said as Stephanie slapped his arm.

They all drifted off to sleep with everyone moving to Bruce's side of the bed as the night wore on.

CHAPTER 19

Dreaming she was in a fire, Stephanie opened her eyes because she was sweating to death. She moved the twin sprawled across her off and kicked the sheet off as she laid on her right side. Stephanie raised her head and looked at the clock. It read 0411. She saw the other twin lying across Debbie. PJ was snoring lightly above her head with a hand in her hair, playing with it in his sleep.

Stephanie laid her head back down, smiling. This was the fifteenth night she had slept with Bruce and Debbie. Just thinking about Bruce, she scooted back toward him as he put his arm across her, making Stephanie smile as she closed her eyes. That was when she felt a hand on her breast. Stephanie looked down and saw her shirt was pulled up to her armpits and Bruce's arm was resting across her with his hand just barely on her chest.

Stephanie thought about how she should handle this. She knew Bruce was asleep by his soft snoring, so this was a complete accident. Stephanie pulled her left arm out and placed it over Bruce's. Then she put his palm on her breast and pushed it down on her breast. Bruce pulled her toward him and squeezed her breast. She bit her lower lip, swearing she was fixing to have an orgasm. After the sensation passed she continued biting her lower lip as she snuggled into Bruce. She dozed off, having dreams of Bruce holding her.

Feeling something pat her cheek, Stephanie waved her hand across her face. Feeling it again she said, "PJ, I will get you a bottle in a minute." Then she heard a whispered voice, "Don't move fast or you will wake up Bruce."

Stephanie's eyes popped open to see Debbie leaning over her. Stephanie looked down and Bruce was still holding her breast. Her heart started racing. *Holy shit, Debbie is fixing to kill me*, she thought. She started to move as Debbie leaned over again, whispering, "Move slow or you'll wake him." Stephanie moved slowly like she was told. Debbie must want to kill her and not disturb Bruce. Well, she'd asked for it. She slowly moved out from under Bruce.

When she extracted herself from beneath Bruce's arm she pulled her shirt down and sat up. Stephanie turned toward Debbie, who was sitting on her knees and smiling at her. Stephanie leaned toward Debbie and whispered, "Make it fast, please." Debbie cocked her head to the side with a bewildered expression on her face, not knowing what she was supposed to do fast. Stephanie leaned forward and whispered, "When you kill me, make it fast please."

Debbie's stifled laughter caught her off guard. Debbie moved out of the bed and motioned for Stephanie to follow. Stephanie crawled over the twins and when she felt her hair get pulled, she unwound her hair out of PJ's hand as she got out of the bed. Debbie headed to the bathroom as Stephanie followed her. When they were in the bathroom Debbie closed the door.

"Stephanie, why would I want to kill you when Bruce felt you up in his sleep?" Debbie asked in a hushed voice.

"Debbie, your husband had my breast in his hand and you aren't mad?" Stephanie asked, taking a step back.

"Shhh, keep your voice down. No, I'm not mad. But if Bruce would've woken up and found your boob in his hand he would feel guilty. Today will be the twelfth straight day he's been out on patrol and he is starting to get tired. I want his mind on staying alive, not feeling guilty about feeling you up," Debbie told her.

"Debbie, what is going on with you? What would you say if I told you I woke up and Bruce's arm was across my shoulder barely touching my boob? Then I pulled his hand to my chest forcing it on my breast. He squeezed it when he pulled me to him and I almost had an orgasm. Now what do you have to say?" Stephanie asked her, expecting a hit. Debbie reached up, grabbed her face and pulled it down, kissing Stephanie on the lips then letting her go. Stephanie just stared at Debbie, thinking she was still asleep and this was a guilt dream.

"Stephanie, was it good?" Debbie asked. Stephanie took a step back, trying to wake up from this dream. Debbie took some towels out, laying them on the floor; then she sat down, crossing her legs and motioning

Stephanie to sit down. When Stephanie sat down Debbie asked again, "Well, was it good?"

Stephanie looked down at her folded legs and told Debbie the truth. "Yes Debbie, it was good. I have dreamed that dream so many times. Not Bruce feeling me up but holding me like he does you. I have dreamed about that moment since the first day I met him and it has only gotten stronger. Debbie you are the best person I know in this world. You're just like Bruce. You see the good in people and take them in expecting nothing in return. That's why it makes me feel so guilty when I think about Bruce.

"Every day since I have slept in your bed waking up next to Bruce is a dream come true, but I have cried each day knowing I have betrayed you." Tears were hitting Stephanie's legs as she talked.

"It took everything I had to admit to you that I loved Bruce. Then I find out everyone knew, except Bruce. I know Bruce loves me but not like he loves you. When you asked me to sleep in here to help with the kids, I almost passed out. Even now I think this is a dream. You caught your husband with his hand on my boob and me just smiling in bliss." Stephanie finished, tears falling off her downturned face.

"Stephanie, look at me please," Debbie said. Stephanie looked up at Debbie. "I know what it took for you to admit to me that you love Bruce. That's why I asked you to sleep in here with us. There are several other reasons that are my own and in time I'll tell you. But when you told me, I knew then how much you thought and cared about me. You were willing to leave here knowing you would probably die just because you thought you had hurt me.

"Now, I want to tell you something. I feel very sorry for you because you deserve someone like Bruce. If anyone deserves a Bruce, it's you. I have watched you over four years gawk at him like a lovesick teenager. I thought at first it was just infatuation but then I saw what was in your eyes. I see the same thing in mine for Bruce," Debbie told her as she reached out and held Stephanie's hands.

"Before the world ended I thought you might find someone like Bruce. Granted, they were very few but they were out there. Now that the world has collapsed, the odds really suck. What would you say if I told you that you could have Bruce and I will step out of the picture?" Debbie asked.

"Debbie, I couldn't do that to you or him. Y'all love each other too much, I'm just the odd step child here," Stephanie told her.

"Stephanie, I want to tell you something, but don't get mad at me," Debbie probed. "I know you had a one-night stand with some guy before you left for Atlanta. You cried yourself to sleep the last three nights you stayed here. Danny heard you crying and woke me up. I went in Mary's room and rubbed your head as you cried and you talked in your sleep. I know the only reason you slept with someone was to try to forget Bruce, which was very stupid. I really hope you used protection," Debbie finished and Stephanie looked at Debbie dumbfounded. That was the worst secret of her life and Debbie knew.

Stephanie started crying again as she said, "I'm a slut."

"Say that again and we will have a problem in here," Debbie warned her with iron in her voice. Stephanie stopped crying at the change in Debbie's voice. "I wouldn't invite a slut into my home, then ask a slut to help with my kids and offer to share my family. Don't disrespect me or yourself like that again please," Debbie said.

"I'm sorry," Stephanie said.

"Now, I'm willing to share Bruce with you but you take both of us. Do you accept that?" Debbie asked her. Stephanie just looked at Debbie like she had lost her mind. "Stephanie, would you do the same for me if the roles were reversed," Debbie asked her. The question caught her off guard. She thought for several minutes then answered.

"I don't know Debbie. I do know if Bruce said to I would," Stephanie told her.

"I thought you might say something like that. Stephanie, you have to get some metal in your spine. Mama runs the house, and if she doesn't, then Daddy goes crazy. You can't just follow Bruce around blindly. I tried that and almost lost him. He's still a man and we have to steer them a little. Not control but just steer them to the right choices. Do you understand what I'm saying?" Debbie asked.

"I think so, but Bruce is too good for that," Stephanie told her.

Debbie dropped her head. Stephanie had Bruce on a pedestal that he could never be knocked off of. She would try to show her. "Back to my question, do you want to share Bruce with me? I'm not giving him up but I will share him with you," Debbie told her.

"Debbie, don't tease me like that. I can't take it," Stephanie replied, not believing Debbie.

"I wasn't kidding," Debbie said with a serious face.

Stephanie just stared at Debbie then blurted out, "Fuck me!" She slapped both of her hands over her mouth with a look of shock, not believing she said that.

Debbie smiled at Stephanie asking, "Is that the first time you said that word out loud?"

Stephanie shook her head no. "Second then," Debbie asked and Stephanie nodded.

"Take your hands off your mouth," Debbie said and Stephanie complied. "Well, do you want to share Bruce with me?" Debbie asked her.

"I will take anything you give me," Stephanie told her with tears of joy in her eyes.

"Okay, now Bruce can never know this. We can tell him in a few years, but not now. We have to warm him up to the idea, taking it real slow. Bruce doesn't like to be led around, so you have to make him think of it," Debbie told her.

"Bruce said that about boys on page 146," Stephanie told her.

"Okay, now I want you to listen to that book and that is how you guide a man, not just make him happy," Debbie told her. Stephanie lunged forward, locking Debbie in a hug and knocking her back on the floor. Stephanie kissed her all over her face.

"Thank you Debbie," Stephanie said, crying and hugged her.

"It's okay, Stephanie, now stop crying. You're one of Bruce's women and we have to be a tough breed," Debbie told her.

"I'll be tough," Stephanie said, letting Debbie go and sitting up. "Debbie, I want to tell you I saw Bruce naked," Stephanie told her.

"Okay," Debbie said, waiting on the rest of the story.

"He was coming out of the shower when I was bringing the kids in here to bathe them," Stephanie said.

"You didn't run away screaming?" Debbie asked giggling.

"No," Stephanie said.

"First, Bruce doesn't feel ashamed of his body and will run around naked. Our kids have adopted that habit and it has spread to Mike and his kids. Nancy is a borderline prude. It took me two years to get her to wear a bikini," Debbie told her.

"Well, he shouldn't be ashamed of it. His body is fabulous," Stephanie replied.

Debbie smiled at Stephanie. "How much do you want to bet Bruce will shower with you?" Debbie asked, knowing Bruce didn't care who was in the shower.

"You just said we have to take it slow with Bruce," Stephanie said.

"You weren't listening. I said he doesn't find anything wrong with being naked," Debbie said.

"He won't do it," Stephanie told Debbie, secretly praying she was wrong.

"If I win, no more guilty thoughts from you. Okay?" Debbie said, standing up.

"Deal," Stephanie said, standing.

Debbie went into the bedroom to find PJ assaulting Bruce with his empty bottle. Debbie grabbed PJ, then started shaking Bruce.

"Bruce, the alarm didn't go off. Go get the shower ready for the girls," Debbie said as Bruce jumped out of the bed. Bruce looked at the clock, Debbie, and Stephanie, then ran to the bathroom. Debbie woke the girls and told them to head downstairs.

Debbie went to the bathroom, "Bruce, I'm going to feed the girls first. Let Stephanie take a shower with you so she won't have to be cramped in with us later, and don't burn her with the water," Debbie told him. Bruce just gave a halfhearted "Okay, whatever." Debbie walked by Stephanie kissing her on the cheek as she walked out the door.

Stephanie walked into the bathroom and closed the door feeling like she was still in a dream. If this was a dream, when she woke up she was going to be pissed. She stripped down and opened the shower door and just stared at Bruce.

"Well, come on in and shut the door," Bruce told her.

Stephanie stepped in, shutting the door, watching Bruce wash his body. When he got to his back Stephanie took the rag and washed his back for him. She could feel the muscles rippling across his back.

She wrapped both arms around him, acting like she was rinsing the soap out of the rag, forgetting that there were three heads in the shower. When she let go Bruce turned around, rinsing the soap off of his back. Bruce held out his hand and Stephanie just looked at it.

"Rag please," Bruce told her. Stephanie handed it to him feeling very lightheaded as she stared at Bruce. Bruce put soap on the rag.

"Turn around so I can wash your back," Bruce told her. Stephanie almost said no because she couldn't see him then. The decision was taken from her as Bruce spun her around and started washing her back. When he was finished he held the rag under the head, rinsing the soap out. Stephanie turned around and leaned toward Bruce.

Bruce thought she was falling and grabbed her, pulling her into his chest. Stephanie wanted time to stop right then as Bruce held her.

"You okay. Little Red?" Bruce asked her.

"Just got lightheaded," Stephanie replied.

"You locked your knees out. Stephanie, you never stand with both knees locked," Bruce told her as Stephanie put more weight on him. Bruce picked her up off her feet, putting her arms around his neck. Stephanie's feet were inches off the floor but her head was in the clouds as Bruce held her with one arm trying to turn off the shower with the other.

"Stephanie, can you help a little? I don't want to drop you," Bruce stated. Stephanie wrapped her legs and arms around him to help out. Not exactly what he had in mind, but Bruce would take it. Be damned if he was going to let her fall and hit the shower floor. He would never hear the end of it from everyone. "Eww she saw your tally whacker and passed out, huh Bruce."

Bruce stepped out of the shower with Stephanie stuck to the front of him. *She may not be able to stand but she can sure hold on,* Bruce thought. "Stephanie, let go so I can dry you off and lay you down on the bed," Bruce told her. Stephanie shook her head no. Bruce wished Debbie would walk in to see what she'd caused. Bruce grabbed a towel and dried off Stephanie's back.

"Stephanie, stand up. I will hold you up, okay?" Bruce asked and Stephanie let go with her legs and slid off Bruce. Bruce held onto her, holding her up, then he just gave up. Bruce picked her up in his arms, taking her to the bed. He laid her down and dried her off. Then Bruce dried himself off and headed to the closet to grab some clothes.

Bruce dressed himself then kissed Stephanie on the forehead, "You okay?" he asked her.

"I'm good, Bruce. Thank you for not letting me fall," Stephanie replied as Bruce left.

Bruce walked into the kitchen and saw Debbie in her chair feeding PJ. Debbie looked up at him smiling and Bruce smiled back. He walked over and sat down in his chair and told Debbie, "Go check on Stephanie." Debbie just looked at Bruce, not knowing what he was talking about.

Bruce took the look as disbelief. "I'm not kidding," Bruce said. Debbie stood up and handed PJ to Bruce and headed upstairs.

Debbie walked into the room and found a naked Stephanie lying on the bed. Debbie walked over to her and relaxed beside her on the bed. "You have teeth marks on your lower lip. If you tell me Bruce did that, I'm goin' to kick his ass," Debbie told her.

"No, I did it to myself," Stephanie answered then told Debbie the whole story about everything she did.

"You had orgasms with him just holding your body?" Debbie asked, just a little jealous.

"I bit my lip so I wouldn't yell," Stephanie admitted.

"Wow, I'm glad you didn't try for more," Debbie told her.

"I'm not ready," Stephanie said.

"No kidding, we would have to do CPR on you and I would have to tell everyone I set my husband up with his new wife that he doesn't know about yet," Debbie giggled.

Stephanie laughed then repeated, "I'm not ready, Debbie."

"Stephanie, it's not that different than with another guy. Granted it will mean more because you love Bruce. Besides your little one night stand, how many guys have you been with?" Debbie asked her. Stephanie just looked at her, not answering. "Are you fucking kidding me? You lost your virginity to some asshole on a one night stand?" Debbie asked, sitting up. Tears started rolling out of Stephanie's eyes. Debbie hugged Stephanie. "Stephanie, why didn't you tell me sooner that you loved Bruce? That was supposed to be special," Debbie said, holding Stephanie as she cried. "You're going back on your promise, so stop it," Debbie told her. Stephanie slowly stopped crying.

Debbie changed the subject, "Well, did you enjoy it?"

"That was the best thing ever," Stephanie told her. "You're the best friend I've ever had," Stephanie admitted.

"I'm not your friend anymore, I'm your wife," Debbie told her.

Stephanie kissed Debbie and said, "Well, that explains it then. I just kissed my bride."

"We have to get downstairs and see what stud muffin is planning today. He didn't get a workout, so he might be bitchy." Debbie got off the bed, headed for the closet, grabbed her clothes and vest and put them on.

"I'll be down in a minute," Stephanie said.

"Come down, we'll write in our journals after breakfast. I'm not allowed on this patrol," Debbie told Stephanie as she headed back to the kitchen.

Debbie walked over to Bruce who just smiled at her. "She's okay, baby," Debbie told him.

"That's good," Bruce replied.

Bruce handed her PJ as he stood up, "Okay, the community building is complete. Today we are hitting the school to get tables, and a restaurant to get a stove and refrigerator for it. I will be taking out a patrol to shadow the scavenging group. We have twenty-six more people we have found on patrols that have joined us. Let's make them feel at home. Danny, Jake, Matt, Mary and Buffy; you will be staying here. I'm taking out a new patrol," Bruce told them and he paused for the complaints he knew were coming.

Not surprised, Bruce saw Danny was the first one up. "What do you mean I can't go? I'm the one that found those six people yesterday and I can kick ass. You can't make me stay here, Daddy," she told him.

Buffy was next. "Daddy, since we've been together I have always watched your back. Now I can't?"

Jake and Matt stood up and Bruce held up his hand, "I'm not saying now, nor have I ever said, any of you were not good. I consider all of you to be top operators, but you are showing signs of exhaustion. In the last few days, each of you have gotten sloppy. Not clearing a room right, loose patrol formations, or not pulling into the correct ambush. If this keeps up, one of you will make a mistake, causing either your death or that of a team member," Bruce told them as Stephanie walked in and sat down at the table.

Unsurprised, Bruce saw Danny still standing. "Daddy, I'm not tired. I can keep going, you need us out there with you. Even the soldiers here don't know what we know."

"Danny, yesterday when we cleared the school you just walked the halls and looked inside the rooms. I had to remind you and several others to keep alert. Clear buildings like you've been taught, never relax," Bruce told her.

"Okay, so I might've gotten a little sloppy but I knew nothing was there. I could feel it, Dad," Danny admitted.

"That's good, trust your gut, but it could've been wrong. Never let that be your lone answer. I've made that mistake and lost team members for it. This is a very unique situation now. Our army is our family, as well as our friends. Danny if you lose a teammate it could be your brother, sister, dad or mom. Everyone makes mistakes, Danny, but mistakes from exhaustion can be avoided, and that's what we're doing," Bruce tried to explain to her.

Then Buffy started in. "Daddy, I know Danny is better than me but I have been beside you since you saved me. Danny and I can keep going."

"I said no," Bruce told her.

Danny and Buffy started talking at once to Bruce. He closed his eyes and started rubbing his temples. He could feel two headaches coming on. One was seventeen, the other one was twelve. Bruce slammed both fists down on the table, causing everyone to jump and shut up. He looked at Danny and Buffy with anger on his face. How could these two do this to him? He did need them out there on patrol but they were going to get hurt if they kept up this pace. Bruce did not trust himself enough to talk so he just walked out and headed to the machine shop.

Danny headed to the door to follow but stopped when Debbie spoke, "Danny, don't bother your father right now."

"Mom, he has to understand," Danny told Debbie as she grabbed the door handle.

Debbie stood up, tucking PJ under her arm. "Danny, if you open that fucking door I will break your leg."

Chairs scraped across the floor as everyone on that side of the table tried to get to the other side, seeing the look on Debbie's face. Stephanie was the only one heading towards Debbie. Not to stop her but to get PJ out of her arms. Grabbing PJ from Debbie, Stephanie cleared the area, grabbing the twins who were still in their chairs and watching with open mouths.

Not believing what was happening, Danny took a step back, caught off guard, but quickly brushed it off. "Mom, I have to make him understand. I'm tough enough," Danny told her as she grabbed the door handle.

Debbie put her foot at the bottom of the door. "If you open that door, I'll break your leg," Debbie repeated in a flat voice.

Thinking she'd heard wrong, Danny just looked at her mom. Danny knew she was bigger and stronger than Mama and could take her nine out of ten times sparring. She really did not want to hurt her mom, but she was going to set this straight with Daddy. "Mom, I don't want to hurt you, so move before I have to move you," Danny told her.

Danny never even saw Debbie's hands come up, double palm striking her chest, pushing Danny back several feet. Danny narrowed her eyes as she turned her body sideways into a fighting stance, ignoring the pain from the strike.

"Mama, move. I'm going outside. I don't want to hurt you, but I will if I have to," Danny warned her.

Debbie was just standing in front of the door with her arms at her side. Her body was relaxed but when you looked at Debbie's face everyone could see she was pissed.

"Danny, if you threaten me again, I will break both of your legs. I will care for you afterwards because you are my daughter and I love you, but I will break both of them," Debbie warned her.

"Move, Mom," Danny said through clenched teeth.

"You are not going to bother your father. So you can stay in your stance all day, my mission is accomplished," Debbie told her.

Danny turned her body toward Debbie. She lunged forward to double palm strike Debbie in the chest and push her out of the way. Debbie saw the attack coming. Again, Danny never saw her mother move.

Debbie snapped out with her right foot into Danny's abdomen, forcing all the air out of her lungs and stopping her momentum. As Debbie's right foot was pulling back, she jumped off her left foot, snapping a kick into Danny's chest. If Danny would not have had on her tactical vest, the kick would have broken ribs. Enough force came through the vest to send pain into her chest, reeling Danny's body upright. Throwing out her arms, Danny tried to stop her movement backwards.

Debbie, seeing Danny throw her arms out, rushed forward, grabbing Danny's right wrist. Debbie rolled her body under the arm, pushing her hip into Danny's body. Flying over Debbie's back, Danny landed on the table with a loud crash, sending plates and glasses across the room.

Still holding Danny's right wrist, Debbie moved forward, pushing Danny's wrist into her armpit. Debbie put her right forearm under Danny's elbow with Debbie's right hand holding her left bicep. With her left hand,

Debbie grabbed Danny's right ear and a handful of hair. Then Debbie leaned back, applying pressure to the arm bar. When Danny tried to roll out of it, Debbie twisted her ear.

"Stop moving, Danny, or I'll hurt you. Daddy has taught me more and longer than you," Debbie told her in a forced calm voice that held tremors of anger. "I could've hurt you more than you will ever know. You are my baby. But don't think I won't rip off your arm and beat you with the bloody end of it. Now, you will listen to me. If you move or interrupt, I will break your wrist, then your forearm, elbow then shoulder. Then when you stand up, I will break both legs because that's what I promised you." Debbie released Danny's ear and hair. "Look at me," Debbie told her.

Danny rolled her head toward Debbie with anger on her face. Debbie moved forward, lifting the arm bar. "Wipe that look off of your face or I will do it for you," Debbie warned her. Danny tried not to scream as pain shot through her arm and shoulder.

"Are you ready to listen and respect your mother?" Debbie asked.

"Yes, ma'am," Danny told her, fighting the pain.

"If I tell your father you disobeyed me, then attacked me, he will spank you but you will no longer be his princess. Yes, he will love you but you will not be on that pedestal any longer as his little girl. This would kill Daddy, that his baby girl attacked her mama," Debbie told Danny. Tears formed in Danny's eyes, not from the pain but from the words, knowing Mama was right.

Debbie let go of the arm bar now that she had Danny's attention. Taking a step back, Debbie tried to release the tightness and tingling in her back. Since she had stood up she could feel the rage build but she did not want it trying to corral Danny.

Debbie took a few deep breaths before speaking. "Buffy, sit down in your chair and Danny, you sit beside her." Danny and Buffy moved slowly toward the chairs, Buffy from fear and Danny from pain, until Debbie screamed, "Now!" They dropped into the chairs, looking at Debbie.

"Now, you little princesses," Debbie said sarcastically. "You two have really hurt your daddy today more than I've ever seen. Danny, you should know better and set a better example for Buffy and the twins. The princesses should be the first to follow an order from Daddy. Everyone here knows what your daddy is doing to protect us from this fucked up world, but you two ..." Debbie paused, trying to keep calm. "You girls are trying to get

Daddy killed, along with everyone in this family. Let me lay out a scenario for you. Daddy takes you on patrol, you're tired and don't see an ambush and get wounded, either shot or bitten, it doesn't matter. Daddy will wade in like a horseman of the apocalypse trying to save his princesses. The boys are here because they listened and learned from Dad," Debbie told them and turned to the rest of the family.

"Which of you would go to try and help Bruce as he tried to rescue his daughters that treated him like shit and one that attacked her mother," Debbie asked them. Everyone raised their hand.

"You two just killed this entire family. Daddy knows what you're capable of, but, more importantly he knows what you're not capable of. This isn't the end of the world, just the beginning of a new one that is more violent and dangerous. We need Daddy at top form at all times, so quit your little girl games with him. Danny, if you would've gone after Daddy, he would've given in, you know it and I know it," Debbie told her.

"I don't always get my way," Danny said, crying, trying to defend herself.

Debbie looked at Jake and Steve, "Third party referee here."

"She's spoiled and Dad would have taken her along," Steve said.

"Yeah, Dad would have given in and tried to cover for her on the patrol," Jake agreed.

"Danny, Daddy doesn't love you more than the others but you're the baby girl," Debbie told Danny as tears rolled down Danny's face. Debbie turned to Buffy. "I'm really disappointed in you, Buffy. You were immediately moved to princess in Daddy's eyes and you didn't listen to him." Buffy threw her head on the table crying, then got up, running to Debbie and hugging her. Debbie hugged Buffy as Danny came over crying to join them.

Debbie pushed them back. "I want both of you to know this: 'Mamas run the family but daddies are the rock of the family.' I got mad because you hurt my rock," Debbie told them.

"I'm sorry, Mama," Danny told Debbie, hugging her again.

"I'm sorry, Mama. I won't be bad again," Buffy told Debbie, hugging her waist.

"Don't make promises like that, Buffy, you aren't even a teenager yet," Debbie told her. Then Debbie looked at both of them. "Girls, Daddy is never to know about this. Am I clear? Neither of you could handle the demotion from princess in Daddy's eyes. When he is an old man you both can tell him, but not before," Debbie told them and made them promise. After they promised, Debbie told them to find Bruce and tell him they were sorry and make him happy.

As the girls ran out to find Bruce, Debbie looked around to see everyone staring at her. Debbie took her pistol out of the holster and laid it on the table. "Let me just say this, nobody better talk about what happened here. If I gave birth to you, I will shoot you in one knee. If I didn't give birth to you, I will shoot you in both. That's the end of the discussion," Debbie told everyone.

Stephanie ran over to Debbie, putting an arm across her shoulders. "I will stab the ones she did not give birth to after she shoots you," Stephanie said, then leaned to Debbie. "I can't hurt your kids, so you're on your own there, but I still have your back," Stephanie told Debbie, making her smile.

Nancy walked over, putting her arm around Debbie also. "If any of mine say anything, I will nail them to a tree in the front yard after they're shot and stabbed."

"Don't piss the mamas off. Lesson learned," Conner said from the den, causing a round of laughter.

Debbie started picking up the dishes off the floor but Millie and Lynn came running over to her. "Leave it baby, sit down," Millie told her as everyone started cleaning up and Debbie sat down.

"They all do it, baby. I did it with two of my three daughters and my husband taked all but one of the boys outside. My mama put a beating on me with her own two hands when I thought I was too big for my britches," Millie told her.

"Millie, I just bodyslammed my daughter on the table," Debbie said, almost regretting her actions.

"Yeah, but she earned it. Debbie, you could've done worse but only did enough to keep her attention like my mama did to me and I did to my girls. You and Bruce teached her how to fight like a man so it hasta goes up a notch. Danny may be a teenage girl but she can beats most men I know. Debbie, you could takes all de men I know. Teaching Danny to fight is more valuable than all the gold in the world now," Millie told Debbie.

Debbie looked at Millie. "Thank you, I needed to hear that."

"I just hopes your boys don't go tryin' to challenge Bruce," Millie told her.

Debbie just smiled at Millie then leaned forward, looking down the table at Steve. "Too late," Debbie told her. Steve just looked away, ignoring his mama. Tonya was asking him what happened but Steve acted like he didn't understand English.

Debbie shifted her gaze to Jake. "What? I haven't been to the backyard. I saw what happened to Steve," Jake told her, then added, "If Dad tells me to squat and shit, the only thing I'm asking him is what color he wants."

Debbie looked at the clock. It was 0740 and it felt like they should be getting ready for bed instead of starting the day. PJ crawled across the table from Stephanie to her. Debbie picked him up, giving him kisses. She realized that no one was going to work and then it occurred that they were waiting on Bruce. She made small talk with everyone until Bruce walked in with the girls and everyone became quiet.

Bruce moved to his chair at the head of the table. "I am canceling the patrol and the scavenging group today. We'll move tomorrow," Bruce told everyone.

Mike stood up. "Bruce, we're pouring the slab for the storage area tomorrow and putting the walls up on the barracks. We'll have to send the scavenge group to get the rest of the cement tomorrow. We haven't seen a blue within twenty miles of the farm. The only movement we've seen is over at Marcus's farm. Your patrol was going to be five miles from the group on horseback. Even if something were to happen to the scavenging group, backup from the farm would reach them before you on horseback," Mike told him.

Conner spoke next, "I'm not disagreeing with you, Bruce, but we need to stay with the schedule. We'll have two Strykers and two Hummers with the protection team."

"I think everyone is ready to spread out to eat. If we get the supplies today, two days from now we can eat together in the Center," Alex said, wanting the Community Center open.

Mike looked at Bruce. "Bruce, you spent two days in Saline clearing the town almost house to house. If we get hit, there's no avoiding it. You've told us we're going to lose people and be attacked. I'm not saying let's just do it, but you are right. We just can't stay here trying to stack all the odds in our favor. Bruce, you can't keep pushing yourself like this, trying to pacify an entire area before we move in to gather supplies. Too many people are depending on you. Not to fight all the battles but to lead and guide us."

Mike laid it out for him so he'd see that the others were willing to take the risk.

Bruce took a deep breath, knowing Mike was right. "Alright, the op is a go. Mike, you'll run it from Mission Control. Conner, you'll command the patrol; set up commanders for your protection detail and scavenger team. Jake, Matt, Danny, Mary, Buffy, and Debbie, all of you in the den, we're the backup team. I want each of you laying down and resting. No games, but you may read, and no leaving without my permission. Gear check in twenty for my team then it's inside all day. Conner, you're to leave at 1000. It should take you only four or five hours, but done or not you're back at base by 1700. Let's get it done, people," Bruce told them.

The protection team had fourteen assigned to it and the scavenge team had twenty-eight. It would be one of the largest patrols they had sent out but they were going after a lot. They would be emptying a restaurant of its kitchen appliances and supplies. Then heading to the school to get the large folding tables and dishwasher and anything else they found useful at each site.

Even with the preparation, the specter of battle had turned its eye upon the clan.

CHAPTER 20

The supply group had left thirty minutes ago. Bruce was lying back in his recliner, reading the notebooks the three idiots had filled out with lists of supply stockpiles. Matt and Jake were going over the laptops that they had gone back and gotten from the overrun camp. Bruce was marking places in a road atlas of locations while the boys printed copies of inventory list from the sites. The lists were very impressive and they had located hundreds of millions of rounds and stockpiles of weapons that the government had stored around the country.

Laying his notebook across his chest Bruce looked around. Danny, Mary and Buffy were asleep on one couch. Debbie, Stephanie, PJ and the twins were on the other couch sleeping. Bruce looked at the boys where they were working the laptops over and smiling. Bruce had asked Jake and Matt if they wanted him to ask for the passwords. They just looked at him and told him no, that would ruin the fun.

"Matt, Jake," Bruce called them, "why don't y'all take a break and get some sleep?"

"I'm good, Dad," Jake told him.

"Me too," Matt replied.

"Sunday we're going to have a report that will knock your socks off, Dad," Jake told Bruce as Bruce drifted off to sleep.

Bruce felt a hand shake his shoulder and he opened his eyes to find Mike standing over him. "They just left the restaurant heading to the school. The UAVs haven't seen anything. The school shouldn't take as long so we should stay on schedule," Mike told him as he headed back to Mission Control.

Bruce lifted his arm and looked at his watch, reading 1420. *Damn, the restaurant must have been a bitch*, Bruce thought. He looked around; the girls were still asleep on the couch but Debbie and Stephanie were chatting quietly together on the couch while they watched PJ crawl around on the floor.

Bruce stretched his arms over his head. The recliner was normally very comfortable but with a full tactical vest on it wasn't. Bruce finished his stretch as Millie held out a plate of food for him. Smiling at her, Bruce took it and started to eat, finishing it in minutes. He Bruce got up and took his plate to the kitchen, grabbed another glass of tea and headed to Mission Control.

Walking into the room, he saw Pam at the radios and monitors. A teenage boy was at the UAV station taking orders from Mike. Mike was watching the large monitor and looking at a map in his hand. Bruce went over to stand by him.

"I have the UAV on the perimeter now making circles. They have all the tables that we need. They are dismantling the dishwasher, grabbing books and food. Conner said another hour and they'll leave," Mike told him. Bruce nodded his head. When the patrol came back, he was going to bed.

"We're under attack!" came over the radio. Mike ran over and grabbed the microphone.

"Repeat your last," Mike called.

"We're under attack, taking fire from the north across the road. Have several wounded," Conner replied. Bruce could hear gunfire in the background.

Bruce walked over to the monitor as the teen flew the UAV to the school. The school was in the middle of a field with the north side facing the road and houses on the other side. Bruce could see gunfire coming from several of the houses. The Strykers were blasting away at the houses with the big 50s blowing large holes in them.

"Debbie, get the team up and ready. Jake, come here now!" Bruce yelled. In a few seconds Jake was in the room.

"Jake, get another UAV up and fly it down the road to Saline then take the road north," Bruce told him as he watched the monitor.

"Mike, tell Conner to fire the Mk-19 and level those houses," Bruce said and Mike relayed the message.

"The Mk-19 gunner is dead; have tried to replace him but a sniper is covering the Hummer and two more have been wounded," Conner called back.

"Conner, tell everyone to fire whatever they have in every direction and someone get on that weapon or you're dead," Mike told him.

They watched on the large screen as everyone started firing and a lone figure ran to the Hummer which had the automatic grenade launcher only to be cut down. Bruce told the kid at the UAV console to turn the camera to thermal.

"Sir, thermal runs the batteries down real fast," the kid replied.

"I don't care if the damn thing crashes, find that sniper," Bruce told him.

The fifty-inch TV went to black and white. Everyone saw the person lying prone on a roof way down the road that ran in front of the school. Mike called out the sniper's position and one of the Strykers swung their weapons around and unloaded on the house.

"Dad, here we are," Jake told Bruce, looking down at his small control station flying the second UAV.

"We're ready, Bruce," Debbie told Bruce, hurrying into the room.

"Wait, this isn't right," Bruce told her as he watched the little monitor in front of Jake. After a few minutes, Bruce pointed at the screen. "There, circle there," Bruce told him.

"What do you see?" Jake asked as he circled.

Bruce pointed at a small hot spot beside the road, "That's an explosive device. You can see a small stripe going back to the house. Mike, ask Conner if anyone has advanced on them to overrun their position," Bruce told Mike and he relayed that to Conner.

"Negative, we have taken out the houses and we're only receiving sporadic fire. I'm fixin' to call a withdrawal," Conner called back.

"No, tell him to stay put, there are ambush teams out there blocking off the escape routes!" Bruce yelled.

"Found them!" Jake hollered. Bruce walked over to the little monitor.

"They are in these houses and back in the tree line here." Jake pointed out three houses on each side of the road.

"Good work, son, now head north and see where that one is at," Bruce told him. Turning to the group, he said, "Debbie, go tell everyone to stop working and get their weapons and start putting people around the property. Get the kids into the basement. Danny, Buffy and Mary help her." As Bruce barked out orders they all just stared at him. "Either our farm or Marcus's farm is fixin' to get hit, now move!" Bruce told them and they took off running.

"Oh shit, Dad look!" Jake said. "I'm eight miles north and I count at least forty," he finished.

Bruce looked at the screen. The group was on the outside of a curve in the road and spread out along the side of the road back in the tree line. "Shit!" Bruce said as he walked to the desk and picked up the chart of code words they used with Marcus over the CB. Scanning the list, Bruce found: Attack Imminent=Snowball.

Bruce grabbed the CB. "Jake, watch that group to the north," he said as he keyed the CB. "Weather Station, this is Sunny Sky," Bruce hailed the Marcus farm.

A female voice called back, "Hi Sunny Sky, this is Weather Station."

"Weather Station, Snowball, I repeat: Snowball," Bruce said into the CB. In his mind's eye, he could picture the woman going through the list and freezing at what she found.

She came back on, her voice trembling. "Copy, Snowball."

"Tell the big man two snowballs that shoot, and they're big ass snowballs. Sunny Sky out." Bruce threw down the CB mic.

"Dad, these guys are going ape shit here and more are pulling up to the road out of the woods. It's over a hundred now easy, I'm guessing closer to two hundred," Jake told Bruce.

Bruce looked at Mike. "They're listening to the CB. They know about Marcus; I'm not sure about us. They attacked the patrol and are waiting on the backup to come and they're going to ambush it. With a lot of the fighters gone, they can just waltz in and take over the compounds."

Mike looked at him. "How can you know that Bruce?"

"It's what I would do. Hit the supply team; when the strike force with your best fighters in it comes to the rescue, knock it out," Bruce said.

"What about our people? We can't leave them!"

"The road south will probably have a smaller ambush. I would put just a small force there to catch those trying to escape. When you find it, tell Conner to load up and when they get close, unload on the area and bring them home," Bruce told him. As Mike started to call Conner, Bruce stopped him. "Tell Conner to make sure everyone is accounted for. Those assholes probably want to capture someone to find out about us," Bruce told him and Mike relayed the plan and about the ambushes in place.

After Mike finished with Conner, he looked at Bruce. "What are you going to do?"

"I'm going to talk to them. I want to know how they found us. I didn't invite them," Bruce said as he walked out of the room, and Mike ran after him.

"Bruce, we can't repel an attack if you take your team out. That'll leave us with a lot of people here that can barely shoot," Mike told him.

"I'm going alone," Bruce replied as he grabbed his pack and weapon and headed outside.

"Bruce, don't go, we need you here," Mike begged him.

"Mike, run the battle. Quit thinking civilized and think like a criminal," Bruce told him, then headed out back.

Bruce keyed the radio. "Debbie, meet me at the machine shop. Jake, get me a number on the ambush to the west of Saline." Debbie didn't answer but Jake copied.

Bruce hopped on one of the four-wheelers that Paul had muffled down. Debbie came up to him.

"Where are you going?" she demanded.

"I'm going to talk to them and find out how they found us. They make for poor company," Bruce said.

"Let me come with you then," Debbie said.

"No, I'll have to move fast. If they hit us, it'll be hard and they'll be throwing a lot of firepower. You'll be needed here. Remind Mike that wounded will be coming in with this group. Use the Community Center," Bruce told her then added, "I love you, sugar mama."

"I love you too, you better be careful and come back," Debbie said as she kissed him.

Bruce started the four-wheeler and sped off. Once he cleared the gate, he opened the throttle. As usual, the tires made more noise than the engine as he rolled down the road. The ambush was eighteen miles by road from the farm. Bruce figured he could stop half a mile away and move up on foot.

Twenty minutes later, Bruce pulled off the road into the tree line and turned off the engine. Mike called him over the radio.

"Bruce, I've been calling you for the last five minutes. We found the ambush site to the south. Conner just leveled it and is on the way home. I sent a UAV to Marcus's farm and we found an OP (observation post) but I can't tell him. Hold on, Jake wants to talk to you," Mike said.

"Dad, I've counted sixteen, two on the north side of the road in the house sitting alone. On the south side of the road all fourteen went into one house when Conner left," Jake told him.

Bruce walked into the woods on the north side and started jogging to the ambush site. Then he asked Jake, "Why do you think they did that, son?"

"I think they were in place to stop the patrol if they tried to escape, and now that the patrol has escaped they are just shooting the shit," Jake told him. Then Jake asked, "Dad, the patrol rolled right through that ambush site to get to the school; why didn't they hit it then?"

"You tell me," Bruce said, slowing down

"The patrol was too big and they wanted to get the ones sent to rescue them because that would be a smaller force but have a lot of fighters," Jake guessed.

"Very good, son, but the site to the north was the primary ambush site. It's the direct route to Marcus's farm. This group was to stop the supply convoy when the main group ambushed the relief convoy. I'm here," Bruce whispered, feeling the rage build, the tightness in his back and the chill bumps on his arm starting to come up.

"I can see you. The two-story house to your right, on the second floor, room closest to you overlooking the road is where I saw two through the window," Jake told him.

"What about the group to the north?" Bruce whispered from the tree line in the backyard of the house. The back door was open and two Harleys were by the back door.

"About twenty went to the school and Conner and his team killed a lot of the ambushers. We counted twenty-seven bodies laid out. The rest just stayed up north; the count up there is a hundred and fifty-four not counting the twenty that left. Stephanie is in here and she can count fast," Jake told him.

"Watch your Daddy's ass, I'm going in," Bruce said, feeling the wave.

"Area around the house clear," Jake said.

Bruce pulled out his XDM. Feeling great, he ran across the yard stopping at the doorway before he went in the back door. Not hearing anything, he leveled his pistol and went in. The first room was a kitchen that opened into a living room with a hallway on his left. Not seeing anything, he slowly walked forward toward the hallway.

The first area he came to was a circular stairwell. He could hear voices upstairs. He continued down the hall, finding a bathroom, office and a master bedroom, all empty. He moved back to the stairway, keeping to the side of the stairs. With his pistol aimed up, he slowly moved upstairs and the voices started getting louder.

Reaching the top, Bruce could make out two voices coming from the right where Jake had seen two through the window. The hallway at the top of the stairs ran the length of the house. Bruce looked quickly to the left and saw two doors, one on each side of the hall; both closed. Looking right he saw only one open door on the left side of the hall.

Bruce moved into the hall, aiming at the open door as he eased down the hall. Stopping at the door, he could hear two people arguing about why they didn't get to kill someone. Feeling a bit brash, Bruce decided to rush the room. Swinging around the doorway, he saw two men staring out the window; one had a pair of binoculars, the other one was just looking out the window and he was closer. Bruce moved toward him and launched his boot toward the man's face.

The target must have sensed him, because he started to turn just as Bruce's boot caught him in the mouth, sending him into the wall then sliding to the floor. The target with the binoculars was turning toward them as Bruce brought the pistol down across his nose. Bruce felt the bone crunch as he drove the man to the floor with another hit. The first target groaned as Bruce walked over and stomped on his head, knocking him out. Then, turning to the other peeping tom Bruce kicked him in the side of the head, making sure he was knocked out.

Bruce zip-tied their wrists and ankles then he zip-tied their thumbs. Reaching in the bottom pocket of his pack, he took out the fix-it-all for every man alive, a roll of gray duct tape. He wrapped tape around their head, covering their mouths. Then he quickly frisked them, pulling out knives and pistols. Standing up, Bruce looked around the room. On the bed he noticed an AK-47, an M-16 with a 203-grenade launcher and two saddlebags with ammo. Looking at the window, Bruce saw five charging claymore detonators. He disconnected the detonators, throwing them on the bed. Then Bruce looked out the window at the house directly across from him. It was a single-story brick house.

"That was good, Dad," Jake told him.

"What about the others?" Bruce whispered, not knowing if the house was clear as he moved out of the room.

"The ones across from you are still in the house. The group to the north is staying put. Those at the school went south but everyone there is dead," Jake told Bruce as his dad cleared the rest of the house.

"We'll send them some flowers," Bruce told him as he headed back into the room with the bikers, holstering his pistol.

"I'll take the flowers to them. It's the least I can do," Jake said.

"That's nice of you, son," Bruce said as he looked around the room again. This time he saw a large black duffle bag. Bruce opened it, finding a shitload of claymores, C-4 and detonator cord. Bruce closed the bag and took it downstairs with him. He dropped the bag by the bikes at the back door. The bag had to weigh over a hundred pounds. *It was really nice of these guys to bring me new toys*, Bruce thought.

Bruce ran into the woods behind the house. Turning to his left, he ran forty yards then moved to the road. Bruce saw two houses, a small house then the target house down the road to his right. He darted across the road. Running to the first house, Bruce stopped on the wall.

"That's the house half of those guys came out of," Jake told him.

"Checking it out; watch our friends," Bruce said as he moved to the back, finding the door kicked in. Bruce searched the house, finding only whiskey bottles and drug paraphernalia. "House clear," he called.

"I think our friends are shy, Dad, they don't want to come out. The back door is open and I can see several in that room," Jake told him.

"Well, let me go and talk to them," Bruce said as he ran toward the side of the house, stopping between two windows.

Bruce had his back to the house and he eased to the backyard, ducking under the windows. Then he looked around the corner into the backyard. Bruce saw over a dozen bikes tucked in the tree line behind the other house in the backyard. He noticed a small shed on the far side of the yard. Looking down the back of the house, Bruce saw three windows.

Aiming his SCAR at the open back door, Bruce eased down the back wall of the house. Looking in the first window, he saw it was a bedroom and could not see anyone. The next window was frosted so he guessed it was a bathroom. Moving to the last window, Bruce could hear the voices real good now. He slowly stood up, easing his left eye to the window, then kneeled back down, watching the back door.

The room was a kitchen with a dining room on the front of the house. It looked like all of the bikers were in those rooms, drinking. Bruce pulled two hand grenades off his vest and straightened out the pins and pulled them.

Bruce let the safety spoons fly. After counting off his three seconds, he ran past the open door. The grenade in his right hand he threw into the front of the house and the other he threw in the kitchen as he passed the door. Then Bruce dove, covering his ears. As he hit the ground he heard the explosion behind him. Bruce rolled over, bringing his SCAR up, and ran through the back door into the kitchen.

The kitchen was covered with body parts; there were no complete bodies. Bruce moved into the dining room and found more body parts, but did see a couple of bodies. The dining room opened into a living room with a hall. Bruce moved to the hall and found a biker crawling on the floor and stomped on the back of his head. Then he opened the door he thought led to the bathroom. A man was laying on the floor, moaning and holding his ears. "Are you okay, sir?" Bruce asked then stomped on his face twice until he shut up.

Bruce cleared the rest of the house, not finding anyone else. He tied up the two he found with zip-ties and duct tape. Then he moved back to check on the bodies in the living room. Bruce found one alive, but he fixed that problem. The weapons in the two rooms were wasted.

Bruce stepped out the back door as Jake called, "That was awesome, but isn't that cheating?"

"Not in my game, I have good rules," Bruce told him, heading to the shed in the backyard.

"I like your game. Can I ask you something, Dad?" Jake inquired.

"Sure," Bruce said as he stopped at the shed and found what he needed on the side. A lawn trailer for a lawn mower or, in this case, Bruce's four-wheeler, to haul shit home.

"Are you riding the wave?" Jake asked.

"Oh yeah. What are their friends doing, son?" Bruce asked as he headed to the bikes.

"Nothing, just hanging out. I don't think they could've heard the grenades. They're six miles away," Jake said.

"I wasn't worried about that; the house is brick and contained the concussion real good. If their friends show up, I just want to make sure that I have party surprises for them," Bruce told Jake as he looked at the bikes.

He found one with keys in it, started it up and took off to his four-wheeler. Pulling into the woods where he'd parked his ride, Bruce just dropped the bike as he climbed on his ATV and went back to the single-story house. Heading to the shed, Bruce hooked up the lawn trailer and headed to the house.

"Dad, I wanted that bike," Jake told Bruce as he headed into the house and picked up his new friends, dumping them in the trailer.

"Sorry son, I just dropped it," Bruce said as he drove back to the first house.

Bruce grabbed the two from upstairs one at a time and dumped them in the trailer on top of the others. Then Bruce went back to get the gear. The weapons he strapped to his front rack. Then he went to the front yard to collect the claymores by the road.

The claymore mine Bruce had seen from the UAV was sitting by the road. The branches and leaves had blown off of it. That was the only reason he had seen it. Looking up, Bruce told God, "Thank you," as he grabbed the claymore and tracked down the others. Over the next half hour, working fast, he set up some surprises for his new friends. Bruce really hoped the targets enjoyed his work.

Finished setting up the presents for his new targets, Bruce walked to his ATV. Seeing one of the bikers looking around, Bruce kicked him in the head. "It's naptime, asshole," Bruce said as he climbed on, started the ATV and headed home.

Turning down his road, Bruce called ahead for the gate to open and for someone to have the bay door on the shop open. Bruce pulled through the gate then drove to the shop. Bruce pulled the ATV and trailer, with his party guests, into the bay. He got off and walked toward the Center where people were gathered around. Debbie came running up to him and wrapped her arms around him as she cried.

"What's wrong, baby?" Bruce asked.

"Bruce, three were killed and seven were wounded. Mike has stabilized them but he thinks we're going to lose two more." Debbie told Bruce.

Then she looked up at Bruce, eyes damp but steely. "Alex was killed. He was on the Mk19 and they shot him first."

"Where's Angela?" Bruce asked, suppressing his anger.

"She ran to our room when she found out. Stephanie is with her," Debbie told him.

"I will talk to her tomorrow. I have one more errand to run and then I have to play with my new friends. I really want these guys to appreciate what I do to them," Bruce told her. "I have to check in at Mission Control, then I'm going to Marcus's. You go help Mike."

"Why are you going to Marcus's?" Debbie asked.

"He has a peeping tom problem," Bruce told her as he headed to the house.

Bruce walked into Mission Control to find Jake and Matt at the UAV station. "Keep one UAV on our friends. I left some presents for them and I want to see if they like them," Bruce told them. Then he said, "Show me the ones at Marcus's."

Jake played the recorded flight over Marcus's farm and Bruce saw where the enemy OP was at. "Jake, get a UAV ready to follow your dad again. After I take care of these two, I want you to call Marcus and tell him to meet me at the gate, in code of course. Give me our backup home radio. I'm giving it to Marcus," Bruce said and Jake gave Bruce the box with the backup home radio. It was not foolproof but it was like the radios they used to carry. It operated on different frequencies and was encoded thanks to the geeks. Bruce was not really worried about a gang cracking the military radios they carried now. The government however, was a different story.

Running down into the basement, Bruce grabbed the last thermal scope and headed back outside to the shop. Jumping on another ATV, Bruce took off. The sun was touching the horizon as Bruce slowed down to fifteen miles per hour and eased down the dirt road and past the driveway. Once Bruce was past the field, he eased the ATV into the woods and climbed off.

The two he was after were six hundred yards in the woods at the edge of the field. Bruce pulled out his NVGs and put them on his head and entered the woods, moving very slowly.

"Dad, they're still in the same spot. Why are you moving so slow?" Jake asked.

"Savoring the moment, son, never rush. You must enjoy the finer things in life, and sneaking up on a sniper is one of the best," Bruce whispered back, switching his radio to voice activated.

It was dark as Bruce reached the area where the two were hunkered down; he carried his pistol in his right hand and his knife in his left. It took him a few seconds to find them with his monocular on. They were hiding under camouflaged netting, otherwise known as a ghillie blanket. Bruce kneeled down and crept forward silently. One was looking through a thermal scope on a Barrett M82 fifty cal. The spotter was looking through an NV scope. The spotter picked up the radio and reported to someone then sat the radio down. Bruce lined up the site and squeezed the trigger. The .45 caliber slug hit the spotter in the back of the head, blowing out his forehead. Before his head hit the ground, Bruce put the suppressor on the back of the sniper's head.

"Need I say more?" Bruce challenged. The sniper moved his hands away from his weapon.

"Behind your back real slow," Bruce told the sniper as he put his knife up. Keeping the pistol to the back of the man's head, he pulled out a zip-tie. Just as the man's hands came together, Bruce eased the zip-tie loop over his hands, careful not to touch them. Bruce yanked the loop tight, dropping his knee on the man's back. "I know that move, boy. Try anything like that again and fuck what the boss says, you die," Bruce warned him.

"I'm dead anyway," the sniper said.

"Boss seen you out here and told me to 'bring in the sniper.' He wants to see if you wanted new employment. That's why you're alive and your spotter isn't," Bruce lied.

"You serious?" the sniper asked with relief.

"Why do you think you're still breathing, dumbass?" Bruce told him.

"Well let's go and see the boss," the sniper replied in a grateful tone.

"Not so fast," Bruce said as he zip-tied the sniper's thumbs together then frisked him, removing two knives and a pistol. Bruce packed up the equipment, hanging some of it off the sniper. The only thing he left behind was the spotter's naked body.

"Head to the road and don't be stupid, I really don't want to kill you. Boss is givin' me a fine bitch for bringing your ass in," Bruce told the sniper.

"Boss pays in women?" the sniper asked in amazement.

"What the hell else would you get paid in? You can choose drugs because the boss grows a lot, but I need to keep my edge," Bruce told the sniper.

"Damn, man, lets go and see Boss, I'll work for him," the sniper said, picking up his pace to the road.

"Hold on, you don't work for Boss yet," Bruce told him as they walked out onto the road. Then Bruce led him to the ATV. He took all the equipment and put it on the front rack, strapping it down. The M82 stuck out on each side of the ATV.

Bruce grabbed the sniper and laid him on the back rack and zip-tied him to it. Then Bruce zip-tied his ankles together. "That isn't necessary," the sniper said.

"Shut up, I'm tired of talking to you," Bruce told him and called Jake on the radio. "Call Marcus, I'm moving. Let me know when you get a reply," Bruce told Jake.

"Already did that, Dad. Your voice mic was still on and let me tell you, Dad, I think you could sell ice cubes to an Eskimo," Jake told him.

"Thank you, son," Bruce replied to the comment.

"They're waiting on you, Dad," Jake said.

Bruce jumped on the ATV and headed to Marcus's house. He approached the gate slowly, looking at the log fence that surrounded the house and barn. Jake came over the radio and told Bruce that two people were lying in the ditch beside the gate, not moving. Bruce stopped twenty yards from the gate and pointed his SCAR where Jake said they were at.

"If you two aren't part of this farm, Carroll's garden is fixin' to get fertilizer," Bruce said.

Darrell stood up from the ditch. "Bruce, is that you?"

"Who the fuck you think it is? The Easter bunny?" Bruce asked.

"I thought you were a trick or treater, it's almost that time," Darrell said as the log gate opened and Marcus and Carroll came out.

Marcus and Carroll walked over to Bruce, each carrying one of the M-4s Bruce had given them. "It's good to see ya, Bruce. What's goin' on?" Marcus asked.

"Marcus, I don't have long. A very large group knows about ya. This asshole was on the edge of your field watching you. They thought my supply patrol today was your people and hit it. We lost several, including Alex," Bruce told them as the sniper yelled, "You fucking lied!"

Spinning around, Bruce rained down blows, beating the man unconscious. Satisfied and feeling better, Bruce turned back around and handed Marcus the radio and thermal scope. "This radio is hard to listen in on and the case holds a thermal scope so you can catch any more peeping toms. I need to get back. If I was you, I would stay in a few days. Let me talk to our new friends and find out where they live. I'll pay them a visit," Bruce told them.

Carroll came over and hugged him, "You tell little Angela my prayers be with her n' Cade. When this's over, we comin' visitin'."

"I would like that Carroll, but now I need to go. Just another thought: You may want to keep half of your people awake at all times," Bruce told them as he sped off down the road.

Driving like a bat out of hell, Bruce headed back to the farm. The monocular eye piece made it very interesting. It was like driving with one eye closed, the other looking through a soda straw. Bruce called for the gate to open then he drove to the shop and just left the ATV parked in front. Before he went inside, he taped the sniper's mouth shut. Then Bruce pulled out his pistol and shot the sniper in the foot. The sniper woke up screaming, but wasn't doing a good job with his mouth taped shut.

"Just making sure you're awake. I wanted you to know, I'm a liar and an asshole," Bruce said as he walked to the house, carrying the M82.

"Hurry Dad! They're heading to your presents!" Jake called over the radio. Bruce ran inside the house and people were everywhere. They parted like the Red Sea for him.

Bruce walked into Mission Control and Jake pointed at the fifty-inch screen. Bruce counted twenty-one bikes moving down the road, with one in the lead and the others riding two by two. It was going to be close, but Bruce thought they all might like his presents. The bikes started to slow as they approached the houses. When they were forty yards away the screen went white. Then Matt panned out with the camera.

Several fires were burning in the road, but Bruce had gotten all the bikes with the claymores. Bruce smiled as the screen changed and he realized he was looking at the group to the north. People were running for bikes, heading toward the present area.

"Oh, this is too good," Bruce said. He couldn't count the number of bikes as they sped down the road. Several stopped at the explosion site then moved toward the second house, pulling into the backyard. A few moved toward the first house, pulling around back. "House one just got turned on," Bruce said to himself, smiling.

At house number two where Bruce had thrown the grenades someone entered the house and the screen went white for a brief second; then they could see the carnage. The bikes at house one attempted to leave and the screen went white again, then explosions started going off along the road. When the explosions stopped, Jake started panning around. They could see a few crawling but none walking. The screen switched again to the group up north. They saw everyone hop on bikes or pile in trucks and speed off, leaving the dead and wounded behind to the east.

"Jake, can you slow that down later and tell me how many got away?" Bruce asked.

"Sixty-seven motorcycles and four trucks," Stephanie said from beside him.

"Hey, hot stuff. How many did I get with my presents?" Bruce asked, really wanting to know.

"Twenty-one in the first group and thirty-six in the second," Stephanie told him emotionlessly.

"Son, make me a copy of that. I may want to spank the monkey to that later," Bruce said.

"I was going to do that, Dad. And you're married," Jake shot back.

"Make two copies and here, I brought you a present," Bruce said, handing him the M82.

"Oh, hell yeah! Thank you, Dad," Jake told him, grabbing the sniper rifle others called a cannon.

Bruce left Mission Control, heading to the shop. Outside the shop, he stopped and closed his eyes, taking deep breaths. Bruce locked his heart and reminded himself that they were not human, just targets. Then he cut the sniper off the ATV, threw him over his shoulder and walked into the shop.

One of the four from the wagon had gotten out and inchwormed over to the shop tables. He had a piece of metal and was trying to use the edge to cut the zip-ties, but success was evading him with his thumbs tied. Bruce dropped the sniper on the table and walked over to the inchworm.

Bruce took the metal rod from him and looked at it then leaned down to the inchworm. "You need a knife for that," Bruce told him, shaking his head. "Here, you can use mine," Bruce said as he drove his knife through the front of Inchworm's right thigh, leaving the tip sticking out the back of his thigh. "All you had to do was ask, dumbass. See, now ya have a knife," Bruce told Inchworm over his muffled shrieks.

Walking to the far side of the shop, Bruce hummed a tune as he grabbed some ratchet straps. Moving to the table, he strapped the sniper to the table from head to feet. He looked up to see Mike standing in the bay door. "How long have you been there?" Bruce asked as he took the sniper's boot off of the foot he'd shot.

"Since you let that asshole borrow your knife. Bruce, he never told you thank you," Mike said, walking over to the table.

"You're right, I will talk with him about manners later," Bruce said vivaciously as he went through the sniper's pockets.

"This guy's foot is bleeding pretty badly. He'll probably pass out before long. I can fix that," Mike offered.

Reaching back, Bruce grabbed a blow torch and lit it. Then he held the flame over the top of the man's foot, then the bottom. The sniper tried to scream and move but couldn't do either. Bruce turned the torch off and put it back after cauterizing the wound.

"It's fixed," Bruce smiled.

"I want to help," Mike requested.

"No, Mike," Bruce told him. He walked walking around the table, grabbed his arm and led him out the bay door.

When they were outside, Bruce looked at his best friend. "Mike, this is on me. I know you think you want to, but trust me, you don't. That won't make Alex come back and it'll only make the hurt worse. Take these packs inside and go through 'em; they belong to the sniper and spotter. There's a radio in one, so go away, I have work to do."

"Why do you always get to be the hero?" Mike asked.

"Hero, Mike? I'm fixing to go in this shop and destroy a piece of my soul. With the shit I've done in this life, I have no hope of ever seeing heaven. But I can make sure this family can, plus I can make sure the family remains safe while here on this farm," Bruce said.

"Bruce, everyone looks at you like you are a god. You always do what needs to be done. Let me help," Mike begged, and Bruce studied him.

"Mike, you lie for shit," Bruce told him. After studying Mike's face, Bruce knew Mike was saying anything so Bruce would let him help. "I miss Alex too but I can't think about that now. You're bringing me down, Mike, and making this harder for me. I can't let the anger rule me. If I stay out here much longer, I'm going to have to use anger to do what needs to be done. Now I'm begging you, leave me alone please."

Mike turned and headed to the house. Before Bruce turned back to the shop, Mike called back, "You're wrong, Bruce, you've done more than any of us to get into heaven. You're willing to sacrifice your soul for this family and clan. If that's not good enough to get into heaven, then I don't want to go."

Bruce stood there for a moment and wished he could believe Mike. Taking deep breaths and pumping the wave up, he told himself, *You can do this, you've done it before and you can live with it afterwards.* His breathing picked up and the tightness spread across his back. Bruce smiled as he crested the wave before stepping into the bay door. Closing it behind him, he walked back to the table and looked at his targets.

"Where did we leave off? I have so much to show you," Bruce said, smiling and rubbing his hands together.

CHAPTER 21

The next morning, Mike was sitting at the table trying to eat breakfast. Two of the wounded had died during the night but the other five should make it if they didn't get an infection. Mike chuckled with that thought. Infection had a totally different meaning now, and the only joy he felt was from hearing the screams coming out of the shop.

Looking around the table, Mike stared at the chair where Alex used to sit. Angela was still in Debbie's room with Cade, who would stay with her for a little while but then leave; he would come back and ask Angela where Daddy was. Then Angela would try to explain again to a two-year-old that Daddy was gone. Cade would cry with Angela then leave; an hour or so later he'd come back and it would start all over.

Hate was in Mike's heart like he had never felt before. They just wanted to live in peace, and living humans had killed good people. Hundreds of millions of infected wanted to do that but no, it was living humans who had killed members of the clan. Tears rolled down his cheeks as he thought about it. He wanted to barge into that shop and make Bruce let him help. Then a part of him was glad Bruce had made him leave.

Stephanie walked in and sat down across from Debbie. "How is she?" Nancy asked. Stephanie just looked at her with a blank stare.

Stephanie turned to Debbie. "I want to help Bruce," she told Debbie. Before Debbie could answer, Mike did.

"No, leave him alone. Bruce is taking care of it," Mike said as Paul came in the back door. They all heard a loud scream from the shop. Paul closed the door, cutting off the scream.

"Let's give everyone a day off, Mike," Paul suggested.

297

"We'll talk about it later, Paul," Mike replied as Angela walked in, carrying Cade. Mike jumped up, pulling out her chair.

"Thank you, Mike. Cade wanted to come down and eat," Angela told him.

"What's that boy wanna eat?" Millie asked.

"Cakes," Cade said, clapping his hands.

"Pancakes, baby?" Millie asked, causing Cade to jump up and down in Angela's lap. The cook staff went into high gear to make the baby some pancakes.

Mike sat back down in his chair as Paul came up beside him. "Mike, the night crew is going out of their minds out there. They've worked the past twelve hours listening to those screams."

"I want to hear the screams," Angela said. Paul went to the back door and opened it up, letting the screams come in. Angela closed her eyes, savoring the screams. Debbie saw the look on Angela's face. It was pure hate and anger but filled with a dark joy.

"Paul, close the door please," Mike said and Paul closed it.

"No, leave it open," Angela said.

"No, Angela, I need to talk to you. We need to bury Alex today," Mike said firmly.

Angela looked at Mike and tears started rolling down her face as she answered, "Alex wanted to be buried in the evening. He said he wanted to go down with the sun, and when the sun came up the next day, he would be watching over us."

Mike looked at Angela as she wept silently. Mike could tell she was fighting the grief and losing. "We'll bury him at sunset today then. Father Thomas will perform the service," Mike told her and Angela nodded her head as Millie sat down a plate of pancakes for Cade.

Everyone turned to the back door upon hearing heavy metal music getting louder. Bruce opened the door and walked inside; he was shirtless and carrying a ghetto blaster playing AC/DC. Bruce closed the door and turned the volume down, but not off, and set the boom box by the door. The smell of burnt flesh and blood filled the room. When Bruce turned around, they could see he had dried blood over his body and noticed the front of his pants were soaked in blood as he sat down in his seat.

"Hey woman, what's for breakfast? I'm hungry," Bruce asked Millie.

"What'cha ya want Bruce?" Millie asked, smiling.

"Food. As long as I don't have to catch it, I don't care," Bruce replied as Millie fixed him a plate. Bruce looked around the table, bobbing his head to the beat of the music coming out of the box. Everyone was gazing at him with blank stares. Millie set a plate of food down in front of him and Bruce just shrugged his shoulders and started eating. Then Bruce looked up at Angela. "Little Foot, we'll talk tomorrow," he told her. Angela smiled and nodded her head.

"We're burying Alex at sunset. You'll be there, won't you?" she asked.

"Yes, I'll be there," Bruce promised.

A man came out of the dining room and stopped behind Mike. "Bruce, is that really necessary?" he asked.

"Dude, this is AC/DC. If you don't like it, I will have to kick your ass just on principle," Bruce threatened him.

"Not the music, the screams," the man explained.

Bruce looked down at his plate as he slammed his palms on the table. Then slowly he pulled his fingernails across the table top, leaving grooves in the surface. As his hands rolled into fists he fought the urge to beat the shit out of this man. When Bruce looked up his eyes were filled with pure hate. "If you mean, do I have to get information from those sacks of shit before the rest of that gang finds us and kills worthless motherfuckers like you, then the answer is yes. They were almost three hundred strong before yesterday, but I got me some and it was good. Watching those fuckers die like that gave me serious wood. You can go and wipe your pussy off now. Ask me another stupid question and I'll cut your balls off and feed them to you. Do you want to ask me another question to see if it's stupid?" The man shook his head and ran back into the dining room. Bruce turned to Angela. "Don't worry, they'll pay." Then Bruce looked at Stephanie. "I need you to do something for me and it'll be hard."

"I'll do whatever you need me to," Stephanie said.

Bruce reached into his pocket and pulled out a digital recorder and laid it on the table. He grabbed both sides of Stephanie's face. "Those aren't people on there. Now say it," Bruce told her.

"Those are not people on there," Stephanie repeated.

"Again, like you mean it!" Bruce yelled at her. Stephanie repeated it, stunned at the yell.

"I want you to type it up. One of them, the sniper, gives a very detailed description of the base. I want an accurate drawing," Bruce told her.

"I will have it done by this afternoon," Stephanie promised.

Bruce looked at Debbie. "Get me another recorder, please." She nodded and left the room.

"Where are the twins and PJ?" Bruce asked Stephanie.

"Upstairs with Danny."

Bruce nodded his head as Millie put another glass of tea in front of him. He drained the glass and stood up, heading to the door. Grabbing his boom box, he turned to Mike as Debbie walked in and handed him another recorder. For a brief second everyone saw the rage leave Bruce's face, leaving a look of sorrow and guilt. "Mike, be happy I made you leave. It's worse than I remembered, but thank you for wantin' to help me," Bruce told him as he walked out the door.

Paul looked at Mike as he asked, "You wanted to help him?"

"Yes I did, and would be out there now if he would let me!" Mike yelled. "Everyone get in here!" he yelled at the top of his lungs.

There was not enough room in the kitchen but everyone did their best to get in. Mike cleared his throat. "I want everyone to hear this so there is no misunderstanding later. That gang that attacked us yesterday? They want the women and kids. They'll rape and torture them just for pleasure then kill them. They sometimes do the same to men, but usually torture and death is what a man can expect. We have to kill them before they kill us. Not only do we have to fight infected, we have to fight these assholes. I only saw a few that wanted to follow Bruce yesterday to protect us. Now some of you are even questioning Bruce as he is doing what needs to be done. He is finding out about them, where they are and how many. You can't ask them 'please.' These are hardened criminals, not Girl Scouts wanting to deliver cookies, you stupid mother fuckers. If you don't like Bruce's methods then go take over for him or fucking leave!"

Mike looked at Paul. "Paul, do you want to watch your wife and son get raped? You must, because you want Bruce to stop. I never thought that about you. Tell your wife and son we'll protect them. Take your balls off and wear a tampon."

"That's not what I meant, Mike!" Paul yelled.

"Bruce is out there now doing what needs to be done. I could see it in his face, it's eating his soul. Let me tell you something, Paul, I'm glad he's doing it and not me. The difference between you and me is I'm willing to take Bruce's place in hell for protecting my family," Mike told him. He

Mike looked around before saying, "Bruce is not hurting us, he's defending us. There are a few here that know the type of animals that are out there. Bruce rescued them from the same type of animals. I'm not going to point them out and cause them embarrassment, but they are here among us. This is a family and when you stop protecting it, you aren't family anymore."

Conner stood up on a chair. "He's telling you the truth. Bruce rescued me. I watched those trash torture my platoon. They cut off their balls, then dragged a knife across their bellies and left them screaming. I watched as an infant was held over its mother and cut with a knife while she was raped, and they did it just to cause her more pain. I will die before I'm ever taken again, and I will take those I love with me," Conner told everyone.

Mike spoke again. "People, we are going to have to kill to protect ourselves and some have already died defending us. We'll have to do things to ensure our safety that you never would've dreamed of. This is real and you can't call time out or 911. You don't have to stay here; you can leave. We told you that when you got here. If you stay, you must fight, and some of you may die. At least here you have a chance. Now, there will be no supply run today but the work is to continue. Now get to it."

Nancy went upstairs with Angela as the crowd dispersed to their jobs. Most agreed with Mike; very few didn't but kept their opinions to themselves. Mike watched the group leave and then turned to see Paul standing by him.

"Mike, I didn't mean what I said. I'm scared. The thought of anything happening to my family terrifies me," Paul told him.

"Paul, the old way is dead. You're going to have to kill men sooner or later to protect your family, and you might even die for them. The only assurance I can offer is that they'll be taken care of if you do die defending them, as mine will be if I'm killed," Mike said.

"I'm sorry, Mike."

"No need to apologize, Paul. I'm sorry for calling you out in front of everyone," Mike said.

"No, I needed that to let me know what we are fighting for. So our kids can have some type of future. I'll always stand with you and Bruce," Paul promised Mike. And from that moment on, Paul would do what was needed.

"Thank you," Mike said.

"Well I'm going to make some coffins for our people," Paul said as he left.

Mike watched him leave and noticed Debbie and Stephanie at the end of the table looking at him. "What?" Mike asked.

"Thank you for defending Bruce," Debbie said quietly.

"Debbie, I almost told everyone but a select few to leave," Mike told her.

"They would've died," Debbie pointed out.

"I know, and for a second I didn't care," Mike said.

"Bruce is right, he needs your heart to guide him."

"Debbie, I want to fight beside him," Mike told her.

"I know, Mike, but don't force it. You could lose that piece of yourself that Bruce needs to maintain control. If Bruce loses that, I believe he will become one of the monsters we are fighting," Debbie confided.

"Debbie, he doesn't need me to keep him sane; he has you and the kids," Mike said.

"I don't have it anymore, Mike, and the kids are too young. I know what Bruce meant by the price of the wave, now, and not thinking rationally. Bruce needs a man to show him when it's time to quit and fall back, or when it's time to unleash hell on earth, sacrificing everything," Debbie told him.

The response sent a chill through Mike. The thought that Bruce depended that much on him made him proud and scared at the same time. "Thank you, Debbie, I thought Bruce believed I couldn't fight."

"Mike, you know better than that. Just remember that Bruce needs that part of you. Your humanity, so keep it close. When you do fight beside Bruce, don't follow him in rage, because you will lose it, even if you follow the rules. That's the price you pay for the wave; you lose the ability to see everyone as human," Debbie said.

"Well, Debbie, that's what I have you here for, to remind me," Mike told her.

"I'm telling you now, Mike, because I might not be there, I could die."

The certainty in her voice frightened Mike as he responded, "Debbie, if you die then Bruce will die beside you, defending you."

"What if I'm defending him or the kids while he is defending us? I can think of a thousand different ways," Debbie told him.

"Debbie, if something happened to you, Bruce would die. He may not physically, but his heart would die."

"That is why you and I are talking now, Mike. You can't let that happen. I know Bruce has to survive for this family to live. We need his knowledge of war and his ability to fight. We need his ability to think outside the box and do what needs to be done."

Mike swallowed before speaking. "Debbie, do you think you are going to die?"

"I know I'm going to die, Mike, just like you, but I don't think I will see old age. That really doesn't bother me, to be honest. The safety of this family and Bruce does. I really believe if Bruce dies or becomes a soulless killer, this family and humanity dies with him," Debbie told Mike as Stephanie put her arm across Debbie's shoulders.

"Have you talked about this with Bruce?" Mike asked her.

"You know I haven't, because it would consume him. We all know how much he loves me. The only thing I know for sure he won't sacrifice for my safety is the kids, ours or yours, but I think everyone else is fair game. We can't let that happen," Debbie told him.

Mike stood up. "Debbie, you have to tell him. You're basically telling me you know you're going to die. I can't live with this secret," he pleaded with her.

"I'm sorry, Mike, but you'll have to for the survival of this family. Are you willing to sacrifice it for me? I'm not," Debbie told Mike as he sat back down and put his head in his hands.

She continued. "Mike, just remember to hang on to your humanity. It's very important. I love you, Mike, and so does Bruce."

Debbie led Stephanie out of the kitchen as Mike sat at the table, crying for an hour. He would keep this secret from Bruce for the sake of the family. Mike stood up, wiped off his face and headed outside.

CHAPTER 22

The clan gathered outside the northwest livestock pasture for the funerals at sunset. Only those on duty were absent. Several huge oak trees shaded the area. Bruce came running up in clean clothes before Father Thomas started the service. Bruce moved to the front to stand by Debbie, Stephanie, and the kids.

Five graves had been dug, and the coffins were sitting beside the graves. Only one coffin had people standing by it and that was Angela, holding Cade and looking down at Alex's coffin. Bruce sighed when he saw little Angela holding Cade. Cade was almost half her size but she held him close.

Bruce whispered to Debbie and Stephanie then he walked over to Angela, taking Cade from her. Angela knelt beside the coffin, kissing Alex one last time; then she stood up, wrapping her arms around Bruce's waist.

Grabbing Emily and Sherry's hands, Debbie walked to the second coffin with the twins and stood beside it. The rest of Bruce's family filed past Debbie and the twins. Stephanie, holding PJ, with Buffy beside her, stopped beside the next coffin. Danny and Jake went to the fourth coffin, and Steve with his new family stopped at the last one. Now each person who had made the ultimate sacrifice for the clan had someone to witness their last journey.

Father Thomas gave a nice service and went to each group and said a prayer. He came back to Bruce and Angela. "Bruce, will you say some words for our fallen brethren?" Father Thomas asked him.

"Not today, Father, I'll say something tomorrow," Bruce told him. He could feel the rage in his blood. He was still riding the wave, knowing he had broken the rules.

"Please Bruce, talk to the clan. They need to hear from you," Father Thomas urged.

"Okay, Father," Bruce told him. He Bruce took a step forward, Cade on his hip, and pulled Angela with him. He cleared his throat before beginning. "We've lost good people here. They gave their life so we could live. They knew the dangers yet went forward to help others here survive. Some went thinking no one would remember them or be at their side on this last journey. They now see they were wrong; they have us with them and they *will* be remembered." Bruce stopped to control his breathing and keep the rage in check.

Then he spoke in a loud voice. "Know this, everyone. If you fight for this clan, you will be honored. If you provided for this clan, you will be respected. If you die for this clan, you will be avenged." The crowd erupted in cheers. People started hugging each other.

Angela looked up at Bruce with her arm still around his waist. It was like hugging a rock; Angela could feel the energy radiating from him and it was intoxicating. Looking at Bruce's face, a shiver ran down her spine then she smiled. Hell was coming and Bruce was going to deliver it.

Bruce let Angela go and knelt by Alex, patting his chest. Then Bruce stood, wrapped his arm around Angela as he moved to the next coffin and patted the man's chest. Then Angela leaned down and kissed his forehead. They repeated the gestures at each coffin, and when they had finished at the last coffin they looked back and the entire clan was stopping at each coffin, kissing or patting the fallen heroes.

Tears rolled down Bruce's cheeks. He did feel loss but these were tears of rage. He had fed off the anger, unleashing the hate. He knew he shouldn't but he hadn't cared as the wave surged through him with each scream of the gang members pushing the wave higher. He'd wanted them to feel pain just for his own joy, for hurting his family. He had been awake for over thirty hours but he felt strong and ready. Bruce wanted to kill and bring pain on those that had attacked this family.

When the last person finished paying their respects, Bruce led Angela to the Community Center. Alex had wanted the Center open so the clan had gotten it ready to serve its first meal for Alex's and the others' wake. Bruce pulled Angela to the table that he'd moved from the house to the Community Center. He set Angela and Cade down and went to go get them a plate, but Millie was already bringing them to the table.

Bruce sat and ate and then just watched as everyone ate and talked. Seeing his chance, Bruce got up and left, heading to his room. Lying on his bed was a notebook that Stephanie had transcribed from the recorder. Bruce started going over the notes then pulled out the map, studying it. Debbie and Stephanie were the next in the room. They came over to the bed with Bruce. Danny, Mary and Buffy came in next, followed by Mike and Nancy. Matt, Jake, and David joined the family to prepare for war. Steve and Conner were the last two in, leaving Tonya and Susan watching the kids.

Bruce stood up. "Okay, let's go over this again. The small island is a hundred yards off the bank. Matt and Jake will provide sniper cover, with Mary watching their asses; they are team three. Team one, my team, will be me, Buffy and Steve. Team two will be Debbie's team: Debbie, Danny, and Conner. The park is on the west side of the lake on a peninsula with a fourteen-foot fence cutting the area off. That part of Lake Bistineau still has water, so the only way for blues to attack is at the fence. There are ten sleeping cabins; each can hold forty people for sleeping and one large hall where they eat and party. Cabin nine and ten hold the hostages, cabin four houses the leader and his captains, cabin five houses weapons and supplies.

"Now, thanks to the information the sniper was kind enough to give us, we know from my attack and Conner's blowing out of the ambush that we killed a hundred and thirty-six gang members. If that wasn't good enough news, those groups had most of the military members. The leader and his captains are just gang members, ruthless and dangerous, but undisciplined." Bruce stopped as the door opened and Angela walked in and stopped in her tracks.

"I'm sorry, I'll go to my room," Angela said, turning to leave.

"Angela, stop and close the door," Bruce told her. "You're part of this family. I was letting you have time to grieve, but you're here now. Watch us plan revenge."

Bruce continued the briefing as Angela quietly joined him. "They may be undisciplined, but they're vicious. Now the bad news: There are a hundred and twenty-five left. We will be out numbered fourteen to one, but we can handle those odds easily. We will set charges on buildings one through four, six, seven, eight, and the hall. Then we will pull back to the water's edge and blow it to hell. If something happens, pull back to the water. Team one, our rally point is the north; team two, yours is south. If charges have been set, keep them in the buildings until we blow them. Each cabin will get five, four-pound charges and the hall will get ten charges. Place your charges on windows or doors, not on the logs, or you just make an escape hatch. Remember, we are going there to kill the gang members, not rescue hostages. If we can, we'll rescue them, okay, but if it goes to shit you will mow the hostages down to kill the enemy. There are anywhere from fifty to eighty hostages. All of the people I talked to agreed that the gang kills them and replaces them so fast it's hard to keep track.

"Now, if we rescue the hostages, Mike will send a convoy for us. If it goes to tee-total hell, we kill everything there and leave the way we came in. Use your claymores around your rally point. Matt and Jake, you will have to provide your own cover, and Mary, you must cover their asses. The gang does send patrols out on boats so stay alert. Attack will start at 0300. I want charges set by 0330 and fireworks by 0350. Mike has operation control. David will run the UAVs. Backup will be the convoy with the Strykers and Hummers, which will be under Nancy. She will brief her team at midnight. Questions, comments?" Bruce asked, finishing the briefing.

"Why not take more of us?" Nancy asked.

"Nancy, for this kind of attack you either go in heavy or light. We don't have the manpower for heavy, and light is one squad," Bruce told her.

"Don't you think twenty pounds of C-4 per building is a bit much?" Mike asked.

"No, I want them dead. I can't do what I want to them, so this will have to do," Bruce told him.

"Okay, that's good enough for me," Mike said, and no one else spoke up.

"Get some rest. We leave at midnight," Bruce said.

Everyone left to get ready for the attack. Bruce lay down in the bed. Debbie lay on one side of Bruce and Stephanie the other. Angela climbed onto the bed and looked at Bruce.

"What is it, Little Foot?" Bruce asked her.

"Bruce, you're different. This is nothing like I've seen from you before," Angela told him and Debbie shook her head at Angela, telling her to drop it.

"I'm ready to kill some assholes," Bruce told her as he drifted off to sleep.

At 2300, Debbie woke Bruce up and he got dressed, checked his vest then his weapons. Then he headed downstairs and tried not to step on anyone laying on the floor as he went into the kitchen. The dining room table had been moved to the kitchen, freeing up a lot of room for people to sleep. Blocks of explosive were laid out on the table.

Bruce checked the blocks to see if they were wired up correctly by his kids and all were ready. Everyone loaded packs with explosives and headed outside. They piled in to Nancy's SUV and started off toward the lake. Everyone had NVGs on, so they drove without lights. Taking the road that followed the east side of the lake, they stopped directly across from the park on the west side of the lake. The lake was barely three-quarters of a mile wide there since it was mostly drained. With the equipment and teams, Bruce was figuring twenty minutes to paddle across the lake in three rubber rafts.

When the SUV stopped, everyone piled out, keeping alert. They were now way out of the patrol zone and blues were about. They moved down to the lake and inflated the rafts using the CO_2 cartridges. Putting the rafts in the water, the teams climbed in and started moving toward the other bank.

Bruce thought it would be hard to find the camp, but he could see fires and lights on the west bank where the park was located. They were either very brave or very stupid, Bruce thought. He favored the latter. The gang was surrounded by infected and had been hit hard a day ago, yet they still left the lights on.

Buffy was in the middle of the raft with a thermal scope on her M-4, scanning the far bank to see if anyone was watching the lake. Buffy just shook her head no. Bruce flipped the voice switch.

"Big Daddy Two, talk dirty to me," Bruce said softly.

"I charge $4.99 a minute; do you have a major credit card?" Mike answered smartly.

"Damn, you better be good," Bruce replied, grinning.

"I'll make you melt," Mike said, breathing hard in the microphone.

"Okay, now I'm horny, Big Daddy Two, better shave your legs. What are the party poopers doing?" Bruce asked.

"We have the three roving patrols with two guards each, and six on the fence just like the sniper said," Mike reported.

"Mama One, what does your gut tell you?" Bruce asked Debbie.

"These guys are idiots," Debbie replied.

"Big Daddy Two, send the UAV a little further inland," Bruce told Mike.

Five minutes later, Mike called back. "Oh wise Kung Fu master, you were right. A mile down the road there are fifteen bad boys in ambush."

"Okay, so they did change something. Not so dumb. Bring the UAV back and watch the camp and lake," Bruce told him.

"I have two on station now and will rotate them out with the third," Mike said.

Matt and Jake pulled into the lead to get set up on the small island and cover the land teams. Bruce steered toward his rally point. There was a boat dock with several party barges and ski boats in the middle of the rally points. When Bruce's raft stopped he got out, followed by Buffy and Steve. Steve pulled the raft up on land. Bruce could hear music coming from the large hall. He glanced at his watch. It was 0231.

"Mike, where're the patrols?" Bruce whispered.

"One is heading for you now, following the fence and water's edge," Mike told him.

"Steve, you take right, I'll take left. I fire first," Bruce said as he raised his pistol up.

It took the guards several minutes to make it to them and Bruce rested his sight on the head of the guard on the left. Bruce squeezed the trigger when the guards were ten yards away, followed a split second by Steve's suppressed fire. The guards dropped to the ground like their strings had been cut.

"Debbie, did you hear that?" Bruce called on the radio. Debbie was a hundred yards from him.

"Hear what?" Debbie asked, answering Bruce's question.

"Mama One, patrol headed your way," Mike called out.

Several minutes later Mike was on the radio. "Nice shot, guys. Why didn't you wait for them to get closer?"

"I'm ready to hit these fuckers," Debbie growled. Bruce smiled. Mama was on the wave.

"Where is the third patrol, Mike?" Bruce asked.

"Just sittin' behind cabin number three, smoking," Mike said, making Bruce smile. Cabin three was on his side.

"Everyone hold, I have 'em," Bruce said and he ran up behind cabin nine. He worked his way up to cabin five and stopped. There were roughly thirty yards between cabins and that was a long shot or a long run. *What the hell, let's walk*, Bruce thought.

Casually, Bruce stepped out, holding his pistol behind his leg and walked towards the two guards. The guards noticed him at twenty yards and called out to him in quiet voices. Bruce just waved with his left hand and the guards started smoking again. When Bruce was five feet away he raised his pistol and shot each one in the head. Then he headed back to the rally point for Steve and Buffy.

"What the hell was that, Bruce? Why did you just walk up to them and shoot 'em? You can do that from a distance. You do have a gun and it shoots over a distance," Mike informed him.

"Thought I knew one of them and he owed me some money. I was gonna get it before I shot 'em, but it wasn't him," Bruce told Mike.

"Oh, well that's okay then," Mike replied. "Are you going to execute the mission early? It's not even 0300 yet."

"I sure as hell ain't going to wait. It's not my fault Debbie beat the kids to make them row faster, throwing off my timetable. They just have to die sooner," Bruce replied, almost back to his team.

"Tell her not to drive the kids that hard, that's our job. Go ahead and kill the bad guys early then," Mike called back.

Bruce rejoined Steve and Buffy then radioed Jake. "Jake, do you and Matt have shots at the guards on the fence?"

"Yep, we have all six," Jake responded.

"What's the distance?" Bruce asked.

"The closest is three hundred eighty yards and the furthest is four hundred twenty yards," Jake replied.

"Take 'em," Bruce told him. The words were barely out of his mouth when Bruce faintly heard the first cough of two rifles. The coughs were followed by successive shots in rapid successions.

Jake called over the radio, "All down."

"Team two, let's move," Bruce called over the radio.

Team one moved along the north side placing charges, while team two moved along the south. They placed the charges along the hall then moved toward the cabins. Most of the cabins had the doors and windows cracked open, which made the teams' jobs a lot easier. In twenty minutes the teams were pulling back to their rally points.

Mike called out, "One coming out of cabin five."

Followed by Matt calling out, "He's down."

The teams reached the rally point and Bruce pulled out the remote detonator. Then he called out over the radio, "Get low and cover your head and ears. This is gonna be loud." Bruce lay down and flipped the switch, setting off almost two hundred pounds of C-4 spread out among the cabins.

The charges went off together as one in a thunderous *ka-boom*. Then the shock wave hit him, pushing the air out of his lungs. As he tried to take a breath, Bruce felt a sharp pain in his left shoulder as debris landed around them. Bruce shook his head and looked at the area as the dust started to clear. The buildings with the charges were all collapsed, and cabin five was missing a door and all its windows. Cabins nine and ten were intact but the windows were gone

Bruce called out, "Sweep the area. Get the hostages to stay down, but don't risk yourself." He Bruce stood up and started to lift up his weapon when pain in his left shoulder sent him to his knees. Looking down where the pain was coming from, Bruce saw a six-inch piece of wood sticking out of the top of his shoulder. Reaching over, he felt the wound. The piece had hit him in the deltoid and Bruce could feel the other end where it had come out the back of his arm, right above the triceps. It felt like it missed the joint but it still hurt like hell. When he tried to move his arm, he wanted to puke, not to mention the end of the stick would hit his face.

"Steve, come here," Bruce told Steve. Steve crept over to his dad.

"Break off the end but don't pull it out," Bruce told him.

"Let me pull it out," Steve cried out, looking at the chunk of wood sticking out of his dad.

"I'll bleed to death, dumbass. What's left behind in the muscle will help control the bleeding. Now break it off," Bruce said, gritting his teeth. Steve grabbed the shard of wood and applied pressure to the end sticking out of Bruce's shoulder, sending stars shooting across Bruce's vision as Steve tried to break it off.

"It's a fucking stick. You can't break a fucking stick?" Bruce yelled at him.

"This is a tough fucking stick," Steve snapped back just as the six-inch shaft sticking out of Bruce's shoulder broke off. Steve looked at Bruce. "Tiddy baby," he said, turning toward the cabins and feeling sick. He didn't want his dad to see him puke.

"You're not going to kiss it and make it better?" Bruce asked as he followed him, the throbbing in his shoulder almost making him pass out. Steve gave him the finger without turning around, still trying not to throw up. "I'm your daddy, boy," Bruce called after him.

"Then quit actin' like a bitch," Steve called back, making Bruce laugh.

Team one advanced to cabin nine to get the hostages as a man came out, dragging a teenaged girl by the hair. Bruce flipped his SCAR to auto, fixing to send a wave of hate toward the two, when the man's upper torso just vanished. The arm was still holding the girl's hair and the lower torso from the belly button down was still standing; then they slowly fell back. A loud boom rolled toward Bruce from behind him. Another man came running out and his upper body vanished but the lower torso actually took another step before falling.

"What the fuck are you two shootin' them with? Artillery?" Bruce called out over the radio to Matt and Jake.

"My present," Jake replied as Bruce heard two more loud shots come from the fifty cal sniper rifle. Bruce didn't see anyone disappear so figured Jake was taking out targets elsewhere.

"And you said I cheat," Bruce replied.

"Hey, you make your own rules, so that means I can too," Jake muttered over the radio and Bruce heard another loud report.

Bruce's team had advanced to the cabin with the hostages. Steve took right and Buffy took left, both firing short bursts as they entered. Bruce was fixing to tell them they only had to shoot the hostages if the enemy was close, not just blow them away.

"Two down," Steve reported.

Followed by Buffy reporting, "One down" as Bruce came into the cabin. Bruce saw naked women and kids staggering around the long cabin. Several had cuts and were shaking. They all turned their heads toward Bruce as he walked in.

Bruce yelled out, "Get in a line, we're rescuing you! We have pissed your hosts off big time, so please do what we ask so we can get the hell outta here. Now follow my daughter; she'll stay with you to protect you while I talk to your hosts about your abysmal treatment." The group just looked at Bruce like he was insane until Bruce added, "Unless, of course, you want to stay here."

As one, the group formed lines between the rows of bunks. "Buffy, you take lead and get them to our rally. Steve, you watch our ass," Bruce yelled as Buffy grabbed the first woman in line, pulling her to follow. Bruce flanked the group as he heard several loud shots from Jake. Then Bruce heard full auto suppressed fire behind him. Turning around to help Steve, Bruce saw two figures fall and three more behind them disappear as he heard three loud successive shots.

"Jake, that's fuckin' cheating now, at least let me shoot one every now and then!" Bruce yelled over the radio.

"Shut up, Dad. This is fun," Jake called back as Bruce heard a shotgun blast to his left. Bruce dropped back down as he turned toward the shot.

Bruce saw a man wearing only blue jeans aiming and firing a shotgun at the island Matt and Jake were on. *You are a dumbass,* thought Bruce as he raised up his rifle, ignoring the pain in his shoulder. Bruce shook his head. *You're shooting at snipers one hundred and fifty yards away with a shotgun. Good luck with that.* The shotgunner's right thigh vanished, causing him to fall over screaming and dropping his mighty magical shotgun. *He really thought he could hit someone a hundred and fifty yards away with his magical shotgun,* Bruce thought incredulously as the man grabbed the stump that remained of his right leg.

Bruce stood up. *This just has to be addressed.* He strolled over to the screaming man, stopped and unbuttoned his fly and pissed in the screaming man's face as the teams continued taking down stragglers. Bruce buttoned up and ran back to his team, leaving the wounded man behind as the screams became softer. His sleeve was soaked in blood but the wound was clotting off as Bruce looked down at his shoulder. "I have business to attend to, you better keep working," Bruce told his shoulder.

Mike called over the radio, "The group on the road is comin' back. They're in four trucks."

Bruce called over the radio, "Team two take south, Buffy stay with the hostages. Steve, we have north. Conner and Steve use the SAWs. They will probably ram the gate and try to stay mobile so take that away fast. Wait until the vehicles are inside the fence before you engage."

Bruce kneeled down at the corner of the remains of cabin one, hearing the trucks approaching. The gate was about fifty yards away and looked pretty impressive to Bruce. It was a chain-link gate that ran on tracks to slide open but there were a lot of metal plates attached to it. Making a rough guess, Bruce was putting the weight at over half a ton. *Surely they are not that stupid*, Bruce thought, hearing engines roaring toward them.

The first truck hit the gate at seventy miles per hour and did manage to knock it down, but the truck flipped forward, catapulting the people in the bed of the truck through the air. Bruce watched in amazement as one flew toward him, flapping his arms like he was trying to fly. The man hit fifteen feet in front of Bruce, feet first. Fascinated, Bruce watched as the six-foot man shrank to four-foot as the bones in his legs shattered in hundreds of pieces. "Cool!" Bruce said out loud as he shot the new dwarf in the chest then swung his rifle toward the gate, still ignoring his shoulder.

When the second truck sped past the downed gate, Bruce sent a 40mm grenade through the front window. The grenade exploded in the cab, killing the occupants in the cab. The steering wheel cut to the left, sending the truck into a roll toward team two and stopping ten yards from them.

Bruce reloaded the M-203 as the third truck sped in and was greeted with a rain of full auto fire. The two SAWs racked the front compartment with tracers arcing off into the night. Truck number three rammed into truck number two, sending the passengers in the back over the cab. Debbie actually had to drop down as one sailed over her.

Truck number four had slowed down to forty as it entered the gate and two people jumped out of the back, breaking several bones in the process. *These guys have watched too much TV*, Bruce thought as he fired the 40mm, hitting the front windshield. The round exploded in the cab. The truck coasted toward them as it was raked with gunfire.

Bruce stood up to kill the wounded and heard groaning from the new dwarf. The man was holding his chest where Bruce had shot him. "You're one tough mother fucker," Bruce told the man as he shot Dwarf in the face.

While the teams finished off the wounded, Mike called out, "You have blues coming."

"How many?" Bruce asked, shooting wounded gang members.

"A lot; the guards report that they heard the explosion here very well and we are over thirty miles away," Mike told Bruce.

Bruce looked at the destroyed gate. *Well those fuckers might have killed us anyway,* Bruce thought. "How long do we have?"

"Ten, maybe fifteen minutes until the first arrive, but the UAV is up to three thousand feet and there are a shitload headed to you," Mike told him.

"Jake and Matt, get over here and see if you can get some of those party barges started. If you can't, we're going to have to paddle them across the lake. Buffy, get me a count of hostages we have to give a ride out of here. Team two, watch the front gate; Steve, you help them," Bruce called over the radio as he ran to the dock.

Reaching the dock, Bruce saw three party barges, two over twenty feet long. Bruce ran to the closest big one and didn't see the keys so he ran to the other and it didn't have keys either. Bruce had never hotwired a boat but he was fixing to try. Looking at the end of the dock, he saw team three running toward him.

"We're going to have to hotwire them," Bruce told them as they came closer.

"No we won't, Dad, you can start them with a thin-bladed knife," Jake told Bruce.

Bruce, knowing better than to doubt Jake, replied, "Well do it then. I really don't want to be here when the blues get here."

Matt and Jake each went to a boat and went to work as Bruce called Buffy, "Buffy, how many and where are you?"

"Fifty-two, Daddy, and I'm at Mama's rally point," Buffy replied.

"Grab the paddles out of Mama's boat and bring that group here and put them on the boat Jake is on. I'm getting the other group," Bruce told her, running toward his rally point. He ran to the raft, grabbed the paddles then ran to the hostages.

"Stay in a single file and follow me. We have infected coming and have to leave fast," Bruce told them and headed back to the dock with the hostages in tow.

"Debbie, get everyone back here to the dock. We're leaving," Bruce called over the radio.

"Debbie, move your ass! The closest group is less than a mile away!" Mike screamed over the radio.

As Bruce neared the dock he could see the group Buffy had gotten filing onto the party barge. The last of the group was on the boat as Bruce hit the dock, leading his group to the other barge. Stopping and pointing at the barge, Bruce told the hostages to jump on, spread out and leave Matt alone.

Bruce headed back to the other barge, pulling out his machete. He cut the lines and pushed the boat out into the marina. Bruce turned toward the camp and could see four figures running toward him.

Mike radioed, "The first group of blues just entered the gate. You really need to move." The four took energy from Mike's words and sprinted full out toward the boat.

Bruce looked at Jake's boat and it had drifted out into the marina. The four hit the dock in a dead run and Bruce pointed at the barge as they jumped on. Bruce heard the engine on Jake's boat start to fire up, causing several roars to erupt from the camp. Cutting the lines, Bruce pushed the boat with everything he could muster, sending it away from the dock. His shoulder was screaming in protest with the effort. Bruce jumped across the widening gap, landing on the boat as it drifted out.

Bruce dropped his machete on the deck and raised his rifle up as the first of the blues headed toward the dock. Bruce started to squeeze the trigger, firing bursts off. Bruce dropped eight as he ejected the empty magazine, slamming in another one as the first blue hit the dock. The party barge had only drifted back twenty feet from the dock and was slowing down as Bruce sighted in on the lead blue and fired a burst.

He emptied the magazine and dropped the SCAR to hang from its sling as he pulled his pistol out. A blue hit the end of the dock and leapt toward the boat, roaring in midair. Bruce started squeezing the trigger, hitting the flying target in the chest, neck and finally the head as the blue hit the front of the boat and slid into the water.

"He tried to fly," Mike said over the radio.

"If they start flyin', I'm givin' the fuck up," Bruce replied back over the radio.

"Yeah, like you could do that," Debbie said from behind him.

Steve stepped up to Bruce's right and opened up with the SAW and Danny opened up with her Galil from his left side. The weapons did have suppressors but it still scared the shit out of Bruce. Matt finally got the engine to fire up, put the boat in reverse and created some distance, then put it in forward and pulled out of the marina.

"Keep it slow, men, the lake is low and a lot of logs are out there. I really don't want to swim across," Bruce told them over the radio.

"You're turning into a sissy in your old age, Dad," Jake said.

"Yeah, he would've made us swim the lake for this assault in his younger years," Steve said, standing beside Bruce.

"You two can still swim if you keep it up," Bruce said, turning toward Steve.

"What's that, Dad? You're breaking up real bad," Jake called over the radio as Steve headed to the back of the barge, smiling.

Bruce smiled as he watched Steve walk off, then heard suppressed shots from the front. Turning around, Bruce saw Danny leaning over the side, aiming back toward the dock. Bruce looked at the dock and saw blues dropping with Danny's shots. When her mag ran dry, she stood up, replacing it as Bruce looked at her. Danny had a small grin and her eyes were filled with ecstasy; her breathing was shallow and steady. Bruce smiled at her as the wave rushed through Danny's system.

"Save it, sweet pea. We have started a world of shit and will need every round," Bruce told her. Danny just broadened her grin and found a place to kneel down.

"I want a dick," Bruce heard Debbie say from the back of the boat. Several of the hostages looked toward her with shocked expressions.

"Baby, we are a little busy and have a lot of company," Bruce told Debbie. Bruce could care less about the hostages but his kids were here.

"I didn't say I wanted yours, Bruce!" Debbie shot back.

"Whose dick do you want?" Bruce shouted back with malice in his voice.

"I don't want anyone's. I want my own. When you pissed in that biker's face that was freaking awesome. A woman can't do that," Debbie said.

"Sugar mama, you can pee on my face whenever you want to," Bruce assured her.

"See, that's what I mean. A woman squatting over a man's face pissing on it is viewed as sexual. When a man does it's totally different," Debbie told Bruce.

Danny spoke up, "She's right, Dad. If we pee on someone's face, it's not like when a guy does it."

Bruce spun around, looking at Danny. "Young lady, if I see you squatting over someone's face I will blister your bare ass on the spot," Bruce snapped at Danny, pointing his finger at her. Several of the hostages were laughing at the discussion.

"See!" Debbie yelled. "Even you see it's totally different, baby. I want my own."

"Baby, you grow a dick. We will get a divorce. It's that simple," Bruce told her.

"That's not even fair!" Debbie shot back.

"If you want to piss on someone, tell me. I will let you hold it and aim it at 'em. Now quit talking about growing your own," Bruce told her and turned to Matt, who was steering the boat. "If you let Danny piss on someone's face, I will break one of your arms," Bruce told Matt. Matt just looked at Bruce with shock. "I'm not kidding, Matt, after I blister her ass I'll break your arm," Bruce warned him. Almost all of the hostages were laughing now. Bruce called over the radio, "Stop the boats."

They were in the middle of the lake as Bruce called Mike. "Talk to me, brother," Bruce said, taking off his vest and dropping it to the deck. His shoulder was screaming in pain and threatening to go on strike because it was tired of being ignored. Bruce waited on Mike's reply.

"Wondering when you were going to call. The west side of the lake looks like a European soccer rally. If there aren't over five thousand at that camp right now I'll kiss your ass. It looks like there'll be around ten thousand in an hour. On this side it isn't as bad, but we have a lot of movement. A group of thirty or more is right where y'all left the SUV," Mike finished.

"Great, I hate this lake and we're stuck in the middle of it," Bruce said, taking off his ACU top and t-shirt.

"What are you doing?" Debbie asked Bruce as he struggled out of his t-shirt. Then Debbie saw his shoulder. "What is that and how did that happen?" she yelled, running to Bruce.

"Shrapnel from the hall, I suspect," Bruce said, looking at his shoulder as Danny came over to check on him.

"Bruce, there's four inches of wood in your left shoulder and you didn't tell me!" Debbie screamed, looking at the wound.

"Well, there *was* six inches sticking out that Steve was finally able to break off," Bruce told her.

"Good boy for not pulling it out, Steve," Debbie told him.

"Oh, he wanted to," Bruce said.

"Steve," Debbie said, looking at him in disappointment. Steve just looked away.

"Well, what's going on?" Mike called over the radio.

"Shut up, Mike, Bruce is hurt, talk to you in a minute. Jake, bring me the first aid kit Mary is carrying," Debbie said over the radio.

"You need me to come—" Mike started to say as Debbie cut him off.

"Mike, in a minute. A woman can only listen to one man at a time. Men usually say stuff to piss us off and we need to know who to be mad at," Debbie said over the radio as Jake brought the other barge alongside.

Danny grabbed the pack as Jake, Steve and Matt tied the barges together. "I need a flashlight; these monocular NVGs suck for first aid. Everyone, turn them off," Debbie warned as she turned on her flashlight, blinding everyone.

"Damn," Bruce heard Danny say. Bruce turned to look at his shoulder. The shard was about half an inch in diameter and the skin around the edges of the shard was purple.

"It's not that bad," Bruce lied, looking at the wound.

Debbie slowly looked up at Bruce. "Say another word and I'll cut your arm off and throw it in the water." Bruce didn't think Debbie would do it, but he wasn't sure with that look on her face so he shut up. Debbie examined the wound, pushing on the edges and sending pain shooting through Bruce's body, but he didn't move. "Does that hurt?" Debbie asked, probing the wound.

"Fuck yeah that hurts!" Bruce yelled out.

"Well, you didn't move or say anything," Debbie shot back. Bruce raised his right arm, holding his hand up.

Debbie just looked at Bruce holding his hand up till she realized what he was doing. "What do you want to say?" she asked him.

Bruce lowered his hand. "You want me to tell you how to fix it?"

"I'm a nurse too, Bruce," Debbie snapped at him.

"You birth babies," Bruce told her. Debbie just looked at him.

"Sometimes I could just slap the shit out of you but it would only hurt my hand. Okay, tell me what you would do."

"Get the hemostats, grab the shard, pull it out the front. Get the twenty cc syringe and irrigate the wound with saline. Then wet some gauze and pack the wound. Then lay a gauze dressing and wrap the shoulder tight with an ACE wrap. Mike will have to irrigate it when we get home and we can't let it close," Bruce said.

"Baby, that's really going to hurt," Debbie said in a concerned voice.

"Well, you won't have to slap me."

"Baby, I was only picking," Debbie told him, her voice breaking up as she fought tears, thinking Bruce had taken her seriously.

"I know you were playing, baby, just hurry and do it. This really hurts," Bruce told her, trying to ignore the pain and losing big time.

"You can hold my hand, Daddy," Danny offered.

"No baby, I might break it. Help your mama," Bruce said as Debbie gathered the supplies.

When Debbie began pulling out the shard, Bruce almost passed out as the pain flooded his system. But Bruce barely moved as Debbie pulled it out, blood flowing down his arm. Then Debbie started irrigating the wound. Every time she shot saline into the wound Bruce wanted to throw up. Several of the hostages did, but Debbie continued the irrigation. When Debbie started packing the wound Bruce was sweating despite the cool night air. Debbie put the dressing on and stepped back.

"Thank you, baby," Bruce said as he reached down, grabbing his ACU top and t-shirt and throwing them to two naked teens sitting across from him. "They're a little bloody but put these on," Bruce told them, fighting the nausea from the pain.

Debbie watched the teens put on the bloody clothes, "Everyone, take off your tops and t-shirts and give them to the youngest ladies first. If anyone has spares, pass them out. Danny, Mary and Buffy, keep your sports bras on," Debbie told the teams as they started stripping. Bruce reached toward his pack to get extra t-shirts out as Debbie slapped his hand.

"Sit back and don't make me tell you again," Debbie said as she reached in his pack, grabbing the clothes.

When they were finished, only eleven were still naked. Jake started digging in the storage area on his boat, pulling out shirts and shorts. Steve started looking on their boat. When they were finished again, everyone at least had a shirt on.

It was 0350 when Bruce radioed Mike. "Well, has our situation improved any?"

"Are you alright, brother?" Mike asked with concern.

"I'm good, brother," Bruce told Mike, lying.

Debbie keyed her radio. "He's lying, Mike. Wake every mother fucker up and roll a convoy to get us."

Bruce looked at Debbie with hard eyes. "Debbie, quit it," he said, then keyed his radio. "Mike, she's exaggerating. What's going on?"

"There are several really large groups passing the SUV but they are circling the lake. When I say really large, I mean a thousand plus. If you can hold on, by dawn the area should be clear enough to get you without starting a war and some following us back," Mike told him.

"That's good Mike, we'll wait," Bruce said as he laid down on the deck. The night air was starting to get him cold.

"See you at dawn, brother," Mike replied.

Bruce looked up as the teenage girl he had given his ACU top to stood up and took it off. She kneeled down. "Put this under your head, sir," she told Bruce.

"That's okay, little one. I'm just going to lay here looking at the stars until we can go home. You put that on so you don't get cold," Bruce told her as she just stared at him, not used to kindness anymore. The teen kissed Bruce on his head, stood up and put the top on before sitting back down. Bruce closed his eyes and drifted off to sleep.

CHAPTER 23

Bruce opened his eyes as Debbie called his name. What Bruce did not understand was how Debbie was calling his name through a tunnel. It was early in the morning; which morning Bruce did not know but he knew it was early on some morning. Blinking his eyes, he saw Debbie leaning over him.

"Marcus has a team at the bank and Nancy is on the way. The group of blues wouldn't leave where we left the SUV. Marcus brought a team down to take them out before Nancy got here. They're going to ride back with us. Are you okay to move?" Debbie asked.

"Hell yeah, I can move. I'm not some invalid," Bruce told her as he sat up. Pain shot through his shoulder, almost sending him back down.

"Bruce, you're running a fever. I changed the dressing and packing an hour ago after Mike told me to. You never moved and the wound is infected," Debbie told him.

"I'm fine," Bruce said as he stood up to prove his point. "What time is it?" he asked, not wanting to lift his left arm up. It was being a total asshole, trying to go numb on him.

"0610, baby," Debbie answered, noticing Bruce was not moving his left arm.

Bruce looked toward the bank and could make out several people there forming a corridor with two rows to the road. As they got closer, he saw Marcus and Carroll standing in the middle of the two rows. As he reached down to get his vest, a wave of nausea hit him, making him stagger. Debbie ran to him as Danny grabbed his vest and weapon. Bruce held out his arm and Danny put his vest on him. Debbie helped guide his left arm in because Bruce was not about to move it. Danny zipped and

322

buckled the vest and put his weapon across his vest. Bruce moved for his pack but Danny stopped him.

"I'll get it, Daddy," Danny told him, grabbing his pack.

"Give it to me, Danny."

"I'll carry it, Daddy," Danny insisted, looking at him with determination.

"Danny, if we get hit I need your hands on your weapon, not my pack. I can't shoot worth a shit now and Daddy's little girl can throw out a wall of lead," Bruce told her, grabbing the pack and sliding his right arm through the strap. He was not even going to try for the other arm. It was being an asshole and not listening to him.

When the boat hit the shallow bank, Marcus walked to the front of the boat. Steve helped the women and girls down as Marcus and Carroll helped them to the bank. When the hostages were safely on dry land, Bruce went to the front to get off. Marcus looked up at him. "Give me your pack," Marcus told Bruce, holding out his hand.

"I have it, Marcus," Bruce told him. Bruce's pack weighed over seventy pounds.

"Boy, don't make me come up there," Marcus said firmly. Bruce sighed and handed him the pack. Marcus grabbed it and slid it on, not showing any sign of the weight.

"Aren't you and Carroll a little long in the tooth to be out on a patrol?" Bruce asked, jumping down and almost passing out when he landed.

Carroll came walking up to him, wearing jeans and a flannel shirt with an M-4 across her chest. "I told ya, I know my age and I don't need ya remindin' me. I've a good mind to find a switch right now," Carroll told him.

"Beat the shit out of him, Carroll," Debbie said as she grabbed Bruce's face, turning it side to side, then laid her hand on his head. Next she placed it on his chest.

"Yep, you gots the blood poisoning," Carroll told him. Bruce just looked at her dully, wanting someone to shoot him.

Mike came over the radio. "Nancy is almost there, save the chit chat."

"Mike says Nancy is almost here," Debbie said because none of Marcus's team had radios.

Bruce started to the road as Debbie put his right arm over her shoulder. Bruce was going to say something but admitted to himself he liked the support. As they reached the road, Marcus pointed to eight people and told them to get in Nancy's SUV and follow them once the rescued hostages were safe.

"How did you get here?" Bruce asked Marcus.

"Walked," Marcus said. "You had thirty hidin' around your truck. They was waitin' to ambush ya, so we snuck up on them and wiped 'em out." The convoy stopped in front of them and the women and kids were directed into vehicles.

Bruce was led to the back seat of Debbie's SUV. As he tried to climb in, Steve was in the back seat pulling him in and Conner was lifting him in. "I can move," Bruce told them, trying to help but now his right arm didn't want to listen.

"Sure, Dad," Steve said pulling him in.

"Bruce, shut up or I will find that lady a switch," Conner said, trying to straighten Bruce out as Debbie climbed in beside him.

"I'm not a baby," Bruce slurred, looking around with eyes that wouldn't focus then passed out, falling over on Debbie.

"Drive!" Debbie screamed.

Nancy stomped the gas, spinning the tires and pulling a one-eighty on the road. Everyone jumped in vehicles and followed.

"Mike, he passed out," Debbie called over the radio.

"Debbie, I'm already set up in the kitchen. I have a stretcher team ready," Mike told her.

"Nancy, kick this piece of shit in the ass!" Debbie screamed out. Nancy punched the pedal down to the floor. The SUV lunged forward, the engine roaring down the road and leaving the rest of the convoy behind.

Debbie rubbed Bruce's face. His skin was so hot under her fingers. "Baby, it's okay. We're almost home, fight for me, baby. You always do what I ask, so please fight for me," Debbie begged, tears rolling off her face and hitting Bruce on the face.

Nancy yelled "Hold on!" as she stomped the brakes, power sliding the huge SUV onto their road, and stomped the gas again. Barreling down the road then turning into the farm, she headed toward the front door where Mike and several others were waiting.

Mike ran to the back door and grabbed Bruce by the legs, pulling him out. Mike and several others laid Bruce on the stretcher and carried him to the kitchen table. The kitchen had been turned into a mini trauma room.

When Bruce was on the table, Debbie grabbed an IV and started one in Bruce's right arm; Mike told Debbie to put in another one. Danny turned on the cardiac monitor, grabbing the leads and blood pressure cuff on the monitor and putting them on Bruce like she had seen him do at work.

"He's dehydrated and lost a lot of blood. Nancy, Steve is his blood type, get a unit from him. Debbie, get two liters of saline into him!" Mike yelled out then shook Bruce. "Bruce, open your eyes! We aren't at the hospital, you have to wake up!" Mike yelled at Bruce, slapping his face. Then Mike grabbed Bruce's shoulder and squeezed it. That woke Bruce right up.

"Fuck! That hurts!" Bruce yelled out, slurring the words.

Mike slapped Bruce in the face. "Bruce, it's Mike. Stay awake. I can only breathe for you for so long, so stay awake. I can't give you anything for pain. Your pressure is too low and it will depress your breathing."

"Mike, how did you get here? Be careful, Carroll is around here," Bruce told Mike in a lucid voice. "I think she is looking for a switch. Don't tell her, Mike, but that woman scares the shit out of me," he said, closing his eyes. Marcus and Carroll laughed from the den along with several others.

Mike was undoing the dressing. "Bruce, Carroll said if you don't stay awake you're in trouble."

"Just let me rest for a minute, Mike," Bruce replied softly.

Carroll came up to the table. "Bruce, open your eyes right now!" she snapped at him.

Bruce's eyes shot open. "Yes, ma'am," he answered, feeling lightheaded.

"I already have a switch here, Bruce. Marcus is holdin' it fer me," Carroll informed him.

"I thought Marcus liked me," Bruce cried out.

"He does like ya. I already used it on him ta make 'im hold it," Carroll told Bruce.

"I told you, Mike, she's going to beat the shit out of me," Bruce said, looking at Mike wildly.

"I'm going to hold you down so she can if you don't listen to her," Mike told Bruce as he pulled out the packing from Bruce's wound.

"You too? What the hell did I do? Debbie!" Bruce yelled as pain shot through him.

"I'm right here, baby," Debbie said, holding his right hand as Danny changed the empty IV bags out.

"They're going to let Carroll switch me," Bruce whined.

"Baby, if you don't listen I'm pulling your pants down," Debbie threatened as Mike started digging out small pieces of wood, making Bruce yell.

"Hey fucker, that hurts!" Bruce told Mike as Carroll grabbed his face, turning it to her.

"Say tha ABC's, Bruce," she told him. Bruce looked at her like she was insane. "Marcus!" Carroll yelled over her shoulder.

"A, B, C, D ..." Bruce recited the alphabet as Mike dug out small pieces of wood and trash out of the wound. When Bruce had said the alphabet several dozen times, he started closing his eyes as he recited.

"Say them backwards now," Carroll told him. Bruce looked at this mean evil woman who he thought he'd liked at one time.

Debbie slapped his hand. "Do it Bruce or I will get the switch from Marcus myself."

"Z, Y, X, W ..." Bruce struggled to recite it backwards. When he messed up Carroll made him start over. Nancy brought the blood in she had taken from Steve and started running it in.

"Get some IV Benadryl and give him 25 milligrams in case he tries to develop an allergic reaction. The IV bags of antibiotics are in the sink, in the bowl of water. They should be thawed out. Hang all three, and after that third bag of fluid is in, stop the fluids. I don't want to overload him," Mike told Nancy and Debbie as he started irrigating the wound. After the blood was in, Bruce started to feel a bit more human.

"Mike, I feel a lot better. Carroll, can I please stop with the ABC's backwards," Bruce asked in a normal voice.

"Yes, Bruce, ya can stop," Carroll told him, patting his chest.

Mike finished the irrigation and dried Bruce's shoulder off for the dressing. "Your heart rate is down and your blood pressure is much better. You were going into septic shock, brother. A few more hours would have been too long."

"Can I have some drugs then," Bruce asked with a smile.

"Sure," Mike said then turned to Nancy. "Get him some Tylenol."

"I hate you," Bruce told Mike, then turned to Carroll.

"Did I kill your kittens or something? Because if I did, I will find you some more," Bruce said.

Carroll rubbed Bruce's shaved head. "No, but you was needin' ta listen and your poor little wife was too distraught to make ya, so I filled in for her," she told him then kissed Bruce on the head.

"Carroll, I really like you and probably love you but you scare the shit out of me. I've killed thousands of infected and hundreds of men, but when you threaten me I want to wet my pants."

"That's okay, Bruce. I love ya but you're a rambunctious man and Debbie's such a little woman," Carroll told him, kissing him on the head again. Bruce smiled mischievously and looked at Mike out of the corner of his eyes. Mike saw it and slid his chair back.

Bruce turned to Carroll. "Carroll, Mike hasn't been letting me eat much."

Mike jumped out of his chair as Carroll pointed her finger at him. "Carroll, he's lying. I have no control over how much Bruce eats," Mike said defensively.

Carroll patted Bruce's chest. "I'll getcha somethin' to eat, Bruce, dontcha worry none." Carroll headed off to the refrigerator. Danny and Buffy went with her to help.

"Dude, that was cold," Mike told him.

"You won't give me drugs. You don't get any tonight either," Bruce said smugly.

"You get me in trouble and I don't get lovin," Mike said, coming closer to Bruce. He grabbed Bruce's head and kissed him on the mouth. Bruce raised his right arm to push Mike off. He felt better but was still real weak. Mike finally let Bruce go, and Bruce rolled over, spitting.

"Dude you licked my tonsils," Bruce yelled out. Everyone in the house started laughing and someone opened the back door to see what was going on. Seeing Bruce awake, they turned around to the patio full of people, yelling to them that Bruce was okay. Everyone started cheering at the news.

Debbie hugged Bruce as he continued to spit out Mike's slobber. "You asked for that one, baby," Debbie said.

"I feel like shit," Bruce admitted.

"Come on, let's go upstairs," Debbie told him.

"I want to pee and eat somethin'. In that order," Bruce said as Carroll walked over.

"I was gettin ready to fix ya somethin', but a woman came in sayin' lunch was ready in the Center. She said she'll bring ya a plate," Carroll said.

"Danny, go tell Millie I'm eating out there, after I pee. Carroll, will you and Marcus eat with us?" Bruce asked, trying to sit up, then stopped. "What do you mean 'lunch'? What time is it?" Bruce asked, afraid to move his left arm to look at his watch.

"It's almost 1400, baby," Debbie told him. Not believing her, he moved his left arm, pain flooding his system, only to discover his watch was not even on his wrist.

"Your watch is in the sink," Mike told him.

"It was just dawn," Bruce said, bewildered.

"Baby, we've been working on you for over seven hours," Debbie said.

"It's still Tuesday, isn't it?" Bruce asked, a little worried.

"Yes, baby."

Bruce stood up carefully, feeling lightheaded. Debbie unhooked his IV and led him down the hall to the bathroom and helped him. Then she led him outside to the throngs of people who started clapping and cheering upon seeing Bruce up and about.

Emily and Sherry screamed "Daddy!" and ran to him, hugging his legs. Bruce slowly knelt down and gave each a hug and kiss. Mike and Debbie helped him stand back up and Stephanie came over to him, holding PJ.

"Where have you been, boy?" Bruce said to PJ, who clapped his hands, saying, "Dada, Dada."

"Well, it's about time," Bruce said, kissing PJ then kissing Stephanie.

The crowd moved with Bruce toward the Center. Bruce went to his table that already had plates waiting on him. Bruce sat down in his chair and looked at Mike.

"Can I get the IVs out?" he asked.

"No, you'll be getting IV antibiotics until Friday," Mike told him.

"That's three days," Bruce said grumpily.

"At least you can count," Mike said, taking a bite of food.

"Of course I can count, but for some reason I really hate the fucking alphabet right now," Bruce said in disgust, shaking his head. Everyone at the table started laughing. Debbie then filled Bruce in on what had happened.

"Marcus, will you and your crew come down this Sunday for the briefing? I want to go over some plans," Bruce asked, trying to get food to his mouth but the IV in his right arm hurt when he tried to bend his arm. Debbie picked up Emily and sat down in her chair. Then Emily and

Debbie took turns feeding Bruce. Sherry felt left out so she stood up in her chair to help.

Carroll laughed at the three feeding Bruce. "If you do what Mike and Debbie tell ya, we will come. We have seventy-six peoples now. Can you feed that many?"

Mike answered. "Carroll, we built this Center to feed over two thousand at a time. With the group Bruce brought in we now have one hundred and eighty-four. We can hold everyone."

Millie came over and put a towel over Bruce's chest and tied it behind his neck like a bib. "You scare me like that again and I'm findin' a belt," she said, kissing the top of his head with tears in her eyes. Bruce just shook his head.

Carroll looked at Millie. "You over tha kitchen and you feed Bruce?"

"Yeah, the other women voted me head of tha kitchen," Millie told her.

Carroll reached in her pocket, pulling out a ziplock bag, "This be herbal tea my mama gave me the recipe for. It helps with tha blood poisoning. I'd give it ta Debbie but I thinks Bruce could whine his way out of drinkin' it with her because it doesn't taste good. Two teaspoons to one glass of hot water; let it sit for twenty minutes then filter out the leaves. Three glasses a day for four days," Carroll said.

Millie grabbed the bag and headed to the kitchen. Debbie scowled at Carroll. "I would've made him drink it."

"Debbie, years ago Marcus cut his hand. He whined somethin' fierce and I quit makin' him drink it. We had to take 'im to the hospital two days later. We have a soft spot for 'em so it's better to let someone else be mean to 'em," Carroll told her. Debbie nodded her head in agreement.

The group made small talk and thirty minutes later Millie came back, carrying a glass of tea and a flyswatter. "My granny made medicine tea likes this. She never taught anyone else 'cause she died suddenly. It do works, but it don't taste good. Bruce, you'll drink it," Millie told him, tapping the flyswatter on her leg.

Bruce just looked at her and laughed, then asked Debbie to give him a drink. Debbie picked up the glass and Bruce took a sip. Bruce could feel his toes curl up backwards as he yanked his head back from the glass. "Shit!" he exclaimed, wanting his tongue out of his mouth. Millie took a step toward him.

"Hold on, woman. I'll drink it, just let me work up to it," Bruce told her. Millie stopped moving toward Bruce. "I would rather lick a dead elephant's butt. Debbie, just pour it down me," Bruce told her. Debbie put her hand on the back of Bruce's head so he couldn't pull away and Bruce drank down the whole glass. When Debbie lowered the glass, Bruce wanted to cough his testicles up on the table.

Once the taste subsided and his toes straightened out, Bruce felt better and his shoulder had quit throbbing. Marcus gave him a sympathetic look. "It took me two hours to drink each glass. It did make me feel better, but the taste was something awful."

"It's not that bad," Bruce told him, smiling. Bruce felt drunk and happy as his head wobbled on his shoulders. "I want to go to bed. I can feel the rotation of the earth," Bruce told Debbie, grinning. Debbie looked at Mike.

"He can sleep. His next dose of antibiotics is at 1800," Mike said as Bruce looked blearily at him.

"Dude, there are two of you," Bruce told Mike, grinning.

"Carroll, do you have the recipe for that tea?" Mike asked her.

"Of course I do," Carroll said.

"Will you show it to me? Medicine is going to get short."

"I'll bring over Mama's books on Sunday," Carroll promised.

"Alright let's dance," Bruce said, trying to stand. He waved his left hand around. "Look, it works again."

"Come on Bruce, let's get you upstairs," Debbie said, grabbing his arm and trying to guide him.

Bruce staggered around drunkenly. "Fuck it, I'll sleep right here," he said, pointing at the floor.

Staggering a few steps sideways, he said, "Nah, I'll sleep here," pointing at the new area of floor. Then Bruce looked at Carroll. "Your mama makes good shit." Bruce gave her the thumbs up while trying to walk a straight line but not even coming close.

Jake, Steve, Buffy and Danny ran to help Debbie guide Bruce out of the room. The twins went to help but Stephanie grabbed PJ and ran toward the door to grab the twins, keeping them out of the way. They managed to get Bruce to the bed and he just collapsed. The twins crawled into bed, wanting to sleep with Daddy.

"Girls you can't sleep with Daddy tonight. Now go with Danny and Buffy and help them take care of PJ. Do that for Mama because PJ will want to lay down with Daddy too and he will keep him awake," Debbie told the twins. Danny grabbed PJ before the twins could and led them out and everyone followed.

Bruce sat up and looked at Debbie and Stephanie. "I can hear the solar winds," he shouted and fell back on the bed.

"What the hell was in that tea?" Stephanie asked in amazement.

Debbie was wiping sweat off her face. "I have no idea but I want some. Stephanie, go down to the kitchen and get a big bowl so we can clean him up."

Stephanie took off to the kitchen as Debbie untied Bruce's boots. Stephanie was back before the first one was off. The two struggled to get Bruce undressed. Debbie fought the urge to just cut the damn things off but didn't. These were his 'tiger stripes.' After stripping Bruce, they started washing him off.

Bruce opened his eyes and looked at his body. "Hey I'm naked," he told everyone.

"We know, baby, we took your clothes off," Debbie said as she and Stephanie washed him off.

"Why aren't you naked?" he asked Debbie.

"I'll get naked later, stud muffin," Debbie said as she held up Bruce's leg so Stephanie could dry it.

"Stephanie, why aren't you naked?" Bruce asked as he wiggled his fingers in front of his face in total fascination.

"I'll get naked when Debbie does," Stephanie said.

Debbie crawled onto the bed and kissed Bruce on the lips. "Baby, I want you to close your eyes and count to twenty, and when you get there we'll be naked," Debbie told him. Bruce closed his eyes and didn't make it past five before he was snoring.

Debbie turned to Stephanie and asked, "You still want to be a part of this marriage?"

"Hell yes," Stephanie said, her feelings hurt.

Debbie smiled and said, "You'll do. You might need a little help, but you will do."

CHAPTER 24

The week flew by. After the first morning, Millie brought Bruce breakfast to his room. She watched Bruce slam the tea, all the while making making funny faces. At noon he did the same thing but Millie never even waited to see if Bruce drank it. Bruce was forced to stay in bed and he started throwing a fit until Debbie told him no more tea, then Bruce shut up.

He stayed in bed, playing X-Box and waiting on his tea. It was Friday evening when Bruce did not want to drink the tea anymore. Debbie almost let him skip it then decided to make him drink it. Saturday, Millie had to stay until he drank it down all three times. When Bruce finished the last glass, he told everyone what they could do with that damn tea, in very graphic detail. Millie just walked out, smiling.

Sunday morning Bruce got out of bed at 0330, feeling better than he had in weeks. Looking back at the bed, Bruce saw Debbie, Stephanie, the twins, PJ and Angela curled up with Cade. Bruce sighed as he looked at Angela. She still cried herself to sleep with Debbie and Stephanie holding her and Cade.

Bruce walked into the closet, grabbing some fatigues and a vest. Getting dressed, he grabbed baby SCAR and headed downstairs to the kitchen. Fixing a pot of coffee, he poured a cup and headed outside. With a cloudless sky the stars and moon provided more than enough light for him to see the farm. He saw a group of people working on the barracks and the storage area. Bruce headed toward the barracks, moving his left shoulder around. It hurt a lot but the pain was dull, not sharp.

Bruce walked inside the barracks. The rooms were done and the crew was painting the walls. Bruce walked upstairs and it too was done. The walls just needed paint. Bruce left the barracks and noticed another frame up for more barracks. Feeling out of the loop, he walked to the storage area. The floor was laid out and ten people were putting up the steel beams for the roof. Looking at how big it was, Bruce was glad the girls had made them settle for eighty thousand square feet. It was huge. Be damned if he would tell them that though. Bruce walked down into the area to the work group.

"I thought we didn't have enough concrete to lay the floor," Bruce mentioned.

"We got the rest of the concrete Thursday," one of them told Bruce. Bruce thanked them and walked out, looking at the fence. A sloping earthen berm ran the length of the property. Bruce whistled in amazement and climbed to the top of the embankment, where he looked out to the area to the west. The heavy equipment was out there in front of a big-ass hole.

"Hey Bruce," he heard behind him. Bruce turned to see Paul walking up to him.

"What's with the pit?" Bruce asked, pointing to the hole outside the fence.

"It's a surprise," Paul told him.

"What are you doin' up so early?" Bruce asked.

"I get up several times in the night to make sure the night crews are doing okay. I just let them go and get cleaned up. Father Thomas is givin' a service today and I wanted them to be able to go if they wanted to," Paul told him. Bruce nodded his head. "Come on, I'll show you around," Paul said and led Bruce around the property.

The fence was almost complete. The bulldozer would dig the sloped ditch in front of the fence next week. The only weaknesses were the gates. They had walled off the gate on the back of the property so they had the south, east and west gates. Paul told Bruce they would park heavy equipment in front of the east and west sides so they could not be rammed, and Mike had put claymore mines on the road and at the front gate. They could be fired from the fort or Mission Control.

When they walked into the front, Bruce stopped, staring at the chicken house. "Paul, the chicken house grew," Bruce said.

"Bruce, we have over four hundred chickens now, with three hundred hatchlings," Paul told him.

"Paul, I have only been out of the loop for less than a week," Bruce said.

"Sorry Bruce, but Debbie and Stephanie wouldn't let anyone talk to you. I tried to go in after Debbie left your room only to find Stephanie standing over you. Bruce, she threatened to shoot me in the leg and if I didn't crawl out fast enough, she would shoot me in my 'pee pee spot' – her words," Paul informed him.

"That's okay, show me what else," Bruce replied with a sigh.

Paul showed him the rest of the improvements and they parted at 0600. Bruce headed to the house to find everyone in the kitchen dressed and drinking coffee.

"You look good, baby," Debbie told him.

"I feel like a million bucks, not that it means a lot now," Bruce said, getting another cup of coffee and walking to his place at the table, kissing Debbie as he walked by. Then he leaned over to kiss Stephanie. They both smiled at him as he sat down.

"Why are y'all dressed so early?" Bruce asked.

Mike answered, "Marcus and his clan will be here in a few minutes. We told them Father Thomas was giving a service and they asked if they could come over."

As if on cue, the intercom went off, "The guests have arrived."

Mike walked over to the intercom. "Let them in," he told Mission Control.

"Hey Mike, I went to the shop and our friends are gone," Bruce said, referring to the gang members.

"Yeah, Paul let them go," Mike told Bruce.

"He let them go?" Bruce asked in disbelief.

"Yep, he put 'em in a wheel barrel and took them to the scrap pond and let them go. Those gators don't really care if their food is yelling or not," Mike told Bruce, then added, "There are over a hundred gators in that pond now and we won't even talk about the creek behind the property."

"Well, I guess it's okay that he let them go," Bruce said, drinking some coffee as PJ started yelling.

"Let's get this boy something to eat," Debbie said, getting up and heading outside to the Center. She stopped as Marcus's clan pulled around and parked.

Marcus and Carroll got out of an old pickup and people started jumping out of the back. People got out of the other vehicles, all carrying boxes of food.

Bruce came up to Marcus, giving him a hug, then motioned to the people carrying boxes. "Marcus, we have enough food here. Why did you bring more?" Bruce asked.

"Carroll said for ya ta ask her," Marcus told him.

"That's alright," Bruce said quickly, making Marcus laugh.

Carroll walked over and hugged Bruce, then said, "Let me see tha shoulder." Bruce never said anything, just lowered his vest, pulling his shirt open. Carroll lifted the dressing, looking at the healing wound then put the dressing back on. "You drank the tea," Carroll stated.

"I'm not talking about your tea," Bruce said, redressing.

"It got real bad on tha last day, didn't it?" Carroll asked, cackling.

"I'm not saying anything about that evil concoction, because a switch would be in my future," Bruce told her, turning around and walking away.

"We almost had to pull a gun on him to make him drink it," Stephanie said, making Carroll laugh more.

They all walked into the Center. It was the most people in one place they had seen in a long time; well, that weren't blue anyway. The group ate breakfast, introducing themselves to each other. After breakfast, Father Thomas gave a good sermon, which made everyone feel better, and then led the group in prayer. After the prayer, Father Thomas looked at Bruce.

"Bruce, you want to start the briefing?" he asked.

"Paul, you start," Bruce said.

Paul walked to the front with a stack of papers then turned to the room. "First, the barracks are done." The room erupted into a thunderous roar. Paul held up his hands for everyone to quiet down. When everyone had settled back down he started again.

"Nancy and Stephanie have the room assignments. The priorities are those with kids and couples. No one has a room by themselves. With the extra people Bruce and them brought, the barracks are full. I want to ask you, Bruce, if I can section off the dining room to make ten bunkrooms that will each hold two people? With that we will have a spot for everyone just for now," Paul requested.

Bruce looked at Mike, Nancy and Debbie, who all nodded their heads. "We don't care," Bruce said.

"Thank you. Now after the supply area we're building two more barracks just like the one we built. We already have the frame up for the next one. As fast as we build them we fill them up," Paul said.

"We're saving humanity, Paul," Bruce said.

"Amen," Carroll said.

"I know, Bruce, that's why we're building two and have plans for four more. The pit that was dug in the west is for fuel tanks. There is a company on the other side of Shreveport that manufactures eight-thousand-gallon tanks. We are getting four, when the weather allows us. One of those trucks that we took from the truckstop was loaded with batteries. We are making another battery house to offset the drain we are putting on the two we have now. The fence is almost done, and we are putting in raised platforms that we can fire from in case of attack. That's it from me for now," Paul said, and several clapped as he walked to his seat.

"Lynn and Millie, you're next," Bruce hollered.

Not expecting to be called, they argued with each other until Millie finally walked to the front. "Bruce, you could've told us you wanted us talkin to these folks," Millie said nervously. Wiping her hands on her apron, she began. "I just want to say we've been having trouble with people helpin' in tha kitchen. Now we're starting to serve a fourth meal at midnight. We're puttin' out a small food area for snackin'. If you get caught takin' a lot you'll get spanked, and you won't be gettin' any more from it. We have ta remember there're a lot of us here, so be actin' right. That's all I got to say," Millie said and ran back to her seat.

"Matt and Jake," Bruce said.

The two boys went to the front of the room and Jake pointed a remote to a wall. Bruce looked at the wall and saw the HD projector from the house. "Jake, what is that doing out here?" Bruce asked.

"Mama and Daddy Mike said we could put it in here yesterday. We can watch movies in here now. Movie night was canceled last night and moved to tonight," Jake told Bruce. Bruce just looked at Mike and Debbie, who both refused to look at him.

"Go ahead, son," Bruce said, just a little unhappy.

"Alright, first we have to tell everyone the government is still functioning underground and several military units are active," Jake said and a lot of people started clapping. "That is not good news, people. They are starting a totalitarian society. They have forced labor camps and any woman of breeding age is forced to get pregnant. The copies we got off the government computer gave us the locations and we hacked in via satellite to confirm it. Matt and I put a sleeper virus in their network to notify us if they try to use satellites to study us, and it'll white out the screen if they try to focus on us. I'm not worried about them coming after us, only bombing us. They only have a force of ten thousand military in Colorado and half that in Pennsylvania. The Navy ships that didn't make it back have gone to Australia. Matt, get the lights," Jake said and Matt complied.

The projector showed a satellite photo on the wall. "This is the area north of Dallas," Jake said and hit the button, throwing up another photo this time closer. It looked like the land had spots over it. "This is a photo of a mass movement of infected. What we have heard on the radio referred to as a horde. There are over three million in this photo. They just move in a group, disperse, then form up again move and do it all over again. The northeast is a lot worse." Jake pushed the button, causing another picture to come up. "This is in Ohio and this one group has seven million. They move like locusts, slowly gathering then moving to a new area to hunt. We have noticed that those infected in the north are starting to hibernate. This has been confirmed on the short wave radio. Several groups have been in the path of these mass migrations and just laid low. Some were passed by but others were overrun. I didn't want to show this, but Dad said this clan has no secrets. We have no groups like this near us. The closest is the Dallas group and they are heading west. Any questions?" Jake asked and no one asked any.

"Now I want to show everyone what this group can do when we attack," Jake said, pushing another button. The screen showed a UAV video of the trap Bruce had set for the biker gang. "This is what my dad set up for our biker friends." The bikes drove down the road and the screen went white. Then the next group came in and disappeared. Several people started clapping. Then Jake showed the attack on the camp, including Bruce pissing on the biker. After the video, Jake called for the lights.

"This is what we can do when we work together. We need everyone to train harder and give it everything you have. When you're asked to go out, we want you to come back, so you need to learn how to fight. That is all I have for now. Matt, you need to add anything?" Jake asked and Matt said he was good.

Bruce got up and walked to the front. "Good job, son," he said. Then Bruce turned to the room. "Okay, now again. Good work everyone on the training and getting the buildings up so fast.

"Marcus, the reason I wanted you here today is this: when the first frost hits we're gonna hit the military bases for supplies. I want you to pick twenty people from your group. We are committing forty plus security. We will take ten eighteen-wheelers and start filling them up. When five are close to being full, five more will leave from here. This way we can keep a convoy running here with supplies. We are taking heavy weapons, assault rifles, ammo, clothes, and anything else we find. Debbie wants to send a group to Shreveport to gather supplies like clothes, food, and storage containers. We will only be training from now on; only current constructions projects will continue. Nothing else until the weather turns cold. After the cold snap ends then we will finish putting everything up. It will be assholes and elbows when it gets cold. I don't want to worry about ammo, and I want everyone here and at Marcus's farm to have three assault rifles each. If more assholes show up, they will fear us, as the blues around here will start to. Marcus, what do you say?" Bruce asked.

"November fifteenth will be a two-week cold spell. Then it'll warm up again until Christmas and'll stay cold 'til the end of January. I like your plan and want to thank ya for including us," Marcus said.

"How the hell do you know when it's going to be cold?" Bruce asked in a shocked voice.

"Farmer's Almanac," Marcus replied. Seeing Bruce's skeptical look, Marcus added, "It's only wrong by a day or two, Bruce."

"Well then, on the fifteenth we move. I expect it will take us ten days of steady work to move what we need from Polk to here. Marcus, can your group start on a large storage area?" Bruce asked.

"Already have. After we saw yours, we started one, and a barracks too," Marcus said.

"Well, if it's any consolation, I like your fence better," Bruce told him.

"Our fence only covers twenty acres, but we're working on that too," Marcus replied.

"Marcus, if we get hit by one of the masses they call a horde, will you bring your clan here to make our stand?" Bruce asked.

Marcus leaned toward Carroll, Darrell, and Eric, quietly conferring with them. Then Marcus turned to Bruce. "That's a good idea. With more guns shootin' we stand a better chance of survivin'."

"Is there any way you can make pens for your animals where they can't be heard, with enough supplies to hand to survive three days with food and water? My guess is if the blues don't hear food they won't even bother trying to get in. If they do, we can resupply you, but let's not throw away good livestock," Bruce said.

"If it can be done, we'll do it," Marcus said.

"Okay, when the weather turns cold, we'll secure solar panels for your farm as well. I want to make a rule that we don't use fuel for electricity unless it's for emergencies. It's in short supply. We do have plans to make some but it will not be in quantities for power production," Bruce told everyone. They all nodded in agreement. Those that had been out in the world had lived for months without it. Now if they had it, they just accepted it anyway they could get it.

"Okay, since movie night was canceled last night we will watch movies after lunch. Marcus, your clan is more than welcome to stay," Bruce told him.

"Thank ya Bruce, we'd enjoy that," Marcus said.

Bruce left the front of the room and sat down by Marcus. "Marcus, thank you for coming to get us," Bruce told him.

"My pleasure, and I still have that pistol of yours," Marcus said, reaching to his back.

"Na, you keep it for saving a Ranger that got careless," Bruce said.

"You weren't careless, maybe a bit reckless, but Rangers like you aren't careless," Marcus told him.

Bruce just studied Marcus for a minute then asked, "You were in 5th Special Forces group, weren't you?"

"Yep, Nam '64-'68 highlands," Marcus replied.

"Thought so. You used that .45 a little too easily, and when I was showing you how to make suppressors you understood the concept way too easy," Bruce told him.

"That was a long time ago, Bruce. I'm surprised you didn't go green," Marcus said, referring to the Green Berets.

"I might have, but I had to choose and I'm happy with my choice," Bruce said, looking at Debbie talking to Carroll in the corner alone.

"Yeah me too. I came home after my fourth tour and the girl I'd dreamed about my whole life came over to my house. When I answered the door, I almost fell over. Carroll asked me why I hadn't come over and asked her to marry me yet. I hung my beret up that day and done what my daddy taught me," Marcus confided as he looked over also. The two just stared at the women talking.

After the meeting, Debbie and Carroll had moved over to sit down in the corner to talk. After about twenty minutes, Carroll looked at Debbie closely then asked, "Why are ya letting Stephanie get close to your marriage?"

Debbie was totally taken back by the question. One minute they were talking gardening and the next, this. Debbie just looked at Carroll, trying to think of a reply. "Well—" Debbie started.

Carroll shook her head. "Debbie, the truth, please. We both grown women who married insane men. I ain't judgin' ya, I just wanted to know. That girl's sweet and kind. I don't think she's got a mean bone in her whole body. She looks at you almost tha same way she lookin at Bruce."

Debbie took a deep breath and looked up at Carroll with tears in her eyes. "I'm making sure Bruce has someone there in case something happens to me," Debbie told her.

Carroll just studied Debbie for a few minutes. "No, you know somethin' gonna happen," Carroll corrected her.

Debbie nodded her head in agreement then asked, "Please, don't tell Bruce?"

"Ain't my place to," Carroll replied as she looked around the hall then back to Debbie. "But I think I know why you haven't. You're scared of what Bruce'd sacrifice for ya," Carroll stated. Debbie nodded her head in agreement again. Carroll sighed. "Well, you're right about that. The only thing I don't see him sacrificin' be tha kids," Carroll replied matter-of-factly.

Debbie just stared at Carroll. Then she looked at Marcus and Bruce and the way they were talking to each other. "Marcus would do the same for you," Debbie said.

"Yeah, he would, as I'd sacrifice myself for him," Carroll replied.

"I can't let him do that, Carroll. Too many people are dependent on him," Debbie stated.

"Who visited ya in your dreams?" Carroll asked, looking at Debbie.

"How—" Debbie started as Carroll spoke again.

"My sister knowed. Our granny come to see her in dreams and told her it was almost time over and over again for many months. My sister told me about it and I just laughed. Several months later she was helpin' Pappy workin' on the tractor and it fall on her. Debbie, you have the same look on your face," Carroll explained.

Debbie wanted to run away from Carroll; she didn't like someone who could read her like a book, but she wanted to talk to her so bad. "Carroll, this is my choice but when it happens, Bruce is going to be hurt real bad. I can tell by the way Marcus and Bruce are talking Marcus was in the service and is a warrior like Bruce. The worst part of Bruce can't stay. He may save the world but he'll be alone, and that hurts me more than anything. All of the kids, they will be fine but Bruce will follow the wave and have a cold lonely heart until he dies. I don't want to know where he will go if he follows that path. I have some hope that if I get someone close to him now, he won't shut out the whole world. Then that one person can bring him back," Debbie explained.

"Well, I can't say I wouldn't try the same thing, Debbie. You'd think after forty plus years I'd not get weak in the knees when Marcus looks at me but I still do. Do ya have any idea when?" Carroll asked.

Debbie shook her head no. "Carroll, I want to ask several favors from you please?"

"If I can, I will," Carroll promised.

"If Bruce ever acts like he hates me, talk to him for me," Debbie asked.

"That man's not capable of hatin' you," Carroll informed her.

"We'll see. Next, the one he chooses, guide her until she gets her bearings. One is so lovestruck with him I don't think she would rein him in if needed. The other, well—" Debbie said, leaving it open.

Carroll laughed and nodded. "You don't have to ask all your requests now, especially if ya think you've time," she told Debbie.

Debbie nodded again, looking Carroll in the eye. "Thank you then, and I'll ask you for more later," Debbie said, "and Carroll, I dream about my dad."

CHAPTER 25

That evening, Bruce was the last out of the shower. Looking at the bed, Bruce fought off the temptation to just lay down on the floor. Debbie, Stephanie, Angela, Cade, the twins and PJ were all playing in the bed. Bruce walked over to Angela and grabbed her feet, pulling off her socks.

Stephanie looked at Angela smugly. "Told you he wouldn't let you keep them on."

"Bruce, my feet get cold," Angela told him in a pouty voice.

"Angela, last night you and Cade burrowed under everyone to my side. How, I don't know. When I feel socks touch me, I think a hairy caterpillar is crawling on my body. I know your feet get cold because you put them on Stephanie and she rolled on top of me. Then I felt two little caterpillars on my chest," Bruce told her.

"I didn't know I was that bad. Cade and I will sleep downstairs," Angela told Bruce, moving toward Cade.

"Get out of this bed and I will duct tape you to it," Bruce threatened her.

Debbie leaned toward Angela. "Told you duct tape would be involved."

"Debbie told me today that you let Susan and Conner have your room. Where would you go? If you say the Center, I'm getting a belt." Bruce said, crossing his arms across his chest. Angela just looked at Bruce, trying to think of something to say.

"You and Cade will stay here until you are ready to leave, which means until Debbie thinks you are ready to leave. I've seen you smile again and I like that, as does everyone else. I'm not saying you don't miss Alex, but you have felt a little guilty that you have rushed through the stages of grief. Angela, in this new world, we have to take any joy we can. We could be overrun and dead in an hour by blues or a gang. Don't feel guilty; Alex wouldn't want that and neither do we," Bruce told Angela, who had tears in her eyes.

Bruce laid down across the end of the bed. "Angela, we know you miss him. It's okay to be happy though and not feel guilty about it. I feel we will have enough guilt in the years to come. The most important thing though," Bruce paused and Angela leaned toward him, wanting the advice, "is don't wear socks in my bed." Angela slapped his shoulder, laughing with tears in her eyes. Stephanie and Debbie knocked Bruce on his back and sat on top of him as the twins and Cade joined in.

"Emily, get that sock," Debbie said and she and Stephanie struggled to keep Bruce down.

Bruce acted like he was struggling hard as Emily ran to Debbie, carrying Angela's sock. Bruce grabbed the sock and threw it at the head of the bed. Angela grabbed the sock and put it on her right foot. Then Angela scooted down to the group, holding her foot up.

"Get him, Angela," Debbie said.

"Don't you dare," Bruce warned her as Angela then lowered her foot and started rubbing it on his chest.

Bruce screamed, "Caterpillars!" They only tortured Bruce for a little while then let him up.

"Don't mess with us," Debbie warned Bruce.

Bruce looked at her then at PJ, who was sitting up on the pillows. "You could've helped," Bruce told PJ.

"Dada," PJ said, clapping his hands.

"I know who I am," Bruce told PJ, who just squealed and shook his head. "I see where your loyalties are, boy."

Everyone was getting situated in bed when a soft knock sounded on the door. "Come in," Debbie said.

The door opened and Danny, followed by Jake, walked in. Bruce jumped out of the bed. "Oh no. You are *not* sleeping in here," Bruce told them.

Debbie turned, snapping at Bruce. "Shut up Bruce, if they want to sleep in here then they can."

"Debbie, Jake hasn't slept with us since he was two and he gave you a black eye then. I don't want to know what it would be like now. It's like a full contact death match sleeping with Danny. I'm surprised that Buffy's still alive," Bruce said.

"Bruce, if they want to sleep in here then they can," Debbie told Bruce, letting him know it was not open to discussion.

Stephanie asked, looking at the open door, "Who is out in the hall?"

Jake turned and waved. Matt and Mary came into the room, staring at the floor. Bruce smiled upon seeing all four together. Jake turned to Bruce. "Dad, can we talk to you outside?" he asked.

Bruce smiled at Jake. "Son, your mom knows."

As one they all looked at Debbie, who was just smiling. Mary turned and quickly closed the door. Danny elbowed Jake, telling him, "Told ya he would tell Mama."

"He only told me two weeks ago," Debbie informed her.

Upon hearing her mother's words, Danny looked at Bruce. "How long have you known?"

"Known what?" Angela asked, looking at Debbie.

"Shush Angela, you deny everything you hear," Debbie told her.

"Depends by what you mean. If you mean that Matt stood little chance of getting away from you, or do you mean that the four of you were boyfriend and girlfriend?" Bruce asked, ignoring Angela and Debbie.

"Huh, t-that Matt—" Danny stuttered then said, "Let's start with us four first."

"Wait, do my mom and dad know?" Mary asked with fear in her voice.

"No baby, not unless you told them, and contrary to what your mother says, I never told her. I only left open questions for her," Bruce told Danny.

"Bruce, you did—" Debbie started to say then stopped in thought. "You dirty son of a bit—."

"Debbie," Bruce stopped her, "you have kids beside you." Debbie looked at Bruce with a scowl on her face. Now Bruce was glad that Stephanie and Angela were sleeping in here after all.

Bruce looked at the kids. "It's not my place to tell others as long as you acted appropriately."

The four just looked at Bruce in shock. Then Jake shook his head. "Dad, how long have you known?"

"Since the paintball field, the day the girls trapped both of you. I realized they had set a trap for you two when this group of boys just happens to show up to play with us," Bruce told Jake as Danny and Mary started blushing. "The girls had been acting weird the week leading up to paintball day. I didn't put it all together until we got to the field. I really thought until then they were planning on sneaking out. That's why I told everyone every morning at breakfast that Mission Control can record."

Bruce stopped, looked at the girls then continued, "When I saw that group of boys waiting and how both of you girls let both Jake and Matt know that they were there waiting on you, I knew something was up. The girls were making you two jealous. From the reaction you two showed, it worked."

"Is that why you tried to kill them, Daddy, because they were making Jake and Matt jealous?" Danny protested.

"Hell no! Those little freaks of nature were scoping out my little girls. They had to pay for the thoughts in their dirty little minds," Bruce snapped at Danny.

"Don't worry, Dad, we took care of it," Jake assured Bruce. "Especially after that one slapped Danny on the butt," Jake finished and Danny's face drained of color.

"What?" Bruce said, his face turning to stone.

"It's okay, Dad, Matt threw him down and shot him thirty times in the chest, standing over him until the blond baby started crying," Jake told Bruce.

Debbie gasped. "I thought Bruce did that."

"No Mama, Matt did. I tried to drown the one going after Mary in the pool," Jake admitted.

Bruce looked at Matt. "I love you Matt, but when Danny is in gear and you—"

"*Daddy*," Danny said, cutting Bruce off.

"How did you know?" Mary asked, still amazed.

"Your plan was way too complicated," Bruce told her, then continued. "Let me guess; the boys came to you the next day. Then the boys set out your rendezvous and such like going to the catfish pond in the middle of the night and kissing up a storm." Bruce winked at them.

"That's impossible, I set the video to loop," Jake said and Matt agreed with him.

"Actually, I was outside waiting on the pigs in the field and heard laughing. Thinking it was Mike and Nancy, I snuck closer and boy, was I surprised. Let me tell you, it's really gross seeing your kids like that," Bruce told them as they all blushed.

Danny looked at him, pointing her finger, "You remember that when you and Mom talk about sex. That's so gross." Bruce laughed at her and Debbie just glared at him. He'd never said anything about the catfish pond.

Matt looked at Bruce. "Daddy Bruce, how do you know it was Jake and I setting up our meetings?"

"They were simple. That is why your mom and Debbie never caught on," Bruce told them as Jake and Matt gave each other high fives. Then Bruce deflated their bubbles. "If you two had started this whole thing I would have never known. I was on the lookout for stuff different about each of you. Jake has on Mary's necklace, and she has his class ring on her necklace. Danny has Matt's bracelet on her ankle while Matt wears her charm bracelet on his ankle," Bruce told them.

Danny crossed her arms, looking at Bruce. "Daddy, sometimes I think you know more than you let on. Just to see what will happen."

"If I wouldn't have known, then I couldn't have covered for you, now could I," Bruce confronted her.

"How do you know we haven't done anything?" Danny almost yelled, angry that Daddy knew.

"You haven't because none of you want your parents fighting with each other," Bruce told her plainly.

All four teens' shoulders slumped at once as they stared at Bruce. Then Mary broke the silence. "Daddy Bruce, the reason we wanted to talk to you alone was we were going to ask you if we should quit seeing each other."

"That is not my decision to make, guys. I will say this, if someone doesn't quit looking at my daughter in combat gear—" Bruce stopped as Debbie yelled, "Bruce!"

"Debbie, he looks at her like she's wearing a bikini instead of full combat gear," Bruce exclaimed.

Matt blurted out, "She's so hot in full gear."

Bruce clapped his hands over his ears. "I don't want to hear that my daughter is hot in combat gear. I'm fixing to get a water hose," Bruce told everyone as Danny kissed Matt, then started jumping up and down shouting, "I'm hot!"

"Debbie, make her stop. I'm fixing to spin off," Bruce said, looking toward the bed, his hands still on his head. Stephanie and Angela were hugging each other, trying not to laugh, but not doing a good job.

Debbie told Danny to stop as Bruce took his hands off his ears. Danny just smiled at Bruce. He looked at Danny and said, "Would you like me to tell you the real reason you came to me?"

The smile fell off of Danny's face as a look of disbelief washed over each face. "You were going to pretend to say you were going to break up, knowing it would make me feel like shit because I love each of you so much. Y'all were going to try to make me sell this to the other parents. Danny was going to play the biggest part. You girls came up with the plan and the boys wouldn't go along until Danny assured you that she was goin' to play the daddy's little girl routine," Bruce told the four. Danny stumbled into the dresser as the others wanted to just disappear.

"How?" Danny asked, not really wanting to know.

"Daddy's little girl wields power over Daddy because he allows it. He wants the best for her. Daddies don't worry so much about the boys. They can fight their way ahead in the world, but daddies don't want that for our girls. But I trained you for it anyway," Bruce answered Danny. Then he asked, "Well, was I right about why you came to me?"

Jake nodded his head yes then Bruce asked, "I just want to know, did Danny or Mary come up with this? I think I have the right to know before I talk to Mike and Nancy." Jake, Matt, and Danny looked at Mary, who just looked down at the floor. "That makes sense," Bruce said.

"Why?" Debbie asked.

"A teenage girl that hangs around Mindy has been following Jake around. I figured that Mindy asked David to put in a good word for her friend to Jake. Of course David knows about you four and told Mary. You two are twins after all, so he would've told you first. Today in the Center, I almost took Mary's weapons from her. Every time Mary looked at that girl, I thought she was fixing to bust a cap," Bruce told Debbie.

"Now I know where Buffy got 'bust a cap' from," Angela whispered to Stephanie.

"I'm going to cut that bitch," Mary said with determination.

"Mary," Bruce said.

Danny leaned toward Mary, saying, "We can shoot her and throw her in the scrap pond."

"Danny, that's enough. Turn down the testosterone," Debbie said, then turned to Bruce. "That's your child. I had nothing to do with her birth."

Bruce looked at the four. "Okay, I will talk to Nancy and Mike. Do you want me to do it slowly over weeks or just get it over with?" he asked.

"Don't let my daddy kill me, Daddy Bruce," Mary pleaded.

Bruce just looked at Mary in disbelief. "Mary, your dad won't kill you."

"Well don't let him kill me!" Jake exclaimed.

Bruce stared at Jake, not believing what he was hearing, "Son, did I kill Matt for drooling over my daughter in combat gear?" he asked as Matt said dreamily, "She's so hot."

Bruce covered his ears. "I don't want to hear that!" Jake, Danny and Mary started slapping Matt, telling him to shut up. When they were finished, Bruce removed his hands.

"Just tell them but break it slow," Matt said.

"Okay. Go down to the kitchen, I'll get them," Bruce told them.

"You are goin' to tell them in front of us?" Mary almost cried.

"Yeah, that was how Debbie figured it out. If they see you in front of them, they can't get mad at you about it. I had to tell Danny about Matt—" Bruce stopped as Debbie interrupted.

"Don't say it, Bruce. Matt has it bad," Debbie said. Matt just smiled as Jake put his hand over Matt's mouth.

"Dude, don't say it, we are really close here," Jake told Matt. Then he turned to Bruce. "We'll be in the kitchen, Dad." The four filed out of the room.

"Debbie, go to the kitchen with the kids. I'm going to get Mike and Nancy," Bruce said, putting on his lounge pants. Debbie got out of bed and headed to the door as Angela picked up Cade and Emily.

"I'm not missing this," Angela said, then looked at Stephanie. "Get the other two and let's go." Stephanie picked up PJ and Sherry and they ran out the door.

Bruce walked to Mike's room and knocked on the door. He heard Mike say, "Come in." Bruce walked in and saw Mike and Nancy sitting up in bed, reading.

"Hey brother, what's up?" Mike asked, putting his book down.

"Hey Mike, I was wantin' to know if I could sleep with your wife tonight?" Bruce asked with a serious face.

Mike looked at Nancy then back to Bruce. "Sure, brother. Just don't make a lot of noise. I'm reading." Mike picked his book back up.

"What?" Nancy cried in shock, looking at Mike.

"Baby, I slept with Bruce last night and I'm sore so it's your turn," Mike told Nancy. She slapped Mike's arm as Bruce and Mike laughed.

"Hey guys, I want to talk to you in the kitchen," Bruce said.

"Can't it wait until tomorrow, Bruce? We were fixin' to go to sleep," Nancy said.

"No, we need to talk about it tonight. I promise it's better than your books. It concerns the kids," Bruce told them.

"Okay Bruce, but it better be good because I just talked Nancy into playing around," Mike told him.

"You were just going to give me away," Nancy pointed out to Mike.

"Nah, just sending in the warm up before the pro gets there," Mike told Nancy, kissing her.

They followed Bruce to the kitchen to see the group at the table. "What're Stephanie, Angela and the kids here for?" Nancy asked with an inquisitive look on her face.

"I can't miss this," Angela said, smiling. Stephanie just stared at Mike and Nancy, then reached an arm around Angela's shoulders and put her hand over Angela's mouth.

When they were seated, Bruce stood at his spot at the table and leaned over with his hands on the table. "Mike and Nancy, I have to tell you something," Bruce said gravely, staring at Mike. "My son is in love with your daughter, and my daughter is in love with your son." The four teens just looked at Bruce in shock. That was breaking it easy?

Nancy laughed. "Bruce, really what is it?" she asked. Bruce was still looking at Mike.

"I'm serious, they've been paired up for some time now. I knew from the beginning and didn't say anything because I approved," Bruce said, not taking his eyes off of Mike.

Danny almost fell out of her chair as the other three continued looking at Bruce in shock. Bruce had just taken all the blame for allowing them to see each other. Debbie was watching Bruce stare at Mike and Mike stare back at Bruce.

"What? How? Why? When?" Nancy faltered, looking at the kids then to Bruce, who was still looking at Mike. Mike smiled and nodded his head at Bruce. Then Bruce turned to Nancy.

"That pretty much covers everything, Nancy, and I will answer it in a minute. The kids have behaved appropriately, but give me a minute first," Bruce said then turned back to Mike.

"When did you get suspicious?" Bruce asked Mike.

"First week in September," Mike replied. Debbie snapped her head toward Mike.

"Which one?" Bruce asked, smiling.

"Matt, then I started watching the others," Mike replied.

Nancy looked at Mike. "What about my baby boy?" she demanded.

Mike said, "Baby, every time Matt looks at Danny in combat gear—"

"She's so hot," Matt said, looking at Danny. Danny just smiled and blushed. Bruce turned away, groaning.

"That's what I mean. I almost took a water hose to him last week," Mike told Nancy, pointing at Matt.

Angela fell out laughing. Nancy glared at Angela and said, "I don't think this is something to laugh about."

"I'm sorry, Nancy. I'm not laughing about the kids. I'm laughing at Mike and Bruce. They are so much alike it's scary," Angela said as she tried to stop laughing.

"Spill it, Bruce," Nancy told him, not very kindly. Bruce told her what he knew and had suspected over the next hour. Then he just looked at Nancy.

"Debbie, why didn't you tell me?" Nancy asked Debbie with tears in her eyes.

"I told her not to," Bruce told Nancy from where he was standing at the end of the table.

"Nobody can 'tell' Debbie not to do anything," Nancy shot back as Bruce sat down.

"He can if he tells her it would really hurt his heart if she said anything to anyone," Bruce told Nancy, shaking his head back and forth.

"That's not fair, Bruce," Nancy said.

"It wasn't her place to say. It was the kids," Bruce told her.

"You are telling it now," Nancy pointed out.

"They asked me to," Bruce said.

"So, I'm the only idiot that didn't see it?" Nancy wailed as Debbie went over and hugged her.

Bruce sighed. "Nancy, you did suspect it. That day in the field when Mary wanted to go to Jake you stared at them for a long time. I saw it on your face. Then when we sit down to eat, you looked from kid to kid. You just blocked it out. That's why the kids were scared to say anything," Bruce told her, smiling.

Nancy looked like she was starting to doubt her own memory. "What—No, I didn't—Well, maybe." Nancy tried to put the thoughts in the right order.

"See, told ya. It's not our fault you doubted yourself," Bruce told her.

"Okay, so maybe I did suspect it!" Nancy yelled. "What are we going to do about it?"

"There is only one thing we can do about it, Nancy," Bruce told her as he stood up straight, cracking his knuckles then turning his neck from side to side and making it pop. He looked at Mike and stated, "My son wants to ask for your daughter's hand in marriage."

Mike slammed his hands on the table and jumped to his feet, "Now hold on a minute, Bruce!" he hollered. Chairs scooted back from the table as everyone, even PJ, looked back and forth from Mike and Bruce, awaiting the clash. Mike gave Bruce a look that could've cracked ice. "My son wants *your* daughter's hand in marriage," he growled.

Bruce squinted his eyes at Mike. "I put up my truck for dowry," he told Mike, rounding the table and walking toward him.

"I offer *my* truck as dowry for my daughter," Mike said, walking toward Bruce.

When they got close to each other, they embraced each other in a bear hug. The tension left the room as everyone breathed a sigh of relief.

"Can I borrow your truck?" Bruce asked.

"If I can borrow yours," Mike answered.

They turned to Nancy with arms across each other's shoulder. Debbie, who was still hugging Nancy, was staring with her at the two insane men who had stolen their husbands.

"Well, it's fixed," Bruce told Nancy. Nancy just mumbled gibberish.

"I know she speaks English, I've heard her use it before," Bruce said to Mike.

"I think English is her second language," Mike answered.

"I'm going to kill both of you with a heavy blunt object," Nancy replied in an angry voice.

"I'll help you," Debbie assured her. The four kids ran in front to the daddies, offering themselves as human shields.

"We can't hurt the kids," Nancy said. She looked at the girls. "You could have told Debbie and me. We would have listened. Now come tell us all about it."

The girls ran over to the mothers, hugging them, then sat down beside them and started talking. Angela and Stephanie went over to join in. Matt and Jake stood up, shaking their daddies' hands.

Mike grabbed Matt. "Son, that's how you look at a girl in a bikini, not full combat gear. And don't say it," Mike stopped Matt.

Bruce put his hand on Matt's shoulder. "Son, it really wouldn't bother me as bad if Danny was wearing a bikini when you look at her like that."

Matt looked at them. "Danny is always beautiful, but when she is decked out, man is she—" Mike put his hand over Matt's mouth. "Son, I will find a water hose," he threatened.

The family talked till 0100 until finally Bruce declared it was time to go to sleep. Everyone bunking in Bruce's room grabbed a sleeping kid and headed upstairs. They all piled in bed, Debbie on the right, with Cade and Angela beside her, then Stephanie and PJ with the twins beside Bruce.

Debbie sat up and looked toward Bruce. "I don't know if I'm ever talking to you again, Bruce."

Bruce sat up. "What the hell did I do?"

"I sat and watched you convince Nancy that she knew when she didn't. Then you totally disarmed her like you do me and anyone else you want to," Debbie said, throwing her head down into her pillow.

"I didn't do anything," Bruce lied.

Stephanie spoke up. "I think Bruce handled it great."

Debbie sat back up. "Stephanie, you're supposed to take my side."

Stephanie looked at Debbie. "Well, he did great and everyone was happy in the end."

"Stephanie, Bruce doesn't walk on water," Debbie said sternly.

Laughing, Stephanie answered, "Of course he can't, Debbie. If he could, he couldn't swim."

Angela laughed and snorted at the same time, finally getting out, "Debbie, Bruce did do good."

"I didn't even see how he did it," Debbie said, throwing herself down on her pillow. "How did you know Mike suspected? Don't say you saw it on his face because I was watching it," Debbie added.

"Debbie, Mike has the worst poker face in the world," Bruce answered, laying back down.

"That was great. Is it like that all the time up here?" Angela asked, still giggling and snorting.

"This room is drama central," Debbie admitted.

"Oh, Cade and I have to stay now," Angela said.

Debbie turned over, kissing Angela. "You can stay as long as you want and remember, we love you but you have to take my side."

Angela looked at Debbie, frowning, "Let me take his side this one time."

"Okay, this time. Tomorrow we'll move your clothes up here. Stephanie shares the closet with Bruce, so you'll share mine," Debbie said, turning over.

They all drifted off to sleep. Around 0300 Bruce woke up, screaming, "Caterpillars!" and scaring PJ awake. Throwing the blankets back, he saw Angela's little socked feet on his leg. Reaching down, he pulled her socks off, throwing them on the floor, then laid back down, grumbling. PJ started hitting him in the head with an empty bottle. Not in the mood, Bruce just closed his eyes, ignoring PJ and falling back to sleep. PJ gave up trying to wake up Dada and crawled onto his chest and went to sleep.

CHAPTER 26

It was November first. Bruce sat in his chair drinking coffee after his workout. His shoulder only hurt with certain movements, but he could lift the same amount of weight he did before the piece of wood tried to kill him. Looking at his watch, it read 0610. Bruce looked around the Community Center to see people coming in after workouts. The night crew was eating before heading to bed.

The storage area and fence were complete. They were putting up several raised platforms along the fence to shoot attackers. The clan had been broken down to ten-person groups and were learning the ways to survive.

Bruce's groups were the kids. His first class was going to be the ten to fourteen year olds. Bruce loved teaching the kids because they loved to learn, if you made it fun. Bruce was going over his lessons in his head as the rest of the family came in, grabbed some coffee and sat down.

Debbie and Stephanie kissed Bruce on the head before they sat down. Debbie looked at Bruce as she sipped her coffee. "Bruce baby, can I ask you a favor?" she asked, looking at him.

Bruce wanted to say "Hell No," because when Debbie asked for a favor it was always something big that he didn't want to do. Bruce knew better than to say no because he still had to sleep in the same room with her. "Sure baby, what do you need," Bruce replied then gritted his teeth.

"I want you to talk to the women and girls we rescued from the gang's compound. Some are having a real hard time adjusting. Some just look like hollow shells. Your talk with Mindy really helped her a lot. I think you can really help some of the women and girls. I know it's a lot to ask and I wouldn't if I didn't think it would help," Debbie told Bruce.

"You're kidding, right?" Bruce asked, not believing what she had just said.

"No baby, I'm not kidding," Debbie replied, knowing Bruce was fixing to dig in his heels.

"You talk to them, you're a girl," Bruce told her.

"I have, and so has Nancy, Angela, Stephanie, Millie, and Father Thomas, but we are not getting through to them," Debbie answered.

"Well, then, I can't do anything," Bruce replied, hoping to end the topic. Boys just did not talk to groups about that.

"Bruce, come on, please," Debbie begged.

Then Stephanie started in. "Bruce, you could help most of the women. Please, just talk to them," she pleaded.

Bruce just turned and looked at Stephanie; then Angela chimed in. "Bruce, just try it once."

Bruce turned to Angela then looked back at Debbie. "Boys don't like to talk about that stuff," he said as Stephanie replied, "Page five, emotions."

"What?" Bruce asked her.

"Nothing," Stephanie said quickly.

"This isn't fair, all of you ganging up on me like this," Bruce told them.

Debbie smiled at Stephanie then looked at Bruce. "Please baby, for me? If it doesn't work then I will know we tried everything to save them."

"Okay, I'll try one time but that's it. When do you want me to do it?" Bruce asked, giving in.

"Tonight after supper. We will clear the Center out so you can talk to all of them at one time," Debbie answered, glad she was not going to have to pressure Bruce into talking to the women.

Bruce nodded his head as Millie brought plates over serving breakfast. Bruce shoveled the food down before Debbie could ask for anything else. Standing up Bruce kissed Debbie and Stephanie then kissed Angela on the head as he left to get dressed.

After Bruce was dressed, he headed to the machine shop for his first class. Bruce had five .22's with suppressors attached lying on a table behind the shop. He waited for the kids to show up. Bruce sat up targets at twenty and fifty yards. Then Bruce laid out five M-4's with suppressors and magazines as his first group arrived.

Bruce pointed at the ground and told the kids to sit down as he started. "First, let me tell you a gun will kill you if you let it. It is just a tool, you are the weapon. If you accidentally shoot one of the clan, it will be your fault not the guns. If any of you do not listen then you might kill one of your friends,"

Bruce told the kids looking into their faces. Bruce saw he had their attention.

"You are the weapon not the gun, so you must be trained not the gun," Bruce said then held up his right index finger. "This is your primary safety and the only safety you will ever trust. Machines fail so do not trust your weapon's safety. Your finger is never to be on the trigger until you are ready to shoot something. When you shoot at something, you shoot to kill it, because if you wound your target it will kill you in return," Bruce told the kids, getting a lot of alarmed faces.

"I will teach you how to survive and use a gun; I'll turn each of you into a weapon. If you don't have balls, you will have them after I'm finished with you," Bruce told them, getting several giggles.

"I'm not kidding. I'm training you so others out there can't kill you or worse. I want your attention and respect. If you have a question, then ask. The only stupid question is the one not asked. Now let's get started."

Bruce started with the .22, explaining how to shoot with iron sights and the basic workings of a firearm. Then Bruce paired them off, showing them how to shoot the .22s. After an hour, Bruce moved to the M-4s. Bruce showed them how to take them apart and put them back together.

The kids enthusiastically took the M-4s apart and put them back together. Then Bruce showed them how to shoot the M-4. The gun was big to most of them but they tried, always keeping muzzle discipline with the guns. At 1000, Bruce led the kids to the shop and explained the basics of close quarter combat (CQB). Bruce stopped at 1130, leading his group to the Center for lunch.

The kids ran to the line to get some food as Bruce headed to his table. He was the last from the family to arrive for lunch. Danny and Buffy were wearing karate gis since they were teaching hand to hand. Well, Danny was teaching and Buffy was helping.

Bruce sat down as Millie brought a plate over to him. Bruce looked up at her, drawing in a breath to say something but Debbie cut him off. "Shut up Bruce, you lost the bet. Until she stops, you will sit and eat what Millie brings you," Debbie told him.

"I just want to get my own food once, Debbie," Bruce replied.

Mike looked at Bruce from the opposite end of the table. He rolled up his sleeve, showing Bruce a red mark. "I tried today to get my own plate and she popped me with that damn spoon. Millie told me your bet was for the whole family, not just you, Bruce," Mike said, rolling his sleeve back down.

"Sorry, brother," Bruce apologized. Mike just grunted at him.

Bruce turned to Danny and asked, "How is hand to hand coming, sweet pea?"

"Good, Daddy, but I have to say most of these women are stupid. They think a woman can't fight a man and I have to show them in each class," Danny admitted, shaking her head.

"That's what most are taught, baby," Debbie told her.

"Well I'm glad I had my daddy and not theirs. Daddy always told us the only person that can beat you is the one you let beat you," Danny replied.

"You are being nice while teaching class, right, Danny? These women don't need some teenage girl telling them they're stupid," Debbie stated.

"No Mom, I'm being good, even if they are stupid. It's just hard taking that out of their head," Danny admitted.

Bruce spoke up, wanting to stop the two. "Danny, how is Buffy coming along?"

"Great, Dad, she is ready for her black belt test in Kenpo," Danny said in between bites.

"Danny, don't you think you're exaggerating a little? You've only worked with her a few months," Bruce responded.

"Dad, Buffy is my sister. How would it look if she was not a total bad ass, like me? I mean come on, I have worked with her every day. She has gotten really good but still has trouble with the hand weapons," Danny stated.

"I really wish I would've been there when you gave birth to Danny," Debbie said, smiling at Bruce. He just shook his head.

Bruce turned to look at Buffy. She was just looking back at Bruce, in disbelief that he doubted her training. "Buffy, get out beside the table. I am going to call out moves and for each one you get wrong, Danny owes me ten pushups," Bruce told her. Buffy just looked at Bruce in shock. Danny just kept eating; she wasn't worried.

Bruce watched Buffy move to the other side of the table; she was wearing her black gi with a white belt. "Kata 1," Bruce called out. Buffy started the movements of the kata, moving in fluid motion. When she finished, Bruce called out another kata. After Buffy completed it Bruce started calling out punches, blocks, and kicks. When Buffy performed all of them, Bruce started calling out techniques for different attacks. Bruce continued the test for an hour. Everyone in the Center had stopped eating to watch the little girl go through her test. When Bruce stopped, Buffy was drenched in sweat as she moved to her chair.

Bruce looked at Danny as Buffy sat back down, breathing hard. "Danny, I have to admit you taught her well. Why is she still wearing a white belt?"

Danny looked at Bruce. "Daddy, you're sifu, not me."

"Danny, you will present Buffy with her belt. You taught her, so the honor is yours. I'm very proud of you, sweet pea." Bruce was filled with pride.

Danny ran over to Bruce, wrapping her arms around his neck and kissing him. "Thank you Daddy."

Bruce looked at Buffy, "Buffy, you did very well and I'm proud of you also." Buffy ran over to Bruce, hugging him and Danny.

Danny told Buffy to head to the gym while she went for a black belt and the girls took off.

Debbie just looked at Bruce. "We have a preteen and a teenage girl that can beat the shit out of most men. Don't you think that is just a little scary, Bruce?" she asked.

Bruce put his arms around the twins sitting on each side of him. "Just think, you have two more to look forward to," Bruce said as Debbie stared at him. Then she got up and left the table. Bruce just thought Debbie believed he was being a smartass. He didn't see Debbie wiping tears from her eyes as she went back to her shooting class.

Bruce met his group of kids under the fort. He gave each kid a sheet of paper with a list on it. Once the kids read through the list they all looked at Bruce.

"This is a list of things each of you will put in a backpack when we bring in some. This list is for your go bag. This bag is to stay packed and by your door at all times. You can add more stuff, but be careful because you will have to carry it if we have to leave suddenly. Now for the first items: fish hooks and fishing line," Bruce said, then reached in one of the pouches on his vest and pulled out a small plastic box. "I keep mine on my vest, in case I'm separated from my pack," Bruce told the kids.

Then Bruce showed how they could use the hooks to fish, catch birds, or set traps. Bruce went over each item on the list and showed them how to use each one. At 1700 when the call came over the radio for classes to end the kids groaned. They were having fun with Bruce. He promised them that they would continue tomorrow but their brains needed rest now.

Bruce led his group to the Center for supper. Debbie came over to Bruce, wrapping her arm around his waist. "Don't forget, you promised," Debbie said.

"I'll do it baby, for you," Bruce replied.

Debbie stopped and Bruce looked down at her. "Thank you baby. This means a lot to me. I want those girls to have a life," she told him.

"You know I will do anything for you," Bruce assured her as he leaned down to kiss her.

"That's why you're my stud muffin," Debbie said, smiling and tilting her head back.

Bruce swept her up in his arms. "Come on, sugar mama, let's get some food."

He Bruce carried Debbie into the Community Center and headed toward their table. The family gathered around to eat, laughing and talking over the day's activities as was most everyone else. Debbie, Stephanie, Angela and Nancy left the table during supper; they walked around the tables, whispering in the ears of certain women and teenage girls. Then they returned to the table.

At 1900, Debbie walked to the front of the building and yelled for everyone's attention. When the talking died down, Debbie spoke. "I would like for everyone to head to the patio. Mike is going to go over the teams for the big runs we're going to do when it gets cold. The people Nancy, Angela, Stephanie, or I spoke to, will you please stay in here? We want to talk to you."

The clan left the building and headed to the patio, leaving fifty-four females in the Center. Stephanie closed the door and locked it. Debbie looked at the women and teen girls around the room.

"I have someone who wants to talk to you. Before he comes up here, I want you to listen to someone who has gone through what you went through," Debbie said and pointed at a table. Bruce was shocked as Mindy stood up and walked to the front of the room and faced the group.

Mindy took a deep breath and Debbie moved beside her, holding her hand. "I just want to ask each of you to please listen. He really helped me and opened my eyes. I have put what happened to me behind me in the past where it belongs. He doesn't sugar coat anything and he tells you just how to see the world," Mindy finished and Debbie hugged her before Mindy sat back down.

Everyone looked at Debbie. "Bruce, will you come up now?" Debbie asked. Several women gasped, realizing Bruce was walking to the front of the room.

Bruce took off his rifle and laid it on a table, stalling for time as thoughts raced through his mind. Debbie walked over to him. "Speak from your heart, baby," she said, then sat down.

Bruce looked at the group and started to speak. "I don't know if what I have to say will mean much to you. I've done a lot of bad things in my life but I think I've done some good also. You can never let the bad drag you down. I don't know what each of you have been through, and to be honest, I don't want to," Bruce said, getting a lot of shocked gasps from the crowd.

"Not because I would think less of you, but because I would want to go get a chainsaw and move through the world delivering medieval justice. I or someone in this family killed those responsible for hurting you, but there are others out there. What I could do to them would make a dark angel cry out in fear," Bruce admitted.

"I know everyone in here has lost loved ones. Kids, husbands, moms, dads, and grandparents, the list goes on and on. If you die then the memory of those die with you. They deserve better than that. The way I see it, as long as *you* live they live through you. If you want me to promise that you'll never go through that hell again, I can't. What I *can* say is this: If more show up we'll kill a lot of them and teach you how to fight them."

"That little girl you saw today doing martial arts in the back? She learned all of that in less than three months. She can use several different guns to fight. She knew nothing when I found her. Several men were raping her mother when I found her, and they were making her watch," Bruce told the group receiving shocked looks.

"She could have lay down and died, but she chooses to fight and live. Each day brings a new challenge. Sometimes it's sorrow but sometimes it's joy. She misses her mother every day, but has found a new one along with a new family. Will we replace her old one? No, we won't, but she has a family now as you can too. You can sit here, feel sorry for yourself and relive what was done to you every day. If you do you are giving those assholes we killed power over you even though they are dead."

Bruce continued talking to the group for two hours. When he finished almost all came up and told him thank you. As each one came by Bruce could see something on their faces he hadn't seen before: hope and determination. Looking around the room as the group hugged him, Bruce saw five women still sitting down at the tables. Each still had the lost look in their eyes. He memorized their faces and over the next several days would talk to them one on one. With his speech, Bruce reached all but one, a woman in her mid-thirties. She would hang herself three days later.

Bruce left the Community Center and found Mike talking with a group of people on the patio by the swimming pool. Mike looked up as Bruce approached.

"Hey brother. How'd it go?" Mike asked.

"I don't know. I only did it so Debbie would leave me the hell alone," Bruce replied, sitting down in a chair.

"Bruce, I hope you gave it your best shot. Those women need help," Mike said, grabbing a chair next to him.

"I just spoke to them. Hell, they're women. I don't know what to say to them to make them feel better. If it would have been guys I would've told them to suck it up, life is hard, you never get ahead, nothing is fair, sometimes the bad guys win, no one is special, and trouble is always one step away waiting to step on your balls. We are born cold, wet, and hungry and it only gets worse and the light at the end of the tunnel is always a train," Bruce replied.

"Well, I'm proud of you for trying Bruce," Mike confided as Stephanie came running over, jumping in Bruce's lap and wrapping her arms around him.

"You were great, Bruce. Most of the women are actually smiling now and talking to Debbie and Nancy," Stephanie informed Bruce as she squeezed him tight.

"Stephanie, I really didn't say much," Bruce told her.

Stephanie leaned back and looked at Bruce, her mouth hanging open. She managed to get out, "What?"

"I didn't say much," Bruce repeated.

"Bruce, you talked about love, hope, honor, compassion, pride, and determination, and the list goes on and on," Stephanie told him with a joyful smile.

"Stephanie, I basically told them to reach down, grab their balls and live their life."

Stephanie's smile vanished as she stared off for a second thinking, then looked back at Bruce. "Well, yeah, from a boy's standpoint, that is what you said."

"Anyone could have told them that," Bruce said.

"No, Bruce, you can say it so a girl can understand how a boy would deal with a bad situation," Stephanie replied.

"Whatever," Bruce said.

Stephanie stared at Bruce, a frown marring her lovely face. "I now know why Debbie wants to slap you when you say that."

"Just because you sleep in my bed doesn't mean you can slap me," Bruce warned her.

Stephanie leaned toward Bruce slowly. Then she quickly licked Bruce's face from chin to forehead, jumping out of Bruce's lap before he could react. "Ha, now what do you have to say," Stephanie challenged.

"You are so going to get it, girl," Bruce replied, wiping his face off.

"Do anything and I'll tell Debbie you were mean to me," Stephanie threatened, seeing Debbie walking toward them from the Center.

"You wouldn't dare," Bruce replied, calling her bluff.

Grinning, Stephanie looked at Bruce and glanced toward Debbie. As she got closer, Stephanie called out, "Debbie, Bruce is being mean to me."

"Bruce!" Debbie yelled, coming around the end of the swimming pool and heading toward Bruce.

"Debbie, now wait just a minute—" Bruce started as Debbie cut him off.

"I was coming over here to tell you how proud of you I was and to thank you. Only to find out you're being mean to Stephanie?" Debbie popped off, coming to a stop in front of Bruce with arms crossed.

Bruce pointed at Stephanie and started stuttering then managed to get out, "Debbie, she started it, all I did—"

Debbie held up her hand. "Bruce, you expect me to believe Stephanie started it? I know she was coming over here to say the same thing I was and then you were mean to her?"

362

Bruce just sat back in his chair, looking at Debbie. Debbie cocked her head to the side as she returned Bruce's stare. "What?" he asked. Debbie nodded her head toward Stephanie.

Bruce just looked away until Debbie started tapping her foot. Bruce looked at Debbie with alarm on his face. Then he turned to face Stephanie. "I'm sorry, Stephanie." Bruce apologized for something he didn't do, but he just wanted the wrath of Debbie to go away. Mike busted out laughing beside Bruce.

Debbie smiled at Bruce and jumped in his lap. Stephanie joined her. They both started chatting about how Bruce did such a good job. Bruce never heard a word either one said as they chatted away to him. Staring straight ahead, Bruce just blurted out loud, "I'm such a pussy." This sent Mike into another round of laughter.

Debbie and Stephanie just stopped talking and looked at Bruce. "What?" Debbie asked.

"I'm such a pussy," Bruce repeated. Mike was having trouble breathing, he was laughing so hard.

"Well, we will get you a douche so you can be a clean pussy," Debbie told him as she kissed his cheek. Mike slid out of his chair and hit the ground laughing, trying to breathe.

"Get up, please," Bruce requested. Debbie and Stephanie got out of Bruce's lap as he stood up. He kissed each on the cheek then stepped past them to glare at Mike on the ground. "You could've said something," Bruce told Mike, who just lay there looking up at him, grinning.

"Are you kidding? That was great," Mike managed to get out before laughing more.

"I'm going to put on a tampon," Bruce told everyone as he stormed into the house. Angela and Nancy walked up in time to hear Bruce's last comment as he went inside. Mike was pounding the ground with his fist, howling.

"I so came in on that conversation at the wrong time," Angela said.

Nancy looked at Mike then to Debbie. "What happened and why is my husband laughing so hard he's fixing to pass out?" Nancy asked.

"I had to remind Bruce who his boss was," Debbie replied.

Nancy nodded her head and looked down at Mike. "Mike, do you need a lesson as well?"

Mike coughed and struggled to his feet, holding in the laughter. "Sorry baby, it's just so refreshing to see Bruce punked down by little Debbie. He didn't do—" Mike stopped as he looked at Nancy's stern face. "You're right, baby, I wasn't laughing. I just have a bad case of gas. I'm going to walk it off." He headed quickly toward the shop and made it about halfway before collapsing to the ground again, laughing.

"Boys!" Nancy exclaimed.

"They never interrupt or take sides when a buddy is getting chewed out by their spouse or girlfriend. It's poor form and they don't want to get in trouble with their own spouse, page fifty-six," Stephanie stated. Nancy just looked at Stephanie with a questionable stare as Debbie started giggling.

"You are truly trying to use that book. I'm proud of you. Let me guess: Bruce really wasn't being mean to you?" Debbie asked.

"Well, not really. He did say 'whatever.' I wanted to shake him hard," Stephanie admitted.

"So he was being a smartass. That's just as bad. That one expression has pissed off more women than anything else," Debbie stated.

Angela asked, "Why is Bruce going after a tampon to wear?"

"He thinks, he wimped out," Debbie answered.

"Bruce wimp out? Look in the dictionary under big boy, you'll find a picture of Bruce," Angela predicted.

"Sometimes I have to remind Bruce my balls are just as big as his," Debbie replied.

"Oh, that's different," Angela agreed with her.

"Come on girls, let's make sure the kids are ready for bed. It's 2100 and class is tomorrow," Debbie said, heading toward the house.

The women rounded up the kids and headed upstairs. Debbie, Stephanie and Angela had their small posse of kids. As they walked into the room, they found Bruce sitting up in bed writing in his notebook as he went over the supply list that the boys had gotten from the judge and the congressman. Bruce looked up as the small army entered the room. *I'm putting another bed in here*, Bruce thought.

Debbie smiled at Bruce. "Did you get it taken care of, baby?"

"I'm not talking to you right now, but to answer your question, I found a super absorbent one to put on," Bruce replied as he continued going over his notes, making changes here and there. The women just giggled as they helped the kids get ready for bed.

Angela came out of the bathroom with Cade and headed toward the bed. Bruce just stared at her psychotically as she walked across the room. Angela noticed his stare but tried to ignore it until she got to the end of the bed.

"Oh, alright, Bruce," Angela said exasperatedly before reaching down and taking off her socks before she climbed into bed.

"I jumped out of bed last night when caterpillars crawled up my leg, and I hit my head on the damn nightstand," Bruce told Angela.

Angela snorted as she stifled a laugh. "What is it with you and caterpillars?" she asked.

Bruce raised his right arm up, showing Angela a three-inch-long one-inch-wide scar in his armpit. "I got this from a fuzzy caterpillar when I was a little boy. It burned like acid and continued to hurt for weeks. And yes, I still have nightmares about caterpillars."

"I'm sorry, Bruce, I thought you just had a foot fetish and I wanted you to work to see my feet," Angela replied with a serious expression. Debbie started laughing as she climbed in the bed.

"I told you I did but those feet are on the other side of the bed," Bruce replied.

Emily and Sherry jumped in the bed, crawled up to Bruce and showed him their feet. "We don't have socks on, Daddy," they said in unison.

Bruce kissed their little feet, saying, "That's because you love Daddy and don't want mean caterpillars to get him." The twins jumped on Bruce, hugging him and covering his face with kisses, then climbed under the cover.

Stephanie followed the twins into the bed. "That's cool, Bruce, I didn't know you had a foot fetish." This sent Debbie into a fit of laughter as she buried her face into her pillow.

"Shut up Debbie, that's between us," Bruce told her. The warning only made her laugh harder.

Stephanie pulled her left foot up to her chest. "I have ugly feet compared to Debbie and Angela," she commented.

"No Stephanie, you have very pretty feet," Bruce said as he continued going over his notes.

"You've looked at my feet, Bruce?" Stephanie asked, smiling at him.

"Of course I have," Bruce answered, causing Debbie to start kicking her feet as she laughed.

Angela rolled over to Debbie. "You have got to share this with us," she pleaded with Debbie. Then suddenly they heard a bloodcurdling scream coming from Mike's room down the hall.

Next they heard loud banging coming from Mike's bathroom on the other side of the wall, and Mike yelling at the top of his lungs, "Goddamn it Bruce!" Followed by another bloodcurdling scream, "My balls are on fire!"

The three women jumped in fright and then, as one, they turned toward Bruce. Bruce was just reading his notes, smiling, his body shaking as he laughed silently. They heard running footsteps out in the hall heading toward Mike and Nancy's room.

Bruce looked toward the door and said, "Be careful when you put on my boxers for the next few days. Mike doesn't have much of an imagination so his retaliations are to reciprocate in kind."

As Bruce finished speaking, Nancy busted into the room, breathlessly demanding, "Bruce, what the hell did you do? Mike ran to the toilet and started splashing water on his balls, screaming. After he used all the water, he jumped into the shower, turned on the cold water and is doing a handstand so the water hits his balls."

Bruce's shoulders shook harder as he laughed silently, still holding it in, then he gritted out, "I didn't know Mike could do a hand stand."

"He never has before. All of a sudden, he started yelling at me to blow on his balls. I didn't know what was happening and told him to forget it. That's when he ran for the toilet," Nancy said.

Bruce struggled to hold in the laughter then informed Nancy, "I put Icy/Hot in his underwear. The burning will stop in a little while."

Nancy just stared at Bruce before replying, "Bruce, I'm not in the mood for another practical joke war."

Stephanie stated out loud, "Retribution is mandatory when a buddy does not help a buddy out with a spouse and laughs when they get in trouble. Page fifty-nine."

Bruce looked at Stephanie. "What? Page fifty-nine of what? How do you know this stuff?"

Stephanie looked at Bruce with a blank stare and replied, "The male brain secretes more dopamine related to serotonin production when the molecular structure of testosterone alters—"

"Never mind, stop right there," Bruce said as he gathered his notes, setting them on the bedside table.

"Bruce, no more please," Nancy pleaded as another high-pitched scream came down the hall. Then Mike wailed, "My balls are on fire!"

"That's up to Mike. We're even as far as I'm concerned," Bruce said as he lay down. Nancy ran back to see if she could help Mike's balls.

Debbie just shook her head. "Bruce, I agree with Nancy, no more, this war stops now."

"Mike has had his payback. I can't say that for others," Bruce replied with his back to Debbie.

Debbie's eyes widened. "Bruce, I'm not in the mood for your jokes, so drop it."

Stephanie looked at Debbie then spoke. "Bruce, you can't do something like that to Debbie."

"I never said she was the only one, now did I?" Bruce replied as Stephanie scooted away from him toward Debbie for protection.

Angela spoke in a tiny meek voice, trying to sound small and fragile, "Bruce, I didn't do anything."

Narrowing his eyes, Bruce just said, "Caterpillars."

The three women put the twins, Cade, and PJ between them and Bruce. They stayed awake until Bruce fell asleep and was snoring softly. They even touched his back a few times to make sure he was asleep. Feeling safe, the three huddled together and fell asleep.

At 0120, Bruce's wristwatch vibrated, waking him up. Bruce eased out of bed, headed to his closet, grabbed several blankets and spread them out on the floor. Moving to the bed, Bruce gently moved the kids to the pallet on the floor, then covered them up.

Bruce started doing jumping jacks at the foot of the bed, gulping down air. Then he walked around, shaking his waist. Finally he moved to the bed, tucking the comforter under the mattress around the bed. Smiling, Bruce eased back under the covers, pulling the comforter over the girls' heads and holding it down with his arm.

Bruce started squeezing his abs and making himself fart, continuing to fart for five full minutes. He heard gasping and coughing coming from under the blankets. Debbie was the first to wake up and began fighting to get out of the toxic air. She pushed against the blanket but there was no give. With tears in her eyes, having had experience with this in the past, Debbie crawled around the bed looking for a way out.

Stephanie and Angela woke up as they felt Debbie crawl over them looking for a way out of the noxious fumes. Stephanie yelled out, "Have we been attacked with poisonous gas?" then started coughing and gagging.

Debbie crawled around the bed, pushing on the edges, but the blanket wouldn't give. Trying to hold her breath as she searched for an escape route, Debbie almost passed out when she had to take another breath. Starting to gag, Debbie yelled as she moved towards Bruce's side of the bed, "Damn it Bruce, that's enough."

As Debbie crawled toward him, Bruce let out a loud fart that shook the bed. Debbie screamed and backpedaled to her side of the bed, putting as much distance between her and Bruce as she could. Angela and Stephanie just started kicking the covers, trying brute force as their eyes continued to burn. Feeling pity for them, Bruce pulled the covers back to let the girls out and they lay there gasping for air. When the smell hit Bruce, he almost felt sorry for holding them under for so long. Almost, but not quite.

Debbie got out of bed and collapsed on all fours on the floor, coughing and trying to expel the toxic fumes from her body. "Bruce, you know how much I hate the Dutch oven," she managed to tell him.

Stephanie looked at Bruce with her bloodshot, watering eyes and smiled. "That was a good one, Bruce," she said with a dry, raspy voice.

"Good hell, that's why women don't have nose hair," Debbie replied, still on all fours beside the bed.

"My eyes are burning," Angela said then looked around before asking, "Where're the kids?"

"They probably chewed a hole through the mattress to escape," Debbie replied.

"I wouldn't endanger kids like that," Bruce said.

"Bullshit, you've done that to each of the kids several times. The only reason you quit was the kids' doctor thought Jake was developing asthma. Strange that you quit and his lungs improve," Debbie said, standing up shakily.

"I only did it to them once or twice," Bruce shot back.

"Bruce, I just tried to breath out of my tits. Once is too much," Debbie replied, heading toward the bathroom.

Angela giggled. "I didn't realize just how important clean air was," she said as Debbie walked back out, spraying air freshener. When Debbie finished Angela stated, "It smells like someone shit vanilla."

Everyone laughed as Bruce got out of bed to grab the kids. Debbie stopped him. "Bruce, just let them sleep down there. The fumes are not that toxic on the floor."

Angela looked at Bruce. "I promise that I will never ever wear socks in your bed again. Bruce, I think something crawled up your ass and died."

Bruce smiled. "I usually get even, Little Foot."

Debbie looked at Bruce then said, "Bruce, get in the middle of the bed. Stephanie, get on his left side, I'll take the right. Angela, lay on his chest. If he gets up, get a bat and hit his knees."

Everyone piled on Bruce and drifted off to sleep, ruining Bruce's next payback.

CHAPTER 27

When Bruce woke up to the alarm clock it felt like the world was on his chest. He tried to take a deep breath but he couldn't. Struggling to open his eyes, Bruce saw Angela's head on his right shoulder and Cade lying on her back. Emily was lying on his left chest beside Angela. Looking over Angela, Bruce saw Sherry on top of his right arm and Debbie's chest.

"PJ," Bruce called out, hoping he was not under everyone, and was rewarded with a whack to the left side of his head. Bruce tried to pull his arms out but couldn't as PJ wacked him again, then hit Emily and Stephanie in the head with his empty bottle, playing drums on everyone's head.

"Stop it now!" Bruce yelled out. PJ dropped the bottle, Bruce's yell scaring him. PJ clasped his hands together and started to frown. Then he started to poke his lips out as tears rolled down his face.

"Oh, you are good," Bruce said, feeling like shit. PJ let out a wail, his feelings hurt. Twisting his body back and forth, trying to get from under everyone, the others waking up from Bruce's yell, PJ crying and the alarm clock, Bruce was finally able to extract his arms and climb out of the pile.

Moving to the side of the bed, Bruce turned off the alarm clock. Then he growled and picked up a crying PJ. Setting PJ on the side of the bed, Bruce knelt down in front of him. "PJ, if you hit me with that bottle again, I am going to hit you with it. I hit harder," Bruce said in a calm voice. PJ stopped crying, looking at Bruce with wide eyes.

Debbie sat up. "Bruce, quit talking to the baby like that."

Bruce just shifted his gaze from PJ to Debbie and said, "Back off woman."

Debbie just sighed and laid back down. It was too early to get in a debate with Bruce even though she was on Bruce's side; that damn bottle hurt. She was not in the mood, so PJ was on his own.

Bruce picked PJ up and sat him on the pillows above everyone's head. Bruce picked up his bottle and gave it back to him. PJ grabbed the bottle and hit Stephanie in the head. Bruce grabbed the hand with the bottle and lightly popped it. Then, taking the bottle away, Bruce tapped it on top of PJ's head. Stephanie raised her head up.

"Lay back down!" Bruce snapped. Stephanie put her head back down; she didn't want Bruce to hold her under the covers and fart some more.

PJ was just staring at Bruce, holding out the hand Bruce had popped like it was broken; his lower lip was trembling. "It won't work on me, son," Bruce said, putting the bottle in PJ's lap.

PJ picked up the bottle and raised it over his head as Bruce barked, "No!" PJ released the bottle, dropping it on his head and looking wide-eyed at Bruce. Picking the bottle back up, Bruce laid it on PJ's lap again. PJ just looked at Bruce like 'I'm not touching the damn thing.'

Bruce just stared at PJ as PJ reached out to get Bruce to pick him up. "No," Bruce said. PJ dropped his hands and grabbed his bottle and held it to his chest.

"Good boy, PJ," Bruce said. Hearing the praise, PJ squealed in delight. Bruce picked him up and sat him next to Stephanie. Bruce put PJ's hands on Stephanie's back, then Bruce rocked PJ's body, pushing Stephanie. "Stephanie, acknowledge PJ then lay back down," Bruce told her. Stephanie did as Bruce asked. Then Bruce praised PJ. The lesson went on for another ten minutes until PJ quit trying to beat people with his bottle.

Bruce picked PJ up, giving him kisses and making PJ laugh as Bruce headed to the bathroom.

Stephanie sat up. "Don't you think that is a little overboard? He's just a baby," she pointed out.

"He'll learn. I'm the Alpha male and what I say goes," Bruce replied.

"Are you going to urinate on him now to show your dominance?" Stephanie asked, moving to get out of bed to get PJ. Bruce looked up at the ceiling like he was thinking about it when Debbie sat up.

"Bruce," Debbie said.

"It works in the animal kingdom," Bruce pointed out.

"Bruce," Debbie said in a low grumble.

"We're going to take a shower," Bruce said, closing the door to the bathroom. The twins jumped out of bed in a dead run for the shower.

When the twins closed the door, Debbie reached over and grabbed Stephanie's arm. "Stephanie, don't do that again. When Daddy is disciplining the kids, Mama has to stand with him, not question him. That is teaching discipline. You act like Bruce was beating PJ with a knotted rope. That lesson just taught PJ to quit hitting us to get what he wants. Why do you think the kids in this family act like they do?

"I know you have read those stupid ass books saying not to spank. Look what they did to this generation of kids. Kids must be taught that if you do wrong, punishment follows, and punishment is never good. I'm not saying grab a tree trunk and break bones. A good spanking will suffice. Did your parents spank you?" Debbie asked.

"No, the nanny did," Stephanie answered.

"Do you still love your nanny?" Debbie asked.

"I still love Ms. Jordan," Stephanie replied with a voice that resounded with love.

"Are you still a little afraid of Ms. Jordan?" Debbie continued the questions.

"Oh yeah, if she came in here right now and said pick up the toys, I would find some to pick up," Stephanie replied.

"You love her because she cared enough about you to teach you right and wrong. Reward you for a job well done and punish you for doing bad. It's the job of a parent to teach their kids. It's not the government's place to tell a parent how to raise a child; they are not there. Not the doctor's to give the kid a drug to get compliance; that is the job of the parent," Debbie told Stephanie.

Stephanie looked at Debbie in shock as the pieces fell in place. "Oh shit," she said. Laughing and squealing could be heard coming out of the bathroom, along with the sound of the shower running.

Cade climbed down off the bed, pointing at the door. "Mama wa wa," he said.

"Cade, we'll take a shower later," Angela told Cade. He ran to the door, stretching on his tippy toes trying to reach the door knob as the twins started laughing again. "Mama, wa wa peese," Cade yelled in desperation.

Debbie got out of bed and walked over to Cade, took off his shirt and diaper then opened the door. "You have another one, Bruce!" Debbie yelled into the bathroom as Cade took off to the shower.

"Come on here, boy," Bruce said as Debbie closed the door and sat on the end of the bed, looking at Stephanie.

Stephanie stared at the floor. "I screwed up big time."

"No Stephanie, you're a new mama that needs guidance. Now, go help Bruce wash the kids and tell him you're sorry that you made a mistake. This is stuff learned over a lifetime and not from a book. You should have learned this from your mama. Now go, we'll talk more later."

Stephanie got off the bed and went to the bathroom to help Bruce. Debbie got up and headed to the closet then noticed that Angela was staring at her with a shocked expression. "What?" Debbie asked.

"Stephanie is taking a shower with your husband," Angela pointed out.

"You're very observant, but you forgot there are four kids in there also," Debbie replied.

"I know, but Stephanie is—" Angela faltered.

"Beautiful," Debbie finished.

"Well yeah, not that you're not, Debbie, but she is just—" Angela stammered to a halt.

"Close to perfect," Debbie helped and Angela just stared at Debbie. "Angela, do I have to worry about Bruce?" Debbie asked.

"No, any fool can see that man worships you. But—" Angela replied, looking for words.

"Can Stephanie throw Bruce down and rape him?" Debbie asked.

"Well no, but Bruce is a boy," Angela said. Debbie just cocked her head to the side. "Okay, no, she can't," Angela answered.

"What do I have to worry for?" Debbie replied.

"It's just weird," Angela replied.

"Why don't you go help them? I'm fixing to, because Bruce can't wash the girls' hair for shit. Stephanie is not much better," Debbie said. Angela just stared at Debbie like she was in a trance.

"Are you scared of Bruce?" Debbie asked.

"No!" Angela replied.

"Well, you sit out here and think about it. I'm going to help," Debbie patted Angela's leg then headed off to the bathroom.

Angela sat on the bed, listening to the group laughing. She got off the bed and went into the bathroom to find a naked Bruce chasing a naked PJ, who was crawling around the bathroom floor. Angela reached down and picked up PJ, who was covered in soap.

Bruce took PJ from Angela. "Thank you, he escaped when Debbie opened the door," he said, turning around and heading back to the shower. "Emily, don't put that in Cade's hair!" Bruce barked at Emily, who was holding a bottle of shampoo over Cade's head.

"I have to wash his hair like Mama does mine," Emily said.

"You can't even wash your own hair. Let Mama do it," Bruce told her. Emily threw the bottle of shampoo down on the shower floor.

Bruce looked at her sternly. "Pick that up right now!" Emily just crossed her arms defiantly.

"Emily, Daddy told you to pick it up. Do it now," Stephanie said. Emily looked up at Stephanie then to Debbie; seeing she had no allies, Emily picked the shampoo up, putting it back.

"Very good, Emily. Since you want to do someone's hair, you and Sherry can shave Daddy's head," Bruce told her. The twins yelled with joy and tried to leave the shower. Debbie and Stephanie each grabbed one.

"You have to finish your shower first, then you can help Daddy," Debbie told them.

Bruce put PJ on the floor of the shower where he started to slap the water into submission. Bruce turned around to Angela. "Are you going to help or just referee," he asked, then squeezed into the shower.

Angela quickly joined the group. After the twins were done, Bruce let them shave his head. They only nicked his ear once. When everyone was out of the shower, they dressed and headed to the Center for breakfast. Heading to their table, they were the last to arrive for breakfast and the sun was still not up yet.

Mike just growled at Bruce when he walked by. Bruce raised his eyebrows at Mike. "Something wrong, brother?" he asked, smiling broadly.

"Dude, that was not even cool or funny by any standard," Mike answered, wanting to throw something at Bruce.

Bruce sat down as he replied, "You thought it was funny when Debbie neutered me last night. You knew payback was coming."

"Payback yeah, not boiling my nuts!" Mike yelled, causing a silence to fall over the Center.

"I wanted to make sure you didn't laugh at me again when I was getting a reaming from a five-foot-tall woman. You could have spoken up for me," Bruce informed Mike.

"Bruce, I'm not saying that some form of payback wasn't called for," Mike said, then yelled, "I tried to dunk my nuts in the toilet for God's sake!" Several smirks could be seen around the table and the room. Mike glared at everyone then started yelling again, "I did a fucking handstand in the shower to try to save my balls! I've never done a fucking handstand in my life! Your kids and mine came running into my room with weapons loaded to save me. What did they find? Me, in the fucking shower, doing a handstand, trying to blow on my balls and get them closer to the water. That's just wrong, man. Matt laughed so hard at me he peed on himself."

Bruce was trying not to laugh as he replied, "Well, you did learn how to do a handstand."

"Mother fucker, I would've levitated if I could have. I was in a handstand for twenty minutes. You know why I wasn't in one longer? Well let me tell you, when you are upside down trying to blow out the acid someone put on your balls you hyperventilate and your arms give out. You drop like a brick, but do you pass out? Hell no! Your balls are trying to pull up inside your body but your body won't let them in, because they are covered in acid. I sat my naked ass down in the bottom of the shower, plugging up the drain and letting water run out on the bathroom floor and I did not give a damn, as long as my nuts were in cold water. That is how I sat for over an hour!" Mike finished screaming.

Bruce couldn't look at Mike anymore because his mind was going into overload providing him mental pictures of Mike's plight. Looking at the table, Bruce said, "Okay, I might have gone too far."

Mike screamed, "Might have gone too far! Bruce, at the end of the hour I couldn't find my balls. I thought they went down the drain when Nancy made me unstop it. You know what, I didn't even care, they could go and hurt somewhere else!"

Nancy just laid her head down on the table putting her arms over her head as her body shook with laughter.

Mike looked at Nancy then back to Bruce. "Dude, you need your man card taken away after that," Mike said in a normal voice.

Bruce jumped up. "Brother, you've gone too far with that!"

"Dude, you cooked my nuts!" Mike exclaimed.

"Okay Mike, I went too far and I apologize to you and your balls. You want me to come down there and blow on them for you, because I will," Bruce said, walking toward Mike.

"Dude, you stay the hell away from my balls! You don't get to look at them or touch them!" Mike said, sliding his chair away from Bruce.

Bruce wrapped his arms around Mike and rubbed his back. "Don't be that way, you're my bareback cowboy."

Mike tried to push Bruce away. "Get the hell away from me! My balls are pulling up into my throat. They know you are near and are trying to hide."

Bruce put his leg behind Mike's leg, taking him to the floor, "Come here, Twinkie man, let me rub on your balls and tell them I'm sorry," Bruce said, then Mike flipped Bruce off of him and tried to put Bruce in a headlock.

"You play with your own balls. You tried to kill mine," Mike said. Everyone in the Center gathered around to watch the two wrestle each other as they laughed at the dialog shot back and forth.

Bruce slipped out of the headlock, trying to put Mike in an arm bar. "Come on, let me rub them. I'll be gentle." Bruce was struggling to get loose while holding back the laughter.

"Gentle? My nut sack is peeling!" Mike cried out and Bruce couldn't help it anymore. Tears rolled down his face as he laughed. Mike seized his chance and spun around, putting Bruce in a full nelson then wrapped his legs around Bruce's waist.

"Tell my nuts you're sorry!" Mike demanded.

Bruce tried to get air into his lungs to comply with Mike's request but was having trouble, he was laughing to hard. After Bruce took a breath he yelled, "Mike's balls, I'm sorry for hurting you!"

"They don't believe you. Say it like you mean it!" Mike yelled, trying not to laugh.

Bruce yelled out, "Oh Mike's big hairy balls with the peeling nut sack! I'm sorry for hurting you. I wanted to pet you and make you feel better, but Mike has taken away my visitation rights!"

Mike released Bruce, not able to hold on any longer. Mike rolled around on the floor laughing with Bruce. Everyone in the Center was laughing at the two. When Bruce could breathe again, he looked up at the table and Steve was the first person he saw.

"Steve, come here and help us up," Bruce said. Steve walked over and helped Mike up. Then he walked over to Bruce with his hands over his crotch.

"Dad, my balls are scared of you and won't let me help you," Steve said, sending everyone into another round of laughter.

Bruce pulled himself up and staggered to the table to sit down. When the laughter died down again, everyone went back to their chairs to attempt to finish breakfast. Bruce looked around the table and went over the class assignments for the day.

After he finished, Debbie said, "Bruce, it smells like it's going to rain today. Do you want us to move inside to continue or just postpone until tomorrow?"

Bruce looked at her, all signs of laughter gone from his face. "None of the above. No training is postponed unless we get severe lighting or a tornado," Bruce replied.

"Bruce, it's fifty degrees out there now. It only reached seventy-five degrees yesterday. For the rest of the country that's great weather, but here that's freezing. We could be asking for trouble getting people sick," Debbie pointed out.

Bruce nodded his head to Debbie and stood up. "Everyone, listen up!" he yelled out and the Center became silent. "If it rains we train! If it snows we train! Our enemies will be out in it and they could attack us in bad weather. Everyone here, young and old, boy or girl, will learn to ignore weather, hunger, exhaustion and fear." Bruce looked around to make sure he had everyone's attention.

"Conner, you will take over my classes from now on. I will be moving from group to group to teach each of you. Do what I say, I will never push you until you die no matter how much you think you will. Your body might tell you that but ignore it and do what is required. There will be no lunch today," Bruce said, receiving a lot of groans.

"See you counted on something. Don't ever count on getting food or rest. When you get either, cherish them as it could be your last. If you don't want to learn how to fight then leave, we don't need you. Everyone here has to trust each member in this clan. That is who you trust and count on, your teammates. When they falter, give them courage and the will to move on. In one month, each of you will become bad asses. By three months each of you will be warriors. Do what I do and do what I say and you will become the master of your destiny. With your team, you will be unstoppable," Bruce said, his voice echoing across the Center.

"Before any ask, yes, even with training you can still get killed, but you will take a lot with you before you go. That level of training doesn't exist. Me and my family will train you. Any one of my family could put on a Ranger tab right now. After you are trained, some of you will be moved to permanent jobs but you will always stay trained. If you don't use the training, you will forget it. Now everyone out, let's go!" Bruce yelled.

He looked at Debbie, expecting to get a pissed off look but saw a smile on her face. Seeing Bruce's surprised expression, Debbie said, "I was wondering when you were going to quit pussy footing around and train these people." Bruce smiled at Debbie and waited on her to stand up and walk with him outside.

The rain started at dawn and continued for two days. Bruce would move from group to group, making the entire group drop down and do pushups and sit ups then crawl around in the mud. The only groups that did not catch total hell were the ten through fourteen year olds, but they still caught a lot. Around 1000, Bruce found a group huddled under a tree trying to get out of the rain.

Bruce ran up to them and made them low crawl a hundred yards, and they had to yell that they were tough. That evening, the clan gathered at the patio waiting on Bruce to tell them they could eat. Bruce walked to the front of the crowd.

Bruce yelled just to be heard over the rain, "When you go inside, do not go to the food line. Stay with your team and move to a table, stand behind the chair and wait for my orders. Now move!"

Bruce followed the last ones in, then moved to the front of the room. "Listen up. Those of you with weapons will clean them before you eat. Your guns are your primary attack and you will treat them as such. You are the weapon, the gun is just an extension. Those of you without weapons will help those with weapons get them cleaned. You can't eat unless your team is ready. We live together or die together. Now when I say, I want everyone to strip down to their underwear. Those not wearing any will find shorts at the back of the Center." Bruce heard several gasps. He pointed to a young man up front.

"Why did I say to get down to underwear?" Bruce asked him. The young man just stuttered. Bruce yelled to the back of the hall, "Danny, why did I say strip to underwear?"

Danny yelled back, "Outside our clothes offered us some protection but in here with no rain falling on us they are just drawing away our body heat."

Bruce nodded his head then pointed to a girl at the front in her late twenties. "What's another reason we are all going to underwear?" he asked her.

"You told us to and we're all teammates," she replied with a soft voice.

"Very good. Next time grab your balls so everyone can hear," Bruce said, walking back and forth along the front. Most of the people in the hall were shivering. "You are not cold, it's only in your mind. Picture a fire burning in your body and push its warmth out," Bruce said and heard movement behind him.

Bruce turned around to see who'd snuck off but saw the cooking ladies coming out of the kitchen, pulling off their shirts. Then they started taking off their boots. Millie looked at Bruce as she was untying her boots. "What? We can't be waitin' for you to tell us to strip, we hafta feed this army," Millie told Bruce then said, "We're part of this clan too. Each of us would've been out there runnin' around in the rain but someone has ta get food ready. When they get trained, someone is takin' our place so we can learn too."

"You got that right, Millie," Bruce said, smiling.

"You may be takin that back seein' me run around in my bloomers," Millie said, kicking off her boots.

"You, Millie? Some parts of my body haven't seen the light outside of a bathroom in thirty years," Lynn said, taking off her pants and gathering her clothes up.

"What the hell are you two talking about? I see some sexy hot mamas in front of me. Lynn, I've seen you run around naked before and that was hot," Bruce said, making both women look at him like he was on drugs. Then Bruce winked at them, blowing them a kiss.

Lynn laughed. "Keep on, Bruce, and I'm gonna wrestle Debbie for ya."

"You can take her," Bruce told Lynn.

Millie walked over to Bruce and kissed him on the cheek. "That's why everyone follows ya, baby. You can be hard but say somethin' to make us feel better. All I have ta say is you better be glad I'm not a little younger," she said, then headed back to the kitchen.

"What the hell does age have to do with it?" Bruce asked as the oldest cook, a woman in her late eighties, came over to him.

"You made this old woman feel good again," she said, grabbing Bruce's hand and kissing it. Bruce reached around, hugging her then kissing her. When Bruce let go, she shuffled to the kitchen, cackling.

Bruce turned around and saw everyone looking at him and smiling. "I never said smile, you're on my time," he said. The smiles dropped off everyone's face and they snapped their eyes forward.

"When your teams' weapons are cleaned you can eat. Now strip," Bruce said, walking toward his table. Bruce couldn't wait to get out of his cold, wet shit but couldn't show it. He might be the king of boys but he hadn't felt his toes in the last hour.

Stopping at his spot at the table, he dropped his gear to the floor then leaned toward Debbie and whispered. "Get Nancy and Danny, then all of you inspect the weapons before letting anyone eat. Tell the girls to ignore the cold; they will be watched. Each of you will have to lead by example. Now tell them quietly. I will clean yours and Danny's weapons."

Debbie nodded her head as she moved to each one, whispered, and then the four moved off. Debbie stood at the front of the line as the other three moved around the room like drill sergeants. Looking at Debbie walking around in panties and a sports bra, Bruce thought he'd never had hot instructors like that.

Each group had ten to twelve people in it and in most groups half were armed. The ten to fourteen-year-old group also had armed members: the five kids Bruce and Mike had brought out of the school, since they'd been checked off on weapons. It was also the largest group at sixteen. The others were just sitting at the table, shivering and trying to help the five clean their weapons. Bruce stripped and cleaned baby SCAR in record time then stood up and walked to the kids' table.

"What are you doing?" Bruce asked.

"We're cleaning our weapons, Mr. Bruce," Marty jumped up to tell him. Bruce looked at him approvingly. When they'd found Marty he was a very chubby boy, but now he was lean with good muscle definition.

"Well, how's it coming?" Bruce asked. The kids could strip and clean the weapons, but they were slow. Several in the group were weaving back and forth in their seats clearly wanting to go lie down.

"We will do it, sir, it just may take us a little while," Marty admitted.

Shaking his head, Bruce looked at everyone at the table. "This is my team and I would like to eat sometime tonight. I know you know how to clean them. Now weapons on the table and sit up straight. Watch my hands," Bruce said, moving to the first weapon. They had given the kids civilian versions of the M-4 from the checkpoint.

Bruce's hands flew over the weapon; he stripped it down then dried the gun off. Bruce cleaned it then reassembled the gun and moved on to the next one. The kids tried to follow his hands but they moved too fast. When Bruce had the second M-4 reassembled, Jake walked over to help. When Bruce looked at him Jake just said, "This is my team also." Together they had the group done in ten minutes.

"Those with weapons to the front of the team, let Debbie inspect your weapon. If they're good you can eat. Once you have finished eating you are off duty. I would advise you to get some sleep," Bruce said, heading back to his table.

The kids filed through as Debbie checked the weapons. Bruce could tell by Debbie's face that even if their weapons had been caked in mud she would've let them through. Bruce sat down and finished his weapons then started on Debbie's. Bruce looked at the first adult group heading toward Debbie. Bruce smiled as Debbie dropped the group and made them do pushups after inspecting the weapons. As the group headed back to the table, Bruce started on Danny's weapons.

Mike stood up after finishing his, Nancy's and Mary's weapons. "I'm going to help them," Mike said, heading to the closest table and joining Matt. Bruce nodded as he finished Danny's weapons. Walking over to Buffy, Bruce saw she was finished. He checked her three weapons and each was spotless.

"Buffy, Danny has taught you very well," Bruce said.

"Don't forget you taught me too, Daddy," Buffy replied.

"You clean just like Danny does. The total opposite of me, but thank you. Will you go help those that are having trouble?" Bruce asked her.

Buffy stood up in her chair, hugged Bruce, then headed to the groups. It unnerved several as the little blonde-headed girl grabbed their gun and took it apart, but they took any help they could. Bruce walked over to Angela to help her.

"I can do this, Bruce," Angela said, not wanting help.

"Angela, I want to eat tonight so stand up please," Bruce told her. Angela stood up but she didn't like it.

Bruce sat down in her chair. "Sit on my lap," he told her. Not understanding, Angela sat down. "Put your hands on the back of mine," Bruce said.

"You can't see the gun, Bruce," Angela said.

"It doesn't matter, Little Foot," Bruce said as his hands moved over the gun, taking it apart and cleaning it by touch. When Bruce was finished Angela got out of his lap.

"So that's how you do it so fast," Angela said and Bruce just nodded.

Bruce moved over to Stephanie. She had her M-4 broken down and was cleaning it. Bruce asked her to stand up and sit in his lap. After Bruce sat down, Stephanie got in his lap, but unlike Angela, Stephanie didn't learn anything new. She was just in a dream state sitting in Bruce's lap. When Bruce asked her to get up, she did so reluctantly and moving slowly. For the first time, Bruce noticed that Stephanie took a long time to stop touching him. Needless to say this made Bruce a little nervous.

Bruce smiled at her, kissing her on top of her head. Then Bruce grabbed his, Debbie's and Danny's weapons to take them to get inspected and get some plates for them. Millie yelled across the Center, "Bruce, you come up here to this line and I'll get my wooden spoon." In midstride, Bruce spun around and headed back to the table, laying the weapons back down.

Millie and Lynn brought plates over and sat them down.

"You can't be pullin' one over on me that easy," Millie said. Bruce just looked down at the table, afraid to look at her in case she'd brought that damn spoon. Bruce started formulating a plan to steal the damn thing and burn it. When Millie left, Bruce looked up to see everyone eating and the family heading back to the table.

Millie and Lynn were bringing more plates and glasses of tea. When they reached the table, Bruce asked Millie, "Where are the little kids? They were in here earlier today."

"Susan, Pam and one of the older ladies moved 'em to the house this afternoon and continued school'n over there. I didn't think they needed to be here when you finally got this army in here," Millie told Bruce.

"That's good, Millie," Bruce said, missing the twins and PJ. He looked up at her. "I want you to tell Jim to get the three stooges in here and clean this place top to bottom every night after supper. I want that to be put on the work list for them every day. When I come in the morning, I want to be able to eat off this concrete floor. You are to check them off every day and you will carry a radio from now on. If they don't do the job right, call me. Next, if they eat any food that isn't for them, you're to break a broom handle over their head."

"Oh hell yeah!" Millie said, trotting toward the door. Reaching it, she threw it open and yelled, "Jim, gets in here now." Bruce was pretty certain they heard her in New York.

Bruce started eating and saw Debbie looking at him. "We don't have time to babysit them, and Millie does. I don't want them to think of any ideas. Mitch and the trooper are the only ones that'll need a lesson or two," Bruce told her.

Bruce yelled out across the Center that when they were finished eating they were off duty. Roll call was at 0500 in the Center. When the family finished, they headed to the house. Bruce asked Stephanie and Angela to check on the kids and that he and Debbie would follow shortly. Bruce told them he wanted to make sure the stooges did not cause any problems. They nodded and left, both too worn out from the day to argue. When they walked out only Debbie and Bruce were left in the Center.

Bruce looked at Debbie and said, "Okay, I think you're right. Stephanie's in love with me."

The shocked expression on Debbie's face would have been no different if Bruce would have told her he was really Elvis. When she regained the power of speech, she asked, "What finally made you see?"

"When I was showing her how to clean her gun fast. She wasn't paying attention and when I asked her to get up she did it real slow, like she just wanted to touch me," Bruce admitted, a little concerned.

"Over four years and it took the end of the civilization for you to finally see that," Debbie said, laughing.

"I really don't think it's funny Debbie," Bruce told her.

"Yes it is baby, you're the only one here that hasn't seen it," Debbie replied, giggling.

"Well, what're we going to do about this?" Bruce asked.

Debbie stopped laughing when she saw a look of uncertainty, panic and a little fear on Bruce's face. Debbie reached and held Bruce's hand, asking, "What are you talking about 'do about this'?"

"Hello in there," Bruce said, looking at Debbie, "she's sleeping in our bed. Stephanie has even taken a shower with me and saw me naked."

Disbelief hit Debbie and she fell back in her chair, letting Bruce's hand go. "Modesty, from you?" Debbie said, not believing she was using modesty with Bruce in the same reference. Shaking her head to get her brain working again, she said, "Bruce, you walk around butt naked without giving it a second thought. Hell, a few years ago at the nurses' convention in Las Vegas you stripped naked on the dance floor if memory serves me correctly."

"That was different. I was drunk and those women weren't in love with me," Bruce said, defending himself.

"Bruce you made over four hundred dollars stripping on a fucking dance floor. There were over three hundred women there and ninety percent of them would have jumped your ass in a heartbeat. I told you I had to threaten to kill several people that night," Debbie told Bruce in a serious voice.

"Did that embarrass you?" Bruce asked out of curiosity.

"Embarrass me? I thought it was funny as hell. If you remember correctly, I was the first one yelling take it off. You're mine. I don't mind showing you off. Especially since you don't have a shy bone in your body," Debbie said then continued. "The only time it has embarrassed me was when we came home to visit my parents that first year we were married. You come out of the hallway bathroom drying your head off, butt naked, meeting my mother in the hallway. I thought my mom was going to die on the spot."

"I told you I was sorry about that. I was still used to showering in the barracks," Bruce reminded Debbie.

"I know that, baby. So what's the problem here then?" Debbie asked.

"Stephanie loves me," Bruce said as if that explained it all.

"And?" Debbie asked, wanting more.

"There's no 'and'," Bruce replied, not understanding this void of reaction.

"So, you want to throw Stephanie out because she loves you?" Debbie specified.

"No, just get her to sleep somewhere else. The kids have told us they are couples now; your plan worked," Bruce told Debbie.

"That will be a big NO!" Debbie snapped.

Startled, Bruce just looked at Debbie then said, "Debbie, this is really freaking me out. I'm telling you a woman who's sleeping in our bed loves me more than a friend and you aren't freaking out."

"Bruce, I have known since the first time I saw Stephanie that she loved you. Hell, everyone in this house knew it," Debbie said.

"Knowing that, how could you let her sleep in our bed?" Bruce asked.

"Yeah, like what have I got to be scared of? Are you going to leave me for her?" Debbie asked, waving her hand in the air. Bruce tilted his head, looking at Debbie like she was stupid. Debbie asked, "Well?"

Bruce took a deep breath before replying, "Debbie, you really think I could leave you? I really don't think I could function without you."

Debbie smiled, grabbing Bruce's hand again, "I know that baby. Bruce, don't get mad when I say this. You love me so much you don't notice how other women act towards you. Girls do see that better than boys."

"No they don't. I've seen guys hitting on you since we've been together. You are so fine it's not funny," Bruce informed Debbie.

"Thank you, baby," Debbie said, smiling, then asked, "So what is the problem with Stephanie?"

"It just feels weird," Bruce admitted.

"Bruce, what if I told you Stephanie is happy just being near you. Stephanie may be thirty and smarter than everyone here put together but socially she's still a teenager. I've talked to her and know her better than you do and her childhood sucked. Sure, her parents were rich, but she grew up alone and being as smart and pretty as she is didn't help. At the private schools she went to, Stephanie was ostracized because of that. So she lost herself in study. You, the 'mighty Bruce' were the first person that treated her like a normal person, just to talk to her and be a friend. Not because she was pretty or smart, just because she was a person. Then you taught her stuff she didn't think girls were supposed to know like shooting guns, hunting, fishing and stuff." Bruce stared at Debbie as she continued, "I'm not going to lie, Bruce, the first time I saw her I wanted to get rid of her. I even told Stephanie that when she finally told me she was in love with you."

Bruce slid his chair back from the table. "She told you?"

"Yes, she told me. Then she said she was going to leave the farm, knowing she would die out there or worse." Debbie answered then continued. "She wanted me to know because she felt I would be mad at her. Stephanie almost died when I told her that I already knew. That's when I told her if she tried to leave I would beat her ass."

"So you then told her she could sleep in our bed?" Bruce asked, not believing what he was hearing.

"More or less," Debbie replied.

"Why was I not informed?" Bruce asked, feeling like a pawn on a chess board.

"Well to be honest, I reckoned you'd never figure out that Stephanie was in love with you," Debbie said.

"Thanks," Bruce replied dryly.

"Baby, I didn't mean that to be ugly. Stephanie is just happy being close to you," Debbie replied.

Bruce looked at Debbie with a flat expression. "What if she wants sex?"

"It takes two to tango," Debbie said.

"Exactly, and this tango boy already has a partner," Bruce replied in a sassy voice.

Debbie laughed. "Bruce, you are one of the few men who believe in monogamy. But I do remember a time when you asked me something."

"We aren't talking about that time. I got popped, remember. And bullshit, Mike does also," Bruce shot off.

"He does now. Mike had an affair the second year they were married," Debbie told Bruce. He just looked at Debbie in abject horror.

"He never told me. I'm going to kick ass. How could he do that to Nancy?" Bruce said, standing up.

"Well, she was having one at the same time. Mike told her and Nancy told him. They put it behind them and moved on," Debbie said, grabbing Bruce's arm and pulling him back to his chair.

Bruce just shook his head as Debbie brought him back to topic. "Back to Stephanie. That first night you had your arm around her in your sleep when she woke up. Stephanie told me she had dreamed about that for years and I could see that it made her happy. Bruce, I have your heart so I'm not worried; why are you? She just wants to be a part of both our lives. I thought Stephanie would find someone like you, but then this virus screwed that up. Unless you have a twin, you are the only way Stephanie can have a little happiness. I'm willing to share a little bit of you with her. Can't you?"

Bruce narrowed his eyes, looking at Debbie. "Who are you and where is my wife?"

Debbie laughed, answering, "Right here." Then she became serious, "Bruce, I'm going to tell you something. Right before Stephanie left for Atlanta she had a one-night stand with some asshole she met at a bar. Stephanie did it just to see if it would make her forget about you, which it didn't."

"So?" Bruce said.

"Bruce, that was her first and only time to have sex," Debbie replied.

Bruce jumped back out of his chair. "Holy shit!"

"Exactly baby, so can't we give her a little bit of happiness?" Debbie said with a pleading look.

"So all along you were doing this because you felt sorry for her and not so the kids would tell us?" Bruce asked.

"Kind of, but I have other reasons," Debbie replied.

"Well what are they?" Bruce asked.

Debbie dropped the smile off her face. "My reasons," she replied in a flat voice.

Bruce held up his hands in surrender upon seeing the wrath of Debbie near. "Okay."

Debbie apologized, looking at the floor. "I'm sorry baby, but I think you can only handle so much at one time. I will tell you the other reasons some other time. Okay?" Inside Debbie was smiling.

Bruce sat back down. "I can live with that because I'm now in sensory overload."

"That's okay baby, I will always be with you," Debbie, said patting his hand.

Bruce looked at Debbie, asking, "Is Angela in love with me too?"

Smiling, Debbie replied, "Not yet." Bruce just wanted to run and hide. Seeing Bruce's reaction, she continued. "Bruce, Angela has always loved you as a friend, but losing Alex has made her scared. When Angela found out Alex was gone, she grabbed Cade and ran to our room. There was no one there, Bruce. She went there because she felt safe with her baby there, in our room. She knows we'll protect her and Cade at all costs. I never asked her to stay, but be damned if anyone is asking her to leave."

"Well, let's see if we can slowly get her in the barracks and maybe find someone to fix her up with before it happens," Bruce offered.

Debbie stood up with a pissed off expression. "Bruce, I'm going to act like you never said that. She's accepting the loss and hasn't cried herself to sleep in days. Angela will leave when she wants to. If she asks you to strip and run barking at the moon, then I better see a white ass running around in the dark and hear you barking. If you hurt either of those girls' feelings, let's just say you will see my wrath and it won't be pretty."

Bruce bowed his head in defeat. "Okay, whatever you say, baby."

Debbie walked over to Bruce and rubbed his shaved head. "Thank you baby. Does it really bother you that much?"

"It's weird, but no, it doesn't bother me that much. It's just with those other women in the bed I can't get lovin'," Bruce told her.

Debbie lifted his face up to look at her. "Bruce, you've brought four kids into this family, three of which are still in our bed."

"Yeah, but I could lock them in the closet. That's kind of hard with Angela and Stephanie, they know how to open a door," Bruce replied.

"Come on, stud muffin, let's get some sleep," Debbie said, turning to get her wet clothes off the floor.

Bruce grabbed her, pulling her in his lap. "We're alone now."

Debbie kissed Bruce then told him, "Bruce, how can you think about sex now? I'm freezing."

"Three things first. I always think about getting some lovin' from you. Second, you're in bra and panties now. Third, I know you're cold," Bruce said, looking at Debbie's chest.

Debbie playfully slapped his arm then kissed him saying, "Bad boy," as she got out of his lap. Turning around, she said, "Bruce, I have mud in the crack of my ass because you wanted to go G.I. Joe today. I'm filthy."

Bruce gave up and helped get all their clothes and gear together. They both took off running through the rain to the house. Making it inside, they were soaked again. Nobody was downstairs so they headed to their bedroom.

Angela, Stephanie, the twins, PJ and Cade were all asleep in the bed. Debbie and Bruce laid their wet clothes on the floor and headed to the bathroom. They jumped in the shower, washing the day away. As they were drying off, Debbie grabbed Bruce and pulled him down to kiss him. Finally Bruce got him some lovin'.

CHAPTER 28

Training continued over the next two days as it rained, finally stopping the third morning. Bruce was woken up by a soft knock at the door. He growled as he got out of bed. The clock read 0523. *This better be good,* Bruce thought. He had moved wake up to 0700 to give everyone some extra sleep. Bruce opened the door to find Millie there.

"Bruce, I'm sorry to wake ya early but we need ya out back in the field where the cows be," Millie told him.

"Okay Millie, let me get some clothes," Bruce said, leaving the door open and heading to the closet. Millie looked at the mass of bodies in the bed, smiling as she waited on Bruce. He came out with his vest on but not buckled up, wearing shorts, no shirt and flip flops and carrying his rifle, and led Millie down the hall.

Millie fell in beside him, asking, "How can you sleep with all those people in your bed?"

"It's not easy," Bruce replied, yawning.

"You and Debbie be really good people," Millie told him. Bruce just scoffed as he opened the back door and the cold damp air hit him.

Bruce shivered as they headed across the patio. "What is it?" Bruce asked Millie as they headed to the back of the property.

"A woman hung herself last night," Millie said.

Bruce stopped. "What?"

"We was a' goin' to milk the cows and found a girl hanging in a tree in the pasture," Millie told Bruce.

"Did you tell the guards?" Bruce asked, heading to the field.

"No, because all they'd do is get you," Millie replied.

"You could've gotten Mike," Bruce informed her, feeling cheated out of sleep.

"She's already dead, we don't be needin' a doctor," Millie answered.

Bruce shook his head, giving up, and asked, "Who is it?"

"I don't know. It's one of the new girls that y'all rescued from the bikers. Late twenties, early thirties, white, brown hair," Millie said.

"Well, what do you want me to do about it now?" Bruce asked as they passed the barn.

Millie stopped, causing Bruce to stop. "Bruce, you's whining like'a bitch, now stop it. What are we going to do with the body and what are we goin' to tell everyone?"

Bruce chuckled as he turned, heading to the field with Millie in tow. It was dark, damp and cold, which did little to improve Bruce's mood as he opened the gate. Seeing flashlights, Bruce headed to them. As he approached, someone shined their light at him.

"Get that fucking light out of my eyes!" Bruce barked a little harsher than he intended.

"Sorry sir," a young male voice replied.

Bruce walked over as the young man shined the light on a woman hanging from a tree limb. Pulling his light off his vest, Bruce shined it around on the ground. He saw a small stool that was used for milking the cows on the ground. Shining the light on the body, Bruce did not see anything suspicious.

Bruce turned to the young man and Millie. "Who found her?" Bruce asked.

"Lynn and I did. One of the dogs was here barkin'. Thinking one of the cows might be hurt, we came over here," Millie answered.

Bruce looked toward the fence, realizing the roving guards wouldn't have seen the body since they stayed along the fence. He looked at the young man and asked, "Who are you?"

"Joe," he replied.

"Now, Joe, what are you doing out here?" Bruce asked in a pissed off voice.

Millie answered. "He's on kitchen detail today, Bruce. Don't be mean to him, Joe didn't do nothin'."

"I know that Millie. She did it herself, that's what has me pissed off," Bruce said, grabbing his radio. "Control, this is Big Daddy One, you copy?" Bruce called.

"This is Control," a female voice replied.

"Have the roving guard wake every son of a bitch here up and tell them Community Center in fifteen minutes," Bruce said, dropping the mic.

"Millie, go finish, I can handle this. Joe, go get one of the electric buggies and please run," Bruce said, turning to the body.

Joe took off in a dead run and Millie walked back to the kitchen. Turning around, Bruce looked at the young woman. Her skin was already bluish-gray and her eyes were bulging. Giving a sigh, he grabbed the stool and cut the rope as he stood on the stool. The body crashed to the ground. "I hope that hurt," Bruce said, grabbing the body, throwing it over his shoulder and heading to the gate. Halfway there, Bruce saw the lights from the buggy coming toward him. Bruce threw the body in the back with a thud, making Joe cringe.

"Don't be a pussy. This bitch wasted our time," Bruce said, climbing into the buggy and adding, "Community Center. Front door. Move."

Joe stomped on the pedal. Spinning the tires, he headed out of the field to the Center. The buggy was not even stopped when Bruce jumped out. Bruce turned around upon hearing his name called. Mike was running off the patio in shorts, flip flops and a vest, carrying Cassandra in one arm, rifle in the other, followed by Nancy carrying Joshua.

"Both of 'em still sleep with you?" Bruce asked.

"Cassandra rarely sleeps with Susan anymore and Joshua wants to be with us too. It's fair, so Susan can have a break. You know she watches the clan's kids every day and we want her to have some time with Conner alone," Mike replied, coming to stand by Bruce, followed by Nancy. Nancy looked in the back of the buggy and screamed, pulling her pistol. Hearing Nancy scream, Mike spun around. Seeing Nancy pull her pistol, he raised up his SCAR.

"She's dead, that's the problem," Bruce told them as they lowered their weapons.

"How'd she get in?" Mike asked with his heart beating a hundred miles an hour.

"We let her in, Mike," Bruce answered, looking at them like they were crazy.

"Who the fuck let a blue in the farm? I'll shoot them myself," Mike yelled as Bruce looked at the body again.

"Watch your mouth, Mike," Nancy snapped.

"Damn, she does kinda look like a blue," Bruce said out loud. Mike and Nancy turned to Bruce.

"She's not a blue?" Nancy asked, finally lowering her pistol.

"No, she's one of the girls we rescued from the bikers on the lake. She hung herself in the pasture. Millie and Lynn found her this morning. Just guessing, I figure she did it around midnight," Bruce told them as the rest of the family came up. When everyone walked over Bruce filled them in.

"Poor girl," Nancy said.

"Poor girl? This bitch wasted our time and resources. This family risked its safety to rescue her. It would've been easier to just blow up all the buildings," Bruce yelled.

Debbie looked at Bruce. "Baby, we don't know—"

"Debbie!" Bruce shouted, making everyone jump back, except Debbie. "Don't try to justify this. You live or die. If you want to die, don't waste our time. She could've just stayed and waited on the blues when we rescued her. It would've been one less to cover and would've given the blues something to do while we escaped. There's no more babying people, that's what let this shit get out of hand. Everyone wanting someone to take care of them, not wanting to do anything for themselves and just depending on the government and others," Bruce yelled at everyone.

Debbie just shook her head. "It's okay, baby, go throw your temper tantrum. Just don't shoot anyone unless you talk to me first please." Bruce was fixing to kick the body then realized he had flip flops on so he just stormed into the Center. The family followed him as Debbie grabbed Angela and Stephanie.

"When he's like that, don't argue with him. Let him throw a temper tantrum and let it drop. If you try to rationalize with him, he gets mad at you. That was pissed off Bruce. Can each of you tell the difference between irritated and pissed?" Debbie asked them and they nodded that they could tell the difference. "When Bruce goes past pissed to asshole, just leave. Not because he might hurt you but because you might shoot him. I'm so glad we don't have elections now. Every four years, I really considered moving. I agreed with Bruce on the topics but, O-M-G, he would look for reasons to fight," Debbie told them as she moved to the Center.

Stephanie grabbed Debbie's arm, stopping her. "Don't you feel sorry for her?" she asked, pointing at the body.

"No, Bruce is right. She wasted our time and resources. Do you feel sorry for her, Stephanie?" Debbie asked.

"Well kind of, she was a human being," Stephanie replied, looking at Debbie for guidance.

"Stephanie, Bruce almost died rescuing her. If we would've blown up all the buildings he might not have got hit with shrapnel or we could have gotten here faster. This is how she repaid us and we almost lost Bruce," Debbie told her.

Stephanie's eyes widened as she took that in. Then, looking at the body, she said, "Stupid bitch," and headed inside.

Debbie smiled at her then looked at Angela. "Don't look at me, I agree with Bruce," Angela said as she headed inside. Debbie smiled as she thought *either one will do fine*. She followed them inside.

Bruce was at the head of the room, pacing with his flip flops popping, waiting on the guards to tell him everyone was there. When the guards came in with the last group, they told Bruce this was everyone.

"Someone open up a radio so those on guard can hear this," Bruce barked. "First, last night a woman hung herself in the back pasture. Now before anyone goes 'aww poor girl' let me just say fuck that bitch. I have a good mind to follow her to hell just to kick her ass." Bruce stopped as a woman stood up and said, "Language, we have kids here."

Bruce looked at the woman with something close to malice as he yelled, "Shut the fuck up and sit down unless you want to run this Mickey Mouse shit show!"

Debbie leaned toward Angela and Stephanie. "See, that's why you leave him alone. He will continue until he wins, and he will win because he does not shut up. He's now in full asshole Bruce mode. If she's smart, she'll sit down." The woman sat back down with a look of shock on her face.

Bruce looked at the room. "Yes I'm pissed off. She had a chance at survival and life. If you survive you carry on your family's and your friends' lineage. That woman wasted our time and resources with her rescue, feeding her, guarding her, and trying to train her. Let's get something straight here and now. If you commit suicide, you'll not be buried here. Your body will be taken off and thrown on the side of the road and your name will be stricken from our record. You will not be buried with those that gave their lives to protect and provide for us. If you feel depressed, talk to someone or reach down, grab your balls, and squeeze 'em hard. I get depressed, everyone does, that's life. If something bad happened to you guess what? If you kill yourself, the fuckers that hurt you win, dumbass. I don't care if it was blues, a gang, or the fucking Easter bunny. I know any family members that aren't here on this farm are dead. None of them prepared for shit. I couldn't go and get them, so they're dead. Am I hurt? Yeah, but be damned if I'm going to kill myself. That just means the infection won." Bruce stopped because he was yelling and his throat was dry.

Millie ran up to him with a bottle of water. Taking a drink, Bruce thanked her and set the bottle down. "Tell you what," Bruce declared, "if you want to die, come up here right now. I'll shoot you in the back of the head. This way you will not interrupt others going about their work tryin' to help us survive." Bruce took out his pistol. Several people looked around at each other, not believing what he'd just said. "Come on, don't be shy. If you want to die, come up, I'll help you. I give you my word. If you come up, you can say goodbye and I'll cap your ass," Bruce said, holding up his pistol and looking around the room for takers.

Father Thomas stood up. "Bruce, I think everyone here wants to live, if for nothing else than to be entertained by you." Giggles could be heard around the room as people nodded their heads.

Bruce put his pistol up, saying, "Thank you Father."

"Bruce, can I please request that she be buried here? She was one of God's children," Father Thomas said.

"No Father, that is one rule that will never change. The only way you get buried on this soil is defending or providing for this clan. If you dive on a grenade, hold an area for others to escape, get run over by a tractor or shoot yourself because you are infected, then you are protecting the clan.

"Otherwise, you get dumped on the side of the road. If you want, you can pray over her, but after I eat the body's gone. If any knew her, don't use her name around me," Bruce said.

Father Thomas just looked at Bruce. "Bruce, we're better than that. She may have lost her way but we haven't."

Bruce closed his eyes. "Okay Father, she can be buried in the far field but not inside the fence." Father Thomas nodded his head, thanking Bruce, and headed to the door.

"Now kids, don't use the language I use. I will allow it if your guardian does, but it better be used in the right context. I'm the boss, I can say what I want. Now, since I came out like the rest of you, to do battle in shorts and flip flops, I'm canceling training. It's cold outside in case you didn't notice. I'm thinking Marcus may be right. The fifteenth is just days away. I want those that have been taught to drive the big rigs to make sure they are ready. I want the ATVs to go with us; we're going to get some forklifts also. Security team, we will be down there until we are finished. The salvage team will rotate out every twenty-four hours. A Stryker and Hummer will protect the convoy there and back," Bruce said, looking around and seeing several blank stares.

"The team lists have been up for days. If you are on the Shreveport teams you will be coming home every day. Security team, I want a meeting with you this afternoon to go over maps. There will be twenty on the security team. I'm breaking it down to four five-man teams. Now let's eat," Bruce said, heading to his table.

He sat down in his chair as Debbie said, "I need a camera. Someone, get me a camera, hurry." Bruce thought she was going to do something to him until he noticed she wasn't even looking at him. Following her line of sight, Bruce saw PJ standing up, holding a chair across the room.

Bruce was fixing to tell Debbie nobody carried cameras now when Stephanie said, "Here," pulling one out of her tactical vest. Debbie grabbed the camera, snapping pictures as the family watched PJ. He was just standing there and he appeared happy with that.

"Bruce, go make him walk," Debbie said, snapping pictures.

Bruce looked at her like she was insane. "Debbie, I can't 'make' him walk."

Debbie spun around in her chair. "Damn it Bruce, the kids always do what you tell 'em. Every kid walked for you and not me, and I have pictures to prove it. Now get your ass over there before I start throwing shit at you."

Bruce jumped out of his chair in case Debbie was serious, and from the look on her face, she was. When Bruce was five feet from PJ, he looked up at Bruce. "Hey little man," Bruce said, stopping and not getting closer.

PJ reached out with one hand to Bruce. "Dada."

"That's right, it's Daddy. Come here," Bruce said, making PJ laugh. Bruce clapped his hands, "Come on PJ." Out of the corner of his right eye, Bruce saw Debbie snapping pictures as fast as her finger could push the button. Bruce finally realized why they had over a hundred family albums.

PJ looked at Debbie and grinned goofily. "Ma-Ma." Debbie stood up, putting her hand over her mouth.

Bruce looked at PJ proudly. "That's right, that's Mama, but don't look her in the eye, she's crazy." Debbie popped Bruce on the butt, making PJ squeal and laugh. Out of the corner of his left eye, Bruce saw Jake moving around with a digital video camera, then he saw Matt pass Debbie holding another one.

"This isn't a football game, guys," Bruce said.

"Bruce, shut it," Debbie said, still snapping pictures.

Bruce looked back at PJ, who had grabbed the chair with one hand again. "You don't need to hold that chair, boy. Come to Daddy," Bruce said. PJ started to sit down and Bruce said, "No, no, stay there." Bruce made funny faces at PJ and he remained standing, laughing at Bruce. Bruce kneeled down. "Come here, boy, let's get some food, then let's go blow something up."

PJ yelled out in delight, letting go of the chair and clapping his hands and Bruce clapped his hands. PJ lifted his right foot, stepping toward Bruce and clapping his hands. When his foot hit the ground he took another step coming closer to Bruce. Then his steps got faster as he started losing his balance. On his seventh step, he started falling forward and Bruce leaned forward to catch him. Grabbing PJ before he fell, Bruce lifted him in the air, making PJ squeal with delight.

Thunderous applause and cheers scared the shit out of Bruce and PJ. Bruce pulled PJ to his chest and looked around. The entire clan was in a huge circle watching PJ taking his first steps. Bruce held PJ up for everyone to see. PJ didn't know what this was about but he liked it as he clapped his hands.

When Bruce brought PJ down, Debbie was there to get him. Bruce took the camera from her and started taking pictures of them together. Stephanie ran over to hug PJ and Bruce took pictures as Debbie handed PJ to Stephanie. The twins came over to Stephanie and Debbie. Debbie picked them up, hugging them, and Bruce kept the camera rolling. Then the camera beeped at Bruce; he looked at the screen and saw: FULL.

Not even thinking about it, Bruce just stepped over to Jake, handing it to him. Jake handed the handheld video camera to Bruce as he replaced the memory card. Jake took his camera back, giving Stephanie's to Bruce.

Bruce continued to snap pictures as he asked Jake, "You and Matt carry video cameras in your vest?"

"Yeah Dad," Jake replied.

Thinking about it for a second, Bruce asked, "Son, can you get me one to put in mine? Better yet, I want the sports cam you have. Then I will just mount it on my boonie hat."

"No problem, Dad, I will have you hooked up this afternoon," Jake said.

The pictures continued for ten more minutes then everyone settled down at the tables. Debbie, Angela, Nancy and Stephanie were huddled together looking at the pictures and videos as Millie brought over plates. PJ was sitting in Bruce's lap, still clapping and wondering why nobody would join him. When PJ saw the food he didn't care about clapping anymore.

After breakfast everyone sat around treasuring the down time before going to do the chores Bruce had called out. Stephanie turned to Bruce and asked, "Why am I not on a team, Bruce?"

Bruce looked at Stephanie, fixing to feed her a line of shit. Remembering what Debbie had said, he told her the truth. "You're too valuable to the family and clan to risk."

"Me valuable?" Stephanie exclaimed.

"Yes," Bruce replied.

"How am I more valuable than anyone else, especially you?" Stephanie asked.

"Would you like me to list it alphabetically, numerically, or just give it to you straight?" Bruce answered.

"Straight," Stephanie replied.

"You're too smart to risk losing you. The teams may be attacked, have a wreck or have a meteor fall on them. Here you are safer and of much more use to us," Bruce answered.

Stephanie looked at Bruce with tears in her eyes. "I'm not that smart. I want to help too."

Bruce reached over, grabbing her hands. "Yes you are. Stephanie, you read, remember and understand stuff faster than anyone I've ever met, heard of or read about. This family is not punishing you because you are smart. We need your knowledge to help us survive and more importantly, to live. Look around the table. You'll see they agree with me." Stephanie looked around the table to see everyone nodding in agreement with Bruce, and the tears rolled down her face.

Stephanie looked back at Bruce. "I've trained with this family for years. You yourself taught me guns."

"Stephanie, come here." Bruce patted his lap. Stephanie crossed her arms and looked down at her lap, pouting. Bruce got up, stepped to her chair and picked her up in his arms. When he sat down in his chair, she had laid her head on his chest.

Bruce wrapped his arms around her as he talked. "Stephanie, I know what you learned with us and I don't think it's enough to risk you outside the farm. I made this decision and everyone agreed with me. Look at it from my side. Let's take the refining information I had you look at. That took up almost two and a half months of my time. We are not going to talk about everyone else's. You did it in hours. Stephanie, you told me you would do what I ask to help. Do you remember?"

Stephanie closed her eyes, thinking, then her shoulders slumped. "Yes the day you handed me the flash drives."

Relief flooded through Bruce; he'd been hoping she had said that. He continued, "This is what I need you to do for the family. I need you to get the supplies we bring back stored. Not just thrown on the floor and stacked haphazardly. We will run out of room and lose supplies. Debbie is bringing storage containers in but we will have to set them up before we can use them." Debbie reached over and rubbed Stephanie's shoulder.

Stephanie sniffed. "I just want to do more than be smart. I don't want to just stay in here reading while everyone else fights for me."

"Stephanie, we need you here now. I never said you were going to always stay here. I said you did not have enough training to risk you right now," Bruce said, hoping he got it right. Stephanie thought for a minute then looked up at Bruce. He smiled at her. "I let you sleep next to me even though you don't shave your legs, don't I?"

Stephanie reached down to feel her legs. "They are too shaved!"

"Made you smile though," Bruce told her as she slapped his chest. "Stephanie, ask Debbie why I wouldn't let her go out at first and I knew she had the training. I wanted to make sure she would use it. I have to weigh the risk and benefit for everyone I send out. Right now, for you, the risk is too great."

"When?" Stephanie asked, looking up at Bruce.

"If you are serious, when this supply run is over I will start training you with the help from each one here. When I feel you can go with a reasonable amount of safety, then you'll go out with my team only. The 'when' will depend on you and how fast you learn what we teach you. I do have books but you need hands on training," Bruce told her.

"Okay." Stephanie gave in.

"Stephanie, this family loves you. We're not the people from the old world who treat you different. If anyone else here could do what you do it would make it much simpler. I would just keep one of you here at all times, but there isn't," Bruce told her.

Stephanie hugged him. "Thank you, Bruce." The rest of the family left as Stephanie hugged Bruce, thankful she had given in.

When Stephanie let go, Debbie came over and joined her in Bruce's lap. "He's telling you the truth. You're really valuable to the family," Debbie told her as she hugged her.

Bruce leaned forward and whispered, "Not to be crude but I have two fine women sitting in my lap in shorts and t-shirts. I can tell both of you are cold and let's just say I'm getting really hot." Stephanie and Debbie released their embrace and looked down. Stephanie covered her chest with her hands. "Why'd you do that? I was enjoying the view," Bruce said, raising his eyebrows up and down repeatedly.

Debbie laughed and hugged Bruce. Stephanie looked at them then hugged Bruce also, telling him, "It's okay, you can look."

"Oh yeah," Bruce said as he heard a baby yell from the floor beside his chair. Bruce leaned his head over to see PJ crawling toward his chair. "Hey boy, you see me with some fine women? Go play," Bruce told him. PJ sat up on his knees, jabbering and shaking his head no. "You don't tell me no, boy. What are you doing crawling? You know how to walk, so get up. This afternoon you will run at least once around the fence," Bruce told PJ. PJ blew raspberries at Bruce as Stephanie sat up.

"Bruce, he just learned how to walk, he can't run yet," Stephanie said.

"We'll tie a rope to him and pull him around behind one of the buggies then," Bruce told her.

Stephanie jumped out of Bruce's lap and turned toward PJ then stopped. She turned back around and sat back down in Bruce's lap. "I'll get the rope," Stephanie said.

Bruce and Debbie hugged her, laughing as Debbie said, "See, you make a good mama."

"Okay, I need to get up but I have a problem. Can one of you walk in front of me toward the door?" Bruce asked with a pleading look. Stephanie looked down then at Debbie with wide eyes.

Debbie laughed. "Bruce, stand up and turn around. Stephanie, jump on his back for a piggyback ride and cover the mighty Bruce. Get off when he reaches the door. The cold outside will take care of the rest. My legs aren't long enough."

As Debbie got off his lap, Bruce told Stephanie, "Be careful with your feet." Bruce stood up, turning around as Stephanie jumped on his back. Grabbing his rifle, he headed to the door and Stephanie jumped off as Bruce took off like a rocket toward the house.

Debbie picked up PJ and she sat back down as Stephanie came back to the table. Angela turned away from watching the twins play chase with Cade. "What was that about?" Angela asked.

"Bruce would've been embarrassed, so Stephanie helped out," Debbie told her.

Angela scoffed. "Bruce embarrassed? Impossible."

"Let's just say he got excited and his shorts were not cooperating," Debbie told her, smiling.

Angela smiled and started giggling and snorting. "Why didn't you tell me?"

"I just did," Debbie said.

"Can I pick on him about it tonight, just a little bit?" Angela begged.

"I don't care," Debbie told her laughing as Angela made devious faces.

Angela stopped making faces and looked around. Not seeing anyone by them, she asked Debbie, "Debbie, the night Bruce tried to kill Mike's nuts, what were you laughing for?"

"I don't know. What were we talking about?" Debbie innocently replied.

Stephanie looked at her. "Bruce said your feet were his fetish and you started laughing and he said that was between you and him."

Stephanie sat down as Debbie started laughing. Catching her breath, Debbie related the story. "Bruce was fifteen and I was fourteen and we were at a pool party. That was the first time Bruce saw me in a bikini after I had filled out. He was watching me like a hawk, and let me tell you, I thought I was hot stuff too. Most of the time when boys look at you, it's from the corner of their eyes but not that day. Bruce was almost drooling over me. He never even glanced at another girl, which I can say made my head get big. When I walked up to him, he would so check me out.

"It was so bad he would not get out of his chair, if you understand. I asked him to come swimming several times but he just stayed in his chair, drooling. So I pulled up a chair beside him so he could get a good look. I put my feet in his lap and he actually started to tremble. With that, let me tell you I thought I was the best thing since sliced bread. I was so fine I could make my boyfriend tremble," Debbie related to them as they giggled.

"Now my mom and dad were at this party also, as chaperones. On the way home, I was lying down in the back seat and my parents thought I was asleep. My dad tells my mom he didn't like Bruce anymore. My mom loved Bruce and told dad that. Dad said, 'You didn't see the way he was looking at her.' My mom said she thought it was cute. My dad stopped the car and looked at my mom and said, 'He was looking at her feet.' My mom didn't believe him and neither did I at the time. So the next day when Bruce came over, I wore a skirt and t-shirt but no shoes. We were out on the back deck and my dad was grilling hamburgers. When Bruce got up to help him, I wiggled my toes and Bruce walked right off a five-foot-tall deck and hit the ground face first. I ran to Bruce to find him laid out on the ground, not moving. I thought he was dead and I had killed him by wiggling my toes at him, but he was only knocked out cold. I screamed at my dad to help. Dad just shook his head as he looked down at Bruce and me beside him crying. Then he went to the back door and yelled inside, 'Make your daughter put on some shoes, the foot freak just took a nose dive off the deck.'"

Stephanie and Angela were laughing so hard tears were running down their faces. Debbie continued, "After that day my dad made me wear tennis shoes anytime Bruce was around. When Bruce was allowed to spend the night, my dad made me wear my shoes to bed. One night, I heard my dad tell Bruce, 'Son, you're weird. Debbie runs around half-naked and you just stare at her feet. Part of me likes that but another part wants to put you in a mental institution.' Bruce looks at my dad and says, 'Her feet are so hot.'"

When Debbie caught her breath, she finished the story. "Even after we were married, my dad made me wear shoes around the house even though Bruce and I were sleeping in the same bed."

Angela and Stephanie were both on the floor laughing, having fallen out of their chairs halfway through. Once everyone could breathe, Angela and Stephanie climbed back in their chairs. "That was great. So that's the reason he doesn't let anyone wear socks," Angela stated.

"No, the caterpillar is true. If you sleep in the same bed with Bruce, you lose your socks. Bruce and Mike went on a hunting trip to Ohio. They shared a bed at the motel and Bruce wouldn't let Mike get in the bed until he pulled off his socks. After that they started getting rooms with two beds," Debbie told them.

Angela looked at Debbie. "Debbie, thank you for letting Cade and I stay with you, Bruce and Stephanie. It has really helped me a lot. I know I just invited myself in with a kid but you and Bruce make me feel safe. This family is totally awesome and your bedroom is drama central. If you want to know what is going on, just stop by your room every night. I asked Paul to find Cade and me somewhere to sleep."

The smile fell of Debbie's face as she stood up, saying, "If I remember correctly, Bruce very clearly stated you couldn't leave until I said you could. I don't remember saying you could."

Angela couldn't look at Debbie. "I don't feel like I belong there, even though I love it."

Laying her body across the table with her face in front of Angela's, Debbie asked, "Why don't you feel comfortable? Did someone say something?" Angela wouldn't look up at her. "Who said something?" Debbie asked her. When Angela didn't answer, Debbie told her, "If you don't tell me, I will whoop every person's ass on this farm until I get to them."

Not looking up, Angela answered, "No one said anything. I just keep getting looks from some of the women around here. They stop talking when I walk up, then ignore me or they'll talk but it's just one or two words. It's like they don't want me around."

Debbie looked at Stephanie, her eyes blazing with anger. "How about you?"

"I don't want to move out," Stephanie answered quickly, just to set the record straight.

"That's not what I meant, Stephanie. Are you getting treated badly by others here?" Debbie asked her.

402

"Not that I know of, and I don't care. I don't want to move out," Stephanie acknowledged; she really could care less what others thought about her.

Angela looked up at Debbie. "They're worse to Stephanie. Since she really only talks to the family, she doesn't notice it."

Stephanie lifted her chin and looked at Debbie. "I don't notice it and don't care if they do. I don't want to move out."

Debbie smiled and giggled at Stephanie, "You can't go anywhere, Stephanie, I told you that already so don't worry." Stephanie sighed with thankful relief. Debbie turned to Angela. "Do you want to move out?"

"No, but I don't want people to think less of you, Debbie," Angela replied sincerely.

"Who's thinking bad about Debbie?" Stephanie yelled, jumping up and ready to fight.

Debbie held up her hand. "Put it back in your pants, Stephanie." Still looking at Angela, Debbie asked, "Are you happy with us?"

Angela nodded her head as she answered, "Yeah, I feel normal again. When Cade asks where Daddy is, I don't feel alone anymore. I have you, Stephanie and Bruce behind me to help and just be there. Y'all treat Cade like he's yours and make both of us laugh and feel like we belong."

"Angela, let me tell you something about little Debbie. I don't care what people think about me, except my family, and they care less than I do what people think about them. We won't even mention Bruce and how he feels about what people think of him," Debbie said, making Angela laugh and snort.

"I care what they think about you and Bruce. Bruce rescued us. He could've left us but he took us with him. When we get here, you go out of your way to make us happy and part of the family. I'm not knocking Mike down because he and Nancy do the same. I think Mike believes Cassandra is his daughter now," Angela replied.

"Angela, I don't want to use force but I will if I have to. I can kick your ass and will. Then I'll drag your whooped ass back upstairs," Debbie told her.

Angela sighed with relief as if the weight of the world had been lifted off her shoulders. "Thank you," she told Debbie.

"Don't thank me. Besides, I think my husband likes your feet," Debbie said. Angela snorted and started blushing. "Angela, are you blushing?" Debbie asked.

"No," Angela said, covering her face with her hands and making Debbie laugh. Debbie glanced at Stephanie, seeing her smile.

"Angela, Stephanie thinks she's not pretty," Debbie told her.

Angela took her hands off her face and looked at Stephanie in disbelief. "Are you mental, girl? I look at you and wonder where the castle is at. On the way here from the hospital, I asked Bruce who else was here. I had met the rest of the family. He described you as the smartest person he knew and the prettiest. I was thinking he was exaggerating, you know how boys are. Then I saw you and I wanted to go and hide, feeling like a troll. Stephanie, you're perfect."

Stephanie smiled at Angela and Debbie. They thought she was pretty, "Thank you, Angela, but you and Debbie are much prettier than I am. I'm just smart," she said.

Angela looked at Debbie. "I'm going to hit her."

"I'll hold her," Debbie offered.

Debbie jumped off the table as Angela bolted toward Stephanie. They grabbed her, taking her to the floor. "Raspberry her stomach," Debbie told Angela as she pinned Stephanie down. Angela lifted Stephanie's shirt and started blowing raspberries, making Stephanie scream with laughter. The twins and Cade saw what was going on and went to help. PJ started crawling over in high gear. He wanted to play too.

After torturing Stephanie for ten minutes, they let her up then gathered up the kids and headed to the house to join in the planning. That afternoon, Debbie gathered Nancy, Danny and Mary and told them about the treatment of Angela and Stephanie.

True to form, Danny wanted to shoot someone, shank two people and throw the rest out. Debbie just told Nancy and Mary that Bruce gave birth to her. Danny confirmed it, saying that's why she had such big balls. Debbie laid out the plan of attack for supper and the group broke up.

At 1800 everyone was at the table except the four. Bruce looked around and out the window but did not see them. "Stephanie where is Debbie, Nancy, Danny and Mary?" Bruce he asked.

"Debbie went to the bedroom. I don't know where the others are," Stephanie replied, smiling at Bruce. Just then, Danny and Mary came in wearing their leather trail-riding dusters. The dusters covered their whole body down to their ankles.

They walked to the table and sat down without taking the dusters off. "What's with the dusters, girls?" Bruce asked.

Danny looked at Bruce. "Nothing Dad, but I have a message for you from Mama. You are to stay in your seat no matter what." Bruce just narrowed his eyes at her but Danny was not forthcoming with answers.

A few minutes later Debbie and Nancy came in wearing their dusters also. They didn't walk toward the table but to the front of the room. Danny and Mary got up and went to the back corners of the hall. Bruce smelled a rat coming.

Debbie stopped in the front of the room with Nancy beside her. Nobody was talking, just staring at the two women that looked like cowboy bank robbers with their dusters on. Debbie cleared her throat. "Can I have your attention please? Unlike my husband, I can't use a voice that shakes the earth." Several laughed then quieted down. "It has come to my attention that several in my family have not been treated kindly by some of the females in this clan. If I remember correctly, one of the clan rules is 'everyone is treated equal and to each his own.' Unless it hurts the clan, then it does not matter.

"I really didn't think that someone who was brought here and treated as an equal could do such a thing. Walking around today, I saw different with my own eyes. Unlike my husband, I don't like to threaten with physical violence, but I will. This is just a talk today. The next time, I will move to threats then acts.

"I noticed a group of twenty or so women that love to gossip and put others down to make themselves feel better. Myself, I don't care what you say." Bruce stood up and started to walk up there as Debbie held up her hand.

"Bruce, I think you received your instructions." Bruce stopped, looking around the room. Everyone could see the anger in his eyes and got nervous. Bruce turned around and went back to his seat. "Thank you, stud muffin, sugar mama has this," Debbie told him from the front of the room. She looked back at the room and dropped her coat, followed by Nancy, Danny and Mary. They were all wearing string bikinis and combat boots. Danny and Mary climbed up on tables in the back corners of the room. Danny was on a table ten feet from the family table. She was wearing a camo string bikini and Matt's jaw hit the floor.

Debbie smiled. "Now that I have your attention, you can see I don't care what you say about me. I know if you talk about me, I'm already better than you. I know this group of women is only doing it out of jealousy. We have what you want. I know who you are, so do you. Don't say anything else bad about my family."

Matt let out a primal yell as he jumped on the family's table, pulling out his knife and screaming, "Who's talking about my baby doll?! You die tonight!!" Matt was breathing hard with drool coming out of the corners of his mouth. Standing in the center of the table in a fighting stance, Matt held his knife out, scanning the crowd. Everyone, including the family, was scared to move thinking Matt might see it as a sign of guilt.

Bruce slowly leaned over so he could see past Matt's legs and see Mike. He inquired softly, "Mike, can you control your son please?"

Mike looked at Matt then back to Bruce. "He's going to be your son in law, you do it."

Bruce looked up at Matt, seeing him frothing at the mouth and breathing heavily. "Uh no, you've known him longer," Bruce said but Danny solved the dilemma.

Danny jumped off her table and walked over to Matt. "Matt, get off the table please," she said.

Matt just kept looking around the room for signs of guilt. Danny shouted, "Matt!" and Matt looked at her. "Baby, get off the table, but only if you love me," Danny told him. The feral look erased off his face. It was replaced by one of unfathomable love as he just stepped backwards off the table and landed on his feet.

"I knew you loved me. Do you like it? I made it just for you," Danny said as she spun around, showing off her camo bikini. Matt's knife hit the floor as he just babbled. The only one that understood him was PJ and he thought it was funny. Danny blew a kiss to Matt and asked, "Baby, I put my boots on too tight; will you help me take them off later?" Matt fell back in his chair babbling and Bruce started banging his head against the table. Danny waved at Matt and skipped up to the front with her mother, quickly joined by Mary. Angela made Bruce stop hitting his head against the table.

After they joined Debbie, she spoke again. "As you can see, the boys really love us a lot. They also love the ones with us."

It hit Bruce like a brick. Someone had hurt Angela or Stephanie's feelings, maybe both. Bruce stood up, unbuckling his vest and dropping it to the floor. Every head turned toward Bruce when his vest hit the floor. Bruce scanned the eyes of everyone in the room and twenty-three women turned away.

Debbie smiled. "Well, if a boy could figure out what I was saying, then the women should have no trouble. This is the only warning you will ever get. This goes not only for my family but the entire clan. If you can't say something good then shut your fucking mouth! Nancy, do you have anything to add?"

Nancy said, grinning, "Oh yeah. I'm just going to clear the air. If you want to talk about someone say it to their face, not behind their back. Women are much worse than guys with gossip. We are not saying don't talk. We are all family here, our clan, fighting against incredible odds. Don't talk to belittle people, trying to make yourself feel better. Those people may be the ones that save your life, again. If I ever hear of this again, I will hurt you myself then I will throw your carcass over the fence."

They grabbed their coats and walked to the family table. Millie stepped in front of the group holding the biggest meat cleaver Bruce had ever seen. "I have a good idea who you are. You should feel ashamed of yourselves but I know you don't. I will use this on you long before they gets to ya," Millie said, holding up the cleaver from hell, then walked back to the kitchen.

Nobody moved in the entire hall. Most wanted to know who had pissed off the women to earn such threats, and the others were just scared. When nobody stood up to get in line to eat, Bruce cleared his throat.

Seeing he had everyone's attention, he spoke. "I now know who the troublemakers are. I'm going to forget this night, but I suggest you remember it. My wife was very wise to keep me out of it because I would have thrown you out. You would have died for childish behavior on your part. Now everyone, let's eat. We survived another day."

Bruce sat down as Debbie, Nancy, Mary and Danny reached the table. Danny went to Matt, kissing him until he stopped babbling. With everyone sitting down, Bruce felt like this day would never end. Shoveling the food down that Millie sat in front of him, he stood up and kissed Stephanie, Angela, and Debbie. Then Bruce grabbed PJ and the twins; seeing Cade was running around with the other kids, Bruce left him and headed to bed.

Bruce stopped outside to look up at the sky. Kneeling down, he let the twins get on his back as Matt, Jake, David, Danny, Mary, Buffy and Mindy came out of the Center. They walked up to him as he stood up with the twins on his back.

Jake laughed, "Piggyback ride, huh."

"Yeah, like all of you, they love them," Bruce said.

"Hey Dad, we're going to watch movies. Let Emily and Sherry come with us?" Jake asked. Not waiting for an answer, Jake grabbed Emily and Mary grabbed Sherry, each putting them on their back. PJ let out a yell like 'hey what about me.'

Danny clapped her hands and PJ leaned toward her. "We're not going to forget the little man who walked today," Danny said as she took PJ out of Bruce's arms.

Each of the kids kissed and hugged Bruce as they walked by heading to the house. Bruce just watched the group head inside, feeling left out. Shrugging his shoulders, he went to his room and took a shower by himself, the first one in a long time. Getting in bed, Bruce looked at the empty bed. It looked really big without all the people in it.

He grabbed his notebook to go over the plans again. Looking up occasionally at the door and feeling very lonely, he just laid his notebook down. Reaching over on the nightstand, Bruce went over the controls on the action digital camera Jake had given him. Bruce had put it on his boonie hat and Jake gave him a mountain of memory cards. Thirty minutes went by until he heard voices coming down the hall. Bruce picked up his notebook as the three walked into the room.

Debbie stopped in the door. Seeing Bruce in bed alone seemed weird. "Where are the kids?" she asked.

"Jake and them took 'em to watch movies," Bruce said.

"That makes sense. Mindy came back to the Center and grabbed Cade, saying she didn't have anyone to play with," Angela said.

They started getting dressed for bed and when Debbie took off her bikini Bruce said, "I was wanting you to wear that to bed."

"If I wear one to bed, they do too," Debbie said, grinning.

Looking at the women, Bruce shook his head. "No that's okay, you need to be comfortable."

After getting undressed, they climbed into bed. No sooner than they had laid down, Angela leaned over Stephanie and looked at Bruce. "Bruce, Debbie's feet hurt. Rub them for her," she told him.

Bruce looked at Angela strangely before replying, "Maybe later, I'm busy right now."

Angela ripped the covers off the bed, exposing everyone. Then she turned around, grabbing Debbie's legs and pulling her over to Bruce by her ankles. Angela straddled Stephanie, setting Debbie's feet on Bruce's chest. Then she grabbed his notebook, throwing it to the floor.

"Come on Bruce, they're right there, rub them for her," Angela said, grinning.

Bruce looked at Debbie's little feet. "I'm really tired, maybe tomorrow."

"Oh come on Bruce, look at her little toes. Don't you want to rub them?" Angela said, rubbing Debbie's foot on his chest. Bruce reached down and grabbed the blankets, pulling them up to his chest.

"Oh no you didn't," Angela said, grabbing the blanket and pulling it off. Bruce quickly flipped over on his stomach.

"Angela, I'm not kidding. I'm really tired and cold. Give me the blankets," Bruce begged.

Angela stood up in the bed and spun Stephanie around so her feet were beside Debbie's on Bruce's back. Debbie was laughing hard as Angela sat on Bruce's legs.

"See, now Stephanie's feet hurt. Rub them too," Angela said, trying not to laugh.

"Angela, I'm not kidding, get off of me, this hurts," Bruce said in growing pain.

"Bruce, your head is turning red. Are you blushing?" Angela asked, giggling.

Debbie leaned over Bruce, putting her mouth by his ear. "You surrender yet?"

"That does it," Bruce said, flipping back over and Angela screamed trying to get away. Bruce grabbed her, pulled her back and started tickling all three. He stopped when Angela peed on herself and the bed. Bruce got out of bed and went for some towels.

Turning back, he said, "Angela, I can't believe you wet the bed. I guess we need rubber sheets now." Angela just flipped him off as he put the towels on the bed and left the room to get the kids. Bruce tapped on Jake's door and opened it slowly. Kids were lying everywhere asleep. Bruce closed the door, smiling, and headed back to bed.

Walking back into the bedroom, Bruce found all three asleep. He arranged the bodies so he could get in the bed. Once he was settled, Bruce lay on his side looking at them for a while. Finally, sighing, he pulled all three close as he fell asleep.

CHAPTER 29

Marcus and Farmer's Almanac were wrong about the cold front. It hit three days early on the twelfth. Bruce waited till the thirteenth. When he woke up to frost on the ground, he called a go. Bruce left the farm at 0800 after the twenty-man security team and the twenty-man scavenging team mounted up. A new scavenging team would be brought down every morning.

Bruce was hoping for ten truckloads a day to be taken to the farm, with each truck carrying twenty tons. Keeping the trucks rotating, five would always be on the road with a security convoy. The trip one way was two and a half hours so when a convoy left from the base, Bruce estimated it could be back in seven hours. Then the five trucks there would leave as the returning convoy was reloaded. The only teams that would not be relieved were his security teams. Bruce had worked out a rotating down time where tomorrow three teams would be up while the fourth provided security.

Bruce was in the passenger seat of Debbie's SUV with Jake driving. The ten members of team one, Bruce's team, and team three, Conner's team, were riding with them in the SUV. Looking around the vehicle, one really could not say it was riding. It was more like being shipped, as tightly packed as they were. Behind them was Nancy's SUV with Mike's team two and Bill's team four. They had left the Beast for the Shreveport teams.

Bruce looked in the rearview mirror and saw the long convoy of ten semis with box trailers and two with flatbeds. The flatbeds carried the forklifts, fuel, and a ramp so the forklift could drive up into the bed. They had four regular forklifts and one boom lift. Bringing up the rear was the hummer with the Mk-19. Turning to look out the front, Bruce stared at the taillight of the Stryker in the lead.

411

Looking at the dash thermometer, which read twenty-two degrees at 1000, Bruce smiled. *This is way weird for Louisiana in November*, he thought, *but I'll take it.* Ten miles from the base, the convoy stopped and Bruce traded places with Jake. Jake threw one of the little Ravens up and jumped in the SUV. When the UAV was five miles in front of them, Bruce radioed the convoy to maintain forty-five miles per hour, matching the speed of the UAV. Ten minutes later, they reached the gate and drove through.

Jake flew the UAV ahead but he didn't see anything except wildlife. They were heading to the back of the base to the ammo storage area. They would pass within four miles of the main post. Bruce told Jake to swing the UAV over it as they drove by.

As he drove, Bruce glanced at the little screen, seeing bodies everywhere. When Bruce heard Jake say, "Holy shit," Bruce looked at the screen. He saw a large building in the center of the screen, but surrounding it was a huge pile of bodies. Bruce just stared, mesmerized at the sight. *That's tens of thousands*, Bruce thought as he looked at the screen.

"Bruce, are you going cross country or what?" Mike called over the radio. Bruce looked up as the SUV drifted off the road. He Bruce slowly guided the vehicle out of the ditch so they wouldn't flip. "What the hell are you doing up there? You're driving like a bitch," Mike called back over the radio.

After Bruce was back on the road, he replied, "Jake has some good images on the computer."

"Are they wearing high heels?" Mike asked.

"Nah, that site wouldn't take our credit card. The Raven is only showing a lot of dead bodies," Bruce replied.

"I prefer them dead, saves me the trouble," Mike replied back.

Jake guided the Raven to the ammo storage area and didn't see anything. Stopping at the gates, they cut the locks on the first one. The second gate was an electronic sliding gate. They cut the gear chain and slid the gate open. When the vehicles were in, Bruce called for the gate to be closed.

In front of them was a field of earthen-covered buildings. Stopping the convoy, Bruce got out and the cold wind hit him hard. Grabbing an acetylene torch from the trailer off the back of the SUV, he went to the first building and cut the lock. Opening the door, Bruce shined his light in and caught his breath.

Crates of supplies were stacked in neat rows. Walking in, Bruce saw this building was mainly ammo. Bruce was feeling lightheaded as he walked down the main aisle. He turned around, yelling, "Daddy has a new pair of shoes!"

"I hope they're warm," Mike called from the front of the building.

Ignoring Mike, Bruce keyed his radio. "Team four, security at the gate. Team three, rear security. Team two, loading security. Mike, mark the rows we want, scavenge team start loading. Team one, grab torches and let's see what Santa brought Daddy."

Team one headed to the SUV trailer. Danny, Jake and Steve grabbed cutting torches and flashlights and headed to buildings. Buffy stayed with Bruce and he taught her how to use the torch. After the third one, Bruce let Buffy roll the torch around to cut off locks and he pulled security. Two hours later they had unlocked all eighty buildings. Putting the torches back, they started looking inside the buildings.

Bruce was finding things that he had no idea what they were or did, but some at least were going with them. Running into each building, Bruce would jump up and down, yelling with joy. Then he run up and down the rows then out the door to another building. The rest of team one just followed, laughing and watching Bruce.

At 1400, Mike called over the radio, "First five are ready for convoy to leave."

Bruce stopped yelling in the building he was in and keyed his radio. "What?" The first convoy was not due out until 1700.

"Bruce, we're just loading crates. That doesn't take shit. Most of the scavenge team is just trying to stay warm," Mike reported.

I didn't think about that, Bruce thought as he keyed the radio. "Load the others, flat beds too. Tell the convoy team when they get close to have ten semis leave the farm. We will up the convoys from five to ten. Get the convoy relief up to help."

"Some of those drivers were for the Shreveport team," Mike reported.

"There're more than enough people there that can drive a truck and what the hell do you mean stay warm, I'm burning up," Bruce told Mike. Bruce wanted to take off his coat and heavy gloves.

"Bruce, I can hear you up here running around yelling and screaming in each building. If you open up anything before I can join you, we will have a problem. I'll start the loading here. Team two out," Mike replied sharply.

Bruce looked at his team; they were all smiling at him. "Am I acting that badly?" he asked them.

Jake answered. "Dad, this is awesome. You're acting like we did when we were little at Christmas. Except I think you're more excited."

"Aren't you excited?" Bruce asked.

"Well yeah, but you're so stealing the show," Jake said, then Bruce saw he was holding his video camera.

"You're videoing me, son?" Bruce asked, not liking that.

"We all are, Dad," Danny told him. Bruce looked at all four; even little Buffy had a camera in her hand. Before Bruce could say anything else, Danny added, "Dad, I think the next building holds some Stinger missiles."

Bruce forgot what he was going to say, yelling, "What?" He took off at a dead run with his film crew in hot pursuit. By 1700 Bruce had run through all the buildings and was walking back to the loading area as the convoy pulled out. Bruce was carrying his coat in his hands. Bruce walked over to Mike.

Mike just looked at Bruce. "Dude, it's twenty-eight degrees and you don't even have a coat on."

"Mike, checking out these areas takes some work," Bruce replied.

"Maybe if you did it without so much yelling, screaming, running, and jumping up and down you might not get so hot," Mike pointed out.

"Whatever," Bruce told Mike, then he got serious. "Mike, I'm taking teams one and three to the motor pool to get some vehicles. Then we will take team one, two, three, and the scavenging team to the armories. We will load them up and pull it back here while team four holds down the fort." Bruce laid out the change in plans.

Mike thought about it then replied, "I like that better than the original. I just never liked the idea of the big semis just sitting in the middle of the base getting loaded."

"Okay, we'll be back shortly," Bruce said, calling the teams to join him.

They drove out to the closest motor pool. Bruce giggled, looking at all the military vehicles. Cutting the lock, they drove in as Bruce looked around. He could tell a lot of vehicles were missing but there was still more than enough for them.

"Team one, we'll take back five Strykers," Bruce started to say but was interrupted by Buffy as she started jumping up and down yelling, happy that she was getting to drive one. Bruce continued. "Team three, get two more ready and some transport trucks for gear. I don't care what you get but I want it big and able to move a lot of gear," Bruce finished. Conner called back he would get some ready.

It took thirty minutes to slave off the five that team one was taking. They climbed in and headed back to the ammo storage area. Buffy did a real good job driving back so Bruce told her to stay in her spot. Buffy let out a big "Woohooo!"

Bruce jumped out of his Stryker as Bill walked up. Bruce told him, "Bill, keep two Strykers here for back up and evac. The weapon is not loaded nor is there any ammo in the back, but I think you can find some lying around here. As you can see, my kids are already fixing that problem on theirs." Bruce pointed at the kids loading ammo on the Stryker. Looking back at Bill, Bruce told him, "Keep a low profile but stay ready, this is where we will change out guard."

"Go get some more stuff; just don't yell and run around so much this time," Bill told Bruce as he grinned at him.

Bruce turned around, heading to the Strykers. "I'm going to act like I didn't hear that."

Matt came over to Bruce. "Daddy Bruce, Buffy flipped me off and said if I sat in the driver's spot she'd duct tape me to a tree naked," Matt tattled to Bruce.

Bruce never got to say anything as Danny barked at Matt, "Matt, Daddy told her she could drive so you leave her alone. So just get in one and shut up."

Matt replied instantly, "Yes baby."

Bruce put his hand on Matt's shoulder. "Sorry, son, it doesn't get much better. They love giving us hell."

"I heard that, Daddy, I'm telling Mom what you said," Danny yelled back.

Bruce smiled at her threat as he and Matt jumped in a Stryker. They pulled out and stopped at the motor pool. Conner had five HEMTTs with trailers and two more Strykers ready. Bruce dropped drivers off for the vehicles. They left as Conner took them to the closest armory. After getting through the fence they had to cut the door down. The lock was electric and the lock was bolted into the door. It took ten minutes to burn around the lock and Bruce kicked the door open.

Bruce told everyone to be careful and not to touch the edges. He walked in and yelled for Mike. They started picking the locks of the cages, throwing them open. Bruce stopped picking locks after he opened the first one up. He ran in and started jumping up and down, then ran out to see the other cages. Mike was just walking up to a door and getting it open in thirty seconds.

When Mike opened one door Bruce almost knocked him over as he ran in, yelling, "Oh yeah, I want that, and that, holy shit I have to have this. Oh shit, I want two of those!" Mike just shook his head, fixing to walk to another door when he noticed Jake with a camera on Bruce.

"I want a copy of that," Mike told Jake.

"I can hook you up, Daddy Mike, but this is so going up on a movie night," Jake said, grinning and watching Bruce hug a mini-Gatling gun. Mike laughed before reaching out and covering Buffy's eyes. "I think he's going to mate with it," he said then headed to unlock the rest of the rooms, pulling Buffy with him.

It was 2000 when they started loading up racks of weapons on the trucks. Around 2030 everyone heard Bruce let out a rebel yell as he found the room Mike had unlocked that was loaded with thermals and NVGs. To put it mildly, Bruce was next to worthless as they loaded the trucks. When the trucks were loaded, Mike had to literally drag Bruce out of the armory.

Bruce knocked Mike's hands down. "Dude, leave me here. I'll wait until you come back. This is the coolest shit ever. I'm putting one of those mini guns on my truck. I'm goin' to road warrior someone's ass. That is some sexy shit. You're in charge." Bruce turned to head back inside as Mike grabbed his arm and spun him around.

Looking into Bruce's face, Mike realized he used to see the same look on his kids' faces as he pulled them out of a toy store. Except this was a big ass kid. Mike looked at Bruce. "Bruce, the trucks will be here soon. We'll come back for the rest. I promise the guns will be fine until we come back. I need you to stay in charge, okay."

"They might get lonely and cold," Bruce whined, stomping his feet.

"We'll close the door. Now come on, the guns could use a little peace and quiet after all your yelling," Mike told Bruce, while pulling him to the vehicle. Mike pushed Bruce in the Stryker, telling Buffy to raise the ramp. Mike held onto Bruce until the ramp was up.

The ten trucks pulled in before midnight. They loaded them and had them back on the road by 0300. Bruce took off running for the Stryker and climbed in, popping his head out the turret.

"Come on, let's go to the armory. They probably think we've forgotten all about them. Come on, let's go," Bruce said, dropping down. A few seconds later the Stryker fired up.

Mike pinched the bridge of his nose, shaking his head. He was getting a major headache and it was in a Stryker yelling for them to move. Bill walked up to Mike and asked, "Who's lonely at the armory?"

"The weapons we left," Mike answered as Bruce started yelling from the Stryker. "I want a tranquilizer gun," Mike said, then noticed Danny with a camera pointed at him. Mike looked at the camera. "You have no idea what I've put up with for this family and clan. I'm ready to go home right now. I want a vacation." Mike stopped as Bruce jumped out of the Stryker and ran over, grabbing his arm.

"Let's go, come on," Bruce said, pulling him until Conner spoke.

"Don't you want to see the SOCOM armory?" he asked.

Bruce spun around. "There's a SOCOM armory here?"

"Yeah," Conner said. Bruce let go of Mike, ran over, grabbed Conner and threw him over his shoulder and carried him toward the Stryker.

Mike stopped Bruce, asking, "What about the other armory? I thought you didn't want them to get lonely?"

"You said they'd be fine. Come on, it's SOCOM, they have cool toys," Bruce yelled out, putting Conner down on the ramp and shoving him in. Team one followed Bruce as did team three since he'd taken their leader.

"What's SOCOM?" Buffy asked.

With his camera still pointed at Bruce, Jake replied, "All Special Forces."

Mike yelled out, "Load up or he's going to leave us." Everyone headed to vehicles except team four, who were feeling a little left out.

Bruce was pulling out and the rest of the vehicles followed. Mike radioed Bruce several times to slow down but Bruce replied back with many unkind carnal verbs. Stopping at the armory's gate, Bruce climbed out through the driver's hatch, bolt cutters in his hands. Cutting the chains and throwing open the gate, he ran to the armory yelling at the top of his lungs while everyone just stood at the gate watching him in awe.

"How does he expect to get in?" Conner asked.

"Ten bucks he chews through the door," Jake said, filming his dad.

"No bet," Mike said as Bruce reached the door and began hitting it with the bolt cutters.

Screaming at the door, Bruce dropped the cutters and ran back to the Stryker, passing the crowd watching him. It was fourteen degrees but no one was bothered by the cold as they watched Bruce wheel out the torch unit. Thinking that was too slow, Bruce picked it up over his head and trotted back to the armory. Bruce cut the door open as the crowd walked up to the armory.

Bruce finished cutting the lock, kicked the door open and ran inside, yelling out like a kid. They could hear him beating the shit of the cages inside, trying to get in them. Bruce ran back to grab the torch as Mike stopped him.

"Bruce, you can't use the torch. Let's pick the locks," Mike said. Bruce looked at him like, "That's such a good idea." Bruce ran back to the first cage, reaching for his picks. Mike pushed him aside. "Let me do it, you'll break yours." Bruce was standing behind Mike and kept bumping him as he looked in the cage. Mike yelled at Bruce, "Quit bumping my arm, damn it."

Bruce stood still until the lock opened. Then he bowled right over Mike, knocking him to the floor. Standing in the room, Bruce started yelling, "OH yeah toys! I fucking love this shit, I'm putting all this shit in my room!"

Mike stood up and turned to Danny. "You and Buffy keep him in here until I get the rest open. Conner, pull the vehicles up."

Danny and Buffy at first tried to block the door but soon realized that wouldn't work. Then with one of them on each side of the room, they would point at a gun and yell. Bruce would run over to see what they had found. The ploy worked long enough for Mike to open up the rest of the armory.

Mike came back to the front as Bruce ran by him. Mike looked at the rest of the team. "Let him go crazy, let's move this stuff out of here." When the first cage was empty, Mike yelled for Bruce. Bruce, thinking they had found something cool, ran to him, panting. As Bruce stopped, Mike said, "You can help. What we don't get we'll have to leave." A look of horror crossed Bruce's face and he ran to the cage behind Mike, picking up a rack of rifles over his head. Mike was going to help him since it usually took two people, at least, to carry one of the racks, but he just moved out of his way. "Whatever floats your boat, dude," Mike said as Bruce ran past him with the rack over his head, still yelling. Mike bent down, picking up two cases to load up.

Conner's team held security while the armory was emptied. It was 0700 by the time they were done filling all the trucks, trailers and Strykers. Mike knew Bruce wouldn't leave anything so he told the teams to take everything including the room of uniforms and the three desks with chairs. Mike drew the line at the file cabinets but would be shocked weeks later when he saw them in the basement. Bruce rode on the back of one of the trucks. Mike tried to tell him the temperature was in the teens. Mike just gave up as he looked at Bruce's grinning face. Bruce rubbed the weapons and talked to them. Secretly, Mike hopped Bruce would get mild hypothermia just so he would slow down.

The convoy pulled back into the ammo storage area and Mike's hopes of Bruce slowing down were soon dashed. Bruce jumped off the truck, yelling for everyone to unload so they could get more. Mike started rubbing his temples; his headache was turning into a migraine and that migraine was unloading trucks and moving at an incredible pace.

Bill walked up to Mike. "When's he going to slow down?"

Mike looked at Bill. "He loaded almost one HEMTT by himself."

Bill watched Bruce pulling racks off by himself, putting them in neat rows. "If you don't mind, my team will stay here and keep this area secure," Bill said, watching the bald Energizer bunny.

"Thanks," Mike replied dryly. "I'm leaving half of the scavenging crew here. The trucks should be here soon. I know Psycho won't wait for the next convoy. The trucks this afternoon should have the relief crew." Bill just nodded his head, in a trance, watching Bruce as he unzipped his vest and pulled off his shirt. Throwing the shirt on the ground, Bruce zipped up his vest and returned to unloading.

"Should we tell him it's not even twenty degrees?" Bill asked Mike.

"It doesn't do any good," Mike said, rubbing his temples and not even looking at Bruce.

The trucks were unloaded by 0900 and Bruce immediately was in a Stryker, yelling at the top of his lungs. Mike took something for his headache, knowing it was useless. He would have to knock Bruce out to make his headache go away. Mike jumped in and they pulled out, passing the convoy as they left. They returned to the first armory to finish taking everything. Mike stopped Bruce once when he saw him carrying a mortar out. "Bruce, do we really need mortars?" Mike asked.

A wide-eyed, smiling Bruce replied, "Man, we so need all of these. We can hit someone miles away. It'll be great. I'll teach you how to shoot 'em. Don't worry, we can play with 'em."

"That's cool," Mike replied in a tired, yawning voice and Bruce took off. *Having mortars around will be pretty cool*, Mike thought as he continued to help load the trucks. Mike put team one without Bruce on guard with his team. Bruce was just wearing them out.

They had two trucks loaded when Jake called over the radio, "Contact to the west. Looks like sixteen in a single file patrol. All armed; several appear to be soldiers. Three hundred yards away. Want me to engage?"

Mike closed his eyes, visualizing the area. The west was the rear of the armory. There was a parking lot outside the fence with a pedestrian gate. Mike radioed Jake, "Are they heading here?"

"Yeah, they're coming straight here," Jake replied.

Bruce walked up to Mike. "Let's kill 'em. They probably want the guns."

"No Bruce, what if they're just survivors like us?" Mike said as Bruce scoffed. Mike added, "They might know where more stuff is at."

"Good thinkin'." Bruce keyed his radio. "Wedge ambush, I'm center. Jake and Matt, get in sniper position and work from the back to the front. Buffy, Danny, Mary and team three, work from the front. The rest of team two stay in reserve in case they flank or have friends. I'll challenge at twenty yards; any hostile action, kill everyone. I'll take one alive to see if they know where more weapons are." Bruce took off running out the door. Mike nodded his head at Bruce's plan. That's why they needed him. Mike felt a little bad as he ran out back for wanting to hurt Bruce earlier. Bruce was already behind a Hummer with Buffy beside him. Mike ran behind a large SUV beside them; lying under it he could see the field.

Waiting a few minutes, Mike saw the line of people walking toward them. Someone in the line pointed at the vehicles beside the armory. The line was heading to the open pedestrian gate. Mike's palms started getting sweaty as the group got closer. When they were twenty yards away, Bruce jumped out from behind the Hummer, followed by Buffy. Bruce yelled,

"FREEZE." The group froze on command as the bald psychopath wearing a tactical vest with no shirt held them at gunpoint. Steam was coming off his body, giving Bruce an evil appearance as he pointed his gun at them with the little armed blonde girl at his side. "You're in a kill zone and if you move you'll die. They're mine! You can't have them, we found them. They were all alone and scared!" Bruce screamed at the terrified people. Mike dropped his head to the ground, wondering how mad Debbie would be at him if he just shot Bruce.

The man in the front of the line held up his hands and said, "Man, whatever is yours that you're talking about, we won't touch it. It's yours."

Bruce just eyed the speaker, wondering if he should shoot him as Mike stood up and walked to stand beside Bruce. Looking at the line of people, Mike said, "Like he said, we have more than enough weapons on you, so don't move. We aren't going to hurt you unless you try to hurt us." Bruce just growled.

"Sir, we heard the engines and thought it was a rescue. Would you tell Mr. Clean we don't want whatever he has that's lonely and scared. I don't know who left them or scared them, but I want to kill them for doing it," the man said.

Mike felt no hostility from this group. "Bruce, go and load the truck, I'll talk to them."

Bruce never took his eyes off the group as he growled, "They may be bluffing."

Mike replied, "Bruce, we have several other armories to go to. Get this one loaded."

Bruce looked at Mike eagerly. "Really?" Mike nodded his head and Bruce took off running, hooting and hollering.

Mike looked at the group. "Just because he's gone don't think you're not covered."

The man up front replied, "Mister, I can see your snipers and the people on our flanks. I know. If you'll let us go, we'll leave and you will never see us again."

Mike radioed for the line to pull back but for Matt and Jake to stay, put then turned to the man. "Is that better? I'd like to talk to you," Mike said.

"Thank you. May my people come up so they can hear also?" the man asked.

"Yes, they can move up and put their hands down. Just don't grab your weapons."

They put their hands down and moved around the leader as Mike asked, "You have a name? Mine is Mike."

"I'm Willie," the man said, reaching out to shake Mike's hand. When Mike shook his hand the entire group sighed with relief. Willie looked behind Mike and, seeing Bruce carrying a rack of rifles over his head, said, "You should tell Mr. Clean that those racks are supposed to be carried by at least two men. They weigh over two hundred pounds."

Mike shook his head. "Don't go there right now, I'm not kidding. What are you doing roaming around?"

"Like I said, we heard trucks and thought rescue had come," Willie told him.

"We're here only for supplies. We have two secured areas outside of Shreveport on farms and a fence around them. The kids can actually go outside," Mike said, seeing several people get real interested.

Hearing a yell from behind him, Mike turned around to see Bruce, by himself, carrying a weapon he had never seen before. And the weapon was big and looked really heavy. Then Willie said, "That man has a serious hard-on for weapons."

Mike shook his head as he turned back to him. "You have no idea. Willie, if you and your crew want to, you can come with us. We do have rules: no stealing, everyone has to work, respect others, defend the group from any attack, and a few others. Basically no free rides for anyone."

"You're awful trusting to someone you just met," Willie pointed out.

Mike chuckled. "I don't feel hostility from you. Next, you have women in your patrol so I know you're not one of the gangs we've fought and wiped out. Plus, if you tried anything, I'll tell him you want his guns."

Willie looked at Mike, chuckling. "Yeah, I could see him killing everyone with a butter knife. If you take us, you take all of us."

"How many we talking about," Mike asked.

"Seventy-four," Willie answered.

"We can handle that easy. It may be cramped until we get you a barracks built. But with that many, you'll have to wait until we're done here," Mike said.

"Let me talk to my group," Willie said.

"That's fine. Come on up if you decide to come. Just leave if not, and if that's the case, good luck," Mike said, shaking Willie's hand and then heading back to the armory.

Willie and his group came up as they were almost finished loading the contents of the armory. Bruce was out front shoving food down his throat, because Mike, Danny and Buffy had threatened to call Debbie if he didn't eat. He was covered in sweat, steam boiling off his skin in the cold air. He warily watched the group come up. Mike waved at a growling Bruce as he walked over to Willie. "Well, you want to come?"

"Yes, we'll ask the rest of the group but this group wants to go," Willie said.

"We can drop y'all by the motor pool so you can get some vehicles. We're at the far ammo holding area," Mike said.

"Vehicles? Are you crazy? The blues will be all over us," Willie said in shock.

"Nah, they hibernate when it's cold," Mike informed him.

"If that's the case, there's a motor pool behind us with buses," Willie told him. Then he asked, "I know of another group, it's about thirty-five, mostly women and kids. I couldn't bring them to us. We had no more room in our building. Can I ask them also?"

"We'd be very disappointed if you didn't," Mike said.

Willie and his group left as the scavenge team loaded the last of the boxes from the armory.

They piled on the vehicles and headed back to the storage area. Mike had really hoped the excitement had left Bruce but that hope ended as Bruce jumped out and started unloading the trucks. They were almost unloaded when three buses and a Hummer pulled up to the gate and were let in. The Hummer pulled up to Mike and Bill. Willie stepped out and Mike introduced him to Bill, as Willie said, "Mike, you have a tight crew here. You must be a good commander."

"I'm number two," Mike said, watching as Bruce pulled off another huge rack of guns.

"When do I get to meet the one in charge?" Willie asked.

"You already have," Mike said, still watching Bruce as the last piece was taken off.

Following Mike's gaze, Willie said, "You're fucking kidding."

"That is the toughest, smartest, craziest, kindest and most cold-blooded son of a bitch I have ever met," Bill said, watching as Bruce poured a bottle of water over his head, making all three shiver.

"Well, he's hardcore that's no doubt," Willie said as Bruce walked toward them then stopped in front of them with steam still pouring off his body.

Willie showed Bruce his palms, saying, "I won't touch your weapons."

Bruce just looked at Willie then said, "Well, if we're attacked I don't want you just standing around holding your dick."

"Well, I could drive it through a few skulls before they take me," Willie replied.

Bruce narrowed his eyes, studying Willie then spoke. "Well, Captain, when were ya at Benning?"

Willie looked down on his jacket and shoulder in surprise. Neither had rank or tab. "How did you know?" Bruce just stared at him, waiting on the answer. Willie replied, "I graduated eight years ago with the tab."

"You'll do," Bruce said then continued, "have your people make a list with names so the farm can get ready for us. It is totally up to you but I'd like for you to send the small kids and women back to the farm with the next convoy. I would understand if you have reservations, but know this: you're part of this clan and I'm in charge. The reason I'd like for them to go back is everyone keeps bitching that it's cold."

Willie smiled. "Yeah, a couple of my people have mentioned it's cold. I was really thinking about going for a swim." Bruce smiled as Willie continued, "I concur; we're joining your group but if those women and children are hurt there will be a big problem."

"If someone hurts them, I'll eat their liver, making them watch," Bruce promised.

"That'll do for me," Willie said.

"How many people, and of those how many troops?" Bruce asked.

"One hundred and eight in total. Of those, twenty-four are soldiers. Ten more have time in service," Willie answered.

"Put someone in charge of your group; they'll report to Conner. Send all the women and children on the buses. My men don't ride buses. You'll come with us as we finish shopping. We leave in ten minutes," Bruce said then turned around and left, steam still pouring off his body.

Willie smiled, turning to Mike. "I like 'im." Mike groaned, thinking, *Not another one.*

Willie carried out his assignments then headed toward the vehicles for the scavenging group. Bruce motioned him over. "Take us to another armory," Bruce told him.

"Okay, but first I have some place a lot better if you like. Real boy toys," Willie said.

Bruce grinned from ear to ear. "Really?"

Mike wanted to cry but put on a brave face.

Loading up, they headed onto base, passing the building that was surrounded by bodies. Willie told them it was the gymnasium and it had been where they'd made their last stand. Last month they'd been hit by a group of infected they estimated at a hundred thousand. They continued driving, finally pulling into a group of large buildings, stopping at the one Willie pointed out. It was huge. Willie told them they would need the torch. After cutting the door, Bruce kicked it open. They walked in and Mike headed to a door with his lock picks. Willie told him to stop and opened the desk in the corner, pulling out some keys, then unlocked the only door in the room. They walked inside to see a huge warehouse. There were trailers with small buildings on them and huge stacks of boxes. Bruce stood still and let out a loud yell before taking off running. Stopping here and there, Bruce let out a yell each time.

Mike just dropped down to his knees to the floor, moaning. Then beside him he heard two more yells and turned to see Jake and Matt yelling. They took off to a stack of boxes. Looking at each other with excitement on their faces, they screamed again. Mike just lifted his arm up. "Great, now I have three of them." Mike felt someone rub his head. Looking up, he saw Danny holding a camera.

"It's okay, Daddy Mike, I still love you even with all these cool toys," Danny said.

"This is the electronic warfare storage area. It houses the Grey Eagle and Reaper UAVs, Puma and Raven micro UAVs, remote ground units, FLIR systems, and a lot of other goodies," Willie said as the boys ran to another stack of boxes.

"We need more vehicles," Mike said as Matt and Jake let out another scream.

"There's another motor pool on the other side of the building," Willie said, walking further into the warehouse to join Bruce and the boys.

Mike sent Bill's team to get more vehicles and they started working.

This was how the days went. Willie would take them over the base, emptying the areas with the supplies they needed. It was day six at 0700 when the fun stopped. They were at the ammo storage area when the convoy pulled in and the convoy leader walked over to Bruce, handing him a letter. Bruce read the letter. When he was finished, he started cussing. When Mike asked what was wrong, Bruce handed him the letter. Mike read it.

Dear Bruce

I know you are having a lot of fun down there but enough is enough. You have sent over four thousand tons (literally, I'm not joking) of stuff up here. The underground storage is full, as is the barn, all storage sheds, most of the house, the barracks, half of the community center, and Marcus's barn. We are now stacking equipment around the property. We have enough for now. Stephanie just did a rough calculation and puts the total number of ammo of all calibers over three hundred million. Half is 5.56 so please quit and come home. We need to build more living quarters and storage areas.

I love you and no more convoys are coming after this one so it's time to come home. There are things we have to talk about. I love you and Angela and Stephanie send their love also.

Love Debbie
P.S. Get the yelling out of your system before you come home.

Mike was thankful Debbie had done what he couldn't. Smiling, Mike looked up from reading to find Bruce looking back at him. Bruce had a smile on his face and Mike's smile fell off his. "Bruce, don't do something stupid," Mike warned him.

"Mike, load these trucks up and pull to the north gate. Wait until we get there to leave," Bruce said and called team one, three, four, plus the soldiers and half the scavenging team to him. Bruce gave them orders to empty the last armory, the PX, and the supply issue area, the mess halls they had passed and two other areas he had seen, then they dispersed. Bruce and Buffy jumped in Debbie's SUV and sped out. The other vehicles left, following Bruce.

Mike just shook his head and told everyone to load the trucks. When they were done, Mike led them to the gate in Nancy's SUV and waited. The temperature was still in the upper twenties so he told them to leave the engines running to stay warm.

Bruce headed to the motor pool with his team and half the soldiers. They started loading vehicles up on heavy transports. Bruce pointed out five RGLs that he wanted also. Leaving one heavy transport open, he walked to the back of the motor pool. Buffy ran up to him. "What are we getting, Daddy?"

Bruce pointed ahead.

Looking where he was pointing, Buffy screamed, "A tank!"

"Yeah, BB, a M1A1," Bruce said, walking toward the tank. Buffy took off running then stopped and pointed at one, yelling that that was the one she wanted.

Bruce loaded the M1 on the transport then went and grabbed equipment from the maintenance area. He told Buffy to get in a Stryker and follow him. Bruce pulled out with a long line of vehicles. Bruce called on the radio to check on teams three and four. They told Bruce they had already left and were loaded.

When Bruce saw the convoy at the gate, he radioed Mike. "Let's go, Mike, we're ready."

Mike pulled off and the convoy followed in the afternoon sunlight. Then he radioed Bruce. "I see over thirty vehicles with you. Several heavy transports also." Then Mike looked in his mirror. "Did you get a tank?"

"Yeah, ain't it cool?" Bruce replied.

"Bruce, I don't see Debbie's SUV," Mike said.

"I'll come back for it. I'll let her drive the tank some," Bruce said.

"I better be able to drive it too," Mike almost yelled back.

"Of course, brother," Bruce said.

They reached the farm at 1700. Bruce told the semis to pull in to get unloaded. He pulled the rest down to the end of the road and parked them. They all got out and walked the mile home. Walking onto the farm, Bruce was shocked at the stacks of equipment everywhere and he was only in the front.

Walking around the house, Bruce's jaw dropped. Everywhere he looked he saw equipment. Beside the barn were stacks of storage containers stacked five high with eight rows. Bruce could hear heavy machinery from the back of the property and saw work going on behind the barracks. Looking at all the stuff, Bruce thought Debbie may have been right.

Bruce headed to the Center and noticed a sign above the door that read: Alex's Center. Bruce smiled as he entered. He didn't even have the door closed before the twins jumped on him. Bruce picked them up, hugging them.

Emily leaned back, wrinkling her nose. "Daddy, you stink." Sherry said, "You have stickers on your face and head."

Putting the girls down, Bruce told them, "Daddy hasn't showered or shaved in a week."

Debbie held her hand out. "Stop. I know you love me but I know what you smell like when you come out of the field. I've already told Stephanie and Angela, so no kisses for you," she told Bruce.

Bruce walked around and sat down in his chair. Willie came in with Mike and a woman ran up to him, carrying a toddler, and hugged him. They talked for a few minutes and the woman pointed at the table Bruce was at. Willie grabbed her hand and came over to the table.

Stopping beside Bruce, Willie said, "Bruce, I would like to introduce my wife Maggie and my son Jason."

Bruce shook their hands and introduced the rest of the family to them then asked them to sit down. The kids were not there, as they'd wanted to take showers first.

Willie sat down with his family and turned toward Bruce. "Nice setup here. My wife told me you are true to your word. Bruce, I want you to know that I am grateful my family is a lot safer and two, I'm not in charge of my group."

"Oh, you are so kind," Bruce said sarcastically.

Willie laughed. "I walked around looking and only saw a fraction of what you have here. Don't you think it looks a little greedy?"

It was the family who laughed as Bruce spoke, "Willie, what do you and your family have? Let me guess: the clothes on your back, maybe one change, as does everyone here. The ones here before you did get some ACUs and most got two pairs of boots. We did have supplies here for our family. We only prepped for us; then one thing led to another and as you can see we have company. We were out of toothbrushes, toilet paper and such. They went to secure stuff from Shreveport. As you guessed, we were after protection. As you well know, we also brought back truckloads of clothes, all military. That is what I want everyone to wear just in case a gang spots us. I don't want them to pick out females. They tend to rape and kill them and we've grown quite fond of ours here.

"We can only go out while it's cold without being molested by the blues. Gangs are another problem; we have tied up with two and wiped both out. Now you may see this as cheating, but when I go into a fight I want all the odds in my favor. That's why I got carried away at the base. Sooner or later we will run across a gang that has military weapons and the knowledge to use them. Then there is the government to worry about, but I will tell you about them later. I want more than they have and not have to worry about ammo. It may look greedy, but when it warms up, I don't want to have to go for supplies. Way too risky," Bruce finished.

"I hope you don't think I was being judgmental. I was just saying. That only confirms my choices to come here, you're thinking several steps ahead," Willie said.

"Nah, walking in I had to tell that to myself. I don't think I've ever seen so much shit," Bruce said.

"Wait till you see behind the barn," Angela said. Bruce just looked at her. "If there isn't six thousand tons of shit out there, I'll kiss your ass," Angela said.

"You said I only sent four thousand tons back," Bruce said, turning to Debbie.

"She lied," Stephanie said. "You had ten trucks making runs; they made at least three runs in a day. Two days they did four. If you would have been loading to federal limits, you would have been around four thousand tons but you way overloaded those trucks. When I saw the first trucks come back, I almost died. I radioed the convoy that left and told them on the return trip only one truck on any bridge at a time." Stephanie shook her head as she continued, "Your average load was forty tons per truck. The first two flatbeds you sent on the first trip I put at fifty-four tons each. Bruce, they have weight limits for a reason. I put your total haul around eight thousand tons not counting your additional convoy. And with over fifty trucks in one haul we are not talking about it right now. Debbie and Nancy reached about five thousand tons before they stopped. Now Debbie has something to tell you," Stephanie said.

Debbie nodded at Stephanie then turned to Bruce. "We had a shoot-out in Shreveport, well actually on the outside of Shreveport, two days ago. We were clearing out the last of the super sports stores and were fixin' to head back to the other group that was getting the cargo containers. Before we got in the trucks one of the scouts reported he saw people running between some houses. I pulled everyone out and we went to the other crew in case it was a two-pronged attack. On the way there, I pulled into an alley, letting my group get ahead of me. A few minutes later two motorcycles drove by. I pulled out behind them and they shot at me, so I ran their asses over. I'm sorry, baby, but your new truck is kind of dented up and has a few bullet holes."

Bruce grabbed Debbie's hand. "That's okay, we'll go get another one. What happened?"

Debbie took a deep breath before she continued, "Well, I stopped to make sure they were okay. One was fine; he stood up but Stephanie fixed that when she shot him, telling him to stay down—"

Bruce interrupted. "Who shot him?"

Debbie looked down at the table. "Stephanie," she answered.

"Why weren't you in the Beast?" Bruce asked.

"I let the other team have it to scout around. They emptied out the warehouses before going to get the shipping containers," Debbie said, still not looking at him.

Bruce looked at Stephanie and she was looking down at the table, as was Angela. Bruce asked Debbie to continue.

"Well, the other one was not hurt that bad, only his leg was broken. We asked him nice to tell us what they were doing but he didn't want to tell us. Stephanie started jumping on his broken leg while Angela and I stomped on his arms and chest. Then he told us his gang was going to hit us on the highway after we left the storage yard. Nancy shot him in his good leg and we left to warn the other—"

Bruce stopped her. "You left an enemy combatant alive?"

"Well, I kind of ran over him when we left. He was moving a little when we left," Debbie admitted.

Bruce took a deep breath. "Go on."

"I called on the radio and told them to hold. I told everyone we were going to get hit, made a plan and left. The security teams pulled off like they were leaving. Then, when the gang attacked, the teams came back, attacking the gang from the rear and we wiped them out," Debbie said, smiling.

"What are you leaving out?" Bruce asked.

"Well, one circled around and jumped Stephanie, hitting her a few times before I shot him. We did find forty-two more survivors," Debbie replied, trying to distract Bruce.

Stephanie quickly said, "I'm okay, Bruce, don't be mad at Debbie. It was my fault."

Bruce started rubbing his temples. "I'm getting a headache."

Mike slammed his fist on the table, scaring everyone as he stood up and began to yell, "Doesn't feel good to have fuckers act like idiots, does it? Motherfucker, that's what I've dealt with for SIX fucking days! You're the motherfucker in charge, but oh no, we open the first fucking door and you start acting like a bitch in heat." Nancy stood up, looking at Mike and pointing her finger at him and Mike yelled at her, "Sit the fuck down. Did you put up with him? Hell no, so don't say jack shit to me, understand!" Nancy just sat back down, her mouth gaping in total shock as Mike continued. "You'd think he would've gotten tired, but hell no. I had to threaten to tell Debbie about the few times he snuck off, scaring the shit out of me to find Bruce gone." Father Thomas came running toward Mike to see if he could help.

"Father, you come up to me right now saying 'be calm,' I'll knock you the fuck out! You want to do something, cane that motherfucker!" Mike said, pointing at Bruce. The family was just staring at Mike with mouths open. The kids came in, having heard Mike from outside, and they just stood at the door in amazement. Mike never acted like this. That was Bruce's job.

Mike continued yelling. "You acted like a complete asshole, you son of a bitch! Did you ever think maybe I wanted to look at some of that stuff? Could I? Hell no, you'd take off running around yelling and screaming, leaving me in charge, doing your job!" Mike grabbed his stuff off the table and turned to the door. Seeing Matt and Jake, Mike yelled out, "Then these two join Bruce in the 'acting like bitches in heat.' I wanted to look at that shit too, but fuck no, you two had to act like that motherfucker back there.

Bruce, I hope you get a migraine from hell because I still fucking have mine." Mike's voice faded as the door closed behind him. Everyone in the hall just watched the door to see if he was coming back so they could run and hide if he did.

Bruce broke the silence. "He's so pissed. Nancy, go give him some and wear high heels, he likes that."

Nancy looked at Bruce, glowering. "I know what he likes. I should make you sleep with him for pissing him off like that."

"He doesn't want any from me. Debbie, go give Mike some and make him shut up," Bruce said.

"I'm not going in the house until he calms down. Nancy, if you wait till he calms down I'll go with you," Debbie promised as the kids came over to the table, sitting wherever they could.

Paul leaned over the table and looked at Nancy. "I've talked it over with Cheryl, and we'll go with you. It's time for us to get kinky anyway. Just please don't let Mike force me to wear high heels."

Bruce looked at Paul in admiration. "About time you joined the family."

Conner spoke up. "I'm not going in there with Mike. Y'all made me go in with Bruce last time and it hurt. I really think he punctured a lung. I'll let Susan stand in my place though."

"Oh that's good," Debbie said, nodding.

Nancy stood up, heading to the door. "Good night, everyone. Would someone ask Millie to save Mike a plate?"

"I've never seen Mike so mad," Angela said as Nancy ran out the door.

"He's never been that mad before," Mary confirmed.

Debbie looked at Bruce, shaking her head. "You shouldn't have done that to him."

"Mike has to learn to take the bull by the horns again. After the time he got hit by that mob at the camp he hasn't wanted to be put in charge unless it was here in a static defense. I felt we weren't in danger so I let myself go. Mike was exaggerating some about my behavior," Bruce told everyone.

"No he wasn't, Daddy. You were acting crazy, but I liked it," Buffy replied, grinning.

"Well, it doesn't matter; Mike knows he can do it again. I even turned my back on an armed encounter with an unknown subject," Bruce said.

"You did what?" Debbie yelled, jumping out of her chair.

"He jumped out, stopped an unknown patrol, then left Daddy Mike and me with them," Buffy said then added, "Daddy Mike did tell him to go. I think Daddy Mike was worried that Daddy was going to shoot Mr. Willie."

"Why was Daddy going to shoot Willie?" Debbie asked her.

"Daddy thought Mr. Willie was going to take his new toys," Buffy answered.

Willie spoke up. "Debbie, if I may. It was a misunderstanding; Bruce was under the impression that I was not going to let him procure some firepower for the protection of this group. Mike merely let Bruce go back to collect the weapons as we discussed the movement of my people up here."

Willie's wife Maggie looked at Debbie, "When he talks like that he's bullshitting you. When he came back, Willie told me he needed to change his pants because a huge man with a shaved head had scared the shit out of him." Willie told Maggie she was supposed to be on his side. Maggie told him not when he was bullshitting another woman.

"Why was he mad at the boys?" Debbie asked.

Bruce smiled. "Willie took us to a huge storage area that had tons of electronic ..."

Jake started. "Mom, you wouldn't believe the stuff in there. We got real UAVs that can stay up for days at a time. More of the micro UAVs like the ones we have and Talon Swords, the UGV. Unmanned ground vehicles like the Warlord we built but with the range of a mile. Then—"

Mary jumped out of his lap, squealing. "Jake, that's only supposed to happen when you think about me." Everyone laughed as Jake blushed.

"Mary, as long as that doesn't happen when he is talking about other girls it's okay," Debbie told her. Mary accepted that and sat back down in Jake's lap.

Bruce smiled then asked Paul, "I take it you have night work going again?"

"Yeah, I have forty out now plus a ten-man crew working on one of the new storage areas. Stephanie came up with the design. We dig a hole, concrete the bottom then put twenty storage containers in it. We'll have ten containers on each side with the openings facing each other and a twenty-foot aisle between 'em that leads to a ramp so we can drive forklifts down to 'em. Then we cement a roof and cover them up with three feet of dirt. The others are working on the barracks," Paul answered.

433

"Today is Thursday; when will you have the next barrack done?" Bruce asked.

"Tomorrow afternoon," Paul said. Bruce just looked at him in disbelief and Paul added, "Bruce, the foundations were already poured and when you can have forty around the clock, work moves fast. The second one will be ready next week, Tuesday at the latest."

"Okay, I'll take your word. How long would it take to double the size of this table? I want it to hold thirty," Bruce asked.

"A couple of hours; if you want it real pretty, a day," Paul answered.

"Can you have it done by tomorrow morning?" Bruce asked.

"Sure," Paul said.

"Okay then, tomorrow at 1000 I want the whole family here. Paul, you and Cheryl plus Conner, Susan, Millie, Lynn, and Willie, you and Maggie bring a notebook. I take it everyone has a place to sleep tonight?" Bruce asked, receiving nods. "Okay, until tomorrow. Right now I'm gonna shower. Willie, I'm sure they've fixed you up as well; if not, top of the stairs, take a left, first door on the right. That's my room. Y'all can bunk with us until you get a room," Bruce said, grabbing his pack and leaving.

Walking outside, Bruce saw a crew unloading a semi from Polk. Bruce smiled. Just the truck he was going to look for tomorrow. Bruce opened the door, reached in the cab and pulled out two duffel bags. He jumped out of the truck, closed the door and headed to his room. Throwing the bags in the back of his closet, Bruce stripped down, heading to the shower.

Bruce took a long shower, burning the filth off his body. He shaved then got out, drying off and turning on the vent fan to remove the steam so he could see. Stepping in the bedroom, he saw all three women sitting on the edge of the bed. Bruce just walked to the dresser, grabbed some boxers and turned around.

"I really don't want to talk about it tonight," Bruce informed them.

Debbie stood up. "It's my fault."

At the same time, Stephanie said, "I wouldn't drop it."

Angela stood up on the bed and said, "I kept bugging her till she gave in."

Bruce held up his hands for quiet and was stunned when he received it. Looking at Stephanie, he scowled. "You used too much makeup to cover the bruise, and your ribs and left knee must hurt like hell."

He walked over and moved Stephanie's hair out of the way to see the left side of her face. The makeup told Bruce the bruise covered most of her face. He opened her mouth and felt her teeth to make sure her jaw was okay. Next, Bruce pulled her shirt and sport bra off, revealing a huge bruise on her right chest. Shaking his head, he ran his hands along her ribs, finding two knots. Pulling down her pants, Bruce saw Stephanie's left knee was twice the size of the right.

Bruce went to the dresser, taking out one of his t-shirts and boxers then grabbed an ACE wrap. He put the shirt on Stephanie, then picked her up, laying her on his side of the bed. When he started undoing her boots, Debbie and Angela helped. Bruce headed to Debbie's closet and grabbed extra pillows. Returning, Bruce wrapped her knee and put her leg up on the pillows. Then Bruce left the room, going to the kitchen and grabbing ice. After making an ice bag, he returned to the room; Debbie and Angela had changed and were in the bed when he got back. He put the bag on Stephanie's knee.

Bruce walked to the end of the bed and Debbie was fixing to say something. He held up his hand. Debbie stayed quiet and Bruce asked, "Where're the kids?"

"Danny and Buffy are watching them," Debbie said.

"That's not fair to them. I worked their asses off," Bruce said.

"I didn't want them in here when you yelled at us," Debbie replied.

"I'm not going to yell at you, baby," Bruce told her.

"You're mad at me, Bruce, I know it," Debbie replied, waiting on the torrent to start.

"No, I'm not. I'm disappointed," Bruce told her and that hurt Debbie more. Bruce looked at Angela and Stephanie next. "At all of you." They all had tears in their eyes because each just wanted Bruce to yell at them and get it over. "You acted reckless out there," Bruce said. Then he explained, "You put four beautiful women in one vehicle with no men. I'm not saying you can't handle yourself. But that's a target a gang would risk a lot of men for. Look at it from an enemy's standpoint. I take women out but I always disperse them so if we are seen they can't target a group of women. They will try to take you alive if they think they can. I want you to remember that. They will take huge losses to get a group like you. Then you were in a regular vehicle. You were the commander and should have been in the Beast or at least a Hummer," Bruce continued, looking at Debbie,

"If something would have happened to you and them I would've moved through this land killing everything. I'm not saying you didn't do well but you know better and you got cocky. Debbie, you told me these two are a part of our family now and I have accepted them. It wasn't hard, I already loved them as friends."

Debbie looked up with tears on her face. "I'm sorry."

"I know you are baby, and so are they," Bruce said as he walked over to Debbie. He bent down and whispered in her ear; when he was finished Bruce stood up and Debbie just looked at him.

"Go ahead," Bruce said.

Debbie whispered in Angela's ear then Angela whispered back in Debbie's. Debbie repeated it with Stephanie after which Stephanie whispered back in Debbie's ear. Debbie hugged both of them then kissed them.

"She asked you both the same question and you both gave the same answer," Bruce told them. Then he asked, "Angela, what was the question?"

"Why are you sorry about disappointing Bruce?" Angela answered.

"Stephanie, your answer," Bruce asked.

"I love him," Stephanie said.

Angela crawled over the covers and moved to the end of the bed and turned around. Kneeling down on her hand and knees, she lifted her butt in the air. Bruce looked at her small butt stuck up in the air at him. "Angela, are you mooning me with your panties on?"

"No, I'm waiting on my spanking," Angela replied. They all started laughing and Stephanie was trying not to laugh hard because it hurt.

"Angela, your butt is too small to spank," Bruce told her.

"Well, I'll move it around to make it bigger then," Angela said, shaking her butt.

Bruce laughed and then left the room to check on the kids. Debbie looked at the others. "Thanks, you two."

"Thank *you*. We're a team here, girl. We stick together," Angela said.

"Yeah, we're a good team," Stephanie chimed in.

Debbie held out her hand. "Let's make a pact. If one of us is hurt or worse, the other two will pick up the slack for the family." Stephanie and Angela grabbed Debbie's hand, saying, "Agreed."

As Angela climbed back in bed, Stephanie asked, "Does that mean all of us are married now?"

"Yep," Debbie said.

"Thank God. I didn't think I could take care of the kids by myself," Stephanie said.

Bruce reached Danny's door and knocked softly. Hearing Danny yell, "Come in, Daddy," Bruce opened the door.

"How did you know it's me?"

"You're the only one that knocks and waits for me to say come in," Danny replied.

Bruce looked at Danny, Mary, Buffy, Mindy and the twins; they were all painting fingernails and toenails. "Where are PJ and Cade?"

"Jake and Matt took them. They are mad at us because we put makeup on them. They said we were destroying their manhood," Danny told him.

Bruce agreed with the boys but did not voice his opinion. "You want me to get the girls?" Bruce asked.

"Dad, we're doing nails," Danny said as if that answered his question.

Buffy looked up at him. "Daddy, this is important stuff. Go away."

"Sorry," Bruce said, closing the door and heading to Jake's room.

Bruce knocked and opened the door when Jake yelled "Come in."

"Hey Dad," Jake said. He was sitting on his bed playing a video game against Matt, who was sitting on the floor. Bruce saw PJ and Cade asleep on the bed. Bruce reached to pick them up and Jake stopped him.

"Leave them; they're okay. We got off the makeup and nail polish the girls put on them," Jake said with a little malice in his voice.

"You sure?" Bruce asked.

"Dad, when they're asleep, they're fine. They aren't that bad when they're awake. Cade will just watch me play games, and since I have everything off my floor PJ can only play with what I give him," Jake stated.

Bruce walked back to his room but stopped suddenly. Images of the shop torture came into his mind. He just breathed slowly until he pushed them from his mind and continued to his room to find everyone asleep. Bruce climbed into the bed and joined them, praying for no dreams.

CHAPTER 30

Bruce woke up sweating, wondering who'd turned the heater on. Then he felt something on his chest. Looking down, he saw Angela and Debbie lying on his chest and Stephanie burrowed under his left side. Bruce gently rolled them off and climbed out of bed. Looking at the clock reading 0412, Bruce gave up on going back to sleep. Grabbing his gear, notebooks, laptop and workout clothes, he headed to the gym.

After he worked out, Bruce went to the hall to wait on breakfast. As he walked in, Bruce saw the family table had doubled in size. There were fifteen chairs on each side and one at each end. Looking at his end, Bruce noted the corners were extended out and rounded off. *The twins are so going to love that,* Bruce thought. Walking over, Bruce ran his hand over the middle section. It was lighter than the rest of the table but was a perfect blend of wood. If this was what Paul considered fast and sloppy, Bruce was a shitty carpenter.

Next to the table were two high chairs. Looking at the new chairs, Bruce noted several with booster seats. *That man goes way overboard,* Bruce thought as he sat his gear down, stripped out of his workout clothes, put on his ACUs, checked his camera on his boonie hat and put on his boots. Grabbing his vest, Bruce thought it felt heavy. *Damn, going to have to work out hard for the next couple of weeks,* Bruce promised himself. Picking up his notebooks and laptop, he sat down to get some work done.

Millie came over carrying the biggest coffee cup Bruce had ever seen. It held an easy eight cups of coffee. When she sat it down, Bruce turned it around and saw the word BOSS written on the side.

"A bit ostentatious, don't you think?" Bruce asked her.

"No," Millie said, "I asked 'em if they saw a big mug to pick it up fer me so I could give it to ya. I painted that on the side fer ya. Just so people knows who's in charge."

"Thank you, Millie," Bruce told her, "but maybe I'm getting tired of being in charge."

Millie sat down at the table with him. "Bruce, you hafta stay in charge. We're rebuilding America, rights here and now, the ways it's supposed ta be, only better. You demand the same from everyone without a care for race or sex. Too many people countin' on ya and no one else can do it. We're gonna accomplish sumethin' here, I can feel it. You could just stay here and we could survive but you're going out into the wilderness and bringing in tha lost."

"I have to keep going out in the wilderness because I keep finding more lost," Bruce said, taking a sip.

"Bruce, quit actin' like a sissy girl," Millie said firmly.

"Millie, I'm getting tired. There's so much more to do and I'm feeling wore down to the bone," Bruce admitted to her.

"I knows, Bruce, several of us sees it. You don't hafta do everythin' yeself," Millie said.

"I don't do everything. I barely did any of the construction," Bruce said.

"That's not what I'm talkin' 'bout, Bruce. You goin' into tha wilderness too much. Several people here can survive out there on these runs. That's what's wearing ya out. You have to let others lead out there or what you're trying to avoid will happen anyway. They'll get killed," Millie said.

"Those are my kids, Millie, I can't send them out alone."

"Bruce, I'm talking about the others here, not your family. You're running your family and kids into the ground with ya," Millie said.

"I'll try Millie, I promise."

"That's good 'nough for me," Millie said as she got up. She looked down at him fondly. "You weren't too hard on little Debbie and the girls, were ya?"

"No Millie, even though I should've been," Bruce said, feeling disappointed again.

"That's good. They was hard enough on themselves. I did try to talk 'em out of it but even us big girls do stupid stuff sometimes. You boys don't have the market on it," Millie told him as she walked to the kitchen.

Bruce started working again as people drifted in. Mike came in later wearing workout clothes and sat down at his spot. He looked at the new table admiringly. "Dude, you didn't have to move me so far away. I wasn't really going to hurt you," Mike said, smiling.

"I wasn't so sure," Bruce said, looking up.

"I'm sorry, brother," Mike said.

"I'm sorry too, brother," Bruce replied, looking at Mike. Then he asked, "Nancy wore the high heels, didn't she?"

"The red ones," Mike said, grinning.

They laughed as the rest of the family came in and sat down at the table. Willie and his family came in and Bruce waved them over, telling them to sit down. Stephanie hobbled to her spot on Bruce's right as Debbie sat down on Bruce's left. Angela sat with Cade beside Stephanie. Millie and several other ladies started bringing plates over.

When they had finished eating the family left to get dressed while Bruce finished up on his notes. When everyone returned, Bruce called the meeting to order.

"Okay, I just wanted to meet with everyone because I wanted to hand out jobs. Debbie and Nancy, you two are in charge of personnel. When you need someone for a job, see them. Stephanie, Angela, Danny and Mary, you're in charge of inventory. I want you to get five people to help you and start today. Don't inventory anything until it finds a home. Mike, you're in charge of security here at the farm. Jake and Matt, you two are still the spooks. Let me know what you need to get those new UAVs up and all those cameras you two took down at the base. Willie, I want you to make a training roster for thirty people at a time, and train them for one month to fight. After we train this group we'll select some and advance their training. When they graduate they get one of these." Bruce pulled out a yellow handkerchief.

"Steve and David, you two are in charge of teaching everyone to shoot. Once they're cleared by you, they'll get a pin." Bruce held up a pin that had a small M-4 on it.

"Once they earn these they are to wear them. We are getting too many people to remember who can and can't have a weapon. I want to be able to know quickly who can go on a patrol just by looking at them. Millie and Lynn, I want to know how the food supply is and about the people that are assigned to help. Paul, you're the manager of the farm. Let me know how it's going. Cheryl, you're in charge of produce. Conner, I want you to build me two strike teams of ten men each, but don't use just men; you know what I mean. Nobody in this family can be on them. Bill, you're in charge of policing the clan. If someone has a problem with an individual, find Bill. Susan, I want you in charge of the kids. Get with Maria and get us a school schedule going.

"From now on, this group, the command group, will meet in the house on Friday nights to go over the week's activities and what is said during the Sunday meeting. Now, does anyone have anything to add?" Bruce asked.

Willie spoke up. "I just want to warn you about one family that came with me here. The Greens. The wife, Jenny, is a liberal bitch and was a thorn in my side. She's not dangerous, just a pain in the ass. I've already seen her complaining about kids with guns."

"Thank you. If she causes a problem I'll deal with her," Bruce said, looking for any other questions. "Alright people, let's go to work."

Bruce headed out to the back pasture to help with the second storage area, working through till 1400. Then he headed to the basement armory. He wanted a smaller rifle for when he was working; the SCAR was seriously getting in the way.

Walking into the basement, Bruce stopped. Racks of weapons were everywhere, with a small pathway around the basement. These weren't all the weapons they had gotten, and he called Stephanie over the radio to come to the basement. When Stephanie limped in, Bruce asked, "Where are the rest of the weapons?"

"In the underground storage, barn, machine shop, garage, and game room. And the rocket launchers in cases are under the fort. I put as many as I could down here," Stephanie replied, defending the chaos of stacked weapons.

"I'm not mad, I just wanted the weapons all together," Bruce told her.

"Bruce, you told me ammo was to go in the underground storage to keep it out of the weather. I knew the guns didn't need to be outside so I did the best I could," Stephanie let him know.

"You did a great job. Do you know where all the weapons are at?" Bruce asked.

"Of course," Stephanie said.

"Where are Debbie and Nancy?" Bruce asked.

"In the kitchen," Stephanie replied.

Bruce radioed Paul, asking him to meet him in the kitchen. Paul replied he was on the way.

Bruce headed to the kitchen with Stephanie in tow. Nancy and Debbie were at the table going over schedules and duty lists. Paul came in a few minutes later.

"Paul, how many storage containers do we have left?" Bruce asked.

"Sixty-four," Paul replied.

"I knew there were mountains of them around the farm, but-sixty four!" Bruce exclaimed.

"We wanted eighty more but stopped after the attack. We're going to make four of those storage areas like the two in the northwest pasture. By the way, the guys said thank you for the help. I didn't know you could run a crane and bulldozer?" Paul inquired.

"I couldn't but I was going to. That crane is so cool too, but back to the point. You have four extra containers. I want them for now. Can you have them moved by the machine shop? I'll show you where," Bruce said.

"Okay, let me talk to the machinists that are in the shop; they tend to get a little high-strung," Paul said.

"High-strung? Those are my toys and I agreed to let the machinists use them. I'll be damned if I ask for permission to put shit somewhere I want," Bruce said, heading to the door. He snapped over his shoulder, "Get the containers up here. Debbie and Nancy, get the family here; they should be on this detail."

Debbie jumped up and followed Bruce outside. "Baby, those guys are good, please don't make them mad. They've made a hundred plus suppressors and worked on everything that has broken. We really need them. Besides you, they're the only machinists we have and you have too much to do."

Bruce stopped and looked at her. "Debbie, I love you but not even you will tell me how someone can play with my toys. Now get the family together. I'll explain when they get here."

Bruce walked into the shop to hear someone yell, "Close the damn door!" He thought about leaving it open but decided not to. Not because of the yell, but because he didn't want his machines to get cold. Stepping around the corner, Bruce saw two men in their fifties. They were standing in front of his two CNC milling machines. Looking around, Bruce noticed both CNC lathes were running along with the regular lathe and shaper.

The closest man looked up. Seeing Bruce, he said, "Sorry, didn't know it was you, Bruce, come on in."

Bruce almost spun off but held his tongue as he walked over. The man that had spoken wiped his hands off on a rag and held one out to Bruce. "Name's Joe, Bruce. My partner is Harry. Sorry about yelling out like that but people come in here all the time wanting to see if we can do this or that. I just tell them bring it to us n' we'll fix it," Joe said as Harry walked over and shook Bruce's hand.

Harry replied, "We don't mind the kids, most just sit and watch. Several have the bug, so we give 'em small tasks and they just love it."

"What can we do for ya?" Joe asked.

Taken off guard, Bruce just said, "I'm putting some shipping containers beside the shop."

Joe and Harry looked at each other and moved toward the door. Harry said, "You need our help, huh?"

"No, I just wanted to see how it was coming along," Bruce lied.

Harry turned around and said, "Come on then. Let me tell you first, this is the best private machine shop I've ever seen. I've worked for companies that weren't this well set-up. How did you get all this stuff?"

Bruce smiled. He liked it when people liked his toys. "E-bay."

"No shit? That's amazing," Harry said with astonishment.

"Where did you train at?" Bruce asked.

"Navy, both of us," Joe replied.

"Oh, then you're good," Bruce said, nodding his head. Navy machinists were regarded as the best.

"You know the machine world, I see. Where did you train?" Joe asked.

"Right here, from a book," Bruce replied, looking at the stuff on the tables.

"You're kidding! I've seen your work around here and it's pretty damn good. For a self-taught it's beyond top notch," Harry said and Joe agreed.

Bruce puffed his chest out with the compliment. He really liked these guys. They showed him the projects they were working on and the suppressors they had made. They talked until Debbie called over the radio telling him they were ready. Bruce told Joe and Harry bye but he really wanted to stay and talk.

As he stepped outside, Debbie came up and asked him, "Are they still alive?"

"Well yeah, I like 'em," Bruce said as Debbie just muttered, "Boys."

"Okay everyone, I want to get the weapons in a secured area. I don't want anyone playing with them until they've been trained. If some aren't missing yet they will be soon. If they have been trained on it I don't care if they check one out and keep it. Now the explosives are different. I or someone on the command group have to approve each time some are checked out, and that includes grenades, mines, and rockets, mortars, etc. Does everyone understand?" Bruce asked and everyone nodded.

He pointed out where to put the containers and sent the kids to get ATVs and trailers. Walking into the underground storage, Bruce stopped. It looked so small with all the equipment, ammo and weapons in it. Walking over to the wall with the weapons, Bruce scoffed. He didn't remember getting that many weapons. Not even half of this was going to fit in the containers. As if reading his mind, Debbie said, "There's more in the barn, under the fort—"

Bruce held up his hand for her to stop and turned to look at the family. "Okay, we'll lock up weapons that can be used by one person. The heavy weapons will stay here for now since it's real hard to carry off a mini gun. Let's do it."

It was 1610 when the family started. Millie brought out plates at supper and the family wolfed down the food then continued on. They finished filling the last container at 2200. Most of the rifles and light machine guns were now locked down. The barn was empty of weapons and the cases of Stingers and AT-4s were moved to the underground storage area. The family crawled into the house and to their rooms, falling asleep without any trouble.

Friday and Saturday passed in a blur. The two new storage areas were ready and the weapons were moved to the back, filling up six of the twenty containers in one pod. The explosives and grenades Bruce put in the other storage area. He didn't think it would do much good. Bruce figured they had twenty tons of C-4 alone and one whole container was filled with grenades. If this storage pod blew up they would find pieces of the farm in Idaho. When the forklift put in the last pallet that would fit and Bruce closed the door and locked it, the thought crossed his mind: *Maybe I did get too much shit.*

All the ammo was now underground; most in the main storage. Looking around the farm, he noticed fewer piles of supplies but they were still everywhere. Bruce looked up upon hearing a semi-truck coming to the back of the property. Ten trucks stopped as one of the cranes lifted the containers off. Wondering where in the hell they came from, Bruce called Mike over the radio.

"Mike, where are these containers coming from?" Bruce asked.

"Paul said we had to have forty more to put up what we already have. I told Conner to use one of the security crews he put together and twenty drivers. It got up to almost thirty-six degrees today and I didn't want to lose the cold front so I let them go," Mike reported.

"All you had to say was, 'I sent some people to get them,'" Bruce replied.

"I sent some people to get them," Mike shot back.

Bruce smiled as he headed toward the Center. Tonight was movie night and the command group's first meeting; he'd moved it because everyone was way too tired last night. Bruce was not in the mood for it tonight either. He just wanted to go to sleep, but they had to. Sighing, he figured he would get enough sleep when he was dead. Then after thinking it through, he thought *No, there'll still be stuff for me to do*. Bruce watched the empty semis leave and then walked into the hall.

Heading to his chair, Bruce just dropped down. Debbie, Stephanie and Angela were already sitting down watching the twins and Cade run from PJ as he crawled towards them. Bruce figured PJ thought that was the best game ever with the way he was laughing. Bruce watched the game as the rest of the family came in and joined them at the table.

Matt stood up and walked over to Bruce as Jake walked over to Mike. Matt looked at Bruce and asked, "May I have Danny's hand in marriage?"

Hardening his heart, Bruce looked up at Matt. "What do you have to trade?"

Matt took a step back, caught off guard.

Debbie threw a glass of water on Bruce. He turned to her as she said, "Bruce, be serious."

Bruce looked at her as water ran off his face. "I was." He turned back to Matt. "Matt, sit down please." Bruce nodded towards Sherry's chair. He looked at Matt and smiled. "Matt, I'm glad you asked me and yes, you have my permission. Since I'm covered in water I'm going to make a guess that you have her mom's permission also. Matt, I couldn't ask for anyone better than you for Danny. You honor me with your request. I know you will make her happy," Bruce told him with sincerity.

Matt's face was covered in tears. He lunged toward Bruce, hugging him tight. Danny ran around the table and hugged Bruce, crying. Bruce stood up hugging both of them. They let go and went to Debbie and embraced her. Bruce looked at the other end of the table and could see Jake and Mary hugging Mike.

David stood up and walked over to Bruce and sat in Sherry's chair. Bruce looked at David and said, "David, I love you but if you ask me for Buffy's hand in marriage I will shoot myself right here, right now. I swear to God I will." A look of horror came over Buffy's face.

David looked at Bruce in shock and in a nervous voice asked, "No sir, I want to ask you for Mindy's hand in marriage. She said I had to get your permission."

"Mindy, come here please," Bruce said and Mindy got up from her chair and walked over. Bruce was not in the mood for this. He wanted to go somewhere and cry until he died.

"Mindy, do you know David has asked me for your hand in marriage?" Bruce asked when she was standing beside David.

"Yes sir, Mr. Bruce," Mindy said in a shy small voice.

"We already talked about the mister when you talk to me along with the sir. Now are you willing to stand by David no matter what the cost? Do you think David and you will be happy for the rest of your life?" Bruce asked, not noticing the entire hall was deathly quiet.

"Yes Daddy Bruce," Mindy replied. That was not how Bruce wanted her to address him, but he wasn't in the mood for a debate.

"David, you have my permission, if your parents agree," Bruce said and they both hugged him. Bruce returned the hug. They left to run to Mike and Nancy. Jake and Mary walked over to Bruce and he wrapped his arms around them, picking them up and squeezing them tight.

Tears were welling up in Bruce's eyes. Putting the two down, he wiped them away. Bruce let them go but not before he kissed them both. Bruce walked over to Danny and grabbed her under her arms, picking her up and swinging her around like he did when she was a little girl. Danny giggled like she used to and Bruce's heart was close to breaking wide open. Bruce sat her down and hugged her. Fighting the tears, he put on a brave face like everything was normal.

Bruce beamed with pride at the three couples as Debbie grabbed his arm and put it over her shoulders. He kissed her on the head and saw her face was covered in tears. Mike's and Nancy's were also.

Bruce asked, "Well, when is the date?"

"November the 28th," Jake replied.

"That's three days from now," Bruce replied, trying to keep his smile.

"Yeah, Dad, we wanted to do it soon and together. With all the fights we've been in we agreed we really didn't want to wait too long," Jake said and Bruce's heart fell on the floor. He understood and agreed. They could all die on the farm in the blink of an eye. The kids were old enough and responsible enough to make their own decisions. He would not deny them this joy.

Bruce looked at Mike, whose face was red and covered in tears; snot was trying to escape from his nose but he just wiped it on his sleeve. Bruce nodded his head toward Mike and he returned it.

Father Thomas came over to Bruce. "I take it you need my services."

"Yes, Father, three marriages to go on Tuesday, hold tha cheese," Bruce forced out, trying to stay strong.

"Can I talk to the couples tomorrow after the service?" Father Thomas asked. Bruce nodded his head, afraid to answer.

Bruce turned to the hall to see everyone looking at them. He cleared his throat. "I would like to announce that my daughter, my son, and my adopted daughter Mindy are getting married. They are marrying Mike's two sons and his daughter. The meetings for tonight and tomorrow are cancelled. We want you to celebrate this occasion with us."

The room erupted in a loud cheer and everyone stood and engulfed the family with hugs. Bruce made it to the kids one more time, hugging them each a long time to remember this moment forever. Making his way to the kitchen, Bruce went out the back door. The air was cold but he didn't feel it as he walked to the back of the farm, finally stopping at the fence behind the catfish pond.

Bruce's legs felt numb. He dropped to his knees and cried, falling face first to the ground. He would no longer be the important figure in their life anymore. The memories of their lives flooded through him, making him cry harder.

Two hours later Debbie was looking for Bruce, asking if anyone had seen him. Not finding him in the hall, she ran to the house, thinking maybe he'd gone to the bedroom. Debbie opened the door and found an empty room. Next she ran to Mission Control. They reported seeing someone walk past the fish pond two hours ago. Debbie took off out the front door, jumped on a buggy and headed to the back of the property. She didn't even notice the cold air on her face.

Pulling past the pond, she stopped, got out of the cart and walked forward a few paces. She could hear Bruce crying. Debbie took off in a dead run, finally seeing Bruce lying on the berm of the fence and crying in the moonlight.

"Baby," Debbie cried out and Bruce held out his arms as Debbie fell into them. They held each other tight, crying.

It was 0100 and they were still crying as they supported each other, heading back the cart. Driving back to the house with tears still pouring out of his eyes, Bruce almost hit several objects like the barn and stacks of storage containers. Stopping at the patio, they got out and headed to the door. Bruce stopped, seeing Danny sitting in a chair beside the back door.

Danny stood up and took off running toward her daddy. From six feet away she leapt in the air, hitting Bruce in the chest with her body and wrapping her arms and legs around him. Bruce caught her in a hug, tears rolling down his face. Danny was crying and hugging Bruce. Debbie just couldn't stand up anymore and fell down on her knees. Jake came running out of the house and picked up his mama. Debbie wrapped her arms around him tight.

Danny kissed Bruce on his cheek then buried her face in his neck as she cried. In between sobs, Danny said, "Daddy, I won't get married."

"Yes you will, sweet pea. Daddy will be fine. It's just that losing his little girl and boy hurts," Bruce cried out, wanting to stop crying but couldn't.

"We'll wait then, Daddy," Danny managed to get out.

"No Danny, I want you to be happy. This is one of the best experiences life has to offer. Facing the world with someone you love that isn't your dad or mom, someone that loves you just for being you. You two have made a choice, sweet pea, and I stand behind you in that choice," Bruce told her.

"No, I'll stay your little princess," Danny wailed.

"Baby, married or not, when I'm eighty-five and you're sixty you'll still be my little princess. I'll sit you on my walker and give you a ride. Daddy is just being a big sissy now. I didn't want you to see Daddy cry like this.

Don't get me wrong, I'll cry more later. This just hurts because my babies have grown up and I'm an old fart now," Bruce said, sobbing.

"You're not an old fart, Dad," Jake said, wiping his nose and holding his mama. Debbie and Jake moved over to Bruce and Danny. They hugged each other in the cold for an hour but none of them noticed. Then Bruce told them it was time to go in because he wanted this day to go away. Bruce and Debbie walked the kids to their rooms for the last time as their little boy and girl.

After leaving the kids in their rooms, they headed back down the hall. Debbie thought Bruce was heading to the bedroom and was shocked when he went downstairs. She just wanted to cry herself to sleep but she followed Bruce. He sat down at the table and Debbie joined him. Minutes later, Mike and Nancy came down and joined them. "I feel older than dirt," Bruce said.

"I don't have any more tears," Mike said.

"I lost all my babies on the same day," Nancy told them.

"We now have five more to go," Debbie said in disbelief. *We have to quit adding kids to this marriage*, Debbie thought.

Thinking about what Debbie had said, Bruce started counting off kids: Buffy, Emily, Sherry, Cade, and PJ. "I'm getting drunk," he said, getting up and going to the basement. When he got back everyone had a glass and an extra one for him. Bruce poured a glass and passed the bottle around.

CHAPTER 31

At 0700 the four were still going strong when the kids came down. They all sat down with the parents, who were now laughing as they remembered the past and told stories. Stephanie and Angela came down with the twins, Cade and PJ. Then Steve and Tonya came down with Nathan. They all sat down and joined in, laughing at the stories. When Susan and Conner came through, they grabbed the little kids and with Pam headed to the Center for breakfast.

Seeing the little kids leaving, Buffy reluctantly stood up to leave. Bruce said with a slurred voice, "Where the hell do you think you are going, BB?" Buffy looked at Bruce. "Sit your butt back down in that chair." Buffy smiled and jumped back in her chair as the others left.

"Hey Mike, remember when we took the girls to Dallas for the football game?" Bruce asked him.

Mike finished draining his glass and started laughing and pouring another as Bruce continued, "Before the game we get the girls jerseys, have their faces painted and both have their hair braided in big ponytails on each side of their head. We are on the 50 in box seats. The 'Boys' are down ten to zip and are playing like crap. Little Danny and Mary, two twelve-year-old girls, climb up on the rails." Bruce stood up to act out his story. "They both grab their crotches and yell, 'Grab your balls like this and play some football, ya pussies!'" Everyone started laughing then Bruce tells them, "Hold on, this is the best part. No sooner than the girls get off the rails then Mike's cell phone goes off. When he answers it, Nancy is yelling at him, 'I just saw you letting my little girls grab their balls on national TV! Are you fucking insane?'"

Everyone was rolling as Bruce poured more in his glass then set the bottle back in the middle of the table next to an empty one. Then Mike yells out,"What about when the boys saw Bigfoot?" Then he started slapping the table.

Steve, Matt, David and Jake all start to blush and look around. Matt said defensively, "Dad, I thought that was going to stay a secret?" Mike couldn't answer Matt because he couldn't breathe, he was laughing so hard.

Everyone except the boys turned toward Bruce, who was laughing also. Jake stated, "Dad, I thought this was going to be a secret."

"Son, I think your family needs to hear this," Bruce told Jake as he finally got to take a deep breath. Jake just shook his head no but Bruce started the story anyway. "It was the first camping trip we took the boys on. We were in Montana fly fishing. Well, one night around the campfire Mike and I start telling the boys stories of Bigfoot. How Bigfoot would wait outside of tents at night to catch boys when they go and pee. Mike told them Bigfoot ate little boy weenies so they couldn't become a hunter. We go on like that for an hour or so, then we gather everyone up and go to bed. The reason for the stories was Mike and I just didn't want them to go out during the night without us. There are big critters up there. Well, I don't know how long it took them to go to sleep—" Bruce stopped as Steve spoke up.

"Like forever! My God, I've never been so scared in my life. Daddy Mike snored once so loud Jake tried to crawl up inside my ass," he said and everyone busted out laughing. Then Bruce continued.

"It was a full moon out and kind of chilly so I was snuggled up in my sleeping bag. About 0300, I feel someone shaking me. I wake up and Steve is shaking me whispering 'Get up.' I sit up to see four sets of wide eyes filled with fear looking at me. Now let me tell you that will wake you up real fast, seeing fear on your kids' faces. Steve leans over and said, 'We heard Daddy Mike yell out followed by a growl and limbs being broke.' I look at Mike's sleeping bag and sure enough he's gone. That was when I heard something being dragged through the woods. Then it would stop and was replaced by a rhythmic deep grunting. I grab my gun out of the pack thinking Mike's ass was getting eaten by a bear. I move to go help him, slowly opening the door of the tent, when Matt grabs my arm and says 'Don't leave us.' I turn around so I could see them and tell them I'm going to check on Mike. Looking past the boys on the tent wall, I see a huge shadow moving up the tent. I had no idea what it was but it was big and I must have made a face—" Bruce stopped as Jake interrupted.

"I remember very clearly, Dad, you said 'Fuck me with a tooth brush,'" Jake told him.

Bruce chuckled as he picked up again, "Well anyway, I move around the boys, putting myself between them and the wall. I'm just staring at the shadow moving up the wall when I hear bloodcurdling screams 'BIGFOOT' from all four of the boys. I hear something hit and rip the tent behind me and before I can turn around the tent collapses down on top of me. I crawl around and finally get out the new door that the boys had made as Mike runs past me yelling, 'Boys, stop!' Mike comes over to get the tent off of me and from behind him going up the mountain we hear four boys screaming 'He's coming!'"

Bruce stopped to catch his breath and take a drink as everyone laughed hysterically. Angela and Danny were holding each other on the floor; they were laughing so hard they'd slid out of their chairs. When Bruce had his laughter under control, he continued. "Mike and I took off running after them. Luckily the boys stayed together in one group—" Bruce stopped as Steve said, "It wasn't by choice, I told them to quit following me."

Laughing, Bruce continued the story. "Mike and I are in hot pursuit. I didn't notice that Mike was falling behind until I caught up to the boys. When I got close to Jake I started yelling for them to stop. Then I hear Jake scream in a shrill voice, 'It can talk!' Jake was at the back of the pack of boys, but all of a sudden, my son could fly. Jake passed the other three like they were standing still and moving backwards. I actually started faltering my pace when I saw Jake take off like a rocket. I still thought they were just scared of that shadow. I lean forward to pick up speed and kept yelling for them to stop. I didn't know they were running from Bigfoot. I finally reach the last two in the pack, which were Steve and David. I grabbed them, picking them up around the waist. Let me tell you, holy shit did they start beating the hell out of me, screaming like I was tearing them apart. That was when I hear Matt scream as he ran up the side of the mountain, 'He got'em Jake!' Hearing Mike come up behind me, I turned and handed the two I'd caught to him. That was when I hear twelve-year-old Steve scream out, 'Shit there's two of 'em!' I take off up the mountain for Matt and Jake, who are now neck and neck. They both think Bigfoot can talk, has friends and has eaten their dads and brothers. These two were going up a sixty-degree incline at a dead run with me in hot pursuit, and by now I'm starting to suck wind bad. All of a sudden I hear Mike behind me let out a loud, high-pitched scream, like a woman in a horror movie. I couldn't stop to check on him because I had finally closed some distance with the last two, so I keep going. Just when I get close I'm breathing so fast I can't yell for the boys to stop, and I hear Jake scream, 'I can hear him breathing!' Knowing I don't have much more gas left in my tank, I dove and tackled both of them." Bruce stopped so he could catch his breath and take another drink. He looked around as he sat his glass down. Only the boys were still sitting at the table but even they were laughing now. Everyone else was on the floor having convulsions.

With a loud voice, Bruce picked back up so everyone could hear, "I realize now diving on them was a big mistake on my part. Those two tore into me like fat women eating corndogs. They bit, clawed, head butted and kicked me until I was able to sit on them, holding them down with my weight.

"That was when Jake, with his eyes closed, sunk his teeth in, putting a huge bite on my thigh. That bite made me scream at the top of my lungs just like Mike did earlier. Matt yells out with joy, 'Bite him harder, you're killing him.' Looking down at Jake latched onto my thigh with his eyes closed, I yell out at Jake 'Jake, quit it's Daddy!' Jake opens his eyes, letting me go and says, 'Where did Bigfoot go, Daddy?'"

Everyone was laughing and only Bruce was not on the floor just because he had to tell the story. When the laughter died down and everyone climbed back into their seats, Nancy looked at Bruce. "You told us a bear attacked the tent while y'all were fishing, that's why Mike had to buy another one."

Debbie stopped laughing as a thought came to her. "Your kids put all those bruises and scratches on you, not you falling down the side of a mountain?" she asked and Bruce nodded, making her laugh again.

Stephanie slowed down her laughing and asked Bruce, "What happened to Mike?"

Bruce looked at her and before he could answer Mike spoke up. "I fell down a steep bank when I went outside to pee; I took out several trees and I sprained my ankle real bad. I had to claw my way up the bank and every time I used my hurt foot I would grunt and groan out with pain," he explained, laughing hard again.

When he could talk again, Mike told them, "When we got them back to camp, all four boys jumped in the truck and wouldn't get out. Bruce and I tried to coax them out, and then we yelled at them to get out. They would just roll down the window and say 'Bigfoot' then roll the window back up. After Bruce wrapped up my ankle, he had to pack up camp in the dark by himself because I couldn't do shit. We stayed in a motel the rest of the trip. It took two days to convince the boys it was me they'd heard in the woods and not Bigfoot."

David turned toward Mike with downcast eyes. "Dad, I really am sorry, I thought you were Bigfoot."

"I know son, that one was on me," Mike said, laughing, and David smiled, happy his dad didn't hold a grudge against him.

"What happened?" Nancy asked, seeing David's reaction.

"Well when Bruce handed the boys to me, Steve was hitting me real hard so I put David under my arm. That way I could wrap my other arm around Steve's upper body to make him stop beating the shit out of me. Well, David saw his chance and took it, biting me right on my tit. He clamped down hard and I screamed like a little girl. I tried to drop him but he wouldn't let go. He was actually hanging on with just his mouth latched onto my chest. I let go of Steve, not caring what the hell he did, and grabbed David, trying to pull him off before he bit my tit off. I was screaming the entire time, just wanting someone to shoot my ass. Steve finally realized it was me and tried to help me get David off. Steve was the one who yelled at David, 'That's your dad!'"

Steve looked at Bruce, grinning. "Dad, have you told Mom about you and Daddy Mike tearing up that diner and you punching out a cop in Texas?"

Bruce stopped laughing and coughed. "Ah no, maybe some other time."

"What?" Debbie and Nancy shouted in unison.

"It's nothing, I'll tell y'all about it later," Bruce replied, grinning.

"Aw, come on, Dad, that's a good story. You and Daddy Mike laughed for an hour when we all talked about it last year bow fishing," Danny said, giggling.

"I don't think either mother would find it too funny," Mike declared, wanting the kids to be quiet.

Debbie looked at Bruce, simply stating, "Spill it."

"We got in a fight with some bikers and a cop walked in. When he tried to break it up, I punched him," Bruce replied.

Debbie sighed, looking at Bruce. "Tell the story Bruce-style," she commanded.

Bruce let out a long sigh, knowing he and Mike were fixing to get into trouble, but he grinned anyway. It had been a really good fight. Clearing his throat, Bruce started. "You remember two years ago Mike and I took the kids to that survival training camp in Nevada. You and Nancy went to some resort just to relax."

"It was the Sands in the Bahamas," Nancy told Bruce.

"Whatever," Bruce said, waving his hand through the air. Stephanie leaned over and popped the back of Bruce's shaved head.

Bruce turned and looked at Stephanie as if she had lost her damn mind. Stephanie was just staring at her hand like it had a mind of its own. Looking up at Bruce, she said, "I'm sorry; I don't know why I did that. I wanted to when I heard that 'whatever,' but I don't know why I did." Stephanie looked back down at her hand.

Debbie laughed. "It's okay, Stephanie, that's a normal reaction to that smart ass comment. You'll learn to block those impulses, otherwise your hand is going to be very sore." Then Debbie turned to Bruce. "Hell yeah, I remember. You and Mike were supposed to accompany us but the kids found that camp that trained with full auto weapons and CQB for two weeks. It cost us a pretty penny because they didn't want you to bring kids there."

"Debbie, after they met the kids and saw that they handled weapons correctly we did get reimbursed for the 'extra fee.' Mary and Danny had those old men there eating out of their hands. The old man that ran it brought them both a present every day while we were there. Hell, he still sends them presents on Christmas."

"Mr. Denny," Danny said, smiling.

"I know who it is, Bruce. We've gone back twice every year. You're being vague, trying to stall the story," Debbie said then drained her glass and poured another one.

"Well we only had to pay for one trip a year. Mr. Denny always let us come back and bring our horses so we could ride them in the mountains," Bruce answered, trying to divert Debbie's attention.

"Bruce!" she snapped.

"Okay, don't get your panties in a wad," Bruce told her as he started. "If you remember, after we got the Tahoe loaded up all the kids were wearing their tiger stripe BDUs. They wouldn't let Mike and I wear jeans. They wanted us to wear ours as well so Mike and I put 'em on. After driving for eight hours we were still in Texas, and everyone had gotten hungry and didn't want to eat sandwiches anymore.

"Mike spots this little roadside diner. We stop there, fill up with gas and go inside to eat. We're sitting down at a large round table talking, having fun, when in walk four bikers. They had on patches but I have no idea who they were with. I didn't pay them any attention. We were sitting there having a good time. Danny sees a jukebox in the corner and points it out to Mary. They asked us for change and we gave it to them so they could go play some music—" Bruce stopped as Jake interrupted.

"Okay, Dad that's enough. You're leaving out the emotion because you know Mama's wrath might be on the way," Jake told him as he picked up the story. "Well you know Danny and Mary, when they hear music they get giggly and dance. They go over and start playing some pop song by Brittney and start dancing in front of the jukebox, laughing at each other. One of the bikers yells out 'We don't want to hear that shit.' Danny and Mary stop dancing and look at the biker and both of them flip him off. They turned and looked at our table and Dad's face had turned to stone as he looked at the bikers. Knowing Dad was pissed, the girls calmly walk back to the table and sat down. Daddy Mike looks at Dad and tells him, 'Bruce, take your dick off your shoulder. I'm not in the mood.' Dad just turns to Daddy Mike with a flat stare and replies, 'I want to listen to some more music.' Dad gets up and walks over to the jukebox and puts in a twenty and programs the same Brittney song to play twenty times. Daddy Mike just shakes his head and turns to us saying, 'Y'all stay out of this and run to the truck when it starts.' We all assure him, 'Oh yeah, we'll leave if anything happens,' knowing we aren't leaving for anything. Dad comes back over and sits down as the juke box starts blaring. The same biker turns around and yells at Dad, 'I told you we don't want to hear that shit. Do I have to come over there?' Now inside the diner was about thirty to forty people and they all just shut up. These biker boys were pretty big and looked tough." Jake stopped as Bruce added, "I've had tougher jock itch."

Everyone was grinning as the kids slowly started smirking to keep from laughing as they played out the events in their minds. Jake turned to Bruce, smiling. "Dad turns to the four bikers who are sitting up at the bar. Looking at the one who yelled out, Dad replies to him, 'I like this song. It reminds me of your mama tossing my salad and your sister licking my nuts.' Daddy Mike just put his hands over his face while we just fell out laughing. The biker got off his stool and walked over to us, stopping beside Dad, trying to intimidate him with his presence. Like that would ever work. The biker looked down at Dad and said, 'Boy, I'm going to have to hurt you now.' Dad looked up at the biker and said with attitude, 'I'm really scared if you can't tell. I think I'm going to make you eat the corn out of my shit, then I'm going to give you a golden shower, and after that I'm going to get you pregnant. Your pussy is so big it really makes me horny,'" Jake said as all the kids fell out laughing.

Bruce looked up at Debbie who was just staring at him. Bruce explained, "Well he swaggered over like he had a really big vagina between his legs and I just had to tell him that made me horny. Hell, I'm getting aroused now thinking about it." Everyone that wasn't already laughing started up, including Debbie.

Jake wiped tears from his eyes and continued. "So the biker squared up, facing Dad, and said, 'You need to stand up so I can kick your ass.' Dad, never taking his eyes off of him, shoots back 'If I get up you are at least getting a golden shower.' Hearing that, the biker took a step back. You could see it on his face, he was getting scared. That was when one of his buddies at the bar shouted encouragement to him. The biker stepped back towards Dad and said, 'If you think I'm scared of a family of pussies that dress in camo, you're dead wrong. I'm going to take your daughters—' Well we never got to hear what he wanted to do to Danny and Mary because Dad launched out of that chair like the Space Shuttle, hitting the biker under the chin. That man flew up in the air, and I'm not kidding, it looked like he paused at the top of his arc over the table behind him. The biker sailed over the table and hit the ground and just lay there not moving. I just knew he was dead and we were going to jail because Dad had just killed a man while we watched. Dad hit that man so hard I know members of his family felt it," Jake declared, giving everyone around the table a serious look.

He took a deep breath and continued. "Before that man even hit the ground, Daddy Mike was out of his chair charging the bar with Dad. The three at the bar never stood a chance. Dad launched a kick, hitting one square in the chest. That biker looked like a cartoon character, his eyes bulged out so much. Dad chopped his friend beside him in the throat and dropped him to his knees. Then Dad grabbed the one he'd kicked, picked him up and just tossed him over his shoulder. The biker landed right in front of our table. We all looked at each other like, 'Oh, a present' and jumped over the table and started kicking and stomping the biker."

Bruce interrupted him. "Y'all were monkey stomping him into the ground, son," he declared.

"Whatever," Jake said. Bruce fought the urge to slap him but noticed Stephanie's hand swing out. If Angela had been taller, it would have hit her in the face, but Stephanie's hand just sailed over her head. Bruce made a mental note to watch his mouth around Stephanie until she controlled that hand.

Jake continued, never noticing Stephanie. "Well Daddy Mike launched himself, hitting the other biker in the jaw and dropping him. Now in all fairness Daddy Mike's guy was the biggest."

Mike bellowed out, "Biggest, that son of a bitch was a mountain. He was an easy six-foot-eight and had to weigh at least three hundred eighty pounds. The biggest guy Bruce hit was six-foot-four and two hundred and eighty. The one he hit in the throat was big but short."

Jake ignored him as he went on. "Like I said, he was the biggest but none of these guys were under six foot. The mountain Daddy Mike hit stood back up and started throwing punches at him. Daddy Mike blocked them and delivered a volley of blows but the man refused to go down. The biker Dad had chopped in the throat lunged at Dad, throwing a wild punch and hitting him in the side of the face. Dad grabbed the man's arm and punched it, breaking his elbow. That man let out a scream that sounded like a cat. Dad started throwing punches and knees into the man, driving him up on the counter. Then Dad grabbed him and threw him over his back. That biker landed beside the one we were jumping on. Danny yelled out, 'Thank you Daddy' and we started jumping on our new toy. Then Danny grabbed a large glass sugar dispenser and smashed it over the biker's head that had a broken arm knocking the man out cold. Then Mary, who was standing over our first toy, reared her foot back and kicked the man right in the jewels. That man threw up and I'm sure if we would have looked his balls would have been there. Mary starts jumping up and down, yelling, 'Danny, did you see that? It really works.' We all stop hitting our toys to see what Mary was talking about. Matt, Steve and Danny were on the one with the broken arm, while Mary, David and I were on the one that just had his balls punted to the top of his head. Mary runs over to the man that Danny knocked out and raises her foot way back and launches a kick into his groin. That guy musta slid a foot on the floor. That's where I learned pain will bring you out of a knock-out. That man woke up in a mid-howl and puked," Jake said.

Looking at Danny, he started again. "When Danny saw what Mary did she jumped up and down and ran over to the one Mary kicked first; he was still holding his balls, trying to comfort them. Danny tried to kick his balls but he wouldn't move his hands. The entire time Danny is yelling, 'Move your damn hands.' Seeing he wasn't going to comply with her request, Danny started kicking him in the face with her combat boots. After five kicks, the man did move his hands, grabbing his face. Which I'm sure to this day he realizes was a big mistake. Danny reared back and tried to put his balls into orbit. The man couldn't even yell out. All he did was throw up again. Danny yelled out, 'That is so cool.'"

Stopping, Jake looked around the table at everyone laughing. "I learned two things then. No matter how many times you get kicked in the balls it still hurts. Second, when someone tells you to move your hands off your balls, it's not going to be for a good reason."

Picking back up the story, Jake took a deep breath. "I have to admit Steve, David, Matt and I stopped as Mary and Danny tested out their new powers. We just didn't have the heart to beat them while the girls were kicking them in the face until they uncovered their balls. Meanwhile, Dad moved over to the mountain Daddy Mike was fighting and started talking to Daddy Mike like nothing was wrong. 'Are you going to play with him all day?' Dad asked Daddy Mike. Daddy Mike ducked a wild swing, kicking the biker in the knee and dropping him. Then, grabbing the man's head, Daddy Mike drove his knee into his face. While the man was dazed, Daddy Mike slammed the biker's head into the bar, knocking him to the floor. Daddy Mike looked at Dad and said, 'Mine was bigger than all three of yours.' Dad shrugged his shoulders and turned around, heading to the first biker he'd knocked over the table, saying, 'If you'd break something they tend to stay down.' Daddy Mike just watched Dad then noticed the mountain was getting back up so he started throwing punches and kicks at the biker, driving him into the wall."

"Now Mary turned around and noticed the first man Dad had knocked out and ran over to show him her new powers. When her foot connected with him was when I realized he hadn't died, though I'm sure he wished he would have. That man sat straight up, letting out a raspy groan as he grabbed his balls. By now Mary knew how to make her powers more effective, so she kicked him in the face, snapping his head back. True to form, the man grabbed his face so Mary's foot could have a clear flight path again." Jake stopped, looking at Nancy and his mom laughing.

"I kinda felt sorry for those three," Steve stated, laughing.

"Are you kidding? It really worked just like Daddy Bruce said it would," Mary yelled out, smiling. "That was when I knew what Daddy Bruce and Dad taught us really worked," she declared proudly.

Jake kissed Mary then continued. "Dad walked over to the first guy who Mary was still demonstrating her powers on. Dad grabbed her and told her this one was his. I have to say Mary didn't like Dad interrupting her using her newly discovered powers, but she rejoined Danny with the first two. Dad stood over the man and started unbuckling his pants. Daddy Mike, who had just dropped the mountain again yelled out across the diner, 'What the hell are you doing?' I'm not kidding here, Dad turned around and said, 'This one is fixin' to get a golden shower.'

"Now during this whole fight everyone in the dinner just backed up to get out of the way. That is until they heard Dad declare what was fixing to happen. They all turned and ran for the door. Even Danny and Mary stopped and came over to us. That was when the mountain stood up again and grabbed Daddy Mike and I think pissed him off. Daddy Mike turned around and broke the guy's knee, then drove his elbow into his jaw, breaking it," Jake said and started giggling.

Getting it under control, he started again. "While Daddy Mike is letting the mountain know he's tired of playing and Dad was fixing to carry out his threat, a cop fights against the crowd to get in. He must have only seen Dad because he ran right at him. Now we all yelled for Dad and that was when the cop grabbed his shoulder. Dad spun around so fast he caught the cop in the side of the head with a punch; the cop never stood a chance. That cop dropped like someone threw a switch. Dad just looked down at the cop then at Daddy Mike. Dad turned to us and said, 'Run.' We all took off running at the same time, heading to the Tahoe which was parked on the other side of the lot. When we got there, we all climbed in, followed by

Dad. When we didn't see Daddy Mike get in, we turned around to see him slashing the tires of the cop car and the four motorcycles parked outside. Dad yelled out for him to move it as he started the Tahoe up and drove over to him. When we pulled out, it was with several other vehicles and we could see flashing lights heading to the diner behind us."

"Dad turned around and told everyone to change clothes and do it fast. Everyone was completely changed in fifteen minutes; even Dad and Daddy Mike had changed. Then several miles down the road Dad stopped at a parts store and bought some wide pin striping and decals. We pulled over outside of town and put them on the Tahoe and stayed on the back roads until we got out of Texas," Jake finished.

Debbie laughed as she looked at Bruce. "I always wondered why you put that striping on my Tahoe."

Nancy looked back and forth from Bruce and Mike, who were taking several long drinks. "Well y'all taught our kids how to become fugitives and evade the law," she finally said, laughing.

"Were y'all ever stopped?" Angela asked, wiping tears of mirth from her eyes.

"Yeah in Arizona, but we were let go because we didn't match the description," Bruce told her.

Angela laughed, shaking her head. "Like I said, life in this family is never dull."

"You have no idea," Debbie said, emptying her glass and pouring another one. When she sat the bottle down Angela grabbed it, turned it up and took a long drink out of the bottle. When she lowered the bottle everyone was just looking at her.

"What?" she asked and no one responded. Angela turned to Stephanie, handing her the bottle. "Take a hit." Angela told her. Stephanie just looked at the bottle then at Angela.

"I want some juice first," Stephanie told her.

Angela shook her head. "Don't be a pussy. Just take three long chugs. We have to show them we're just as insane as they are," Angela advised her.

Reluctantly, Stephanie took the bottle and turned it up, taking three long drinks of straight vodka. Taking the bottle away from her mouth, Stephanie gasped for air as her stomach told her it did *not* like that. "Shit, I think my balls just fell off," Stephanie declared in a dry raspy voice, blinking her watery eyes as the table erupted in laughter.

When the laughter died down, Jake looked at Bruce. "Dad, I know we'll get married with the family rings, but I want to go and get some for us to wear afterwards."

Bruce looked at Jake and smiled. "Yeah, y'all are getting married with the family rings and that does mean all of you," he said, looking at Mindy and David, who both smiled saying, "Yes, sir."

Bruce turned back to Jake. "When has Daddy not taken care of business?" Bruce stood up and felt the earth move under his feet. He staggered out to the kitchen to the bedroom and headed to the closet and grabbed a bag. Heading back down the stairs, he fell down the last four and jumped to his feet. "I meant to do that," he said.

Sitting back down, Bruce laid out three boxes, trying to read the names on the boxes but the words wouldn't stay still. "Buffy, come here and read please. The words won't be still," he implored.

Pointing at the boxes, Buffy said, "Danny/Matt, David/Mindy, and Jake/Mary."

"Your mom knew your ring sizes, and thank Mike for not shooting me when I snuck off to get them at the base. I knew you wanted to get married so I grabbed them in case it was summer when you did. That way I wouldn't have to fight a million evil smurfs to get you some rings, but I would have," Bruce said as he slid the boxes to the kids. Then he added, "Don't forget to thank Nancy for calming Mike down by wearing the red high heels." Nancy laid her head on the table.

"Now ladies, take the girls upstairs to have the bachelorette party. The bachelor party is down here. I'm not going back up those stairs; I swear they move," Bruce said.

"I can't see my feet and you want me to walk upstairs?" Debbie asked.

Danny spoke up. "Let's have both here."

Bruce looked at Debbie. "You can do that?"

Jake replied, "We can do whatever we want."

"Get some juice. None of you can drink this straight," Bruce said.

"I can," Steve said proudly, grabbing the bottle and turning it up. He was the first to pass out so he woke up wearing make-up and red glossy fingernail polish on his fingernails. The young couples made it until noon. Bruce went down an hour later, followed by Nancy, Debbie, Angela, and Stephanie. Mike made it the longest.

Through the whole morning Buffy only drank juice as she sat watching, laughing, and listening to her family. She laughed so hard at them for so long her stomach muscles hurt badly.

Watching her family, Buffy realized how much she loved them. When everyone had moved to the living room, Buffy followed. As everyone passed out, some on the furniture, the rest on the floor, Buffy just watched and laughed with them. After Daddy Mike fell asleep and quit telling her stories, Buffy got off the couch and walked over to Mama and Daddy on the floor, lying down between them. Even though it was only late afternoon, Buffy curled up between them and went to sleep with them. She smiled as she drifted off to sleep, remembering what Daddy had said: "Family first." She had a family.

ABOUT THE AUTHOR

Thomas A. Watson lives in Northwestern Montana, but grew up in Doyline, Louisiana and Grenada, Mississippi. He moved to Shreveport, Louisiana to start a family. He graduated from Northwestern University with a Bachelors in Science. Watson's love of reading, which was instilled in him at a young age by his parents, inspired him to begin his writing career.

Working currently as an RN in an emergency room in Missoula, Watson loves the outdoors and taking time off of work.

By the author: The books in my Blue Plague series are no holds barred about the end of civilization and are not for the faint of heart. The language and actions are harsh, even by the main characters. It is my portrayal of what it would take to survive an event of this magnitude. It deals with the harsh reality of those that prey on the weak when no one is around to save and protect them. There is humor, honor, family, and hope in this series, because a world without these is another name for hell. The world has seen small scale deterioration from disasters, but nothing on the scale of this series. If you don't think society would not break down like this then you are sorely mistaken. Bad people are everywhere in our society. If your neighbor was starving or scared, could you trust them to leave you alone or help protect your family?

I wrote this book based on what I saw after hurricanes Katrina and Rita about what would happen if society broke down worldwide.

ACKNOWLEDGMENTS

Once again, I have to say one person cannot write a book alone. It has been so fun to write this series and share it with the world. Walking into a book store and seeing someone reading your work is so cool.

To my family, I must say thank you so much. Nicholas, Khristian, Tina, and Dylan, thank you for letting Daddy lock himself in his study. Next, I have to say thank you to my mom and dad for encouraging me to read and passing that love of reading on to me. See, Mom, that book club you signed me up for when I was a kid paid off. I have to admit; I love telling a story.

Next, I have to address what a few have asked about. The characters appear super-human. I know many people and families that are this active, staying in excellent shape. They have to be to hunt around the world, kayak, skydive, mountain climb, and other extreme sports. Again, I know personally many people that live prepared. They do not consider themselves preppers or survivalists, just people that want to be self-reliant and be prepared for a disaster. These people are more set up than those in the book. To those who want your average couch potato who knows nothing except how to order at Burger King to survive an event of this magnitude, I'm sorry. The truth is they would die, and it would be a short book. My characters are not super-human, just prepared, like I describe in each book. If you read books of this type, then you are building a knowledge base. Granted, it's fiction, but they give readers ideas and scenarios. Knowledge is power to those who seek it. The reason I explain the weapons is because simply saying they have a gun leans more toward pure fantasy. Why not a magic wand? Like the Hollywood actors who never reload. The Blue Plague series' website has pictures of the weapons.

To the Facebook queen, my wife: Thank you for wearing out the computer telling others about my books. I can't forget Christian for the great cover art once again. To the six hundred plus who follow Blue Plague on Facebook, thank you. Hearing from each of you every week really kept this house going. Blue Plague: The Fall has sold thousands and is still going strong; for that, I have to say thank you. I still can't believe how many have sold and are still selling.

To those who are going on this journey with me, I say thank you.

BOOK

PERMUTED
PRESS

PERMUTED PRESS
needs **you** to help

SPREAD (THE) INFECTION

FOLLOW US!

𝑓 | Facebook.com/PermutedPress
𝕐 | Twitter.com/PermutedPress

REVIEW US!

Wherever you buy our book, they can be reviewed! We want to know what you like!

GET INFECTED!

Sign up for our mailing list at
PermutedPress.com

PERMUTED
PRESS

KING ARTHUR AND THE KNIGHTS OF THE ROUND TABLE HAVE BEEN REBORN TO SAVE THE WORLD FROM THE CLUTCHES OF MORGANA WHILE SHE PROPELS OUR MODERN WORLD INTO THE MIDDLE AGES.

EAN 9781618685018 $15.99   **EAN** 9781682611562 $15.99

Morgana's first attack came in a red fog that wiped out all modern technology. The entire planet was pushed back into the middle ages. The world descended into chaos.

But hope is not yet lost— King Arthur, Merlin, and the Knights of the Round Table have been reborn.

PERMUTED
PRESS

THE ULTIMATE PREPPER'S ADVENTURE.
THE JOURNEY BEGINS HERE!

EAN 9781682611654 $9.99   EAN 9781618687371 $9.99   EAN 9781618687395 $9.99

The long-predicted Coronal Mass Ejection
has finally hit the Earth, virtually destroying
civilization. Nathan Owens has been prepping
for a disaster like this for years, but now he's
a thousand miles away from his family and
his refuge. He'll have to employ all his hard-won
survivalist skills to save his current community,
before he begins his long journey through
doomsday to get back home.

THE MORNINGSTAR STRAIN HAS BEEN LET LOOSE—IS THERE ANY WAY TO STOP IT?

EAN 9781618686497 $16.00

An industrial accident unleashes some of the Morningstar Strain. The doctor who discovered the strain and her assistant will have to fight their way through Sprinters and Shamblers to save themselves, the vaccine, and the base. Then they discover that it wasn't an accident at all—somebody inside the facility did it on purpose. The war with the RSA and the infected is far from over.

This is the fourth book in Z.A. Recht's The Morningstar Strain series, written by Brad Munson.

GATHERED TOGETHER AT LAST, THREE TALES OF FANTASY CENTERING AROUND THE MYSTERIOUS CITY OF SHADOWS...ALSO KNOWN AS CHICAGO.

EAN 9781682612286 $9.99   EAN 9781618684639 $5.99   EAN 9781618684899 $5.99

From *The New York Times* and *USA Today* bestselling author Richard A. Knaak comes three tales from Chicago, the City of Shadows. Enter the world of the Grey–the creatures that live at the edge of our imagination and seek to be real. Follow the quest of a wizard seeking escape from the centuries-long haunting of a gargoyle. Behold the coming of the end of the world as the Dutchman arrives.

Enter the City of Shadows.

PERMUTED
PRESS

WE CAN'T GUARANTEE THIS GUIDE WILL SAVE YOUR LIFE. BUT WE CAN GUARANTEE IT WILL KEEP YOU SMILING WHILE THE LIVING DEAD ARE CHOWING DOWN ON YOU.

EAN 9781618686695 $9.99

This is the only tool you need to survive the zombie apocalypse.

OK, that's not really true. But when the SHTF, you're going to want a survival guide that's not just geared toward day-to-day survival. You'll need one that addresses the essential skills for true nourishment of the human spirit. Living through the end of the world isn't worth a damn unless you can enjoy yourself in any way you want. (Except, of course, for anything having to do with abuse. We could never condone such things. At least the publisher's lawyers say we can't.)

PERMUTED
PRESS